THE MUSEUM OF ABANDONED SECRETS

Praise for *The Museum of Abandoned Secrets*

"Many books at the top of the bestseller list today are not necessarily distinguished by the quality of their language. In Ukraine, however, a book that has been the number-one bestseller since it was published is not only an exception to this rule, but quite the opposite. Oksana Zabuzhko's *The Museum of Abandoned Secrets* is so rich and precise in its language, and also so political and demanding, that one cannot help wondering what is different about Ukraine."

—*Kultur Spiegel*

"*The Museum of Abandoned Secrets* is a magnum opus, in which everything that the armory of literature can provide is mobilized against the forces of darkness: strong emotions, the power of pathos, the most compelling images...A novel of power—and a powerful novel."

—*Deutschlandradio*

"Pugnacious, feverish, brilliant—with her 759-page novel about the history of Ukraine in the twentieth century, Oksana Zabuzhko has thrown open a window in her homeland. She is already celebrated as a second Dostoyevsky, but above all she has triggered an intense debate about social relationships and their roots in the past that people have yet to come to terms with."

—*Schweizer Radio DRS*

"As an attempt at the archeology of memory it sets the world on fire, as a romance novel it is touching, and as a vivisection of social and political injustices in late- and post-communist Ukraine it has a virulence that is difficult to surpass."

—*Ilma Rakusa, NZZ*

"Violence and fear lie in the bones of generations of Ukrainians, and what power do the ostracized dead have over the living? Oksana Zabuzhko writes about this heavy subject as lightly and freshly as the main female character talks."

—*WDR*

"This book is a spectacular intellectual success. It is driven by the belief that intellectual and political freedom is the only thing worth fighting for, apart from love, of course. Equipped with an almost megalomaniacal imagination and defiant humor, the author invents dreamlike parallel collateral campaigns, illuminates culture, society, and politics in multiple perspectives, and makes ghostly excursions into the past...With *The Museum of Abandoned Secrets*, Oksana Zabuzhko has written both herself and Ukraine into the scabby heart of Europe."

—*Berliner Zeitung*

THE MUSEUM OF ABANDONED SECRETS

OKSANA ZABUZHKO

TRANSLATED BY Nina Shevchuk-Murray

amazon crossing

Text copyright © 2009 by Oksana Zabuzhko
English translation copyright © 2012 by Nina Shevchuk-Murray

The Museum of Abandoned Secrets was originally published in 2009 by Fact, Kiev, as *Музей покинутих секретів*.Translated from Ukrainian by Nina Shevchuk-Murray.

Published by AmazonCrossing
P.O. Box 400818
Las Vegas, NV 89140

ISBN-13: 9781611090116
ISBN-10: 1611090113
Library of Congress Control Number: 2012946025

For Mom and Rostyk

Regardless of their original functions, objects buried for an extended time underground or under water become archeological artifacts. At the moment they are recovered, their new history begins. Being buried underground often results in damage ... to both organic and inorganic materials.... The goal of preventative conservation is to arrest the progress of such destruction by ensuring optimal storage conditions.

—From "Cultural Welfare: Restoration of
Archeological Finds in Berlin's
State Museums," exhibit guide,
Altes Museum, Berlin,
March 27–June 1, 2009

To know what's happened to us ... wait for us.

—A 1952 inscription on a wall of the Lviv KGB prison,
open to the public since 2009
as the Lontsky Street Prison Museum

THE MUSEUM OF ABANDONED SECRETS
✱ FAMILY TREE ✱

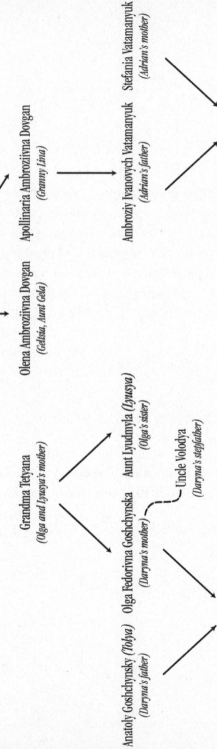

CONTENTS

Room 1. This

And then come the photos: black and white, faded into a caramel-brown sepia, some printed on that old dense paper with the embossed dappling and white scalloped edges like the lace collars of school uniforms, all from the pre-Kodak era—the era of the Cold War and nationally manufactured photography supplies (really, nationally manufactured every-thing)—and yet, the women in the pictures are adorned with the towering mousses of chignons, those stupid constructions of dead and, more often than not, someone else's (ugh) hair. They are dressed in the same stiff rectangular dresses as the ladies in a Warhol film or, as say, Anouk Aimée in *8½* (a film they could have actually seen, or at least had a theoretical chance of seeing, if they endured the five-hour wait in the squeeze of the film-festival crowd, then fought their way into the movie hall, sweaty and ecstatic, with those chignons knocked askew and with dark multicolored horseshoes of sweat in the armpits of the white nylon blouses that one always wore with one's best colored chemises—nationally manufactured, naturally—cerulean, pink, lilac).

But the photos can't show you the chemises or the moist horse-shoes, nor could anyone reproduce the smell of those lines—of bodies still naïve to deodorant, but generously floured with powder and rouge and scented with Indian Sandalwood from the Red Moscow factory or, at best, though no less cloying, with the Polish-made May Be. No one could ever restore that mottled chorus of perfume and the women's hot flesh, and in the pictures—freshly made-up and with their hair just so—the women could easily pass for Anouk Aimée's contemporaries with no Iron Curtain visible from where I stand forty years later.

You know what I just thought? Women are generally less susceptible to political perturbations than men. They pull on their nylon stockings, or later, the hose that were so hard to find in the stores, and smooth them over their legs with the same concentration no matter what—Kennedy assassinations or tanks in the streets of Prague—and that's why it is men who truly define the face of a country (at least the country we once had).

Do you remember the hats the men wore? Those identical furry cubes with earflaps, same for all, like a uniform. Pyzhyk. That's what the fur was called, that's right, herds of silently black pyzhyks lined up in military precision on the terrace of Lenin's Mausoleum on the 7th of November, and it was invariably pouring—as if the whole universe were in mourning—while stressed-out column organizers barked at the marchers like guard dogs at chain gangs because the columns were to pass in front of the mausoleum without umbrellas, bareheaded in the rain or snow, so as not to spoil the picture on TV (not that we had color TVs, our national manufacturers hadn't quite "overtaken" the West on that front yet).

But you protest. Those had come around by the seventies, except they were impossible to find and expensive as hell.

Alright, what's next? This stern-faced rug rat in a romper with pom-poms, that's you, too? And the woman holding you on her lap, who's that? Granny Lina? The picture casts a spell—grips you and doesn't let go—maybe because just as the photographer closed the shutter, the woman lowered her eyes to the baby with that preoccupied and beatific expression that all women have when they hold a child—theirs or someone else's—leaving us on this side of the lens, waiting for her to look up again, while the picture grows more disconcerting the longer you look, especially when you know that the woman is long gone from this world, and we will never know what she would've looked like had she blinked and raised her eyes from the baby that instant.

As if I didn't have plenty of my own ghosts—my own unfading, caramel-shiny brown faces, dappled with the pox of the same raster that cannot be Photoshopped away. Pictures that when scanned lose their soul—like poems translated from one language to another—looking dreadfully pitiful on screen, as if they'd been pulled out of the water and hung to dry on an invisible wire. Raised from the bottom of the sea, one could say, the phrase calling up a subconscious habit of perception: there they were, buried under silt and water, and we found them and brought them back to light—like it's some great favor or something. Where exactly does it come from, I'd like to know, this ineradicable attitude of superiority toward the past? This stubbornly dumb, can't-kill-it-with-an-ax conviction that we, the now, critically and categorically know better than they, the past. Is it from the mere fact that their future is known to us, that we know what happens? (Nothing good.) It's much the way we treat small children—pedantic and permissive at the same time. And we always think of the people of the past—just as we do of children—as being naïve in everything from their clothes and hairstyles to their thoughts and feelings. Even when those people are our own family. Or rather, had been, once.

"What are you thinking about?"

"I don't know. Us, I guess."

This is the difference between a marriage and all other (however volcanically eruptive) affairs and flings—this obligatory exchange of ghosts. Your dead become mine and vice versa. The list of names submitted for All Souls' Mass grows longer: as always, there is Anatoly, Lyudmyla, Odarka, Oleksander, Fedir, and Tetyana, but after them come, like a new orchestra section joining a symphony in a drawn-out, lowering, celloed, and double-bassed andante, Apollinaria, Stefania, Ambroziy, Volodymyra—names that sound as if they belonged to a completely different nation, and maybe it was a different nation after all, the one wiped out in 1933 between Kyiv and Poltava—a tribe whose members have names like Thalimon or Lampia or Porf or Thekla, names that make one think of early Christians and not at all of relatives and kin just two or three generations removed. The Western, Galician, Catholic names from the same time sound alive in comparison, however vaguely—but still there are people who can say, that's my uncle, that's my grandpa, that one perished in Siberia, and this one emigrated to Canada.

That's when you recall, with an addled nostalgic smile that spreads on your face slowly, out-of-focus—like milk spilled on a table—how one day in the early eighties a box came for your family from Canada, from just such a brother-of-a-third-cousin-once-removed uncle. The KGB let it through somehow, either because it was already busy packing up or just plain and simple had lost its grip, like everything in this country that turned loose and flabby right before the finale. A real Canadian box containing no flower-rimmed, square shawl that the diaspora insisted on supplying in great numbers to the Old Country but *jeans*—sweet Jesus!—your very first Levi's, and a denim shirt to go along, and then in the foreign-currency-only Beryozka store your parents bought you real Adidas sneakers and an Adidas backpack, and that's how you arrived at school, every day.

And for an instant I hurt again with a hot cramp in my stomach, with that retrospective, and therefore meaningless, teenage jealousy—as if this picture of yourself that you remember sends me tumbling twenty years back, right along with you, frozen at my school desk, unable to take my eyes off the most hopelessly unattainable boy in our class. You don't even notice me—you wouldn't notice the girl I was then, an acne-pocked, straight-A student with a wet-noodle braid on my shoulder—you never would, except maybe to politely open a door for me. Boys like you from good families, plied with early success, always have good manners because you have no need to draw attention to yourselves with stupid pranks; nothing better than positive life experience to engender friendliness—that superficial, tepid good-naturedness, like a constant body temperature, that is utterly impervious to aggression—or sympathy.

"Incredible," I say, shaking my head, but you don't understand; you're not on the same wavelength, and you continue surfing along on your own frequency, registering my comment as a quick burst of applause for your past triumphs with girls. You toss it, with a small clink, into that twenty-years-ago drawer in your mind; and so we stay, just as we were—each with our own drawers whose contents haven't mixed, haven't even been put out side by side and really compared. And that's what I meant by incredible.

How could we hope to conduct our dead-relatives exchange— to cross these ghostly bloodlines that stretch into the most impenetrable reaches of time—if we can't even manage to marry our younger selves, that boy and that girl who used to fall in love with other girls and boys, who both lay awake at night in different cities without the slightest inkling of each other's existence? And the worst of it is that they are still here—that boy and that girl. They must be if I am still capable of such idiotic jealousy toward your high-school sweetheart—never mind that I met her decidedly in the present tense, precisely so that I could get over it once and for all, because the comparison now was not at all in her favor. She turned out to be a rather dour, prickly, thick-boned, and lumpy-looking matron, like the former project engineers who now have to sell secondhand clothes off cots in street markets; and she had those deep-set eyes—like soot-black hollows—that with the passing of time seem to be increasingly the result of constant crying or no less constant drinking, aging their owner beyond her years.

On top of that, she didn't even smile when we met, which leads me to conclude that *her* life experience thus far has not proved particularly conducive to friendliness—it is quite possible that first schoolgirl love remains her only bright spot—and so I ought to pity her, both as a fellow human being and as a woman. But like hell I can, because I am still not sure which woman it is that you see in there: This current one, or this one and the one from back then, together, a shadowbox backlit with a time-denying glow from another dimension. If it's the latter, the deck is stacked against me because the only me you know is the present-day me, cut with an ax at a year-old whorl—a single thin line, no matter how wonderful the shape it draws.

"You're like a little bird … my schoolgirl …"

"How am I a schoolgirl?"

"It's your body—it's like a teenage girl's. It's fantastic."

"What is?"

"That it has managed to stay this way."

"What a prick!"

"Oh, am I now?" you say, very agreeably, turning me on my back. Your hands' capacity to coax out of my flesh musical tones—so varied in pitch and color, audible to myself alone (a little like the minimalists, like Philip Glass, only this makes Glass look like a rookie; he couldn't have dreamed of such a palette ...)—once again forces me to enter a different kind of listening: with my eyes closed, focused completely on the pictures that flash and flicker on the insides of my eyelids, like a symphony—first come pale fronds of fern, unfurling slowly, as if underwater, with the fluid precision of Japanese prints; then the surface breaks into a rich dollop of tropical emerald green that grows darker and darker until it congeals and hardens into the aching point of my nipple, and at exactly the moment when I am about to cry out with real pain, the pressure releases, spills into a caressing flood, and a round, fiery-orange sun rises triumphantly above the horizon. The joy makes me laugh out loud. I am now all living, spinning wet clay in the hands of a master potter, a musical sculpture.

"You're not supposed to applaud after the overture," you say from somewhere in the dark, as if already inside me, and your hands keep moving with merciless precision—this gift of yours—and I begin to die again, as usual (How *do* you do that?) long before you enter and fill me entirely; and when you finally do, all that's left of me is a form, a mold—warmed with the gentle glow of gratitude, fluid and flexible—into which you pour all of yourself with the desperate force of nature, the all-consuming fire and rock. Oh you, you, you, my love, my nameless one (in these moments you don't have a name, cannot be named any more than infinity itself)—a primordial boom, a flash of newly born planets, an eclipse, a scream. Of course, this is incredible luck; you and I have been unbelievably, unfairly lucky—so lucky it's frightening.

Why us? And what price shall we be asked to pay for this? But just think about it—I murmur in blissful lethargy, my nose tucked securely into your not-yet-cooled neck, with its sweat, with its warm, spicy (Cinnamon? Cumin?), manly scent—millions of people must have lived their whole lives and never experienced anything like this (although, come to think of it, how would we know?—but something inexorably fills happy lovers with this unshakeable certainty that they are the first since creation). And that's why there isn't a single reason (and if there had been, it's been washed away with the tidal wave), not a single good reason, to rewind and reflect upon that "schoolgirl" and the fact that you persist—as if you'd be an idiot not to—in your stubborn, hand-callusing work of merging me—in the sum total of all emotions and sensations, sensory memory included—of binding me in with your first love.

This would be the moment to ask with affected cynicism something like, "What, you're an expert in schoolgirls? Nymphophile? How exactly would you know?" But a question like that would do no more than disrupt the mining machinery of memory—an intrusion as careless as calling after a sleepwalker as he makes his way along the edge of a roof, and with the same risk of having the roused man tumble to his death. No, let it all be; let it go as it goes. I'm not the one to take a wrench to someone else's brain. And really shouldn't I be flattered? Or at least reassured? What more reliable proof of his undying love can a man give a woman than to plug her (to borrow from electrical engineering) into the network of the first female images set into the concrete foundation of his imagination: his mother, his sister, the girl next door? (And women do this, too: all of us plug each other into one thing or the other, ready to replace breakers, find missing wires, and wrap it all thickly with insulation tape until—boom!—the circuit shorts with a jolt.)

Dear sisterhood: Let us all love our mother-in-laws, for they are our future; they are the women we will become in thirty years (otherwise, your beloved would never have noticed you, would never have recognized you). Let us love our rivals, past and present, for each one of those women has something of ours, something that we ourselves fail to notice and prize and that, for him, is sure to be most important. Shit, does this mean I have something in common with that droopy-faced hag with eyes like burnt holes in a blanket!?

And this is just the beginning, Lord. Just the beginning.

Apollinaria, Stefania, Ambroziy, Volodymyra. (How comical these cloche hats from the Jazz Age of the already-past century: these tightly fitted little felt pots, pulled down to just above the eyebrows and banded with silk—you know it's silk because it glistens even in the prints—with tiny brims and round tops; and the women's legs, always in stockings, even in summer. Just think how they must've sweated, poor things.) To shuffle the photos is to greet each one of them silently with my eyes, despite the fact that they're all long dead. I'm the one poorer for it.

It's not just me looking at them—they *do* look back. I realize this in an instant (I couldn't possibly explain this, even to you!) with the same precise and inexplicable certainty as I did one day, many years ago, at St. Sophia Cathedral when I had wandered in, lathered after a half-sleepless night, agitated not so much by any real events but by the much more deeply disturbing premonition of fundamental changes in my life—changes whose advance I could feel from all sides at once and which I knew portended the end of my youth.

The ticket office had just opened and I was the first visitor, all alone in the echoing and alert silence of the temple, where every step on the terrifying cast-iron floors rang all the way through the choir lofts. I stood at the bottom of the honey-thick twilight suspended in half-consciousness by a swirling, tilting pillar of sunlit dust until I suddenly felt a thrust at my chest: from a fresco on the opposite wall of a side nave, a white-bearded man in a blue, richly draped, floor-length cloak looked at me, his dry, walnut-colored palms pressed together. I felt faint—a soft, furry paw brushed me from inside—a shaky shard of a vision slashed through the air. Something stirred. I stepped closer but the man—this monk or statesman with the time-darkened face and those clearly drawn, typically Ukrainian contours that are also soft like the lines of aging mountains and that one still recognizes, so easily, in the faces of the men at the Besarabsky Market—was already looking at something else. Only the eyes— implacably dark and swollen with knowledge—burdened his face, as if not given quite enough room, and it seemed they would turn upon me again at any moment. I couldn't stand it and looked away first, and it was then that I saw what I had never noticed before, as if helped by a sudden shift of light: the cathedral was alive, it teemed with people—every wall and arch was inhabited with dimly silent, time-smudged women and men, and every one of them had the same otherworldly eyes, pregnant with the ecclesiastical pall of all-knowing.

All these eyes *saw* me. I stood there in view of a crowd, only it was not a crowd of strangers. They took me in with such kindness and understanding, as if they knew everything about me, so much more than I could ever know myself, and as I slowly dissolved— like a pat of butter in warm water—in their encircling gaze (I couldn't tell how long this lasted, time had stopped), it was suddenly revealed to me as the most obvious thing in the world that these people did not just live a thousand years *ago*; they had lived *for* a thousand years, taking in everything that had passed before their eyes until their gaze held the quintessence of time—the heavy slow suspension of a millennium, clots and crystals of time squeezed together like tightly pressed atomic nuclei. And I was before them, a mortal, barely nineteen. I wasn't even a woman yet to tell the truth (it was soon after that I became one), so perhaps mine was the kind of revelation classified in theological literature as a maiden's vision or some such. At any rate, never again, in any of the ancient holy places—not at the Athenian Parthenon, nor on the bare site of the Jerusalem Temple, nor in the Garden of Gethsemane—would those, visible or invisible, who persist in a place for ages, welcome me as one of their own. All I ever felt again—even when I managed to be alone with them—was their purposeful wariness, not menacing or defiant but more akin to a held breath, a whisper: *What do you want, woman?*

I must admit they have a point. Indeed, what business do I have with them? Having once accepted a man, a woman passes irretrievably into a different gravitational field—she simply falls into time, into a silt-clogged stream, falls with the entire weight of her earthly body, with her uterus and ovaries, these living chronometers. And time begins to flow through her, no longer pure (for when pure it does not flow at all, it stands still, like that day at St. Sophia; it is a single lake, a placid spill of the radiant dark-honeyed twilight) but *embodied* as she is in her clan—her kin—in the endless chromosomal rosary of the dying and resurrecting genotype that pulses with mortal flesh into that which we call—for lack of a more accurate term—human history, every one of us plugged into a serial circuit and once in, you cannot jump out, you cannot see the whole thing from outside. Unless you're a nun—but it's too late for me now.

And so now I don't know what I'm supposed to do with this new feeling. They look at me from these old photos as if I owe them something—I shrink and shy in their heavy gaze that reaches so far beyond the moment captured by the camera, unsure about what it is they expect of me. It's as if they don't know if they can trust me, like they need to size me up, to see if I am good enough for the family, how serious my intentions really are. (Good Lord, what nonsense am I thinking?!) These women with their cloche hats and their thighs sheathed in sun-spotted Jazz-Age dresses (it is a clear summer day, and there are trees in the background that might still be growing in the same spot, and a dog, his tongue wearily lolling from his mouth) and their buttoned-up, sporty-looking boys in turtlenecks and breeches, and men with black moustaches like butterfly wings above their lips, later called Hitler moustaches (but Hitler hadn't yet come to power, and across the Zbruch River no one had yet stacked mummified-alive corpses like hay, and Lemyk hadn't shot Consul Mailov, and Matseiko hadn't taken aim at Minister Pieracki ...).

And then here are those after the war, in incomparably poorer rags, who managed to live despite it all, the *remainers,* or better, the *survivors,* meaning the nonetheless living. (Which sounds so much kinder, doesn't it?) And here is a tiny snapshot after the deportation, with oppressive, low-slung volcanoes on the horizon (Kolyma? Transbaikal?), and the boy in the foreground is struck with a completely different leanness, not the athletic kind but the thoroughly plebeian, hunger-worn kind. He wears a baggy jacket with hideously padded Terminator shoulders, and so does the young woman with poodle-like curls next to him. Both are laughing into the camera; their heads are close together yet their hands are behind their backs, as if still under the armed guards' command, but laughing joyfully nonetheless, laughing from their hearts—their entire beings so happy about something. What is it, one wonders, that could make them so happy there?

Something painfully familiar flashes in the tight ripples around the man's mouth, like déjà vu or a dream you can't recall in the morning. I must have seen this same expression in your face, must have caught its fleeting, uncanny breath on your features, gone in an instant without a trace, a message from a long-gone soul who has only this one way of reminding us about himself—and if I look carefully (What exactly do you imagine I've been doing here all this time, gulping down eyeful after eyeful?), I can find something of yours in many of these faces, something imperceptibly altered but shared nonetheless, as if an errant beam of an invisible torch-light, dancing over them, flashed you out of an accidental fold of another's features or in a turn of another's head. Here, here it is; it almost coheres but again merely almost, and the dream of unrecognition goes on, growing slowly more nightmarish, as if now I am chasing a fleeing ghost.

"Here's my paternal great-uncle," you introduce with a note of involuntary solemnity, or perhaps it just sounds solemn to me, and I define silently: Paternal great-uncle means the brother of your paternal grandfather. My lips stretch idiotically in the smile of a well-brought-up girl who is working hard to be liked by these adults—pleasure to meet you—and suddenly a blinding, shimmering veil of tears slips across my sight, and I hurry to swallow them, blinking them away before you notice because, like all mama's boys, you automatically interpret a woman's tears as a personal reproach, instantly growing sullen, as if you've been struck, as if, except for you, there is nothing for a woman to cry about in this world. I'm sorry, dear, but I don't have it in me to resist the numbing spread of this insane, universal tenderness that pools under my skin like blood from a thousand wounds—this visceral, glandular, animal pity for these dead, for their youth, their speech, their laughter no longer audible from where we are, their piercingly pitiful, child-like innocence to the impenetrable gloom that awaits them. Or, perhaps, it is the pity I feel for you and me, for the two orphans abandoned to fend for themselves—like Hansel and Gretel in the dark, dark forest—two lonely shipwrecks washed up onto the shore of the new century by the last, life-draining effort of so many ruined generations of men and women whose only achievement in the long run was to bring us into this world. And on this we ought to congratulate them posthumously, because most of their peers didn't even manage that.

"Don't cry."

"I'm not."

"Please, what is it?" (with your brooding, almost injured face and your immediate impulse to hold me against your chest, to stroke my hair, to shush).

"It's okay. It's over now, I'm sorry." Let's go on. To the 1960s chignons and nylon raincoats, to the things that already pop up in our own childhood memories, things that are no longer photographic but fully corporeal, with a feel and a smell: I remember how loudly one of these raincoats rustled when we hid under it in the wardrobe. And, oh, I had a toy bunny just like that, in short pants and a lace ruff! I just can't remember what it did when you wound it up. Beat on its drum?

Looks like I'm still playing the little girl's role; and you've got the adult part this time: You are the ambassador for all your dead.

You do look like you've grown older just in the time spent with them, grown out of the lankiness, the floppy-eared-ness of that loose-limbed boy who walked as if scooping up some extra space, and whom I followed with my eyes from behind my window, until he disappeared around the corner, a thread unspooling, only the thread came out of myself—my own body—like a silkworm's.

Sometimes I am overcome by an almost maternal pride—as if I were the one who brought you into this world, so well put-together, with such relaxed grace in every gesture. The previous generation of "exemplary boys"—those Soviet ones who were destined to be "pioneers," "Komsomol men," and then "Communists" (and turned out exactly so)—moved differently, more stiffly, with the implacable military uniformity of the future pyzhyk hat wearers, still so easy to spot in any international airport that one doesn't have to think twice about coming right up and chatting with them in Russian. And perhaps that's why I couldn't ever stand them—those exemplary ones—and why I—the straight-A student with big bows in her hair—gravitated inexorably to the punks, although, of course, you are no punk, and there is no one to whom you could be compared—there were no such boys in the days of my youth; they hadn't been bred yet. This must be whence my fits of maternal pride, this feeling never known with any man before. Not the "look what I've got" feeling on those mornings when I wake up first and, pulling back the covers, stare with hungry curiosity anew at the man stretched out on his back beside me, and weigh, like a merchant, my life's loot in pounds; and not the blood-bubbling thrill, like a burst of champagne, when I am approaching from a distance and you haven't seen me yet: "And a man like this loves me!" Not the first, or the second, but a kind of a spellbound, puppy-like wonder, as if I've shaken off sleep, rubbed my eyes, and still cannot believe it. Can this be my man, exactly as I imagined him? (And I have always imagined *him* since my now-distant school days!) So alive, so real, so much more unexpected, nuanced, and interesting than I myself could ever have invented; so big and skillful with his *let me do this* and really so much better at every task than I am (even at cutting bread—he gets paper-thin, uniformly even slices, a pleasure to behold, while all I can manage are thick unwieldy chunks, lopsided and saw-edged as if a hungry beast mauled the poor loaf). And most importantly (I boast to my girlfriends silently, and then aloud, no qualms whatsoever), most importantly, he does everything with this amazingly natural ease and simplicity that must have something to do with his infinitely touching grace, like a young animal's—the complete lack of any need, rooted in the body, to pretend to be something other than himself (to march in step, to keep eyes on the head of the man in front, to look the boss in the eyes and lie with an unclouded gaze).

No, I certainly could not bestow upon him this gift of organic dignity, no drawer of my imagination held such a treasure, and never before had I encountered a person who could pass through falsehoods with the same calm ease, emerging utterly untouched by their falsity. Here my contribution amounts to staring in amazement—slack-jawed, like a child at a magician—and pondering how wonderful it is, after all, that it was not I who conjured you! For the first time, practically in my entire life, I can finally say it's great that I have no control whatsoever over what you are and what you might yet become. Even better, I don't want any. I am afraid of it; any intervention on my part would be for the worse.

You, naturally, entertain no such notions. Who knows what kind of notions you do entertain about me? Sometimes I get a bit scared—love generally is a scary thing, happy love no less than unhappy, only for some reason no one ever talks about that.

Fear blew through that very first moment when you—smiling as if at an old friend—set out toward me across the bedlam of the TV studio and the chaos seemed to dissipate before you—to disappear from the frame—so irrelevant was it to you as you stepped over the thickets of tangled cords and swerved around treacherous machinery with the grace of a nocturnal animal in the dark woods, and inside me suddenly surged the intoxicating sensation of a mind at the brink of collapse. As if the invisible wall that separates us from chaos slid apart, and one could now expect anything: this new young man of unclear origins could be a psycho, for example, one of those maniacs who keeps calling and lies in wait at the studio entrance—only psychos don't have such openly childish smiles (and, simultaneously, as if on a parallel track, sped the rueful thought, he must have a girlfriend, a young one, one of those hip ones in a strappy top and tight little pants); and that's when I heard your voice addressing me and froze for an instant, because you dropped this outrageous question as casually as if we had played in the same sandbox, only you'd stepped out for, oh, thirty years or so, but now you're back and ...

"Have you been looking for me?"

That was a hell of an introduction!

"Why would I be looking for you?" I shot back, quite sensibly, as I willed the cracking wall back into place and the surrounding world into a semblance of normalcy, but the world had already turned—like a dress, inside out—and I saw myself through this young man's eyes: still in makeup from the recent recording, as if cut out from a TV screen, which always produces in newbies a staggering effect—like the familiar flat picture has been replaced with a 3-D one and alive on top of that (you can try it on for size, see how this woman fits—how she's just tall enough for the top of her head to brush against your lips). My face like a cream puff, hair brushed smoothly back so that no one would be left ungraced by the sight of my exquisite ears, the rest of me packaged into a leather vest and a white musketeer blouse from Bianco (thanks to the sponsors mentioned in the final credits), with black—and, by the way, seriously tight—jeans. All the cameramen love getting shots of me entering the set from afar, full-length and legs in the frame. You can tell I fixed what I was wearing that day in my memory, forever—that unmistakable sign of all momentous events in our lives—although at that moment, my TV-star getup was strapped on tight like a bulletproof vest, in full combat mode.

What is it you imagine you want, kid? And who the hell are you anyway, for me to be "looking for" you?

"I was told you're looking to make a film about Olena Dovganivna."

Aha.

"And you care because?"

"That was my granny. My great-aunt, actually," you added with a quick apologetic smile.

He does have a sweet smile, I thought then; it lights his face like the sun breaking through the clouds, though his lips move only a little. Something at first made me classify him as one of the Russian-speaking, bracing myself for the forced, just-learned Ukrainian, tight as a new shoe, with foreign phonemes rubbed raw like blisters—"lookedd," "toldd" (for Christ's sake, unclench your teeth already!)—and the cringe-inducing hobbling through phrases as they translate them, word for word. It's like watching a drunk try to stay upright. Our producer talks like that, very deliberately, "I think calls into the air (meaning on-air calls) must be cut short." Or, "We are in need of a stronger show, with unique countenance." Unique what? Oh, content, unique content. Even the young man's purely Galician, "That was my granny," didn't prove anything since the linguistic neophytes eagerly borrowed the Galicians' colorful words—folksy phrases and even the trademark lilting intonations—only to deploy them in most unnatural ways, believing all the while that this is exactly what one ought to sound like when one speaks pure and authentic Ukrainian, which, to be fair, they may never have heard spoken by anyone other than a Galician. And it's not like Galicians can't speak Russian either. As soon as they land in Kyiv, they switch and chirp merrily along, as if they were keeping Ukrainian for their own secret use, behind layers of mysterious rites and seals of conspiracy.

Nor did it matter much that this boy introduced himself as the grandnephew of the Insurgent Army warrior, the woman who has gripped my imagination from the instant I saw her image on a faded archival shot—so radically different from her peasant-faced fellow insurgents, so neat and refined ("smart," as the locals would say), even in her guerrilla uniform, the army-issue belt wrapped around her small waist with such flawless style it wasn't as if she had just climbed out of an underground lair but was simply dressed for a hunt across her family's lands (you could almost imagine a riding crop in hand behind her back and her pack of purebred hounds just outside the frame, straining their leashes and whimpering with excitement).

No, the boy's ostensibly intimate—blood!—bond to her (admittedly, one could glimpse a resemblance in his lips, his eyes) was not, in itself, a recommendation. Our old gang (Where are they now?) remembers all too well how in the early nineties the great-grandson of the legendary nationalist Mykola Mikhnovsky introduced himself as "a thoroughly Russian person" at "democratic" haunts along Khreshchatyk—all those long-defunct "Dips" and "Culinary Cafés"—and could even be prompted to read Russian monarchist poems of his own composition, which no doubt made his ancestors spin in their graves like chicken on a spit. And we won't even say anything about the descendants of the less-notorious historical personages. Ukrainian families changed faiths, languages, and national flags in practically every generation—sometimes faster than fashion, like addicts going through needles: a shot in the arm and toss this one out the window, grab a new one, and so on, for the entire span of our recorded history, beginning, most likely, with Kostyantyn Ostroz'ky who founded the Ostrog Academy to counter the Polish expansion only to see his granddaughter convert to Catholicism and deliver the Academy—lock, stock, and barrel—to the very Jesuits her granddaddy had spent his entire life fighting. This would appear to be our only national tradition that survives to this day—this compulsion to offer ourselves up to whoever rules the day—so you can't expect me to swallow this kind of bait, strung like the Bible on a line of "begats."

And to add to your disappointment, love, I must confess that I did not observe any fateful switches clicking in me to meld your grinning mug with the oh-so-compelling visage of the woman whose story tantalized my imagination, nor did I sense any immediate spiritual kinship, or an exciting twist of fate, or any other such nonsense that could be interpreted, in a pinch, to portend the events that were about to stun us. Hate to break it to you, sweetie, but I felt nothing, nothing whatsoever, even if you don't believe me and get upset, because *How could this be?* Zilch, nada. Aside from the momentary loss of self, prompted by the suddenly parted wall—a feeling akin to a vestibular hallucination, as when you didn't smoke quite enough pot at a party: the world's ablaze but the fear's still with you.

And to be completely honest, I did not really expect much from this new connection to Dovganivna's family—even though I had begun to look for someone, not yet sure who exactly—because experience has taught me that the hero's relatives, and especially those of the once-removed variety, are of little use. The best one can hope to wring out of them, with luck, is a few old photos from the family album if they haven't been lost forever to arrests or searches, and maybe—with some special, incredible luck—a shred of an utterly irrelevant personal memory, something that Mom, or an aunt, or an uncle's sister-in-law (women are better memory keepers) mentioned while knitting mittens or stuffing varenyki—a meaningless, accidental dollop of information rolling around in someone's mind like an unidentifiable piece of a lost gadget or the cap, at the bottom of a drawer, to a long-drained bottle of cough syrup. A useless, random recollection that, say, shortly before his death the now-famous ancestor asked for pear compote, which stuns you for a moment while you search for an appropriate response: Is this something Proustian, a madeleine dipped in tea? Or they might tell you that the dining table on the family home's (destroyed, naturally) verandah was made out of unvarnished planks of wood, rough to the touch in that way that pine is, you know—uh-huh, thank you very much, that's very interesting, but I'm afraid we're running out of film. Meaning that for the last fifteen minutes the director has been making faces at me like he's about to vomit and sawing his throat with his hand, until his histrionics make me laugh and I lose the thread of the conversation—although in fact I find such memory garbage no less compelling than the story that we cut, squeeze, condense, spice up, and serve to the public in a neat thirty-minute package.

Oh, I mastered that kind of cookery just fine and turned out my product with a practiced hand and my own feel for the ingredients. But these unwanted shards of someone else's life, which could be discarded with such casual finality—and which had been so precious and full of meaning while the person was alive and perhaps loved in a way that made every such detail glow as a special gift—never failed to strike me as pathetically frail, like unearthed remnants of vanished civilizations. After all, wasn't this about the only thing that remained *truly theirs*, something that could not be bequeathed or recycled, forged or refashioned to match new ideologies, publicized in newspapers and on TV until the last modicum of the departed person's presence was stomped out, unraveled, lost under a thousand footprints?

After the death of Vlada Matusevych—Vlada whose dear little face with its pointy, birdlike features was posthumously rebranded by glossy women's magazines until after a while even I could look at one of her mass-reproduced portraits without having my heart cramp—I had ample opportunity to learn that it is only such useless trifles of memory that have a chance to remain solidly present, and I kept one for myself: Vlada, the very definition of petite, had the habit of almost touching whomever she was talking to, of insinuating herself into their space with one smooth balletic pas—her back slightly bent and her head held high, looking like an unwinding lasso, or a cat about to leap into a tree—which unsettled even the most recalcitrant political gorillas. And for me, everything that used to be called Vlada Matusevych is contained—like an ocean in a drop of its water—in this one movement.

How could you show this on film? Even if you could, if you found it somewhere, on a friend's cell-phone video or a clip from a birthday, a party, someone's wedding—she was a fashionable artist; she was everywhere all the time, and there had been so much of her that in the first months after her death, Kyiv seemed deserted—even if you had it on film, what would it mean to anyone?

I have come to think that a person's life is not so much, or rather is *not just*, the dramatically arched story with a handful of characters (parents, children, lovers, friends, and colleagues—anyone else?) that we pass on more or less in one piece to our descendants. It's only from the outside that life looks like a narrative, or when viewed backwards through a pair of mental binoculars we put on when we have to fit ourselves into the small oculars of résumés, late-night kitchen confessions, and home-spun myths, trimming and shaping life into orderly eyefuls. When seen from the inside, life is an enormous, bottomless suitcase, stuffed with precisely such indeterminate bits and pieces, utterly useless for anyone other than its owner. A suitcase carried, irredeemably and forever, to the grave. Maybe a handful of odds and ends fall out along the way (a request for pear compote, a sinuous balletic pas like that of a cat about to pounce) and remain to rot in the minds of witnesses and mourners, so whenever I stumbled into one of those lost, disowned scraps I was filled with a vague but insistent shame of my inadequacy, as if this piece, this accidental survivor, contained the key—the lost secret code to the deep, subterranean core of the other person's life—and now I have it, but I don't know which door it unlocks or if such a door even exists.

***

I didn't get this from TV, from the stories and people in front of the camera.

There was the day when, for some reason leafing through an old pulpy book from my father's library, I ran into a note in the margin of a yellowed coarse page (Soviet newspaper stock) in Dad's characteristically dense, thorny script (sometime in the seventh or eighth grade my own handwriting aspired to imitate his, but eventually mellowed out, untangled, and came to resemble Mom's) written next to the apparently innocuous, idiotic critique, "Hamlet's hesitation to act decisively in sight of triumphing evilness." (God, the language! Still struggling to find its way out from under the debris of Stalin's pogroms, limping and dragging on broken-splintered bones.)

He underlined this critique with an impulsive, nearly straight line, and scrawled an equally triumphing *this!!!* with three exclamation marks in the margin. It struck me like a divinely inspired epiphany. In that instant I realized I didn't know my father. He died when I was barely seventeen. I only remembered him the way he was in relationship to me as a teenager, a child, and from those memories, amended with a few cryptic posthumous (and petrified for lack of new material) remarks from Mom, his friends, colleagues, and his students—who seemed to have adored him unless they are all lying—I constructed a mental image: an avatar with the appearance of my father as I remembered him at forty-five, hospitalized and almost at the end of his bleak story, the kind not uncommon for his generation. And yet this man ... no, wait ... a much younger man (I did the math quickly: he would've been younger than I am now!) who read this book sometime in the late fifties or early sixties, before I was here (a mythical formula that inevitably prompts a child to ask, "And where was I?"), and scribbled his enthusiastic *this!!!* in the margins—exactly as I would have done had I found an idea I recognized as similar to my own, sympathetic to something I'd been thinking, turning over, worrying, living—was beyond the contours of the simulacrum I carried in my mind, as if the two—this one and the one in my head—didn't know each other; or rather, I didn't know this other, new one.

This man and I shared, I could tell, a vague but fundamental kinship; I could see so clearly (from inside, as we see ourselves in dreams) how in that instant the pieces of the puzzle triumphantly clicked into place in his mind—*this!!!*—a snap like the sound he might've made with his fingers, the thumb and the middle one, just as I do sometimes, in moments of intense excitement. And suddenly I recalled that he did have the habit of snapping his fingers and that it irked Mom, who told him it was vulgar and a bad example for the child, which made him sheepish—and this was new, too, because I'd never remembered him to be anything but very confident. I don't think I'd ever heard him say, "I don't know" or "I was wrong."

But something had been shaken loose in my memory, and another wave of recollection washed over me: one night I found the bunny I'd drawn in my school sketchbook covered in inexplicable blue spots, and I went bonkers—and Dad, mortified like a little boy caught red-handed, confessed that it was his fault; he wanted to make the bunny gray but just missed a bit with the color. At the time I seethed with righteous indignation; I could not grasp why he would've sneaked into my sketchbook and touched my paints—he who'd never put a drop of paint on a shred of paper in his entire life, who didn't even know how to hold a brush!—and, for a long time, I'd bring up the ruined bunny whenever I needed to one-up him, because it never failed to shame him again. Only now, with this new internal vision, did I see this little prank as it must have felt to him, and realized that it wasn't the act of spoiling my picture (for which I, the incurable perfectionist, still got an A!) that he was ashamed of, but his inability to resist his childish impulse—the sudden spark of curiosity, the urge to watch the paint billow in the jar of water, watch it fill the brush and color the white spots on the paper— and that he, a grown man and a *paterfamilias*, was caught in this momentary, unbefitting weakness.

All of this was unspooling, faster and faster, one thing pulling on another, as if the inky scribble in the margin, like a loose thread I grasped, had led to a vast sunken rhizome—a lace of feathery roots that retained the shape of an entirely different, unfamiliar life, one independent of a daughter, a wife, or any friends—but I had no means of seeing it clearly, up close. He had taken his suitcase with him.

I remember I climbed with my feet into the armchair and scoured the whole book, inventing a new reading method on the spot: not from left to right, or from right to left, but in concentric circles, chewing on the text, like the hungry caterpillar, beginning with the underlined phrase, "Hamlet's hesitation to act decisively in sight of triumphing evilness." I had no other key—no other trin-ket had slipped into my hands from the suitcase that had already been taken away from me—nothing that wouldn't have turned into dust in the twenty years since Father died. So I pondered *this!!!*, so casual in the margin, like detective Columbo scrutinizing a set of uncommon tooth marks on a cigarette holder that he'd found next to the body; the only difference was I wasn't looking for the murderer—I wanted to raise the dead.

What the book was about I couldn't tell you under threat of torture, but by the end of my necromantic investigation I became firmly convinced that my father's long "struggle against the system" (as we Ukrainians have been calling it since 1991)—his desperate knocking on all those imposing oak doors; his countless letters, complaints, reports, and petitions to the Kyiv City Council, the Solicitor General's Office, the Ukrainian Central Communist Party Committee, and the Central Committee in Moscow (three or four bulging folders, held by strings tied into dead, eternal knots and stored in Mom's attic); his trips to Moscow, each of which was supposed to resolve things once and for all, only every time they sent his query back to Kyiv and he had to start the cycle all over again—the whole gory mess that replaced his life and that finally sent him to the loony bin with the then-typical political diagnosis of "acute paranoid psychopathy," stemmed from nothing other than my father's secret knowledge that he, too, shared, like a shameful disease, Hamlet's damned hesitation to act decisively in sight of triumphing evilness. And when the evil imperial machine rolled by, almost but not quite brushing him, it was this knowledge that prevented him from stepping back, that compelled him to throw himself in its path, and made him do so, again and again, each time recapturing the right to self-respect.

And I'm still convinced of it.

The crippled, poorly written phrase turned out to be his watermark, an enduring epitaph to his life, which ended just as crippled: try and fit it into the format of a documentary story and you'll have to close with a drawn-out physical decline—a dimming consciousness, struggling against the clamor of excruciating pain in every muscle caused by the rattling doses of insulin which the Soviet criminal psychiatry (as it later came to light) dispensed especially generously—and you'd have to show that hospital-issue robe, the color of cornflowers, which I remembered him wearing when Mom and I were finally allowed to come visit him in Dinpropetrovsk; and his skinny, yellow legs with bulging joints; and his stiff feet that stuck out from under the robe, like chicken feet from a shopping bag (enveloped in a well-aged sticky smell of urine or unwashed skin); and a slow, murky turn of dull eyeballs without a drop of reflected light, shriveled like an old man's (signs of constant dehydration).

None of this has any heroic or romantic potential, especially when we remember that this dragged on for years, and that's completely unentertaining, which is why such things get swallowed by "Five years later" or, in somebody else's case, "Twenty-five years later." Really, you can't expect anyone to keep watching that long! (There's no other way to make this kind of story into a film, no way to touch the audience—which means there is no story, no pitch, as any producer will tell you, better luck next time.) That's the rub: my father's daily struggles, in and before the hospital, not the days of his research and teaching career, but his battle with what ended it, and then ended him—the floods of letters he'd sent, the useless appointments he'd gone to, the whole absurd and exhausting war that was lost before it had even begun because once engaged, the system would not and could not yield. And that's exactly what he was after, spending year after year in futile attempts to convince quite possibly the same people who had signed the orders he had come to protest that what they did was wrong. The entire narrative of his life, if we were to reconstruct it with documentary faithfulness—capturing all four folders and their knotted-to-death strings—had no point, only bitterness and waste. The point was in the epigraph, in the watermark. In a single, nearly straight line that was accidentally preserved.

There was another reason I knew this to be true. Exactly a year before, on a summer vacation in Crimea, by Kara-Dag, I had sneaked away from the rest of our group and spent half a day climbing the same cliff again and again, like Sisyphus, and leaping into the water below. The day was still and smothering hot, and every time I climbed I sweated like a horse, and my knees buckled, and my heart clattered somewhere in my throat. When I was little, I once hit the water with my stomach and had been afraid to dive ever since.

When I finally stumbled back into our camp at dusk, my legs twisted and turned under me as if I were hopelessly drunk, and it took all I had left to propel my body forward against the resistance of the air. My reputation as a daredevil, a thrill-loving adventure seeker who would do just about anything to get her adrenaline fix, had to have been carved in stone that night, and at dinner the men of the group couldn't take their suspiciously twinkling eyes off me, apparently convinced that any of them could come up with much more pleasurable means of supplying me with adrenaline. A few of their wives turned unattractively skittish, which put a bit of a damper on the blissful intoxication I had achieved with the powerful cocktail of two substances that are so hard to obtain for a professional intellectual (Is that what I am? Can a journalist in our country be an intellectual?): utter physical exhaustion and pride in a job well done. "Whatever did you do this for?" asked the puzzled Irka Mocherniuk, the only person who really cared to know, and I said, "Not what for, but why."

I dove because I was afraid of diving. I spent half a day doing great violence to myself on an empty shore under the blazing sun because the fear, once driven deep inside, lived on somewhere in my body like an invisible iron shackle that wouldn't let me move. I chipped at it with each dive, wore it thin and finally got rid of it. From that day on, my life held one less fear.

My father's note in the margins of that book helped me under-stand that he spent his whole life doing the same thing—climbing a cliff and leaping off. And not because he was some sort of natural hero, in fact, probably quite the opposite: he must've had to force himself do it every time. He had to break the shackles, to overcome "Hamlet's hesitation." At the beginning, he may have even believed that the whole case was a product of a high-ranking bureaucrat's wickedness and, if someone could just remove this evil impulse, like a speck of dust from an eye, the terrible, criminal ruination would stop and he wouldn't have to bear witness to what he called "the turning of a palace into a pigsty."

The Palace Ukraina was completed in the fall of 1970, and we went to the opening celebration as a family—this was the first palace in my life, a reality that finally gave shape to that fairytale word, something that matched the word's dazzling radiance and incomprehensible, immeasurable scale, flooding the shallow lagoon of my child-sized imagination. Since then, Ukraina, the most palatial of all concert halls, was where I imagined all kings and princesses to live, because it was simply the best in its festive 1970 incarnation, grander than anything I've seen to this day—the Klovsky Palace was obviously not fit for even the poorest princess, and the Mariyinksy was still closed to the public. Ukraina was in an utterly different league than all those Soviet-era Happiness Palaces, which I considered to be nothing but pretense since they looked no different from the structures that house winter farmers' markets. I have a vague memory (a view from the back of the crowd—women and children, on such great state occasions, were supposed to stay out of the way) of my father in the immense ocean of light that was the foyer, surrounded by tall (from my five-year-old vantage point), laughing men shaking each other's hands and of my own proud knowledge of my father's importance: "Daddy built this!"

Of course, he didn't really build it; he was just one of the experts who performed the engineering calculations, a newly-minted PhD with a suitably themed dissertation, a humble nut in a great machine really—if he stepped away, no one would have noticed. Several days later the man who actually built the place— the lead architect who had to have been there in that laughing swarm of Very Important Men receiving their congratulations and basking in his glory—left the office of the Central Committee's Secretary, went to the bathroom, locked the stall, and hung himself on his own belt. His palace turned out to be too good for Kyiv. It overshadowed the Kremlin Palace of Congresses, and that was not just indecency and arrogance, but a grave political misstep for which the Kyiv authorities were getting their asses thoroughly kicked, and those asses had to be saved by making steps, taking measures, and finding someone to blame, preferably, by opening a criminal inquiry into the theft of construction materials, but when their best candidate for the role of the thieving conspirator so blatantly refused to play along—going so far as to hang himself in the Committee's very own building—the inquiry, thank God and His new charge, was first postponed, and then disappeared altogether, as if flushed down the toilet, without a trace, so that soon everyone forgot about it, perfectly naturally, considering how often these things happened, impossible to keep track of them all.

Instead, Palace Ukraina was promptly closed "for renovation" and its interior efficiently stripped of the tasteful finishes, and everything—the carefully varnished beech parquet floors; the dove-gray, worsted-wool upholstery; the stained-glass lamps— was replaced with whatever was cruder, cheaper, and plebeian, so that when it opened again, a couple of months later, with the acid-blue armchairs that are still there today, I did not recognize the magical palace of my fairytales: it was gone, disappeared into thin air just as a fairytale palace would if a genie picked it up and carried it to the other side of the world in one night. Only then we at least would have had the emptiness that alone can be a fitting monument for the structure that had perished (as Ground Zero remained for years, an abysmal wound among Lower Manhattan's skyscrapers, but we have seen our share of wounds like that long before—how many of them gape, like knocked-out teeth, in Kyiv's streets, marking the sites of blown-up churches, of which only those whose place hasn't been taken by a grain elevator or a Young Pioneers' Palace are still remembered). But this palace stood right where it had been, obligingly and garishly retrofitted to resemble a humble provincial movie theater, all in one piece, and with the same name, so that one could begin to believe that the other, the original, was a figment of the collective imagination, something we all happily hallucinated together, after too much champagne, but we're sober now, tovarishchi, and that's what reality looks like: just an unfortunate mishap, an old story, really, and not even enough to call it a story—a bit of oversight, the guilty have been reprimanded, back to work.

Mom recalled that at first there were quite a few of them—Father's colleagues from the institute, the Academy of Sciences, and the National Construction Research institute—who were charged with calculating a corrected budget that would demonstrate that the supplies had been overpriced and who had refused to do so, standing by the original calculations. After about a year, during which the whole mess was mostly forgotten, the dust settled, and the Party had a grand time assembling for its annual Congress at the Palace Ukraina, thus providing a conclusive blessing for its humbled innards, and someone especially stubborn had been officially reprimanded, someone else was threatened to be "reduced in force," and some—these must've been the least protected, the poor doctoral students—had to leave Kyiv and go build cinemas (if not cow barns!) in small towns, my father alone remained to brandish, in the shadow of the ax that already hung above his neck, the truth that no one cared to hear. Perhaps, from the vantage point of an imposing paneled office it did look like madness: What the fuck is wrong with that freak? Who does he think he is?

Being, like my mom, a hard-skulled humanitarian, all I managed to comprehend from a cursory inspection of the folders in the attic—touched fearfully, suspiciously, like a clump of dried snake skins—was that after a while the case wasn't about the construction costs anymore: the plot had twisted and coiled on itself, involving more and more agencies, sprouting new limbs, each one more phantasmagoric than the one before, and only Father continued to attach his original reports in defense of the crippled project to every new petition, to show where it all began—with a precision that his addressees must have found very irksome—so his petitions grew thicker as they rolled back and forth in layers of cross-references and official evasive responses and additional evidence and more evasions from higher-level offices and then his complaints about being threatened in a lower-level office and about the anonymous phone calls relating the same threats he'd received at home and about a bizarre fight at the entrance to our apartment building when several strangers beat him up (this, I remember, happened not too long before the loony bin—it must've been the last warning). The case dragged on for years, gathering speed and mass like a paper avalanche, like the nursery rhyme in which every chorus adds a line, growing into a menacing, galactic force—the rat ate the malt, the cat killed the rat, the dog chased the cat, the cow tossed the dog—and the creatures grow new crumpled horns at every turn, and new ones pop up, cartoon-like, bigger and bigger—the cow, the milkmaid, the man, the priest, all the way to a dinosaur, a T. rex—a whole crew of them that one day comes rolling in an ambulance, wearing white coats, what the fuck, what did you want to prove?

And that's basically what happened—and where is the story in that?

This progressive, thickening nightmare could have been stopped at any time. All one had to do was step out, leave the game; other people did. They stayed alive and did just fine—and to them we must wish many happy returns. These were not just the small fish like Father, convicted on white-collar mismanagement charges—their name is legion—but even the quite conspicuous ones, implicated in the most resonant political scandals, ones whose names thundered across the frequencies of Western radio stations, who performed public acts of civil disobedience—shouted from a public stage, say, before the police could pin them to the floor, or threw themselves against the locked doors of an ostensibly public court hearing, or went to the Shevchenko monument on the poet's anniversary, a single moment that could earn enough dissident credibility to last one's life. And then, after 1991, they could write memoirs and book speaking engagements, which is precisely what most of them did, never once mentioning how it was that they got out.

One suspects they didn't get out completely clean, one surmises they did get soiled, just a little: wrote a confessional letter, say, or perchance performed even more intimate rites of contrition and absolution (complete with promises to behave nicely henceforth) behind closed doors. Who today cares to find out? Who cares? They got out and worked, according to their professions; they received promotions, raised children, and improved their living conditions—so somewhere in those fetid infernal corridors there must have been the door, however narrow, with the green EXIT sign above it, a real, tangible way out, indicated on the emergency evacuation plans. After all we're not talking about Stalinism here, ladies and gentlemen; this is the era of Socialism with a human face, which, translated, means if you really wanted to live, there was a choice.

This is why there could not be any doubt that my father tightened the noose around his neck with his own hands, and that's what it must have looked like to the people who ultimately determined his fate, and that's what it looked like to my mother, and that's what I learned to think as well, when I got older—that he didn't leave the already-revved juggernaut any room for maneuver, that he made a strategic mistake, erred, miscalculated. This is sad and painful, but there's nothing we can do, and we must live on. Really, not that different than if he'd literally been run over by a truck.

And another thing: as I grew older, I began to feel ashamed of him. Compared to my classmates in school and even more so those at the university, my father was a loser, not someone I could brag about. When asked directly, as when one had to stand up in front of the entire class and report one's parents' occupations to the teacher, for the roster (and she doesn't hear it the first time, so one has to repeat it, louder), I would squirm and mutter, eyes down, "Group-one disability," and sit down, hearing, I thought, the class whisper and giggle behind my back. Such things are hard to digest—children can never forgive their parents for humiliating them.

His death at home—they let him go home when his kidneys failed after another long course of "treatment"—could do no more than add guilt to the shame: mix a spoon of soda with a spoon of salt, and time kept blending the two together into a thinning bitterly salty mix that nothing could sweeten, neither the increasingly frequent enthusiastic letters (especially post-1991, and even more so once my face became a regular fixture on TV) from his former colleagues and students about what a great teacher he was and how much they all, it turns out, loved him (Where were they then?), nor our producer's very tangible offer to raise the story with Palace Ukraina from its thirty-year-old tomb in the archives and fashion my father a glamorous, albeit posthumous, almost-dissident biography. Here was a real opportunity, a chance to restore to people's minds the forgotten pages of recent history (as if the people in question had any unforgotten pages of history, recent or distant). The idea was not bad, but it was nipped in the bud by one well-known poet—one of those once widely read, with patriotic verses and a vague victim-of-the-regime claim. Interestingly enough, I wanted to interview her on the occasion of her birthday—and found myself in a knockdown: the draft-horse-sized harpy with a bad bite spent the first half hour spraying me with spit, tossing her head to make the few remaining strands of her dyed hair bounce (which about forty years ago may have signaled to some undemanding men both a temperament of a young ogress and the spirit of an indomitable patriot), and making absolutely sure that I realized how privileged I was to have been granted access to a person who only "interacts with very select people"; she then proceeded to relate, in great detail and with vivid illustrations, as if it had happened the day before, how for her first, fifty-year jubilee—the same year, I quickly calculated, when they gave

Stus, also a poet, his second (and deadly) prison sentence—the National Writers' Union didn't even send her a congratulatory telegram, but instead mailed her (imagine that!) an invitation to someone else's reading—the harpy still, twenty-five years later, remembered whose—scheduled, intentionally, no doubt, on the same day, and that's what it was like, being persecuted! I did not manage to get out of her any other details of the persecution. The harpy didn't have a story either, only a personal myth, one that must have been promoted by quite a few men dazzled by the then naturally auburn tress-tossing, so that now the glow of their past efforts could warm her vacuous old age, in which she didn't give a flying fuck about all those friends of her mythical youth who had perished in camps in the middle of nowhere, whose memory, had it survived, perchance would have permitted her to retain some sense of proportion and style.

I left that apartment and fell to pieces. The vision of dragging my father's made-up cadaver into the same carnival tent of "the persecuted," where this veteran martyr held court, soured everything with particular potency, and I proceeded to get most ingloriously drunk at Baraban that night, downing the strongest cocktails like a sorority girl—but they all tasted of soda and salt, and in the morning the hangover reeked of the same, salt and soda. There was no story. I had to make peace with the plain, dumb reality: I was the only evidence that the man had ever existed on this planet. I had his eyes and his blood type. Come to think of it, why would anyone expect anything different? Isn't this the fate of the human race?

this!!!—a scribble in the margins, a bauble that slipped out of the suitcase—turned the binoculars for me. For an instant, as if a flash of lightning cut through the darkness, I saw a living soul, and the strange thing was that it was the same father about whom I, against my best instincts, continued to feel ashamed. His only place in any historical narrative was that of a nameless extra, a statistical value—one of the myriad, if they could ever be counted, whose names were not listed by Amnesty International, who had not been arrested or sent to prisons, but who succumbed, slowly and quietly, in their own beds, to legitimate cardiac arrests and kidney failures, and other disorders, whose causes were clear only to their families if they had any. We could also add those who drank themselves to death and those who killed themselves—the only meaningful history we can craft for the future is the history of numbers, and the more zeros—the better. Six (Or more?) million dead Jews equal the Holocaust. Ten (Or fewer?) million dead Ukrainian peasants equal Holodomor. Three-hundred-million refugees equal the fifty-six local wars at the beginning of the twenty-first century. History is written by accountants.

During the Khrushchev thaw, officials who issued belated death certificates to the families of those executed in the NKVD prisons came up with all kinds of diseases to fill in the "cause of death" field—thus erasing zeros from the number of executions. Another twenty years later their fictional cardiac arrests and kidney failures became real, as is commonly the case with useful inventions, and literally killed people whose fathers and grandfathers they could beset only on paper, post-factum. Another number was made unreal, and with it, an entire generation lost its common story, leaving its descendants no means of detecting a shared fate—from here, they all look discrete, just people who lived, died, things happened, you know ... this one was a decent engineer and a talented lecturer who died from the side effect of a drug, having done his time in a psychiatric clinic with a falsified diagnosis—and that's it, go ahead, tie those little strings into a dead knot. I needed the inadvertent insight to make the puzzle pieces fall into place—the triumphant snap of fingers, the blue bunny in a school sketchbook, the catchy, generous laugh, the charge of energy that filled the man—to see him from inside and recognize, in that flash, what it was that drove him, had driven him to the end, that had not permitted him to back off and make the single required concession that white was really black: his indomitable abhorrence of his own fear, the physiological mandate from his very healthy and apparently very proud soul (and the soul has its own physiology that does not always agree with that of the body) to reject this fear that had been implanted in him against his will, like viral DNA. If you spend years carrying around something you cannot live with, it might just become easier to crash upon the water than to stop diving.

In the time I spent with the crumbly book, I experienced a rush of fierce, bone-piercing bliss, as if soaring on a glider: I could be proud of him. Not as my father—he had been gone too long for that—but as a person I could admire had I met him now. It seemed forever since I'd actually met anyone like that (Did they really all die out?), and the unfulfilled need to be around them—not even to be close; I'd be happy to admire my heroes quietly, from the crowd, if only there'd been someone to admire—pulled on my insides, like hunger, like vitamin deficiency or sexual dissatisfaction, and the discovery splashed my face like life-giving water: How could this be, I muttered half-consciously? How could this happen? I put down the book and stumbled around the room, blindly, as if feeling for something I had lost there, then fell back onto the chair and stared, just as blindly, at the same page, while my thoughts looped on themselves, tangled into knots, refusing to register the real shock: How could it be that I really know nothing about him? And won't ever know—won't ever find any other evidence of his life as he lived it? He didn't write private letters, didn't keep a journal, didn't leave a single impression of his internal self in any material substance I could find, pick up, turn over—nothing, except a random remark in the margin of a random book.

this!!!

***

Since then I have more faith in misplaced trifles than in rehearsed stories, which always feel like something gutted, stuffed, and roasted before being served for me to gobble up. I believe in remembered mannerisms and scribbles in books, accidental scowls caught by a friend's camera, and strange tooth marks on cigarette holders. I am the detective Columbo of the new century—and please don't laugh at me! I know that these excavated remains of vanished civilizations, the many, many civilizations that had once existed under people's names, do not lie. If we have any hope of understanding anything about another's life, this *this!!!* is it. We've heard all the other stories before, thank you very much, and we're sick of them.

I can no more pass up these scattered shiny beads than a raccoon can ignore a broken mirror. And I mean literally: I pick them up and drag them to my lair. I have a whole collection of them already: my own disordered notes in various notebooks, on random scraps of paper, on festival booklets and concert programs, on the backs of press releases, on any other printed matter, and lengths of film from the cutting-room floor, twisted and kept, for reasons unknown, in an old computer box—all in utter disarray. Why, you could very well ask, am I holding on to this poorly scanned drawing by a little girl from Pripyat who died of leukemia and whose strangely unbrokenhearted parents were convinced she'd been destined to artistic fame? It's hard to tell whether this really was the case: all children's drawings are interesting, and, in this one, a brown hippo stands on the shore of a blue lake, rounded toward the horizon. The picture didn't make it into the Chernobyl show (I remember I wanted to keep the program austere, somber, inexorable, no sentiments, no snivels), and the girl's mother was upset with me: I had taken away her role of the tragically lost young genius's parent, and what could I give her in return—a dead child? Still, even if there hadn't been the upset mother and my guilt, I wouldn't have it in me to kill the picture—so I'm keeping it, as if hoping to find, one day, the proper place for it.

Essentially, none of my shows ever grew out of the themes that I so thoughtfully pitched to my producers and colleagues. They were all conceived out of just such small details, some hook that caught my attention and teased with the promise of inaccessible secrets, like a distant glowing window seen at night from a passing train: Who lives there? What are they doing? Why is the light on so late? As a rule, such things did not make the final cut, either remaining somewhere beyond the scope of the lens, or making a brief appearance in the background, so inconspicuous that I alone could find them, like a signature hidden in the corner of the picture. Or, to be completely honest, like a note acknowledging another defeat, equally private, because I hadn't once been able to make something—something I felt it was possible to make if only one had the lost secret code—of my pile of beads and gravel, hadn't managed to turn these pieces so that a single change of light could illuminate someone's life completely, totally, all pieces in their places, hadn't once created *this!!!*.

Which does not mean that one should stop trying.

I have no other method—if this even counts as one. I don't believe in other methods—I think they all have been milked dry. And to do things any other way would simply be no fun.

I don't know what drew me into the photograph where, among five Ukrainian Insurgent Army soldiers, second from the right, stood a young clear-eyed, bareheaded woman ("A unit," Artem whispered, pushing the print across the desk toward me, careful to touch it very lightly with his fingertips as if the picture, if not handled with caution, could explode with a gunshot) with bangs curled into a Hollywood roll, as was the wartime fashion. She seemed to smile at me, this lady whose small waist was cinched so smartly, even whimsically, with the uniform canvas belt, and whose entire posture exuded a calm, self-possessed confidence—not of military discipline, but rather fox hunting on a family's grand estate: here's the young mistress waiting for her horse to be brought up, the pack of purebred hounds straining their leashes and whimpering excitedly just outside the frame. She would look perfectly complete with an English riding crop and a pair of white gloves, and yet her sophistication (so out of place in the middle of the woods) also had a wondrously feminine quality—consolingly cool, like a strong, kind hand against a hot forehead—that must have had a soothing effect on horses and hounds, and young men with automatic weapons. She was the only one among them who smiled, her lips drawn in a barely discernible curve.

"What a beautiful woman," I observed, for some reason in a whisper, although she was not so much beautiful, in the usual sense, as radiant: even in the faded picture, she was surrounded by a visible halo of light, like an Old Master painting of an angel sent to deliver the glorious word—"Fear not, Zacharias: for thy prayer is heard." Artem blinked sideways and grunted either in agreement or, conversely, was simply shocked by my silliness, as any historian would be after he'd just shared a prized archival document with a total philistine—all she can think of is pretty women!

Nevertheless he responded, with his thin, crooked grin that seemed to mock preemptively what he was about to say, somewhat lewdly, "So which one of the four do you figure she slept with?"

"This one," I said, without hesitation, pointing to the guy on the far right, with wolfishly close-set eyes and a crooked nose, letting Artem's transparent implication slip without acknowledgment. (By then he and I hadn't had sex for at least three months; I saw no reason to galvanize our naturally ebbing liaison and found a new excuse every time we ran into each other so that he may well have begun to suspect that I suffered from a mysterious chronic illness, a constant menstruation or something.) The wolfish guy posed with one foot forward, as if on the move, hand securely clenched around the hand guard of his rifle, which he used to balance himself like a walking stick, and my certainty about him was all the more puzzling because had I been that woman, I would have chosen another—that one, standing most apart, the last on the left who looked to the side, as if the whole photographing business had nothing to do with him. Of all the men in the picture, with simple, peasant-looking faces, chiseled by many generations of hard physical work (And isn't war, too, hard physical work?), he alone was truly handsome, a dashing brunet, a perfected and ennobled clean-shaved incarnation of Clark Gable with unaffected, long-buried sorrow congealed in the dark eyes.

Clark Gable couldn't muster such sorrow for the most lavish fees; this was something cultivated for years, not gained in an instant. This was the sorrow that filled our folk songs, all, it seems, in minor key—marches, ballads, doesn't matter, the words don't matter because they can't contain this sadness or explain its origin, only music can—and the brunet had *musical* eyes, eyes that *sang*.

Artem's hand carefully, solicitously stroked my thigh through the slit of my skirt, climbing higher and higher above the knee, and I automatically thought, as I always did, about his wedding ring: I worried about it snagging my hose. I could have just moved away— after three months, that would've been enough—but I remained transfixed, bent over the table and riveted to the picture, where, I was now convinced, a silent secret drama played out between the woman and these two men. Artem breathed harder; his thumb found the crease between my legs and went to work on it through the hose and the panties. He was always a very diligent lover: a scholar and a bibliophile, he did everything as if armed with a solid list of reference materials, which sometimes made me feel like I was a rare artifact equipped with an invisible user's manual, and other times like he was mortally afraid of me, and I'd rush to his rescue, ignoring the taste of long-refrigerated cheese that would linger in my mouth afterward—Artem's beautiful penis, for some reason, was always cold, and so was his whole body.

But in that instant, eyes locked on the picture and nails cutting into the table, I suddenly felt a fierce arousal, much more intense than if I'd been watching porn—unfamiliarly menacing, desperate, and predatory, as if this were going to be my last time, as if a spotlight had found and blinded me, leaving nothing of me but a base, well-deep scream that did not sink, but instead rose, climbed as through a narrow shaft, pushing aside my aorta, breaking through my clenched teeth, and it didn't matter anymore who—or what!—jerked up my skirt from behind, ripped down layers of fabric, faster, faster, I focused myself in the point where my salvation would come—and it came, instantly, like a summer storm—and someone's paw closed over my mouth, and I realized that the scream that thundered in my ears had come from my own throat. I shook my head, refusing the paw, and blinked slowly—murky yellow smears swam in front of my eyes, and the first thing I could see clearly when they began to dissolve was the photograph with the five figures in it: their silhouettes burned with sharp white light, as if on a negative. I had to blink again, and a few more times—until the photograph cooled to its normal condition—and then observed that it wasn't the picture that was shaking but the table, for the important reason that I was folded onto it in a rather uncomfortable pose, with Artem studiously pounding me from behind, while also attempting to keep one hand over my mouth—this was all happening at his workplace, after all, in the library storage basement, and could have turned quite piquant if a coworker peeked through the door, except that he always locked it as soon as I arrived.

It occurred to me in that instant—an inanimate and vacant blob of cognition, not even a real thought—that this was the only thing that attracted me: the unheated basement with its linoleum floors, the soporific yeasty smell of rotting paper, and the conspiratorially locked shabby door lent our pitiful little fling the exciting air of delinquency, like when you're students and fuck like rabbits in every suitable nook, and quite simply erased from my memory whatever attempts Artem may have made to transplant the action into a regular apartment, with a regular bed.

I straightened my clothes quickly, checked myself in my compact mirror, all without looking at the happy, sweaty, and confused Artem, who felt the urge to show some uncalled-for tenderness, which, as the poet Pluzhnyk once said, "is born on the far side of passion," but froze up in the face of my indecent efficiency and monosyllabic grunts. I may have made it look like I was fleeing from the site of shame and dishonor, but my mind, sharpened by the orgasm, ran like a super-computer clicking through an algorithm with maximum effectiveness and minimum use of energy: "You have my 1928 Kyiv guidebook, by Ernst, don't you? You still need it? And would it be okay if I borrowed the photo, just for a while?"

I slipped the photo between the yellow pages of the innocently extracted Ernst, pulled my purse closed around it, made sure I didn't leave anything behind; Artem caught up with me when I was already halfway through the door with his kiss (sloppy) and the warning that he'd call at the end of the week (Why is it that men always have to stake a claim on the future when they say goodbye? Like I wouldn't call him if *I* wanted him?)—and that's it; that was really it. We did not see each other again, and when he called, I complained of how busy I was, said I'd love to, it would be heaven, but I can't, I really can't.... I'm quite good at that if I do say so myself.

Artem (thrilled about a chance to prop up a worn-out romance with a substantive obligation, as often happens when affairs are ending or beginning—when you're lending books, CDs, and pictures, and inventing shared engagements that are hard to evade later) asked me at the door what I was going to do with the picture, and I mumbled something cryptic along the I'm-thinking-to-do-something-about-UIA lines; it's a hot topic (as if I were rehearsing what I'd say to my producer). Of course, this was just a flaky-artist excuse—I wasn't thinking anything of the sort. I was firmly convinced that only Western Ukrainians had the right to write, film, or say anything about the Insurgent Army because it was their families who held, just under the surface, either "forest boys" themselves or someone deported "for abetting," and when someone got deported, the whole village was sent along, just to be sure; so it's a miracle the Soviets didn't manage to pack them all off to the other side of Yenisei, as the Poles did when they cleaned out this side of Vistula. Why on earth would I go try to stick my two cents into what, to some, still feels like a bone crushing?

All I had in my personal history were Mom and Uncle Volodya's, my stepfather's, accounts of the 1947 hunger in Eastern Ukraine: Uncle Volodya (I never could bring myself to call him Papa Volodya, as he and Mom would have liked), then a fifteen-year-old Odessa boy, worked alongside adults netting fish from under the ice and kept his family alive. Around the ice holes, he said, all day long lingered swollen women on elephantine legs, immobile, like ghosts: they waited for the fry to slip out of the nets, snatched them off the ice, and gobbled them down, raw. To get bread—the blessed, salvific bread—both his Odessa and his mom's Poltava communities outfitted expeditions to Western Ukraine ("in Western," Uncle Volodya stubbornly kept saying, as if this illiterate patch on his generally very proper, for someone from Odessa, Ukrainian was inseparable from the events of the past and had to remain uncorrected; "in Western" was his, and "to Western Ukraine" belonged to a different generation). These hunting parties stuffed themselves, like sardines in a tin, into the deranged freight train #500-J that chugged from one station to the next with no order or timetable. Its ghoulish nickname was 500-Joy because it was liable to stop without warning somewhere in the middle of a field and stay there for five hours, or five minutes, and start again just as suddenly, leaving behind a shedding of the unlucky ones who jumped off to relieve themselves. So they learned not to look for cover, and just rolled off the train's platforms and roofs—head over heels, men and women—all in a rush to bare their behinds with a single feverish thought: to make it, and to claw back into one's spot before someone else had taken it. This constant fear of losing the spot was branded in Uncle Volodya's memory, and his spot on that train must've been especially hard to win—a starved teenager shoving and elbowing grown men—but I was captivated by the vision of that sexless orgy of the hurried mass expulsion of bodily fluids and solids along the train, the ease with which people could be transformed into a herd.

Those treks after bread were no safer than the ones undertaken in the name of breadwinning today—migrations after work, to Westerner Europe, the real, Schengen-visa regime Europe, aboard a sooty Icarus across Poland and Slovakia, where every clump of trees might conceal an eager Russian gang, quick to block the road with their Kalashnikovs aimed at the bus. Uncle Volodya, who made the rooftop journey on the 500-Joy in the spring of 1947, remembered a flashlight blinding him in the middle of the night and the icy needle of steel against his throat. "Got money, boy?"

Incredibly, he thought to fold back both sides of his threadbare jacket exposing its empty inside pockets and to squeal the first thing that came to mind, "Going to my brother's," and they left him alone, didn't frisk him; though he did have money—carefully sewn by his mother into his boxer shorts—he could not say the same about a brother. (What he must've had was a dream, a boy's secret dream, an orphan's dream of a brother, an older one for sure, who would come back from the front, beat down every offender, would protect and defend—and the dream did protect him.) In their eyes—the eyes of dirty, famished people who hurriedly washed the railroad embankments with steaming urine—the then newly annexed Galicia—in its eighth year of being whipped, along and across, by frontlines and now a guerilla war—still retained the glow of "Europe," an oasis of unimaginable luxuries. It beckoned much as the new, Schengen Europe beckons today's Ukrainian migrant workers—and to those who were lucky enough to make it, it bestowed generously of its riches: a sack of dried biscuits for some, two bags of buckwheat and a bag of dried peas for others, and for the luckiest ones—a packed, shaken-down, and leveled sack of flour. Mom's older sister, Lyusya, may she rest in peace, managed somehow to carry precisely such a marvel on her back all the way back, with a change of trains in Zdolbuniv, and that's how 1947 did not become, despite the Ukrainian plans of the mustachioed Generalissimo, a conclusive repeat of 1933, so the UIA can be credited with winning at least *this* war, one that's not mentioned in a single history textbook. Not a single food-rationing crew in the late forties would risk going into a Western Ukrainian village to "shake down grain"; if it foolishly did, it would be remembered as last seen on its way to that village, as Uncle Volodya told it, with a satisfied predatory smirk, which still held something of the boy in awe of a friendly power—someone's in for an ass-kicking!—but which also was colored with a tinge of resentment and something a bit like envy, as in, sure, easy for them to fight, they didn't swell on the ice with me, *Where'd they be then?* Swell you did, I could have said to Uncle Volodya (and did, often, in my head, but never out loud), but that time was different from what happened in 1933—there was by then a large and, by all accounts, fairly well-organized army that had spent the previous three years practicing their bread-defending skills on the Germans; this experience kept the country alive.

Aside from the Finland campaign, this was, no matter how you look at it, Stalin's only defeat; and, for forty years after he died, the official Soviet history spared no funds or imagination to pay "the West," as they called it, back. The funding part stopped being a secret for us—the sophisticated kids—in school, when no other topic provoked such heated arguments during the breaks: for our parents, the war was still alive, not something fixed in books, and the families' accumulated memories diverged way too far from what we were supposed to memorize, resulting in a nearly chemical incompatibility, words and memories bubbling and bursting, finally depositing the textbook in the clear and despised category of "Bullshit!"

And that's really all that I personally could claim to know—not much. So the whole UIA thing had nothing to do with anything.

I just *could not* leave the photograph with Artem. It was *mine*—it had become mine. And not just because I happened to have been thoroughly fucked on top of it without putting up much resistance. Instead, I didn't resist because at that moment I was possessed by *someone else's will.* That's what it had felt like. (And for the rest of that day I could barely move, as if I'd been run through a meat grinder.)

The young woman who stood with aristocratic ease among four armed men in the middle of the forest and smiled imperceptibly, the woman surrounded by a halo of light, a chimera of photography, had a name—Olena Dovganivna.

And beyond that, I really knew nothing.

***

"What are you thinking about?"

"I'm never going to make this film. Never."

"Of course you will. It'll all work out," you say with confidence that scares me.

Your family silently looks out at me out from the photographs, all at once. I can't believe it. What did you see in me? (A question that must never, under any circumstances, be voiced, so I bite my tongue anyway, just in case—I wouldn't want *you* to start thinking about it.)

Something I never told you: When you kissed me that first time (actually, it was I who kissed you first—when I couldn't stand for another second to be held in your ecstatically adoring gaze that only lacked a pair of hands folded in prayer—of course you were intimidated, with me being a TV star and all), what shook me most, wrung me more cruelly than ever, was the expression I saw on your face when our lips parted: the look of a man who climbed to the top of the mountain, then turned around to look at the valley, and saw the earth swallow the city where he'd come from. You looked at me as if you didn't recognize me, as if I oscillated and changed shapes every instant, and the flickering of ecstasy and horror on your face mirrored my shape-shifting, and for an instant, before we looked away, I glimpsed through your eyes the ground parting beneath; silently, with the sound on mute, buildings collapsed one after the other, as if filmed from an airplane by an awestruck cameraman.

Since then, the sensation became my own, and every so often I feel its short mournful pang: I am standing at the top of the mountain and you are looking at me, and there's nowhere for me to go if I wanted to leave.

"You'll work it all out," you say, and your certainty sounds unshakeable.

I only now figured out why I felt so ambushed by your Ukrainian when we first met: you move through life with too much confidence. You're too calm and composed, as if you have not the slightest inkling that one could be otherwise. Among those of us over thirty, who grew up with the constant awareness of our Ukrainian-ness, such natural, unconstrained dignity is rare: composure like yours, even posture like yours, requires three to four generations of ancestors unfamiliar with any kind of internalized social humiliation—not something possible yet in post-twentieth-century Ukraine.

Give me your hand. So hot.

You have wonderful hands; the most beautiful hands I've ever seen on a man—strong, finely sculpted, with long, well-bred fingers. Why am I not Rodin, or at least someone in marketing? I'd put your hand on a woman's knee and hold the shot. Buy Hanes hosiery. This must be the limit of my imagination, the best I can do—commercials.

Don't let me go, you hear me? I know nothing—I don't even know if this is what people call love, or if I'm possessed again by someone else's will. Sometimes I think I am. I don't know what to want from the future and whether we even have a future. I don't know anything. Just hold me, okay? Don't let me go. Just like this.

Room 2. From the Cycle *Secrets*: *Contents of a Purse Found at the Scene of the Accident*

Daryna Goshchynska's Interview with Vladyslava Matusevych

[The scene is picture perfect, as intended: Two women, a blonde and a brunette, are sitting at a café table in the Passage on Khreshchatyk. Both are stylishly dressed and well groomed, both sport bare tan shoulders. It's the end of August, when everyone returns from summer vacations. In the background, a waiter appears every so often, dressed in a white jacket and wearing the mysterious smile of unspoken understanding that is the trademark of all Kyiv waiters and the reason they all look like low-rank Hindu deities, while the truth is that few of them really know what they're doing and most are deathly afraid of running into an unusual client—say, someone accompanied by a TV camera that's currently installed between the tables. One notices the lovely play of light as it filters through the blonde woman's hair, making it golden and translucent; in fact, it is darker than it appears but streaked with highlights the shade of ripe wheat to give her pale face, with its masculine cleft chin and small birdlike features, a brighter frame, without which it would certainly disappear in a crowd, despite her wide-set eyes. The colors have been chosen perfectly, and no wonder—she's a painter. In the foreground, more colors contrast with the white of the tablecloth: a glass of dark-ruby wine, a voluminous tankard of Obolon lager with its bridal-veil cap of froth, an ornate pack of Eve Slims—the white-jacketed deity brings an ashtray as big as a soup bowl, but it's black, better to move it out of the shot, take it off the table altogether, it draws the eye too much.] "Does anyone mind? Okay, this looks good; let's roll."

"Vladyslava, we've known each other long enough that I can address you in informal terms even in front of the camera—and take great pride in that." [Both laugh the conspiratorial laugh of women who take pride in their age and are connected by something utterly inaccessible to men, which always inspires a vague unease in the latter.] "First of all, let me congratulate you on your remarkable accomplishment, especially uncommon for a Ukrainian artist—the Nestlé Art Foundation Award for your solo show in, correct me if I'm wrong, Zurich?"

"Zurich, Bern, Geneva, and Lausanne," lists the blonde. [She has the businesslike intonation of someone long and well used to remarkable accomplishments.]

"You must forgive me; you know what it's like for Ukrainian journalists: any foreign cultural coverage comes to us secondhand."

"If not third," the blonde interjects.

"Exactly!" the interviewer agrees. [She's a little too eager, and both women laugh again, this time with a tinge of unanimous menace that suggests a history of shared grudges against various things national.] "There's nothing we can do about that, so you have to tell your story yourself if you want motherland to be informed."

"Remember the old Soviet joke," the blonde says. [She leans over the table, so that her whole upper body faces her interviewer, and she resembles a cat about to leap into a tree. Now the cameraman can appreciate the resolve of her small, sharply featured face with its cleft chin, and he zooms in for a close-up.] "Why is there no meat in the stores?" [The reporter raises her eyebrows in exaggerated curiosity, bursting with a barely contained giggle.] "Because we're making leaps and bounds toward Communism, and the cattle can't keep up. It's the same with artists who gain international recognition—the country can't keep up."

"And not just artists," the reporter agrees, after she stops chuckling. "The same is true for our scientists who get hired into Western universities when their ideas don't interest anyone at home, and for our intellectuals who follow grant money abroad because they've got nothing here. The country's best minds are leaving in droves, and I'm afraid if this goes on at the same rate for another ten or fifteen years, we'll all be running around on all fours by then. Still, Vlada, you and I are optimists, aren't we?"

[The blonde narrows her eyes skeptically, taking aim at the next statement, which will determine whether she will, in fact, remain an optimist. This causes tiny creases to shoot across her temples, and for an instant, her face gains the heartbreaking sculpted perfection that will become fully hers in a few more years—the perfection of character manifest, which makes some women more striking in middle age than they ever were in youth—another two, three years and the blonde, if she remains a blonde will grow into her own and become perfectly, dramatically beautiful.]

"So what if the recognition you've achieved in the West today translates into little more than envy at home? Objectively," [The brunette's poppy-red, Guerlain-lipstick-stained mouth enunci- ates the last word with a sexy air-kiss, draws it out as if in bold italics—she is addressing an imaginary TV audience, not just her friend.] "you still work for the benefit of this nation, even when it can't, as you put it, keep up, and in particular, loses track of its own rapidly changing ideas of itself which, to me, is an important issue." [The blonde murmurs something affirmative; she must find the didacticism boring.] "Ukrainians are known to suffer from chronically low self-esteem, so every time one of 'us' is recognized by 'them,' it's salve for our long-cherished national wounds. So, let's talk about this thing, your show. First, could you explain the title, *Secrets*?"

"Well, the whole idea grew out of a game we played as kids: remember, back when we were little, in the sixties and seventies, all girls made 'secrets'?"

"Of course I do! And here's something—only girls did, no boys allowed, right?"

"Nope, strictly no boys, not even friends, I remember that." [The blonde pushes away a strand of hair that's fallen into her face and with it, it seems, thirty years worth of memories.] "I had a friend like that; we played house. I was Mom; he was Dad, but even he was not privy to secrets …"

"Not to change the subject, but I'd like to ask—when you were little, did you play more with boys or with girls? Because there's this theory that all socially successful women are products of what's called masculine socialization, meaning they were raised more like boys."

"I don't know.... No, I wouldn't say so. No, we girls played like we were supposed to, dolls, clothes for them—I was the prime seamstress in our yard, I liked that a lot.... No, I think something else is important." [She thrusts up her chin resolutely; her eyes flash, cat-like, and change color: a minute ago, as she was searching her memory, they were infant-like, watery-gray, but now, powered by a fully formed, ready-to-roll idea, they oscillate with a piercing steel-blue current—the cameraman must be in heaven. It's not often that you find a face as expressive as this one, whose surface, like clear water, shimmers with light reflected off every motion beneath.] "You know what really made a difference? Being a Daddy's girl. Dad was the key figure for me. He was the one who taught me to draw, you know, then took me to art school every morning; his word was law for me, for a very long time. I still consider him a much-underappreciated artist; some of his pieces are terribly interesting, especially his non-figurative works, but you know what the official take on abstraction was in Soviet times. Actually, this is insanely interesting when you think about it—I think you're onto something here, with what makes women successful. All the girls I know, the ones who got somewhere, they're all Daddy's girls, and you are, too, aren't you, Dar?" [The brunette nods silently.] "You can find this even in folktales: it's always the wife's daughter, Mommy's girl, who loses out, and the man's daughter brings home a treasure—ostensibly because she works hard and the other girl is lazy, but what if the wife's daughter just doesn't know any better? Hasn't been properly socialized, you know? She's got no clue how to behave among strangers, what to do to gain their confidence, how to work behind the scenes toward her goals—she just blurts it all out, like to that sorceress ..."

"The Snake Queen," prompts the brunette.

"Yep, the Snake Queen. The chick turns up in the palace and rattles off her list of wants, as if to her own mommy. She's like a domestic savage, isn't she? It's like, for generations our women didn't have the skills to teach their girls how to behave outside the home—you needed a man for such advanced politics." [Forgetting herself, the painter bites her nails in concentration, but realizes what she's doing and stops; her hand, in contrast to her petite figure, is substantial and strong, with a wide palm and unmanicured nails—an expressive hand, an honest craftsman hand. The nail-biting will get cut when the footage is edited.]

"And if we consider," picks up the interviewer, [She works the idea like a thread, smoothing it out, reeling it around the spool.] "that the nineties gave us our first, for all intents and purposes, generation of single mothers, a generation of women who were no longer ..." [She rounds her mouth again and leans into the word as if pushing against a locked door.] "afraid of raising a child by themselves, what kind of future, do you think, will their—our—daughters experience? Will you be able to ensure that your Katrusya is properly socialized? Enough so," [A professional half-smile, caught in the corners of her mouth, puts the next phrase in invisible quotes.] "that she won't lose her bearings in front of any snake queens?"

"I think so," the painter answers after a moment's hesitation, firmly and without a smile. [It is clear that this was the question she was trying to answer earlier with her fairytale ideas.] "I very much hope so."

"Back to secrets—does Katrusya make them, like we did?"

"Are you kidding?" [The painter waves the reporter off, and laughs, with the shy pride of a parent outrun by her child.] "Kids only play computer games now. And, I must add, I think they do get worn out by being constantly bombarded with visual information—it's like there's this chromatic noise around them, all the time. Think of the world we grew up in—how much grayer it was ..."

"Oh, yeah." [The reporter groans from outside the frame.]

"How hungry we were for color. Remember our collecting craze—and for what? Colorful candy wrappers—the brighter the rarer!"

"And the more precious," adds the journalist [with full professional competence, intent on getting all the facts straight]. "I remember how I envied a girl next door, whose father was one of the few people who got sent abroad every so often and brought her foreign candy—she had the most extravagant collection on our block; you didn't know what to look at first."

"Sure, I have stories like that too. And now, think how you made a secret. First you dug a little hole in the ground and lined it with something shiny, like a foil wrapper from a chocolate bar—and actually, such glimmering backgrounds that provide a deeper perspective are common for folk-art icons, the late ones, from the end of the nineteenth century, when they were being made by factory co-ops. You can still find some out in the country."

"I never thought of that," the reporter perks up. [She is like a bird dog that caught a whiff of game.] "But I suppose it shouldn't be surprising: children's games always retain rudiments of a vanished adult culture. Did you read this somewhere, or is this something that just occurred to you?"

"Give me a break, Daryna, where would I read this? We're still waiting for a complete history of the Ukrainian icon and you want someone to take on little girls and their tchotchkes? But wait, the similarities don't end there. So you have this shiny silver or gold background, and you lay out your design—with leaves, pebbles, whatever junk you could find, as long as it's brightly colored: Candy wrappers, pieces of glass, beads, buttons—there were lots of fun buttons back then, everyone sewed, knitted, crocheted, you had to be crafty. You could add flowers—marigolds, phlox, daisies—usually to make a kind of a decorative frame, a border, which is also a common practice in Ukrainian folk art. So you had a little collage piece of sorts, whatever struck your fancy, and then you took a bigger piece of glass, like the bottom of a bottle—remember that those factory-made icons also came framed and under glass—and set it on top of the hole and buried everything again. Then, when you came back later and brushed the dirt off that spot, you'd see a tiny magical window into the ground, like a peephole into Aladdin's cave."

[The interviewer, who has been enthusiastically nodding like an A+ student at a favorite professor's lecture, opens her poppy-red mouth to offer a suitably insightful comment, but the painter continues to talk, sending the reporter into another fit of vigorously affirmative miming.]

"Of course, this cannot be considered a purely artistic activity, nothing like when children draw or make up verses just because they can."

"That's it," mumbles the interviewer, "that's what I wanted to …"

"A secret's main purpose was not to be beautiful but to be something that no one, except its creators, had the right to see. When you made one, with another friend or two, you couldn't even brag to anyone else about how pretty it was; it was to be strictly private. The next day you'd come to the same spot—which you'd have marked with a broken branch or a rock—and check if your secret was intact. This was a ritual of the girly friendship, a sisterhood rite, something like that."

"I remember how much drama there was around the thing." [The journalist finally interrupts, her voice ringing dreamily with elegiac notes. She shakes her head in amazement as if she is just now appreciating the scale of a past disaster she's survived by sheer luck.] "'Gal'ka showed our secret to Darka!' and for the next three days everyone's miffed and tiffed, and it's such a betrayal that no one speaks to anyone."

"And the worrying," continues the painter [with a sentimental gleam in her eyes], "when someone had come and moved the rock that marked the spot! A pack of little girls becomes wildly preoccupied: counting steps and trying to figure out if some trespasser really went after their secret."

"And if, God forbid, someone did dig it up—well, that was a mystery better than on TV!" [Both women laugh a moist feminine laugh, low and deeply felt, as if they'd forgotten why they'd come together in front of the camera.]

[Two ladies in full bloom, well-kept, Mediterranean-tanned, and boutique-dressed (Morgan and Laura Ashley tops, silk Versace scarves, and Armani skirts, nothing showy, heavens no—not a speck of conspicuous consumption, none of the Moscow-edition *Cosmopolitan* brand of fashion that makes one look like an expensive whore—just pure class and apparent simplicity, the understated style of working women who know their worth and don't need to advertise anything) with instantly younger, clearer faces and that radiant reticence in their eyes, the inwardness that women can preserve even when their souls find the most intimate concord, so that they resemble two young mothers adoring their offspring—as if watching, from the distance of many years, their children rather than themselves, or, even more than that, two suddenly ageless friends who just entered a pact over a secret, enacting an unspoken rite of sisterhood to which boys are not privy. This gives the boys at the scene—the director and the cameraman—an instant and suspiciously unanimous urge to take a break, smoke a cigarette, change the tape, do something to turn down the heat and announce their existence, to restore order to the world—as one does at home when one's wife is too engrossed in a phone conversation with a friend, and one feels the need to let the wife know, in sign language, that she's not the only one who gets to use the phone or, more desperately, by letting a plate crash to the kitchen floor. Take a break, girls, take a break.

After the break, which, like it or not, does drain some of the passion from the women's inopportune lyrical exaltation, the interviewer—like a trotter that broke stride, loped off, and had to be brought back into the race—regains form, returns to her businesslike tone, and unleashes a compensatory flood of erudition to make up for lost ground, like the straight-A student suspected of not having done her homework (although no teachers are found in the picture) and determined to restore her sterling reputation.]

"Vladyslava, what you said makes me re-evaluate the European reception of your show *Secrets*—and we remind our viewers that, before coming to Switzerland, the show was mounted in Germany, at the Deutsches Museum in Munich, as well as at a private gallery in Copenhagen ... more on that later .... I've read the reviews in *Süddeutsche Zeitung* and *Neue Zürcher Zeitung,* and I was surprised to find that the writers hailed, as they put it, your 'innovative use of Byzantine icon-painting techniques,' as if it were the most remarkable thing about your work. I'm no art historian, of course, but I know enough to know that any really innovative uses of icon-painting techniques ended with Boychuk—when he and his students were executed and their works destroyed—and it's difficult to classify you as a new-Boychukist. Your works can be said to trace their origins to Dubuffet, with whom you've also been compared, but your collages on silver and gold, in my opinion, are more interesting."

"Thank you." [The painter smiles, with a professional dose of skepticism.]

"Another artist who comes to mind is László Moholy-Nagy and how he pioneered the technique of layering surfaces to give a painting a third dimension, depth." [The reporter realizes she's monopolized the conversation and, possibly, having run out of her straight-A student zeal—now that she's had a chance to show off—apologizes to the painter with an earnest, almost childish smile that offers a wordless plea, but the painter obviously does not register such subtleties: she is focused on the ideas and waits for the next question.] "Basically, it seemed to me that Western reviewers really didn't have a context into which they could readily fit you: they don't know much about Ukrainian art; Russia is their closest reference, hence all this Byzantine talk. But, on the other hand, maybe they could see something we don't because we see your works from our inside point of view—namely, this mystifying kinship between children's secrets and icons?"

"It's really not all that mystifying, the kinship." [The painter leans forward again, jutting out her pugnacious chiseled chin like a small clenched fist.] "Personally I strongly suspect that the game, when it first appeared, imitated something that adults were doing—burying icons."

[The interviewer gasps, opens her poppy-red mouth, and forgets to close it.]

"Really, I mean it. Early thirties. We forget one thing about collectivization: when those food brigades came, they didn't just clean out pantries or take valuable goods—shearling coats, rolls of fabric, stuff like that. Displaying icons in the home was instantly incriminating. They were either destroyed on the spot or taken away, if they had any value: gold plating would be stripped off and the boards themselves burned. So, if you had any foresight at all, you'd simply take yours down and bury them in a secret spot; it had to have been a popular practice—and there you have your secret."

"That you couldn't tell anyone about."

"God help you, no! Not a word. It's not that far-fetched: our mothers must have spied our grandmothers secreting icons into the ground, and imitated them when they played, as all children do. With time, our generation inherited only the seemingly point-less manipulations with found shards of glass, a fading echo, a sound without a message. And, by the time we had kids, even that was gone, so it's done, forgotten!"

"Grandma told me," the reporter begins thoughtfully, "that they buried Great-Grandfather's entire library then, a stash of pre-revolutionary books: Vynnychenko, Hrushevsky, a history of French literature in Petliura's translation—enough that they were afraid, you know. And then they couldn't find the spot where they put it, and their house burned down in the war ... so it all must have just rotted away underground." [She blinks when a new idea brushes past her and then leaps after it like a hound on a fresh track.] "Don't you think this burying of treasure can be seen as a sort of a recurring motif in all of Ukrainian history? Again, look at folktales and how many tell of buried treasures, from the Kozaks, the Opryshkis, all those other rebels. And a whole stock of dark magic goes with them: how the treasures come close to the surface and burn, appearing as wandering flames above ground, and the Devil guards the treasures, so you have to know how to handle him and what to throw at the burning treasure to make it turn into coins. I don't know if you find this stuff anywhere else in Europe, except maybe in the Balkans. What if our secrets date all the way back to those older myths? The ones about cursed treasures?"

"Nope, uh-uh," the painter shakes her head. [She's already considered this and rejected the idea.] "And you know why not? Precisely because secrets was a girls-only game. It was women who buried the icons—it was their job: one, because they were safer from the authorities—if they got caught, it was no big deal, like what else would you expect from a stupid broad."

"No class consciousness," the interviewer pipes in with the vintage Communist-speak.

"Exactly, and who took the cattle back from the kolkhoz in the early thirties? Again, mothers and wives, and that's how they managed to keep them. Had their men tried to get their horses back, that wouldn't have gone so well; they'd be shipped off to the Solovki the same day. It's like when the women riot, it's not for real. And two—and this is more important—a home's icons have always been a kind of Di Penates, deities of the hearth, and of course, all things domestic constituted the woman's sphere of influence—the man's began outside the door. So when our grannies went digging to bury their icons, they weren't intent on preserving our artistic heritage, but simply protecting the spirit of the home, as good wives and mothers have always done— 'While the icons hang, the home stands,' as the proverb went. It was women's work, Daryna, I'm telling you, and that's why two generations later it turned into a girls-only game. That's the only explanation."

"That's astonishing," announces the brunette, triumphant. [Now she could really use a break to digest the new ideas, but since they've already had a break, albeit not of her own devising, she soldiers on.] "And what about for you, personally—is being a woman something that you feel is important to your work? Do you draw a distinction between men's and women's art? Do you see yourself as an heiress to a uniquely female artistic tradition? Can you name any female artists you consider your predecessors?"

"That's a good question, Daryna, thank you. I feel that with *Secrets* I finally found a style that's truly my own, and I don't just mean the technique of mixing things into a collage, against a patchwork background—all my touched-up photographs and padding with glued-in car visors to create bulk—although this also constitutes a very feminine approach to media. I'm like the woman who makes her borsch by mixing whatever is slowly rotting in her fridge." [The painter pauses, searching for words, and at that moment a sudden gust of wind whips her hair back, extracting her small pale face out of its shaggy gilded frame, leaving it naked and defenseless, and she looks like a serious gray-eyed boy, thoughtful beyond years—an acolyte soon to take his vows, whose entire presence is threaded with a cold, otherworldly light of estrangement, an uncanny, unsettling moment, a hush, as if someone invisible has stepped into the frame. A sudden chill ripples through the interviewer, but that could be the air, maybe a door opened and closed inside the building, or simply the first breath of the imminent autumn; it is, after all, the end of August.]

"I'm sorry," the painter says. [She looks baffled, and attempts to smile, haplessly.] "I lost my train of thought.... Oh yes," [Her voice gradually regains its self-possessed tenor and flows evenly, stumbling only occasionally over the most treacherous twists and shallows of thought.] "it's not just about technique. I work with objects that have been in everyday use, or, rather, what's left of them. The pieces of china that form a mosaic on the canvas are shards of actual dinnerware and figurines. The same goes for the car visors, and the pieces of fabric, burlap, knitting—I rarely use anything new; things that have been in use have a special feel to them, they're warm. So, if you want to talk about my sense of a female legacy, I'm kind of inverting, mirroring something women had done since ancient times—decorating their everyday lives. Traditionally, it is the applied arts, and not studio painting, that has been the feminine domain, especially here in Ukraine, where all ornamental painting has always been done by women. That's the tradition all our primitivists come from—Prymachenko, Sobachko-Shostak—where else if not from the world of painted stoves and sideboards? Even Aleksandra Ekster in the mid-1920s designed patterns for artisan carpet-making co-ops around Mykolaiv, until the government sent them all packing."

"Really?" the reporter croons. "I had no idea ..."

"So yes, there you have it. And I do the opposite—I work with what's ruined, the wrecked home, so to speak—trying to build something new, but different, out of it."

"And succeeding," says the interviewer. [Her sudden response has an unintentional reverence that instantly erects an impenetrable glass barrier between her and the object of her admiration. The painter squints.] "*Contents of a Purse Found at the Scene of the Accident* is, in my opinion, absolutely brilliant." [The painter mumbles incomprehensibly.] "Really, I mean it; it's a postmodern classic! Who bought it?"

"The Lausanne Hermitage."

"Well, how nice for them—they could just go and buy themselves a Vladyslava Matusevych!" [She turns to the camera emphatically, so that no one could possibly miss this. A few sparrows blow off a table nearby, startled by the dramatic pronouncement.] "And we are too poor even to put together a national museum of contemporary art! It is a splendid piece, truly splendid." [She slows her pace to a luxuriant purr, as if savoring the painting's every detail in her mind again.] "And now we'll only have the slide to appreciate." [She looks down and reads from prepared notes.] "The painting visualizes a complete drama, composed of small fragments of evidence that usually go unnoticed. In its own way, the work is highly cinematographic, like a montage in which each cut speaks volumes, so one can spend hours reading it, frame by frame—the broken glasses, the receipts, a customs declaration, a picture of a husband and a child tucked into a notebook, a bronzer with a shattered mirror, and those horrific bloody smears on top of ..."

"That's lipstick, Daryna!" the painter interrupts, laughing. [She is visibly relieved to have the conversation move off the laudatory and on to the technical track.] "The smudges on the mirror—that's actual lipstick, Revlon, I just fixed it with varnish."

"No kidding? Finally, I have a chance to ask—I've been dying to ask you this: Didn't it scare you to make this? Wasn't it unsettling—to compose, literally, a *still life?*"

The painter shrugs. "I was curious," she says after a moment's hesitation. [The word is like a clear spot she's found on an icy sidewalk.] "I've had this idea since that Swissair flight went down over Halifax, remember, back in '98, and for a week divers fished personal belongings out of the water to help identify the victims—what if all that's left of you is your purse? What will it tell people who never met you? And then one day my own lipstick came uncapped and smashed all over my compact in my purse, and that's when I saw what it should look like on canvas. But to say I was unsettled? You should tell me—you've seen the whole series in my studio before it went to Switzerland—did it feel unsettling to look at?"

"That's the amazing thing—it's a radiant piece! It's got this easy energy, like it emanates light—all your *Secrets* do, despite the chaos they portray. It's as if you tamed death, domesticated it." [The interviewer falters, unsettled a little by where the train of thought has carried her, and instantly hurries to explain herself.] "I don't mean it in the way Hollywood horror flicks would have it; there's not a whiff of fright in your work, but—How do I put it?... There's your elegant composition; the warmth of your incredibly vivid, sun-drenched Southern-steppes palette; and your delicate ornamental touches, so sweet and so domestic—it all makes you forget that the whole series is about death, ruination. A piece like your *Contents* would look fine in a living room—not just a museum!"

"And you'd put it there? In your living room?" [The painter leans in, intently, in an upward motion, again like a cat about to leap into a tree, her gleaming eyes wide and expectant, and her lips parted slightly, ready to lap up the words that drop.] "Honestly—would you?"

"Oh my God, are you kidding? I'd kill for it! Only I'm sorry, Vlada, who has the money for such luxury?" [The brunette giggles lightheartedly, electrified like a woman in a jewelry store, giddy at the mere chance to look, touch, even try things on.] "I certainly don't make enough to afford a Matusevych."

[She says this with a clear note of pride—the kind of pride easily recognized by any first-generation career professional in a country where to identify specifically what you cannot afford (a BMW 6 Series, a Tiffany necklace, a Matusevych) is to draw a wide circle around scores of less-exclusive possessions that you can in fact afford, unlike the vast majority of your compatriots, and with the same naïve, neophyte pride of a global provincial dropping the name Vladyslava Matusevych, as meaningfully as the world's art-loving bourgeois utter Picasso or Matisse—the pride of a teenager who feels at home among the grown-ups. The painter, however, is not flattered by this intonation—she appears to occupy a different store altogether.]

"Thank you, Daryna," she says simply. "This is very important for me, what you've just said. I'll give you a painting, no worries, as a present. Not *Contents of a Purse*, of course, a different one, but from the same series, from *Secrets*. You'll come over and choose one, okay?"

[Even under the thick layer of makeup, one can see the interviewer's face grow suddenly darker as she blushes with a breathless thrill—all the way past her ears.]

"Don't shoot this!" the brunette cries out, laughing. [She turns her entire body to the camera to block the shot. The sudden motion makes the silk Versace scarf wound carelessly around her bare neck slip and begin to slide off, and she pins it with both hands against her collarbones. This looks comical in the frame—like an ingénue actress in her first role as a simple-hearted provincial maiden who's just cried out in joy and clasped her hands to her bosom.]

"Vovchyk," she pleads. [The interviewer is now consciously playing the part, sensing she's being adored.] "What did I say? Stop the camera right now! You monkeys, what are you thinking? I'll cut it anyway—the last thing we need is to air a pronouncement like that, I'd never live it down, they'll say Goshchynska takes kickbacks for her interviews!"

[Men's voices rise from behind the frame in a low mutter:]

"Yeah, especially from politicians!"

"Hey, she'll take her men where she can get them!"

"Ha-ha-ha!"

[And that's when the camera stops rolling—at last.]

**

You're a doll, Daryna Goshchynska, a stupid painted doll, she tells herself, having found much to detest, if not altogether abhor, about her bubbly on-screen persona, having pressed the stop button on the control panel and lowered her head onto her arms in the darkness. You're a good-looking woman to be sure; people look at you and think, she's got it. Blowing sunshine all over and up whose ass? You want a medal or something? What the fuck? You forty-year-old bird, compulsive valedictorian, peddler of eye candy and book smarts, you doll, you stupid, stupid doll.

**

Vlada, Vladusya, so small and so indomitable, as if held up by an iron rod—once I caught her working in her studio, her hair tied back with a bandana, in threadbare overalls crusty with paint and chalk, and felt stunned: where was my grand dame, the star of fashionable salons and glamorous receptions? She looked like a teen at a construction site, the flunky sent down the scaffolding to fetch buckets of drywall mud; the studio stank ferociously of varnish (I was instantly lightheaded); Vlada was even paler than usual—her lips bluish-lilac as if with cold, and she gulped milk straight from the torn corner of the carton that stood open on a table, breathing and snorting like a sweaty peasant; her brow and nose were speckled with gold dust—and it was a strange realization that this backstage, dirty, and calloused proletarian existence was her real life.

Later, after she was gone, and the stirred-up viper's nest of the Kyiv bohemia couldn't get enough of the event (not without the schadenfreude at the comforting prospect of things returning to their natural order in which all Ukrainian artists, without exception, are starving and unknown), it became intolerably painful to accept that realization about Vlada's life, especially after the cost of her lavish funeral became the subject of greedy, whispered calculations—"a fortune for the coffin alone!" (The first time I heard this, I wholeheartedly wished, on a swell of pure molten hatred, that the appraiser get one of those coffins for his own use, and wished I could take my imagined curse back when I remembered that the moron had thyroid cancer, and that Vlada herself had bought him some rare drugs from Switzerland, out of her own pocket, of course, because he had no money, and she'd always paid for everything out of her own pocket, the invincible iron girl, except, as it turns out, not invincible, and not made of iron at all.)

Where did she get it—this unwomanlike certainty of hers, the rock-solid confidence in her chosen path? I, who was conditioned to hone in, like a radar, on applause, who withered like a flower in stale water without a regular dose of male admiration (what an idiot!), in the course of our friendship gradually learned to take a mental tally of my actions—for her, first and foremost, and tried my hardest to earn her praise, made only more reliable by the fact that, unlike the approval of men, it had nothing to do with the length of my legs or the size of my rack—to the point where the smallest vexations sent me scrambling for the phone, to cry on Vlada's firm shoulder, and she never once told me to get lost and get a life, as I, undoubtedly, deserved. She seemed so unflappable and solid: her career grew like a cottonwood sap—up, up; her boyfriend shot straight from the launchpad of his shadowy business (I still don't really know what it was that he did exactly, but the money must have come from the kind of sources our nouveau riche prefer not to advertise and only mention in passing, as a joke) into elected office, and just kept going, and Vlada said he was almost done with the mind-blowing mansion he'd been building for the three of them somewhere in Roslavychi, the exurb dubbed "a slice of Switzerland," among pristine meadows and ponds; her Katrusya went to the British Council School, with the children of foreign diplomats, to the tune of ten thousand bucks in tuition per year (Vlada paid). Her life was wonderful and would only keep getting better—and this also gave me security, a firm foundation for the confidence I needed so much, as if Vlada's success promised, by some primitive, inaccessible logic of association, that everything would be similarly wonderful in my life as well, if not today, then tomorrow for sure. What else feeds female friendship if not this associative twinship, this reciprocal mirroring and intertwining, and don't friendships die precisely and only when they run out of such associations?

That's why, when a month or so after our interview she complained to me of not being able to sleep—and she so rarely complained about anything, and always only in the past tense, after whatever difficulty had vexed her had been overcome, the barrier cleared, and the effort involved reduced to a source of comforting insight for a friend in need, as in "I know exactly what you're dealing with, I've gone through the same thing, but see, I made it, and so will you"—I simply missed the alarm, failed to receive the signal, or, more precisely, ignored it like background noise: such signals, apparently, are only recognized by cretins like myself in deep hindsight, after the funeral, when all the heaving and sighing and shaking of heads adds up to a critical mass and reveals that such signals fell around the deceased in her last weeks like hail. How could we all have missed them, under what collective curse?

"Would you believe it, I can't sleep," she'd said on the phone, as if extending an invitation to marvel together at this unusual phenomenon, but at two in the morning the tireless gurgle of her voice bore into my ear like a subcutaneous irritation because I had to get up at six for a live session and was close to falling over as I moved around my apartment, bumping into furniture, half-aware of packing my bag, with the phone against my ear that seemed to be slowly mashed into a bloody mess as she dripped, "I have this idiotic fear, like, if I fall asleep, I will die...."

"Vlada, you're simply overworked," I said, for the sixth time in the last hour, "nothing comes without a price; you've had a hard year, leave it all and go on vacation somewhere far away"—thinking that the newly elected representative also needed some resting, since apparently he had no way of helping a woman fall asleep and was turning into one of his brethren who get from stress to stress by drinking their way through a sea of alcohol, only to be diagnosed with erectile dysfunction by age forty—and Vlada was still babbling, unflinchingly, that yes, I had a point, and they were already planning a trip to Dubai, or Abu Dhabi, one is cheaper and the other more accommodating, and which one she'd recommend in case I decided to get away, finally, too, until I had to plead for mercy and howled, "Vlada Matusevych, would you please shut up and let me get away for the four hours I still have?!"

She laughed—a short, erratic flute scale, strangely melodic but suddenly awkward, as if she just then realized that she'd been keeping me up, and unsettling, too, because I also felt awkward for having flaunted my sleepiness to a friend suffering from insomnia—and it felt like I'd left her to fend for herself at night in an unfamiliar place. The laugh stuck in my ear like water, except that it did not, like water, seep warmly into the pillow as I slept through the short hours, and I woke still hearing its silvery echo, which, should I have had the wits to stop and listen to carefully, would have spelled out another warning signal—a sign that my outburst, which had slipped out of my grip like an ax falling from tired arms, had cut an invisible cable from the great edifice that is life, and it shuddered in response. In Vlada's tinny laugh, high like a taut string's ear-splitting response to an errant touch, razor on glass—that's the dissonance that the four hours I still had must have sent into the widening, humming circles of infrasound vibrations that were already swirling around Vlada, because the truth was that at that point, I had many more hours left than she had; hers were countable, hers were slipping away, hers were almost drained to the bottom, but neither of us could have known it then.

And three weeks after that she did fall asleep—precisely as her late-night fear warned her not to—in the middle of the day, in her car, on the highway to Boryspil, on her way to meet her agent who was flying in from Frankfurt with her paintings; he insisted he'd given them to her and they parted at the airport; but when Vlada's overturned Beetle, crumpled like a tin can around her body, which was speared, hard, by the steering wheel, was lifted from the ditch and cut apart, there were no paintings in it, neither in the back seat, nor in the trunk, and, of course, one could assume that the car was robbed after it had crashed, or one could indulge a swarm of far worse and entirely outlandish suspicions about the accident, of which the only one that retained any vestiges of common sense, and thus could keep the living from losing all of theirs, was the idea that Vlada had fallen asleep while driving and the car had swerved off the wet highway (it had been raining just before the accident), and no one would ever know—this haunted me for a long time afterward—whether in the last split second before impact, as the Beetle flew into the ditch, Vlada was shaken awake in time to realize what was happening (Long enough to be terrified? To scream? To feel the pain? To hear the sound of her own bones crushing?) or if she'd woken up already on the other side, trying, unsuccessfully, to rub her eyes and slowly coming to realize that she no longer had eyes nor hands to rub them with. (This would be better—so much better that I spent many months convincing myself that that's exactly what happened.)

"I killed her," repeated Rep. Vadym, face frozen into a bizarre half-smile, as he sank, fat and red (Vlada, small as Thumbelina, had always preferred large-scale men), into the ottoman; his shirt had come undone and a patch of high-quality underwear stuck out; a bottle of Courvoisier stood on the rug at his feet, and he held his glass with both hands, mechanically swirling his drink and repeating his mantra—"I killed her, I killed her, it's my fault, I should have been in that car"—and this grotesque teddy-bearishness of his was the hardest to take, especially when paired with what he was saying, so inconsistent with reality, so discordant with what had happened—like the sound a razor blade makes on glass—as if he'd been cut and pasted here from a different movie altogether. I thought he was beating himself up for having let Vlada go alone, that he was crushed with the desperate realization that if he'd gone with her, she would've lived—and it was hard to argue with that—but it dawned on me that he was not feeling guilty about Vlada so much as feeling sorry for himself. It took all I had not to scream at him, Shut up!, even though he was not really speaking to me, or asking anything of me, and would've been asking the same question if I weren't there, would ask his drink, and the ottoman on which he sat: "Dear Lord, how am I supposed to go on living?" And then with a precision amazing for his size, he put the glass down on a coaster and hid his face with his hands, half-moaning and half-mumbling something completely incomprehensible and leaving me to stand there helplessly and stare at his fingers splayed against his baby-pink bald head like a bunch of sausages.

It wasn't duty that brought me speeding to his damn nouveau-riche apartment on Tarasivska—just finished, with a penthouse, and a glass roof—I hadn't come to comfort him or to meld with him in shared grief; there was something else I wanted: I was watching him like a slowly darkening mirror that still held Vlada's image, to find on him still-warm bits of her presence from the day before and pick them off him, like lint, to see him—as I realized I'd begun to do—with her eyes, something I'd never done before, when he was just a boyfriend (that's how Vlada referred to him, always in English), not her lover, not her man, her boyfriend; that's why, on some level, my mind put check marks of approval against his underwear, and the unexpected delicacy of his movement as he put the glass down—a quick *aha*, so these paws with sausages for fingers know how to be sensitive—and noted also his dry eyes—Vadym poured much more into himself than he let out, a sign of healthy virile appetites, of a vigorous bladder and other organs (once, when the two of them came over, we spent five hours sipping Courvoisier, but he never once got up to go to the bathroom; Vlada always said they had a great physical relationship, she wouldn't have said anything if it weren't so, so her insomnia had nothing to do with that). But it wasn't like I'd run there to appraise him for an auction and grade his condition either; these things flashed in my mind at random, in double-exposure, I felt neither distaste nor sympathy for this man, and when I told him it was not his fault, I did so not because I felt sorry for him but solely out of respect for Vlada's death, which belonged to her and her alone, and must have been woven according to the unique design of her lifetime. As for Vadym, I instantly and irretrievably cast him the role of the banana peel on which people in old movies slip at fateful moments and crash to their deaths, but real life, unlike movies, sets up its fateful moment long before any banana peels make themselves available, and that's why Vadym's mechanical screeching—I killed her, I killed her—was irksome and offensive: it disgraced my proud and independent Vlada by claiming agency in her life, it reeked of yellowish newspaper clippings, which were, no doubt, to appear very soon, scandal-mongering vultures must've caught the whiff of offal already and begun circling around the house, tomorrow there'd be flocks of them, see if you can hide from the flashes then—but this was also something one had to survive one way or another, and it would all happen later, in the noxious weeks when her death would be deboned, quartered, and roasted with different sauces in a breathless recipe contest broadcast to every household in the nation, until the thing got so frayed and worn that even my heart stopped seizing every time I saw her portrait and the portraits became just pictures of a famous person, an entry in a *Who's Who.*

In those first few hours, there was only one thing I needed, and that's why I came to Vadym's apartment and sat there with him, as he vacantly drank the cognac that refused to do its work, while Vlada lay somewhere on a freezer shelf with a tag tied to her toe—I couldn't shake off the pesky and senseless idea that she was *cold* there and kept shivering myself, ripples of sudden chill shimmying up and down my skin just like that time in the Passage during our interview, when Vlada shape-shifted for an instant into an acolyte on the eve of his vows, someone destined for other-worldliness, only now the chill would not stop; I could not get warm and kept going back to the cognac, and every sip I took, instead of warming me lodged in my chest, solid and unyielding, like the steering wheel—and the only thing I wanted, the thing I came for, was to confirm, right there and then, that Vlada had been happy with Vadym. If I had that reassurance, I'd feel better; I'd be able to craft the horror into some semblance of meaning, like if she herself had showed up and said, with a resolute bounce of her bangs, I've no regrets, you know? None, you have my word.

Again I washed up in her apartment just as I always did in moments of panic and confusion—I'd come looking for comfort that only she could give, in the very apartment she'd left the day before, and then gotten into her sunshine-yellow Beetle. And then slammed the door shut.

Later, someone must've rung the doorbell, or come in, or Vadym finally had to go to the bathroom, because I was left alone in the living room and stood next to the uncurtained window watching a dense, fluorescent Gauloise-pack blueness quicken and solidify outside; during those days, all colors appeared painfully saturated, all lenses focused in all directions at once, and my eye kept tripping on utterly irrelevant frames—on the way to the cemetery out the car window a pair of dogs, one spotted and the other black and shaggy, rolled on a pile of lacquer-glossy wet leaves; and on the subway bridge, as the funeral procession passed under it, a homeless man with a patchwork tote, bowed against the low-hanging sky—with the kind of sharpness that also happens when you're in love and every randomly arranged instance, once it falls into your sight, swells, rounds, and breaks off like a distinct drop of water; so, maybe it's only in love and death that life becomes truly visible for us. Through the window, amid the fluorescent blue, I could see children playing on the sidewalk across the street, sharp moving silhouettes, black cutouts, with only their white sneakers flickering in the dusk like dying lightbulbs; in the foreground an old woman in a tiny knit hat, swaddled like a cabbage in many layers of clothes, searched slowly, with mesmerizing, dendritic stiffness, through the trash cans; and then, very slowly, as if filmed with speed-ramping, a car crawled by, a dark Mazda with blazing lynx-like headlights, and as I stood there in the raincoat that I never did remember to take off, I saw myself from outside too—someone painted into this creaking, straining, but *still unfolding* picture, and also saw, with the same piercing clarity, that Vlada was no longer part of this continuous time. We were being separated by its implacable flow; its forceful tug, so palpable at that moment, dragged me—now only me—blindly along and left Vlada behind, in the yesterday, marooned in the past as though on an ice floe, and the widening gap between us was rapidly filling with a roiling, rushing surge of new frames of life without her. I watched this flood come and knew I *would never be able to tell her about it*—up till that moment, from the minute I heard, and later with Vadym, the whole time, my mind kept addressing her, sharing its shock with her, chastising—Why did you go alone, Vlada? and a million other trifling post-factum warnings—and it was still she I entertained, and soothed, and came to ask: Were you happy with this man?—but it was already like talking into a dead phone, and all I had left to do was hang up and let this terrible, slow current carry me irretrievably forward, without her.

I understood that Vlada had died and I had remained to live.

When Vadym returned and we started talking again—finally, the cognac took effect and memories burst out of him, random and unstoppable—I said "she was" for the first time about Vlada and was surprised at how easily it came and how easy it was to continue, from then on, in past tense.

This must be it, then—ground zero—when a new count is set to begin and a new system of coordinates takes root and reaches outward into the unknown. Time fills you in, layer after layer, like calcium encrusting joints, and the things and places that once bled with the dead person's presence dry up and scab over with repeated daily use in this new time, the time "without": the crosswalk, next to the movie studio where Vlada once sneaked her yellow Beetle behind me and stuck her shaggy, golden-wheat head out the window and hollered, "Daryna!" having been crossed another dozen times, sheds her presence and no longer hurts, becoming just another crosswalk; the windows of her apartment— the ones I checked for light as soon as I came out of the subway, the ones whose glow made me walk faster in anticipation of our kitchen-table talk after she'd put Katrusya to bed—first became the dark windows of an empty home, and then dissolved into a row of other windows, as if swallowed by a crowd, until one day, as I walked by, I realized I could no longer find them—was the first one the second or the third from the corner balcony?—and stood there on the sidewalk struck with my mouth open, like Lot's wife, trying to remember the layout of the apartment, while lines from *Hamlet* swirled in my mind, "My father died within these two hours. / —Nay, 'tis twice two months, my lord." (Or twice two years—does it get any easier?)

Fighting a pile of old letters at home, in another useless fit of resistance against the expanding paper chaos, I recognized the hand on an envelope with such intense emotion that it pinned me to the spot like an animal in a spotlight: *This is from someone I once loved!* And only after I read the return address did I realize it was Vlada's writing. Is it truly not the person that we remember, but only our own feelings attached to them? Does the loss hurt because it leaves us flailing, throwing our severed emotional limbs after something that's no longer there? Only the places that were unsoiled, untouched by subsequent visits retained the memories they originally held: the bench on Prorizna Street, next to Yama Café, where in the fall of 1990 the two of us sat burning our palates with "the double-halves" of coffee from Soviet cups with handles broken off to discourage anyone from stealing them, while below, in front of the Central Post Office, the not-yet-renamed Independence Square roared as a single body—its low drone swelled into one explosive boom after another, reverberating off walls, running quakes and shudders through window panes, all the way across the deserted city to the old Jewish market and the striking trolleybus depots—and the empty trolleybuses, their poles lowered and wires drooping like wet whiskers, stood aligned in two rows along Khreshchatyk, as if readied to be used as barricades; our faces felt the hot breath of stormy, combustible air—the crackling air of unrest that is released from the fissures between epochs like subterranean gases from between slipping tectonic plates, the air that picks you up and carries you along, air you can walk on, run on, shouting and not hearing your own voice. Our lips, parched after a day of standing on the square, burned as we passed our single cigarette to each other; we drank the boiling-hot double-halves and Vlada talked and talked without pause, as though she'd broken through many years of silence—about her divorce, about how things can't go on the same, how life had to change, how it had to begin, finally, for real. "We had no youth, Daryna," she said, meaning the students who'd lain down in the square and no longer got up—the students on their backs, face to face with the sky, their features starved into seraphic transparency, their suicidal headbands with the words "hunger strike" etched meekly in white on their foreheads—and we envied them because, unlike them, "we had no youth."

Vlada's verdict cut me to the quick—it was so brutally true; she always possessed that unsparing clarity of vision, an astonishing degree of honesty for a comfortable Soviet girl. I felt the same as she did, but she was always first to recognize and articulate what it was, and as I listened to her then I felt, for the first time, a stab of another thought, one that I had been afraid to acknowledge—that my own marriage had expired just like hers, and I had to find the courage to tear it apart soon, to sever it surgically before the rot infected the two souls entangled in it. The world melded into a giant, rolling mass; our lives, and the only era we'd known, were falling apart in front of our eyes, and they were being ground down to irreducible solid specs that could then be sucked into the dark maelstrom of history. We had both married very proper Soviet boys, handsome and nice, college and, later, graduate students; and it was only when time came crashing down around us that we realized that these proper Soviet boys, so handsome and nice, feared nothing more than growing up—that an insurmountable horror of the adult life in which one had to make independent decisions had lain latent in them like an incurable virus, and it took nothing less than an utter collapse of the social system that had relied on men just like them to bring it out. Vlada had sensed all this a step ahead of me and was first to jump ship, to paddle her one-woman rescue raft away, with the infant Katrusya at her breast—I don't think I would've had the guts were I in her shoes, but then again, I didn't have the guts to have Sergiy's child either. She had not a shred of fear in the face of the unknown; her whole being hummed, aimed at the future, as though she were set atop a tightly coiled steel spring ready to pop, and the energy she contained charged me, too, giving me some of the same confidence—she was wearing a black leather jacket that day, and I remember thinking with a smile, in a sudden rush of tenderness, Biker girl! All she needs is a white helmet ...

The bench on Prorizna is still there—after they closed Yama Café, they turned the place into a casino so it no longer serves as the perch for bohemian smoke breaks and now sits empty most of the time, on a blank slab of asphalt, no longer hidden by lilac bushes that were cleared to make a parking lot for the casino-bound Mercedes and Porsches—the only surviving monument to that autumn when we were, as it turned out later, still young, so young that we didn't even know it. Because only youth, having found itself straddling a widening chasm between two eras, can leap forward with an easy heart, away from its crumbling past, can send whatever has been to the trash, like a bad draft, and set out, at not-quite thirty, to "live for real"—it is only youth that has the arrogance to cross out the years that have not satisfied its ambition: time teaches you to waste nothing, to savor unhurriedly, like wine, things that years earlier you would've brushed aside on a princely whim, thinking, as young Katrusya said whenever she missed her bus, "Dey'll send us anoter one, bettuh." Time teaches you that no, unfortunately, they won't.

Vlada had ten more years exactly—ten berserk years of living "for real," at the speed of a Harley barreling down a mountain road (with Katrusya in her backpack); ten years in which she, a single mother without any material resources, except the studio on the Andriyivsky Descent that she inherited from her father, transformed herself into a truly accomplished artist, possibly the most successful painter in Ukraine—if you can measure national success in foreign sales, of course (although lately even our homegrown fat cats have begun to warm up to the idea that owning a Matusevych is badass), or in foreign sales and Ukrainian envy, because the latter is far more precise and sensitive than money alone: money, after all, is relative, and no one ever has enough, but envy always circulates in reliably high supply, and the more of it that roils around you, the thicker and more noxious its vapors, the more certain it is that you have risen, damn it, risen above the crowd.

(As if she did it on purpose, as if she'd stood up from the trenches and let the sniper's bullet find her. As if someone up there cared that we shouldn't rise too far above anything, that we should toe the line. Inch forward, slowly—not the way she wanted it, "for real.")

It is always on Prorizna, when I pass the orphaned little bench on its bare knoll, that the stubbornly offended, purely childish thought—It's not fair!—pops up like a forgotten buoy and hits me anew. If there's still someone up there who enforces the rules, then it was even more unfair of him to rip her out of a life that she lived full tilt (literally) like a crock dentist who pries off a good tooth—Oops, sorry, a bit of a mistake here, but you can't put it back, can you?

Vlada herself must have been more than a little cross after she'd been deposited in the next world so unceremoniously: the very first night, while her body lay on a morgue shelf, she appeared in my dreams unusually furious—in her studio, wearing those same threadbare overalls and rummaging through drawers in search of something; she waved me off when I called out to her, desperately, with my whole being—meaning, leave me alone, I'm busy—and said something truly bizarre, something about "a bill of ward" that she urgently needed because "there are too many deaths." I memorized those words exactly because, although the language of dreams is as impenetrable as that of prophecies, it is incapable of untruth and therein lies its central distinction from what we say and hear in daylight; it is our perception that skews the dreamt messages, "instrument bias" as scientists call it, and that's why whenever I manage to preserve something I heard in my dreams until morning I write it down verbatim, even if it sounds a hundred times less meaningful than what I heard Vlada say to me on that first night, especially since, as it later turned out, on the same night in Vlada's mother's apartment, where Katrusya was staying, lights spontaneously went on and off in different rooms, doors opened and closed, and the girl cried out in her sleep, "Mama!"—apparently, Vlada was searching there too, searching for her bill of protection, but against what? And to be given to whom?

At the funeral, the teary womenfolk chatted themselves into the consensus that Vlada must've been looking for the lost paintings, the "many deaths" referring to her subject matter, and one gallery curator, turned irretrievably kooky on canonically dogmatic Orthodox grounds, blurted out what would feed the whispering, watery-eyed gluttons in certain circles for a long time hence: "You must not toy with a topic like that, you know?"—not without a dose of moral superiority, like someone officially tasked with watching over cosmic justice (Vlada couldn't stand these born-again types and called them "the church CheKa"). The men, who generally held more positivist views, found a different interpretation more appetizing right there at the wake, especially after they'd had a couple drinks and the quickest of the ladies joined in and went to work with their knives and forks. To them it was quite obvious that Vlada had been "marked," and for quite a while, "'coz everyone knows you could hire a professional hit man for five hundred bucks on a slow day, and a single one of Vlada's painting would fetch many times as much, enough to whack your own mama—Five hundred, ha!" "Didn't you hear on TV the other day? Just outside Donets'k, someone dug up a grave the day after the funeral to pull ten hryvnas out of the dead man's suit pocket that a neighbor saw the widow put there." "No, that's not what I'm talking about, stuff like that always happens, I mean professionals, for them to slip a car into a ditch, especially off a wet highway, is easier than falling off a log!"

And so the conspiracy theories spread and knotted one over another, growing more incredible the further they spun away from the actual event, and it was no use trying to talk sense into the people who'd never seen, other than on TV, either Vlada or Vadym (whose imposing representative's figure at first thoroughly discombobulated the police; I remember seeing an inspector in the maelstrom of kin and friends, and a few others, all in uniform caps and with identical shifty looks of small thugs caught red-handed). They wouldn't hear that A) no signs of any contact with another vehicle were found on the smashed Beetle; B) the investigation was able to reconstruct, rather competently, the path traveled by the car as it swerved off the highway, which C) made the crash a clear and conclusive accident, to the great relief of the police, who nonetheless purported to keep looking for the lost paintings, although you didn't have to be a genius to guess that they'd never be found, unless, I don't know, someone tripped over them—and what Ukrainian cop, if he still had his wits, would wear down his soles chasing after some "pitures," no matter how many times you tell him that they cost more than some stolen Volga?;

and, most importantly, that D) we do not, thank Lord, belong to the EU, regardless of how hard our anointed leaders thump their gelatinous chests to make precisely the opposite point, and one would be hard-pressed to find a decent art-thieving mafia in the deep ass that is our independent-of-any-rationality nation, where a modest bribe to a local official lets you carve out a piece of a brick wall with any Bruno Schulz fresco you fancy, or any fresco for that matter, anything, really, and the pickings have been slim ever since our last Goya and Ribera were sent to Moscow for "conservation" in the 1960s, never to be returned, just as no one intends to give us back the gems of the Tereshchenko collection that Grandpa Lenin himself traded off to Armand Hammer for his relief effort in 1921; so, no, it's been a good half century since a self-respecting art thief could find regular sustenance on our lands, not to mention the fact that one needs a good network of legitimate art dealers to smuggle things out, and, as our cameraman Antosha puts it, Where the fuck do you find yourself some of those?

Ukrainians, as any preschooler will tell you, focus on much simpler, homely things: arms, drugs, non-ferrous metals, poached Carpathian lumber, girls "for work in Europe"—fail-safe operations, with good cash flow, and who needs academies and shit like that; let things take their course, the country'll find its way; let all those nutty artists and other trash feel secure as they would in their mommies' bosoms for the simple reason that no one gives a flying fuck about them; let them live and graze, if they can find themselves a pasture.

Vlada and I talked about all this a million times, laughing at especially burlesque episodes, such as the time she bought her apartment—a transaction that involved a change of clothes in the bathroom stall at the real-estate trade exchange to release a money belt packed with fifty thousand sweaty dollars from its rather erotic captivity under Vlada's bodysuit; don't let anyone tell you that money doesn't smell, but who would have thought twice about the little woman as she marched down the street, wrapped in layers of baggy knee-long sweaters like an onion? Just like that, Vlada went all over the city, and outside the city, alone with rolled-up canvases in her car because no one on God's green earth would ever want them! Folks, think about it, I wanted to tell all those scandalmongers who wouldn't give up on their murder mystery involving a famous artist and unimaginable wealth (three paintings, in fact, which together might have fetched ten thousand dollars on a good day in our kind of market): What would your hit man do with those paintings? How would he go about turning them into cash? So, of course, I laid it all out—my iron-clad logic of A, B, C, and D, and so on—as soon as anyone mentioned the topic (And the idiots just wouldn't let it rest, would they?); for the longest time their openly disapproving response remained a mystery to me: Why did they always behave like I was taking something away from them? Like I came to steal something precious? At the same time, parallel and yet more outrageous versions seeped out of some dark corners, like water trickling from under the door of a flooded bathroom: one was that the accident was Vlada's way of killing herself, and what shocked me most was that this version was popular not among the casual, nothing-better-to-do observers, but among her own people—the painters she knew, all of whom suddenly felt compelled to voice their personal, unique eyewitness accounts about the last time they saw or talked to Vlada and how they "would never guess anything like that"; the other hypothesis, even crazier in its own way, was that Vlada was killed because of Vadym, as in, someone wanted to send him a message, a mysterious competitor or, God help us, a political rival—as if the dude were the redeemer of the anti-Kuchma coalition or something. But this one stopped me in my tracks for a second once I remembered his desperate muttering of "I killed her," which, let's face it, could have had a different meaning from what I was able to comprehend, with my bovine perceptiveness, at the moment, especially when one recalled that the number of politicians and entrepreneurs killed in car accidents on our country's roads grew longer by the day—a fact that was even deemed noteworthy by *The New York Times*, which doesn't bestow such honor on Ukrainian events very often—and every one of those deaths had been ruled, in official speak, "a misfortunate accident." Philosophically speaking, the ruling had its own logic: there's very little fortune in anyone's sudden death, and as far as accidents go, every single event in our lives is an accident, all of them—or, maybe, none at all—and the very hairs on our heads are all numbered, only we're not the ones doing the numbering, a conclusion that prompts our nation, which had given the world the great philosopher Skovoroda, to settle back, having made a bit of a fuss, every time, into its very Skovorodian stoicism; but to imagine that one of these "accidents" could have been aimed at Vadym, that he was so important that someone would've considered Vlada, his utterly uninvolved-in-his-business girlfriend, collateral damage—this was too much, even for Ukraine. Yet no sooner could one version be dismissed than several new ones appeared and spread in every direction, overtaking, like rising water, every dike reason could put in their path, going under and around in countless trickles, and it took me more than a few months of this to learn not to blush like a ripe tomato and screech mean things, quite without composure, every time someone asked me the question, with its probing emphasis, "Are you sure it was an accident?"—more than a few months to grasp that it was not truth people asked for, whatever it ultimately turned out to be, but a story. Amen. And who am I, who makes a living manufacturing such stories, to judge them?

Against my better nature, I had to admit, nothing is better suited for a story than the sudden tragic death of a brilliant and famous young woman. No young man's death could ever produce the same effect—it's as if men were expected to die, were doomed to die by some silent communal pact, if not in war, then somewhere else, as if the poor things were quite unfit for anything else, and that's why with men, it's not the fact of the death itself that we judge but how well it was performed: Did the deceased meet his fate chin-up, did he take it bravely on the chest, thus fulfilling a man's purpose, or did he try to hide, like a coward, and betray said purpose dishonorably? We must reach one of these conclusions—call it The People's Death Police, if you will—and that's why we will not forget the case of journalist Georgiy Gongadze until we are delivered his tangible, bleeding real death instead of anonymous beheaded remains dug up somewhere in the woods. But no one remembers Vadym Boiko, the face of Ukrainian TV in the early 1990s, who shortly before a blast in his apartment was giddily showing his colleagues a thick file—I've got them all, those old Commies, right here, at last, you'll see it all tomorrow!—and when the smoke cleared everyone saw Boiko's burned body and cracked concrete ceilings. Boiko is quite forgotten because why would anyone bother remembering if everyone knows what happened?

A young woman's death is another matter altogether: it is always seen as a violation of the very natural order of things, since the first thought is inevitably about her brood—when there isn't any (and will never be) and when there is (who will watch, oh, who will care, who will wash my orphan's hair as the folk song mourns, and a million like it, century after century). A story is badly needed here—it alone can help restore the natural order of things; it can focus the frame and present this one death as a horrible aberration, a painful disruption for which someone, somewhere, will have to answer, if not now, then eventually, and if not in a court of law, then to a higher Judgment. If, on top of everything else, the victim was seen as a princess, showered with gifts by fairy godmothers every birthday and Christmas (Which already hinted at a trespass, inserted the required measure of injustice into the equation: Why should she be the special one?), and if she never once in her life acted the victim because she was too proud, or had principles, or for whatever other reason, then it only makes more sense to blame her for everything—let her take it all, if she's so special—and close the case, turn, spit, curse, nothing like this would ever happen to me. A story like that is a chant, a protective spell that seals the other person's death, puts it in an airtight glass sarcophagus, fit for a museum display—you can look, you can walk around it, you can even run your fingers on the glass and tap it with a pointer as you teach the lesson of how one ought not to live, lest one intends to find oneself at the height of one's powers—and six feet under: Always buckle your seat belt, follow the rules, avoid dubious liaisons, don't paint unsettling pictures and, for God's sake, don't rise so far above the crowd. All my dogged As, Bs, Cs, Ds, and so on were no more than a pathetic, wasted, toothless attack at this thick glass sarcophagus—an assault on people's fundamental, self-preserving belief that death, our own or someone else's, must have a sensible reason, that the world is just. And what did I have to counter this—my wimpy, childish, and inconsolable *"It's not fair"*?

As if all this weren't enough, Vlada veered off the Boryspil highway at the same spot where the politician Viacheslav Chornovil crashed in 1999, and Vlada's death stoked a new fire under the old rumors of foul play suspected in his accident; it was after these flared up again that I first had the inkling that her words about "many deaths" did not refer to *Contents of a Purse Found at the Scene of the Accident* and a few other, less funereal, paintings on the theme of death, did not refer to her work at all, but communicated a much more literal—and menacing—insight she had come back to share. The place where she went off the road had long enjoyed a very bad reputation among Kyiv's motorists; it was an evil, fateful spot: at least once every season, someone got into trouble there, lost traction on perfectly dry asphalt and swerved all the way out into the oncoming traffic, or collided with another car while passing it, or had his gas tank explode for no apparent reason—had it been the custom, along the preeminent Boryspil highway, to festoon its flanks with memorial wreaths and flower bouquets, as folks did along more common roads, the rainbow of colors at this spot would announce it from afar, like a cemetery entrance set in a lush bed of florists' stands.

It seemed, then, that Vlada, as countryfolk say, found herself in the wrong place at the wrong time, and was caught on the track laid by earlier deaths precisely at a time when her own life juices were sucked almost dry—she did have a very hard year, but what do I really know about that? What does Vadym really know about that, despite being territorially, at least, the closest person to her? How stunned he was—with a brief flash of a childlike delight, as if at a message relayed from her from a distant land, a sign of a persisting connection—when I told him about Vlada's midnight terror of dying if she fell asleep. "You must be kidding?" Was it because he would've ignored it, would've told her to take some pills—so you're stressed out, no big deal—or because she didn't share with him anything he might have indulgently interpreted as silliness? After all, Vadym belonged to the class of people who were used to dealing with Problems That Had to Be Solved and not with Misfortunes That Had to Be Endured, and this, as they say in Odessa, is a big difference. It is the demarcation line that divides us into the strong and the weak of the world, and the reason why it is the strong who, at the end of the day, are the least equipped to deal with tragedy and therefore collapse dramatically when one befalls them: Vadym coped by drinking himself into a mute stupor and then climbing into his Land Cruiser and driving off into the night, toward Boryspil, as if he hoped to see Vlada somewhere along the way, so he had to be watched and fought nightly into bed, first by his friends, and later by some provincial relatives summoned to Kyiv for this purpose; but, for reasons that defy understanding, nothing ever happened to him on these nocturnal sojourns, except the money he lost paying the traffic cops, or, rather, whatever US dollar bills he grabbed and blindly thrust at them when they stopped him. What followed usually depended on the cops' benevolence: one time they towed him to their station and kept him there for the night, pouring him strong tea from their thermoses and calling every single number in his address book until they roused a friend to come take him home—the ticket must have been especially impressive that night, or maybe he just ran into some really kind cops (Why not? Things happen.), some good folks who listened to him pour his soul out and tell them, over and over, how his Vlada perished, until he fell asleep on a cot, or they finally knocked him out, instantly and professionally, and who would blame them if they did?

It had never occurred to me before that, of the two of them, Vlada was the stronger one. The ancient mythical notion (branded into me since infancy by my mother) that the husband—the Man!—unless he was in jail or in hospital, must be "the leader" and "take care of everything" was apparently more persistent than I had suspected, outliving hell, high water, a ruined marriage, and a broken (multiple times) heart, providing the dusty peephole through which I viewed (without really seeing much) Vlada's marriage as a fulfillment of our poor mothers' ideal: here—finally!—a strongman shielding you from all worldly mishaps with his mighty shoulders, both physical and financial; all you have to do is bloom, look pretty, and pursue spiritual improvement, without a care in the world, other than scheduling your interviews on national TV. The funniest thing is that women like that still existed in our mothers' generation: the ladies who stayed home, cooked borsches, studied esoteric literature, patronized persecuted and unrecognized artists, occasionally penned or crafted something, and were held in high regard as impressive activists by their communities; but the fact that some humble hardworking husbands bankrolled all their activism—their artists, their books, and whatever went into their borsches, too—was never mentioned in polite society, just like it wasn't proper to point out that a person has to piss and shit; the knack these ladies had for arranging their lives so comfortably belongs to the ancient feminine arts that were irretrievably lost by the end of the twentieth century, like weaving on an upright loom or treating hives with herb smoke. By the time we came around, the ladies were in their decline, widowed—their humble hardworking husbands, naturally, having all died first—we found them not grandmotherly even, but as a tribe of mothballed ancient girls who didn't know how to go out alone or where the phone and electricity bills were; they responded to an innocent "How are you?" with a two-hour-long lecture on their existential condition, and generally seemed slightly batty, an impression that could not be alleviated even by the glow of their former glory and that was made all the stronger by how laughable they were, which, in turn, cast retroactive doubt on that much-publicized glory, the times that made it possible, and the incredible persistence of the ideals they embodied.

Only when Vadym collapsed without Vlada, like a sack dropped in the middle of the room, did I see how things really were between the two of them—but it didn't make me feel any better. I remembered her the way she was when she first fell in love with him—it seemed like yesterday, but no, 'tis twice two years, my lord—how suddenly charming she was, as if her face, posture, and gestures were lit with a soft low light, and the lumbering Vadym melted in her presence like butter in the sun, clearly not having eyes for much of anything else, and it was all so darn nice that often, after I'd said goodbye and was alone, I'd catch myself still smiling and feel silly, like I had jam on my chin and no one told me. True love always becomes a source of warmth for the people around it, a small hearth, and I was also happy for Vlada in a purely woman's way—happy that she got so lucky, and juiced, like on an essential vitamin, on the fact that her new affair, no less intense at thirty-eight than it would've been at eighteen, showed me, just as Vlada did back in 1990, during the student hunger strike, that, no matter our age, the possibilities continued to be endless, the future was open and would remain so for the rest of our lives—that it would forever beckon like a gate through which one glimpsed the misty-gold horizon.

No one could give me this feeling like she did, except men, for a very short time during the same period of being acutely in love—before the gates slowly screeched closed again. Where could a feeling like this come from in this eternally despoiled country that still lives according to the kolkhoz-era dictum, that one exhausts one's entire stock of possibilities when young, and once that's done, all one has left to do is live through one's children? Something in me always revolted violently against this massively psychotic urge to hurry up and settle, make a tight nest out of life and curl up in it as if for a good night's sleep; it must have been the memory of mom's swift and sudden descent, after she got married for the second time, into a stolid, shapeless, middle-aged womanhood—so radical for the woman who, with Dad, remained trim and elegant, even through the worst of times, someone men turned to look at in the street. Being a clueless teenager at the time, I promptly blamed her transformation on my stepfather: Uncle Volodya may have be a hero and a saint in his surgery, and I didn't doubt my mom's assertion that he went above and beyond to make Father's last months tolerable—although I doubted that it was necessary to extend her gratitude all the way to marrying the man—but, at home, this knight of scalpel and catgut lived like an absolute slob in old bubble-kneed sweatpants, that inescapable domestic uniform of Soviet men. He shocked me with hospital jokes that came in just above barracks humor on the idiocy scale—he'd say to someone on the phone, "Cunt you slick up?" and that was supposed to be funny. And he was acutely disgusting in every bodily function: he could be shaving in the bathroom with the door open and break wind like he was blowing out rusty valves, could keep on talking loudly from the bathroom over the unmistakable sound of his indomitable peeing, made me blush at the dinner table with his comments about the laxative or constipating properties of the meal; he approached eating very seriously, loved "grub," and after a meal of rabbit stew at a friends' house, while picking his teeth, would offer the insightful eulogy of "Yeah, this rabbit did not die for naught"—and everyone laughed, and Mom laughed, and didn't even look awkward! After my sophomore year, after I took my very first camping trip, with guitars, fires, and sex on a windbreaker spread on the ground as an excuse to hightail it from a home ruled by this, as I dubbed him, "Odessa louse" into a marriage, I still hung on to my belligerent belief that it was he who pulled the plug on Mom; he cut the power, turned off the lights, dragged her down, and debased her to the endless, pointless culinary clucking, "Darynka, dear, I've canned some tomatoes for you and a couple of jars of eggplant, and the jam didn't come out right, must've overcooked it, I'll try again while the strawberries are in ..."—she, who wrote poems when she was young, good ones!

I earnestly believed she was the innocent victim who could no longer be rescued, and that belief hurled me into my own life as if riding a rocket-powered broomstick, armed with the determination not to let anyone, ever drag me down; every hint of settling down threatened to do precisely that, tied my hands and loaded rocks into my shoes, and I needed more than one year, and a whole bunch of bumps and bruises, to come to the realization that a woman is never a victim in cases like Mom's, even when that's what she wants you to believe—that my mother, after she settled down, thank goodness, so solidly and conclusively, had nothing more to look forward to, except Uncle Volodya coming home to dinner, and must have pulled the plug, without much regret, herself—she had no use for it anymore.

All my peers were wired, more or less, for the same purpose: to settle down, soon and forever, as if someone were chasing after them and their lives depended on jumping into a bunker and sealing the doors—all except Vlada. She alone lived without the least concern for what her environment and upbringing dictated—and they dictated a comfortable bunker, and a father for Katrusya, because how could the child grow up without a father, and family friendships, and group vacations that could later be talked about on social occasions, and so on and so forth; an entire carefully knotted net that, by virtue of its own gravity, shapes your life without your participation, and it is only after the net is filled and the life's minimum passing score is achieved that a woman can allow herself to let her hair down a little—have a solo show of her paintings in a trendy gallery, say, with the requisite presentation of a custom-suited husband who gallantly refills ladies' drinks at the reception. Vlada, however, behaved as if she'd gone to a different school where they didn't cover such things: She came and went mercurially, as she pleased, with whomever she pleased and where she pleased, looked fantastic doing so, and painted better and better, so that people began to feel intimidated, especially after she came into money, and it got harder to wave her off, dismissively—"Who, Matusevych? Give me a break! You call that a genius?"—because money, no matter how you slice it, has a way of validating its owner's way of doing things.

For some reason, people had the hardest time recognizing the obvious: Vlada was born with the gift of inner freedom that usually comes packaged with talent and without which talent has no prayer—without it, you'll waste yourself chasing applause—and this surplus freedom, like a topped-off tank of gas, let her rev through any external rules that were put in her way without a second thought; Vadym, once he entered her life, could get into the backseat or could man the pit stops and time her laps, but she never thought of their union as settling down, and was irked when her girlfriends insisted on implying precisely the opposite when they congratulated her on, among other things, making such a rich catch—"I'm no pauper myself," she'd snarl back, incensed. Already then I could see what would be crudely and unattractively revealed after she died: that she was not the only one to whom her inborn surplus of freedom and confidence gave the strength to keep her own council—it nourished everyone around her, all of us, including Vadym. Vadym first and foremost.

Things I wouldn't have noticed before now ached like fresh abrasions—such as the time when Vadym, drunk, sobbed, "How am I going to live now?" like a spoiled little boy who's used to having his every wish instantly granted, rolling in a tantrum on the floor without his pants because there's no one to jerk him back to his feet. "She set the bar for me!" and my mind went on adding businesslike entries to its spreadsheet: Is that so, then? You too, huh? At the funeral he also said, no longer hysterical and instead with measured manly grief, "She was the best thing in my life"—as if this confession could make our good Lord suddenly ashamed of what a great personal harm he'd done to the poor man, and again the ache grated through me: What about her, how are we to make meaning of her life now, isn't that the most important thing? I could, of course, just blame his nonsense on shock: people are liable to blurt utter insanities in a state like that, and men especially—nothing to do about that, they know neither how to birth nor how to bury; life's hardest, dirtiest jobs are reserved for women—and no one would expect perfect style from the grief-stricken man.

I guess I was still storing my perceptions for later, by virtue of habit—collecting and rehearsing them so I could share with Vlada, something I would catch myself doing for months—because at that moment, I recalled, as an animate voice in my internal dialogue, Vlada telling me, way back when, about the time when she was little and her father took her to the village to attend the funeral of his mother, the grandmother Vlada had never met. Vlada remembered waking up in the middle of the night and seeing through the open door the flickering candlelight in the other room: there, people were sitting vigil with the newly departed and the candles appeared to little Vlada to be growing into the darkness of their own accord, like fiery flowers, and she thought these were the fern blooms of the fairytales she'd heard, and even made a wish, only she couldn't remember it; that night she heard the lamentation—"Real lamentation, Daryna, you don't hear it like that anymore, not even in the country!"—she said it was like singing, a single musical phrase repeating itself, rising, sweeping up, as if running uphill, then sliding back down, helplessly, worn out like the van that took her and her father to the village through late autumn mud, wheels spinning on every hill, and this monotony contained a kind of all-embracing uncanny clarity, as if only this, the monotony, could truly express the beauty, and the agony, and the vanity of human effort on this earth. Little Vlada sat spellbound under her massive sheep's wool blanket, afraid to breathe, her every bone gripped by the universal mourn that knew no consolation, and the female voice went on singing-wailing that one phrase, brimming with words, spilling out all deeds and affairs of the departed, listing them to someone intangible who was not in that room, as if it washed over them, one by one, and by doing so transformed them into noble regalia that shone brighter than gold, so that Vlada didn't grasp right away that the song talked about her own grandma, whom she'd never met and who now lay there under the fiery dome of candlelight and would not rise again, no matter how she was implored, with the terrifying urgency of futile pleading that is known to men as despair, "Oh, rise, rise again, my dear, my bosom friend, my sister...." Vlada didn't remember any other words—and they were not meant to be remembered, the lament an improvisation that is only sounded once and is not repeated or recalled—but she did remember a man's low, slightly coarse voice murmuring from just outside her door in approval, "That's some fine lamenting," and that's how the city child learned that the song was a lamentation and that it had witnesses other than herself, that there was an audience that had gathered to appreciate it. In that instant, Vlada said, the magic was gone: the mourner turned into a kind of an actor, and soon after she finished, Vlada caught her voice out of the general low hum of women's voices—very businesslike, common, as if changed into dry clothes; it was answering someone or giving someone instructions about where to drape the embroidered rushnyky and how many. "I went back to sleep with this bitter feeling," Vlada remembered, "as if I'd been cheated."

Now that it was she who lay there, pillowed in a heap of flowers, her name struck me anew every time it was said during the liturgy, as if jolting me out of sleep—Lord, receive the soul of Thy servant Vladyslava, and pardon her her sins, whether voluntarily or involuntarily, whether witting or through ignorance—Vladyslava? This is about her? Lord, Vlada! Vladusya, no!—and tears burst from my eyes like from busted pipes, as I watched them lift her coffin, the one that cost "a fortune" and looked small as a child's—you didn't really notice how tiny Vlada was while she was alive; there was so incredibly much of her while she talked, moved, and laughed, and maybe that is why she looked held down by force in her coffin, not just dead but really killed, beaten in, and held up to be ogled, to expose how really defenseless she was. As she lay there like that and we stood around her and tried to utter something (I did, too!), and all our words were so small and pathetic—who could possibly give a damn about who she was to you, mister?—so ill-fitted, even if you put them all together, to measure the thing that was her interrupted life, the same words people would use to talk about other things, after they got home from the funeral and sat drinking tea in their kitchens, that's when I could tell Vlada I'd have given anything to have someone do "some fine lamenting" over her as they once did over her grandma. I could have told her what we didn't know before: how your throat swells with your enormous, tumorous muteness, when you don't know this forgotten ancient ritual, the only one, as it became clear, fit for minutes like these, the one meant to wash a person's life just as someone washes her body, as common words could never do, to wash—and raise it above the crowd's heads to be seen above the coffin, to make it fine. This is not cheating, I said into the silence of my dead line; this was art, Vlada, only no one knew it anymore, and I didn't either, and the only thing that would come out of me, had I dared to give my soul shape with singing, would be the half-choked mooing of a wounded cow.

And after this—slowly, drop by drop—the forgetting began.

Lord, is this really all?

**

Daryna Goshchynska gets up from behind her desk, walks to the window, and stands there for a long time, looking through the dark glass at the scattered flickering stars of city lights below. How little light there is in Kyiv—and it's the capital. One can only imagine what the country looks like. Dark, dark. How poorly we live, Lord, and how bad we are at dying.

"Daryna?" Yurko, a colleague from the evening news, calls out, puzzled. "Why are you sitting in the dark?"

A light switch clicks and the window pane projects—suddenly, so it gives her an unpleasant jolt—an image of a beautiful young woman; in the partial light that eats up the details, she is really young and extraordinarily, piercingly beautiful; it's almost frightening, this beauty, something pagan, witchy. She's got long, Egyptian eyebrows and dark lips as if sated with blood—this is not her televised self crafted to make viewers wonder about the designer of her suit and the brand of her lipstick. This face is something carved out of the night by the light of a bonfire—primeval, elementally gorgeous. Before she turns back to the world and Yurko, who has been talking at her all along, Daryna hungrily takes in this impenetrable face, both hers and not her own: so this is what she looks like when she is alone—much stronger than she feels.

She draws from this strength to give Yurko a dazzling smile. "I'm sorry; I was thinking … what did you say?"

"I'm saying, a young man just called for you." Yurko's eyes turn silky with insinuation. For a couple years already, their relationship has been balancing on the brink of flirting, which is not much, but no man likes to find himself a herald of another man's arrival, and Yurko lets Daryna use the small pause, if she will, to explain herself, to dismiss, if only with a twist of an eyebrow, the young man as a second-class citizen. She does not, so he grins magnanimously somewhere in the direction of this man, "He was worried about where you were."

"Gosh, I turned my ringer off. Thank you, Yurko."

She glances at her cell. Of course, it's Adrian. Unhappy Yurko retreats out the door. How strange that she forgot Adrian existed. That she keeps forgetting about him—as one forgets about one's own arm or leg. She picks up her phone and calls him.

"Aidy?"

"Lolly?" His voice bursts with unmediated delight, as it always does when they haven't talked for a while, even for a little bit. For an instant she feels the imprint of his hard member, like a silk-covered rock, in her hand and a blast of Adrian's smell (Cinnamon? Cumin?) hits her with such forceful nearness that she must sit down on the edge of the desk, squeezing her free hand, unconsciously, between her legs. Lolly was the name she was called when she was little, before she could roll the r in Daryna, but Adrian didn't know this; he derived the name anew from doll—my doll, dolly—Lolly in keeping with the childishness of his love's language, a characteristic shared by many openhearted men. He couldn't conceive of being embarrassed by it either, and at first she resisted, feeling uneasy—I'm not a doll!—but the Lolly that hadn't been heard for thirty-odd years must have worked its magic, overcoming the momentum of her experience and confirming, once again, the nearly metaphysical expedience of everything Adrian did, as if he had, in fact, possessed some secret knowledge about her, which called for respectful obedience on her behalf, and perhaps it was precisely because he sensed this, that he always called out his Lolly! so triumphantly, like a young dad who's just picked his firstborn's name and is thrilled with the sound of it. And still it unnerves her a little, and the thought that a stranger might witness this shameless profession of his bliss makes her want to put a hand over his mouth—he could be at his office, in a cab, or a store, or wherever.

"Where are you?"

The question sounds like she's worried, and that's how he interprets it, which makes her feel a little guilty, as if she'd toyed with him on purpose, so she tries to focus and listen diligently as he explains how he finally made it to his unpronounceable department at the university where he is still considered to be working on his dissertation, but didn't catch the head of his committee, and the secretary promised the boss would be back soon, and he wasted almost an hour drinking a pot of coffee with that hen—except that Adrian doesn't call her a hen because he never says anything negative about anyone unless absolutely necessary, and even when it is urgently and critically necessary, limits himself to a remark about the subject's one unattractive deed and does not generalize, while Daryna, on the other hand, has long nourished the suspicion that the department's secretary has the hots for Adrian and uses every chance she gets to enjoy his company; it's really shocking what girls will do these days (for fairness's sake Daryna admits that before she was Daryna Goshchynska, a national news anchor, she herself was not above making the first move with men she liked, but this was ancient history, so shrouded in the mists of time that it doesn't placate her now). While Adrian talks, she blinks mechanically at her reflection in the glass—now her usual screen image, only badly lit and with a cell phone pressed against her ear.

Vlada and Adrian—they're separate drawers, parallel channels of her consciousness: she and Adrian met when Vlada was already gone. And now she feels no urge whatsoever to introduce them in her mind to each other—it's a new era, a new calendar. PV, Post Vlada.

Artem, now he knew Vlada. And, Artem marked the beginning of Olena Dovgan's story for Daryna (she smiles at the flashback to the humble basement where the story began and her compromised pose at its inception); Adrian appeared after that, in the second act, so to speak. Artem is now in the past, too, and is unlikely to make another appearance in her life, as if he'd played the role he'd been assigned and left the theater. For a split second, Daryna feels woozy, lightheaded, as if she'd soared above the flow of time on a giant swing and looked down on it from above, like from that enormous Ferris wheel in the park when she was little, reeling every time she reached the very top, where she could see as far as the horizon—Was she scared to face the whole world at once, alone?

There was something illicit about that bird's-eye view of life, of what seemed then like the whole world, like the view from the top of the Tower of Babel; it was something not permitted, something that a human being was not meant to tolerate for more than a slipping tail of an instant—and now she is slipping just like that, unmoored by a sudden meteoric convergence, in her mind's eye, of people scattered throughout time and space, with no connection to each other that a normal, ground-level view could discern into a single, meaningful design, a complete picture, a vista. A mere flash of a vista, really, because the very next instant the picture disintegrates, scatters, just before Daryna grasps a single line from

Artem—through Dovganivna—to Adrian and remains sitting on the edge of the desk with a vision cooling like sweat between her shoulder blades: the sudden knowledge that *everything* around her is threaded with these lifelines, and a hundred, a thousand of them run invisibly through her and into other people's lives, but to discern and comprehend the pattern they draw—a picture so grand, so magnificent, that a single glimpse of it fills you with knee-buckling awe—is impossible if only for the single reason that the lines extend way beyond your chopped-off field of vision, beyond the frame of your life, your short, damn it, short years, threading together people from different centuries—let alone generations—different ages, finding them further and further apart, so far apart you could never see them. This living fabric knits and weaves us together, flows, shifts, loops, and passes, and we have no hope, with our meager few decades of allocated time here, of leaping from its midst to see it from above and discern its infinitely scattered pattern, more intricate than a star map, but we all rub together unknowing—the living, the dead, and the not-yet born—who knows how many of us, and what chimerical knots have conspired to have her sitting here with the voice of the man she loves in her hand—and she can't even see why she loves him, why him and not someone else?

"Hello?" the man in question says gently, as if carefully patting her awake; he has sensed a thinning of attention on her end of the line, a transition, as he would put it, from the solid to the plasma state. "Lolly? Are you there?"

"Uhu ... Aidy, do you remember the ontological proof of God?"

He snickers—not because the question strikes him as absurd, and not because it comes out of the blue, but because any surprise coming from her delights him inordinately, still. She wonders how long this will last.

"I used to, but I can't just give to you off the top of my head. Why?"

"I think I just discovered it."

He laughs out loud, laughs at his clever girl, his tireless inventor. He's happy to find her in a good mood.

"I'm serious. There must be someone who sees the entire picture—the whole thing, from above. Like from the Ferris wheel in the park. Only not just right now, this moment, but all the time."

This sounds exceptionally stupid; it's been a while since she proclaimed anything so inane with such heartfelt conviction. Like a schoolgirl, really.

"Oh, you are so smart!" But he agrees, he agrees preemptively with whatever she wants to say. As long as it makes her happy. As long as there's peace and quiet and good counsel—with the only acceptable exception of her moaning in the bedroom on the king-size bed with a Moroccan silk comforter. He likes it when she moans—"don't stop the music" is what they call it.

For a moment, Daryna is filled with such anguish as if someone has pushed her out of a rocket ship into open space and cut the cord: nothing, nothing, and no gravity. She is alone.

Adrian, meanwhile, picks up her idea from another end, as if with a pair of tweezers, places it on a glass slide under his mental microscope, and sets another on top, until hers is utterly unrecognizable. "I can tell you one thing, from the theory of probability, if you want to know. I read somewhere that statistically the actual number of accident survivors exceeds the projected number by five percent. Consistently."

No, she doesn't want to know anything of the sort. She doesn't even want to make the effort required to decipher his abracadabra—like at a math lesson in school when you know you're going to be called on next and will have to come up to the board and pick up where the previous victim put the chalk down. But Adrian is a kind soul—she's being unfair—he'll explain it all himself.

"Theoretically, the dice should roll fifty-fifty: the number that survives should be the same as the number that dies. But five percent more survive, consistently. These five percent—the X factor, the unknown intervention—that's God. He's mathematically proven to exist."

"No kidding? That's really interesting."

She's not being ironic—okay, maybe a tiny bit—she really finds it interesting, and the classroom is warm, and the lights hum cozily under the ceiling (it's still dark outside, first period, winter), and the piece of chalk creaks on the blackboard peaceably—only it makes your fingers feel funny, like they don't belong to you, unpleasantly woolly and slippery on your pen.... Her earlier reverie is gone, vanished; she's only managed to latch on, like a bulldog, to the word threads, and now it'll spin in her mind for the rest of the day, she'll mouth it absently, threads, thready-threads. Threads. Threads that make up a pattern that we can't see. That's why no story is ever finished, no one's. Death cannot put a period on it.

At this point, it finally occurs to Daryna that this deeply intellectual discussion will add a hefty charge to their cell-phone bills, enough that they could have had the discussion much more pleasantly somewhere nice over cake and coffee. Once again Adrian's yuppie profligacy dulls her own poor-girl instincts: she sees—and apparently will always see—money as a set of opportunities, fanned out in front of her like cards, from which she must be careful to choose only one, the best, and, for Adrian, money is something to be spent on whatever strikes his fancy, here and now. And this, despite the fact that they make almost the same at their jobs (hers pays slightly more), so it's not a matter of numbers—it's about an internal freedom that no amount of money can buy; you either have it or you don't. So it looks like she doesn't, but so what? Let it go already.

"Why did you call me when you knew I'd be at the studio? Just to chat?"

"Actually ..."

His voice changes, recoils as if upset with something, retreats like a scared little snail into the safety of a dark crack. Something happened, Daryna's stomach sinks—but no, it can't be, if something bad really happened (And why does she think it has to be something bad? Why is she always waiting for the other shoe to drop, for the world to come apart, what is wrong with her?), he would have said so right away, instead of dragging things out—or wouldn't he? They haven't lived through a calamity as a couple yet—no accidents, ambulances, or financial disasters—only piddly stuff, the usual everyday vexations, problems that one has to solve and that are amenable to solving, so how would she know how he endured misfortune? Real misfortune.

"Well … I wanted to tell you right away, while it was still fresh. I, you know, dozed off after lunch, just nodded off right in my chair, so weird—that's how I missed my prof."

"Vitamin deficiency!" she laughs operatically, like a diva in the *La traviata* banquet scene—she can't contain her relief: nothing's wrong, everyone's alive and well! "'I fear daytime sleep: it dreams clairvoyant torment,' that's from Tychyna," she throws in on the same breath, gathering momentum, like an ice-skater heading into a sparkling, spinning toe loop of inspired twitter—and slams on the brakes, with a gulp of deflating lungs when she realizes that's not it, he hasn't told her the whole thing.

"That could very well be. I had a dream."

"A dream?" It's as if the word was obscure to her.

"A dream," he repeats stubbornly, which makes the word lose its meaning completely. "Of you and Aunt Gela."

"We are such stuff as dreams are made on," she mumbles, automatically, echoing the meaningless word and groping around for a quote, anything to help her keep her balance as her world rocks: she has no business appearing in his already suspicious dreams in the company of dead people; that's enough to send a chill down the spine all by itself. But she and Aunt Gela—Olena Dovganivna—do exist together in the waking world, connected by a completely reasonable project: that cursed film of hers, the agony of it, and the fact that still, after all the work she's put into it, she can't find the single right turn of the key that will unlock the story, that one twist of the plot that will set the entire mechanism in motion—could it be possible that Adrian, as sensitive and finely tuned to her mind's frequencies as he is, unconsciously reflected her growing, unsettling obsession with Dovganivna?

"And what were we doing in your dream?" She giggles, and her giggle comes out pitiful, tinny—as if he'd told her a scary fairytale and she now needs him to say it wasn't true. And yet she already knows—from her gut, from inside, where it resonates loud and clear—that things stand otherwise: he won't. And it's not about her film.

"First the two of you were in a café, a summer café; you were sitting under an umbrella. It looked like the place in the Passage ... both in summer dresses, you were laughing ... drinking wine."

Aha.

"And then?"

"You know, it was complicated," he gives up suddenly, and lets a genuine, unconcealed plea of alarm for her fill his voice. "I can't remember everything now; that's why I called you as soon as I woke up ... I wanted to get it all across without losing any, but you weren't there ..."

I was, I was, clicks in her head—right when you called, I was looking at the same footage, only with a different dead woman!

"Let's talk about it at home, okay? I'll give you the full debrief, promise.... And, Lolly? Let me come pick you up, okay?"

"No way," she says in her best not-a-care-in-the-world voice—to calm them both down. "I'll get a ride. Yurko will take me."

She does feel a true and urgent need for Yurko's company, for their playful, easy banter in the car along the way, for the juggling of slightly off-color jokes and ironic comments about the day, their regular, pleasant emotional gymnastics, refreshing like a shower or a cup of coffee—one of the well-ordered world's small rituals that give us the sense of security and stability. That's exactly what she needs.

"Don't worry about it, Aidy. It's nothing."

"I'm not so sure. Not so sure at all." She could almost see the way he shakes his head, trying to get rid of the nagging idea that buzzes inside his head like a trapped fly. He looks so funny when he does that, like a boy—and he says, just like a little boy, "Promise me that you'll be careful!"

She gives another operatic howl, more dramatically now, in a mezzo-soprano, out of Wagner.

"There's always that margin of five percent, right?"

She shuts her phone and stares for another second into the blackness beyond the window, at her antipode fleshed out of the night by the trembling glow of a fire. The otherworldly, thunderously beautiful face with elongated Egyptian eyes and dark-blooded lips rises toward her, chin resolutely thrust up—and suddenly shivers with a quick chilly tremor, as if swallowing a sob that's burst from deep inside.

Vlada, Vladusya. Help me.

Daryna Goshchynska turns around, presses the eject button, pulls out the tape with the copy of the interview, throws it into her tote, and yanks the zipper closed. She puts her raincoat on, turns the lights off, and throws the door open.

"Yuurrrkooo!" her throaty, trilling call resounds in the empty hallway over the clicking of her heels—almost like a dove cooing.

Room 3. Adrian's Dreams

Lviv, November 1943

The man with a briefcase under his arm runs hard down the sidewalk, past the locked doors and padlocked shutters on the windows of ground-floor apartments; his footfalls, even on smooth unshod soles, thunder in the emptiness of the early morning, loud enough, it seems, to rouse the entire neighborhood; the cobblestones are wet and slippery under the film of the night's lingering frost. A voice inside his head calls, "Watch out!"—the same voice that's always warned him of imminent danger, that gives plain and concise orders: step off the path and hide under a bridge—moments before a Studebaker full of Krauts drives across it; or "Don't go there!" two blocks away from the safe house—where, as it turned out later, in place of their liaison agents, Gestapo had been waiting for him since the night before. Some in the Security Service felt compelled to wonder if this was too much luck, if, by chance, he was actually the one to "spill" that safe house, having avoided the trap so handily, but to hell with them and their suspicions; everyone knows he'd come out dry, alive, and unscathed from much hotter waters, almost as though he was possessed, and perhaps he is, by this voice that whispers its spell over him, demanding that he obey, that he respond instantly, in his muscles, in his body, like a wild animal, not wasting a single instant on thinking. This is why the second he hears "Watch out!" he opens his briefcase and puts the still-warm Walther pistol inside it. The muzzle is still smoking after the shot, the smell of gunpowder and burned metal all but comforting, welcome in his nostrils; his hand still feels the springy imprint of the recoil that had pushed it up and back moments ago. Grabbing the briefcase by the handle with his other hand, he proceeds at a regular pace, a sparse, focused gait of someone on his way to the day's business—a clerk hurrying to his office—precisely a moment before the milky-gray fog at the corner of Bliaharska expels the black shapes of the military patrol, glistening in their leather coats like wet tree trunks.

Exhibit A, ladies and gentlemen. Adrian Ortynsky, aka the Beast (the alias he had taken for good reason) got lucky again. To walk past them without arousing their suspicion is nothing, piece of cake, done it a million times—the thing is to relax, not to clench up into an anxious knot, but to cease being a solid body altogether and proceed as though it were all a dream from which he could wake at any second, whenever he so chose. The November morning chill biting at his skin under layers of clothes; the particular grip of his hand on the briefcase handle so that he could drop it, should the need arise, simply by relaxing his fingers; the dark cupola of the Dominican Cathedral in the fog-distorted distance at the end of the street, floating weightless high above the ground; the frost-laced damp cobblestones—Katzenkopfstein, the dream readily offers in German—and the synchronous pounding of marching boots on them (iron-shod boots, made to last, made for stomping the will of the Übermensch into whoever is under them, for intimidation, not for flight), the pounding that comes closer, overtakes him—and passes, thank you, sweet Lord Jesus, passes without hesitation.

In that moment of passing—as the patrol leaves the man and his persisting luck behind as indifferently as if he'd willed himself to dissolve, right in front of their eyes, into shaggy strands of milky-white fog—a very important shift occurs in his own consciousness: the bullet he just fired into the chest of the Polish Gebiet Polizei's Commandant when he stepped out of his office into Serbska Street (Kroatenstrasse, as they call it), and his flight along Serbska and Ruska Streets after that (to the young gunmen he schooled he always said the Germans were bears, and one must run from them the only way one can outrun a bear in the mountains—on a crooked path, diagonally uphill; the Magyars, they were wolves and only knew the language of fear; and the Poles, well, the Poles were rabid dogs; he knew that for certain, had known it ever since that childhood day when the Uhlans galloped into their village, dragged his father out of the parish, pulled his vestments over his head, and chased him around with whips, while one of them rode on his back, all of them yelling, "Long live Marshal Piłsudski!"— the Poles were rabid dogs and were to be killed like dogs, with a single shot), and everything that happened a mere minute before he slid as a single mass into the past like a load of dirt slipping off a shovel into a hole. It became just another completed mission, another assassination on Beast's record, while the man himself strolls freely onward with his briefcase, away from it, toward his new, clear, and certain destination: the streetcar stop, his final rendezvous point with the courier girls who would relieve him of the murder weapon.

He glances at his watch—it would be impolite to make them wait—and hastens his step, through the modest park, past the wet tree trunks, their rutted bark like weathered weeping faces, on to Pidvalna, and every hair that stands on its end on his arms quivers as the seconds tick off.

TICK … TICK… TICK … TICK …

This has always come easy to him: parceling out his time, slivering himself up into its fragments. Shedding the just-lived like flakes of dry skin, pulling all his senses up by the root from the past moment and replanting them completely intact into the present. It could be said he really didn't have a past in the sense that other men had, the ones who moaned and talked in their sleep. If it were up to him, he'd send them packing home: a man who calls out to the living and the dead in his sleep can no longer fight. Bullets find him in the next fight, and sometimes even without a fight, they just find him, as if made for the single express purpose of finding and pinning someone's living past. But he is Beast and knows how to live in the fleeting moment alone. And he has luck.

Now he does not fear the echo of his own steps on the park's paved path.

TICK … TICK … TICK … TICK … And what wonderful fog lingers this morning! (He is lucky with that, too.)

In the fog, or at night, or even without a single glimmer of light at all (especially since the Soviet air raids began and only a few ghostly bluish camouflage lamps smolder on the railway station's canopy), he knows his city by touch, in his blood, like a lover's body: wherever he may stumble blindly, wherever he throws his arm out for balance, the city offers itself to him, yields softly, opens a familiar alley, a warm odorous ditch, a moist crease between buildings. Zhydivska … Bliaharska … Pidvalna—it's his lips, his skin, the slippery lining of his innards that rub and burrow and part the lightly breathing folds of stony flesh; it's his city and it will never betray him; it'll guide him through itself like a loving and knowing wife, his faithful one; it'll spread itself open and take him in; if need be, it'll hide him completely—inside, in the swampy, sinewy darkness of its underground passages.

He does not remember how long it's been since he was with a real woman, even in a dream from which a man wakes with the sticky semen on his thighs—but in *his* city whose every cobblestone (every Katzenkofstein, pox on their German whoring mothers) he remembers not just with the soles of his feet but has learned, once and forever, with every muscle and tendon in his previous, long-gone life as a child, a schoolboy, a loafer, and a fop; here, he stays erect day and night, as it sometimes happens in the happiest of marriages—and the city keeps and protects him as no woman could. At times, the German presence in the city infects his own body: the black-and-white blemished eagles and crooked-arm crosses on buildings (Kroatenstrasse, ha!) feel like scabby calluses on a beloved body, a sensation first engendered by the Soviets in '39, by their shabby, kitchen-smelling soldiers in stiff boots, their savage *"Davai, davai,* move on!" their ubiquitous patches of red (just like the German color later) fabric stretched over buildings with their slogans and pictures of their leaders, the entire wood-suitcased Asiatic horde of them that within a few weeks picked every store clean to the bones like an invasion of giant red ants and hatched instead, in the heart of the downtown, in front of the Opera house, a swollen welt of a flea market where the local crowd could be entertained in broad daylight by the sight of their women latched on to each other's hair in a ferocious fight over a pair of satin stockings.

The fear that bred and burrowed through the city, which had never known anything like it, was the surest sign of their foreignness. When the Soviets ran away, this instinctive sixth sense of foreign presence remained with him, and that's why he, unlike so many others, never doubted that the Germans would not stay long either, not even in the very beginning, before the arrests. They were also strangers here, just as foreign, though they maintained the appearance of human beings so much more than those other ones: their officers wore gloves, made use of handkerchiefs, and when they gave their "word of honor," they did keep it, even while they were calmly and efficiently robbing people's homes of anything that had remained after the Soviets. Just like the others, they spun the city into a spider web of fear, and just like the others, they were blind: they had no eyes to see how drastically they did not fit here, that they were a carbuncle, a pimple that the body would expunge, burn off with fever. Against the intimacy he had with the city—and he hadn't really ever been this close with a woman, hadn't ever had one he could truly call his—this innate rejection of the foreign raised in him, when he was on a mission, a sense not even of righteousness but of his own mystical invincibility. He was untouchable. How could he fail when every pebble was on his side? Afterward, he would always pray and ask God to forgive him for his pride, if this was pride—he wasn't sure; he had lost the habit of deeper contemplation when he began living in the running stream of each moment, so in all moral questions he had placed his trust in God: he knew better.

And here's the streetcar stop, a trifle left to do, a few minutes: give the briefcase to the girls, get on the streetcar with them, jump down at the convenient turn off the Lychakivska (*Oststrasse*, man, *Oststrasse!*)—and that's it. He's done.

TICK ... TICK ... TICK ... TICK ... And that's when an invisible wave of heat washes over him, out of nowhere, and his blood thunders in his temples—never mind that his body mechanically continues on its course, at the same brisk tempo of an inaudible lively march. His lips grow instantly dry and he gasps for air like a fish, mouth open wide—he can't breathe.

This is not a signal of danger—something else, something other waits ahead—something is closing the distance between them, heading to their inexorable collision at the streetcar stop, something that could not, should not be there. Something whose presence at today's assassination of the Polish police Commandant is absolutely inconceivable—incompatible by blood type.

He has seen, but he cannot believe: his blood resists, all his many years of honed underground instincts, everything that made him invincible. A single memory shoots through all those years, incinerates everything they contain into ash, throws the heart of the once-lived time: the orchestra is playing tango with Polish lyrics—"I have time, I will wait, should you find a better one, I will let you go your way"—and the smell of a girl's blonde hair under the electric lights, the intoxicating light smell, the sharp torment of unspeakable tenderness that turns everything inside you into a flower, a bloom of animate, tickling petals (and, at the same time, the nagging fear—what if she catches a waft of his sweat and it disgusts her—so delicate, so small and light that it makes him want to fall, drop himself as a shower of petals under her feet). He feels all this hit his chest with a force no lesser than that of the bullet he fired into the police executioner sentenced to death by the Organization—as if his own shot caught up with him in the middle of the street, and Beast goes faint and soft, about to collapse like the man he killed, and he will now see everything he did not stay to watch earlier on Serbska. This painfully clear, visceral realness of the memory is the most surprising part of it all—that it should be so perfectly alive after being pried out of some long-barricaded corner of his past that he considered irrevocably severed from his present: this is the amazement he felt as a little boy when, in the middle of the winter, he beheld the gleaming round smoothness of an apple pulled from the cellar where it had been kept in its underground nest of straw—by what magic did it preserve that smoothness, that deep, slightly bitter breath of autumnal orchards?

He does not collapse; he is carried forward, dizzy with the merciless shortening of the distance between them, and his past melts inside him with brutal, catastrophic speed. He sees himself as one does in one's moment of death—or the instant after dying?—from outside: among all the people out walking on this downtown street at this early hour, he is the most vulnerable, an open moving target. A slow, wet, gaping wound.

TICK … TICK … TICK … TICK …

My name—Adrian Ortynsky.

He is happy.

He sees with great clarity the wet rounds of cobblestones, and the hem of ice at the edge of the sidewalk, and the shiny street-car tracks. He sees before him, growing closer with every step, the two girls' faces: one, Nusya's, as though muted, dim, and the other—yes, he knew, he'd been told that there would be two of them, that Nusya would bring a companion, but Lord, who could imagine!—the other blazes in his eyes like a dazzling flare that remains after looking at the sun; he can't see her features, but he doesn't have to see them in order to know—with his entire being, his whole life at once—it is She.

She.

TICK … TICK … TICK … TICK … "I have time, I will wait," the orchestra plays, and the couples spin on the dance floor. How long he's been waiting—all these years, and he didn't even know it. And now the waiting is over.

Closer. Closer still. Another moment—and his hand would fall into hers. He is not surprised to notice that it suddenly begins to snow—someone up above also waited for this moment to give his signal, to let large white flakes spin in the air, settle on Her hair, the golden curls around the small beret, on Her eyelashes, instantly fuzzy as though bleached. Her eyelashes. Her lips.

Somewhere in the back of his mind a watchful half-thought perks up, as if transplanted from someone else's mind, that snow is bad news, he'll leave tracks when he runs across the park—but nothing of this kind has any chance of rising to the surface of his consciousness at the moment. Does she recognize him? She is snowflaked. Smiling. Serene. Snow Queen—that's what he called her that night when he walked her home, to the Professors' Colony far up Lychakivska, her tall lace-up boots leaving tiny, miniscule impressions in the snow, child's tracks, and when he pointed it out to her, she indulged him with a small laugh, slightly coy, "What fancy is that, Mister Adrian; it's just my foot, it's plenty common." "But I insist, Miss Gela, be so kind as to compare," and he carefully planted his bear paw next to her little delicate trace like an imprint of a flower petal with the minute bud of her heel at the bottom, and it felt as though he were protecting it from a stranger's prying eyes, shielding her with his own imprinted presence—"Take a look, be so kind, I insist"—once, and again, and the whole way home. To see their footprints next to each other, again and again, was rapture beyond compare, like touching her in some mysteriously intimate way, and when she flitted away from him, almost startled, when she drew back her hand and hid in her towered fortress—her eminent professorial villa guarded by a quietly watchful army of relatives and maids, invisible at this late hour, and with doors that creaked like a living baritone in surprise—he remained standing just outside her porch, rooted to the spot where she had abandoned him, without the slightest idea of where he should go next or why.

The sparse garland of petals threaded by her tiny booted feet led away from him and ended, like his thoughts, at the door; then a second-floor window lit up and her shadow swung onto the curtain, filling him with a new wave of joy, so he stood there for a long time not taking his eyes off that tall window, haloed like a beatific fresco in church, where her shadow moved as though on a movie screen: retreating, then surfacing again, and then holding still for a while, allowing him to imagine that she was looking at him, and he could no more stop the flood of whispered insanities he muttered to himself than if he'd been wrung by a fever. He laughed and felt no cold. The window went dark eventually, and it took him a while to realize what that meant—she'd gone to bed, and he told himself so, muttering under his breath, shaking his head and smiling a little, as if he were lulling her to sleep in his own arms, as if he'd just been granted another proof of her incredible closeness, a sign that the two of them belonged to themselves: she asleep upstairs, in her boudoir, the seam of her steps needling up the snow-white stairs; and he, bearing witness to both these marvels, and thus drunk on his ecstasy, remained there guarding her tracks until light, with no recollection of when and how he got home.

And the most amazing thing—he didn't even catch a cold.

The fact that she now approaches—in the same gliding walk instilled by Lviv's most glorious tuteurs (only the legs, my lady, we're moving only our legs!) beside Nusya, his regular courier, and carries toward him that serene, unattainable smile of hers like a discrete source of light in the November cityscape—is equivalent to the heavens collapsing in pieces onto the earth below—he wouldn't blink an eye if they did collapse. Snow falls and carries the smell of her hair, the dizzyingly tender, humid blonde smell; a flake alit on his lips and its featherlight, barely perceptible kiss pulls his mouth into the long-forgotten smile of *that night*, a blissfully silly smile, reflexive like the contraction of muscles when a doctor taps your knee with his little hammer, and instead of letting them both know that he had completed his mission, that everything was okay and went according to plan, Adrian Ortynsky exhales, equally unconsciously, and blurted out like the village idiot, like a green, greener-than-grass rookie ... "Gela ..."

The sound of his own voice brings him back.

TICK ... TICK ... TICK ... TICK ... "Does the gentleman know himself?"

That's Nusya speaking from somewhere at his side, almost out of his armpit—she's such a little button of a girl and always when she's nervous this awkward Polish syntax spills out of her:

she bragged she'd graduated, in the old days, from the Madame Strzalkowska's Polish Gymnasium, and it's a marvel indeed that they hadn't quite managed to craft a first-rate Polish chauvinist out of her—my dear pal Nusya, Nyusichka, who wouldn't love you, you nugget of a girl? He is suddenly gripped by a wild, predatory joy, reckless, drunk, like the thrill that swells his veins in the middle of a street fight, that explodes out of his chest as song, as uncouth howling (once he caught fire as he ran through yards, balconies, and roofs, firing back, and his head roared, like a tavern band getting people to the dance floor. "Tell you once I went to L-viv! Saw me many pret-ty things!"—*wzzz!* a bullet zapped the tin roofing next to him, and a tambourine rattled inside him, answering, and the fiddle squealed higher and faster, rabid, *presto, presto:* "On a bal-cony up high sat a la-dy stool-a-stri-de! Shame to look and shame to see, but she's right abo-ve me!"—dog your mother, missed me, didn't you?)—he's swollen with it; he's lifted above the earth; he could grab both girls under his arms, like a fairytale giant, and make a game of kicking open the trap of time that has closed around them—the three of them, encircled in a single reality available to them, however you slice it: a dead body on Serbska Street, a gun in a briefcase, the briefcase in their hands, and the police will start searching the city any minute if they haven't yet. Tick, tick goes the blood in his veins, counting seconds—they're all tied together into this one sack, and some giant invisible magnet has pulled Her toward him and pressed Her into his chest, and their dance isn't over until the orchestra stops.

So, come on, whoring mother's son, play! Play, damn it, play till your ribs crack!

And before any gentleman who might indeed know himself has a chance to utter a word, copper cymbals slam together in his head, a deafening, thunderous clatter descends upon him, a loose ringing like the sound of a crashing crystal palace, the shattered ice palace of the Snow Queen. A streetcar pulls up, the hoped-for one—everything as it should be, yes, ma'am, everything as the good Lord ordered and the General Staff had planned, and the eye coolly counts, as though through the gun's sight, the doors: let the front wagon pass; it's nur für die Deutschen and almost empty at this hour; people at the stop huddle closer to the rear of the car, mostly womenfolk who can't easily jump up into the middle while the car is still moving, let us climb in now, my girls—please, my fair ladies, go ahead—"Sir, mind your step!"—what a shame, I did step on someone's toes—"Please excuse me!"—a wench in a headscarf, then a lady in a fox fur collar, and that's when you clutch your purse anxiously, blocking the way for the folks behind you, nicely done, a sudden shift, a short commotion at the door—I learned this trick back in Polish times, when I did time on Lontska Street in the cell with pickpockets, but where did you pick it up, my pet, how do you know what to do next?—and it is your narrow gloved paw, not Nusya's, in the midst of swirling bodies that takes my briefcase with the precious Walther, also corpus delicti, in the moment when I'm lifting you onto the step, and then you're up, in the car, catching the swinging ceramic loop in your other hand and regaling the conductor with your easy, luminous smile. The way you clasp the briefcase is so sweet, so femininely helpless, but you have taken on the burden of mortal risk, albeit the lesser share of it because the police don't stop women in the streets to search them, do not subject them to that disgusting groping that always leaves you feeling dishonored, clenching your teeth until your brain cramps.

No, they do not touch the women and, God willing, Nusya and you will get the weapon to its secret cache without any trouble, only no one will tell me if you did, just as no one had told me that you were here—here and not in the safe Zurich where you'd gone to study before the war, and we'd never had a chance to say goodbye because I was chasing lice in the cell on Lontska when you left, and then Poland fell, and the Soviets came, and I had to flee to Krakow because the Poles handed over the lists of their political prisoners to the NKVD, most of them Ukrainians, and our boys started getting snatched again, and of those who did get snatched, none ever came back.

All these years I kept seeing the same dream—I remember it clearly, and I've always thought I don't dream; I was sure I didn't, but maybe I just forgot my dreams as soon as I woke up because my mind, once conscious, bolted the doors to the rest of it, so maybe I did moan and call for you in that dream—the dream in which we are dancing in a great dark hall, like the one at Prosvita or the People's House, only bigger, and at some point you vanish, and I don't even notice how and when, just suddenly realize that I am dancing alone—an instant of abysmal cold, of sticky terror: Where are you, Geltsia? I dash around looking for you, run around the hall like a madman, and the hall is growing bigger; it's not a hall anymore but a giant open space, a drilling field, only dark as night, but I know that you're somewhere here, you must be here, only for some reason I can't see you.… And now here you are, you're found again, my girl, the gears of separated times have locked back together, and we are together and have already executed the first movement of our dance, the pas de deux with a handgun. Somewhere an invisible master of ceremonies is calling out the dances inaudibly as I lift myself into the streetcar behind Nusya, and for another ten or twelve minutes will have the pleasure of beholding your face over people's heads, my brave little girl—this is the kind of music they're playing for us, nothing to be done about that; we must dance until the end, until the last breath as our oath commands—we were always such a glorious couple, the best on any dance floor. They said the two of us were the spitting image of Marlene Dietrich and Clark Gable; all your friends must have envied you, so have no cares and fear not. It's not for nothing that I have luck, and there's always been enough of it to go around, to cover everyone who went with me, and those who went alone and did not come back—Igor, whom the Bolsheviks tortured to death in Drohobych jail so that his mother could only identify the shirt on the body; Nestor, who perished somewhere in Auschwitz after they arrested him in September of '43; and Lodzio, Lodzio Daretsky, the most talented of our class, who went to Kyiv last summer, after the resistance there had already fallen, and one day, God be my witness, I will find that son of a bitch who sent Lodzio there, to be shot like a rabid dog by Gestapo the day after he got there—all of them, and there's more every day, stand in the gloom along the dance hall's walls, or maybe in formation around that drill field, and follow us with their eyes—Igor and Nestor and Lodzio, and God alone knows how many more. In my dream, I run past them without looking because I am searching for you alone, and only now that you have come back and the dream surfaces as a drowned man comes up from the bottom of the Tysa River when the highland pipes sound their call, do I realize that it was they who filled the hall; it had to grow bigger to make room for them all, all who stepped out of the dance and will never come back—but they stand there, mute, and do not move, and watch us, and wait, and this means that our party, Geltsia, is only now beginning.

"Grand rond! Avancez! A trois temps!"

"Time!" the voice urges, shoves, hard, from inside his skull. Gulp, one last time, an eyeful of her face, inhale her, almost taste her on your lips—what fool said you don't drink off a face?—and off you run, brother, à trois temps, trá-ta-ta, trá-ta-ta, trá-ta-ta; the streetcar screeches as it contorts its body through the turn; stones of nearby buildings speckle your vision—jump, you useless fool!

Down, down the hill, ahead of the streetcar, with his hands now free and his eyes slashed raw, heavy as a pound of bleeding flesh severed from her radiant face in the gloom of the crowd, hammered now with endless rocks, stones, cat's heads, Katzenkopfstein, run!

Run. Run. Run. Round the corner … through the gate … park … down the path … trees … trees—black stumps. Is it someone's labored breath behind you? No, it's your own raincoat, rustling. And why are your cheeks wet, and what are these tiny streams running from your nose to your lips—is this sweat, already?

I am crying, flashes in his mind. Sweet Lord, I am crying. These are my tears.

Without noticing, he slows his flight—à deux temps, à deux temps—and touches his cheeks with his hands, with his fingertips, carefully as though it were *someone else's* face. Woe to you, Adrian, pulses in his head, woe and woe and endless woe, you're done, you're finished ...

Why woe?! Everything went just fine!

He blinks at his watch again: the entire operation, from the moment his mark stepped into Serbska Street, has taken twelve minutes. Twelve and a half to be exact. Actually, almost thirteen. Thirteen.

So what—he's never been one for signs—what is happening to him? A premonition? A hunch? What is he afraid of?

"And Jesus, immediately knowing in himself that virtue had gone out of him, turned him about in the press, and said, 'Who touched my clothes?' And his disciples said unto him, 'Thou seest the multitude thronging thee, and sayest thou, Who touched me?' And he looked round about to see her that had done this thing."

He never really understood that Gospel episode of healing the bleeding woman, even when he got older and learned from his friends—in lewd, draffish words that did not accord with the Holy Scriptures—what that meant, that the woman was "bleeding," and it tormented him for a long time, because he couldn't bring himself to believe it. His dad read the Scriptures out loud to him when he was little; later, he didn't dare ask him about it. The story remained a mystery to him: how could He, without seeing, feel that someone had taken of his power?

Now he knows. The Gospel was as precise as a medical diagnosis. You couldn't have put it better. There are no better words, that's it.

That's exactly what he felt.

Something has changed—and he already knows what it is: of those twelve (no, thirteen, damn it, thirteen!) minutes, the last ten remain with him and *do not pass*. The minutes he spent with Geltsia. She remains with him. He carries her inside him and does not want to let go, not for all the treasures in the world. He knows this is how it will be from now on.

All these years without her he sped across the surface of time as though on smooth ice—light, unstoppable—and now it has cracked, opened a hole, given under his new weight. The power that had held him above time has left him.

Adrian Ortynsky, alias Beast, registered as a Fachkursen student at the Polytechnic, also Johannes Weiss by other papers, also Andrzej Ortynski. Twenty-three. Invulnerable. Elusive. Invincible. Immortal.

And, in this very moment, fully and clearly conscious, he is about to die.

His death has already set out for him; it began its countdown to their rendezvous precisely ten minutes ago. How long before it runs out—hours, months, years—doesn't matter; he and death are out to find each other and *will* rendezvous as certainly as lovers who'd set a date.

TICK … TICK … TICK … TICK … The beast inside him reaches for his throat (how defenseless the moving pulsing bulge under his fingers, how easy it would be to crush the cartilage and shred the tendons), throws his head back at the snow-swollen sky, and bares its teeth as though to show his perfect mandibles to the invisible dentist somewhere above.

He may have seemed to be screaming—but mutely, without noise. Or laughing—also without noise. A single living soul under the war's November sky, with his face turned up. The dead can rarely enact such a feat; only the luckiest of them fall down face-up, because, yes, even death has its share of luck to give to its chosen few. The rest die with their eyes down, into the ground. Into the ground.

Kyiv, April 2003

A hospital? White coats, no, not coats, more like white sheets wrapped around people's torsos, very strange … it must be a hospital.

A black Opel Kadett—very fancy—black uniforms, black shiny peaks on uniform caps—Where are they taking me?

Wake up, Adrian.

The vision slips away, as if sucked through a dark tunnel, grows smaller, shrivels into a tiny dot, and is gone.

To lie a little longer with my eyes closed, listening to the noises around me, feeling out the room like a blind man, inhaling its familiar scents: this is my room. The bed—empty; my arm, when I reach out, falls as if chopped off onto a crumpled pillow, nothing else. I hear myself growl in protest, and the noise wakes me up completely: this is my voice. Eyes still closed, I think beyond the doors, listening in my mind to the hallway, the bathroom, the kitchen. All quiet. I am alone. There should be a clock on a bedside table on the other side of the bed; I can reach it with my other hand. Wow. Lolly must've dashed out before dawn. Of course—she's got the early morning show today. Which I have already missed. Slob. Darn it. What is it with me and sleeping these days?

Inside my head like the smarting trace of a needle: the black Opel Kadett full of foreign officers (What uniform *is* that?), a woman in a white coat, or rather a sheet wrapped around her body; a spatula, or what do you call it, being boiled in a shallow metal dish.… To heck with it, shake it off.

Outside it's raining, a nice spring rain that brushes the trees and the grass with a gentle lisping noise. Open the balcony doors and breathe deeply: the air is warm, moist. Beautiful. In the yard below, a smattering of tiny bubbles spreads like a new skin over a silver Mercedes that has a tiny flag on its parliament-issue license plate; my trusty Volkswagen huddles behind it like a village accountant next to the Terminator. The Mercedes's Representative owner lives next door—a quiet type, must be really new, first-term, not a real politician yet.

I know where he lives because someone broke into his flat last year, and the cops went door to door, thorough as plumbers, and had everyone sign a piece of paper stating that we saw and heard nothing. They were the ones who told us, spilled the beans on the Rep., so to speak. Before, when the family from the first floor was robbed, no one came to ask any questions whatsoever; the folks simply put iron bars on their windows. Now, when you're coming home late at night, the sidewalk is divided into regular squares of golden light from their grated windows, like a medieval fortress. You'd think kids would like playing in that light—they'd be fairies, or kings, or knights with their fair ladies—only kids don't pretend things like that anymore. And they should be in bed anyway, which is too bad. Somehow thinking of the kids makes me feel sad—I don't know if it's because I'm not one of them anymore and can't make good use of the fairytale stage, or because when I was little we didn't have such golden-crossed windows. We had a hedge of dirty-gray, nine-floor apartment towers, tiled on the outside like the insides of water closets, the yards between them dotted with the toy-size white huts mysteriously designated "trash-collector"—they stank ferociously, but we still liked hiding there, in between the large trash cans, big enough that if you crouched, no one could find you; and it was in the dark intimacy of that stinking refuge that I learned how girls pee. The girl's name was Marynka, and she wore bright, fire-engine red leggings. Since I could not believe my eyes, she kindly permitted me to investigate by touching the wet furrow between the tiny flaps; I must have had the instincts of an experimentalist already. Experience is experience, even when it's gained behind a dumpster. Nothing is wasted.

Lolly must have been running late: her cup and the spoon she used to stir her coffee tossed willy-nilly in the sink, the squishy grounds in the rusty-brown filter still warm in the coffeemaker. The bowl with unfinished muesli she left on the windowsill makes me go all warm and fuzzy, and I catch myself smiling: I know she stood here, eating, looking out the window into the well of our yard, as she always does when she eats alone. Walking around the kitchen like this, retracing her steps—it's like pulling on a still-warm robe she's taken off and left hanging invisibly in the air; you can wrap yourself in it, you want to rub your cheek against her, Lolly. And the smell—the waft of her perfume lifted off the pillow where she slept, warm with the sweet, yeasty, bread-dough smell of her body—it follows me around, grows stronger by the window where she stood, washes over me at the door where she put on her boots. I press my fingers against my nose and inhale a slightly different version of her—a sharper, saltier tinge like the smell of seaweed drifting in from a distant beach—draw it in, and hear myself moan, unwittingly. What a joke! I'm like a dog left in the house alone, nosing his way around, looking for his master. When she first began staying the night, I did exactly what a dog would do after she'd left: I burrowed into her bathrobe and went back to sleep until she returned. The only social gesture I could muster was to call the office and lazily lie to them about feeling under the weather—I've no idea whether they ever bought the excuse, delivered as it was in a blissed-out drone; and I didn't care, and when you don't care, you're always ahead because no one can do anything to you. I'd lounge in my nirvana bed until noon—sleeping, waking, dozing off again, marveling joyfully at the change of light and the objects in the room that seemed unrecognizable once they'd responded, like salient creatures, to Lolly's vibrating presence—and never had the guts to tell her about it. But it was then, actually, that I started having *these* dreams.

In the daytime, they fade, melt, sink under the surface like shards of cracked ice floes. They're all thin around the edges; I lose the plot, only grasp the biggest pieces, stacked on top of each other but disjointed like pages from different chapters caught by a single wayward staple: the black Opel Kadett, some sort of place like a hospital, the spatula or whatever it is, the white-sheeted torso. Normally that's how it is with dreams, especially when your mind is stuffed fuller than your in-box, and you wake up like someone slammed your face against a table: not this again, damn it, can I please think of something else? But *these* dreams, they were different from the get-go. First of all, they aren't just a fantastical reworking of whatever happened the day before; they've no relationship to anything I could ever have personally experienced. No déjà vu whatsoever. As best I could articulate this to Lolly—because it is always when I talk to her that I can best verbalize my ideas, even when it's the operational principle of a thermionic generator or something else she has no clue about—*these* dreams feel like I've been put inside someone else's closet, and I'm looking at a stranger's clothes, hung around in strange order. What I see and manage to remember certainly means something to someone out there, but I myself feel like the person who accidentally got plugged into someone else's phone conversation.

"Do you mean to say," Lolly then inquired, frowning and biting her lower lip in concentration, "that you are seeing someone else's dreams?"

"No, that's the thing, that's their other distinction: it's more precise to say that I'm dreaming someone else's consciousness."

"Meaning?"

"Um, how do I put it ... it doesn't look like a dream—more like a memory, a very vivid, visceral memory, with touch and smell— only I am absolutely certain that whatever is happening has never happened to *me*. I know it's not *my* memory."

One undisputable advantage of living with a reporter is that with time, thanks to her extraordinary skill of patient questioning, she trains you to explain yourself with great coherence and in perfectly clear language, plus your vocabulary expands to such unprecedented levels that sometimes people think you're the one who writes for a living. So, here's the picture—stuck in my mind after I dreamt it a least a dozen times: a forest in springtime, tree trunks spotted with sunlight, the smell of wet bark and sap, a very green smell, and the man walking in front of me is dressed in a gray-blue military uniform with a Schmeiser over his shoulder, only his belt is not made of leather, for some reason, but woven, with stitching. We are walking through the forest "goose-file"— somehow I know that's what it's called—and this sturdy peasant back, girded with its woven belt, is the last thing I see when a dry stutter explodes from behind the trees; something shoves me hard in the chest, and everything goes black. After that, I don't remember anything—it's gone like a piece of paper in dark water. A bit later, after she'd had a chance to confer with knowledgeable people—she knows more experts in various fields than the State Reference Library, all she has to do is pick up the phone—Lolly, excited as Sherlock Holmes on a case, reported that such woven, stitched belts do, in fact, exist, and have for quite a while—as part of the US Army uniform. You see, that's what I mean—how would I ever know that?

"Okay, what about that Schmeiser? Are you sure it was a Schmeiser?"

"Absolutely, and the forest looked very much like our forests here, not the American woods, and more than that—in my dream, I knew what everything was called, not just the trees but even the bushes: thorn apple, heather, juniper."

"Well, that actually doesn't surprise me at all—you could have picked those up somewhere, in passing, like when you went hiking with your mom when you were little, the time you climbed Goverla, and then just forgot ..."

"But by this logic, is it the same with the American uniform: I knew it once, then I forgot? Is that what you're trying to tell me?"

In response, Lolly arranged her face into one of her proprietary contortions: one lip thoughtfully pursed, brows scrunched together, eyes like a pair of tiny pointy horns—"the silence of the wolves" it's called, when she runs out of arguments but doesn't want to admit defeat (she also has "the silence of the lambs"—with big, piteous eyes, when she's begging for mercy)—and, of course, as always, I had to laugh and hug the little imp. But I also had to wonder: Heck, what if I *had* seen a uniform like that somewhere before, like on one of those shoddy posters in military prep classes? We're all Cold War children after all, and those with technical education especially—all groomed to work for our dear ol' military industrial complex, which, may it rest in peace—met such inglorious demise that I'm the last one of our class who still, at least on paper, counts in the ranks of our profession, although others never relied on it for their bread and butter, and it's good they didn't because it wouldn't get you a single dry a crumb now. I'm lucky I liked playing with Uncle's cigarette holders when I was a kid—who knew I'd start a business out of that, ha!—but I still remember the u-es-es-arr's terrible military secrets, like the fact that the diameter of our noodles matched the caliber of our bullets, and that our cocoa factories were engineered to switch to manufacturing gunpowder in twenty-four hours, so why shouldn't some rotten layer of my collective unconscious spit up a long-forgotten detail about those dirty imperialists we were so keen to fight?

A logical explanation, to be sure, but I didn't like it: it was inelegant. It lacked insight, an inspired suddenness of association that makes everything click together like pieces of a puzzle, with no loose ends left untucked. I can certainly ignore my gut feeling here—no matter how loudly it screams that what I saw in my dream is someone's death as it did, in fact, happen—but I'm still physicist enough to know what makes a good, true solution, and that, Lolly, is elegance; a single inspired maneuver that puts everything into place.

"I understand," Lolly sighed, giving me the lamb look. "It's not only your formulas that work like that."

"That could very well be true, but you know what else? Now that you mentioned Goverla, I'm convinced it was a Carpathian forest."

I really don't want to go shower and wash off her smell, even after I eat. "Sloppy McGrimes!" Lolly teases when we eat breakfast

together: nice natty girl that she is, she won't take a sip of her coffee until she's showered and put on her underwear at least—she
doesn't understand what it's like for me when she's so squeaky
clean. *Stop, right now.*—I'm afraid that is not possible.—*Where's your
willpower?*—Gone, never to be seen again.—*Maniac!*, but raspy,
tender already, eyes misty, my sweet girl, white undies slip down
like a flag of surrender, and then she whimpers softly like a teddy
bear, and it makes everything inside me turn, all over again. "You
know," she said one morning—after we made love like that in the
middle of the kitchen and she sat there on her chair so totally,
unbearably mine, languorous-luxurious, with her hair wet at the
roots, and contemplated her lazily parted thighs—"you know, men
are so doglike in their instincts: always in a rush to mark a woman
as their territory." I could only mumble something back at her
then, like a happy idiot, and didn't feel jealous until later, when
I could think again, remembered the barn door after the horse
bolted, as Granny Lina would put it. Although, really, what's there
to be jealous of? Her memories? Please. Only for some reason,
when a woman hears a man say something like "You women are
all the same," she triumphantly interprets it as more proof of her
being right—"See! I'm not the only one."—and a man, by contrast,
gets all worked up over the mere possibility of just being one in a
lineup of previous offenders.

But hey, I know my way across this minefield; I'm not one of
those morons who ask something like, "How many did you have
before me?" I'm not one to ask questions, period. Lolly and I
mapped out our sandbox a while ago sharing bit by bit, scoop by
scoop, the things that were most important for the other to know;
I even shook hands with Sergiy, her ex-husband, once at a large
party, and I remember I almost liked the guy—he had an open
face and a boyish smile that must still work wonders on women—if
not for his handshake: limp like a dead fish, like all the air had
been sucked out of him a long time ago and he keeps dragging his
shell around because these burdensome social obligations force
him to do so. An aging boy, one of many.

The one thing I really wanted to know I went ahead and asked—"Why did you split up?"—but never got an answer, split up and that's all, as if that in itself was the answer; it certainly was the only answer *she* needed, and she didn't feel like coming up with another one just for me. Okay, that's her right, what can you say? Worse when she lets something slip, a phrase, or a reference, something that sounds sentimental, nostalgic, and when I jump in—sometimes a bit too sharply, I'll admit—before she goes all doe-eyed reminiscing—sure, that one, the guy that you went to the Baltic sea with, the one who taught you to eat lobster—she's stunned, every time, *"Did I tell you that?"* She doesn't remember. Fortunately, the number of love stories in our lives is finite. (And I still don't know how to eat lobster, pick at it like a retarded monkey, no fun at all, just more trash on my plate.) The number of stories is finite, but the number of memories is infinite, and that's a big difference—Lolly mentioned that man because she thought of something completely different from what she'd told me about him before, and that's why she's always surprised: the lobster had nothing to do with it. She doesn't remember, but I can see it all perfectly: the broken red shell on a white platter, the plump, juicy half of a lemon with the lobster's ravished flesh, the ecstatic licking of fingers, the plastic bib the waiter solicitously supplied shamelessly splattered with juices—to eat a lobster it's almost a sexual act, if you know how to do it, of course, and I'm not even talking about the smell that lingers above that table—softly salty, so much like the smell of my girl herself, which, naturally, may not be something that occurs to her at that table at all, but most certainly occurs to her companion if they'd spent the previous night together and if he is not a complete idiot … okay now, that's enough. I've no business in *her* memories. Especially since she wasn't talking about the lobster this time at all, and the number of memories is infinite. Like natural numbers—a countable infinite set. That's the thing.

The thing is, toots, you cannot ever tell yourself fully and completely to another person, no matter how close you are, even to the one with whom you mix your breath by night and share the world by day. I don't know; maybe identical twins can do it, but only for a while, as children.... It's like finite and infinite sets: regardless of how they depend on each other, the first one will have a limit, and the second one will not. End of story. Instinctively, you try to help things along by adding as many shared experiences as you can; you make the woman you love a constant witness to your life—hoping, vaguely, for a purely arithmetical advantage, for strength in numbers: to have the sum total of hours lived together outweigh that of the time spent without the other. (And why hours? Why not minutes, or seconds, or milliseconds? How long does it take you to experience something, to pick up an impression, a feeling that would morph somewhere in the deep dark mines of your subconscious into a memory I have no hope of accessing, like chlorophyll into coal?) Only it's all for naught—*Love's Labour's Lost*, as Grandpa Shakespeare wrote. (Am I right, Lolly? Do you appreciate my English?)

The math doesn't work for the simple reason that even the events we experience together (Remember the time we went to buy our first desk lamp at The Guiding Light, and you were so taken with those tri-jointed arms, playing with lamps all over the store, folding and bending, and I was trying to explain the advantages of halogen bulbs over the incandescent ones, and you listened like a straight-A schoolgirl, so attentive you let your little mouth open a bit? And later, after we left the store with our purchase—not something with a jointed arm, but a totally different, stylish one with a heavy chrome column—you asked just as enthusiastically, on that same brainwave, without even changing your voice, "Didn't that salesman look like a mole?"—and all I could do was stare like a slow-witted goat, not knowing what to say, because the very fact of that salesman's existence had escaped me, let alone what he looked like.), all those things we live through together, Lolly, leave each of us with discrete memories, and the number of these is also infinite.

This, if you think about it good and hard, can drive you nuts. I did go a little crazy with this idea back when I was a student: let's say we have two infinite sets, say of natural and real numbers—how are we supposed to compare them? Which one is "less" and which one is "greater" if they are both potentially endless? It's just like that with us—we have two infinite sets: one is the number of all your memories (X) and the other, the number of memories you share with me (Y). Mind you, there's also the concept of a set's power, as when every member of Y directly corresponds to a member of X, but not the other way around; this means X is more powerful than Y. Example: I remember that there was a salesman at The Guiding Light—that there had to have been one!—but not whether he looked like a mole, a camel, or an ox. And even if I spend the rest of my life holding your hand—which, of course, would cause certain inconveniences—X would still be more powerful than Y, and no feat of my imagination would help me see the man the way you did. So.

Eggs, that's what I want.

What if this is the elemental essence of love: Having a person who shares your life but remembers everything differently? Like a constant source of wonder: world not just there, but *given* to you anew every minute—all you have to do is take her hand. Sometimes, even often, the same idea occurs to both of us at once, and we finish each other's sentences—"that's just it, exactly, that's what I just thought"—thrilling us as if we'd just found a secret door in a shared home, but I bet had we tried to write out our individual trains of thought, separately, and then compared notes, we'd see we weren't thinking *the same thing* at all—only *about* the same thing. The difference is obvious. X remains more powerful under all conditions. That's why it is so rare for two people to dream the same dream.

But they do, don't they? Late Granny Lina told about the time in Karaganda, where they'd been deported, when she and Gramps dreamt the same thing on the same night: that the ice had cracked on the river and all three of them—she, he, and my eight-year-old dad—leapt from one ice floe to the next, holding hands, until they made their way to the shore, where they could see a white house on the green slope, the table draped in a white cloth and set for a meal out on the porch. Gramps then said, "Looks to me, Lina, like we'll be going home soon"—and later it turned out that it was that night (or almost that night) Stalin died, and in about a year they did go back.

It's different, of course, in that I wouldn't want to share a dream like that with Lolly for all the tea in China, thank you; a dream like that is a glimpse of the future when the same danger haunts both. It's borne of a forced intimacy, when you're being squashed into each other by outside forces, melded into a single mind because you've got nowhere else to go. That's some kind of marital bliss, right there. Who knows how they'd fare in normal life. But what if the threat comes from inside, not from the outside? What if it's enough that my girl's memories are an infinite horde, and I have no way of knowing which one of them will turn against me?

By contrast, *these* dreams of mine have become a kind of a shared secret—the kind that married couples have. I've never been married before, so I love stuff like this, probably more than she does; I think it's so cool that she wants to remember these dreams, writes some of them down, generally treats them with the utmost seriousness, like a homegrown Dr. Freud. I'm the same with her cycles—always keep track of them in my mind, so that I can reassure her whenever she worries for no reason. She is pretty good, though; she really studied psychology. When they had the course, she said she spent the entire semester in the reading room, bingeing on specialized literature, even talked her way into an internship at an asylum: first, because the kid must have itched to find out exactly how she got left without a father, but also, I bet, because she was not without doubt—what if something was really wrong with him, the diagnosis not a sham? As a result, what she knows about the discipline goes way beyond the usual intelligentsia erudition, which is, by itself, vastly beyond my grasp—all I know I learned from my sales practicum; I'm a self-made psychologist ("psychomite," as Lolly says). It must have been because of her that I've grown to love *these* dreams. Because they are not just mine, but ours, together.

Although truth be told; they are no one's, and there isn't much to love about them, either.

They just stick in my mind like burrs.

Last night it wasn't the death in the forest (and not so much death, as the back of that guy with his Schmeiser), no, there was something else equally unnerving. All *these* dreams are unnerving—not in their mood, but in their stories. Inside the black Opel Kadett there are people in unfamiliar officers' uniforms, up in front, to the left, and to the right of me; I'm in the back seat, and they are taking me somewhere because I'm a suspect in a murder, but I know that I'm not in any real danger, that it'll all resolve itself somehow. Another image: must be a doctor's examination room in a clinic because surgical instruments are being boiled in a small metal pail on a spirit lamp; I can see very clearly the tiny bubbles as they rise to the surface and burst around the tools like sparks.... And there was a woman there, the one wrapped in a white sheet; I don't remember what she looked like—in the next frame she gets up and walks somewhere with me, down a low-ceilinged corridor, to a ladder, phosphorescently white in the moonlight, where I lean her against a log wall and raise her skirt.... Darkness pulses with widening concentric circles of fire, and a slow female voice, impassive like voice-over, says, "It's never like that, it never happens like that—twice out of three times in a row." This feels piquant. The woman must know such things. Of all things, an erotic dream this one is not. I feel nothing. Not just nothing approximating an orgasm, but nothing at all. Not a thing. I only register the facts, as an outside observer: two fiery contours and it's never like that, apparently, twice out of three times. And how is it, then? With Lolly, I see all kinds of things, but no fiery circles that I can recall.

That's another thing all these dreams have in common and the reason I thought of them as something alien from the very beginning: unlike regular dreams, they're utterly emotionless. No joy, no fear, no anxiety, no arousal, nothing—only stories; the colors, smells, sounds, the feel of things—all there, no problem, all senses amplified like when you're high on something, but the emotions are missing. If these are, in fact, memories, they must come from a disconnected brain. A zombie. The raving of a severed head, as Granny Lina would put it.

Without Lolly, that's what I would've thought, most likely: I'm losing it. So what if it feels good—feels like a glimpse of another world, like in the mountains, when you can suddenly see a distant valley from between the peaks—loonies dig their trips too, no? But Lolly already told me—very firmly—no. She said they are incredibly unhappy, those people, except the ones who go through manic phases, but those spells don't last very long before depression sets in again. This did not describe me at all, and she also told me to quit messing with things I know nothing about. She said it almost like she was offended, like I strayed into someone else's misfortune, a very limited-access territory. Like it was a privilege I didn't have. Sorry, toots. This I understand; I'm not a knuckleheaded lobster-eater eager to take a pretty reporter for a ride around Benelux (the Be and the Ne may be out of my reach, but a nice vacation in Croatia is very much in the offing this summer—Lolly doesn't know yet, I'll tell her in another week or so)—I know there must be some dark things in her memory, especially where her father is concerned, dark and heavy like boulders that she piled into a wall around herself, a fortress of self-preservation locked even to me. A closed subset of memories we'll say—literally and figuratively. Alright, if that's the deal, I don't mind. And I still feel a pang of something, funny human creature that I am: like if I were a full-blown lunatic I'd be more interesting for her, more heroic or something ... as if it really mattered to me to stake a claim on whatever part of her life she'd cordoned off for her father—who, let us be completely accurate, was not really mad either, so you,

Lolly, need to re-examine your self-appointed position as the Crazy People's police. Every man has a right to his own lunacy. Or something like that. You bet I'll exercise mine every chance I get.

The bacon nice and crisp. *Crack-splat, crack-splat, crack-splat*—three eggs into the pan and the kitchen instantly fills with assertive hissing. An inquiry into the fridge yields cucumbers, a disheartened bunch of radishes, and a few shoots of chives. Life, ladies and gentlemen, is not all that bad. Add the Chumak mayo (buy Ukrainian!) and we're a chop and a toss away from a Vitamin Salad, a happy throwback to the era of geriatric socialism. Oh, wait a minute, I'm lying—there was no mayo in socialist stores; we relied on farmers-market sour cream. When we were students, it took a special trip to the Theater Café on the corner of Volodymyrska, on the spot now occupied by the five-star condo high-rise, for the marvel called "egg under mayonnaise": a hard-boiled egg garnished with a teaspoon of mayo. Best bite you could take with a drink. If I ever decided to go into the restaurant business, I'd have a hard-core period place, fierce eighties. I'd call it something appropriate, like Caféteria or Obshchepit, Shcherbytsky's as a last resort, but still, no fads, no frills, no vulgar falsifications like that Co-op chain that's "co-op" in name only. No siree, we'll do it right, and we'll be true to the last archaeographical detail: rickety tables on duralumin-tube legs, always with a piece of folded paper under one of them so you don't spill your borsch; forks and spoons of eternally greasy bendable aluminum, no knives in sight, obviously; and for the napkins in the middle—plastic containers repurposed from the office-supply inventory loaded with hand-cut little squares of dense smooth paper, the kind that goes transparent under the lightest touch, catching your fingerprints better than the cops. On the menu, aside from my favorite Vitamin Salad, of course, we'd have mystery cutlets breaded with prickly stale crumbs, to be served with blue-hue mashed potatoes; fried hake with steel-colored, weapon-grade noodles; pelmeni with vinegar; borsch; and dried fruit compote, always with a dark-brown layer of silt, most likely of plant origin, on the bottom of the glass. Oh yes, and the chopped beet salad. Glasses of the thick-walled, octagonal variety, vodka with beer, and the puzzle of "a choice of desserts" for dessert, represented most often by a sizeable pile of sugar-dusted chopped dough appealingly called Finger-Licks—when I came to Kyiv, in my first year at the university, which, not to spoil anyone's breakfast, also happened to be the Chernobyl year, I lived almost exclusively on these Finger-Licks until I figured out how to cook. For old times' sake, I'd serve "eggs under mayonnaise" too, but only when I got really sentimental, as the spécialité du jour.

Done right, with the walls painted shoulder-high in green oil paint, some vintage-scary posters, light bulbs in only half the lights, and a guaranteed half an hour before a waiter acknowledges your existence—basically, with a full immersion into the period atmosphere—a place like that couldn't keep people out if it wanted! And not just Western tourists, although that's a gold mine right there. I've got to sell it to someone. How about that character with the silver Mercedes, next door? I can't believe no one has done it yet—boys must all be embarrassed about their valiant Komsomol youth; they all want new and foreign stuff, some weird fruits de mer and Château-de-Fleur, they're all gourmands from Konotop—not much better, really, than the hillbillies in the old days, who all craved high-shine East German dressers and made room for them by getting rid of old hand-painted chests and Petrykiv step stools. The grandkids would now give anything to have those back, but tough luck, it's all gone. Now we have to buy classic Kyiv china back from Europe, import our own stuff, and not just the china. And still every auction is packed with the French Empire; it sells like pancakes, and dudes bid each other out of sight, 'coz that's how cool they are, and it makes me want to say—brother, be yourself, whenever did your granny ever lay her eyes on French Empire? Why are you buying someone else's past? Now a genuine Shcherbytsky's setup I could supply in a blink—heck, it'd be the hottest thing in town! It's bound to come around sometime in the next twenty years anyway, so what are we waiting for?

Anyway.

To heck with historical authenticity, I dump about half a can of olives into my Vitamin Salad on a last-minute impulse, it'll be a Greek Vitamin Salad, a post-Communist hybrid; too bad there's no cheese, some feta would be nice, or, better still, some fresh Carpathian bryndza … alright, this'll do. Now, bread into the toaster. Nothing like the smell of toasted bread. Finally, I'm fully plugged into the outside world—and drooling. Time to turn on the TV; it's tuned to Lolly's channel, but of course, inane slob that I am, I've slept straight through her segment and land into the latest news. Which will tell me that Americans are still bombing Baghdad. Fucking blitzkriegers.

No sooner do I settle in front of the TV and stuff a heaping, steaming, awesome forkful of eggs and a bite of warm, crusty wheat toast into my mouth than the outside world mounts a surprise attack: the phone rings. Screams like it hurts. Should have set the answering machine to pick up.

"Gud mornin, Adrian Ambrozich."

It's Yulichka, my busy bee—already up and running the office, bless her heart. If only the sweet soul could find it in herself to speak Ukrainian, so I wouldn't have to lose ten seconds of my life every time this Adrian Ambrozich comes up and I have to merge him with myself (which is, at the moment, chewing). Some clients, aware of my principled distaste for patronymics ("Oedipal complex," I usually explain, kidding, of course, but many still get somber in the face, and go "Oh, sorry, sure thing …") pitch something totally outrageous, like "Mister Adrian"—somehow they think it's the Russian equivalent of saying "sir" in Ukrainian. It's ridiculous and ungrammatical, but really popular—another post-Communist hybrid, like my salad, only far less appetizing. So why should a man have his breakfast interrupted?

"Adrian Ambrozich," Yulichka is clearly excited because she doesn't even apologize when I mumble with my mouth full—"I hev some hick here, from a villadzh, somevere next to Boryspil, he brot a Swiss knaiv, from var-taim, with a small so, in gud condishn. He ses at home he hes a kukoo clock end a walnut wardrobe, used to be his grandpa's, he sed."

Whoa! No authentic cuckoo clocks have been sighted since about a year ago; Bray has scrubbed the market clean of them, no prayer for small fish like me. Is this for real? Yulichka certainly has the nose, that's the main reason I hired her. Walnut wardrobe—that could be anything, but we can't let this redneck out of our sight!

"Hold him there, Yulichka," I hear myself say in Russian. Wow, I didn't think I could: that's what money does to a man—and not even money yet, a mere providential waft of it in the air. Makes me think of Les'ka, we were at the university together: she and her husband went into the gas business under the tutelage of some Petya from Moscow, and later Petya turned out to be gay and would come visit every time he got the itch for Les'ka's hubby—Les'ka would move out to the guestroom then. Do not judge so ye will not be judged, indeed.

At the moment, though, Yulichka couldn't care less about what language we're speaking: We're both breathing hard on our ends of the line, like a pair of lovers (like with Lolly before dawn, I think, irrelevantly).

"I meid him koffi."

"Good job," I say in Ukrainian, having regained my self-control; she does know what she's doing. "Keep him entertained for just a bit longer, I'll be right there," I almost add "just let me take a shower." To heck with the eggs, leave the pair of warm golden eyes to grow cold on the plate, but I have to shave at least—I can't very well roll in all stubby! Have coffee at the office: I sourced me a mean espresso machine, no shabbier than Bray's.

A catch, finally! Man. About time—been scraping by on small stuff for years already, junk, bric-a-brac, whatever I can find, totally like that runaway goat from the nursery rhyme, as Lolly recites, "Ran past a stream—snatched a gulp to drink, ran past a trash heap—snatched a bite to eat." No way to run a business, really.

But now if I could take a spot at a good show, Doroteum's coming up, for one, with a few really nice pieces.… Alright, stop it, enough daydreaming—go already!

Turning off the TV—like clearing the table: erase the picture. Salad into the fridge, the egg dregs glowing with protein—into the mouth after all, albeit on the run, plate into the sink—and I'm in the bathroom, in front of the mirror, with the water splashing and the Gillette buzzing as happily as a bee on my face, when my mind suddenly registers, grants access to the footage that was on TV while I talked to Yulichka, the ochre-and-mud vision of Baghdad that's been on every channel for the last couple days: far below, a bridge in the clouds of sand or blown-up brick dust, and a thread of American Abrams tanks crawling onto it, out of palm-tree greenery, from left to right—from the distance they look like a pride of monstrous prehistoric turtles. This turns out to be the last shot filmed by one of our own—Taras Protsiuk, Lolly knew him—from the balcony of the Palestine Hotel moments before the first turtle, which had already begun to turn its turret toward the camera, fires, and the next shot every TV channel in the world shows is one of Taras's dead body, face down on the concrete with his legs folded under him and arms thrown wide, no longer holding his camera. The sound—I can't remember if I heard any sounds. The guttural menacing growl of the tanks as they rolled onto the bridge—did I hear it on TV, or somewhere in my mind, after the dry rattle of the machine gun, in *that* dream last night?

I go cold all over. I stand in the middle of my bathroom, on the mat, barefoot and stripped to my boxers—and shiver. Something's short-circuited. Something—an idea—illuminated everything in a flash, and I must find it again, hunt it down and catch it before it vanishes into the chatter, into the thick of all other thoughts that came with it and now crowd inside my head like a drunk party in a small living room; shove them aside, look for the one that flashed, not quite whole, snippets of conversations with Lolly. Associated Press pledged assistance to the dead cameraman's family … Ukraine in deep dark ass again, because how can a country demand any sort of investigation of anyone else if it routinely whacks its journalists right at home, and cuts their heads off for good measure, like scalp hunters … Lolly once drank with Taras, may he rest in peace, at some TV-people party of theirs … to the guy in the tank, the gleam of the lens may have looked like a signal for enemy fire, war's war, God damn it, or as some insist, it looked like a sniper—only why would a sniper be a threat to a tank? … the Americans have really gone nuts in Iraq this time around, keep shooting their own like they'd had their heads spun around, as Granny Lina would say, Well, shouldn't have gone a-hunting after those desert demons, should they?; our boys said they lost their wits like that when they were in Afghanistan.… Where the hell is my aftershave? I always put it on this shelf, where did she put it? I hope the Rep.'s ride isn't blocking the driveway, better to just call a cab … phone numbers for Taxi-Lux and Taxi-Blues, damn it, I'm late and the redneck with the cuckoo has nothing to do at the office but add zeros to what he wants for it. A close-up of a weeping Latina reporter in a white T-shirt, it's blazing hot in Baghdad, the coffin with Taras's body being loaded onto the plane, and one of the guys who'd sat with him in the hotel bar just the night before holds the camera steady, and even if he's crying, too, no one will see his tears, because his eye is the camera, and it's outside him, external, impersonal, and pure … Stop. Stop, stop. Here it is; I've got it … slow now, easy, don't lose it.

The image of the tanks on the bridge that Taras captured on film and that now runs on every channel—that was the last thing he saw in his life, right? The last memory fixed by his mind. Only he had a camera in his hands—he was lucky (that's so wrong to say!) to have the whole world see the last thing he saw before he died.

Question: What would happen to that last shot captured by his consciousness if he hadn't had the time to transfer it from the retina of his own eyes onto that other one, the mechanical eye of the camera?

A camera can be turned off. It can be set to play. A camera is a very simple device. But where does it all go from your own, human eyes if it's you who's been turned off?

Why do we choose to believe that it all just disappears, fades into nothingness with the person? Because there's no play button? But we don't get to watch it when the person is still alive just the same. No matter how close we are, how intimate, we've no way to glimpse that footage, as I have no way of entering Lolly's memories. But it doesn't mean it's not there.

The back of the man ahead of me, in the uniform with a woven belt, the dry rattle from behind the trees—and blackness. *After that*—blackness. This picture, this last picture, with the back, the grass and the underbrush, the thorn apple and heather and juniper, the sun bunnies on the tree trunks, the smell of humid earth and soggy greenness—where does it go? To what posthumous vault?

The black Opel Kadett with the unknown army's officers, the spatula boiling in sparkly bubbles, the stairs phosphorescent in the moonlight, the woman's voice keeping a methodical count of our orgasms … I am not mad I tell myself as I try to suppress the shakes; I am not mad. Calm down. I'm not mad. I'm just watching someone else's footage.

Made by a dead person who didn't have a camera.

He doesn't care that I don't deal in *that* kind of antiques.

I know this is true because I am shaking. The puzzle has fit together, no loose ends. Dreadfully simple, elegant really, as it ought to be with the right solution. The only thing missing was this basic, obvious premise: the footage kept in one's mind does not disappear. And why would it? Just because a man didn't happen to have a camera? Please, the camera is incidental; all it does is prove that the film is there.

Just like *these* dreams.

The absolute, inviolable certainty that I am right calls up, for a moment, the half-forgotten sweetness—that blissful, triumphant unclenching of brain cells that used to come in abundance from lab research and that can never be fully replaced by the satisfaction of a well-done business deal, no matter how complex the scheme. Nothing to write the Nobel Committee about, to be sure, but the thrill is just the same—and perfectly sufficient. The world can be explained. Specifically, somewhere out there lies buried a humongous, immeasurable—infinite, that's it—vault, an archive of things once witnessed, of footage that wants to be watched. How, by whom, those details are not important. This, one must admit, is a comforting thought. An idea that offers a man, at the risk of sounding melodramatic, a shot at non-lonesomeness (that's a Lolly word). As in: my memory, in its entirety, I bequeath to Daryna Goshchynska/Adrian Vatamanyuk (choose one). Okay, maybe not in its entirety; that may be too much, but wouldn't this make for a great sci-fi story? I'm full of ideas; I'm shedding ideas this morning. Spawning. A morning of high ideation. A high-yield morning. I'm Ideating Adrian. Mister Adrian Ideatov. No, better, like an emperor—Adrian the Idea Bearer. Wow. Watch out, Boryspil redneck, I'm gonna get your clock and your little cuckoo, too!

Snickering at myself (no one else to snicker at in the empty apartment), I rub into my cheeks a pleasantly cool squirt of silky Egoist (never did find that aftershave)—soon as I get to the office, I'll desire a double espresso from Yulichka. Pull on a brand new, just-out-of-the-plastic, crinkly Hugo Boss shirt—a T-shirt won't look respectable enough—snip off the hateful plastic whiskers that stick in the seams where labels had been attached, straighten cuffs, admire the package; cool and style all around, good to go to Sotheby's, or to a Swiss bank, yes, definitely, Sotheby's first, then to the bank to unload the cash—and then it finally catches up with me, like late-night heartburn, this very simple, little tail end of my earlier idea, sudden and undeniable like a door slamming into a face: Why me?

Sweet Jesus, why me? Why did he, the one that gets shot in the dream, whoever he was, choose *me* to sit through his archival reels—if I didn't ask for it?

And, while we're at it … who was he?

Black Woods, May 1947

"Father," he said, and wanted to say again, *Father,* but his voice failed him and only a low groan came out. Someone shone a battery lamp at him; the circle of its light swung back and forth across the wall, a log wall like that of a village church; and in the shadows, outside this circle of light, he thought he saw a priest's dark cassock. This made him happy: Papa's here, he thought, and the overwhelming joy of it almost brought him to tears—he felt so weak and tender, softened with love and gratitude to his father, so worn out he couldn't even get up to kiss his father's hand and ask for absolution as he'd longed to do: *Father, I killed people, I abandoned my studies back when the Germans first came—how many fell at my hand? I did not forget, Dad, what you said to me when I left, when you gave me your blessing: Do not shame us, son. I was a good soldier and I am clean before Ukraine; forgive me, Father, my blood-spilling sins.* But then he remembered, the gash of the memory clean and sharp in his mind like a knife wound, that it had been three years since they sent Mom and Dad to Siberia, and he moaned again and closed his eyes, still feeling, like a blind man, the tightly packed, hard-breathing human mass all around him. The air was heavy—the animal pall of human flesh mixed with the acerbic tinge of medicine and disinfectant; it wheezed, mumbled, and bubbled; it heaved like a dog coughing up a bone; once, a young voice rang out from the dark, wild and loud, "Throw the grenade!"

"Shhh," a whisper rustled toward the voice, soothing, comforting. He heard clothing move, sensed the air stir around him, and the circle of light lifted from his eyelids, went to the young voice, but still he felt like the Holy Father remained at his bed, not leaving him. The other smell, that's what it was—sap, or as they say around this country, firring, the woods. Pine trees. The logs of the wall, he noticed when he opened his eyes, also seemed fresh, stained with sap. An infirmary then, not a jail.

He was safe—someone was looking after him: his body was immobilized, swaddled and feeble, blissfully freed of the need to move for the first time in many years. Someone worked at his side as he lay unconscious, worked to do good for him—the attention he discerned on the other side of the lamp was also kind and comforting, caring, and his forehead retained the feeling of being touched by a delicate, cool hand. He was so moved by this sweet, blessed peace that had been given to his body that he just lay there enjoying his helplessness, feeling his every cell vibrate with joy, glowing inside, the hot wash of gratitude barely dammed by his closed eyelids: kindness, he was filled with kindness; it flowed through him; it emanated through every pore of his skin; it inundated and washed away his feeble self, his memory, his past, even his name—he was nameless, helpless like a new babe bobbing on the waves of an endless, resplendent ocean, washed on all sides with love so abundant it made him weak with awe and marvel.

Where did it all come from, or had he died already, unbeknownst to himself, and gone to heaven? But he'd had no chance to confess; he'd wanted to confess, but hadn't gained the strength to speak, and yet he felt he'd been heard and forgiven—so this was what it was like to have been forgiven of your sins. He willed himself, for the last time, to open his tear-streaked eyelids, open wide—like the dead eyes of murdered rebels that the NKVD pins with matchsticks when they put their tangled bodies on display in city squares—and from his alien, heavily numb lips happily peeled off the single and most important thing he had to say: "Thank you, Father."

At this, the ocean shifted, and in front of him stood a solid wall of gold, high as the distant heavens, and he knew he had to scale it to get to the other side. This was incredibly hard and he could not hold on—he collapsed, everything collapsed, and darkness fell.

Later still came long, viscous dreams that trapped him like the knee-deep bogs that filled his boots when they'd marched north in spring. Mother came and poured milk from a jar into his mouth; there was too much, it filled his nostrils and he couldn't breathe; he fought and turned away until he saw it wasn't milk at all but cherry liqueur, hot, thick, and ruby red.

Then he was in Lviv again, at Sapieha Palace, and boys marched at him out of the gates of the Academic Gymnasium, while he stood with his hand raised in salute waiting for them to pass so that he could march after them, but he never got to go with them because Lodzio Daretsky called out of the ranks to him, laughing, "You dope, what are you doing walking around in a uniform? The Soviets are everywhere."

"And you," Adrian called back. "What about you? Are you allowed?"

"We've nothing to worry about now!" Lodzio answered and laughed, a free, raucous laugh, such as he never had while he was alive; only then did Adrian make out, next to Lodzio, Myron, who'd blown himself up in a bunker not too long ago so he wouldn't be captured, and Legend, tortured to death back when Germans first came by the Gestapo on Pelchynska Street, and that doctor from the East he'd met a few times in the Red Cross office, Ratai, they called him; he had that Poltava way of rolling his l's so soft, smooth as silk, and he'd perished, they said, this last winter somewhere in the mountains when the Poles dropped grenades into his infirmary. They were all dead, those who marched past Sapieha; they'd never even met each other alive. He recognized some but not others, and could only ask as he watched them pass, "Where are you going, then?"

"To St. George's," someone said, maybe even Lodzio, "to pray for Ukraine. You better get going too, enough lollygagging already!"

He felt shamed, and wanted to run after them, but something held him from behind. He turned and saw it was Obersturmführer Willie Wirzieng himself, the hog with a butcher's jaw—only changed out of his Gestapo uniform into new NKVD rags, with enormous epaulettes studded with living, blinking human eyes instead of stars, and an invisible voice told Adrian that those were the eyes of Ukrainian political prisoners that Wirzieng had personally gouged out—who grinned at him, strutted and hissed, "Never did kill me, did you?" Adrian protested that he tried, twice, and both times the failure wasn't his: the first time Wirzieng unexpectedly took a different route, went the way he'd never gone before, and the other time something else made him abort the mission.

"Alright, try again!" said the one who was Wirzieng, and Adrian opened his eyes at once, as if shaken: above him, a woman's face floated in the dull yellow glow of a lantern, now coming closer, now pulling away. Geltsia!, he thought, thrilled—it had been so long since her last letter he'd begun to wonder if she'd moved out west with one of their convoys, then suddenly remembered he wasn't supposed to call her Geltsia, should have said Zirka, but it wasn't her anyway; the kiss that moistened his parched lips wasn't hers—and in the next instant he knew it wasn't a kiss, either. He was nailed to a cross; he rose and fell on his pierced hands as he fought for air, and every time he lifted himself, a terrible, infernal pain filled his chest and the centurion below shoved at his mouth a vinegar-soaked sponge on the end of his spear. How long can I last like this?, he thought, terrified, and saw below, on the other side of the cross, Stalin, Roosevelt, and Churchill: they sat there like the myrrh-bearing wives in Brueghel's *Crucifixion*, at the foot of a little knoll, and played cards like in Yalta, with cut-up pieces of a map—he strained, against the piercing pain, to see who'd gotten the map of Ukraine, but it wasn't there; he realized it was long gone, played to the bottom of the discard pile, and would never come up again in this game. He wanted to shout in anger at the glib Churchill, who looked a little like Wirzieng, *What about your Fulton speech—didn't you promise to wage war on the Soviets?*—but asked instead, *Lord, why did you abandon me?* The centurion popped up again, bared his teeth at him, and pointed to where Geltsia, no, Zirka, kneeled, bent at the waist, loose-haired, in a fitted uniform overcoat that had parted, very Brueghel-like, to reveal a bit of raw, purple lining that pulsed like freshly skinned flesh. He gathered his remaining strength to call out to her, to catch her eye at least, so she'd know he was there, but she did not see him, someone's shoulders blocked her view, and he couldn't figure out how it was that he could see her but she couldn't see him, and then wondered, with a new pang of horror, if she no longer lived.

"She lives alright, lives just fine," the centurion said in the exasperated tone of a peasant telling his old cow to stand still; Adrian looked closer and went cold: under her coat, Geltsia's body was wrapped in a white sheet spotted with blood.

"And we'll see each other again?" Adrian pleaded, because he no longer feared anything, even a no.

"Sure you'll see her," Roman howled menacingly, for some reason in the Boyko dialect and sounding as though he called from the bottom of a well. "Moy-ye, you'll see her good and right ..."; then, he took aim and hit Adrian between the ribs with his spear, so hard that all the stars tumbled out of the sky and darkness fell again.

And a bit later he clearly heard a woman's low voice say above him, "His fever has broken, Father Chaplain."

And another voice, a man's, padding softly but surely, as if with felt-slippered feet, answered quietly, "Thank the merciful Lord."

This was no longer a dream.

He opened his eyes and tried to move; the same terrible pain rang through his chest, making him hiss and freeze, eyes bulging, waiting for his body to tell him where it did not hurt. The man stood at the foot of his bed dressed not in a cassock, but in civilian clothes, wearing a vested suit and a cravat, and the woman, whom he could guess to be young and swarthy, lingered right above him, so that in the dim light he could clearly see the lush, oblong hillocks of her breasts under her blouse—like a pair of doves, he thought with a sudden lively interest. And at once felt angry at this most inappropriately eager metaphor, and at the even more inappropriate urge to stroke these doves, and his inability to move, and at the next thought that came on the heels of the first: how scrubby, hairy, and foul-smelling he must've grown, a beast of the woods indeed, in contrast to the man at the foot of his bed, who, although no longer young, with large bald spots on his bulbous forehead, was clean-shaven, sharp-collared, and seemed to emanate the unmistakable aura of a good cologne, which made it all the more humiliating to be lying in front of him like this. These were all rotten, sordid thoughts, noxious muck—all occasioned by this woman, her near warmth and scent, and this made him truly and finally furious: Why'd she have to go and stand there?

He was also nettled at the vague, elusive connection he felt between the man and something extraordinarily nice, something precious and joyful—like a sun shower in a glen when he was a child, a veil of gold nuggets thrown over the iridescent green and held up with pillars of sunlight—but what it was—so fine, and perhaps recent—Adrian could not recall, the woman's presence distracted him; he did, however, recall a different glen, and the recollection lifted him above the last traces of his delirium and made him forget the pain that had pulled an iron brace around his chest again: How long has it been, and what about the boys? What happened to them?

They were trekking through the woods and the last thing he remembered was the sunlight spotting the trunks of the pines and the rectangular back of their guide, Roman, ahead of him, outfitted in a homemade uniform and girded with a thick, stitched, woven sash, instead of a regular leather belt—men ragged him about it (the girls liked Roman so much they didn't want him to leave, stole his belt and kept it!), as men in resistance always rag agreeably quiet types. Roman, in response, only smiled his reserved, farmhand smile and kept at whatever he had to do; belt or no belt, he was good at it, his rifle—an MP44, a beauty—was a piece to prize. When Adrian asked him about it, Roman simply said he "borrowed it back in '44 from one SS man," and Adrian liked that about him, too—the way he said it. Anyone who'd seen Roman walk through the woods would also know he was a veteran: he had a light, capacious gait, noiseless as a cat's, not a twig cracked underfoot, not a puddle stirred. Adrian appreciated it right away—this inborn skill of a native who didn't have to learn the woods by camping with Plast Scouts—and tried to walk like that, too, light and agile, happy to have the man lead him.

He'd felt out of sorts since the night before, trailed by a premonition of some vague ill, irritable and distracted, and then the strap on his map case snapped right as they were about to set out—another bad omen—so this sturdy rectangular back ahead of him felt reassuring. Adrian was glad to be looking at it, this dependable construction as though especially designed for the purpose of hefting horse-size loads—carrying sacks of grain, bringing sheep out of a snowstorm into the warmth of the barn, and the wounded, sure, why not dragging wounded friends off the battlefield, too.

Of course you never thought of it like that—you didn't say to yourself, *Let's take this guy with us because he could carry me if I get hurt, or finish me off*—but no combat unit could persist *without* this gut-felt certainty. It was the primeval raw goo, the only substance that could bind a handful of discrete male selves into one—a unit, a pack, a swarm, a hundred—only then could an idea transform them into a working army, a self-propelled force that gathered speed and multiplied its strength, so that one day in '45 a field up north might have turned from rusty-brown to gray with sheaves of rag-doll soldiers that the Bolsheviks kept herding onto it, hundred after hundred, until they had to give up and retreat, never to realize that it was a single swarm of UIA, not even forty souls, that turned them back. The idea, no matter what our political teachers told us, is like yeast and will leaven only the finest flour; and the boys who came from behind the Curzon Line and told stories of how they sang duets, from their trenches, at the Poles on the other side before the fight—"Antko, Antko what are you fighting for?"—"My father Sta-a-alin!"—until one of the Antkos, driven to distraction, would snap back, "No more mine than yours!" which eliminated any possibility of further fighting on the spot, and those boys, proud and very conscious of what they fought for, and by that faith made invincible—were first and foremost good stock, the finest flour that could wrap you like a second skin, so that you and the man before you, and the one behind, and those to your right and to your left, all of you, once mixed together, became one flesh, an army of the people. This was the feeling, lost for several years after the army split up into small groups and went underground, that he experienced again behind the shield of Roman's rectangular back as they moved through the humid early-morning woods, in unfamiliar terrain, goose-file.

There were five of them, too many he thought, but the dark-eyed security-service character with hollow cheeks, Stodólya, had insisted they take two guards where one would have been plenty, and nothing, nothing in him snapped or dropped—no time!—when Roman suddenly froze in his tracks and the next instant they caught machine-gun fire from behind the bushes ... Sweet Lord Jesus, what happened after that?

Who carried him out? Who dragged him to the infirmary (something made him believe it was Roman)? How did it all even happen—reconnaissance said the raids had passed—how did they drop right into the ambush, like a ham hock into stew? And who to ask about it all now—the one the dark-eyed nurse calls Father Chaplain?

Two pairs of eyes, black and gray, gleamed at him expectantly from the dusk. Well, there you have it—he's awake and alive, no worries. And mad as hell—nothing inside him but anger: as though the very refitting of him back into reality, from which he had been so abruptly disengaged, scraped him raw and left him fiercely itching. Doggone it, if only the pain in his chest would let up! He, who had always scorned any corporeal weakness like a mistake in a mathematical equation, now must be compelled to lie hobbled on his cot and wonder if he'll make it up to relieve himself.

The priest coughed gently, as though tuning his voice to a pitch that wouldn't add to the pain, and then smiled—an unexpectedly open smile that made his whole face glow, every scrunched-up wrinkle of it, "Glory to Ukraine, Commander."

He returned the greeting, barely catching his breath before falling into a cruel fit of coughing that made him break out in sweat. He wasn't a commander, just the management adjutant, but they didn't need to know that. Where the hell was he?

"You'll have to stay with us a bit until you get stronger. I am Yaroslav, and this is our nurse, Rachel."

Rachel, huh. Now it would've been impolite not to look at her straight, and, trained as he was in the German days, he took quick stock of her features; his eye gathered and arranged them, like a picture in a kaleidoscope—noticing the unmistakable signs of the persecuted race, small things you normally don't see until someone pointed them out: a meaningful tuck of the plump upper lip, distinct like an Arabian stallion's; the cut of her nostrils; the smattering of freckles on her olive skin; and her large, prominent eyes like jet stones, half-hidden under heavy eyelids. He remembered then where he had seen this face before, now heavily retouched by shadows: it was she who leaned over him to put a cool cloth on his forehead; she who washed his body and gave him water to drink, wiping his mouth and chin dry.

Suddenly and inexplicably embarrassed, he asked, "So it was you who cared for me?"

She laughed and spoke fast, with the melodic Hebraic intonation—almost as if she felt a bit shy herself and rushed to sweep her unease under the pile of words. "Me and our doctor, he's the one who did the surgery, took out the bullet, and repaired your pleura. The bullet came close but didn't touch the lung—you must have special luck!"

"Thank you," he mumbled, disoriented: he was being swept up in the forgotten prewar hustle of the Galich market, the clamor from the Jewish rows where quick, black-eyed merchants outyelled and outclucked each other praising their goods, and he wanted to close his eyes again—this woman had too much life in her; she spouted it thick and heavy as oil and he was too weak. The priest and the nurse apparently understood how he felt and exchanged a quick, short glance—adult conspirators over a small child's head—but he did not get upset with them; he had no more energy for that, and he had to conserve the little he did have if he hoped to find out anything. It was imperative that he keep them there, that he speak to them, so that they wouldn't leave him alone with the picture that had been branded in his mind and still burned there: the sun spots on the trunks of the trees and Roman's rectangular back with the assault rifle and a hand grenade in a holster, girded over his shirt with the homemade woven sash. They did not seem to want to step away from him either, and Adrian read their hesitation. The two of them, no, three, counting the invisible doctor, had fought Death for him: he was their small personal victory and they deserved to enjoy it for a little while longer—and he had to exploit this.

He pinned them to the spot with questions, quick and straight as darts, concise, dry, to the point, Security Service style—not leaving the one being questioned any chance to think—asked in a low voice because his breath barely squeezed in and out of his chest and he was afraid of coughing again. Gradually, however, the strength came and took his side—the anonymous, faceless strength of the Organization, blind as the laws of physics; he managed to claim it again, if only for a few minutes, and he was no longer the patient—he was an officer, and the two healthy, strong, full-blooded people, the man and the woman before him, straightened up and stood at attention without even noticing.

Who brought him to the hospital? Woodsman's men. A zero point zero of new information—of course it was Woodsman's people, who else, those were the men with whom he'd set out. *How many made it out of the ambush?* They didn't know. *Were there other wounded?* Yes, but with light injuries, to arms, shins, nothing serious, thank the Lord. *Killed?* They didn't know this either—but they would have heard if there had been, someone in the surrounding villages would've known. *So they were not in a village?* No, the village was no longer safe, there must be a mole, NKVD came and stayed for a whole month before Easter, searched every house until they found the hideout with two wounded men—they must've known what they were looking for. *And? Took them alive?* No, the boys shot themselves. May their souls rest in peace. This bunker, in the woods, is safe; that's where they did surgery—at the warden's station; the one who carried him out on his back, the guy with the big nose, told them he was severely wounded, said he was an important person, a commander from the district, asked them to do everything possible.

So that's how it was. He was very grateful. He said another thank-you just to Rachel, who rushed off to bring him water to drink, good, spring water; the whole hospital seemed to be very well kept. "Now let the commander rest a bit."

"How much longer?"

"That's for the doctor to say when he comes back."

It seemed they really had nothing more for him to learn. He thanked them again; a record number of thanks per unit of time. He was, in fact, exhausted—limp like a beaten-out rug.

The guy with the big nose—that was Stodólya, obviously: he had a distinctive, elongated physiognomy, with gaunt cheeks that made his nose protrude like a wolf's. He certainly knew his conspirator trade, but he went too far this time: could've left him instructions about communication instead of dooming him to passive waiting. They carried full knapsacks of literature—did even a shred of it survive? Stodólya, huh. Carried him out on his own back, fancy that. Why did he think it should have been Roman who saved him?

It was very good that Stodólya was alive and unharmed. It meant that while he was lying here, Stodólya was doing both of their jobs. Someone had to collect information about the local Bolshevik agents—they really wormed their way into the woodwork here. You should be pleased, Commander.

He was not; at least not as much as he ought to have been. All for the simple and primitive reason he was ashamed to admit even to himself: he didn't like Stodólya. Some barrier stood between them, and neither man had a burning urge to overcome it. Such things were rare in resistance where the spirit of brotherhood and a shared fate united everyone, where you were pleased just to see a comrade alive. It just had to have been Stodólya, of all people. The man who saved his life—Stodólya.

Of the two most readily available strategies for handling an unmotivated antipathy toward someone who's done you good— forgetting the good or identifying the motivation at the core of the antipathy—Adrian instinctively adopted the latter; his memory solicitously offered something he once heard about Stodólya: that he executed a boy who'd fallen asleep while keeping night watch. The boy was a new recruit, arrived from a nearby village the night before; he was seventeen years old. Stodólya did as The Code demanded, and no one would ever hold it against him, but still Adrian did not like to think about that boy and his last moments in front of the firing squad—as if it were he, Adrian, who was to blame for his ill fate.

There was something else, though. These country boys—these hard young men, straight as an arrow, honest as the land itself— always engendered in him an inexpressible guilt. It wasn't the purely military emotion of the officer toward the people he could send to their deaths—it was a more delicate, more intimate sort of emotion, like the desperate impotence of a loving father and husband who cannot protect the ones he loves. He felt guilty about his "high" birth; about his education, which inspired in them the traditionally Ukrainian, near-pious devotion; about the moments of pure exaltation he had experienced in Vienna before St. Stefan Cathedral and in the presence of Raphael's *Madonna with the Blue Diadem*—he felt guilty for having seen the world they didn't know, and would never see before they perished; even a shared death could not ordain them equal. It may have been the burden of this guilt that, with time, had made him more enamored, in a romantically zealous, innocent way, of the mysterious metaphysical force that blazed in those boys like peat fires and filled him with awe and trepidation. It was not rational; it didn't come from books they'd been given to read or ideas they'd been taught—this force came straight from the very land that had borne them and from which they'd been shoved, and stomped, and kicked by rib-cracking Polish, Magyar, Muscovite, and who knows who else's boots; this was the amassed force of its centuries-old, silent, dark ire.

One day in '44 around Kremenets, he and three others stopped at a homestead to ask for water; while the mistress fixed supper and ran to the pantry, which in that country they called by the Polish word spizharnia, the master, a solidly built, not-yet-old man with a face tanned like boot leather, sat them all down in a row on the bench under the icons, like kids in a schoolhouse, and demanded to know what it was that they were fighting for. They pulled out a stack of brochures from their knapsacks, and a few issues of *Idea and Action*; Adrian, worn out and faint with the warmth, food, and domesticity, mouthed the usual, well-rehearsed statements like a somnambulant, hearing his own voice from a great distance and seeing nothing except the three transfixed little faces of the boys who watched them—and listened to them as though to a choir of angels—from the loft above the stove where their mother had ordered them to stay; and when they said goodbye and thanked the mistress for the supper, while she fussed over them and filled their arms with food—"Here, take this, for the road, of Lord's bounty"—bread, salo, and pungent smoked ham, the not-yet-old man suddenly appeared among them dressed in his sheepskin coat, outfitted with an old Russian Mosin Nagant he'd been keeping who knows where, and a leather tote, nodded to his wife, meaning, me too, and when she wailed, "Don't you go buck-mad on me, old fool!" he said simply, "Martha, look, it's *our army* that's come!" Adrian's throat caught at these words and didn't let go. It took all they had to talk the man out of it.

Later, he saw dozens of them, those middle-aged men, often side by side with their sons; he watched them fight—and remembered that lump in his throat. This war wasn't simply fought by people with arms—it was fought by the land itself, fierce and implacable, its every bush and knoll, every living thing. A young village wife in front of her house, arms across the chest—laughing straight into the Reds' faces—while he listened from the backyard, rifle cocked.

"Some hot thing you are, all by yourself—and where'd be your husband?"

"He is, indeed, Officer-sir, somewhere, lest your boys shot him already!"

He froze to the spot, ready for an explosion, but the woman better divined the balance of powers: the others sort of withered right there and, after shooting the breeze for a while longer, just for show, left, retreated.

"Gramps, you got some water to drink?" An old man, white-haired and white-bearded, towering over the fence like the Lord of Sabaoth, watching the crawl of exhausted alien troops, two and a half million of them, an entire front making its way back from Germany, where they'd been thrown, like an elephant against a pack of wolves, back in '45—and too late: "Go on," the old man called, waving them on with his hands almost in blessing, "the Bolsheviks will take care of you." Every fence, every gulch, every haystack resisted. Never before had the land known a war like this one. Even that eternal peasant—bovine—patience and stamina, that had so grated on Adrian in the days of Polish rule, suddenly transubstantiated, like water into wine, into something with a higher, ominous purpose, something far from the dumb fatalism he had believed it to be on the sleepless nights when he, a student then, turned over and over in his mind Stefanyk's blood-curdling vignettes and the caustic lines of Ivan Franko's "Moses," "For you knew yourself to be brother of slaves and the shame of it burned you"—now he burned with shame that he could ever have believed himself to be somehow better, higher than they.

In reality, the power of their self-sacrifice was far greater than his—perhaps precisely because not one of these men ever believed himself to be in any way special, and this innate humility concealed their inner dignity, their immutable core, hard as flint—and ready to strike a fire. Once lit by the blaze of war, they saw themselves, for the first time, inside history—and took it up, with a spit and a rub of their calloused hands, like a plow. "Martha, look, it's *our army* that's come!" The army waited for you, it was ready—it gave you a shot at glory and a band of brothers, "gain the Ukrainian nation or die fighting for it," but also Stodólya and his firing squad, should you fall asleep on watch. Shouldn't have fallen asleep, of course; you couldn't fight a war with men like that. Our army is not just an army, and our cause is a special cause. Who couldn't understand this?

Now, for the first time in years, he had many hours at his disposal and could think about all this. All the time in the world, as the funny English saying went. The shelter was equipped with a radio receiver, and sometimes he caught snippets of American broadcasts, but he only recognized individual words and didn't have the textbook with him that he'd begun to study last winter; his German, against his rather naïve hope, did not help at all. Once he woke up, drenched in sweat, with a lucky guess that the "slaughter" he heard from the radio was the same as the German "schlachten." He must have called it out before he was quite awake, because in the darkness next to him bedsprings creaked and something very dear, a breath of home, bread and fresh milk, brushed hot against his face, and he felt in his hands two warm hillocks like a pair of round-chested doves of the kind he'd kept when he was a boy, and held on to them so they wouldn't get away.

"What is it now, easy, shhh, shhh," the doves cooed their reprove, and he realized, in a flash—It's Rachel!—and meant to beg her pardon so that she wouldn't think ill of him, to tell her how vowel sounds travel from language to language, crawl across great fields of snow camouflaged in white robes, and how he came to unmask them, but she determined otherwise. "Sleep now, sleep," and went to do something with his pillow or blanket; he never learned exactly what because he obeyed her order and sank back into sleep instantly, like a rock into water. And he made no more serendipitous linguistic discoveries after that: the thorny thickets of English pronunciation got the best of him.

Or maybe, he thought in his more lucid moments, when the pain curled up like a small dark animal in his chest and only its slow pulse warned him it was still there, maybe he simply lost the knack for abstract reasoning, having trained his mind to aim for immediate and practical results. For some reason, this made him sad, which, in turn, also proved disconcerting: coupled with his physical debility, the forced mental indolence disrupted his routine and released a host of subterranean emotional currents he didn't know how to manage—he flailed and bobbed in them, ineffectual like a poor swimmer. He couldn't even give them names, label them—he'd always been better at numbers than words; he spent his first year in the woods toting around Krenz's *Collection of Mathematical Problems,* until he finally had to leave it behind at a safe house—now he wished he had it back; it would've helped him keep his wits engaged instead of obsessing about God knows what nonsense.

Beside him, the infirmary bunker hid three other wounded who, for various reasons, could not be placed with village families; one man was brought in after Adrian—gangrene had spread to his leg and, when they unwound the bandage, the small shelter filled with a noxious cloying smell that nothing, not the excellent ventilation nor the nightly airings, could dispel. Once he caught a whiff of the same sugary-rotten-marshy scent on Rachel—it unnerved him: they all liked the nurse; she was so lovely to watch as she worked around them, moving smoothly between their cots, radiating her abundant, blazing aliveness throughout the room, as she cooked their food, or brought fragrant herbs from outside for the brew she boiled on the kerosene burner and poured into small stoups—all without a moment of rest, such a hard worker, bless her heart, and it was so wrong to have this rotten smell connected with her, until he spied her grabbing a roll of gauze before she ducked behind the curtain that cordoned off her bed and suddenly realized where the smell had come from. A hot flush of shame flooded his face then, and he felt like a boy caught spying around the girls' convenience. He tried to forget this episode, along with the night he grasped her breasts, to remove them from his memory, as was his custom to do with anything that distracted him from the mission. The problem, however, was the mission had stayed up above the ground somewhere, outside the infirmary bunker, leaving him to cough and spout like an engine on half its cylinders.

He was no good at being sick. He made sure to communicate that to the doctor, Orko, the first time he saw him, a young man, a student by the looks of him, and always badly shaved—whenever he sat down on the edge of Adrian's cot, the lamp illuminated a few stray bristles on his cheek. Orko was possessed of an attractive innate seriousness, often found among good students from poor families; Adrian appreciated how thoroughly and considerately, as if teaching a class, the doctor described what was going on inside his chest, where the bullet had entered, and what path it drilled—here Orko wiggled his fingers in the air and, failing to locate an anatomic chart or a chalkboard, drew with his index finger a parabola in front of Adrian's nose and stabbed at the space above it. He also confessed they had feared he wouldn't survive the pain of surgery—they had nothing with which to etherize him: ever since many of our people at the district clinic had been arrested, all drugs, not just ether or chloroform, had been difficult to procure, and they'd had to have their alcohol homemade, with an extra round of distillation. But Orko told him he was lucky to have a very strong heart, and a strong, healthy organism in general, knock on wood, so all they had to do now was pray that nothing got infected.

Orko spoke with a mechanistic, crafty practicality, as though puzzling out a fault in a broken mechanism: all parts and their functions were clear to him, and this inspired trust. Adrian would have loved to talk more with him, but Orko had little time to spare on chitchat: he practiced illegally and was called to do surgery almost every day, sometimes at the forest station and sometimes right in an open field, rushing from one village to the next to save whoever got burned, kicked, or mangled. Two villages over, there was a girl orderly, sent in by the Soviets from the other side of the River Zbruch, but the locals didn't trust the sovietka, calling for "their own doctor" instead, and were often right to do so, Orko sensibly observed: the girl knew little beyond mustard plaster, fire cups, and, when she first got here, the Komsomol. Now, after a few conversations with Woodsman, she was thinking straighter, and had started working for us, but she's not much help yet, young as she is and greener than grass. Adrian had to laugh, in his mind, at Orko calling anyone young, although there were, in fact, only a few older doctors with the insurgency—almost all of them emigrated to Europe after the Bolsheviks took over, and even if Orko never had a chance to finish his studies and obtain a proper diploma, Adrian was certainly not one to criticize his professional skills.

It was also a long time since he ate like this: in obeisance to Orko's instructions, a steady caravan of village women passed through their shelter, bearing baskets of eggs, fresh milk, and sour cream. "You'd think we'd moved the market here," the boys joked. He was regaining his physical strength quickly: first he could sit up in bed; then he made his way to the toilet, down a narrow fifteen-foot corridor from the main room, on his own, albeit by holding on to the wall; and then he was able to get outside to stretch his legs. The first time he climbed to the surface, the exertion of it sent him back to his cot, where he lay for a while gasping for breath and watching luminescent green circles spin in front of his eyes. He caught Rachel's dark eyes and read in her gaze a strained, almost painful attention—she even bit her lip as though to fight back a moan, and that's when he smiled at her as he used to smile to the younger, weaker soldiers, to cheer them up, and being able to do so improved his mood dramatically.

He remembered the way she bit her lip—or rather held it with the just-visible edge of her teeth—later, when he sat playing chess with Gypsy, a man from Slobozhanshchyna, an Easterner, who was shot in the hip. Gypsy's face, in the time he spent in the infirmary, succumbed to a tar-black pirate beard that made his incredibly white teeth glisten ferociously from its thicket when he talked—and he talked a lot, a quick-hitting storm of words, choppy like the rattle of a machine gun. Adrian could make out maybe every sixth word or so, because Gypsy peppered his machine-gun delivery with unfamiliar sayings, interrupted, over and over, with the meaningless "ye follow" as if he were mocking someone hard of hearing, "Hey, you, ye follow, wait with your laundry up the stream, let me finish"—with talk like that, no wonder they couldn't put him in the village; he was too conspicuously "not from around here." Adrian found himself taken by surprise when this chatterbox turned out to be quite a competent chess player, who executed such a clever version of the old Indian defense that Adrian, playing black, couldn't regroup and counterattack until mittelspiel.

Nevertheless, the whole infirmary rooted for Gypsy, and even Ash, the lad with the penetrating wound to his leg, raised his fever-thinned voice from where he lay, too weak to get up, "Pin his tail, Gypsy!" "Show him how we do it!" the others chimed in. The Easterner was popular, despite his constant showing off and slightly superior attitude toward the Galicians, to whom he referred, always in the plural, as "Galich-men." ("You Galich-men, you ain't seen a tarred wolf yet, ye follow?") How, exactly, one came to sight a tarred wolf was never clear—for all they knew, this mysterious creature was not unlike the tar-bristled Gypsy himself; his buffoonery always seemed to come from the outside, in third person, whom he alternatively ridiculed and reassured, and the Galich-men took no offense. Gypsy did not hide the fact that he once fought for the Soviet army; he even revealed to Adrian something he'd never heard before—that before sending soldiers into combat, Bolshevik commissars swore to them, "on behalf of the Party and the people," that the kolkhozes would be abolished after the war. Adrian had to laugh at this—how stupid could Stalin really be?

"Easy to say now," Gypsy replied, with new and unexpected vile in his voice that made the room go so quiet you could hear shadows gather in the corners. "What else would I've fought for on the motherfucker's side? For what they did in '33?"

The boys tsked and shushed him, but without conviction, as if instead of shaming Gypsy for his cursing they felt shamed themselves: "Hey, bite it, a lady's listening!" Rachel, who was warming something up on her burner with her back to them, did not betray with a single motion whether she'd been listening, but in that instant Adrian became aware, suddenly and intensely, of how differently they all behaved, all the time—not because they were not well, but because of her. Because she was there.

It only made it worse that he'd never been one of those who took every chance to revile "the skirted army," averring that the "wenches" belonged at home and not in the insurgency, but, at the same time, he had to admit feeling, on multiple occasions, that he would rather manage without female assistance, although sometimes it was simply out of the question. Among the bleakest episodes of Adrian's resistance career was his parting with Nusya, his courier of many years: her puffy red face, her mouth that kept slipping into an ominous twist followed, again and again, by bursts of uncontainable sobbing, and the things she said to him then, as he listened mutely and didn't know how to respond. He was, of course, aware of the possibility that Nusya liked him—but, come on, girls always liked him, all of them, as far back as the Gymnasium he had to put up with all their talk of how much he looked like Clark Gable, and it drove him to distraction because the boys at the Assembly paid him back with pure, unadulterated spite that made it that much harder to win their respect, and later to best them, demanding that he take, teeth clenched, the most outlandish dares and emerge the winner, every time. Nusya's coy, kittenish mannerisms were, in his mind, a direct consequence of her conservative Polish upbringing ("Femininity above all!"), in addition to her having been born an incurable flirt, so it was only after that last, heart-rending scene that haunted him for long afterward that he wondered whether a woman was ever capable of sacrificing herself for an idea—for the pure, selbstaendige idea, an idea that's its own justification—or only one that was embodied in a person she loved, a husband, a father, a son, alive or dead? Even Geltsia—although Geltsia was something completely separate and very different—rushed back home from Switzerland in '41 exactly like her old man, Dovgan Senior, did in 1918 when he left his family in Vienna, and all but walked the last leg to Lviv from Krakow, arriving to catch the last, withering street fights—those for the Central Post Office. Then he spent a year torturing himself for being late—you'd think the only reason we couldn't hold on to Lviv back then was not for the massive Polish reinforcements but for Dr. Dovgan's absence at the front lines, never mind he'd been excused from the Austrian draft for being flatfooted. Twenty-three years later Geltsia also missed the best part—the June 30 Sovereignty Proclamation—but came just in time to see everything else, everything that followed and does not seem to end. In a way, she tied the score for her old man. She's always adored her father.

Women. And yet Adrian had to admit that every one he'd ever worked with remained tough and loyal to the end. Women took risks less willingly than men—that much was true, but they didn't go looking for trouble out of pure bravado; instinctively, he'd always trusted women more than men, as though their dedication to the cause drew extra strength from their devotion to the men they loved and took pride in, the twin bonds mightier than steel. He still disapproved when resistance couples got engaged or married—but only because he believed now wasn't the right time—though no one could deny that the ones who did marry fought twice as hard, as if their wives supplied them with extra energy. Like batteries.

Rachel here—did she have a husband or a fiancé? Why didn't she legalize in the first place, as almost all Insurgent Army Jews did when the war ended and we went underground? Although, that first wave rode the trains to Siberia—that's a Bolshevik thank-you right there, for helping them fight the Germans—the later ones were more cautious, obtaining false papers that could get them over to Poland and from there to Palestine. Adrian heard about only one Jewish doctor, Moses, who refused to leave and perished not too long ago somewhere around Lviv in a raid—blew himself up with a hand grenade when he was surrounded.

Adrian watched Rachel's unreadable back and felt an enormous, monstrous pity fill him—the sort one feels for an orphaned, abandoned child. He never felt this way about the Ukrainian girls in resistance; it stood to reason that they should fight along with the men for the common sacred cause, but why should this Jewish girl suffer? "Come with us, Galya, with the Kozak army, we shall treat you finer than your own mommy," went the song they used to sing at student parties; and Yuzya, the linguist, once told them, swearing on his own mother's grave no less, that the original version had Haya, not Galya—Haya, the young tavern-keeper—and it was only much later that the oral tradition reworked the unusual name into a native one that sounded similar. "By her braids to a pine tree they tied the young Haya ..."—lied to her, lured her, took her with them, and then tied her hair to a pine tree in the woods and set the tree on fire. And she screamed and no one heard her. Like that Ukrainian teacher whom the Soviet partisans tied by each leg to a bent-over birch and then let the trees go—they did say one of them could not take her screaming up there and shot her, half-torn, in the head. "Who comes riding through the woods he will hear my crying ..."—what a horrific song: trees screech, unbending, and you scream, and I can do nothing to help you, girl, only make sure you always have a grenade and teach you to pull the pin out with your teeth when they twist your arms behind your back, before they think to jerk your head up. "Hey, Haya, Haya, green woods left you crying ..."—it even sounds vile, this Haya, Haya ... like gasping for air, not singing ... or are my lungs wheezing? Galya is better.

Adrian didn't notice as he fell asleep, finally. He dreamt of Roman. The guide was the same as before, in his homespun duds and with the MP on his shoulder. Adrian followed him through the woods again, stepping into his tracks just as before, only the forest was somehow stranger, newly washed by the rain and threaded with sunlight, much like the green woods in the song; Roman seemed to be saying something as he walked, but Adrian could not make out any of it, no matter how hard he strained to listen. Then Roman stopped, and very clearly said, "Here's where I live." Adrian looked around him and saw a small, dark hovel, or rather a cabin, empty but for the icons on the wall and a large table in the middle—Roman appeared on the other side of the table, where Adrian couldn't reach him.

"And where is your family?" Adrian asked, thinking that the cabin would surely be too small for anyone else.

"They'll come soon," Roman answered elusively, in his usual reserved way. "They'll all come soon," he said and added, "light me a candle." Adrian was puzzled: Why wouldn't Roman do it himself, if he's not a Jew and it's not the Shabbat? There was no candle on the table anyway.

He woke up from the dream with a vague sense of unfulfilled obligation, but also, for the first time, really rested, refreshed; this made him happy—it meant his body was coming back to him; the elemental, animal pleasure of this erased the inarticulate regret about Roman's request. It felt good; he was good at slipping the grip of the past.

The new sliver of strength would serve him well that day. It was the day Ash died.

For the first time, Adrian watched a man die not in combat, and it proved a lot more difficult. The plan had been to take Ash to the forest-warden's station to do surgery later in the day, cut the gangrened leg off, but he did not live that long.

When he woke up, he felt really well, unusually so, even sat up on his cot and smiled without a trace of delirium. Orko came and said encouraging things to him; Rachel busied herself preparing the tools for surgery. Back from his excursion outside, Adrian stopped next to her burner and stared with a convalescent's eager curiosity at the stubby, oblong metal box: the water in it wobbled a little and glowing sparks of tiny bubbles rose from the bottom, growing more numerous and dense until they sheathed a pair of mysterious-looking metal tongues, not unlike the ones that used to accompany asparagus at Dr. Dovgan's dinner table. Adrian was mesmerized by the interaction of water and metal: he had seen water boil around bullets and shrapnel when they fell, hissing, into the river—but here was the opposite, water heating the cold metal, warming it gradually, peacefully, surreptitiously almost; there was a strange harmony in this, a musical sensibility that held him captive, unable to turn away. The picture would stay etched into his memory along with the melodic word he'd never heard before, *pyemia*. Pyemia, aka death, one of its many aliases. Death is a great conspirator; she changes her names and guises whenever she pleases. So much work to unmask her, find her—and so often too late.

"Girls will love you anyway," Orko said to Ash.

Something new hung in the heavy, stuffy air of the bunker; people lay, sat, and moved as though afraid to disturb this new invisible presence. Adrian asked for some water to drink and saw Rachel's drawn face up close: her lower lip pinned with her teeth, her Arabian-stallion nostrils tense, flared, the tiny smudges of freckles around her nose dark and sharp as never before. Someone knocked on the vent outside, three—one—three: the code. Yaroslav appeared with some ether he procured for the surgery, carried in a tightly lidded stoup he didn't open—the flame of the kerosene lamp could ignite the vapors, it was unsafe—but its availability made everyone, not just Orko and Rachel, feel relieved, breathe easier, as if the priest's offering appeased the invisible force that had nested among them, gnawing at the beams and the walls until they threatened to collapse, a massive, crowded grave. Rachel packed knapsacks, clattering instruments, running Orko through a checklist: "Did they boil the bedsheets at the station? Did the girls bring alcohol from the village? Please pass me that large clamp." Can they go already? thought Adrian, irritably. Let them take it all out of here, and the poor sap with it. Lord, please help, please let everything go well.

But it didn't. While they were packing, Ash turned for the worse, and then worse yet. He degenerated faster and faster, like he was falling off a cliff. And then the agony began.

"Mommy," Ash mumbled blissfully as convulsions shook his body and rattled his teeth. "Go, the bells are ringing … my horse, Bloom …"

"He is not in pain," Orko said quietly to comfort everyone, himself included. "He feels good: the intoxication, the poison in the blood is making him euphoric like strong drink."

Adrian covered his head with his blanket and sweated there, in the dark; the stench grew intolerable and he was afraid he'd have to throw up, and then afraid of coughing. Yaroslav asked a question in a low voice, someone answered, "Ash." The priest didn't know the men in the bunker by their aliases, but for Ash it didn't matter any longer.

"Give me your hand, your hand, Marichka … the music's so fine!"

"My son, you must make your peace with the Lord."

The altered, deep sound of the priest's voice, at once kind and resolute, made Adrian startle and recall, no, regain—because he never forgot it but simply put the feeling away, saved it so that he could retrieve it later and enjoy it fully when he was alone—the sensation of floating, weightless and powerless like a newborn, in an ocean of soft, ambient light—*Forgive me my sins, Father.* It was Yaroslav who took his confession when he was on the brink of death, when they didn't know if his heart could take him through the pain; it was Yaroslav who gave him absolution, and he felt happy, as happy as only one having passed through a great passion that clears the soul can be, like a surgeon's scalpel, of the gangrene of sin, so that one may know God is here, he has not abandoned you … *thank you, Lord, for your mercy has no bounds,* the dark cassock at the foot of the bed, the swinging light of the lamp that was now turned on to Ash—Yaroslav was administering last rites, not waiting for the boy to regain consciousness. Adrian squeezed his eyes shut and began to pray along with everyone else.

And still the end wouldn't come.

Ash now talked to his commanders, reporting some ambush, a "herd" or a "hollow," asked to be forgiven and thanked them for coming to his wedding, being his guests—his speech stuttered like a faulty telegraph, words came in mismatched chunks, but it was still clear: Ash was saying goodbye. His body could no longer hold its contents. If not for the smell, Adrian may have been able to stay there with him instead of standing up and risking his neck by climbing above ground in the middle of the day (although he couldn't tell what time it was—they may have been watching Ash die for hours, days already), but the old Beast, the alter ego he was loath to give up despite the overdue need for a new alias, as secrecy demanded, raised his head and listened warily: outside, everything was clear, the air moved gently, the trees shuffled their fragrant leaves, and a brook rolled on somewhere close with the noise like wind in the treetops. A doe stepped gingerly to the water on her tiny hooves and froze, listening, not far from the lid over the back exit where they'd meant to take the patient, to carry him downstream to the station; she must have sensed the two-legged animal underground; but they were alone, the two of them, and could hear nothing else, no magpies or blue jays, who are always first to signal the presence of strangers, not a mouse disturbed, only the tinkling of cowbells far in the distance—the sweetest music of a clear forest. During raids, the Soviets didn't allow people to take cattle to graze in the woods, so that no one could send word to the rebels. All clear, just a few meters away was life—and here was death, and its colossal mass squeezed him out of the lair, up, up, like a cork. He found an excuse, too: someone had to take out the latrine bucket—high time really, it was overflowing, foul; others had been taking turns to do it, and now he was strong enough to pitch in. Gypsy readily volunteered to help; Gypsy was quiet today—silently got up, silently climbed the ladder (dragging his leg), silently pushed the lid open. A muted heave, like a sigh—*pfff*—and the cork popped out.

Later he couldn't tell how long he sat there, deaf and blind in the green-and-gold carousel, the piercing intensity of colors and smells of life. His head spun; his arms, when he leaned against the ground, trembled. He could barely help Gypsy with anything, leaving him to bury the waste more or less by himself. It smelled of near rain; the yellow genista flowers glowed bright as stars, and a smooth black caterpillar crawled across one yellow petal. Adrian lay on his back to catch his breath and saw the sky: big fluffy clouds, like clumps of down, sped across it. In his temples—the same persistent beat: *no*—like a mad radioman—*no, no, no*. No. A death like that—*no, please, God, no.*

He begged the Lord for a single thing in this hour of weakness; he pled for a single mercy—a death in combat. Under fire, under bullets. *Do not fear the fire that is sent to test you.* If only it were fire alone! The beautiful, noble, honest fire—he trusted it, he'd been in it, fire from machine guns, and artillery, and tanks; he'd learned to kill with a single shot, and that was war he could understand. It was war he knew how to win—and, in his way, loved; the "old warfare" as the Insurgent Army's veterans called it, nostalgically. Now the Soviets brought a different kind of "warfare." More and more often, death at their hands meant typhoid in well water, paralyzing poison in a bottle, gas creeping through the vent into an underground shelter. Before taking your life, this death robbed you of your will and your body, turned you into a sack of pus. Adrian Ortynsky did not fear torture: he knew he could last through it without breaking because, ultimately, it always ended in unconsciousness (or death, he used to add, but after he learned of his strong heart, he became less optimistic). But, Lord knows, this slow, horrific, humiliating extinction—he didn't want it. Did not want. *Weak I am, Lord, take this cup away from me!*

Gypsy sat nearby and smoked. Then he buried the stub and thoroughly covered the spot with moss. Suddenly, he spoke: "My father, he used to do woodwork. Made crosses."

Adrian didn't say anything.

"All his life he'd made crosses and they shoveled him in without one. Threw him into one big dump, and that's that ..."

"The Soviets?" Adrian asked, noticing just then that Gypsy spoke without his usual "ye follow." "Or the Germans?"

Gypsy spat a fleck of tobacco that got caught in his beard.

"Ours. During the hunger. The drag went around the village, picking up corpses. Mother was still breathing, but the driver said, 'She's got a day, no more; I ain't making another trip tomorrow.' So they shoveled her in, too."

They were silent again. Adrian wondered what a drag was. The strange word blocked his mind and didn't let the rest through. But what about Gypsy himself? How did he survive?

"I was gone by then," Gypsy went on, in response to the unspoken question, as often happens between people who share the same bunker. "Grandfather, may he rest in peace, took me to the station when they drove the kolkhoz horses there, to the syndicate, for soap.... Stuffed me into the train car when no one was looking, so I rode all the way to Kharkiv with those horses. They couldn't stand on their own anymore, so they tied them together, front to back ... drove them to the station like that, tied up."

Suddenly, Adrian saw it with absolute certainty—as in dreams or when a difficult problem suddenly resolves itself. "Gypsy—that was a horse, wasn't it? Your horse?" and instantly thought he shouldn't have asked.

The gunman's eye turned at him, glistened strangely. A towering, black-bearded man—like a picture of a highwayman in a children's book. Half-giant, half-bear. Adrian looked back at Gypsy and heard a rhythmic thumping in his ears—his own heart, or the wheels of the train: with a famished, half-dead boy in the car full of starved horses, skins, ribs, ribs and bones. The horses rode to their death. And the boy rode to survival.

"They lifted them up in the kolkhoz stable," Gypsy said slowly; it looked like he was grinning with his very white teeth. "Ran the girth under the belly, like so, and ran it through a block, then pulled to lift them.... And ours, while they still took them out to the field, every night turned to our yard. He'd stand there by the fence and look in. He knew he couldn't come in. A smart horse, he was. I took him my bread, and Mother cried … he recognized me on the train." Gypsy spat off another nonexistent tobacco crumb and bared his teeth. "Gypsy recognized me, ye follow?"

A gnat buzzed thin and high in the air between them.

"He, while he still knew himself, said he had a girl somewhere," Gypsy said abruptly, and without any connection to the previous topic. It sounded like a question, a feeling out. "Marichka she's called."

"'Round here, they've got two Marichkas in every yard," Adrian grumbled, sharper than he'd meant it. Gypsy, however, nodded with almost visible satisfaction, as though it was exactly what he'd wanted to hear. As if it provided further proof for some personal theory of his: for example, that everything in the world is vanity of vanities and chasing after the wind. He must make a heck of a soldier, Adrian thought. A good—a tough—one. The angry ones—those usually burn out fast. But this guy—he's already burned into slag; he'll last forever.

They were quiet for a bit longer. The wordless understanding they'd found for a moment hung between them, then passed, and both felt it go. Gypsy stood up first. "Should we go, or what?"

When they came back, Ash was gone. He left behind his dead body, which needed to be taken out and buried.

That day Adrian really came to appreciate Yaroslav. Without him they would've turned into a pack of snarling dogs—everyone's nerves had been worn to shreds, or, as Gypsy put it, gone to hell in a handcart. The priest served the parastás and stayed with them for the wake. Outside, a generous, thick rain fell watering Ash's fresh grave—it seemed nature itself burst with tears, mourning the boy who couldn't be mourned by a bride or his family; the drip-drop of water into tins under the vents coalesced in Adrian's mind into the same, repeated bit of doleful song: "Neither Father'll cry for me, nor my dear mother, re-la-re-mi-faa-mi," and the next line clawed its way in, "only will cry after me three fair lasses...." Of all things, he could do without wondering who would mourn *him* if he died—he knew, however, that others were thinking about it, too, could feel the morbid, unwanted ideas about the inevitable end to their struggle take shape in their minds; these always came when one of them perished—you bury a bit of yourself—but he didn't know how to change it.

He filled a barrel with rainwater simply to be doing something; Rachel boiled new potatoes, skin on, and Orko, in violation of the ban, mixed a sniff of his alcohol with water—to be drunk in the memory of the departed. Yaroslav told them the news: in such-and-such village they arrested a truck full of people who refused to join the kolkhoz, but our boys freed them in a fight around R., and there were wounded; in the other one, the turncoats wanted to ambush Woodsman, spent three days waiting for him in the village head's house, got pissed as farts, shot holes in the ceiling, and Woodsman never came. Yaroslav purposely conveyed the sim-plest, most common news that everyone was curious to hear; Ash, too, would have been, had he been alive; and somehow Yaroslav made it feel as though the dead man had not left them at all, quite the opposite—could now, having been freed from the burden of his suffering body, join them at leisure and hear something he was curious to know. And Yaroslav kept talking to oblige him. In the same level, soft-as-silk voice, Yaroslav addressed the soul of the departed, inviting it to share their meal one last time; they prayed like respectful children at a village home where the old-est son had gone out into the world and learned something that they, the younger ones, were not yet to know—passed his leaving exams or joined the army.

The candle burned evenly in the corner; spoons clacked, noses ran—from the drink and the rich potato steam savored by Ash's soul, side by side with the living, and a heavy, complacent warmth filled their bodies; without anyone really noticing, Yaroslav tamed Ash's death, made it into something domestic, common and obvious, and the funereal weight disappeared all by itself.

They were a family again, all together and Ash with them. Adrian watched Yaroslav with an adoration he no longer felt the need to conceal; the priest's large forehead, as though made of two separate hemispheres and appearing even bigger because of the bald spots, glistened with tiny drops of sweat, which he wiped, again and again, with a handkerchief he kept unfolded on his knee in place of a napkin. When the moment seemed right, the conversation having found, like a river on a flood plain, new, discrete paths, Adrian acted on what must've been a purely military urge to report observations of anything uncommon to one's superior (regardless of any rank Father Chaplain may, in fact, have held, his seniority was at the moment beyond doubt, silently and unanimously acknowledged) and told him his dream from the night before—about Roman in the tight hovel, his "Here's where I live," and his strange request to light a candle for him. Yaroslav knew Roman; it appeared the man hadn't been seen or heard from since the skirmish in which Adrian was wounded.

"It means," Yaroslav said, "that you were the last to see him alive."

Adrian realized the priest was right—and it was like a hidden light went on in his mind: he realized he had known it all along—Roman died because he shielded Adrian with his body. In the dream, he had no proper home because the boys didn't have a chance to build him one, didn't bury him properly, in a coffin—the NKVD must've taken the body. What was it he said in the dream? "They'll all come soon."

"I will perform a service for the rest of his soul," Yaroslav went on in his quiet and impassive voice, not a trace of steel—and yet it felt like he was building a fortress wall. "His soul is now passing through the twenty ordeals on the way to its judgment, so it's no wonder it asked you for help. Thank you for telling me. May God bless you."

Adrian stared at the flame of the candle, unblinking. His mind, overwhelmed, sputtered random, individual visions of the day: Rachel's ashen face with the lip bitten down, the water beginning to boil in the metal instrument case.... Yaroslav possessed it—this willful softness of water that swallows steel and tempers it into surgical purity.

"In the name of the Father, the Son, and the Holy Spirit, amen."

His father—that's who the priest reminded him of. His father, from whom he'd had no messages since '44—since the day after the Soviets' second coming, when he and his mother were taken on to the deportation echelon. *Amen, I say to you, there is no one who has given up house or brothers or sisters or mother or father or children or lands for my sake who will not receive a hundred times more....* Hundred-fold indeed—for he had yet to happen upon a home where they weren't received as kin, and of brothers and sisters he gained thousands all over Ukraine, and who of them would not shield a brother with his own body? What a great smile Roman had—like a slow, hesitant glow thawed his face. Adrian turned his face away, into the shadows, and quickly drained the remaining alcohol from his cup: let everyone think that his eyes watered because of the drink to which he was unaccustomed.

"Father, pray for my parents, Mykhailo and Gortenzia."

Hearing that Adrian's father was a parish priest, Yaroslav glowed like a child, even his wrinkles smoothed out. With great conviction, he told Adrian that his father was chosen for a rare and great gift of God's love: to provide spiritual consolation during the time of enormous trial—on the echelon, in prison, in deportation—only true shepherds merit such destiny; many are called, but few, as always, are chosen. Something personal lurked behind his words, his own long-borne plight. Adrian wondered for a few moments if he should also ask for a service to the health of Gela, but did not dare, could not let the very name of her leave his lips, as if he feared that once added—like a line to an endless list, to the myriad unknown Marias, Vasyls, Yurkos, and Stefans—it would lose not only its sovereignty but also its invincibility, fall subject to the laws of common mortality.

Yaroslav left first, walked out into the rain without the cloak the doctor had offered him saying, "You need it more than I do," because he had yet to stop at the warden station to tell them the sad news that there would be no surgery, and only then, after Yaroslav had left them, did Orko explain, over the minute squares of paper into which he and Rachel began sorting the powders that the priest had brought, "You know, our Father here asked to be sent with an echelon ... twice. They didn't let him."

"Who?" asked Adrian, confused.

The doctor shrugged his shoulders. "The church authorities, the ones higher up ... the bishop did not allow him, or someone like that—I don't understand their hierarchy very well. First time in '39, after the first Bolsheviks, when His Excellency Metropolitan Sheptytsky himself pled to take up the suffering, thinking he might save us all if he lay down his life, but the Pope wouldn't permit it. That did make an impression on our Father here, as you can imagine: if Sheptytsky himself is not let away, what's a mere parish priest to say? And the second time, as I heard it, he asked of one ... a stigmatic here, right before the Germans retreated. This stigmatic, when he fell into ecstasy, he would go into a trance and speak in other people's voices, so people visited him to ask about their families, if they hadn't heard anything for a long time, and other things, too ... even from the Central Command, they said. Back then I was still studying, looked at such things very skeptically, thought I knew everything—I was young, what can I say. Later I saw things—things no hypnosis-neurosis could ever explain: Why does a man, with gaseous gangrene who absolutely should die, before morning, not die? A doctor, you see, is just a tool ... an instrument in God's hand. Only the instrument's gotta be sharp too—sharp and straight!" He lifted his head at last and smiled ruefully like the skull on a bottle of belladonna, instantly looking as tired as he really was—not with a day's hard work but with old, chronic exhaustion that can't be slept off in a single night. Ash's death struck him as irrefutable proof of his own inaptitude, and Adrian had no idea what to say to him—this was an uncharted realm in which the ignorant were better to keep silent.

"They brought him too late, Orko, that's all," Rachel said. "Had it been even a day earlier …"

"We dallied plenty," Orko said, sharply, turning to Adrian again as if he was the ultimate appellate authority now. "And what can I do, when we don't even have a way to run a blood analysis? I don't even know when the pyemia began! We do everything by feel, groping in the dark; you should see our girls soaking wounds with whey to get the swelling down so that we can actually see what's going on in there! And I haven't had one man die on me yet!" he shot angrily before falling silent, shamed.

He shouldn't be, Adrian thought—this wasn't bragging—and was about to say so, but froze: Rachel, having moved between them, stood quietly stroking Orko's hair—like a master calming a skittish horse, whoa, sweets, shhh—"sha" as Rachel said it. Orko let his eyes close and sat absorbing her touch. Are they … could they be together, somehow? Adrian wondered, feeling an unwelcome stab of something like jealousy on the top of his stomach. But why not, really, it would be quite natural; only how had he not seen it before? He looked around furtively—loath to be the lone witness to their unexpected intimacy, but the boys had all fallen asleep already, or were too exhausted to take part in the officers' talk. Utterly at a loss for what to do, he blurted, finally and awkwardly ("like a fart into the campfire" Gypsy would say), "So what happened with that stigmatic?"

One could think this was his way of calling the doctor to order, and yet Rachel did not move away—she held her place next to Orko, her hand on the back of his head. What if it's just a kind of therapy they have, to keep each other calm? At once, Adrian felt an urgent need to feel her hand on his own head; he could sense her touch on his crown so intensely that his skin crawled, a new current running through it.

"Tough news," said Orko, forcing his sticky, reddened eyelids open again, and sobbed, once, like a miniature seizure. "The Holy Father said he didn't even need to ask his question: the stigmatic knew what he was thinking as soon as he stepped into the room—that he meant to volunteer for a prison echelon when the Bolsheviks came again. So he said to him, 'No, don't even think about it. You must stay.' After that, our Father finally found it in himself to obey, and joined the UIA, as a chaplain. Our gain, I say, no?" He tried again to arrange his cracked lips into a smile. "I figure it's better to have Father here and not somewhere in Siberia.... I am sorry; I shouldn't have said this to you."

"It is good when there is a priest on an echelon," Rachel said, as if chiding him mildly for something they both knew.

Orko faltered, and then busied his hands on top of the table, carefully folding an already folded piece of paper. Adrian looked at the woman as though seeing her for the first time. She stood there, her arms hanging limp at her sides, all of her somehow exposed, proffered, while the words she'd spoken hung in the air like a hand that'd been extended and ignored. What exactly did she mean by that? And to whom?

He felt hot, heard the hum of his own blood in his ears. She stood before him and shone her black cabochon eyes at him, and he caught her smell in his hungry nostrils—raw, milky-fleshy, cheese-and-sour, fermenting, incredible ... the smell of a woman with smooth skin and hot, creased body, rich in fragrant nooks and crannies. Lord.

"Boys fought Rachel off a German echelon, back in the day," Orko's slightly alarmed voice reached him slowly, from a great distance: the voice tried to wedge itself between them, to shush, to gag them with its unnecessary explaining, to turn them back, but it was too late—the woman's eyes revealed that. Her stilled, wide-open look, like a gate flung open—Adrian had forgotten a woman could look like that. Fort comme la mort. To hell with it. To hell with death, with its grinning rotting maw—he was alive; he had forgotten anyone could be as alive as this. Life filled him, swelled in him in one fast, incessant ascent; it pulsed in his groin and in the tips of his fingers that screamed for a feel of that smooth, so-near skin. To hell—he won't die. Not ever. Not now.

Something in him shifted, a lock turned. Something that a moment earlier would have seemed outrageous, unthinkable, nigh blasphemous, now appeared as the only possible event in the series that had aspired, from the very beginning, to gain this singular point: Roman's death, Ash's death, the bunkers, and the raids, and the endless echelons peopled with sorrow and tears—Westbound yesterday, Eastbound today—and the fiery pine, tall as the sky, and the crackle of a woman's hair as it curls on her temples and burns, and the struggle, to the end, no matter what lies in wait for us up ahead; everything suddenly melded together with violent, intolerable intensity like the bright daylight that blinds after the bunker gloom and scorched him, in the hollow of his aching chest, with the terrible and indomitable force of raw life, hot as a naked wire, like a woman's body under a woolen skirt and a Soviet gimnastiorka. He could see the tiny stiff curls at her ears, could see, through the toad-colored blouse, her shoulders and her breasts, and remembered them, somehow, tightly wrapped by a white red-dappled sheet. (Was that during his surgery? But he thought he was unconscious ...) Her body smelled precisely like the body of a woman who is meant for you and you alone. Everything was as it had to be because it could not be otherwise.

He rose to his feet—her gaze his lifeline. "Could I offer you my assistance?"

"We're about finished already," answered Orko, who was not addressed by the question; his voice rang with offense, but it no longer mattered. Nothing mattered. Without looking away, she slowly raised her renascent arms and smoothed her skirt over her thighs: a single motion to bestow herself upon him.

Sleep, sleep—he remembered her voice in the night.

And it didn't matter that the rain had stopped and that Orko stayed at the bunker having no way to go back to the village alone on a moonlit night, and whether Orko did fall asleep, whether anyone was really asleep when the two noiseless shadows, one after another, slipped into the corridor. In the dark, the heat she radiated seemed visible, and her thighs above the rubber-banded stockings were smooth like freshly scrubbed fishes, only hot; the hatch, lifted, let in a flood of moisture-laden, swooning air, and the merciless moonlight poured over the ladder above—only then did she turn to face him and he pressed her, hastily, even brutally, into the rough log wall, not even giving himself a chance to rejoice at how readily she received him, eager, as though she'd been waiting for him a long time, all her life, and had developed the best, most befitting shapes for him so that she could envelop him instantly, like a glove, to enfold him without a trace, with all her pores and orifices at once, into the pulsing fiery gorge that opened before he realized he was inside it and could only growl to suppress his moan—and then it was over. In the moonlight he could see her face, her eyes squeezed shut and her lower lip bitten, and no longer felt anything except the annoying wetness and the urge to wipe himself clean. And shame, too, the same shame as when he went with other Gymnasium boys to a bordello and also spilled right away, after a few awkward, all-but-painful spasms, and the whore turned her head and leered at him over her shoulder, with one eye, like a hen, peering from behind thin streaks of her hennaed hair that hung over her cheeks. *What, kiddo, done already?* He had the same empty feeling then—and this is it. The familiar pain stirred in his chest, making him anxious, and he let go of her legs. Dog your mother, you're no lover-hero—you're a cripple. Another moment—and she would have appalled him, like that redheaded slut. *I loved one girl, then another, and a dozen after—four fair maidens, five Jewesses, and the rest with husbands....* That's it, lady. Back off.

But this wasn't all, and he knew it as soon as she lifted her heavy, puffy eyelids—slowly, as though returning from a great journey—and fixed him in her unmoving black gaze, the gaze of a snake, flashed through his mind. The Snake Queen who lives underground and guards treasures untold.

Two narrow, cool little hands squeezed his face, "How ładny you are…," and she corrected her Polish word, as if through sleep. "Handsome."

The Polish startled him—much more than if she'd spoken to him in Yiddish.

"Are you one of those … assimilated?"

Instead of answering, she buried her face in his chest—he felt she wanted to devour his smell just as she had swallowed his body a moment earlier—and muttered, words he could, incredibly, hear inside him, resonating off his bones, between his ribs, tickling the spot where she had extracted the bullet—"So the Lord God took out one of his ribs and closed up its place with flesh. And the two of them shall become one body." The fast, chanted Jewish intonation vibrated inside him, rocked him like a bridge; this wasn't the intonation of the marketplace as it had always seemed to him—not of trading, but of crying, wailing—how had he not seen that before? This was a dirge, a lament of garments rent and hair pulled out in tufts to fly on the desert wind: Shema, Yisrael, hear my cry! But there wasn't anyone left to hear her, she had no one to cry to. He stroked her hair. Przemysl, she was from Przemysl, where, in the ghetto, her entire family perished—burned in fire, in '42. That was before Germans started shipping the Jews out, before the death camps were built—so they simply set the ghetto on fire, and for a month afterward the whole city and the suburbs smelled of charred meat. And burnt hair. He shuddered—the blazing pine tree stood before his eyes again, the giant torch belching sparks into the black sky—he touched the tiny curls on her temples and found them much softer than they looked, and smelling, as unwashed hair should, of gristle and spice, a feral, raw-life smell. With her braids to a pine tree. Mom, Dad, Grandpa, Grandma, Uncle Borukh, Sister Ida with her husband, little Yuzek-Iosele— all burned alive, no one escaped. And she left her own people: a Gymnasium friend's family, Ukrainians, hid her. And then—then she was caught in a raid, the god of Israel wanted to return her to the dead, but in the train car she prayed to the Crucified like that Ukrainian family taught her to do, and a miracle came: UIA attacked the echelon.

Finally, he grasped it: it was not herself she told him about but her god who had abandoned her. The hard and cruel Jewish god who knows neither mercy nor forgiveness and takes his revenge for disobedience on women and children—it was the place of this god, now vacant, that she offered him, the man she herself brought back to life. Her body yearned for him, begged to receive him—he was her absolution of the sin of godlessness, of the terror of empty death. He felt faint again: no woman had ever granted him such absolute power over her, there was something forbidden in it, almost terrible and therefore magnetic.... As if to confirm his insight, she kneeled in front of him, and he trembled—he gathered his essence into her soft, lamb-lipped mouth, ecstatic in her near-piety, as if performing a mystical rite of worshipping the power she herself was summoning forth from his loins, and the power came, stronger, more lasting than he could ever imagine, greater than himself.

For a while he ceased to exist—brushing off the feeble whisper of her warnings, he passed into dark un-memory, guided by the singular, indomitable urge to move forward, deeper into the supple smelt of burning lava that lapped at the red-hot dome of his skull; and this was impossible, incredible, intolerable, an ungodly sweet dying in arrested time, where there was no light, only the fiery darkness, at which he cleaved and pounded, a subterranean smith, until suddenly the darkness squeezed itself around him into a blissful quintessence of gratitude, a tender ring, like a soul-rending kiss, squeezed—and relaxed, and again, and again, until he could not take it any longer, and at the very instant he fired his handgun with a single triumphant cry and the shot-through body collapsed onto the ground, the darkness shuddered and gathered around the two of them into a dazzling fiery contour—a ring of electricity made manifest—and he fell supine onto the bare dirt floor breathing hard, face in the moonlight, and marveled, now completely conscious, that nothing hurt. Nothing, really, she worried for nothing—a happy, acute calm made his body ring like a well-tempered bell. Gently—amazed slightly at the heretofore hidden, untapped reserves of affection inside him—he ran his fingers over her shoulders; now her presence next to him was pleasant, it made him want to talk to her, stroke her, to keep what they'd experienced with them.

"You are a sister of mercy indeed—time to request you be recognized by a Headquarters' decree: For selfless work at healing the wounded!"

After a pause, she answered, but not with a joke; her voice called back altered, somnambulic (a sound that filled him anew with the happy knowledge of his might), "I would like to die now … for you."

"Fie on you, bite your tongue—don't say that!"

But still he felt flattered.

"No, love, it's true … that would be best. Because it's never like this."

He was still reveling in his new condition. "You know, I don't feel tired at all," he said, and then suddenly realized what she'd just said: not only he, but she too had experienced it for the first time—the fiery contour of electrical current stood before his eyes. "So you saw it, too?" He felt her nod silently more than he could see it, and instantly fretted, as men are wont to, over his newly gained property: "How do you know about this? Who taught you?"

She understood his anxiety and whispered straight into his ear, before licking off a drop of his sweat, like a cat, which sent another luxurious tremble down his spine.

"I haven't known anyone for two years."

This made him happy—it meant Orko wasn't a contender—but it still wasn't enough.

"And before?"

"Let's not talk about that," she asked of him, somber like a well-mannered child. "Listen." She sat up with a heavy sigh, smoothing her skirt over her thighs again in the dark. "I know we will all die …"

"Everyone dies. Haven't you heard?"

"That's not what I mean. The war is over. You can't seriously believe that the Alliance will want to fight Moscow? No one can take any more war."

"We can," he said. His own words resonated, made him shiver, listening, like an echo of a distant march. In different circumstances, this talk would've raised his suspicion, made him wonder if it weren't a MGB provocation, but at that moment he truly loved her—for helping him articulate the simple truth, the mere knowing of which filled him with intoxicating pride, like in that Ólzhych poem he'd loved since his Youth Assembly days: "It fills you to the brim, this breathtaking thrill / Commanding your body and spirit / That death enters humbly and bows at your door, a handmaiden, baffled and timid."

It's true what you say, girl, everyone's been broken, all the powerful, armed-to-the-teeth states wet their pants halfway through, let a half-victory be their cowardly prize, the victory over Hitler, the weaker and stupider of the two, for they have no guts to finish the job—only we do, a stateless band without international support or even Red Cross assistance; we alone did not call the tyrant a victor, and that's our truth, and that's what we'll die for. Sometime, in the future, the generations that will come after us will understand this. That "Westerner," a Frenchman or a Belgian, who manned the radio transmitter up in the Carpathians, the one whose voice on the shortwave broadcast every night—"Attention! Attention! Ici radio diffusser Ukrainienne clandestine"—made us feel like the whole world followed our fates with bated breath, he said so, too: "You are the saviors of Europe's honor."

He stroked her hair, comforting her like a scared child; funny, anytime a woman starts on politics, it's like showing someone nearsighted the view from a mountain, and even in chess they don't see beyond two moves ahead. But what is this madness—he wanted her again, more hungrily than before.

"Come to me."

"Wait, love, my dear, my precious, my ... my, wait, let me say this, I beg you; this is important. I've never said this to anyone, ever. From the minute I saw you, I knew this ... I just didn't know it would be like this, that it could be like this. Listen. If I perish tomorrow, I'll have no regrets. Do you understand? I know now why I was spared."

"Sh-shhh. Don't talk like that ..."

"No, wait ... but if I shall stay alive ... don't be angry, please? I want you to leave me a son. So that you can stay inside me, and I could carry a part of you... in me."

He wasn't listening—what was she saying? Madness. In his mind—like a speeding train running off a bridge, a blazing-white scream *Geltsia!*—Geltsia was the one he wanted to hear say that, why this other woman instead, what had he done to be punished so?—but the train flew, unstoppable, to where the tracks had been blown up, and the engineer could only squeeze his eyes shut against the inevitable, imminent catastrophe.

"Wait, wait ... don't move, you just lie there; I'll sit, like this ... it'll be easier for you."

And it was, in fact, easier—not right away, though; at first it was hot, dark, and moist, as it should be in the underground realm ruled by the Snake Queen—she was magnificent inside, a tightly coiled, elastic snake, and then it felt good, very good, unspeakably good—maybe it really never was like that and he was still dreaming? He felt himself being carried across a storming sea. No sooner did he roll off one giant wave, blissful and drenched, than he was pulled up again, raised with the next surge, higher and higher, to the desperate, intolerable zenith; he wished only that this would never stop, because with each wave he felt stronger as the new feeling took root and grew in him, the feeling that a man can only glean with a woman, and nowhere else—the joyous wonder at his own might, at his untapped capaciousness. He saw the fiery contour of the electrical circuit again, and, adrift on a calm patch between dying ripples, thought through the hum of pleasure that resonated inside his entire body, *If I had been killed, I would never have known this.* This was clearly someone else's thought, spoken to him by something other than his voice, an imprint of her words, *I know now why I was spared,* fed him drop by drop like medicine, to be digested by his mind as slowly and gradually as his flesh soaked in her body's juices (and he'd thought they were the only thing exchanged when people made love!), and the warning signals flashed in his dimmed mind, hissing rockets above a dark battlefield: for the first time in all his years underground, Beast had truly allowed another person inside him.

And that put an end to it all—he returned to himself. Happiness drying him, quickly like a dog, a Beast. Sweat grew cold between his shoulder blades and the crack—the fissure just rammed in his personal wall, the lightly charted, merely suggested zone of openness to another person, a person in her own right, regardless of her service to the common cause—was filled with new, quick-setting cement. For Pete's sake, if he can be a stud like that, what the heck is he doing on his ass in the hospital? All fat and smooth like some Red captain shagging a resort nurse—while the boys are dying somewhere? You lazy bastard!

Before he could really feel them, he worked his limp fingers to button up his shirt. Whatever had passed between him and this woman clumped together with other events of the day and tumbled, gathering speed, into the open abyss of the past, cleaved off his existence in dense layers of wet clay—and the clay-caked pickax that the doctor and the priest had used earlier to dig a hole for Ash, stood leaned against the wall, between a barrel of kerosene and a sack of grain, smelling of a fresh grave.

Rachel kept silent, smart girl; he did like her, but if she'd let something slip right then he was liable to cut her off, say something sharp instead of keeping his peace, and would feel guilty afterward.... But she was a good woman, very good; must've been with the resistance for a long time—she didn't ask unnecessary questions. He, on the other hand, had a question for her, and then a few: First of all, why was she still illegal? Wouldn't it work better for her to get a regular job as a nurse at the district clinic, or in

Stanislav, or even in Lviv, since they needed people everywhere? No, she answered, mechanically as if being interrogated, that was not possible. She was legal already once, in '45, and then last year the MGB arrested her, they knew she'd been with UIA before, and they ordered her to kill Woodsman. She came back with the news to Woodsman himself, told him everything, and he left her underground. So that's how it was. He didn't ask her anything else, figuring he would have a chance to discuss it with Woodsman later, and only asked, for some reason, if they'd beaten her. No, they didn't, only the inspector cursed and screamed horribly, a Jew, too, which seemed bizarre to her—that it wasn't a German who promised to pack her off to the camps, but a Jew; he kept scream-ing at her, How could you, you're a Jew turned Bandera's cunt, what, they … are better than our guys? She faltered; he didn't say anything. It was unpleasant, as if that inspector had come between them and right away found the weak spot, and this moment of hesitation was to him the final proof that they both ought to erase their weakness as soon as possible, ought to forget that desperate explosion of nature that had thrown them into each other's arms, to edit it out from their memories, as the instructions put it: not to remember too much. At the very least, do as was done with the most important documents: put them into a bottle, seal the cork with wax, and bury it deep underground. Sometime later, perchance, he could dig it up and think about it again—not for a second did he believe he'd have that chance—but now he lived again in the fleeting moment alone. The trap of arrested time that caught him when he was wounded sprang open again. He was well.

Already falling asleep on his cot, in the tenuous borderland between dream and reality, delicate like the lamb-soft lips of a woman brimming with love, he startled as if shoved. He could feel the fluffy cloud of her touch enveloping his body on all sides, like cotton padding a precious Easter pysanka, only his hands were tied behind his back and an irresistible, gale force pulled him into the open doors of a black Opel Kadett, the same as the one in which they'd taken him to the Gestapo on Pelchýnska, and Rachel reached out her arms to him, helpless, and her face was white in the moonlight like a round of sheep cheese, and he shouted back to her, over and over, as he was dragged away, lifted off the ground, *I am Adrian Ortynsky!* This was what shook him awake, in terror, sent him scrambling, heart pounding, for a fingerhold in the real darkness of the bunker, where he remembered himself and breathed again: Thank God, it was only a dream—neither one of them ever did ask the other's real name, nor Rachel for his alias.

Completely calm now, he slept—the deep, untroubled sleep of a healthy man.

***

Finally, Stodólya came for him, with a guard and another lad, a local: they intended to move him somewhere to a more distant village, to convalesce on fresh milk in some good people's hayloft, but he refused, declaring he was fully fit for any work already. Orko confirmed that he was out of any immediate danger and only needed the dressing on his wound changed regularly. And as far as convalescence went, really, doctor, nothing makes a man stronger than honest toil, and few things weaken him faster than forced idleness; shouldn't medicine take this into account? They had to admit he had a point; he won. He always won.

Stodólya could tell him nothing new about Roman: no body had been brought to a village to be identified, and none had been put on display in the district town. Roman disappeared without a trace, dissolved into the green smells of a spring forest, became a dream.

Stodólya informed him that they were to spend the summer and fall together, as the Headquarters directed: due to significant losses this spring (he listed the names of fallen officers and the world went dark for a moment before Adrian's eyes), there had been a major regrouping, and both of them were being transferred to newly unmanned terrain. He identified their new regional commander by alias, and Adrian nodded—he knew the man back from the fall campaign of '45, when he led a hundred. "They'll have their hands full, and they'll have a secretary, Dzvinya, my fiancée," Stodólya added—very formally, as if to forestall any potential infringement, like, she's mine, alright?—at which Adrian nodded his congratulations, hiding a smile. Of all things he could imagine, Stodólya to be in love was by far the most outrageous. On the other hand, what did he know about the man? Well, he'd learn more, wouldn't he?

Stodólya, as if reading Adrian's mind, suddenly reached into the chest pocket of his jacket and unfolded a paper packet much worn along the creases to reveal a small photograph, which he offered to Adrian—for an instant, it seemed even his face, always cautiously drawn to a point, with that aiming crooked nose and the sharp eyes set close to each other like a wolf's, softened, warmed from inside, and almost smiled.

"This is she."

But Adrian never saw Stodólya's smile, although he was very curious to find out how an enamored Stodólya might smile. It is quite possible that Stodólya was, in fact, smiling as he held the photo in his hand, but if he was, Adrian did not see it.

The woman looking back at him from the picture was Geltsia.

Room 4. From the Cycle *Secrets: After the Blast*

Hi—hello, sweets. Here—give us a kiss. *M-mua.* Why are you all so, sort of ... discombobulated? You goof, of course everything's fine, better than ever. Yurko dropped me off right at the door, just like I said on the phone, and what did you have to dread? (Such a stupid way to use that word—he says dread whenever he means worry, and I can't seem to break him of this habit. Dread, by the way, is a transitive verb: One has to dread some*thing*, like war or famine, and if one is talking about some*one*, then one can worry, fret, brood, agonize, lose sleep, and dozens of other synonyms, but who speaks like that anymore?)

Here, hang up my coat, would you please? *M-m-m*—what *is* that smell? Hol-y mol-y, what is going on here?—is someone coming? Wow! Look at all this stuff; it's like a five-star restaurant in here, flowers and all.... You—you are really something.... Can I taste it? Straight from your big skovoroda here? Okay, your skillet, whatever, but I must point out that the name of Ukraine's greatest thinker was, in fact, Skovoroda, so it's a perfectly good word.... Alright, alright—quiet as a mouse, watch me, *z-zip*; I'm out of your way, going to wash my hands. Or should I go ahead and shower for such a romantic occasion? Dress for dinner? And perfume myself with something fabulously sexy? By the way, did you know that of all smells men find vanilla the most arousing—don't you think this smacks of some sort of infantile fixation on their mommies' cookies? No, really, I read it somewhere—not about fixation, about vanilla; I figured out the fixation part all by myself, with the help of my towering intellect, what else? O-oh ... Aidy! That's not where the intellect is ... not even a woman's, let go! Very well, good sir, if you find intellectual women so irresistible, I shall henceforth be known by my new pseudonym: Daryna Skillet. Pretty catchy, no?

I'll get myself a column in *Women's Life*. About the big stuff, and such. Only no one would ever know what a "skillet" is.... Aidy, you lummox, did you not get shampoo at the store again?

Chianti? I like *that*! I like it a lot. (Such a *guy* thing to put on this whole show, with wine and flowers, and then forget to get shampoo, which ran out two days ago!) Looks like a decent bottle too—2002—nicely done, Mr. Sommelier.... Oh, come on, the candles—that's too much, that's like something they'd tell you to do in *Women's Life*—have you been reading that crap with a flashlight under the covers? Sure, over in that drawer—there should be a new pack. Yep, that one. Are you supposed to eat this with a fork or a spoon? Aidy, will you get a move on—I'm starving! Oh, it's the candleholder you wanted to show me? Oops, I'm sorry, I got distracted by the candles—so, yeah, let me see ... cool.... What is it, copper? Bronze, huh. And how do you clean it? Or is supposed to be this ... pickled color? More like mold on a pickle, actually—that's exactly the color, isn't it? Super. I love it. Weighs a ton, too! Wow ... it's like in that Lesya Ukrainka story where the lady companion cracks the old baroness's skull with a candelabra just like this! The one in the story is bronze, too. If you take a good aim, and really swing it ... no kidding. A multifunctional piece. Alright, where are those candles? Let's have the picture complete. Hang on, let me turn off the lights ... uh-huh. Doesn't go with our kitchen at all, but in a large house somewhere in the suburbs, where you could put it on a marble mantle—sure, it'll look great. Or like, in a dining room, in the middle of an oak table the size of a tennis court....

Have a buyer yet? And how much do you charge for this beauty? Some more, please, I haven't eaten.... So is that what's paying for the banquet? *Mm-mm*, this is great! Say it again? Gnocchi? I get it—it's like galúshki, only Italian.... Thank you, that's good for now, or I'll get wasted on an empty stomach ... *mm-mm*. Potato dough? And then what—I've got spinach, cheese, garlic—and something else.... Whatever it is; it's fantastic. And you made it all yourself? With your crafty little hands. See, Aidy, it's like I said: you only get better with time.… Thank you! Who's the buyer—that big fat marmot of yours with piggy eyes? No, I actually like him—you can tell the dude's pretty sharp and not completely without taste. He sounds like he's really into antiques and that tells you something right there; he's not like all the other ones, the ones that buy music halls for their sluts … yep, and TV stations. You just had to rub that in, didn't you? Alright—*cin cin*! Nope, prosit is German, and we're drinking Chianti, so you gotta say it in Italian.… Smell that! This wine's alive and kicking, I tell you what.

(Please, I can't cry now, not now—he's been so sweet, I don't deserve all this—and why do I have to wind myself up like this. I'm like a vibrator, pardon my French, with the off switch busted—just buzzing, buzzing all the way home, and why, one wonders? So what, he had a dream? People dream things all the time—it's just a dream, nothing special about it; so what if his subconscious replaced Vlada in my footage with his great-aunt Gela? Put a known entity in place of the unknown one, that's perfectly natural—all it means is that he thinks about me even in his sleep, looks for me, feels where I am and what I am doing at the time—because he loves me, my Adrian, sweetheart, sunshine, darling.…)

You know what? Your ears move when you chew. I swear they do! Do like this … see, see! That's hilarious. Not true at all—not everyone. What, now you're gonna say mine do, too? No, I don't believe you, wait, no, let me see it in the mirror.…

(Why did I forget—how could I forget, so it only now comes back to me: Vaddy—that was how Vlada addressed her Vadym, not in public, of course. God forbid. And not when she spoke about him in the third person—she was always fastidiously proper, buttoned-up like a graduate of a young ladies' pensione, not for her the vulgar familiarities of mere mortals—she always referred to him by his full name, and I only heard this domestic one once or twice, when she let it slip accidentally, like when you lean forward too far, and a button comes undone on your blouse, and everyone glimpses your underwear. One of those times may have been the night when the two of them came to visit, and Vadym brought a bottle of Courvoisier, which he proceeded to drink by himself because Vlada and I preferred wine. Something irked her enough that she forgot herself for a moment and addressed Vadym as she did at home, in private—"Vaddy!"—followed by something really sharp, angry, nothing like the nice-but-firm tone that women use to put a check on husbands who may be enjoying themselves a bit too much, those half-jokes designed to preserve the company's good spirits and decorum. To hell with decorum! This was raw, this would make you look away to avoid staring at the exposed patch of underwear, and since I was the only one present and had absolutely nowhere else to look, I think I giggled or blurted something inappropriate. I don't remember what exactly, only how awkward it was.... Had we been alone, without Vadym, had he gone to the bathroom, or out to the balcony for a smoke, everything would've been cleared up right there and then, but Vadym sat between us, rock-solid, like he was bolted down to the floor, chair and all, like the bed meant for the next victim in *The Hound of the Baskervilles*—sat there like it was his singular mission not to leave Vlada and myself alone even for a minute, no matter what, even if his bladder burst, and this monumentally benevolent solidity of his transformed our girlfriend chirping, whether or not it contained any trifling dissonance or mutual concern, into a sort of organic white noise, little waves lapping innocently at the foot of the rock, too insignificant to cause the rock any manner of discomfort.

Before that night I hadn't had much opportunity to observe powerful men at close range—men with the kind of great power that comes from great amounts of money. All my previous experience dictated that a man brought by his paramour to be checked out by her girlfriend should fan his tail like a peacock and deploy the full arsenal of his charms, real and imagined, so I was ill-prepared to deal with the strategic advantage Vadym had instantly gained on us by holding down his position at the table, next to his cognac, and maintaining the indulgent expression of a charitably minded giant. He had complete and undeniable control over the terrain on which his relationship with Vlada unfolded and did not allow me a single peek into that realm—left Vlada and me in the dust like greenhorns, to put it simply.

Could this be precisely what she loved about him—the cold-bloodedness of a professional player, the chess-master's logic applied to human pieces, and the fierce, single-minded focus on the results, which artists so chronically lack? An artist is totally different; he or she is forever doomed to wandering, mind and body, in tangential details, sinking into obscure complexities, into colors and shades, patches of knitting and shards of porcelain, and put before people of action, with their unwavering pursuit of "Ready! Aim! Fire!" and the jackpots hit as a consequence, must inevitably feel like a teenager in adult company—and that's exactly how I felt with Vadym that night.

Vlada had to have felt that way, too, and for a lot longer, only she thought it was really cool—we're always attracted to those whose souls ooze vital enzymes we lack most desperately ourselves. Actually, I don't even know why Vlada wanted to see me that time: something must have been grating on her, something she'd come to doubt already, but somehow we spent the whole five hours conscientiously discussing sociopolitical issues—Kuchma and Gongadze, the shake-ups at the top and the rein-tightening we felt in television, the Venice Biennale, and how profoundly Ukraine managed to fuck it up, and what a redneck pig-farm manager our deputy PM for humanitarian programs showed himself to be—all those things that Ukrainians always talk about, whether they're friends or just met each other a minute ago, forever marveling at the breakneck speed with which their ne'er-do-well country hurtles off yet another cliff, like the farmers in the joke about the cart full of melons that breaks on their way to the market and they stand there, gaping at all their melons rolling down the hill, and one says to the other, "Hey, look, the striped one's ahead."

That's how we spent that night—bemoaning whatever striped things were getting ahead—even though beyond all that usual nonsense, Vlada—and by extension, I—did sense something unsettling, unsolved, something that must have been the reason for her bringing Vadym over. Something that made her seek out, hope secretly for a moment of truth, for that late-night hiccup in personal machinery when, warmed with alcohol and easy banter, one feels the need to call off one's internal guards, loosen one's tie for a moment, and become oneself—for the alchemic brew that induces confessions, unlocks closets, pulls out drawers, drags up long-buried secrets and extracts declarations of old, age-old love—or equally old envy—all those stunning stories you never even suspected to be hidden right under your nose, like lions sleeping in savannah grass; such séances don't last long, a witch's count—from the first roosters till the second—but they are the zenith of every party, its catharsis. A party without them is like sex without an orgasm; they are the living knots that make the threads of friendship stronger, and if someone only taught those poor Americans not to go home at ten, but to hang around for two or three hours longer and let things take their course, they'd save a fortune on therapy.

They left right after midnight that time because Vadym had to fly out, at some ungodly hour before dawn, into the boondocks, to Dnipropetrovsk, or Odessa, to the nonexistent pipeline "Odessa-Brody." So in the end, it was Vadym, again, who set the timer on our little soiree; he was the one who had constructed the whole evening and controlled it, from start to finish, making sure nothing got loose—all guards posted, all buttons buttoned, ties knotted, and nothing, nothing, about it gave him the least bit of bother, except maybe his bladder that had to hold five hours worth of cognac, but that was the price he was perfectly willing to pay for his victory, hands down, over us. When Vlada called me the next morning, ostensibly to share impressions, or, as we called it, to debrief, it was already a new day, with new troubles and concerns, and if she had ever intended to tell me anything that would've been, in Vadym's opinion, undesirable, the moment for it was gone, lost forever. Flushed, you could say, down a pipe ...)

I'm coming, Aidy, just a second … I'm trying to wash my mascara off, got a clump in my eye.

(… because how could anyone ever imagine that a man can replace a woman's best friend—that's just silly, and it shouldn't ever work that way anyhow. And yet every man, in his heart of hearts, holds the opposite conviction most dear: they all believe that as soon as we got one of *them*, we no longer need anyone else in the great wide world. But even when he's such a sweetheart, and really wants to understand you because he truly loves you, and you love him too—really love him, not just bang him—even then, you can never hope to fall into that perfect and complete sync that exists between two women; and he will always begrudge you that, albeit just a little and in secret even from himself, and that is why love is always and inevitably war. Love is War, how Orwellian—and it is war, a special kind of war, one in which the winner loses it all … I'd rather be dead before I win one of those, that's what I'd tell you now, Vadym, Vaddy—now you actually use that name yourself; I've heard you do that, now that there isn't anyone else to call you by that name—after you've seen your victory dead, quite literally, in an oak coffin with brass handles, so why are you still beating on a dead horse, Vaddy?)

Just … a … moment! Can't you wait another second? I can't hear anything in here, stop talking—you and your habit of hollering across the apartment like it's the open range or something!

(That's another one I can't seem to cure him of—I've pointed it out so many times and all for nothing … Aidy's just like his old man: when we took the crew to interview him, he didn't hesitate to bellow at us, myself and the cameraman, from another room—never mind that we were perfect strangers to him. Every man turns into his own father, so does that mean that I—what?—am I turning into my mother, too? Ugh, that would not be good....

Now Vlada, she never resembled her mother in the least bit; it was more like Nina Ustýmivna was a sort of an aging child for her, an adopted and really obnoxious child—Vlada rarely even left Katrusya with her, only when she had no other choice—but actually she managed her mother rather elegantly, unlike yours truly, she knew what buttons to push. Whenever Nina Ustýmivna took a deep breath to launch—with that heavy, theatrical sigh that instantly made my skin crawl all over—into her favorite oratory about what hard, sad, hopeless lots Vlada and I drew in this life— meaning the absence of certified-and-stamped husbands, because, of course, Nina Ustýmivna's mantra, "a dead husband is better than no husband," was her holy and regularly professed creed, and she never did really accept her daughter's divorce, of which her daughter, smart girl that she was, informed her only after she had the paperwork in hand, saving herself from several valium-mediated dramas—no sooner could Nina Ustýmivna begin one of her "cello solos," as Vlada called them, than Vlada would raise her eyebrows and respond, very solemnly, in the same grave cello tones, "What husbands, Mommy? Please, we can't be bothered, nous sommes les artistes!"—and for some impenetrable reason, the French exerted on N.U. had the same effect as a crack of a whip on an old lesson horse. Her whole affect would change into a collected, grandiose kind of posture, monumental in a vaguely imperious—imperial—way, as if the woman suddenly remembered that she was "an artist's wife" and must bear this time-honored designation with the utmost dignity. And the funniest thing was that N.U.'s real name, the one on her passport, was not Nina, but Ninél, an anagram of Lenin, not something one acquired with a high-bred childhood and French governesses—and really, it's not like there were any governesses left in the USSR in the 1930s— but proof, quite to the contrary, of the wild and raucous youth of Vlada's Komsomol–activist grandma and her Bolshevik-minted (one of twenty-five thousand) Ag teacher grandpa, who, as Vlada sarcastically pointed out, had to have run roughshod on plenty a kolkhoz-resistant "location" before they decamped for Kyiv in 1933; so, she added, we're lucky it's Ninél and not Stalína, Octyabrína, or some other Zvezdéts you'd never shake off.

I suspect that it was in Nina-Ninél Ustýmivna's rigorous school of behavioral management that Vlada acquired her benevolent, gracious, ironically indulgent attitude toward the "professional wives"—that breed of belligerent females with the eyes of bored ewes who always lurk, like security guards, in close proximity to their husbands, aiming for a chance to grab, à la the unforgettable Raisa Gorbacheva, their own share of limelight when you are having a professional conversation with their husbands, all the while communicating to you with their every grimace and gesture exactly what a hopelessly inferior creature you are as you stand there all alone, with no man in sight whatsoever. I can't help myself around them: *If not for your VIP beefcake, I'd pack you off where the sun don't shine, bitch!*—but Vlada found them as entertaining as an exotic animal species, like the white rhinoceros, and she almost felt sorry for them somehow, just like for those poor rhinoceros that are so easy to spot and shoot in their bright white skins.)

Phone, sweetie! Can you get it? Here—it's your cell.... Yes, you left it in the bathroom—and tossed a towel on top of it, too.

(What I really like is to listen to him talk on the phone—it's just like watching him out the window, or in the street, in a crowd, when he doesn't see me, smiling to myself on the sly. Once I eavesdropped on a parallel line for almost the entire conversation, listening to the two men's voices like to a radio play—if the other voice had belonged to a woman I would've hung up of course, instantly and instinctively, otherwise it would've looked really bad, like I'm a jealous harpy or something, but with another man on the line it was really cool. I could listen, against the shadowy background of the other man's low *boo-boo-boo*, for the eager sprout of his lithe, pleasant voice, growing like a beam of light, and for his laugh with that little snort, like a young horse, that always makes me want to stroke him ... and it's always fun to watch guys talk to each other when there is no woman around to constrain them or make them want to preen. Men's conversation has a different rhythm: it's faster, more aggressive; they throw lines like punches; they spar like schoolboys at recess; they don't let their emotions crawl all over the place like we do—they keep them tight and focused inside their sentences, like fists, which, when you listen in, does sound like they're jousting a little.

"I even went to Crimea once with that Kápytsya guy," grumbled the base, a fellow physicist in his previous life, apparently. "Should've taken a woman instead," retorted my mensch. "I would, but they all leave me in May," the other explained, with a glee I thought unexpected. "Seasonal allergy!" diagnosed mine. "Yep, that's what it is, and I can't make it before July …"

I put the receiver down at that point, because they were making me laugh. Later, Adrian told me about the guy—they were in the same class at university, roomed together in the Lomonosov Street dorms in the late eighties, and the room was right across the communal kitchen where the Vietnamese students fried hot-cured herrings every day, so the boys knocked out their window to get some air, and then had to nail a padded quilt over it in winter. In his telling of it, this all sounded downright hilarious, like a well-pulled-off prank, and clearly that's how they thought of it at the time. And now this buddy of his was out of work, his lab due to be shut down, separated from his wife, and out of luck with women in general—always had been, but I knew that much already.

He gives me full and very detailed reports about his friends, of whom there always seem to be more. I haven't even made it through the whole list yet; it boggles the mind, really, how he managed to acquire so many. It's like he hasn't lost a single pal in his entire adult life—he's still trailing people from all the way back in middle school—and somehow, incredibly, he manages to hold the whole mob in his mind, remembering all their domestic troubles, fights with parents, snafus at work, abortions, and divorces. Lets them all cry on his shoulder when they need to, listens to everyone, makes helpful phone calls, deals with funeral homes, hospitals, and car mechanics. I can't even keep their names straight because once he's introduced someone to me he refers to them as if they were our common friends and not someone only he knew, as in, "Igor called."—"Which Igor is that, the one that's losing his hair?" And every time I evince such considerable powers of retention it makes him go all sunny—"Yep, that one!"—and of course it never once occurs to him that the shedding Igor may not at all appreciate having me, or any other sexually relevant woman, privy to the embarrassing details of his personal plight. But men have always delivered their brethren to women they love without so much as a blink—bald heads, binges, erectile dysfunctions, and marital affairs included—the way a woman would never hand over her friends—her self-preservation instinct wouldn't let her, unless, of course, she's a complete idiot. That, and that fundamental feline neatness of hers, the one that demands she hide her blood-soiled pad where he'll never see it, that she pluck those naughty hairs from her chin, that she smarten up and wash between her toes. Anything so unseemly honest you might betray to your man about your friend today might come back to haunt you tomorrow, as if you've unwittingly opened his eyes to aspects of female nature he, with his manly shortsightedness, never noticed before, had no inkling existed at all. And that's why, generally, women's solidarity is much stronger than men's—women guard what unites them far more jealously.

Whatever I tell him about my friends has already passed a kind of censorship, whose partial objective, let us be honest, is to dim the ladies' stardom a bit, turn them into a courtly entourage befitting my own queenly persona, into a kind of an organically coordinated flowerbed, a magnificent backdrop against which I can cut an all-the-more-compelling figure. Any details that might claim a disproportionate share of his attention are in this process corrected and retouched, while the most flattering light is turned upon Me the Magnificent.

But this is different from what men do; this is women's business as usual, the game we've always played, ever willing to change parts to help each other out—your turn to be the queen today, mine—tomorrow: around Vadym, I was Vlada's lady-in-waiting, just like she was mine when I was seeing Ch., for instance, or D. before him. So when you think about it, this is just another manifestation of our feminine solidarity; guys wouldn't know where to start—they're forever falling over each other to stomp one another out to impress you, like bucks or elephants or some other animal before a female, and without even a specific goal in mind, such as, for example, actually stealing you from the other guy, just for pure art's sake.... Alright, sounds like he's finished his conversation, and I think my eyes look almost normal again. You can't tell I've been bawling ... a little puffy, but I'll tell him it's because I had to rub the mascara off, with cold water, that's it. Shit, I bet the food's all gone cold in the kitchen by now!)

Vaddy—gosh darn it, I am so sorry—I meant Aidy, of course ... can't talk today. Who did you say called? Oh that one.... (He doesn't see it; he sees nothing—neither puffy, rabbit-pink eyes, nor my anxiety over this Freudian slip—he just goes on shining like a new penny, because of what he's just heard on the phone. He's rushing to tell me, now, right away; he's eager to share and, of course, to get the benefit of my encouragement and approval: our candelabra just got another buyer, can you believe that? Some hotshot, hot enough to desire his own independent appraisal; he's got an expert too, flies him in from Moscow because he doesn't trust our homegrown Ukrainian ones.) So does that mean you can have them bid against each other—your marmot and this new one—set up a little private auction of sorts? Is that how it works? Wow, that's awesome, Aidy! Congrats!

(There are more details; he keeps piling them on with that same forthright, barnstorming tempo of male business talk, and it takes all I've got to scrape together enough attention to hang on, almost wrinkling my forehead in concentration in order to stay with him, but I feel such a heroic effort is beyond me. I am really tired. I can't muster the grace my mind needs to leap from one thing to the next, one stone to the next across the stream, especially when I know what dangerous craggy rocks lie hidden under the surface, and how hard it is to lift them from the bottom. He doesn't even notice. He's just chirping on, a merry little bird, oblivious, like he isn't the reason I'm suddenly able to see underwater with this bizarre second sight that catches glimpses of the terrifying depths we skim so innocently. He is just a guy dreaming his mind-twisting dreams; he unloads them on me and goes on with his day. He is always at ease when I'm around, within reach, but as soon as I make to leave the room, I hear his indignant *Where are you going?* behind me, as demanding as the howl of an unattended baby. Although, maybe, there's a bit of a protective instinct in it too, and a touch of that anxiety that you always feel when you let a piece of yourself go into the unknown, like if you forget a document folder in an empty train compartment, or something like that. For as long as I'm out of reach he is prey to all kinds of fearful troubles, like the hordes of hungry-eyed men he thinks of, as he once confessed to me, every time he goes out without me—he notices them in the crowds, these pushy, preda-tory types with their teeth-baring leers, ready to sink their fangs into their pretty prey, and always shudders at how many of them prowl out there, and how I have to walk among them like Little Red Riding Hood in the woods.

And that's why he is only truly content and happy when I am at his side. It's even true when he sleeps: when we are in the same bed, he either doesn't dream at all or get the same regular crap I do, just like everybody else, stuff not worth retelling, but when I'm gone, even if I get up and leave without waking him up, that's when Adrian Vatamanyuk's private screenings begin. Click—and a tape of unknown provenance slides into his unattended head; up until now these have featured totally unfamiliar characters in a period drama, but now, apparently, it's my turn to star since the most recent installment has me interviewing Olena Dovganivna—and that's just perfect, what can I say, a real séance. Like a hundred years ago, before people had TV, and various loons also set up interviews with the dead, spinning tables and all, "Spirit, spirit, are you here?" To which any self-respecting spirit naturally responds with "Fuck off," or something along those lines, and rightly so, because really, leave the man, I mean the spirit, alone. You'll all be there, in your own good time, and will certainly find out whatever it is you're after.

I'm totally with the spirits on this, only our situation is a tiny bit different, a rather big bit, actually, if you really think about who started it and who doesn't leave whom alone. I personally never bothered anyone, no spirits, no nothing. I've got enough trouble without them, and so does he, by the way—he's running around with those antiques of his like a chicken with his head cut off. Thank God, he's banking a bit of change here and there, but it's not like I can't see how much he misses his physics, all those alternative energy sources he can't bring himself to part with, can't quit on that dissertation of his even if no one else gives a flying hoot about it. He keeps futzing with it just so he can keep one foot in that door, not even a foot, a toe, a pinkie, even after his business started making enough to pay the bills—but still not enough, I don't think, to move out of these boonies into a decent neighborhood, not to mention any murky plans regarding our future.

I don't know really—one could, I suppose, get a loan to buy a place, but that takes connections at the bank. Maybe one of his clients could help—all our banks start their own collections these days. What about this new candelabra candidate who's supposed to be such a hotshot, what if? Aidy may have had the same idea, that may be why he's so wound up about it, why he's so inspired to keep on about all the details of the deal he'll make, while it takes all I've got just to keep staring at him, as if opening my eyes wider will help me hold on to at least the gist of what he's saying.

And where, I ask you, do spirits fit in all of this? In what itty-bitty crack? It's no wonder he just dumps them all off on me, shakes them off like a dog come in from the rain—watch out when they fly! It is my job, after all, nothing to be done about that, and the film about his great-aunt is also mine to make—no man would ever make that movie, wouldn't even think of it. It's like Yurko said—he's our Bluebeard who, whenever he's not embroiled in the many challenges of his domestic life, likes to show off his feminism like a rented Brioni suit—"Who's that poor thing you've

dug up? If you were going to mess with UIA, go find yourself a real
ace, some daredevil who mowed down the bad guys like hay, first
Germans, then ours, pardon me—Russians—and then roused a
revolt somewhere in the Gulag. Now that would be something—
and you picked some wallflower with a typewriter. What kind of
story is that?"

Sure, I agree, not much there, but I'm not the one who did
the picking you know—*this*, the story, picked me, knocked me
down and had me, did, in fact, have me quite literally, which, of
course, I shall never tell Adrian, and of all my friends could only
maybe tell Vlada—she would appreciate it, but by the time this
happened Vlada was no longer among the living, and now it's all
guys all around me, at work, at home, wherever I turn, that's just
the way the cookie crumbled, and I go around censoring myself
to accommodate them.

So there you have it: I'm smiling and nodding at him, all duti-
ful, because I know he needs my encouragement, and support,
and regular watering, weeding, and feeding. Every woman must
cultivate her little garden with the proudly erect phallus at its
center, like a Mexican cactus—these are very demanding crops,
these phalli; they wither and die without constant care and attention, and if I need to call off my guards, let my hair down, and
just be myself for a little while I have two options: soak myself into
a pruney-fingered blob in a pine-scented bubble bath, or, more
radically, perfume myself with vanilla all over, pounce on him, and
drag him to bed growling like a panther to buy myself a relaxing
half hour of complete abandon. Only, unfortunately, the second
option is not really an option when I'm exhausted like now—the
kind of exhausted that wears your nerves down hair-thin and
makes you want to cry—and I would really be happiest right now if
I could just sit with you, Aidy, without either of us saying anything.
I'd sit and finish this Chianti you found—it's really wonderful—
pour more for myself, and you won't even notice—the wine glows
beautifully in the glass I hold against the candlelight, burns with
a dark garnet fire. I know you can be quiet, Aidy.

You're one of the few people with whom it's been easy and natural from the start to be quiet—there was never anything foreign or alien in your presence. And that may be what I love most about you—a man with whom it is nice to be quiet, what a gem!—because there are things you really can't talk about with men, and all these things settle in us, accumulate and calcify like scum inside pots or plaque on teeth, and itch and itch, and then begin to oppress us—vaguely, so we can't even name them and don't even know what's wrong with us until one day we die and no one ever finds out what it was that gnawed on us as we lay on our deathbeds....)

Aidy? Aidy, listen to me.

No, I didn't understand any of that, I'm sorry. Honestly? I wasn't really listening. I was thinking about something else entirely. Don't be upset. You know what it was?

Here, cin cin, to us, and let everything be great. Let it all go smoothly, you know—with your deal, and generally ... listen.

It's your dream that made me think of this, the one you had earlier today—about me interviewing your great-aunt Gela at a table in the Passage. Actually, I brought you a tape to watch with an old interview of mine—take a look at it later, okay? It's in my tote, in the hallway. You can turn the sound off, so it doesn't distract you, the picture's the thing—you'll see what I mean when you watch it ... Aidy, listen, I'm serious. Something's going on here—both with my film and with these dreams of yours. They're connected somehow. And the two of us are somehow involved in it all.

There's another plot behind all this, a different story. I am sure of that, dead sure. Feel it in my gut. No one really knew her, this Gela Dovgan. Even while she was alive.

How do I explain this ... promise not to laugh at me, okay? All that stuff we recorded with your dad, what he remembered his mom and Grandma Apollinaria telling him—it's all very good, no doubt about it. I can use a lot of what's on those three tapes we have of him talking: Gela's childhood, the Gymnasium, her joining the Youth Assembly, the Ukrainian student community in

Zurich, and then the whole family going to the gulag "for Geltsia," and your dad's own memories of Karaganda, when he was little—how they rode the train for a month—it's all important; I'll use it, and all the family photos are really cool too. I'm just thinking about going to the woods to shoot some footage of old bunkers that are still there, but that's when I have the shooting script—I'll read it live against the backdrop of the woods.... Nah, no worries, I won't climb into any bunkers, nothing'll cave in on me—would you quit being like my mom, talking to me like I'm five! Only all that doesn't quite cut it, Aidy. It's all wonderful, but it's not it. Not quite. She wants something different from me.

What do you mean who? Gela, who else? Olena Dovganivna. Olena Ambroziivna Dovgan, may she rest in peace.

You don't think I'm losing it, do you? Thanks, 'preciate it.

Please, don't take it the wrong way—I am really grateful to your dad and to you, for coming with me—he would've been totally different with me if you weren't there, wouldn't have talked to me like that, relaxed like with family—but your dad had seen her once in his entire life, and he was mostly asleep in his cradle when she came to see them in the middle of the night that time.... You see, Aidy—only, please, don't laugh, this is really serious. I mean it. Basically the entire time she was in the underground she was among men. Except maybe those radio operators' courses in '44, but that was still under the Germans, and from then on, until she died in '47, it was all woods and bunkers for three years straight—without a female soul beside her. And I'm not even talking about their draconian conspiracy in which they didn't even know each other by name, never mind sharing anything personal.... That she presumably confided to the family during that visit about some guy she'd secretly wed doesn't change anything, Aidy. Does not, trust me. Whatever kind of guy he was.

She had something in her heart—and no one to tell. Something only a woman would have understood.

You said it. Exactly. That's exactly what I'm thinking.

Yes, please, a bit more. Thank you.

I think it's still tormenting her—whatever this thing is that she died with, not having told anyone. And she wants me to help her unburden herself.

She needs me. And you too, Aidy. That's why we're together.

Well, of course it's not the whole reason. I remember it perfectly—you were smitten at first sight by my legs in black jeans, a first-round knockdown, a kick in the gut, of course.... Only I am not kidding, Adrian Ambrozievich. I am as somber as a fresh-cut tombstone.

So about the tombstones.

I wonder if it is time we dig into exactly how she died. Under what circumstances. 'Cause it would be a crying shame to stick into the film that sorry claptrap of an MGB excuse you guys've been hanging on to since '54; that's one. And two—no one has really looked into it yet: after 1991, when you finally could, there wasn't anyone left, was there? Grandma Apollinaria had passed already.... No, sweets, stop it. I'd never mean it like that—of course, there's always something else; that's life. It's what always happens when there's no immediate family left—the children, they care what actually happened to their parents, because it affects them directly, it ricochets into their lives, although even then, depends on the children.... And who's she to you—Grandma's sister, big deal, plenty of families don't even remember kin like that. You should thank Granny Lina that she managed to pass it on at all! Oh absolutely, you don't even have to mention it—of course Lina looked up to her since she was little; Gela was her icon, the older for the younger—sure thing. Gela's brilliant, Gela's beautiful, Gela joins the Plast, Gela joins the Youth Assembly, boys tail Gela in packs wherever she goes— that kind of stuff stays with you for the rest of your life; even if Gela had lived, and she became a hero and died heroically on top of all that.... Basically, you got lucky. No, not with her dying and all—with Granny Lina, she could've kept mum, you know. Secure a happy Communist childhood for her grandson. Many did, nothing wrong with that.

So, Aidy. We've no other choice; we need intel. Not from the family, but from the twilight zone. The other side of the moon. From the underground, yep. From her last years. That's where we gotta dig.

We've got the lead, too. A tiny one, but enough to latch on—her death was recorded by the MGB; we know this from that '54 epistle. I bet you anything a few folks earned themselves new stars for that operation. That's where I want to start: where, when, under what circumstances did she die. Documented precisely. And then we'll go from there. It'll work.

This, naturally, won't be easy. Nothing's easy in this ghetto country of ours. But at least it's not 1954, and our own Ukrainian Security Bureau does give up their archives bit by bit at the rate of their honorable retirees' relocation to the Lukyaniv Cemetery, or wherever it is they bury them these days.... Yep, to avoid traumatizing anyone.... You can scoff all you want; I think they must be really vulnerable right now. If you're gonna break women's fingers in the doors or, you know, crush testicles with your boots, you've got to be, among other things, a hundred percent sure that you would never *ever* be held responsible for it, and by the time you're old, after you've lived all your life with that certainty—heck, the idea alone'd give you a heart attack!

Okay, whatever, to hell with those—let their underworld colleagues take care of them, the ones with the pitchforks.... These archives, basically, have the same setup as the spetskhran storage in the good ol' USSR, when you needed to read some pre-Brezhnev issue of *Pravda* "for work," and you brought a note certifying that you were a PhD in history, and that was your topic, so this was something the government actually tasked you to do—go read *Pravda* from such-and-such year. (Wait, how do I know all this? Oh yeah, from Artem again.) Only here instead of *Pravda,* or some writings by Hrushevsky, or whoever, you've got the basic biographical data for the person you need: Dovgan Olena Ambroziivna, year of birth—1920, place of birth—Lemberg/Lwow/Lvov/Lviv, year of death—1947, place of death—and that's where we appeal to you, our kind and valiant record keepers.... It's like, you know, it'd be nice to find Grandma's grave, do it all up neat and proper. I've heard they let the family have the case files without a fuss; Irka Mocherniuk's mom made an inquiry about Irka's gramps, what, five years ago maybe, and got to take it all home, with all the denunciations written about him bound neatly. Said she learned all kinds of interesting things about old family friends.

Because if I try to go there with an official letter from my channel—all doe-eyed and innocent, I'm just looking to make a movie here, I won't be any trouble at all, can I just take one little peek in there, please?—they're sure to go all hot under the collar and turn vigilant on me like they've been taught in their KGB school. They'll sift through the case and cut out anything that could compromise their colleagues who are still alive, and all I'll get instead of a fat binder will be a manila folder with two pieces of paper glued into it. You can bet your life on that. You, as a direct relative—her, you could say, descendant—have a much better chance.

So, whatddya say? Can we hold 'em up or what?

Aidy, Aidy ... you're my bunny rabbit ... warm and fuzzy.

Nope, you don't have to go anywhere—it should all be in their central archive, here in Kyiv, all the important UIA cases are here, I've asked. The files on the Supreme Command—those got shipped to Moscow, they took loads of Ukrainian archives, in 1991 most recently, after August 24, right after the independence—cleaned the stacks out like in '41 before the German army, people say, burned papers right there in the yard for several weeks—covered their tracks, you know. Of course there are things we'll never learn—but it doesn't mean they didn't happen. It's not like they went anywhere; we're still living with them. Only it's like walking in the middle of the night through someone else's place—you keep bumping into furniture.

Speaking of which—we should blow out these candles. Could you turn on the light, please—not the main one, just the pendant above the table?

Yeah, I am ... really tired.

O-oh, fuzzy-duds … you're so warm …

No, before we turn in, would you mind watching that interview of mine with Vlada? Yes, that's the one I told you about—you didn't see it air, did you? That was before our time. I didn't have *Diogenes' Lantern* then—my pieces ran as individual interviews with some editorial cuts. And here on tape it's all raw footage, as it went. No, I'd rather not; I've seen it today already. I don't want to do it again. Just don't have it in me, Aidy. Honestly. Watch it alone, in the bedroom, okay? I'll go ahead and accept my fate—do the dishes here.

That was a glorious dinner you fixed. Thank you, toots.

You're so nice—what would I do without you?

Just leave it, leave it. I'll take care of it.

Aidy, Aidy, did you play with girls when you were little?

No, I just wanted to ask if you remembered this game we used to have—dig a little hole, line it with flowers, tinsels, beads, make it like a picture, cover it with a piece of glass and bury again? A secret, it was called.

You don't, do you?

***

UIA SOLDIER QUESTIONNAIRE

1. RANK AND ALIAS: Officer cadet ~~Zirka~~ Dzvinya
2. LAST NAME NAME: Dovgan Olena
3. NATIONALITY: Ukrainian
4. DATE AND PLACE OF BIRTH: 1920, Lviv
5. EDUCATION: Three years of physics at the university in Zurich
6. DESIGNATION: Radio operator/radio engineer
7. SITUATION: Unattached (single)
8. SERVICE IN OTHER ARMIES:
9. TERM OF SERVICE IN UIA: Since March of 1944
10. PROMOTIONS: [response illegible, form stained]
11. COMMENDATIONS: [response illegible, form stained]

12. WOUNDS AND HOSPITALIZATION: [response illegible, form
    stained]
13. DISCIPLINARY ACTIONS: [response illegible, form stained]
14. BLOOD TYPE: [response illegible, form stained]
15. SUPERIORS' OPINION: [response illegible, form stained]

***

Her name is Anastasia, and she's my intern—I've got interns now, can you believe it? That's how it all begins, isn't it? And then one fine day you realize that everyone around you is younger than you are, and not just younger, but like a pack of teenage wolves—nipping at your heels waiting for you to make room for them. They are the first generation that won itself the new Europe—the one whose tender minds, their young and gelatinous brains, got steamrolled by the whole megaton bulk of American media. It's just like in the old days with the poster of the glaring Red Army soldier pointing his finger at you: "Have you enlisted in the Army?" Only the questions are different now: "Have you vacationed in the Canaries?" "Have you bought a Mercedes?" "Are you shopping at Gucci?" And they fall over each other in their mad rush, wherever the gigantic finger on the screens sends them at the moment, snapping whatever seems like an obstacle in their way. I can just see the spike on the suicide graph that this Internet generation will deliver our sociologists in ten years or so—*whoosh*, like the Independence Square fountain.

This one's decked out in a Gucci blouse, a pair of Bally boots, and a tote bag to match the boots. She's a pointy-nosed little doll with eyes like a pair of plastic buttons and a permanently gaping mouth, already marked with a pair of lines emerging on each side, a bit soon for her very early twenties, but I bet that sensuous little mouth of hers has worked over more thick masculine stubs than I have in my entire life. Unless, of course, it's Daddy who dresses her. Actually, the two are not mutually exclusive.

Whenever Gucci Nastya aims her moist gaping beak at me (at me!), I have to fight back a strong urge to inquire, with great concern, whether she, by chance, is suffering from severe sinusitis. Such is the new crop cultivated for the profession by the Journalism Institute right under our noses, here in the old Syrets' neighborhood, in the snow-white sarcophagus the Communist Party built for its own spawn right before the ol' USSR's demise, because their old place on Rylski Street, also a not-too-shabby Secession villa with lions, which Gucci Nastya and I happen to be passing right now, was getting uncomfortably crowded for the Party's lush cabbage patch.

The villa is now a bank and the lions have to sit encircled by pink granite, as if in the middle of a skating rink. I ask the future Ukrainian journalist if she knows what this building housed a mere fifteen years ago—not that distant a past, really, she must've been going to school already—if she knows that her alma mater is genetically related in the full sense of the phrase to the establishment that used to rule from here and, judging by the prostituting proclivities of national journalism, a place's karma is indeed something that gets passed on like genes, only I don't tell her that.

Anastasia (that's how she introduces herself—by her full name) keeps me in the crosshairs of her plastic-button eyes and her blow-job-ready little maw—no, she doesn't know what used to be here, and it is obvious that she doesn't give a flying fuck either. But I am the one who will sign her TV-internship report, and later she'll be telling everyone that she interned with Goshchynska herself, so, after a momentary hesitation, she dares to offer an obsequious giggle—meaning, that's cool. Guppy. Goldfish in a bowl. Why, for God's sake, journalism? Why not some business management, with the prospect of a job at a foreign firm where she could marry someone Swiss, or Dutch, or, worse comes to worst, American? Why'd she choose this?

"Nastya," I say tenderly, "would you mind me asking why *you* decided to become a journalist?"

I can almost physically sense the balls my question sets in motion as they roll and clack inside her skull—she's calculating which answer would score the most points. Like in a computer game. A small, agile, ferreting kind of a brain, tuned to promptly locate food.

"I've always been good at writing."

See *Business, Natalie, Elle Ukraine*—the advice column: How to Succeed at a Job Interview. Be confident; try to convey the impression of a person who knows the value of her professional accomplishments. And, of course, the American TV shows—*Melrose Place, Project Runway*. And I have to put up with all this because she's attached herself to me like a piece of chewing gum on the sole of my shoe, because I, when we left the studio together, was foolish enough to offer the child a ride downtown, and then the child climbed out of the studio car with me, and to my tactful "Where do you go from here?" twice already responded with "I'll walk with you," not blinking an eye. What was it that Russian said: my generation's shit, but yours is something completely incomprehensible.

"Writing—meaning spelling?"

I'm not holding back anymore.

An actual emotion finally flashes through the plastic eyes—anger, a lurking predatory enmity, even her little lip instinctively pulls up into a snarl—only the growling is missing. Alright, we've got contact now. In another year, armed with her diploma, she'll write in some toilet-paper-yellow tabloid that Goshchynska hates women. Especially young ones, beautiful ones. And intelligent ones, naturally. And, if on top of that the girl gets paid a couple grand a month, she'll see no difference between herself and me whatsoever, except the fact that I am older and thus, in her understanding, of lesser quality, like yogurt past its use-by date.

The more I watch them—this savage new undergrowth—the less motivated I feel to have a child. And all the more relieved that I haven't had one yet—you can't keep them, protect them, from this. You can't lock your flesh and blood in a room and feed them organic spiritual product through a little window in the door. I can't imagine how the ones whose parents did manage to raise them like that navigate this jungle. Especially if, God forbid, their parents can't quite shoulder Gucci and Bally.

"Journalism, Nastya, is not just good writing."

Who gives a damn? Why am I saying this? To whom?

The important thing is that here, next to Bohdan Khmelnytsky monument, I really have to shake her off in a hurry; I am about to cross paths with Aidy, who should be just leaving the Security Bureau's public office on Volodymyrska Street (the former townhouse of the Hrushevsky family, by the way, I think automatically—How'd I get on this "former" properties trip?), and least of all do I wish to have this future golden quill as a witness. Only I've run out of ideas of how to rid myself of her gracefully. What a stupid mess.

"Excuse me," I say, and pull out my cell, pressing, underhand, Aidy's button. He sounds busy, responds monosyllabically, something's not going according to plan over there; and here I go, with my idiotic, utterly unnecessary questions about where it's best for me to wait for him, complete bullshit, but I can't very well just tell him that the single purpose of my call is to allow me, once I press the end button, to turn back on my intern (I do wonder which one of those bosses of mine saddled me with her?) and extend a polite yet decisive hand.

"Well, Nastya, it was a pleasure to take a stroll with you, but someone's waiting for me."

Without the cell—that helpful crutch—I'd never have disentangled myself with such dignity. That's what cell phones are for—to mask our rapidly progressing helplessness vis-à-vis the real world when we find ourselves face to face with it. A kind of a safety net for interpersonal communication without which we can't really make a single step anymore—have to hang on to it at all times. Like babies in playpens.

Rejected but indomitable Nastya struts off down Sofiivska, swinging her little tush, packaged into two discrete halves inside her pants. (I bet she's already got early cellulite in there, physically

all these kids are somehow incredibly rickety, the Chernobyl generation—maybe that's where their wolf grip comes from: snatch
off your share in a hurry, because in another ten years you won't
have anything to snatch with?)

I turn onto Volodymyrska, its first hundred yards cheerful
along St. Sophia's white monastery wall under old chestnuts, and
the next hundred gloomy—a shadow cast diagonally from the
opposite side of the street where the KGB's, now the Ukrainian
Security Bureau's, gray facade rears up at the top of the block,
splattered on the face of the hill like a monstrous toad that's
pulled itself upright to St. Sophia, squatting in the middle of the
city's historical center, in the heart of Grand Prince Yaroslav's
ancient city. And I could have told Nastya that as late as the 1930s
a charming little church stood here, St. Irene, dating back to the
thirteenth century, as radiant and feminine as St. Sophia, white-
walled under a dark-green chaplet of its dome (I've seen pictures).
But the monstrous toad with a jail in its gut squashed it, crushed
it with its weight till its bones—its walls—literally cracked, and
today the only trace that remains of the little church is the name
of a side lane—that's all we get, names; that's all that's left to us,
like rings with precious gems pried out of the settings.

Only Nastya, of course, doesn't give a damn about all that,
and in any case her interests will always be aligned with whoever
did the crushing and not with whomever got crushed, because
the crushed, as she learned from her mommy, daddy, school, and
television, are the losers, has-beens, and screw-ups, so I can take
my little church and go hide in a dark, quiet corner. I don't like
walking on that side of Volodymyrska—and I'm not the only one.
In the Soviet days it was always empty, vacuumed clean—people
have loosened up since then, lost the bit and the rein, but I still
don't like walking there. I'll have to, though.

And right there, on the crosswalk before Reitarska, my cell
rings: Aidy.

"It's not here," he says, and I'm almost run over by an especially
nervous Toyota that jerks off before I quite make it all the way to

the sidewalk. (I stick my tongue out at the driver.) Their archives, turns out, are not here but across the street, on Zolotovoritska. And that's where he is right now. And that's where I am to go; he'll tell me everything.

"They're all going to lunch now; I just made it!"

I turn around—like the indomitable Nastya, like a tank; I dash between moving cars not waiting for the green light. Zolotovoritska is a street I like: cozy, quiet, one of the few streets in the center that retains its true old-Kyiv charm, and even the recently sprouted cohort of granite-plated bankomorphic high-rises can't do anything to destroy its spirit. And right on the corner of this agreeable street, in front of a flowerbed, on a little knoll, in the sun, stands my good lad—like a beacon to show me the way—and it's instant: a hot wave of utterly inane joy at the sight of his lanky-colt figure, his close-cropped head, his smile that beams from afar like a discrete source of light in the cityscape. He's seen me!—but I did first! I did!—and while this distance between us—this bisector not found on any maps of the city, called forth for just this minute beside this flowerbed, this line that's made this empty corner of Zolotovoritska and Reitarska alive, buzzing and pulsing for this one minute, shrinks at the speed of the intercepted glance (the knee-buckling, head-spinning kind that makes your heart drop into bottomless tenderness), while this "crosswalk," invisible to all but the two of us (and no city in the world has road marks more important than these!)—counts down the seconds that remain between us—seven, six, five, four—I see, with peripheral vision (like a black gangster-mobile that pops up out of nowhere in a cheap action flick, and next a window'll roll down to let out the muzzle of a submachine gun)—an incursion onto our bisector, from somewhere behind me on the sidewalk, of someone else's black shadow. Not a casual brush but a frontal attack, resolutely aimed to wedge itself between the two of us, keeping us both in its sights. And when I step onto the sidewalk, a step away from Aidy, instead of touching him, finding him in a quick tangle of hands, shoulders, cheek, I run into the wall of that foreign look, sprung up suddenly beside us, short and hard, as if from under a frown. Prominent black eyes set in fleshy eyelids, an appraising look, but not in the usual men's way, different, so that you want to shake it off right away, like a black spider; before this instinctive impulse can reach my brain, the look scrambles its aim by leaving only a vague unsettling residue, a slimy trail—and Aidy, taking his hand off my shoulder in an interrupted gesture, turns his head and smiles starchily in that direction as to someone he knows—barely, but enough that the person deserves a few niceties, even if he'd turned up at a bad time.

"Going to lunch?" the man asks.

This sounds like a send-up for a recently concluded conversation to which there is nothing to add, and it's not hard to guess who this type, stuffed into his mass-produced suit like into a corset, might be—that very same archive's employee who left the office on Aidy's heels and should've kept going instead of coming to loiter around us. The mister's head hovers at about Aidy's shoulder, and the rest of him is not much to look at either—the rump significantly outweighs the top, legs sort of stubby—but his bearing and face are remarkable: a strong face, he must've been a real hottie when he was young; schoolgirls doodle such Mephistopheles profiles in their notebooks, only he's not my type. I don't like those Mediterranean-swarthy, sepia types with eyes that become more prominent and black the more white strands they get in their black wool, and something vaguely hawkish in their features—the whole aging Arab terrorist look. Or Israeli military. For some reason, I think they must be constantly sweating—like someone used too much oil paint on them and forgot to daub the painting. And he's got military bearing alright; they all carry themselves like that—even when all they've got is an archive job. What's his rank, I wonder?

Aidy cleverly makes a point of not introducing us. A cow would get it—go on, move right along, nothing to see here—but this forward-chested stub of a terrorist is much less perceptive than a cow; he's about as sharp as my Nastya, and he proceeds to shower

Aidy, verbosely, paternally, solicitously, with patronizing notes, with some utterly unnecessary details, belaboring the already belabored—that it's better to telephone them, anytime after tomorrow, the more time they have for the search the better, not all cases have been cataloged yet, priority is given to requests for rehabilitation of which there don't seem to be getting any fewer, not at all, quite the opposite, much has been done already, but there's still at least as much to do. And there he stands, good and sturdy, with his thick, oily eyebrows and his hawkish profile, and bullshits and bullshits, and does not intend to shut up anytime soon, and I catch him glancing at me again and it finally dawns on me: he recognizes me! (Is that why he stopped?)

Shit, of all things, we could really do without this. Dude, why couldn't you just go to lunch? Damn television—soon as you stick your nose out in public, someone's always staring at you, liable to ask, "Is this really You?" And not even to get an autograph, but just because, to confirm they're right. I keep mum like a real Ukrainian partisan, not a peep, standing beside them as if we're on a subway and not in the middle of the street, and focus on breathing through my nose, keeping my face straight as a passport photo—it's not actually your face people recognize as much as your expressions and, especially, individual intonation, so I stubbornly drag out my pause, long, endlessly long, folks'd be shuffling and coughing already if this were the theater. And he has no desire to wait forever either; it is his lunch break after all.

"I'm sorry; you're Daryna Goshchynska, aren't you?"

Here we go.

"And I'm sorry, who would you be?"

Aidy makes a grudging entrance—like a double base in a jazz band, "Pavlo Ivanovych, from the archive."

Pavlo Ivanovych, sure. A purely KGB way of introducing oneself. I heard this from my mom: they were all either Pavlo Ivanovyches or Sergei Petrovyches, all those operatives, "guardians," men without last names, just name and patronymic. For no reason I can grasp, this gesture of loyalty to the age-old traditions of his guild suddenly pisses me off—I mean really pisses me off. I go blind with a rage that's rushed to my head—or maybe I'm just slow to react today and there is a whole cocktail of accumulated ingredients exploding now, all my aggregate irritation beginning with Gucci Nastya (or maybe it was Nastya who infected me); but at this particular moment, I am just as ready to bare my teeth and growl—so furious my jaws cramp.

"In that case, I am Daryna Anatoliivna!"

"That I knew," he says, regarding me as if a fed condor atop a tall cliff: the heavy, wrinkled eyelids half shield his unmoving protuberant eyes—eyes fit for an Oriental beauty, velvet and languorous, a pair of jet stones. What are they doing on him? A prank of nature. With a very slight emphasis, just a skosh of pressure, exactly enough to make sure his words don't go unnoticed, he repeats, "I know it's Anatoliivna."

Am I supposed to fuss, fawn, and flip right over? Gosh, wherever from, how, pray tell, I'm dying to find out? Piss off. Jackass.

"Your matinka still alive?"

That's exactly what he says—matinka. In Russian, this would've been matushka—appropriate, even respectful. That's how they used to talk among themselves—matushka, and also supruga, as in "Send my regards to your good supruga," never "wife"—"wives" were something the people they interrogated had, men not to be considered or given regard. But for their own: matushka, supruga—the jargon of power, the victors' argot. How did I not notice that he is translating from Russian in his head?

If he and I were iguanas, we'd be set in a perfect shot for *Planet Earth* on Discovery Channel: face to face, rearing with angrily unfurled hoods, waiting to see who strikes first. Or cobras—those also sway in the air before darting at the enemy, a lightning-fast whiplash. (I do also have Aidy on my side, calm like a boa constrictor, wise to keep his peace, and this, undoubtedly, gives me extra strength, but we'll leave him outside the frame.)

"Yes, she's well, thank you. And yours?"

Did I imagine this, or did the other iguana shudder, slump on its feet a bit?

"Please send my regards to her," he goes on—not one to be knocked off his course, that's another habit of the powerful—ignoring anything out of line, letting it slide as if it never happened. Canceled as being not in effect. Except, if your matinka's off limits for me, then why the hell should you be messing with mine?

"Regards from whom?"

"Boozerov," the iguana finally cracks and names himself, and it sounds unexpectedly intimate: the hood falls, the frill folds, there are worn loose sacks around his eyes, sagging jowls of well-cured skin above his shirt collar—a man in his fifties, and deeply so—with liver spots on his cheekbones, troubles with digestion and very likely his prostate, too, his career mostly played out, and obviously not too brilliantly, ahead of him only retirement with its pension and the constant worry that it'll be cut, and what has he done to be snarled at like that?

"Pavlo Ivanovych Boozerov," he confides further—almost embarrassed as if he were whispering something lewd into my ear, a man pestering a woman in the street, following her—and is transformed right before my eyes, this poor, ill man, just think about living with a last name like that, sheesh, that's quite a favor his mom and dad did him! A serious name—earnest, genuine Ryazan-Tambov vintage—the kind often found among old army retirees, like the unforgettable lieutenant colonel Plankin who taught PE and history at our school and was rumored to have become Plankin after he took his wife's name, having himself been born Dillrodov. So Boozerov is actually not that bad, could be worse—unless, of course, Pavlo Ivanovych is pulling my leg, because he looks no more like an authentic Boozerov from Ryazan marshlands (Tatar cheekbones, gray eyes, a general watery indeterminacy of color) than I look like Osama bin Laden. The casting's all wrong. Is he expecting to hear how pleased I am to meet him, or what?

"Just say it like that, to your dear matinka—Boozerov, Pavlo Ivanovych. I think she'll remember me. Our paths crossed."

"It's a small world," Aidy observes philosophically, inserting his head into the frame, and, thankfully, right on time—I have not the slightest clue what to say to Pavlo Ivanovych's lyrical pronouncement. Really have no desire whatsoever to learn when and under what circumstances his path may have crossed with my matinka's, and thus proceed to say nothing, obtusely and not politely at all. Over and out. And anyway Pavlo Ivanovych's digestive juices must be trumpeting their call to battle: I see two yellowish-white streaks curdled like old sheep-cheese in the corners of his mouth and get genuinely queasy. Pavlo Ivanovych, on the other hand, feels quite the opposite.

"A pleasure," he helpfully voices the line I missed—if no one's serving, he'll help himself. "A pleasure to know that she's raised such a ... famous daughter (last word spoken with the Russian stress). I myself often watch your shows, although it's not always easy for me to find the time. And my daughter (with the Russian stress) just worships you."

This stiff little stump in his corset suit smiles for the first time. What a surprise—an awkward, meager smile, à la Shtirlitz from the classic Soviet TV series. It looks as though he had to engage untrained and long-calcified facial muscles; maybe that's what they did in their Cheka schools: set everyone's faces to the same standard, one mold for all, but still—at the mention of his daughter, the smile works, comes out warm, likeable, brightens his face—he's basically a handsome man, even exotic-looking, so what if his shape let him down a bit.

And I do smile back and say thank you, and that it's very nice to hear: an automatic reaction like a camera's flash once you pushed the button, but wait, it's not over yet; he reaches into his chest pocket (No gun under his arm!—then again, should there have been?) and pulls out a notepad and shoves it at me, opened to a blank page of checkered graph paper. His daughter (with the Russian stress!) would be so thrilled to have my autograph. A loving dad—how nice. I'd be happy to, of course, only I would need a pen, too. And something for her personally, he mutters. Just a few words, one line. Of course, my pleasure. What's her name? Jeez. Very nice ... thank you ... me too.

Sheesh, that was it?! All this sending of mysterious regards to my matinka (but I'll make sure to ask Mom what his deal is, if, of course, she remembers him), all this drawn-out hanging on, and five minutes of utter bullshit—all just to get an autograph that's given to anyone free, just for the asking?

Either I'm missing something or this customer's really a little off his rocker. Not an iguana, maybe, but a different form of life for sure—the kind you have to study purposefully or you'll never figure out what's going on in its head.

"Call," he says, by way of parting, putting his precious notebook back inside the pocket of his frock, "if you need anything."

As if it were I who'd been the petitioner, and it is now I who'll be extended the privilege, as one of "their" people—of the private, backdoor access, far from the hassle of the public entrance, whenever I call, as is only right and proper among "our" people. It's like he doesn't even see Aidy anymore, doesn't look once in his direction—as if Aidy hadn't been here, and his name's not on the list, and his relatives don't merit to be sent any regards (like, for example, Dovgan Olena Ambroziivna, year of birth—1920, year of death—1947, place of death—unknown).

"Your friend ..." (a blitz pause, a double take, a quick stab of eyes: How much of a "friend" is Aidy to me really?) "has my office number. Call anytime."

I just didn't know any better and like an idiot sent Aidy down the straight and narrow honest path, through the turnstiles and security checks up front—could've saved us all a world of trouble just by using my national name, and not for official business at all, imagine that! Who'd have thought that *Diogenes' Lantern* would turn out to be Security Bureau employees' favorite show? Or, rather, the favorite show of Veronika Boozerova (poor kid, she must've gone through hell in school with a name like that!)—a Conservatory student and a future musicologist. Wow. I gotta admit sometimes it is useful to work in television; it has its perks, not just irks.

Nonetheless, we shall do just fine without any handshaking (judging by his momentary hesitation, the idea did occur to Pavlo Ivanovych). His hands, surprisingly, are not plump and stubby-fingered, but quite cultured, intelligentsia hands, but still—they must sweat. And no matter how stiff and upright he stands, his body is plain unmanly—everything sort of slipping down into the hips, pear-like. Can't find a suit coat that could hide his butt—it is too well padded, and sticks out. A woman's butt. I must be having an expressive-butt day.

Finally, we're alone. A few more steps toward the Golden Gates (without speaking, we both head for the café next to the fountain)—and Aidy hooks his arm around my neck and lets it ride there, heavy like a small hungry animal with a mind to dart, nip below, and just as instinctively, I hug his torso, fall into step with him, let my side gnaw into his, and feel his warmth: the law of communicating vessels, as he says. And if Pavlo Ivanovych Boozerov is compelled by the incorrigible habits of his trade to watch us from around the corner (or whatever it was Shtirlitz always did), that's his own problem. Let him go choke on his chops.

"He, when he saw you, couldn't get his pants down fast enough!" Aidy laughs. "You should've heard him in his office, before he signed my request: Who are you, and where from, and what for, and who's she to you, and where did you get this information—a proper interrogation. By the end of it I began to seem suspicious to myself ... and then—what a change!"

"Behold the power of a father's love."

"And Lolly's popularity, let's not forget that!"

"Yeah, especially among the SB types. By the time I go on air, he's out like a log, I promise you—I've no doubt he goes to bed right after the news. A fan—please!"

"All the same, Lolly ... you're a TV star, a celebrity, and that pulls some weight—you can't deny it. He must've had to make up that whole send regards to Olga Fedorivna thing right on the fly, just to rub elbows with you."

"You think?"

"Bet my life on it. Anything to show that he's not some pencil pusher, a no-name mutt. You'll see; call your mom—I bet Olga Fedorivna will be very surprised."

"Boozerov—how would you like that for a last name?"

"I almost lost it when he introduced himself. Took all I had not to crack."

"What'd he say back in the archive? Just stick to his Pavlo Ivanovych?"

"I'm telling you, he was too good to look at me back there. As friendly as a rhino in heat."

"But at least he signed your inquiry, didn't he?"

"He signed it alright, said they'll look, but they give no guarantee whatsoever that they'll find anything. There's only hope for those who enter here ... something like that. At least now he'll get his ass out of his chair."

"God, and Veronika Boozerova—who names their child like that! And what, I wonder, do they call her at home—Vera? Nika? Rona?"

"Nika probably. Rona—that's too high culture."

"Well, he's not a cop, after all—he's, like, intelligence service, no? Daughter a Conservatory student ... and did you see, he's got quite decent hands?"

"I've met cultured cops, too. Once ..."

Aidy launches into a long and funny story—the story itself may not be all that funny, but the way he tells them, all his stories, is very funny, or, rather, he knows how to infect you with the sense of fun he has with whatever he's talking about. He's got the power of suggestion, the gift of puppies and small children, reserved only for the truly talented among the adults, people of beautiful and pure soul. And I am laughing my head off listening to how the charitable Aidy and his friends taught a cop to play bridge on a computer when said cop showed up in the middle of the night in response to a call from their highly obnoxious neighbor, while they were having a rocking good time, and what came of that. His stories are often raw, bratty, full of street-smart gallows humor that's irreverent, irresistible, and always draws you in, with its youthful excess of vitality but more with its organic innocence, its unfamiliarity with the darker sides of life, or maybe, the carefree disregard for them that borders on courage and most often turns out to be precisely that.

Somehow, incredibly, Aidy retains this purely boyish, friendly openness toward everyone he meets—as if the only things he ever expected from them were new and exciting adventures. People usually sense this, and the waitress who comes to our table to take the order, a blonde as pale as a flour weevil, also falls under his spell and begins to radiate friendliness, even throws in something in Ukrainian although the language doesn't come smoothly from her lips. It's always like that with Aidy, everywhere we go; I noticed this when things were just starting with the two of us, back when we were still on formal terms, and everywhere—in a line at the post office, in a taxi, at a video-rental kiosk—we goofed around and hollered and laughed out loud, and I saw the way everyone reacted, the loosened-up smiles that would spark around us, as if everyone remembered something nice, private, something long sunk in their memory; and that's when I first realized that I wasn't just imagining what was going on between us, that others could see it too.

The fountain splashes, drops of water fly out and land on us, the sun crawls out, adding color to the world, and the people around the other tables become somehow instantly more glamorous. Aidy finishes his story about the cultured cop, then reaches out and carefully extracts a miniscule shriveled leaf out of my hair. The weevil brings our beers, places the mugs on the dark-green rounds labeled Obolon, and timidly offers, "Nice and sunny, ain't it?"

We unanimously decide to consider Adrian Vatamanyuk's first raid on the SB archives a success and its unplanned finale especially remarkable. Spontaneity, Aidy declares with feeling, that's what one needs to appreciate more in life—a deflection of an electron that determines the fate of a universe. The deflected electron—is that supposed to be Pavlo Ivanovych? The comical Pavlo Ivanovych, the middle-aged squid drilled into military shape, with the eagle's profile, eyes of a harem prima donna, and the name of a hereditary Ryazan boozer, a twelfth-generation wino.

"You know," Aidy says, "I can't shake off the feeling that I've seen him somewhere before. Something about his face looks familiar ..."

"With a face like that—you couldn't forget the man if you wanted to!"

"It's really something, isn't it? Extraordinary. The eyes especially."

"Do you think that's why they stuck him in the archives? Couldn't be an operative with a mug like that—they were all supposed to be plain nobodies ... unrecognizable."

May Pavlo Ivanovych hiccup gently over his lunch.

A pigeon lands, shakes himself, businesslike, and scampers between the tables looking for something to eat. Must be local, this is his spot. Them pigeons, they must have the place divvied up like the mob—who gets the park, the square, the café. You could make a separate map—the pigeon Kyiv—with flight trajectories, high points where a decent pigeon can take five, and, of course, the places where they can always find some grub. Plus the warning signs: cars, cats—you see so many dead pigeons in the streets, so lazy they can't even bother to lift their butts from under the wheels.

"Still," Aidy says, shaking his head stubbornly as if trying to chase off a fly that's buzzing inside, "I've seen him somewhere before, I swear."

"You're just like Mykolaichuk's Vasyl in *The Lost Letter*: 'Listen, dude, where'd I see you before?'"

All of a sudden Aidy slaps himself on the forehead, and his eyes light up with mischievous little sparks.

"And what did we forget, huh?"

"What?"

"Des-sert!" He makes horrified eyes. "We forgot about dessert!" And, twisting, he waves at the waitress. "What's on the tray today?"

***

The phone rings. (Not a bad opening for a script, Daryna thinks, half-asleep, anchorwoman at a still-independent TV channel—wait, nope, no longer independent, two days already not "in-"—and here a hot twist, a turn of the corkscrew in the pit of her stomach wakes her up completely. The previous day's conversation with her boss rises in her mind. She didn't dream it—but her train of thought keeps rolling, automatically, on its no-longer-necessary filmmaking track, not a bad opening for a script: it's dark on screen, and in this darkness, the phone is ringing, an antique, prewar sound, *tiling-tiling-tiling*, like Alpine cowbells—you're the cow, stupid, what antique sound? Those are the bells from the Milka commercial. Shit, brain's stuffed so full of rubbish she can't dig up what she's really thinking from under all that. And why, in the name of grace, would anyone rouse a person at this ungodly hour—crap, it's not early at all, ten o'clock already!)

The phone is ringing, and she slowly forces her foggy head to face it with a sense of deep hatred for the whole world—whatever that world may have contrived for her during the night, she does not expect it to be anything good: it hurts everywhere her thoughts turn. Like she's been beaten. Well, isn't that what they did? Stripped and pummeled her like a no-good, truck-stop whore and tossed the body under the trees in the windbreak. Only there isn't a dog out there who'd call the police if he saw it.

The number comes up: it's Mom. Oh no. Please, not this, not now. With Mom it's even worse than with strangers: she has to parade in full splendor of your success the same as for everyone else, but somehow feel vulnerable as a cornered rabbit the whole time. And it doesn't get more vulnerable than this, now.

Nonetheless, she picks up obediently and presses the answer button: filial duty, nothing to be done about it. Hasn't called her mother for three days—pay up.

"Hi, Ma." (God, just listen her voice—she sounds like a crow!) "How are you?"

This question always elicits the same response: her mother starts talking about her husband's complaints—Uncle Volodya is slowing down, little by little. He's got arthritis, can't really bend his knee anymore; he'll need surgery; his sugar is elevated, needs another round of IVs—aging has recently become an all-consuming topic for the elder Goshchynska, and the younger treats it with the sympathy of a devoted sports fan, albeit one currently following a different league. It is really not unlike a match—only drawn out in time, with its own rules, which no one explains ahead of time, and, unfortunately, with a predetermined outcome: you're being shoved, at first with small, and then increasingly more debilitating blows, off the highway and into that same windbreak. Your withering body, as it prepares to become earth, rehearses its decomposition through a collection of infirmities, sore spots, and affected organs; breathing and moving become tasks that demand undivided attention; the morning evacuation is an event that sets the tone for the rest of the day; and all this makes the participants of the process members of a closed club, with its own champions and underdogs. And Uncle Volodya, by design, should've belonged among the former, should've proven a professional of aging—what else did he spend his life training for digging around in people's innards, in the gaping flesh of rotten and damaged meaty fruits, where there should be no surprises left for him?

But it didn't work out like that: Uncle Volodya whines like a child, resenting the slightest physical discomfort; the disloyalty of his own body, which is turning into an enemy minefield—one wrong step and you're in the ditch—is experienced by him as a personal affront, an injustice that he, of all people, most certainly does not deserve, and in which his wife appears to be somehow complicit. He hasn't given up enough to trust that she is on his side; he still believes he can go it alone; he is still kicking, creaking along, the old stump.

What Daryna fears and expects, with subconscious dread, to hear every time her mother calls is the news that Uncle Volodya hustled up an affair with some young nurse or assistant, his last mad love—with the packing of suitcases and, God forbid, division of property, and her mother's tumble into the prospect of lonely old age. These things happen more often than you think; every fading man's battle with his own body unfolds according to the same unchanging plan, and the appearance of a woman thirty or forty years his junior in it is as inevitable as menopause is for women. And when this stage of events is late in coming, you begin to worry, against your better nature—come on, already, you bastard, go ahead and do it, and get it over with! But the bastard seems to be taking his sweet time, and for today, it appears, red alert shall also be postponed. At least that's one piece of good news in the last twenty-four hours (if one considers no news to be good news).

Mom is babbling cheerfully as usual, rattling off drugs she's planning to buy, and also, it seems, something's grieving their cat (a varmit that entertains himself by leaping onto guests from the top of a wardrobe or lurching from under a couch and sinking his teeth into your leg, but Mom and Uncle Volodya fawn over him like proud parents over their firstborn). "Go have him fixed already," Daryna drones flatly as if uttering someone else's lines, as she always does—a certain set of phrases is repeated in every conversation with her mother as if on a recording. (Or does this also belong to the rules of aging—same words, same things, same scratchy records: avoid all changes in the environment because the ones going on inside your body are enough to drive you nuts alone?) "Cut 'im and live in peace." Who does she have in mind when she says that: the cat, or Uncle Volodya? Or, perchance, R. and their sordid story, as a delayed reaction to what she'd heard from her boss yesterday?

The mere memory of it is like a burn in her brain—she almost moans out loud again, you bitches!—but stops herself. She's got it under control already; she's awake, good morning, Ukraine. Lord, she used to be so proud to say those words on air. The last thing she needs now is to start bawling, so Daryna, teeth clenched, breathes hard through her nose, short and quick, in-out, in-out—until the stifling wave ebbs, retreats, and her eyes blink off a pair of tears that tickle her cheeks as they run down her skin. Olga Fedorivna, meanwhile, says she can't do it—feels sorry for the living thing, meaning Barsik, the cat, what's he done to be crippled like that?

But she must be sensing something uncertain on the other end of the line—or maybe she's unnerved by the pause that's stretching too long. The boundary of acceptance—the line of demarcation plowed between mother and daughter once and forever a long time ago, the flagged strip of no-man's-land along which they stroll, each on her side, smiling to one another from afar like border guards of friendly nations—is not something Olga Fedorivna has ever dared cross. Generally, she is not a woman who crosses lines, clinging instinctively to every chilling interaction protocol instead, as if she feared that left to her own devices she'd melt into a little puddle on the floor. Like a snowman brought indoors.

Once when she was little, Daryna did bring one of those in—a small, doll-sized, and very dapper (as it seemed to her) snowman she made herself—and wanted to show off to her mom, and what stayed in her memory—the next frame stamped into her mind—was her mom wiping away the puddle on the kitchen floor, wringing out the rag into the sink and crying. That was the first time she'd seen her mom cry, and she didn't grasp right away what was happening—at first it looked like she was laughing, only somehow not her usual way. What happened there, in the interval between those two frames—why was she crying?

Mom—Retired Snow Maiden. The long-established script dictates that it is she, the daughter, who must supply prompts in their conversation—lines like ready-made molds that the mother eagerly fills, scooping up snow with both hands. And this pause that is now spreading in the receiver like the puddle on the floor (Daryna even remembers the floor: plank, painted brown with oil paint, with pale crescents of scratches where a table had been moved), while the daughter hurries to swallow her tears and mentally wring herself out into an invisible sink, regaining her ability to pretend, this pause is like a flood, rising quickly, quickly, ever quicker under the neutral strip they'd constructed between them. Another moment and the whole pile will shift, slip, and slide, and the daughter won't be able to babble that everything's fine (couldn't be crappier, really—meaning, it could, of course, but someone'd be calling an ambulance then). It's just that she was still asleep, and she hasn't called because she's been busy, tons of work, barely keeping her head above the water. (No worries, she'll soon be unemployed and free as a bird—actually, what is she going to do then? Hang out online for twelve hours a day? Have Mom teach her all her recipes and wait, dinner on the table, for Aidy to come home? Aidy told her not to worry, that he could support them both—said it with a proud note in his voice even, or at least that's what she heard, and she got upset, because she saw the typical male egotism in it: Couldn't find another time to boast your financial potency? Boasting probably couldn't have been further from his mind; it's just she, oozing her wounded suspiciousness of everything and everyone, like toothpaste squeezed from a tube— the defining characteristic of all the defenseless and humiliated. How quickly she takes on this role!)

All of a sudden, Daryna becomes truly scared: she sees herself in the emptiness of a moonlit landscape, in the zone of absolute loneliness, like Uncle Volodya with his arthritis—your misfortune isolates you, and afterward you have to learn to live anew, and with the people closest to you as well. How will she manage that?

In 1987, during Daryna's pre-graduation field studies, she was suddenly summoned into the chancellor's office, and from there taken to the First Department where a shortish KGB captain with shifty black eyes (*swoosh*—the red ID fold-up card opened under your nose; *slap*—closed, no time to see a damn thing, except maybe the captain) prattled about who-knows-what for two hours straight, like wind blowing sand at her from all sides at once, and then offered her an opportunity to "cooperate." By that time she was so worn out by her futile attempts to pin down the direction of their schizophrenic conversation—no sooner did she feel she'd almost grasp it than it slipped through her fingers again—which jumped from vague mentions of her departed father, who, it was never quite clear, was either "not guilty of anything before our government" and all but paved the way for perestroika, or somehow posthumously obliged her, Daryna, to correct his mistakes (Which ones would those be exactly?), to heavily loaded, ratty hints about her classmates, the friends with whom she hung out at Yama Café on Khreshchatyk, and then abruptly to a completely fantastical "underground organization" that the captain's institution, ostensibly, had uncovered at the university. The captain himself didn't even pretend that he believed any of what he was saying; it seemed his only goal was to determine how much and what kind of hogwash he could dump on her.

In the whole two hours, she never once managed to catch his eye, as though the little black orbs moved by their own logic, different from that of regular people—the way, they say, you shouldn't look shepherds in the eye because the dogs take it as a challenge and might just lunge for your throat. All in all, it was like having a conversation with a lunatic, when you don't dare call the nurses because you know the head doctor is mad himself—and as she fought through the quicksand of shaken reality, half-hints, and half-lies into which she sank deeper the more she tried to clear them up, she thought, with sickening horror, that this was exactly how they once talked to her father before handing him off to their mad nurses. And the fact that times had since changed (Did they really?), that it was spring of '87 outside the window and anticommunist protests whirled across the city, did not mean anything in this distorted world; and even if it did, then only inasmuch as it supplied this other side of the looking glass with new material for new schizophrenic distortions.

All of it wore her down so much that when the captain finally concluded his soliloquy (because he'd talked almost nonstop the entire time) and suggested she write some monthly reports for him, she, instead of telling him to eff off right there and then, agreed to "think about it"—compelled either by the student habit of not turning things in until the last possible moment (to win time to prepare, time to dress her refusal into an impeccably worded formula, although that was something they most certainly wouldn't give a damn about!) or by the instinctive impulse to step away from the scene of an accident first, like when you break a heel walking, and only then catch your breath and assess the situation.

That it was a mistake, she realized right away, by how obviously and instantly happy it made the captain—but the gravity of it took time to fully manifest itself, specifically the three days that would pass before their second, and final, interview. She realized she never got out, never stepped away from that terrible office—quite the opposite: it was as if she'd chosen to take on its burden, hefted it onto her own shoulders, the silly little caryatid, and schlepped it around the whole three days, more or less delirious—having the conversation with the mad nurses inside her head the whole time. *And what if … no, like this … and I'll say to him … and he'll …* (and the shortness of breath the whole time).

Later she would recognize this infestation of mind in dissidents' memoirs: people lived like that for years, wired, as if into an electric grid, trying to untangle something that by definition could not be untangled—drawn into a chess match with a schizoid. But at the time it felt like she was the only one left in the world. Her husband, Sergiy, couldn't tell her anything helpful except recalling that his mother had also been approached by the KGB with something like this once, but who hadn't been approached? Millions of people went through the same trials, and yet no collective experience emerged from it, and every rookie had to start from scratch as though he (or she) were the only one in the world—a metaphysical state, almost, like in love or in death when no other person's experience is of any use to you, and no book has words for what is happening to you, the One and Only, with the sole difference that this whole thing was sealed under the massive lid of solid, shamed silence—this was not an experience people liked to share.

Sergiy was left outside, behind the looking glass, and his inept efforts to cheer her up resembled the unnaturally lively gesticulations of people seeing someone off on a train, before it departs: those outside wave, come close to the windows, tap on the glass, make faces—and those inside are already thinking about which of their suitcases has their slippers and toothbrush in it. When the train pulls out, both sides breathe a sigh of relief.

In a few more years, she and Sergiy pulled away from their shared platform never to return, but it was during those three days that she got on the train: the experience she lived through in isolation only added to her loneliness and put more distance between her and those she had considered to be her closest people—and about this the books also said nothing.

She's always told both herself and her friends that she learned not to trust collective experience then, none whatsoever, because it was all slop and bullshit meant to befuddle the working class, and the only thing one could rely on was individual people's stories. She used her example with the captain so often—in smoking rooms at work, at populous parties (appreciating, with a secret satisfaction, the instantly soured mugs of ex-informants—although why necessarily "ex-"?: good help is always in demand)—that she wore it to the bone. Apparently, there was another thing she learned from that experience: when someone humiliates you, you must return the blow instantly and with force—it's the only way to stay on your feet. Any hesitation, moping, or attempts to explain what a good girl you really are automatically turn you into your enemies' accomplice, before you've even had a chance to catch your breath.

No, she could find no faults with her performance in yesterday's conversation; she did everything right. Daryna turns onto her stomach and presses the receiver against her ear—like a gun to her head.

"Mom."

The puddle standing still on the plank floor, the wet glare of the kitchen light like the eye of a giant fish. It was a neat snowman.

"Mom, I'm quitting my job."

A quiet rustle of fright rises in the receiver, the sound of air leaving a punctured tire. Daryna begins to comprehend, as if for the first time and with utmost clarity, that her mother has lived her entire life in anticipation of bad news. That for Olga Fedorivna good news has always been a mere interlude, a postponement. When on September 11 the Twin Towers in New York collapsed on the TV screen, Olga Fedorivna was certain that the Third World War had begun—the one she'd expected forty years earlier, during the Cuban Missile Crisis. And she wasn't the only one: Ninél Ustýmivna was so sure that stand-off fifty years ago was going to be it that she had an abortion (Because who has a child when war's about to break out?), so Vlada actually wasn't her first. The generation of being ready for the worst.

What if they hadn't been all that wrong, after all? What if that's how you should live—always prepared to see the little world you painstakingly erected like a tiny industrious ant disintegrate before your eyes, ready to start from scratch again, just as pains-takingly—pebble by pebble, twig by twig, scrap by scrap?

"That's what I figured," rumbles Olga Fedorivna, already drag-ging the first twig to her construction site, "that something was wrong, because the whole morning's been so gloomy, so queasy somehow, everything just falling out of my hands!"

This touches Daryna, surprising her—"queasy" is an amazingly apt word. She does feel foul inside, poisoned.

"So what happened, why, how?"

"What's been long time coming already. We've held out long enough anyway. They sold us, Ma."

"How?"

"The usual way, like everyone else, packed us up and sold us. The whole village, our entire channel. With all its indentured souls, including my own. We've run free long enough—time to come in."

Olga Fedorivna, a consumer of finished televised product, only allowed to peek into the production kitchen every now and then when her daughter cracks the door open, wonders naïvely to whom they'd been sold, and whether it might be possible to arrange with the new owners for *Diogenes' Lantern* to remain on air. "You might as well take a lantern if you're looking for shows like that on TV. Soon there'll be nothing to watch at all—if it's not soap operas, it's those stupid talk shows everywhere; honestly, how stupid do you have to be to watch those? One feels sorry for the hosts; and the rest—click all the channels you want—are elections, elections, elections. Let them all get elected to hell already!"

Daryna can't help but be amused by such fervent support and catches herself mentally calling, her boss, or rather, her ex-boss, as her witness: here you go, feedback from a common senior citizen! (And how long is it going to take, exactly—for her to leave *yesterday's* office, to shake off the sticky coontails of their conversation?) And where, in the name of God's grace, do they all—especially those who'd gotten to big money—get their unshakeable certainty that the audience is a herd of sheep that need only have the most insipid laboratory-protein chaff poured into its trough?

Ratings, their boss used to say piously (in the old days, back when they were a team, when they stayed up into the wee hours, high on instant coffee and their own arguments—Lord, did it all really happen; it wasn't a dream?), ratings are the objective indicator of what people want, and there you have it: entertainment, and more entertainment, and of the kind that doesn't overload the circuits upstairs. Malarkey! she'd fire back (that's when her opinion was still worth something, when it could, she thought, change something); people consume whatever they're being fed, simply because they don't have another choice. The same way you go to Big Pocket and buy those plastic-looking apples fit to hang on Christmas trees—they don't rot, don't dry up, and they'd still shine a year later—but that doesn't mean you wouldn't like a living, breathing, fresh-off-the-tree Simirenko, nice and juicy and with a real little worm inside, just that you wouldn't find any in the supermarkets, only the tin Granny Smiths—eat all you want—and there you have your rating.

Their arguments ended—a long time ago. What happened yesterday was just a line drawn under the emptiness, dead air that's been running for who knows how long, rustling with the blank frames of the played-out film. No more movies for you. She, Daryna Goshchynska, has been discarded as, by the way, many before her. Decommissioned, my dear, decommissioned, your place can always be filled with fresh meat, more agreeable and always willing to please—with a moistly open little maw and ecstatic whimpering when it's being had through every hole.

Olga Fedorivna, meanwhile, is busy spinning her own thread of thought—mother and daughter run their parallel courses like two rivers divided by the hilly terrain of incommensurate experience, making inept swerves toward confluence and missing each other time and again.

"You've been sort of edgy for a while, Daryna. I even wondered if maybe things weren't working with you and Adrian; I've been worried about you. I could see you were all nerves...."

Of course, if it's "all nerves," then it must be men troubles. Mom's logic is ironclad. But the funniest thing, Daryna thinks, is that they both guessed wrong. She, for one, has been blaming all her tension of the last year on the film about Dovganivna, like an ostrich with her head in the sand—nose and ears plugged to avoid paying any attention to the stupendous shitstorm that raged around her, muck first pooling around her ankles and then rising to her knees, making it harder and harder to move, never mind breathe: live debates were disappearing from prime time; news people complained about receiving daily thematic instructions from their channels' owners, prescribing exactly how they were to present each piece of news and about which they were to keep mute as fishes. Original programming sank under the tidal surge of Russian imports, as if life were being replaced by slipshod alien simulacra slapped together on a desktop by a sophomoric nerd— the dusk of reason falling all around. But she thought she had found a niche where "it don't flood," as Yurko liked to say; they all thought so, everyone who stayed with the channel to the end, stubbornly refusing to notice that it does, in fact, flood. Until, that is, it flooded absolutely everything in sight, and it became clear that there were no more niches—only those who pay and those who deliver the goods. Meaning, that's how those who were paying saw things, and to them it looked like the natural order of things. The unnatural part was that there appeared to be no one who would object to that view.

"That's what they offered me, Mommy, one of those imbecile talk shows."

"Instead of your *Lantern!?*"

"If you can imagine that. A show for young people. The producer said 'we're revitalizing the channel's brand.' They're betting on young audiences, and I'd get, as they saw it, a mega bonus: the youth talk show. You know the drill: Just say no to sex without a condom; we met in a karaoke bar, and so on," she stumbles, swallows the lump that's come up in her throat (assholes! assholes!) to finish. And then there's the *Miss New TV* beauty pageant—but no, she'll leave out that new part of the programming; it's not fit for Mom's ears—one shouldn't tell such things to museum workers of advanced age.

"What carry-oakie bar?" Olga Fedorivna asks, dejected.

Once again, Daryna feels her eyes fill with tears. What's the point of rubbing it in like this—for her mom, or for herself? Of all people to whine to.

"Doesn't matter, Mom, that's just an example. They want me to wear braids. Revitalize my image, you know, make it easier for the target audience to relate. You've seen those commercials: generation jeans, everything and at once?"

"Did they all lose their cotton-picking minds?"

Olga Fedorivna's voice prickles with sharp, rejuvenated notes that bring on, in a hazy fade-in, a vision in Daryna's mind from more than thirty years ago: a trim brunette in a bright yellow dress marching across the kindergarten yard beside a flummoxed teacher to whom she is reading the riot act, while little Darynka looks on through the window of the dining room, where she'd been locked up after dinner to finish the hateful sour cream—a whole glass of goo that she, in desperation, forever abandoned by everyone, sits straining, with disgust, through her puckered lips, which does nothing to lower the level of the white gunk under her nose. She looks on and a blast of joy shoots through her both for the knowledge of her imminent liberation—Mom's here!—and the shock of her first experience of *seeing from outside*: this is my mom—how beautiful she is! If only you could always remember your parents the way they were in their best years. But there's never time for that, because you've got bigger fish to fry—your own best years, which, just like theirs, pass, damn it. They pass.

The thing that really got her was that her producer never, not for a second, doubted that their offer would flatter her, that she'd be delighted by the mere fact she'd been deemed suitable for a youth talk show. And worse yet—she did, for an instant, feel flattered. Like when the driver of the car next to her at a stoplight sent her air kisses, like when men in foreign airports occasionally turn to look at her (and she could be completely sure that they didn't recognize her, that the lit-up looks and the uncontrollably loose grins were meant not for a TV star but simply for a beautiful woman, because at home you could never tell the difference—men look at attractive women and celebrities in the same way), like when a black Lexus sped up and slammed on the brakes next to her in the street, sending a fan of water into the air, so she barely managed to jump out of the way, and from behind the rolled-down window appeared the mug of a boy umpteen years her junior to say, in a leisurely Russian, like a restaurant order: "Leave your phone number, miss." (And only when she laughed into his face, could she see by his changed expression that he recognized her, fired up with a different, more preemptive interest—here it is, the power of the media: "Wait ... don't you ... don't you work on TV?")

Such things always pleased her, she won't deny it; they gave her new zest. For a moment, she was almost hypnotized, listening to her boss tell her about herself: they'll style your hair into braids, for a "frisky," as he put it, look, and dress you more casually, youthfully, from Benetton, something informal, a little top, shorts and over-the-knee boots, a miniskirt. What paralyzed her was not so much his tone of an old seducer as her own eternally feminine eagerness—to submit, spellbound, to the hands of a designer, stylist, makeup artist ... anyone who would make her different, better; and the audience, ready to appreciate their efforts, is right there. The salesgirl hands you a few more skirts that go, in her opinion, with the jacket you're trying on in the fitting room, while the man sits with his newspaper in an armchair waiting for you to come out and sashay around the store, turning in front of the mirror and smoothing the skirt over your thighs and behind, as though molding your own body—you're your own Pygmalion, the outfit your marble: What do you think? For that one moment, in yesterday's entire conversation, she did feel ashamed, but she won't tell her mother about it, no way, and her mom wouldn't understand it anyway. She's never set foot in an expensive boutique and, really, it's not like Uncle Volodya could sit in that armchair waiting for the shape-shifting séance with the Sphinx smile of a man who will pay for everything in the end. No, their generation did not get to experience as many of life's joys as ours, and isn't this precisely what makes us, in our heart of hearts, look down on them?

"That's right, Mom, and that's exactly what I told him—and that I won't be made into a public spectacle."

That was not what she said, not what she said at all. She only knocked him off his tone—a bed-broker's business tone in which he proceeded to wrap her up and tie her with a bow. She went to the edge of his desk and perched there like a stripteuse, jerked up her sweater, flashed him with her bare belly and asked him in that angrily ringing voice whose cracked shards can still—who knew—sometimes be heard in her mother's voice, "And how about my navel—have it pierced, or are you chicken?"

He broke off, forgetting to shut his mouth, dithered, and waved her off, meaning, stop it—but got back on track right away, regained his balance, glibbed with a chuckle, "Yum, I'd like a piece of that!" But from that moment on, spoke with her as with an equal, an accomplice. (How apt that old actress had been who told her once, after a session, when they were sitting in the old woman's pauper kitchen drinking tea with biscuits that had obviously been diligently scrubbed clean of mold before being served: "When push comes to shove, sweetie, it is better to be a whore than *a thing*.") All she did was shove him a step off the top of the mountain where he'd clambered and stood, triumphantly, engrossed in self-admiration, and then rolled, rambling, down all by himself, dragging her with him and scraping her bloody along the way; but that part—about her boss, about R.—was not for telling Mom either, that was for her to figure out on her own.

"And what did he say to that?" Olga Fedorivna persists, apparently still clinging to something, something that looks to her like hope. Daryna feels a small stab of annoyance. When she was young, her mother's insistence on using details to shield herself from reality, this clinging to small things (after Daryna's father's death she kept telling everyone how well he ate the day he died—porridge, carrot juice) used to drive her to distraction, made her want to slap her mother: Wake up, already! Youth has no idea yet of the effort the art of survival demands—it is an incredibly vacuous age. And we're at such pains to stretch it out for as long as possible.

"Mom, you're like the sheriff in *Natalka Poltavka*: and what'd you say to that, and what'd she say to you?"

It's not like she could tell her how the boss went on to explain to her, as an intelligent woman, all the obvious advantages of the new course. First playing to her weakness (no one could say he didn't know his personnel!)—her incurable need to be liked, the curse of the good girl (with, of course, what else, big bows in her braids) that's been hanging around her neck her entire life; to have people applaud, to be praised, wow, Darynka's such a smart girl, did such a nice job reciting that poem!—and then appealing to her ambitions, of which there are plenty. How else? Who would ever agree, if they had no ambition, to dunk their visually rounded mug like a goldfish into millions of living-room aquariums twice a week: This is *Diogenes' Lantern*, and I am Daryna Goshchynska.... We'll be back after a break ... (The cosmic blackness on the other side of the studio floodlights aimed at her—effectively blinding her—seem to be populated, like a giant auditorium stretching out to infinity. It's as if millions of eyes are looking at her from there, and every time, even after seven years on air, it seems people are sitting out there, very still, waiting, ready to creak their chairs, cough if she strikes a false note, even though there are no chairs in the studio except the one under her; she can feel that populous held breath in the space between her and the screen, the eyes of those to whom she speaks—they hold her up as water holds a swimmer.)

Boss leaned hard on the new "scale"—another ace slapped onto the table (the table in his office was now imposing, oak, fit for a game of pool)—and the scale did impress: prime-time promotion, billboards and ads on the subway; they'll make her into a cult figure of the new generation. What the hell else does she want? He strutted; he was proud of himself—it occurred to her that it was he, in fact, who wanted to earn her praise, as would any man from a smart and beautiful woman, but still something was off: something was gnawing at him; there was a gap, a hole he wanted her to help close.

Just recently, about a month before, they were celebrating his housewarming—he'd moved into a new apartment, a magnificent, newly renovated, two-story next to the Opera Theater. It had to have set him back half a million bucks at least—the expansive living room with a brick fireplace, the marble-finished bathrooms like Roman thermae. And it was there, while the guests were touring the pantheonic bathrooms, to their happy laughter (pierced, time and again, like expensive upholstery with stubbed-out cigarettes, with uncontainable, hissing ahhs of envy), that Antosha, their cameraman whom they'd dubbed Occam's Razor for his fast adherence to the principle of finding the most basic explanation for every human action and for being almost never wrong

("If your cynicism is what's called the wisdom of life, Antosha,"
she used to say, half-kidding, "then I wish to die stupid." And he
answered with his latent alcoholic's suggestively loony half-grin,
"You should be so lucky, hon!"), grunted, quiet and short, like a
spit: "That's it, the boss hit some big-ass pay dirt; time to jump
this rig." Meaning their channel, which was already sinking fast,
turning, like all the others, into a corporation, a front for some
uncouth money-laundering enterprises, and their captain, their
boss and breadwinner, their producer and co-founder, drenched in
sweat, as if he'd come from the shower, darted, like a halfback on
a football field, across his cavern of a living room from one VIP to
another, desperately ingratiating himself: *Pyotr Nikolaich, have some
sushi. You like it, don't you? Aleksei Vasil'yich, a drop of vodka?* (There
weren't many of them at the party, those men of Vadym's ilk, with
identical occiputs sunk into soft cushions of fat that make their
heads resemble pool balls dropped straight onto their shoulders;
Daryna knew almost none of them—there weren't many, but a
single type like that is enough to spoil an evening.)

And at some point, after another one of his bendings-over-
backwards, the boss must have caught Daryna looking at him—
probably sneering a bit. But no, she must've been still sympathetic,
because at the time she still thought this was all for the channel's
sake, that the boss was slavering the movers and shakers for their
collective sake, for the cause, to keep the channel afloat—ate shit,
bless his soul, every day so that Goshchynska could grow flowers
on the air. Well, flowers always grow on shit, and television is no
different from a beautiful woman: Does anyone blowing her kisses
through his car's window wonder about the inner workings of her
guts, about the smack of fecal matter inside her intestines, whose
regularity, by the way, is directly responsible for her radiant complexion? Except that here it wasn't fecal but financial flows that were
being pumped and someone did have to insure their regularity.

That's what she thought, pinching her delicate little nose,
because in that gigantic tele-organism the role she was meant to
play, after all, was not that of the colon but rather of the radiant

visage, "the face of the channel." And under that understanding look of hers, extended to him over the well-fed shoulders and masticating heads, the boss, as if waking up from a dream, suddenly looked triumphantly, conspiratorially, over his smoke-filled cavernous salon, literally smoothed the salon over himself—just like a woman, out of the dressing room, smoothes a new skirt over her thighs—gathered it all in, weighed it, and offered it to her, the whole thing with himself in the middle, with the same feminine inquiring anxiety in his look: What do you think? As if she were the one who held the controlling interest, as if the whole show would instantly lose its meaning without her approval.

She remembers it seemed really funny to her at the time, and she laughed at him from across the table (she'd had too much to drink), saluting him with her glass in a mute toast: Cheers, sweetheart, here's to you! And Lord, how he bloomed in return, glowing as if she'd lifted a rock off his shoulders, lightened his burden! And she had no clue that by then the channel's fate was, must have been, already decided. Antosha, as always, had been right, and the controlling interest was being passed into someone else's hands entirely—the ones that took her by the throat yesterday, using her boss's hands to do the work. The same boss who saw her as an accomplice and continued to need her approval: You're on the right path, comrades! Kiss my ass, asshole.

It's hard to believe, isn't it?, she asks in her head—not of her mother (she doesn't talk to her mother in her head) but of Adrian, with whom she is also unlikely to share this observation out loud because it's not the kind of thing that you share with anyone, period—where do they all go, these observations that no one ever shares with anyone and that just gather dust in the dark corners of people's brains? It's hard to believe how much in this life is determined, sometimes, by a single accidental phrase, a single look—a conspiratorial glance, an encouraging expression across the room, just like that—and someone picks it up eagerly, grabs your hand, and drags you into their cabal, lifting the lid on such a teeming subterranean nest of worms that you would have preferred not to have seen, never even wanted to know existed.

And it all starts with the commonest little misunderstanding—you were simply misunderstood. The world is full of crossed signals, and no one really understands anyone anymore. Such scale, such opportunities, such a leap in her career—what is wrong with her? The boss really could not understand, and if he were pretending, then only very little. And what about her project, her unfinished film? He blinked when she asked about that, as if trying to remember: What film? He'd forgotten already, he had erased that file from his memory—some people are lucky like that, they have the serendipitous gift of forgetting everything unnecessary. "The one about the UIA or something?"

"You know what he said to me, Ma? About my *Lantern*? He said no one needs my heroes. That they are not the heroes in touch with the times."

In touch with the times, how wonderfully apt—it slashed her like a blade. Pyotr Nikolaich, Aleksei Vasil'yich—they've bought this time, just as they bought airtime. They thought themselves the major figures, no, the only heroes of life's written drama; they believed, especially for themselves, and they lived their lives with this belief—until the last control shot to the head. But the boss, the boss! He's not one of them; he's not of their breed. He was a talented journalist once; he made that fantastic film in the early nineties, about the little Chernivtsi kids who'd gone bald. (A rocket fuel spill at a nearby army base, wasn't it? The city should've really been evacuated—wait, wait, but the story somehow got hushed down after that, never came up again, and, just a minute, if she recalls correctly, the man who was investigating the cause of the disaster, a local, didn't he disappear, die quietly under mysterious circumstances?) If she's not mistaken? It's hard not to be mistaken, hard to keep it all straight in her memory, when the memory's long overburdened, the system's overloaded, and her head has long ago turned into a computer box, cluttered, with snippets of film, with frames of unidentified provenance, shots of who-knows-where and faces with names unstuck from them (this has happened a thousand times: the face—you recognize, the person—no). And she tells herself she's delivering information to people, but all she actually does is add to the piles of snippets in their heads and so help them *forget* because she doesn't remember squat herself, except whatever's blinking right in front of her, on whatever narrow strip is cleared of rubbish to fit in what's due today.

Shit, what if she is really in the wrong business?

"They're the ones out of touch," Olga Fedorivna responds, bitterly, and Daryna vaguely registers that she invests these words with something private, invisible, and inaccessible to her. And then her mother adds, though it's not clear about whom, "Roaches."

A rickety bridge is in those words, a narrow plank thrown from one bank to the other. Daryna can sense it but has no time to listen to it; she's riding her own current—and not only out of the pure momentum of an active life that never really hears those who'd dropped out of the system (Because what could they possibly tell us—the retired, the jobless, the homeless, the bankrupted, the crumpled wrappers swept to the edge of the sidewalk where we click-clack so dashingly along in our brand-new Bally heels that they'll never be able to afford?) but because she is, quite simply, overrun with indignity, great and intolerable. She's got a fresh hole gaping inside her, and she's just begun to mend it. She's too busy attending to herself, like Uncle Volodya with his arthritis. (The conversation with the boss, retold to her mother in a slightly different edition from the one for Adrian the night before, acquires new contours in her mind in the course of retelling, in being fit together; this is the only thing that's important to her at the moment—to re-dub and edit yesterday's footage in her memory into such form as can be turned into an asset and lived with from now on.) All she needs is a grateful audience with supportive oohs, but her mom keeps falling out of character and darting off track, still somehow failing to grasp into which molds she's supposed to fit and to turn into ice. She's getting old, that's a fact: losing her flexibility, losing her quickness. But "roaches"—there's something to it: Mother does have a feel for words, not for nothing did she write poems when she was young, but then again, who didn't back then, in the sixties. The boss now strikes Daryna as not unroach-like at all, despite the fact that he never wore mustache. It would fit him. A sort of neurotic jerking of the nose, which became more conspicuous the more nervous he got yesterday—like he's constantly smelling something disgusting. Antosha even maintained, for a long time already, that the boss had to be doing cocaine, and after last night Daryna was inclined to believe it. A man can't just live in that cloaca; he's got to do something at least about the smell.

"You know what I'm really sorry about, Ma? That story I had planned for next week, did I tell you about it?"

"You never tell me anything."

Here we go—the guilt trip.

"That's not true, I do. The story was really heroic, no spin—about a surgeon from a district town in Donets'k Oblast, one of those, you know, mining ghost towns where every living thing has fled, and three-room apartments go for three-hundred bucks, and whole city blocks stand vacant. The surgeon's salary is two-hundred-and-forty hryvnas, less than your pension. So, he gets called to emergency surgery in the middle of the night, and runs out—the streets are dark, no lights—and falls into a hole, and breaks his leg; then crawls like that, one leg broken, all the way to his hospital somehow, where he does the surgery. And only afterward lets them take him to the trauma unit—they had two gurneys ready after the surgery, one for the patient, and the other for his doctor. Men like that still live in this country. Tell Uncle Volodya so at least his colleagues will know."

What she does *not* say, because it smarts like a fresh cut, is how she'd spoken to the man on the phone just the other day when arranging for the film crew. He had a wonderfully kind voice, cozy like felt slippers, and he stuttered a bit, must've been taken aback—imagine that, TV was coming all the way from Kyiv to talk to him.

And right after that they called her into the boss's office. What Donets'k Oblast? Who cares? Forget it! Boss even switched to Russian as he always does when he loses self-control. The Donets'k Oblast was now to be portrayed as a land of sweeping prosperity, practically Switzerland, or better still, not portrayed at all. And then he said that thing about her heroes—that no one needs them; the show is cancelled. How to look that doctor in the eye now?

And Mom, having ooh'ed at her daughter's every word with hungry attention, proceeds to rub salt into the fresh wound. She waxes poetic that exactly, exactly the people like this surgeon are the backbone of this country—like she's tapping her pointer on an exhibit for the benefit of an invisible tour group: "These are the kind of people who hold this world together, have held it since creation, and they must be known! Because when you don't know such people are out there, it is very hard to go on living."

She is speaking about herself, Daryna suddenly realizes. About how she once had to go on living without that knowledge—for how many years? Seven? No, more than that—living as the wife of a certified schizoid. Engineer Goshchynsky had also once crawled like that at night along his very dark street with a broken leg—until they broke his spine, too. And all around, everyone else was normal, and no one crawled anywhere—people bought furniture and went on vacations to Sochi. Like we go to Antalya now. Those who didn't go did not have a voice then and don't have it now, and we're better off not knowing they exist at all.

A museum worker made eighty rubles a month. Uncle Volodya, a rich man by Soviet standards, after the wedding also took his Olya to Sochi. They wanted Daryna to come, too, but back then she was so angry that she signed up for the student harvest brigade instead and bedded Sergiy on the second night of the trip, on his windbreaker spread out on the sand. He had to throw it out afterward. From that first time, the thing she remembered most vividly was the draft between her legs, when she lay under the sky with her panties off. That, and the triumphant knowledge that she and her mother were now equals, that she couldn't be told what to do. It's possible that if it weren't for Sergiy—if the windbreaker didn't unfold into long nights of wandering, poems on a boat, and her tears on his chest (wet stains on his T-shirt—she was marking the poor guy from all her glands)—she would've slept with the whole brigade that summer, would've erected a paling of phalluses between herself and her mother, not knowing then, in the blindness of her youth, that it's not a way out. There is never a way out from one's mother; it's life without parole.

For the first time in her life, Daryna realizes she had never tried to imagine—as if she passed a door a thousand times and it never occurred to her to peek inside—how, in fact, her mother lived all those dark years that were now stored in her attic in the four bulging folders knotted shut. How did she endure, frozen into Snow Maiden's trim, upright form, Father's entire hopeless struggle, and the crushing bulk of her environment, and the fear creeping under the doors, the bandits in the stairwell, vans with red crosses on them, the Dnipropetrovsk asylum, and afterward—three years of wandering in and out of hospitals with the urine-soaked remnant of what once had been the man she loved, without the knowledge, back then, that he was not the only one, that others were also crawling into their own dead ends, a whole, uncountable in the dark army of defeat's heroes?

And then she married again—and got heavy within a year, like all of her folded, suddenly crumbled, even her face. Uncle Volodya taught her to eat well, unlocked her dormant culinary talents. In the years her father was committed, those talents wouldn't have been of any use; the two of them mostly lived on boiled potatoes. Daryna loved them when she was little, and still does—mashed, peasant-style, with sour milk, sprinkled with parsley if you have some—what's not to like? A teenager has other problems, and adult children do, too, and you always miss your parents in time. And generally, living side by side with someone does not mean bearing witness to his or her life. But how did she endure, all the way until Father's death, *what* held her?

Daryna recognizes very clearly that this question is now directly relevant to her own life: yesterday she, too, closed a door that no one will be in a great rush to open in order to find out how she's doing in there. She's already felt the grip of emptiness, the air of solitary confinement—yesterday, after leaving boss's office, when she curtly informed her guys that *Lantern* had been cancelled and that she would not be working in the new format she'd been offered. (But nothing about the *Miss New TV* show!) She was not, of course, expecting the guys to rouse the whole channel to a general strike in protest. (Or did she, in her heart of hearts?) Besides, everyone's been waiting for something nasty like this for a long time and this turbid anticipation weighed on them. Even the jokes in the smoking rooms were getting blacker and dirtier by the day, and while the storm clouds gathered on the horizon, folks began cutting out, resigning, scampering away like little mice, but something else stung her: that the guys, after they cursed and vented their shared bile (because the *Lantern* was their common brainchild, conceived and gestated together, a hacked-off chunk of their lives) and asked her if she was really going to leave the channel (and whether she had her eye on anything, oh yes, they were most curious about that), were suddenly no longer with her— she felt it: they withdrew inside, let her slip from the grip of their attention. Every one of them was already busy assessing his own prospects, scheming which way to paddle and how to recalibrate himself, and she was already outside the circle, standing there with everything she left unsaid scrunched into a crooked grin on her lips like one hose leg pulled on.

Vovchyk, her director of so many years that they were basically family, even he made this unpleasantly preoccupied face, as if he'd just remembered some very important business, when she said the thing about banditry and whoring—that she was not about to be part of that, and she realized that Vovchyk *would* stay, under whatever ownership, and *would be part* of that, and was offended by her determination *not* to, by her instantly taking away his one shot at not feeling like a piece of shit while he did what he was going to do. Here's the first person who's *happy* to see her go; start the count, who's next?

Of course, she was in no danger of eating mashed potatoes for lunch and dinner—she was merely in the same danger that awaits all outsiders: the danger of loneliness. Sit at home with your man (and thank the Good Lord that you have a decent man!) and eat your moral superiority all you want, while life races on without you. As soon as you disappear from the screens, everyone'll forget about you—better people have been forgotten. It's not the movies, hon (as Antosha says), not some classic locked into a vault, with a small chance of coming back to light one day—this is television. The show must go on. And she's always been in public and with the public; she loves the public and is used to being loved in return—and how's she to endure all this now, on moral superiority alone?

And, almost surprising herself, not thinking about the words, just the way it bursts out of her, head first into the deep end, Daryna asks her mother, "Mom, did you believe in Dad?"

Pause.

"I mean, when they took him away?"

Mom understood the question—remarkably she is not surprised by this turn of their conversation; she is simply looking for words she doesn't have readily available; she's working through the thickets of the many years of silence inside her.

"I knew that everything he was doing was right."

"Did it make things easier for you?"

"Sweetie, is 'right' always easy?"

This comes out with such overwhelming, ancient sadness that for a moment Daryna is petrified. Her mother may not be a hero, but you couldn't call her stupid either.

"No. Not always."

Both grow silent then, sensing themselves on unfamiliar territory and hesitating before the next step. Olga Fedorivna suddenly chuckles softly—from afar, as if really from the other side of thirty years.

"You know, I never told you this … when Tolya was in Dnipropetrovsk …" (This Tolya startles Daryna like a tang of a string: usually Mother says Father or Dad, but now she is talking about a man she had once loved, and not to her daughter but to a grown woman, maybe even to herself.) "in daytime I could somehow manage to keep my mind busy—at work, the tour groups saved me, and then I had to find food; back then it was another full-time job, to stand in all those lines. I remember on a Sunday once I'd gone to every market—Zhytni, Sinny, Lukyanivsky, Volodymyrsky—no meat anywhere, they all sold out before dawn! And you had anemia then, and the school doctor said …" (How strange, Daryna thinks—she remembers none of that, only remembers that her period started later than other girls' and for a long time she was troubled by the feeling that she'd suddenly slipped from the top of her class in everything to the bottom, and when she finally "had visitors" she was so thrilled she bragged to another straight-A student, Oksana Karavayeva, "I'm a young woman now!" and Oksana sneered into her face and said, "So go buy yourself a medal!") "you had to have meat, even if just a little, even mixed with bread into cutlets, and it was all just empty shelves all around. I'll try the Besarabsky Market yet, I thought; that's a chance. So I went all the way there, and it was getting dark already—and they were locking up, right under my nose.… I just fell against a wall and wailed out loud! That I cried, that was the first time—after they took Tolya, for a long time I couldn't. Went all hard inside, a piece of wood. At night, after I was done cleaning, washing everything …" (Daryna's memory helpfully retrieves the long-forgotten: the humid haze of laundry in the apartment, steam from the sheets being boiled on the stove, windows in the kitchen fogged, and the wooden handle from an old butterfly net with which her mother, hair wet and face glistening with sweat, like a dockhand, turned the bedsheets, which distended into giant bubbles above the rim of the enormous pot. Did she do laundry almost every other day on purpose back then, to help her forget?) "after I make it all clean, and you're already asleep—that's when I was fit to climb up the wall! And no sleep, none, no matter how much I'd worn myself out. I better figure something out lest I lose my mind, I thought. So I thought this up: I'd lie down and close my eyes, and start playing movies in my head. I'd lie there and imagine Tolya's come back already, so handsome, finer than before, and that they restored the Palace Ukraina the way it was at first—I'd see every little piece of parquet in my mind, how they're laid out, like shadows, this chimerical optical effect it made—and that they're giving Tolya medals up on the stage, everyone thanking him for saving such beauty, saying it's all his work, he did it.... Everyone rises, and applauds, and they bring in flowers, big basket arrangements, and set them on the proscenium like on an opening night—and I'm sitting in the box, in an evening gown with open shoulders; Tolya used to say I had Bryullov shoulders and it was a sin ever to hide them, they were a national treasure ..." (Daryna remembers her mom's bright yellow dress, also, yes, with a portrait collar—her high neck, hair done up; the dress had lasted until she met Uncle Volodya, who must have also decided that such shoulders shouldn't go to waste—Mom must've worn that dress for at least ten years, not much room for new clothes in eighty rubles a month with a teenage daughter.) "and I'd lie there like that, and dream, and dream, all so nice, like I'm putting a spell on myself—until I fall asleep. All the while knowing perfectly well, crystal clear," Olga Fedorivna chuckles again, as if confessing to some childhood mischief, "that I'm making it all up, that it's not there and won't ever be—but it still feels better. Like a sort of drug."

"Daydreaming," Daryna squeezes out, trying to make it sound considered (all diagnoses always sound considered, even the deadly ones). "It's a term in psychology."

"Really?" Olga Fedorivna responds absentmindedly. The fact that a secret game she'd invented for herself and never told a soul in thirty years (One wonders, what does she talk about with her current husband?) has apparently been classified, named, and filed in the corresponding drawer with a label on the front, fails to impress her.

Generally speaking, Olga Fedorivna has little patience for generalizations, an instinctive distrust of them whether they are scientific terms or political concepts—she doesn't hear them, doesn't remember them, still doesn't know the difference between liberalism and democracy or what a civil society is—they're all men's games for her, only relevant to her own life inasmuch as they can one day ruin it.

It occurs to Daryna that she's inherited from her mother much more than she's used to thinking she has. Her ability to play movies, too, it would seem—only Daryna's movies have always been played for a wide release, always with the question of how to transfer them to the screen and show others, and her mother's were produced for an audience of one.

Now that's a show she'd love to make: Wouldn't it be something to capture on film all those fantasies people spin inside their minds to help them survive? Daydreaming on screen—television of the future! A great project, one has to admit, especially for a retired anchorwoman. Well, now that she's been retired (No, after she has retired herself; let's be clear about that!), she'll have plenty of opportunity to dream up, without any constraints, like her mother once did, as many wonderful, sleep-inducing projects as she pleases, never worrying about bringing them to life. She'll be the creator of her own private virtual reality, protected from everyone's dirty hands. Clean ones too, unfortunately. A magnificent prospect—might as well go hang herself right now. Really, not that different from getting on the needle.

Still, something in what she's just heard gnaws at Daryna, something's stuck, like a fish bone between the teeth, and she stubbornly keeps pushing her tongue there—to pry it out.

"Daydreaming can be dreaming while awake. Or dreaming with one's eyes open. Dreaming in a conscious state."

"Of course it's conscious, that's what I'm telling you," confirms Olga Fedorivna, as if she's surprised that her daughter hasn't taken her words on faith and needs to have something translated from somewhere else as further proof, while she, the mother, has already told her everything essential. "It's not like hallucinations or something, God forbid!" (Oh yes, Daryna recognizes this, too; it's their family legacy, the fear in their blood: it only takes one certified nutcase in the family, with a firmly affixed label—never mind that's it's fake—to keep them forever spooked, seeing the menacing shadow of insanity at every step. The "acute paranoid psychopathy" label they'd affixed to her father may not have implied any hallucinations, but "having obsessive ideas" was certainly enough for a diagnosis; and the kind of ideas considered obsessive were the ones you wouldn't give up, even with such persuasive entreaties as a blow to the head on a dark stairwell.) "It was just me, thinking up this beautiful, beautiful fairytale for myself, just like the ones I used to tell you before bed when you were little. And I got so used to it sometimes, even at work during the day, I'd catch myself thinking that something really nice was waiting for me at home that night—the way it had been with Tolya."

Oh, so that's the way it had been with Tolya. Daryna knows well this joy of a day brightened through, in every detail, by the anticipation of a night of lovemaking—only for some reason her mother's naïve confession (which instantly opens the door to a whole pressing mass of other far-reaching speculations about her sexual life, with Uncle Volodya included, and her mother obviously doesn't know how much she's just revealed about herself, more than in the whole twenty years of their diplomatic negotiations) instead of moving her, reverberates in Daryna as a dull pain: an echo of her old filial revolt, perhaps, from which she emerged armed with an unassailable youthful certainty that she would never, under any circumstances, let any man dominate her, or maybe a vast, accumulated sympathy for her mother then and pity for her now, all at once.

Daryna's always known that she was a love child, and, as she got older, in her own relationships with men stumbled upon just such pieces of direct evidence, loosened up from the depths of her childhood memories, that her parents had been very happy together. For decades, those childhood impressions lay preserved inside her, waiting for the searchlight of adult experience to bring them out of the dark: here's their family, coming home from a walk, and Dad lets Mom go ahead of him on the stairs, remaining to stand, with the little Daryna, below, his head thrown back, looking up, and then rushes, laughing, to catch up with Mom, jumping over two steps each time, and they tussle and giggle somewhere up there, on the next floor, forgetting in that moment about her completely. The way Adrian loves chasing her up the stairs now. Though it's Sergiy to whom she owes this discovery; he was the first to confess he couldn't help himself when her watched her move from behind (back then, before she knew men, she received this information with acute curiosity, and instantly recalled the expression on her father's face when he stood on the landing with his head tossed back).

It took her until about second grade to wrap her mind around the notion that Mom and Dad at one point actually met each other as complete strangers, who may not have met at all, and then she wouldn't be here—and then she set to deposing them with a pros- ecutor's persistence about exactly how they met. You could say it was her first interview, and she remained quite unhappy with it as with all her interviews before today (yesterday, yesterday!). She was after nothing other than a ready-made story that would have shown conclusively that Mom and Dad did not meet by accident at all, that it couldn't have been otherwise, and that they'd fallen in love at first sight and for all time. And Mom and Dad, like a pair of high-school punks, stole the initiative and took the game in their own direction, incomprehensible for an eight-year-old. They goofed, shot, outdrawing each other, completely irrelevant, as they seemed to her, details, like snowballs, interrupted each other glee- fully, mocking. *And you said …*—No, it was you who said …—*Pish, I'd never. Who d'you think you are?*—Yeah, right, you just keep saying that after you couldn't take your eyes off of me! Mom giggled like a girl who got a note from a boy in class—something she had no, in little Darynka's furious opinion, mommy right to do. Exactly as

Aidy loves recasting their first meeting in humorous terms, loves improvising, in jest, new treatments for the same plot—how he barged into her studio, and she hissed at him like a cat, but her legs, hey, he took good stock of those legs right there and then, and resolved he mustn't let them slip by!—and she giggles exactly the way her mom did, and tosses snowballs back at him. Now she knows what a bottomless source of renewal it is for every love to return to its origins, to the beginning, and how all this play reaffirms in you the sense of having triumphed over life (because you can only play with what's yours, yours alone, what belongs to you and what no one can take!).

Now she's sorry she was such an inept interviewer back then. That in her demands for a story she failed to remember the *details*—only retained a general vague image, like in a snow globe: her parents are young; they're laughing; and their faces, back then, half-buried in the snowdrifts of time, are like a source of light inside the glass.

"Why are you quiet?" her mother asks, across the span of thirty years.

Why? Because that love's gone, and nothing's left. Unless, of course, you count her, Daryna Goshchynska. (Who was it that just recently addressed her by patronymic, and with a kind of suggestive emphasis, too?) Daryna Anatoliivna Goshchynska, a retired television journalist, not quite forty years of age, who is languishing in bed at eleven a.m. like a log, with cheeks wet with tears, and has nowhere to go—not exactly a great, when you think about it, contribution to humankind. It is foolish to think that children set something right somewhere, do some sort of justice, supply the crowning achievement, or a purpose for anything. Love has no purpose beyond itself—every love has its own life and its own biography; it is a separate creature.

Once upon a time there had been a love in this world, Olya and Tolya—"Otollya" as they used to sign postcards to friends—had been and then stopped being. Just stopped, for technical reasons—in conjunction with one signatory's departure. And that's it? Just like that? You leave life, disappear from the screen, and that's all it takes for your love to vanish, too? The love that had buoyed you up for years?

She doesn't say anything because she doesn't know how to ask her mother: What did she do with her love? Did she archive it somewhere inside, tying the strings into a dead knot? Or, did she switch its tracks like Kyiv's streetcar drivers used to do back in the in the seventies—by hand, with an iron hook—and set to finish loving Uncle Volodya with the same underlived, interrupted love that was so cruelly mangled halfway? Was it really possible that it was *the same love* that still went on for her? Because all that savage energy of the soul that is called love—the one that can cut you down with the force of a direct blow when you're dusting the desk on which he used to unroll his blueprints, or when you find in a drawer an old scarf that still holds his smell, or simply anywhere, for no visible reason—cuts you down, the tidal wave of it knocks you off your feet and all you can do is fall where you stood and howl like a beast without words: Where is he? Why is he gone?—all this energy cannot possibly just disappear, it has to go somewhere, doesn't it?

When she was young, Daryna did not think about these things, of course; back then, her only desire was to escape as soon as possible from her crippled family, which couldn't do better than to hatch Uncle Volodya and his moronic medical jokes—one big taunt like a fart into navy sweatpants. And without any of that "Hamlet's hesitation to act decisively" that once caused her departed father so much trouble. Unlike Hamlet, she acted, for being only nineteen, rather decisively. (Told herself as soon as she spotted Sergiy—this one!—and when, the following night, he, inflamed by her hurried, eager availability—take me, I'm right here!—drilled into her, thrown onto the sand, with his unexpectedly hard and hot member, she couldn't help herself, even though she'd squeezed her eyes shut like she was at the dentist's—so as not to see the instruments—and yelped with pain. Poor Sergiy all but got a stutter from the shock of this being her first time, enough to traumatize the boy for life. She was lucky it turned out okay—Sergiy was very moved, stroked her hair, and whispered "my baby" to her, and that's when she burst into tears, burying her face in his gray, as she clearly remembers, T-shirt, into his chest, because after her father this was the first man's hand that had stroked her hair.)

Hamlet, to be totally frank, had a much easier time being decisive. After all, his father died a king, and the son had all the right to shove the two portraits into his mother's face and point out: this had been your husband, and this is your husband, and tut at you, dear Mother. What assets did she, Daryna, have, except perhaps these memories of her early childhood, still warmed with love, elusive and tingling like a dream you can't remember in the morning but that makes you ache with the sense of irreparable loss? And then, right away, the next frame: the yellow knobby bones with the feet sticking out from under the robe, the permanent, inextinguishable smell of urine around the home where you couldn't invite any of your friends. (In the first months after the asylum, Father could only talk with great effort; his speech later returned, more or less, but the unpleasant strain in it remained until the end, like a person who's crawling above an abyss and is afraid to lose his footing.) Nothing regal, nothing heroic at all—only the long, inescapable shame of a repressed teenager. And in this version of the play, Gertrude then tried, in vain, to make her daughter understand how much Uncle Volodya sacrificed when he left Father to die in the hospital and spared no painkillers for him: usually such patients were discharged, so they wouldn't spoil the hospital's stats with another exitus letalis. A perfectly fraternal act on her stepfather's part, nothing like Claudius's: all men of the same woman are in a way brothers (oh no, not all, she refuses to imagine R. and Aidy have anything in common; Aidy's done nothing to deserve that!).

"Mom, what if I asked you what Dad and Uncle Volodya have in common?"

"He's kind," Olga Fedorivna responds instantly, as if she'd been waiting for this question for twenty years. "I've always told you—make sure a man's kind, that's the most important thing. Seriozha was kind. And Adrian, too."

For the first time this morning Daryna can't stifle a smile: the ease with which her mom ties into the same circle her own and her daughter's men—the ones she knows—makes her forget, for an instant, the bottomless bog her boss had tried to drag her into last night. Images of her life's kind men spin before her like in the Hutsul arkan dance—they're all brothers; they all must be introduced to each other, so they all become friends. The circle flickers gathering speed, faster, faster, as it blends into a single being, a collected radiance of a single gaze that glows with tenderness—this lasts no more than an instant, and the vision disintegrates, but, how strange; she feels ever so slightly better, consoled. Somehow, her mother has managed to break her out of her gloom, alleviate the fear of loneliness. No, she won't bend over for them, hell no. What her boss offered last night was more horrible than solitary confinement. Much more.

***

Once, in Polissya, Daryna got to see a quag—an unnaturally, acidly bright, motionless pool the color of light pickle mold in the middle of a marsh. From the distance, its utter stillness awed her: a blind, piercingly green eye of death. She remembers her sudden, intense urge to throw something into it—anything, just to break the spell of that uncanny stillness, to see, with her own eyes what it was like, what an end like that looked like, when the darkness sucks you in and there's nothing to grasp on to; the mere thought of it makes everything inside go numb with terror, but still it lures, beckons to peek in.

There was a moment in the conversation yesterday when she felt that same mucid disorientation. For as long as her boss kept trying to appeal to her ambition, the only emotion she felt boiling inside her was rage. Her ambitions were on a completely different plane, and the boss, while he may have been using the same word, had something completely different in mind. It was as if he stubbornly insisted on calling, say, a table a glass (like the one into which he kept pouring himself cognac, while she barely tasted hers, only felt a headache coming on) and expected her to do the same. He tempted her with access to a humongous—at least thirty percent!—audience, bragged about the channel already buying meters to measure ratings in cities of a half a million people and up—and that's just to start with, the one hundreds were next—and all she wanted to spit back was: What the heck for? *Ukraine's Got Talent?*

He was burying all her professional aspirations alive and had not the slightest inkling of what he was doing. He never felt the studio darkness expand into infinity on the other side of the cameras; there was no one sitting in fear for him, ready to cough and creak their chairs in response to any falsity; he couldn't care less about what he put on the air. Professionalism, for him, meant how, not what, and if the Insurgent Army theme was better left alone for the time being, then it wasn't worth bothering with at all, and anyway, entertainment programming was the safest niche—he said it exactly like that, using that word, and it made her cringe, and then laugh with all the spite she had in her: ah, the niche again!

Nose already twitching with the nonexistent roach whiskers, he assured her she would be protected from politics, all that dirt, he gave his word. Sure, she's "the face of the channel," and it was never her business to care about the provenance of substances that bubble in its guts, so why should it start being her business now? That's only logical. And then he told her—intimately, a little wearily almost like he'd had enough of her tetchy jibes, her crooked half-grins, and her little bitten-down lips, all of which had the singular purpose, as any idiot could see, of drumming up her price, a pretty woman's usual ritual resistance before she gives in and takes the hardened dick into her mouth—how much she would be paid. Cash, of course, in an envelope, off the books.

She gasped silently, unsure of what face to make so he wouldn't notice anything: she felt naked—no one had heard of such salaries in Ukrainian television before; the ceiling was five grand a month, unless, of course, you count those who got their kickbacks in envelopes, directly from their political clients, and their channel was never among the wealthy ones. She'd been getting two, and was fine with that. That's when it went to her head, spinning, dizzying, for an instant: they could buy an apartment downtown if they sold Aidy's digs—and better still—oh the impossible dream!—a small house in the country, in some near-Kyiv quaint alpine hamlet; it's all "Alps" around Kyiv, everywhere you turn—hills, meadows, lakes, ponds, and not everything's sold yet, although the prices are stratospheric indeed, but all they need is a little patch of land, like in Roslavychi, where Vlada had been planning to live with Vadym. And right away, with dazzling, sobering clarity, it occurred to her that Vlada's death was also connected to this hidden churn of financial flows—with the invisible gigantic intestine where blood and oil mixed in the same pipe: Vadym was into oil, and Vlada was into Vadym, and she got the blood. What was it she said in that dream—"too many deaths"?

Frozen, Daryna felt the breath of the subterranean bog—its invisible vapors rose against her skin, fogged her mind. Bank accounts' credit columns endowed with cell-like, self-replicating ability, the flickering of mysterious numbers on computer screens and stock-market monitors: all this was alive—it rose, throbbed, grew, moved. "I'd be curious," she said to the boss, "I'd be really curious to know—where's the mother lode?" Boss took it as an expression of admiration and winked, with bravado, just like that time at his housewarming party. "I mean," she said, not yet aware of how close she'd come to lifting the manhole cover and seeing the blind acidly greenish glimmer below with her own eyes, "don't get me wrong; I know I'm an expensive woman,…" (he gave her a sleazy snigger) "but I'm also aware that free cheese is only found in the mousetrap—braids don't fetch that kind of dough!"

That was her swerving off road and cutting straight through the rough—she no longer cared; she knew her cause had already been lost and wanted to have one last satisfaction: to know the mechanism that was behind this, let it be her last journalistic investigation; she's a professional after all, isn't she? (For the fall, the anniversary of her friend's death, she'd planned to make a separate film about Vlada, for *Lantern*—and for Vlada, too. Yep, and apparently Vlada's no longer in touch with the times, and Vadym's been showing up on TV more often, generally looking like he's got his act together and is doing pretty well; *why* should we mess with the dead if we've got living people lining up, cash in hand?) The Donets'k surgeon, Vlada, Gela Dovganivna, whom she kept postponing, unable to find the key to her story—Lord, how proud she was of her show; how much she loved her heroes, always had butterflies in her stomach when she went to the website to read the viewers' comments the morning after a new episode had aired. What's happening to us, how low can we fall, what are we letting them do to us?

No, she did not burst into tears right there, in the boss's office; she'd held her face screen-proof—like a cream puff, because fury was boiling inside her, and fury demanded action, immediate action. She interrogated; she went on the offensive; she cornered him; she didn't know she had such breathless pace in her; she rode it like a witch on a broomstick, and he did not realize that this was merely a doomed man's attempt to extract from his executioner the law that had sent him to the gallows—no, he looked at her with growing respect, as at a woman who was expertly, professionally raising her price. Good job. (She's run so many times into this astonishing shortsightedness in otherwise intelligent people that she long stopped marveling at it: it was like a virus, increasingly widespread, that affected not only politicians, businesspeople, and members of her own journalistic tribe, but also artists of whom one commonly expects a more complex spiritual organization. Instead of living, people were scheming, playing out their combinations, and anything that was not part of their scheme was simply blocked in their consciousness, as if they had a blind spot.)

Boss really valued her, even the tip of his nose was all sweaty with tension she noted gleefully—she wasn't the only one on whom the conversation was taking its toll! Alright, he sighed, about to slap his last ace, the joker up his sleeve, onto the table in a grand, bighearted sweep—cards down! He might be able to negotiate a bigger sum for her, he said, he'd do his best—if it works, they'll "take her in" (he said this in Russian, when the talk turned to money, he switched completely into Russian) on the profits from the *Miss New TV* show. Is that so? It's a very serious project, he warned, nervously twitching his sweaty nose (and *Diogenes' Lantern* was NOT serious, she dictated mentally to her invisible attorney— the boss's every word scorched her like a flame), only this must remain strictly between the two of them, okay? (This reminded her of someone else—oh yes, her captain from that office with fake leather doors of 1987 vintage: he also asked with the same sepulchral import for the conversation to remain between them.)

This was in her own interest, by the way, because he had Yurko pegged to host the *Miss New TV* pageant (Yurko!—she yelped inside—and Yurko will agree?), but only on an official salary— Yurko's not in on the profits. How about that? They do value her!

"And what kind of show is that?"

"The usual kind, just another show, the main thing's to select and sort the girls who applied, and then they'd be passed on to a different agency."

"Meaning what?"

"Well, only a few finalists will appear on the show, you know," he explained.

And where would the money come from?, she almost asked like the last idiot—and that's when it finally dawned on her.

"Motherfucker," she said. "Jesus fucking Christ."

She thought she was smiling as it sometimes happens to people in shock. Boss's face hung still before her in close-up, as if someone had hit the pause button (he'd never heard her utter such profanity; the words popped out by themselves, as if they were the last pieces needed to complete the puzzle). And under her gaze, this face, confirming her guess, was collapsing, slipping like a wall in earthquake coverage—from his eyes, where the inquiry (Is something wrong?) was replaced by the flash of realization (She won't be his accomplice!) to the fright (What has he done?!), a moving shadow, to the deathly bleached wings of his nose, and then to the chin that somehow instantly lost shape and dropped like a clump of wet spackle. In the fraction of a second that she experienced as endlessly long minutes, this man seemed to have disintegrated right before her eyes, and she saw clearly what he would look like in his old age—if, of course, he lived that long. She could smell his fear as one smells the odor of a long-unwashed body. No, this is not a mistake, there's been no mistake; she understood everything correctly—what kind of "a different agency" it was, and from where the profits were planned to come.

"So, we're retraining into slave traders?"

"What are you talking about?" Eyes skittering, gathering his face back into a fist, "I haven't told you anything."

"And will you tell the girls? Will you tell them what kind of show they're being invited to?"

"Oh please, give me a break," he snarled, happy to find himself on solid ground again, on well-trodden territory. "What, you think those girls are all unspoiled goods? Half of them are turning the same tricks for free in their shithole towns and can only dream of being paid for it. They're the ones signing up in droves in response to those ads for dancers in Europe. You think they don't know what kind of dancing they'll be doing? Those floozies'll be thrilled to get out of their pig farms ..."

She didn't listen after that, something clicked in her ears like when the reel gets chewed up in a tape recorder. He sounded as if he'd memorized this text in advance and had only been waiting for a chance to unload it on someone—after all, one always needs to justify one's own actions, and blaming the victim is always the murderer's simplest excuse.

Yurko once managed to interview a professional hit man; they ran the footage with the man's face hidden, but the killer was unexpectedly articulate, and when Yurko asked what it was like to murder people—what it feels like in action—the man responded with the same memorized preparedness, took it straight out of the gate: "I am not a killer; I am a weapon; I am simply a gun in other people's hands." She was astonished, then, to learn that a killer, too, could have his own brand of morality. Did Yurko know what role he'd been assigned? Or, would he repeat, when he found out, his usual joke about "Sergeant Petrenko, father of four"?

They say this legendary Petrenko does, in fact, exist, and appears every so often, like a ghost, on the Boryspil highway where he actually introduces himself that way to the drivers he pulls over: "Sergeant Petrenko, father of four!" Looking on, expectantly, as his victim opens his wallet.

Yurko actually has four kids from three (Isn't it?) previous marriages, and supports all of them as a decent man should—always looking for side gigs. So does she really have the right to pin him against the wall and force him to choose by revealing the origins of the windfall that's about to drench him? She tried to remember how many of Yurko's kids were girls—three, or all four—but for some reason could only recall one of them, the fifteen-year old Nadiyka, who once came to the studio—perfect age for the sex trade, and also with braids, a blonde little thing ... a sweet child.

Easy for you to say, Daryna, Yurko might reply, and if he didn't say it, he'd still think it: you've got nothing tying you down; you do with your life as you please; you can slam those doors behind you whenever and wherever you want—and he'd have a point, of course; they're far from being in the same boat. Still, something has to be done—not police, perhaps, but she's got to find some resources to publicize this information—to make sure that the fifteen-year-old twits who'll rush in herds from Zhmerinka and

Konotop tomorrow to send their bikini shots into the contest on TV will know what kind of show, damn it, is planned for them!

The boss repeated again that their conversation had to stay inside the office. "And that is something I cannot promise you," she said—still compelled by her team instinct, her atavistic reflexes, a recurrence of a partner's duty: cards down, fair play.

"I would not advise you to make a fuss," the boss answered, with unconcealed hostility. "I rather strongly would advise you not to. Trust me at my word."

"Or else what?" she said cheerfully. (Looking him straight in the eye, straight in the eye just like dog trainers tell you not to do—as if for seventeen years she'd been spurred on by that captain's elusive look, which hemmed her in, stitch by quick stitch, in another office, the look she never managed to crack, no matter how much she wanted to peek inside it, see, touch whatever it was that stirred in there, underneath.) "You'll whack me, too?"

He recoiled as if she'd struck him. Maybe I shouldn't have said that, flashed in her mind. She herself would not have been able to explain why she blurted it out—like a line from a long-accumulated case built for the prosecution. At that moment, she was not thinking at all—forgot all about—that old case in Chernivtsi that had launched the boss's career, about the uninvestigated death of someone or another. She just flipped open, automatically, in response to his threat, her own hidden blade: pure bluff, improvisation in a fit of inspiration. Her advantage lay in the fact that during the entire conversation she'd felt surreally fearless—as if all this were happening to someone else, as if she'd landed inside a sci-fi movie, no, a Russian gangster miniseries, where she moved with dreamlike lightness.

And that's when the boss began to scream, as is the custom of all weak and frightened people when they are defending themselves. In the first instant, she wondered if he, perchance, had lost his mind, raving that she ought to know better than to come here and lecture him all Mother Theresa–like … as if they're all in shit and she's the only one white and pure, as if she doesn't sell the goods just like everyone else ... when all it took for her was to bang someone like R. and voila, she'd won the channel a lump-sum loan that went, to the last penny, to underwriting her show, so that she could fuck it all up and leave them to clean up the mess ... *aha*, and don't look at him like that, fucking princess, some star she is ... the nation's conscience, is it? ... cunt ... he'll have her know he's just as good a professional as she!

Have some water, she counseled through her teeth. The sight of a man's hysteria prompted in her nothing but a cold repulsion, and the drivel he was sputtering at her appeared at that moment so outrageous that it didn't affect her at all. She had long ago relegated her short, wild affair with R. (who at the time had a seat on their sponsoring bank's board of directors) to the archives and wished to recall none of it—neither their heavy, dark lovemaking that filled her body with a dull and joyless, bovine satiety (like the feeling one got sometimes after anal sex, only with R. it was every time), nor its worst final chapter when she was doing everything in her power to get away from him, and it was proving to be not at all as easy as she'd thought.

As soon as R. caught a whiff of her intention to desert, he turned aggressive like a bulldog with a bone. Once, he caught her arm and, with a lupine grin, squeezed it hard with two fingers, leaving a bruise that she had to cover with a tennis sweatband for a week afterward.

He hunted her, caught up with her in the worst possible places, brandishing his owner's right to her to everyone around (he knew this infuriated her the most and hit where she was most vulnerable), ambushed her after work, took her "home" from receptions, where he arrived with the resolute look of a husband who'd come to make a scene (and she tottered out after him, choking on her hatred, like an obedient heron in her high heels, to assault him in the car, later—with her fuming tirade, breathlessly gulping her cigarette, the classic domestic horror).

Weeks after, exhausted and edgy, she finally yelled at him, in a kind of a haze, right in the middle of the street, everything she thought about him and ran in tears into the subway (for some reason the subway seemed the safest place to her—it was impossible to picture R. there). For months she was afraid, when she came home at night that she'd see his Grand Cherokee with its headlights turned off, like a sleeping brontosaurus in the darkness, next to her apartment building's door.

Her initial infatuation, short-lived and addling like a jinx, took root in her acute curiosity about a breed of men she'd never encountered before: the ones who turn over big money and for that reason radiate an unassailable certainty that they're also the ones who make the world itself turn on its axis—men of Vadym's type; she thought she'd finally understood Vlada then.

She probably wouldn't have fallen for R. so hard if it weren't for Vlada. As though by doing so, she was walking in her tracks, following her, posthumously. Vlada lay in the overcrowded Baikov Cemetery, where one had to squeeze between graves to get to her like on the subway at rush hour—and Daryna, heart pounding and no underwear in sight, sped in the studio car to the meeting at the bank (back then, the boss always took her to these meetings with him), took a seat next to R., found his hand under the table and pushed it discreetly under her skirt, and listened, giggles and arousal swelling inside her, to his breath change as he fought to control himself so that no one would notice. (Once, finding a moment, he ran after her, shoved her almost brutally into the bathroom, threw her, breasts down onto the sink, and, entering her from behind, roared out like a sea lion in heat, "What a bitch!")

This game was much more addictive than anything at a casino (where R. had also taken her), and in the early days she was pretty strung out—high on the ease of the power she had over this man, at her bidding to run after her, nose to her crotch like a dog, mowing down, like roadside markers, all the rules that had taken him to the top, and she thought she'd discovered for herself the same feeling that must have attached Vlada to Vadym—the joy of giving a man who used to think himself omnipotent a taste of freedom he had never known before. Only that was as far as any joy went for her with R.: she could never feel herself as just a woman, as one should in honest sex—just a woman, and just a man, the same thing for thousands of years, and new every time. R. never reached that level of freedom.

In a sense, he remained for her as he had begun: a specimen of a different species. At first, their feverish coupling—in his jeep, at his dacha, once even at his friend's house, in a dark room lit only by the porn flickering on the TV screen—dazed her like a kind of a perversion, like sex with King Kong or Bigfoot, although there wasn't really anything perverted about it, unless one counted his habit of photographing her in various intimate poses. (She asked then, half-kidding, whom he intended to blackmail with those pictures—because she didn't give a damn. She was free to sleep with whomever she wanted and didn't plan to run for Parliament; R. answered, unsmiling, don't be so sure, leaving her with an uncertain suspicion that he was not, in fact, just shooting his own porn, but planned to keep a file on her just in case, to give him control over her, and in this there was also something acutely arousing, sinfully titillating.)

The turning point came in Holland, where she'd agreed to go with him on a two-week vacation and every morning, when she woke up next to him, felt like she was sticking her head into a bag—and neither the museums, nor the sea, nor the wonderful little seaside restaurant with lobsters, nor the low Rembrandtesque, phantasmagoric light of that country, reflected everywhere by water, could rescue her from that bag: R. loomed before it all—a heavy, dark mass without air holes.

One morning, having climbed out of bed before dawn and smoked a cigarette, on an empty stomach, by the window open to the gentle glimmer of the wet, scaly tiled roofs in the fog, she realized very clearly that she needed to excise this man from her life immediately—like a rotten tooth or a malignant tumor. R. was simply emotionally obtuse—packed hard inside, like dry ground.

You can't tell such things by sight; they only really come to light in bed. This must be the fate of many of the nouveau riche, and generally anyone who spends too much time with the same kind of pressure applied on the same, very narrow range of emotions: it's as if parts of their soul atrophy. Life had pressed R. into a total spiritual impermeability, a chronic constipation of sorts—and she, Daryna, was his laxative.

He needed her because he needed the aerating, the breaking and turning of his petrified soil, both in sex and in his everyday life: that's what casinos were for and racing his car, cutting lanes on the Zhytomir highway, and saunas with masseuses and sex-tourism to Thailand and a whole repertoire of other aids, all at the client's disposal, that could stimulate the emotional peristalsis—having acquired estates, people now spend them on anything that makes them feel alive. She was for R. just such an aid, and that's what she felt herself to be, after all their mechanical orgasms, she felt it in her ass, like she'd been screwed there.

This was, give or take, what she yelled at him in the end in the middle of the street, seeing nothing around her, and she knew she hit the bull's-eye, that he'd disappear after that, excise himself from her life like a cankered growth—men like him did not go back to the site of their defeat. The thing is, though, that they don't ever forgive those who were there to witness it.

And this was the fact she had overlooked: R. wasn't simply her past, wasn't simply a lover she'd left—much more brutally than she would've preferred. (She couldn't stand violent breakups with sordid scenes and did, in fact, nurse at the bottom of her heart that idiotic notion of all her men somehow constituting something like a single extended family—she was, for instance, frightfully pleased to introduce Aidy to Sergiy and watch them shake hands; she loved them both at that moment.) He wasn't someone with whom you could part and not see again for years in a city of three million, where you couldn't swing a dead cat without hitting a banker, or a journalist, for that matter (and they didn't, fortunately, all frequent the same watering holes); R. was her enemy.

And he took his revenge in the simplest way available: first by giving the channel money and then by cutting it off; goodbye, we regret to inform you that our priorities have changed. Read: If I can no longer fuck your anchor, I'll fuck you. Did he think that perhaps the channel's bosses would then deliver her to his door-step rolled up into a rug like an Oriental slave girl, and he'd be able to walk all over her in some uber-cynical manner? No, that's unlikely—it was probably just his good business sense at work: What's the point of paying if you don't get anything in return? Simple as that, and no need to, as Antosha (or Occam's Razor) says, multiply redundant essences.

"And don't you pretend," the boss hollered—much more confident now that he'd spotted her confusion, with decidedly more spiteful indignation—"don't you even try to pretend like you didn't know anything!"

But she did not; she knew nothing—that was the rub; there were lots of things she didn't know and wished to continue not knowing: she shut her eyes and pinched her nose, just like everyone else. Silly little Daryna, little Red Riding Hood, climbing into bed to play with the wolf thinking him her grandma. There's your sex with King Kong.

Out loud she laughed at him—because what else could she do—*eww*, how disgusting! The primitive, dumb as a tank, logical force of this whole edifice crushed her; how easily these two, the boss and R., had robbed her of her private life behind her back—what she used to consider her private life (as she said to R., oh so lightly: I sleep with whomever I please—and he did warn her, didn't he—don't be so sure)—converting it into dollars and cents, like they'd translated her into a hard, solid language they could understand. Knocked off her accuser's high ground, she finally saw the anchorwoman Goshchynska through their eyes: an expensive woman, to be sure (and with a price tag attached!), what a bitch, a sexy cunt, a walking ad for contact lenses—I use them and toss them without regret. (What if that's what R. thought—that she'd used him to get money for the channel?) "Unshakeoffable" as the boss had once complimented her comically, not knowing how to say "irresistable" in Ukrainian, and thus capable of being useful on screen: braids, a little top, welcome to our whorehouse; that was how they saw her, and that was the version they admired—that was the version they were willing to pay for, even to "take her in on the profits," whether from the election carousel or the slave trade, whatever's in season.

They saw her as one of them, and she had nothing with which to shield herself. Her work, all her professional accomplishments by themselves meant nothing to them but instead lay beyond the reach of their assessment scale, in the "blind spot." They were just fun and games on the margins of the big business—aspirations for television with an intellectual gloss, celebration of heroes no one's ever heard of—well, that's nice, fit for an international contest somewhere, where it can fetch an award to hang under glass on the wall in the boss's office, but essentially no one gives a flying fuck.

R., when she talked about her work (told him about her heroes, the idiot!), would smile a Buddha smile and say that her enthusiasm made him insanely horny (and would pull her hand into his pants, so she could see for herself). The same effect was produced in him by the enthusiasm with which she sucked delicious shreds of lobster flesh out of the shell in the little Dutch restaurant: an erection was another hard (doesn't get much harder) language, tangible like money, into which they translated what they didn't understand. And she had nothing else to show them as proof of her identity; she worked with them, she lived on the money they paid her, even—and she couldn't strike this from her résumé either—occasionally slept with them (a woman's curiosity can lead all kinds of places!). She was inside the system and felt quite at home there. Had she told her boss that after seven years on air she still felt the darkness in the studio of an audience extending to infinity on the other side of the screen—full of people to whom she was accountable, could even feel their breath—this confession, most likely, wouldn't elicit even an erection from him: he'd just laugh and counsel her to spend more time outdoors. He had also become a different biological species—she'd been refusing to see it for too long.

It occurred to her that he really wanted her to stay with the channel. He wanted her to be the way they saw her; he was willing to fight for that. Not just for the profits, or for the "face of the channel." This mattered to him: that they become equals, two of a kind, professionals, and he no less (better even—because he's the one paid more) than she—to erase between them any gap that could not be translated into clear, hard language. The gap irked him.

And, exactly as with R., only without the screaming (on the contrary, dreadfully slowly and quietly because rage was choking her and made it hard for her to speak, even the room grew darker around her, as if dusk fell suddenly), she said things to him that she hadn't intended to say and that would've probably been better left unsaid, because it's not wise to be so old-fashioned as to declare war—like Prince Oleg to the Khazars—right in the face of the person you intend to war with (she knew she would do everything imaginable to kill their dastardly show). But, just as with R., telling the truth to the eyes of the person facing her was, in that moment, the only thing she could do to separate, to shield herself from their sticky grasp, like lowering the manhole cover on the cloacae below.

"Do you realize," she said to the boss, "that you're contagious? You're like the guy with TB who goes around spitting into other people's soup. Like in vampire movies: you've been bitten, and now you must bite everyone else so they become like you. And that sucks, brother. Big time."

Amazingly enough, he kept silent. Then muttered in Russian, obviously working over something in his mind, "You're insane."

"Aha," she said, rising to go, straightening to her full height in front of him on her high heels (he was short, a small man with a Napoleon complex), stepping like a hot-blooded racehorse—unshakeoffable. "That's right, insane. It runs in the family, don't you know?"

***

She only tells her mother the triumphant part, in an edited version, without too many details. Olga Fedorivna suddenly chimes in. She remembers that fifteen-year-old film that propelled the boss into big journalism—sure, sure, it was on TV—children in Chernivtsi struck down by a mysterious illness, terrible shots: a hospital room full of little girls and all of them bald as old men. You bet, a picture like that stays with you: science fiction, banshee purgatory. The kids would wake up one morning, get out of bed, and all their hair would stay on the pillow. Soft baby hair, a tiny silky scalp.

"That was right after Chernobyl, wasn't it," says Olga Fedorivna, delighting in her good memory.

"No, Mom, that was later. And it's got nothing to do with Chernobyl."

A typical merging effect: the greater horror subsumes the smaller one. Chernobyl, Chernivtsi—they even sound similar, both start with Ch, easy to mix them up. Mix them up and then forget. Do they teach this in the Journalism Institute now: How to present information in the manner that makes it easiest to forget? And then paste over the poignant image in people's minds with something from *Star Wars*—plenty of bald-headed little monsters in that story, all over the place really.

Boss had made his name with that horror clip about bald children, but no one remembers this fact anymore, and he himself never brings up his early days. Another man died then, his body the roadblock to any further independent investigations. Another man paid for the boss's career.

But she didn't even remember this, wasn't thinking about that story at all during their conversation! The precision of her aim was something akin to what a body does in a moment of danger, when it knows which way to duck, all by itself. You just poke with your finger, not looking—and lose the whole arm to the gooey mess with the requisite dose of someone's blood in it.

That time in Chernivtsi, Daryna explains to her mother, it was, presumably, an accident at a military plant to which the authorities never granted access. Moscow managed to close the case just before the Union fell apart. A rocket fuel spill, most likely. Who knows whose security services were involved—Moscow's or ours—the fact remains that someone badly needed to have the whole story hushed up, whatever it took.

"So what you are saying," Mom says, straining to digest the information, "is that the gentleman who was investigating the case was, in fact, murdered? And that your producer knew about it—and kept quiet?"

Why is it, exactly, that she finds this so hard to believe? Daryna feels something like her old filial exasperation.

"Mom, you're like from Mars, or Venus, or something! What, Father's colleagues didn't quietly make their careers on someone else's blood? When they'd driven the architect to killing himself—and then made him the scapegoat—and they all, except Father, signed the denunciation like good boys." Now, wouldn't it be interesting, flashes through her mind, to meet with those people now, whoever's still alive, and see who they'd become. Do they also moonlight in human trafficking when business is slow? And while we're at it, let's see how their kids turned out, an instructive little show indeed—and suddenly she sees what she could've done with her father's plot in which she could never find the story. Now, when she can't make anything, barn door closed and no horse in sight, as Aidy says. "You've lived your life with all that, and now you're surprised?"

"Yes, but that was *then*!" Olga Fedorivna protests. "Times have changed!"

It's like generational egoism in reverse. Everything bad has already happened to us, and our children start from a clean slate. And the children cheerfully trot off into the world convinced that that's exactly how things'll turn out, and the parents egg them on: go on, kiddo, we've done our time, but you'll have the good life now—lots and lots of it, all you want. And the kids, aside from this blessing, are armed with nothing, go bare as a bone. Stripped naked, that's the thing.

"We all thought so too, Ma."

If only one could know where "then" ends and where "now" begins. And how stubbornly blind this self-preserving human faith is—the faith that a clear watershed divides them. That it's enough to turn the page—start a new calendar; change your name, passport, seal, and flag; meet and fall in love with a new man; forget everything that had once been and never (even alone with yourself) remember the dead—and the past will be made null and void. But there is no watershed, and the past pushes at you from every pore and crack, mixing with the present into dense inseparable dough—and you have very little chance of flailing your way out of it. Only we keep on consoling ourselves with our childish illusion that we can control the past because we can forget it. As if our forgetting would make it vanish, go away. Like Irka Mocherniuk's rug rat when he got angry at her for slapping him and threatened, "I'm gonna make it all *dalk* for you now!" squeezing his eyes shut as hard as he could.

Still, Mom can be forgiven, Daryna thinks—she did spend her working life in a museum, after all, got used to a cataloged kind of past, ordered and pinned to the corresponding dates, like a collection of dead butterflies: here's "then," and beginning from this point it is "now," all nice and tidy. When Daryna was little, she loved visiting her mother at work. Back then, all the exhibits in the museum's halls were above her head, glassy glimmers up there, mysterious and unattainable, and one of the adults would always pick her up so she could peek at the pictures under the glass—there were many, immeasurably more than in any book, she couldn't dream of getting a good long look at all of them, and the incredible riches the adults possessed made her swoon delightfully—and that's what it meant to be an adult: to have access to all the pictures in the world, like Ali Baba's treasure caves, and she wished to grow up sooner, faster. And, well, it all came true just the way she wished, didn't it? Of all things, she's always had plenty of pictures.

And again, a wave of scorching pain swallows her, so hot she has to bite into her lip so as not to moan out loud: rot it all to pieces; she really *was* good at television! What happened, that it was no longer important—being good? Young journalists don't even use this word anymore; they don't say that someone is good at what he or she does; they say successful. A thief—if he has millions in offshore accounts—is a successful entrepreneur; a hopeless talentless putz—if his face is on every channel—is a successful journalist. And it's us they learn from, Daryna thinks dully. Boss talks like that too, and not just about shows, but about people too. And he also says professional—that's the highest compliment from him. Alright, let's say so-and-so is a professional—and what about everyone else? Who are they? Amateurs? Then why the hell do they still have their jobs?

They had been a team once—when was that? So long ago. That was her real youth, first and foremost because of its sense of unlimited possibility: the wild nineties, free-sailing—just show initiative and money took care of itself; suburban mansions popped up and burst as merrily as bubbles on the puddles under a spring downpour, but the air was thick with ideas, the air swirled and roiled with them! In their old studio, their very first one, set up in a rented factory warehouse (the factory had shut down, let them have the space for a song), they'd pull up their chairs and sit up into the wee hours of the night, drafting the program grid, arguing and yelling at each other; the crumpled stubs of unfinished cigarettes spilled from overflowing ashtrays onto the table, and when the smoke got so bad their eyes watered, someone, most often Vasyl'ko in his nerdy bug-eyed, fogged-over glasses, would finally get up to open the window, throwing a jacket over her shoulders on his way back. Where are you now, Vasyl'ko? On what meager Canadian pasture do you nibble your bitter grass?

Last she heard from him was an e-card sent in late 2002, from some total armpit, Manitoba, where in winter the temperatures fall, like in Siberia, to twenty below, and the air's so dry your lips crack to blood. What the hell was he doing there, in that desert? What was he wasting his life on? He was a natural—no one could draw people out like he did—he'd talk to a post and have it spilling its guts before you knew it. He had that effect on everyone, even the president, or, actually, back then just a candidate. (A remarkable show it was: that redneck never caught on that he was being stripped to his dirty laundry in view of the entire country and went all soft, started bragging about his poor postwar child-hood and how back in '55, dressed in his only threadbare suit coat from his native village, he rode in a coal car to take the institute entrance exams because he had no money to pay for a passenger ticket—and he shone, glowed with the sated pride of the victor who can now show the world a whole warehouse of suits in place of that old coat he'd ruined, and fine suits indeed!)

Vasyl'ko was the first to locate this little spring that powered, as it eventually turned out, the whole wind-up mechanism of our so-called elites—their deep, lusty thirst for revenge for all those Soviet-time humiliations, and to hell with the cost: back then, in the nineties, no one could yet see that the only thing these people desired, as they took their seats in our TV sets with an increasing sense of entitlement, was to climb Kyiv's hills (knocking a few floors off the old buildings—so they don't block their view of St. Sophia) and throw, right there on Yaroslav's grave, the triumphant feast of new nomads. Vasyl'ko wasn't after some deep social analysis, and never forced any conclusions upon his audiences—he just knew how to *listen*; really, it couldn't be simpler; how to listen to what people were telling him and hear the incredible volumes they said about themselves, without noticing, when someone listened to them the way Vasyl'ko did. He could repeat any conversation, even one overheard by chance, almost word for word, and now everyone's just yakking away over each other's heads and nobody hears anybody.

The new crop—they're totally checked out, blank, like they were born with the earbuds in. Nastya the intern, while her guest is talking, keeps herself entertained by rehearsing the different angles of her supermodel smile, waiting for him to finish until it's her turn to voice the next question. While Vasyl'ko, a communica-tion genius, who even in a ninety-second vox pop could present any random passerby as a one-in-a-million precious soul, is observing

Canadian sparrows through his binoculars somewhere at the end of the world. That e-card he sent sported a bright-yellow-chested creature with a tuxedo-black tail, and Vasyl'ko wrote that it was a new hobby of his: bird-watching. Bird frigging watching.

And such stories were myriad; they were legion; they were everywhere you looked. People emigrated, disappeared, dropped off the radar; old phone numbers when she called, thinking—he's the one I'd love to bring in for the new show!—were answered by strange voices. *No, so-and-so had sold the apartment, and didn't leave a forwarding address*—as if an invisible tornado swept through their ranks, leaving only a few of them who had once been called the first echelon of the Ukrainian journalism, those who still remembered Vadyk Boiko and the first show he wrote and hosted on the only Ukrainian channel that was on the air back then. The whole country watched it, streets on his nights empty like after a flood, and then one winter day in 1992, Vadyk, very happy, bragged to a colleague about a pouch of papers he was about to publicize: "I've got 'em Commies right here. I'm gonna drop a bomb on them!" And forty minutes later a bomb exploded in his apartment, where they later found his burned-alive body plastered to the floor. The authorities announced a few theories that all boiled down to the victim having burned all by himself, and without anyone's help whatsoever; they closed the case, and no one would bring up Vadym Boiko's name on the air after that, as if he'd never existed.

Maybe if we had spent the rest of the nineties speaking and shouting about him, if we had kept reminding each other about him, if we'd gathered for an annual wake and aired it live every winter, all for one, in solidarity, on every channel while that was still possible, maybe then it would've taken them longer to take care of us? And the thing is, we all went so quietly, without a peep or a fight, and the Gongadze case doesn't count: by the time Giya's head (literally) rolled at the close of our wild nineties, the bitter and magnificent age of aspiration and hope, of skyrocketing careers and buried projects, of daily self-congratulatory banquets where we went to graze with a laugh at first—here, give me today's wire; let's see who's got a release for dinner tonight—and later more and more selectively—ugh, I won't go there, those bastards never have booze (The boozeless bastards were the last surviving holdouts of the Helsinki group who were still talking, mostly to themselves, about the lustration problem, but who cared about them anymore?)—by that time, although we still picked and chose our clients and put on superior airs negotiating the price of white-washing some rotten company's reputation, we were already tame as guinea pigs—we'd gotten used to beer at Eric's, and jazz jams at 44, to flying to Antalya and Hurghada on vacation. We had already partaken of designer boutiques and our first discount cards. We were well-fed, well-groomed guinea pigs, with glossy fur—those of us who managed to find our way to the flood of money cur-rents—we had no instinct for danger, and that, perhaps, was the main mark of our generation: bare as bones, armed with nothing but our parents' blessing of go-ahead-kiddo-and-you'll-have-the-good-life, we stuck our heads into the trap happily and with an easy heart, even with a sense of our own relevance; we took pride in our glossy furs, in being paid, and being paid well—for being talented and insightful, of course, what else?—and then it was too late. We went along, thinking, in our naïveté, that we were shaping the new television landscape—we measured our ratings, thought up new shows, and, like children, felt unbelievably cool when we said "in Ukrainian here for the first time"—and what we really did was dance on blood, and that unavenged, unreprised blood ate at us from inside, insidious as lead-laced water.

"What came of us, oh, what came of us?" squealed Irochka Bilozir on every channel—another burnt-out star of the nineties, relegated soon after to the faceless infantry ranks of synthetic Russian pop; her helpless squealing, as it later turned out, was the true chorus of that era, only no one heard it when they should have been listening: Something wrong was really "coming" of us, but so inconspicuously, day by day, drop by drop, how could anyone notice?

People were changing—they didn't just drop off the radar, out of the country, out of the profession, lost to the margins, to the Internet, to small-town newspapers that no one ever reads, to radio frequencies barely buzzing along on foreign grants and dying almost before you could find them on the dial—even those who stayed on the radar were no longer the same. Something broke in them, their internal resistance disappeared: where you could, not so long ago, a mere two, three, five years ago, find a solid, good shoulder to lean on, things suddenly slipped and lost shape—softly, viscously, with eyes shifting and hiding in the hangover swell of the eyelids. "For free, Daryna, only your mom kisses you; let's make a deal: you show me what you've got and I'll show you mine"—and the especially principled editors put five-fold markup on the especially libelous dirt on their own pals and would not budge a cent, all in the name of their sacred friendship. "Don't take it personally, bro," they'd say afterward to the victim, "how'd it be if we ran an interview with you?"—and the victims agreed.

The multiplying personnel gaps were then filled, like a karst cave with water, with the watery-green teenagers, who had absolutely no clue, wanted to know even less, and were only too eager to take on the most blatantly partisan political product. Oil barons enthroned their mistresses in the so-called Lifestyle Interest sector, morality and culture included, and the hordes of serf souls delivered the shows for their silicone-lipped, porn-shells turnkey, so all the ladies had to do was roll in and read prepared text at the camera. And the same guys who once, in the early nineties, broke their backs to raise, like proverbial barns, the most resonant media projects (which later sank, quietly, noiselessly, into the pile of rubbish, and smashed crippled shadows crawled out from under the ruins for a long time afterward, limping to reception buffets where they could eat for two days in advance), the guys who in 1990 lugged bundles of the first independent Ukrainian newspapers from Lithuanian printers and took the police clubs to the kidneys for their efforts—these same guys, saddled with premature beer bellies and bald spots, went to earn their living as whipping boys for parliamentarians—as press secretaries to various political roughnecks who were liable to bid them fetch their mineral water in thunderously unprintable language right in front of the press corps. And the whipping boys quickly learned to affect permanent holy-fool grins that were supposed to evince their complete philosophical invincibility against the whole vanity of vanities of this world, full-contact Buddhism as Antosha used to say, listening askance, like whores to an inappropriately chatty client, whenever Goshchynska got on her soapbox about her heroes—as if calculating, in their minds, what kind of money was paid for the box, and how much of it they could hope to snatch for themselves.

At some point all professional topics just expired, suddenly and at once; people stopped talking seriously about what they did, because no one did anything seriously anymore except make money. At some point—What did it look like? When did it come?—very suddenly, they all stopped caring, as if the once-released virus of the latent disease that had been eating away at them from inside finally did its job, and the only thing left to do was to record the rigor mortis. And not even rigor but a viscous, boggy mass that sucked you in everywhere you turned, and the sense at yet another dinner that the people mobbing the tables with their plates and glasses, slurping in unison, clattering table-wares and getting instantly drunk (many never sobering up again) were not living and—no sense denying—yet rather successful in this life, these corpses, decomposed into the already-runny, porridge-like consistency: reach out to touch them with your hand and the goo would swallow your whole arm. This vision came to Daryna more than once or twice—a hot, scorching thrust at the nape, the cerebellum, like a blast from a champagne cork (or a gunshot—straight at the nape, into the pituitary, muzzle pressed into the hollow between the hemispheres).

Once, soon after Vlada's funeral, it came again—at a restaurant, at some celebratory occasion, at the point when the tables are stripped down to the soiled dinnerware, sweating waiters stumble splashing dessert onto the parquet floors, and the conversations lose coherence, scattering into a chaos of solo monologues, a lady of Balzacian age resolved to speak about Vlada and kept squawking, peacock-like, like whizzing a saw through a log, "I can't, I can't, I can't believe that she is dead!" And one of the men, totally wasted, grunted peaceably back at her, a deep echo rung from a bell, "Who of us is alive?" Daryna remembered the cold shiver and, at the same time, the scorch of fire that burst into her nape like a bullet, and instantly sobered her up. Pushed her, like a cork, to the surface of the general chaotic noise, as if lifting her up to the ceiling from where, as she looked disengaged at the stirred-up maelstrom of people and leftovers, she thought with superstitious horror that it's true; he's right—there are no living souls here—this is the underworld.

Vlada—how did she know this? And this angle, this point of view from the ceiling? She had a painting, in the *Secrets* cycle, titled *After the Blast*. It was a view from above, and in the middle, a splattered circle of light like a multistrand crystal chandelier spun fast on its hook, shattered into animation-sliced circles like ripples spreading on water. Vlada was always fighting stasis; she used to say the Old Masters' work already contained both animation and cinematography, and, in comparison to them, we gained in technique and lost in imagination: we've grown lazy and forgotten that one can communicate everything, absolutely everything by painterly means alone, even sound, as Picasso did in Guernica, the noise of the air raid brought across with dimmed lights and swinging lightbulbs. And that's what Vlada also achieved to a degree in this painting: Her blazing circle of light was like a multilayered wheel knocked off the chariot of the terrible Advertisement God, spun with raging, blend-into-a-single-blot speed; and beneath, a field the color of rot was peppered with a dense black confetti of tiny human shapes like remnants of a defeated army—each with a logoed shopping bag (the bags were shrunken photographs glued onto the canvas). Hugo Boss, MaxMara, Steilmann, Brioni—a brand-name spill.

The critics commented acerbically that Matusevych painted "an explosion at a shopping mall" and should demand remuneration from all those brands for advertising them. But in fact she had painted *a war*—the one we were losing every day, without ever knowing it, as we sped, helter-skelter, across that rusty rotting field. And as it turned out, it was only our bodies that kept moving. We were running in the underworld. We'd been blown to smithereens somewhere along the way. We didn't know there were mines, no one had told us: we kept running, panting, clutching our brand names to our chests, our apartments, our cell phones and automobiles—and still thought we were alive, because no one had told us we were already dead.

"Too many deaths," Vlada had said in Daryna's dream—and really, it's like someone had knocked the bottom off the fairytale barrel, and a legion of deaths had broken free. Something happened to death itself at the century's turn, a transformation that had gone unnoticed for too long: like a new note from the orchestra that at first seems an accidental false noise and then grows to redefine the whole symphony, a new form of death swelled and took root—death without cause. Up until then it was commonly believed that people died of illness, of old age, in accidents, or at someone's hand—that a matter as grave as the cutting short of a life must always have *cause* and death had been quite accommodating, finding new pretexts for itself every time. But at the turn of the century it suddenly quit playing by the rules, lost its mind, and among the old, still comprehensible deaths squatted with growing impunity this new death—a death deranged.

Young men were killed in their sleep by their hearts, which had never ached and then suddenly stopped; young women drowned silently in shallow bathtubs, under the shrouds of still-warm bubbles; a person tripped, fell on a sidewalk—and did not get up again. As if all it took were a single casual breath, a single careless tap of death's fingers—and several lively, busy little shapes with logoed bags in their hands fell with phantom ease, like in a computer game. People did not notice that they ceased being shocked by the news of a classmate one hadn't seen for several years no longer alive, a colleague one could finally pay back for that old loan long been buried. "Darn!" Yurko once griped. "He'd promised a tutor for my kid!" Death stopped being an event—people reacted the same as if the deceased had moved out of the country, making sure to erase the old addresses from their contact lists; death no longer demanded an explanation. Somehow, all at once, the tethers that held one to life grew loose—rotten threads that could pull apart any moment. As if in all the crowds that flowed through the streets, that flooded offices and cafés, supermarkets and stadiums, airports and subways, there was no longer, in all those people together, enough total life to require any kind of effort to pry a physically healthy person out of it. On the contrary, it took an effort to hang on to life. And to remain alive was a feat achieved by only a few.

You prepared us for nothing! Daryna wants to yell at her mother. You, the slave generation, submissive daydreamers with eyes wide open—what did you give us? What the hell is it good for, all your survival experience, your lifelong struggle in lines for a piece of meat, for imported boots and an efficiency flat with a separate room for your children, if the only thing with which you managed to arm us is your faith that the page had been turned—stomped out, forgotten, and now your children will have the good life, because we can earn as much as we want wherever we want, and no one will start a KGB file on any of us just for speaking Ukrainian? You couldn't imagine a better world and so obediently buried your dead for it, without a shred of dignity, except maybe the tears you swallowed somewhere in a dark corner at night, and you did not even teach us to take pride in our dead—you silently acquiesced to the very thing that was demanded of you: to admit that they *lost* because they *perished*, and the winners were the ones who had stayed alive, with apartments, dachas, and Sochi—the successful ones, as we say, we who'd gotten this virus from you—to despise those who'd been left behind. You gave us nothing else, nothing at all, nothing but the pride in our own bank accounts and our own faces on TV—you launched us into life, light as puffballs, and we blackened and burst as soon as our youthful vigor began to flag; you loaded us with emptiness, and now we're passing it on to the next generation.

All this could have been screamed blindly, with the inspiration of hatred that, once ruptured, shoots far in every direction, like an abscess that'd been swelling with pus for years: *It's you, you; it's all your fault!* And what a relief that would have been—to find, finally, an entity of which one could demand the account! But Daryna is silent. She resists the urge to leap upon this slippery surface and speed along with a surfer's breathtaking ease—dear Lord, how many times has she witnessed scenes just like that between mothers and daughters? What terrible things were confided to her by the same old Irka Mocherniuk, who always said that her mother had castrated her father, and had screamed at her mother, at the peak of her own marital problems, that their entire generation should've been sterilized like they did in China so they wouldn't have had any children? And Irka's mother called Daryna and cried on the phone telling her all this, begging her to "influence" her Irochka, as if Daryna and Irochka still went to school together and sat at one desk. But Daryna herself is resolutely incapable of forcing anything like that out of her throat: it gets stuck. Unlike her friends, she no longer feels entitled to judge as she had when she was nineteen. And not because it's been twenty years since then—there are no statutes of limitations between parents and children. It's because, in her case—as she realizes very clearly—it would be unfair to judge her parents: they did give her something.

She is lucky: she is "insane," and it's hereditary.

She really had no inkling, before yesterday, of how powerful the instinct of resistance to evil would prove to be in her—more powerful than any desire or longing, than any possible temptation. And it wouldn't have been this strong if her father hadn't died because of it. And if her mother hadn't approved of his choice.

Incredible, but that's how it was.

Daryna feels a new, detached kind of respect, as if they were strangers, for this couple, Olya and Tolya. Otollya. Erased, shattered, destroyed—like the fairytale palace clad in gentle dove-gray shades of the interior, adorned by ornate shadows, the parquetry, the lamps.... Everything's gone, nothing remains—nothing you can touch, show on TV, price out in hard currency. Utterly incomprehensible how this force could have passed into her. They didn't even tell her anything explicitly when she was little, her parents; they didn't exhort or admonish, just as all her classmates' parents rarely dared confide to their children anything that did not fit with the commonly accepted modus vivendi. (Irka was only told in 1990 that her grandfather actually died in the Gulag and not at the front; and Vlada remembered, not without irony, how Matusevych Senior very secretly whispered to her, in the eighth grade sometime, that he was actually for socialism, but without Russia, but she had to keep mum about it, or else—this was enough to pack you off to the camps, people got seven years for less!) Daryna's parents were no dissidents by any stretch either, and no textbooks would ever mention their names. They merely had the strength to do what they thought was right—and take the full measure of what one had to take in that country in return for doing so, death included.

And somehow (How?) this strength of theirs—the one that seemed so wasted because it hadn't translated into anything tangible—turned out great enough to confer upon their child her own margin of safety. So that in a different era, in a different country, packed with deaths like a can with sardines this child would remain alive.

That much was true: she was alive, and no one could take it away from her.

What was it Grandpa Nietzsche said? What doesn't kill us makes us stronger? Okay, maybe not everything. But sometimes, the thing that does kill us makes our children stronger.

Still, she never wanted to have children of her own.

And that's when she suddenly remembers—all but slaps herself on the forehead, a habit of Aidy's she's adopted—breaking the flow of her mother's consolatory monologue (which she hadn't been listening to anyway, tuned it out, something about how "now" is not the same as "then," and that things have a way of figuring themselves out). She remembers from whose lips she recently, this fall, heard that abrading, inappropriately official Anatoliivna. Amazing, actually, that she'd forgotten to ask her mom, totally crossed her out of that story with the Security Bureau archives where Aidy had gone a few more times, and all for naught: they kept saying they couldn't locate Great-Aunt Gela's case, and now what, no more movies for her, so what's the point anyway? She remembers clearly, painfully, as if from a previous life, the sun-drenched corner of Zolotovoritska and Reitarska, their first assault on the newly built archives, her own single-minded focus on her quest and feels astounded by how happy she had been so recently—and how many unnoticed details she let scatter away from her sight in her happy single-mindedness, like pebbles from under the hooves of a racehorse barreling around the track—but there it is, the tiny rock, wedged into the cracked hoof, never would've thought of it if they hadn't reined her in.

"I'm sorry, Mom, can I interrupt you?"

Olga Fedorivna obediently stops talking.

"I keep forgetting to ask you about this one thing. Does the name Boozerov mean anything to you?"

Silence.

"Mom? Hello? Can you hear me?"

Did they get disconnected or something?

"Boozerov?" Mom finally responds—in a very surprised, young alto, the voice that had once belonged to a brunette in a bright-yellow dress. "That was our curator's name. How do you know him?"

"What curator?" Daryna thinks she must've missed something: The job didn't exist back in Mom's day, did it? What was there to curate if there weren't any independent art shows or private galleries, none of it?

"The KGB curator, who else? Every Soviet institution had its own KGB curator, it was a special job they had."

"Oh."

So in some way times have changed a little—if the meaning of the word has changed.

"Boozerov, what do you know," Mom mutters. "What was his name? Gimme a second, I'll remember ..."

"Not Pavlo Ivanovych by chance?"

"That's it! Pavlo Ivanovych, Pashenka we called him. He was young, younger than me, he couldn't have been thirty then; he was born after the war already.... Such a hottie!" Mom's voice takes on a refreshed but clearly vintage tart disapproval as if being a "hottie" was an aggravating circumstance for a GB man. "He had that dark complexion, you know, and those big eyes like olives.... He should've gone into movies instead of the KGB; he looked like Omar Sharif. How do you know him?"

"Met him at the Security Bureau's archives, when we went look-ing for Adrian's great-aunt's case. He's still got those eyes—like an Arabian stallion's. He sends his regards."

"Fancy that, he hasn't forgotten me!" Olga Fedorivna marvels tartly again. "So he's at the archives now? No more tracking people for him?" She's regained her composure already, like she's fixed up, with both hands, her still-lush hair, fluffing it up with her fingers— a mannerism of hers, and Daryna can almost see her do it at this instant. "He used to have these long interviews with me, back before they took your father in for the psychiatric assessment—wanted me to, you know, influence your father. Latched on to me like a leech. We had a small staff at the museum, nothing really for a curator to do, so he worked me to pieces trying to earn his star.

"Once, I remember, I got really pissed at him; I was at the end of my rope already. What's the point of your meetings? I asked him. What do you want from me? It's not enough that you ran my hus-band to the ground; now because of you my boss is giving me three kinds of hell—our directress then, we used to call her Ilse Koch among ourselves, was on a tear, ran my life like in a concentration camp: anytime I all but dashed out for ten minutes to buy a pretzel on the corner, I had to write an explanatory report! I just couldn't do right by her. She wanted me out of there—must've freaked at a black sheep in her flock. Well, he sort of looked a bit ashamed then. Swore he thought very highly of me, and wrote a very good report about me. And maybe he wasn't lying, because just after that the directress relaxed a little, left me alone. And he disappeared after that—they transferred him somewhere and I heard our museum had a different curator, but he never contacted me and I didn't see him. I figured our Pashenka made a slip somewhere, because he was all sort of droopy and mopey in those last days. Said to me then that he wished he had a wife who'd stand up for him like I did for Tolya."

In her mother's voice, as if plumped up from inside, Daryna clearly hears notes of pride. Perhaps, she thinks, that's what kept her going all that time when she was alone? The sign, sent to her through Pavlo Ivanovych, that she was also doing everything right?

"Whatever did they want from you? They only wanted to pin mismanagement on him, not subterfuge."

"Like you could ever tell with them, Daryna! They just had to get into everything, and spoil it all. Kept asking me if my husband had an irritable temper—he must've been collecting material for their psychiatrists, but I didn't think of that until later ... and wanted me to make Father take back all his petitions. 'Don't you want to live in peace?' he asked. I told him of course I do, but I also want to respect my husband, and my husband would never agree to such abomination—libel an innocent person, and posthumously! I remember he blinked at me in this stunned way and said, 'So that's the kind of woman you are!' I wondered, a little," Mom adds sheepishly, "if he'd taken a bit of a shine to me."

"Hey, that's violation of procedure! The valiant Soviet CheKa men were strictly prohibited from having any sentiments toward their charges. There were special instructions about that, I've read those."

"Your matinka still alive?"—"And well, thank you, and yours?" Daryna feels herself blush at this memory, the way she snorted, snapped, stomped her foot like a little Billy Goat Gruff. And what do you know, Pavlo Ivanovych is basically family! Somewhere in the same archive where Olena Dovganivna's case is buried, sit Pavlo Ivanovych's reports about Goshchynska, Olga Fedorivna, year of birth 1939, Ukrainian, unaffiliated, married, husband—no, that's no longer relevant, it's best to skip that field.

"A pleasure to know that she's raised such a famous daughter"—with the Russian stress. Because what—she might not have raised one? The retired terrorist, doe-eyed Pavlo Ivanovych Boozerov with his substantial behind and liver crusts in the corners of his mouth, loving father of a Conservatory student wrote, thirty years ago, when he didn't yet have those crusts and was making his career in the so-called field operations, a good report about her mother. Are we to understand that if he had written a bad one, Mom would've been, just like Dad, thrown out on the street, or, worse, would've gotten a prison sentence? And what would've happened then to her? God knows, but nothing good, that's for sure—political prisoners' children didn't even get access to higher education until after the Soviet Union collapsed. She'd have landed in some horrible children's home, most likely. Or maybe Aunt Lyusya would've stepped in, taken her to live with her in Poltavshchyna? Even then, her chances of growing up to be famous would've been zero; that's probably why he said what he did. She's not going to stay famous for long, though, and, generally speaking, it is not at all clear what she's supposed to do with herself from now on—but that's not Pavlo Ivanovych's fault.

And at once she's overtaken again by that same, vestibular-like, short-circuit dizziness that happened to her once before, in the spring, the day she stayed late at the studio watching her interview with Vlada and Adrian called to tell her about his dream. For a fraction of a second—this can't last longer, a living human being can't take this for much longer—she is carried upwards by the speeding elevator or a giant Ferris wheel—not above space as in Vlada's painting, but above time, above yesterday's office with the boss's gesticulating little shape inside it, and reflected from it, in direct retreating perspective, the other, 1987 office with fake, leather-padded doors, above the wet highlights of the Dutch tile roofs behind the hotel window, and still further, through an enfilade of rooms opening into each other, where a seventies' kitchen boils with the pot of bubble-swelling laundry on the stove and the puddle that had been the snowman spreads on the rust-colored painted plank floor, and her young father stands on the landing with his head tossed back; from above, in bird's-eye view, for a slipping tail of an instant, she sees it all pulse together, set into motion like cracked-off hummocks in the world ocean, plugged into some giant, boundless power field, and sees the thin—flickering and countless—dazzling threads running through it all, piercing her life—and stretching beyond it, beyond the horizon of the visible to compose a deliberate, no, deliberating, living design, Dovganivna—Adrian—Boozerov—Mom—herself—Vlada—R.— boss—captain.… Another moment, whose very imminence fills her with knee-buckling awe, and it seems they all, living and dead, will push their times together like chairs to a table, will take their places in the plugged-in map of the stars and everything will become clear—what, everything?—but nothing.

The moment passes, the whole picture, without ever having come together, scatters into pieces, into flat shards of memories with which you could never erect the Tower of Babel, and Daryna is left sitting on her messy, crumpled bed, blinking at the curtain brightened by the sunlight to egg-yolk yellow with the shadow of the window frame on it like a cross distorted in a magnifying glass.… Threads, her mind turns over belated like a hard, sticky piece of candy that won't crack. Threads, thready threads. Mom— herself—Boozerov. No, that's not right: Dovganivna—herself— Aidy—Boozerov. No, she can't bring it back; it's all gone. Again, like that time in the spring—it flared and died.

But she does retain one thing from this flare: the being above—in relation to what happened the night before as well.

She's broken free of the boss's yesterday office; it doesn't oppress her anymore. She does, in fact, feel better.

"Thanks, Ma," Daryna says into the receiver she is still clutching in her hand; her knuckles stand out as if made from mother-of-pearl. "I know now what I have to do."

She'll go to Boozerov herself. And she will bring Gela's case to light—to heck with the film, if that's how things turned out, it's not about the film—she needs to find out where these threads that run through her life come from, whence this capillary lace of human destinies. And she'll also meet with Vadym: he's the only elected representative with whom she could be considered almost friends—they have Vlada in common. He is her only immediate chance of undercutting those bastards' show with which they plan to cover up someone else's slave trade. This is what's really important.

And what she's to do with herself, where she's to look for work, and whether she's to look for a job at all—that's all like scree underfoot, the common rubbish of life's prose, in the same department as what to make for dinner tonight. That's how she is seeing it at the moment—in big, clear terms, with her vision corrected—and she knows it's the right way of seeing.

"See, I know you're my smart girl!" her mom brightens up. "You'll see; it'll all turn out okay."

"How else, Ma?"

"Only do be careful!" Of course, Mom is Mom.

Daryna barely contains herself before she responds the same way as to her boss last night, and can't help but smile, "I'll do my best, Ma."

"Alright, you take care of yourself now!"

"You too, Ma. Call if you need anything."

That's a ritual phrase between them, and it means if you need money. This time, for the first time it doesn't sound completely heartfelt: her savings, Daryna hopes, will last her a while, but how long can they actually last if she also needs to help the old folks? Aidy, after all, also has a dad on an engineer's salary—it's enough for the food, but not for the medication he needs. That's how it all begins, that's how they leak and flood, our little cardboard houses. Nah, to hell with it, she doesn't want to go slopping around in all that again.

After she puts down the receiver, Daryna rises and, just as she is, in her flimsy nightshirt, goes to the window, throws the curtains open, and gasps with surprise. So that's where her clarity came from, that's what lit the curtain with the yellow light that she barely noticed for the entire hour she was on the phone: It's the snow! The first snow came in the night!

Spellbound, she looks at the instantly lightened street, at the heavy white lashes of trees in the park next door and the roofs turned white, turned Christmas-y, like a picture in a children's book: smoke is rising from one chimney, and the whole view looks as though the city had drawn a deep breath and stayed still in the blissful smile of relief. Her city—they can't take that away from her, either.

"So," Daryna says out loud, addressing no one in particular. "Let's fight back, shall we?"

Room 5. An Evening for Two

Half Past Five

ACQUIRED THIS MONTH:
1. *Polish military cross for Monte Cassino (inscription on the medallion "Monte Cassino Maj 1944"), bronze, with suspension ring, no ribbon, award document missing.*

Could send out a feeler to our military collectors about this. Be better to find a Polish contact, though—for them, it's got historical value, too.

2. *Commemorative badge issued on the 150th anniversary of Skovoroda's death, made from tank-grade steel, with the philosopher's portrait and inscription on the medallion ("Grigory Skovoroda 1794-1944").*

More from '44, huh? Bulk supply. Must be a sixty-year cycle or something. I'd read something once about the cyclic model of the universe—not much of a scientific hypothesis, but it does make you wonder sometimes how history makes itself known in roundabout ways.

3. *Tin-glazed earthenware ocarina, Kyiv region, mid-20th C.*

I don't remember this. Where'zd it come from? What does it even look like, this ocarina?

I'll leave my office, go sit in the subway, and play my ocarina … make this pitiful sound—there was a little old dude I saw in the subway once, playing a sopilka fife on the escalator landing. Never heard anything sadder in my life. Our folk music is not especially happy to begin with, and underground, laid bare by that frightful resonance, it cut like a knife, like the wail of an abandoned child. The voice of people that cryeth in the wildernesse. An abandoned sound—exactly what I feel like right now. Where the heck is that ocarina?

Let's get married, I said to her. I'm thirty-four already, and I've never said this to any woman before. My dad, in his day, took

Mom out to a restaurant expressly for this purpose, and Mom got so emotional she splashed wine on herself. But on Lolly it made no impression at all. Meaning, she snorted, the way she does, like a filly, and tossed her head just like that and said, "So that what? There'll be the stamp in the passport? So I'd be officially a home-maker instead of unemployed?"

I was going to protest—what's that to do with anything? Sure, I understand—what happened to her on TV affected her much more deeply than she admits even to herself: she has no concept of herself outside of her work. She simply doesn't have an alternative role at hand; shake her awake in the middle of the night and ask, "Who are you?" And she'll say, "Journalist!" She's got all her eggs in one basket, as they say, and now that she's had the basket taken away, my girl feels like she's had her whole life stolen and can't think about anything else. I understand exactly how she feels; I'm not an idiot. How could I not, really, after I'd gone through the same agonies myself—alright, maybe not exactly the same. I was twenty-five then and it actually seemed kind of cool to try something new, dabble in antiques—why not (just for the time being, I thought!)? Lolly's situation's totally different, and when you're staring down forty there's nothing cool about it.

But only when she snorted her filly's snort and said the thing about the stamp, which she'd already had in her passport once before, and then what am I doing (she didn't say this but she might as well have) filling my—and her—head with this nonsense when she's got some real problems on her plate, did it dawn on me that our notions of marriage are totally different. I am a Catholic, after all; never mind I haven't been to mass in ages. And that for her it's like this part of life's been painted over with oil paint—like the window in our school bathroom that was painted halfway up and we boys used to scrape out various inanities on it with our penknives; then at the university, I remember, the bathroom window, exactly the same, and someone had scratched, "God is dead. Nietzsche," on it and below an oval that was supposed to be a head, with a humongous mustache and hair standing on end, a thicket of straight lines—a portrait of Nietzsche maybe, or maybe the God that was dead.

4. *Two Russian copper coins, "denga," 1708, and "altyn," 1723, both in good condition.*

Jeez. How'd I fall for this junk? Hoboes do better picking through trash—they'd laugh at this "business" of mine....

I should've explained to her, like to a child: I'm not after the stamp, Lolly—I want us to be wed. In church, at the altar. I, Adrian, take you, Daryna, as my wife; I, Daryna, take you, Adrian, as my husband. In sickness and in health, in joy and in sorrow, till death do us part. That's it, and what's so fucking mysterious about it? And I would also like it, I would, Lolly, to be totally honest, like at confession. (Which you also did not understand that time I'd gone, why I'd done that, and kept asking like an anthropologist: What does it mean that you felt the need to go to confession? Did you mess up somewhere?) I'll tell you straight, I would, in fact, like to have a little Lolly-tot race a tricycle around our place raising a ruckus and looking like you and me both at the same time—doesn't matter a boy or a girl. I would like to hold his little hand in the street, and help him collect his toys scattered in different rooms, and sit at his little bed and read to him, and teach him everything I've learned in my life—even if I haven't learned all that much. And that's it. And Nietzsche, if I'm not mistaken, died in the loony bin after he'd first spent ten years eating his own shit.

What are you afraid of? You tell me. What?

You little terrified girl with tight little fists, determined to betray none of your fear—I saw you. I knew you to be that girl from that first moment, as soon as I'd spotted you among the backstage chaos of the TV studio that looks like a factory floor and a fossil dig at once—among turned-off cameras, dead like pterodactyls, and the twisted cables underfoot that slithered out of nowhere like pythons in the jungle—where, on the brightly lit stage familiar from your broadcasts, you, just done, were unpinning your microphone and talking to your crew, and all of you steamed with a kind of hot, feverish charge—as if you'd all just tumbled out of a nightclub and didn't know what to do with the rest of your artificially pumped-up high.

Back then I didn't know yet that this was the condition required for creating any virtual reality, and the one on the screen above all: to be real, it demands from its creators a constant energy feed, new logs for the fire, new kilocalories of living exhilaration—same as with a lie that has to be refreshed, fed all the time, even if it only means keeping it at the front of your mind with a constant mental effort because left to its own devices it would instantly deflate like any parasitic form of life, like mistletoe when the tree it sucked dry finally falls.

You belonged to the army of those who feed it—with their own blood, the gleam of their eyes and the freshness of their skin, and with time I learned to detect in you and your crew this short-lived, drug-like, camera-induced high; I watched you all come down from it outside the lens's reach—some faster, others slower, and still others, after several years on TV, turned lethargic and limp, like they'd been unplugged, and came to life only on camera; under the lights, they'd flip their tail a few times, like a fish thrown back into water, and then go back into suspended animation.

Back then I knew none of this, and the only thing that stunned me, blinded me, was your sharply lit shape, like an Egyptian figurine in tight black jeans. Before, I had no idea how blatantly the screen can lie: how close-ups make everyone's faces look equally wide, when in real life you are so fragile and fine—delicate, as Granny Lina liked to say, the highest compliment she could pay a woman. And you seemed to me then not the queen of that other-side kingdom but the opposite—the girl sacrifice, a lamb with your eyes and lips blackened à la Monica Bellucci, like a child who'd painted herself with her mother's makeup. When I came closer, the crown of your head came exactly up to my lips, and it was like someone gave me a push in that instant, saying into my ear, *Here, Adrian, is a woman made to your measure.*

I should protect you now, but I don't know how. That's the thing, my girl. More important—don't know if that's what you really want. In all your childhood photos that I have seen—from the little Lolly with a big bow perched above her comically Socratic forehead, to the teenager with mouse-tail braids, who is, everywhere, shying away from the camera like a small animal wanting to hide (as if you could sense, even back then, that the camera lies)—your little hands are squeezed into fists. As if you did all your growing up like that—in the constant state of red alert. My little warrior. These fists of yours—thumbs tucked under the folded fingers—are all I see these days: you've squeezed yourself into a fist, just like that, folded yourself in, and locked me out. Some work is being done in there, inside you, and I am not privy to it.

Can anyone ever understand a woman completely? And do women even understand themselves?

It's not like you've deliberately pushed me away from your problems—no, you told me about what happened in great detail, and you listened very intently, without your usual "contortions," when I tried to demystify for you how business works in our godforsaken country where government itself is merely a kind of business, and television is also business, and your entire journalistic guild serves, as even I can see from the sidelines, as a mere tip of the iceberg, one of the many means the real players have of laundering their dough—a plug, in a word. A gag. You didn't like that word; you bit your lip, winced with a pained expression, and recoiled too abruptly in the next instant, when I, stirred by tenderness, reached out to stroke your cheek. You were already closed before me, tense and cocked like a gun, and this short wordless exchange cut me to the quick, almost as if you'd rejected me as a man. And maybe even worse.

There's one thing I realized, Lolly: you're a strong woman—much stronger than you appear and you think yourself to be. It is only people of real strength who, on the ruins of their lives' script, do not rush to grasp the hand extended to them but instead react the way you did: instinctively isolate themselves, escape inward, like a sick wolf that leaves the pack and runs into the forest—to find the herb that can heal him or to die trying. You poor little wolf, what are we going to do with you, huh?

I know you need to find new footing, build your razed little hut anew, from the foundation up. If I hand you the building materials you need, you'll take them, of course—from me and from anyone else, from anywhere, as long as you can make use of them. And any other kind of help I can offer you'll also accept gratefully: you'll drink, say, the bedtime tea with honey I make you, nuzzle my shoulder, and tell me I'm sweet. But you won't come to *my* little hut, which, by the way, wasn't built overnight either and took just as much work as yours—you won't come live in it. Mine or anyone else's.

Build Me a House of Straw but One I Can Call My Own. That was the title of this really nice piece I found last summer, a wonderful folk-art painting—from the Cherkassy region, the traditional "a kozak and a girl near a well" subject, circa 1950. Could've been late forties even. I did fine with it, primitive art is in vogue these days. And the piece was a real classic, fit for a catalog: the kozak in a long red zupan, the girl wearing a wreath with ribbons, the well with a sweep, the white dappled horse, white house on a green field, and below, yellow on green, in naïve unpracticed lettering— that title. Blows your mind when you think about how people lived back then: kolkhozes, slavery, stone age; wore trousers made from tent-capes; ground a handful of pilfered grain on a hand mill to keep from starving—and when they had a free moment, they still ground alizarin crimson and ocher into thinned poppy-seed oil and painted the world that no longer existed. A world they'd had taken away from them, left only in a line of a song. The abandoned voice, the cry in the wilderness, like the fife in the subway at night. Build a house of straw. There's some silent tenacity in that, like there is in those tightly squeezed fists: as if to say if there isn't a way to build even with straw, I'll at least paint that house of mine—paint it and put it up in my room. The last territory to call one's own: 30 by 20 centimeters, in a homemade frame, from here to here—this is mine.

I know—you're of the same ilk as those nameless village paint-ers. You're one of those who wish to change the world—not adapt to it.

And I, it would appear, am a conformist.

And that's the way the toad farts.

Shit, the fuck I want those fucking coins!

Adrian Ambrozich, as my Yulichka says (She still wears a mini-skirt over her G-strings. Is she still nurturing the hope that one day I will lose it and lunge at her with a hungry growl, or does she consider this to be appropriate dress for a secretary at a success-ful firm?), Adrian Ambrozievich, you're an asshole. Yes, my dear, and man enough to admit it. And don't you go consoling yourself with the fact that everyone else is just the same, or even worse. If they're not assholes, they're goons. Either one or the other, and sometimes both. Take your pick, as they say. And tick your ballot accordingly, damn it.

Because really, what's this house I call my own? When the Soviet military-industrial complex went down the drain, taking all our science with it, all I managed to catch was a different train. That's if I tell it like it is, as at confession, instead of strutting my feath-ers the way I keep doing for Lolly—keep fanning my tail, not too much, but who wouldn't want the woman he loves to think him just a bit better than he really is? Praise me, Lolly, let me know you're proud of me—such a cool cat I am, got everything running just so.

The truth is that back then, in the nineties, I simply got lucky—took me years to appreciate how lucky I got. I was lucky to have contacts among the people who later learned to call them-selves art dealers, was lucky that I'd grown up knowing my way around the junk they were picking up for a song every Sunday at the Sinny Market—you wouldn't believe what turned up, what wonders could be had for a few pennies. Back in his National Bank days Yushchenko went there every weekend, like he was on the clock, and now he's got one of the country's best collections of folk antiques and is running for president (and God help him because those bitches got us by the balls already!—every day a new rule from tax inspection, they'll squash us, small businesses, like bugs for these elections!).

And my guys dragged stuff from that weekly dump without looking, like raccoons, often not even knowing from which side to open a snuff box, or that a Secession writing table, albeit crippled into a legless bench (which was what they thought they were buying), could have a secret drawer (like the one where we found a sheaf of yellowed old letters, which I guessed in a flash to be love notes—the letters were from before WWI, written in Polish, and that's how we stumbled into a whole other Kyiv, one the Bolsheviks thought they erased without a trace: the one of Polish nobility that had lived there since the fifteenth century and thought the city their own, and for whom, at the dawn of the twentieth century, Vladislav Gorodetsky set out to build on Vasylkivska Street a new cathedral with the fashionable concrete puffery, only they never got any use out of it. I could not really read those letters, but I had this strange feeling they'd been written to me, personally—back then I was dating Tatyana and kept getting ready to say to her what she kept waiting for me to say—that I loved her; I'd even convinced myself that I did, in fact, love her, but left her apartment every time still not having said it, and when I found the letters something inside me cracked—I got this hunch, that ran wider and wider like a fissure, that the true love of my life was still ahead, and not that far, actually: the letters promised Lolly to me).

For me, it is the world of objects I grew up with—I recognize their musty smells, the traces of tallow drips on their surfaces, the black dots on ineptly polished silver like dirt under the nails—as if I'm back in my grandpa and granny's apartment, crowded with cracked ancient chests of drawers, and for that reason always sort of shadowy. When they returned to Lviv in 1955, they couldn't live in the family's townhouse on Krupyarska because it'd been taken over by a KGB mayor and his brood, but our family still managed to preserve some of its furnishings and wares—and in that, too, I was lucky.

When the university sent me, with a kick in the ass, into the big world, after the instruments at the research lab where I worked got cut off for unpaid electricity bills, never mind paying anyone's salaries, and I didn't even have enough for cigarettes, and one day caught myself watching for butts as I walked, it was then I got scared, scared to a cold sweat: I had no idea a person could be debased so easily and that this person could be me! The entire social matrix in which I'd grown up burst like a soap bubble, and the only solid thing I could latch on to, to keep from going down with it, was that world of old things that my ancestors had pre-served—my family legacy, why not? There it is, finally, the right word: I began to live on my legacy; I am, basically, just another rat-ass rentier—not a self-made man. I was simply lucky enough to discover I had a legacy—that the knowledge and skills that had quietly imprinted themselves on me when I was little suddenly acquired real value, measured in hard currency.

Cigarette cases, candle tongs, pocket watches, lidded ink-wells, and carved umbrella handles (ivory, be so kind as to observe!—I would say to customers in my grandpa's voice)—I knew it all by touch. I could even sew on a Singer foot-pedal machine because I'd fixed one of them for Granny Lina when I was a teen; and before the market sorted itself out, in the boggy chaos of the time, I somehow came to command the reputation of a freaking guru, and once acquired, a reputation's as hard to shed as it is to get. By the time the bog solidified and set like concrete, I was already on the inside and had my own two feet to stand on. Had I started a few years later, I wouldn't have gotten as much as a sniff at the business without some venture capital, so yet again—I got lucky.

And I got unbelievably, fantastically lucky with one of my first partners, our department's ex-Komsomol organizer, Lyonchik Kolodub, who out of the goodness of his big heart gave us his philandering digs, a one-room efficiency on the ground floor of an old-Kyiv townhouse. He'd bragged he bought it back in 1991 for two grand, exactly one-hundredth of what it's worth today, but back in 1991 two grand for a regular person was as mythical a sum as a million bucks is today; it was never clear whence it could have come to a man like Lyonchik Kolodub—rat, boozer, womanizer (or, as he would tell you—a hero of the sexual battle front), and an absolute zero as a physicist who, ever since his freshman year, had aimed at a Komsomol career for the single reason of being utterly unfit for anything else.

The puzzle solved itself when one day Lyonchik vanished in an unknown direction, taking, rumor had it, the former district committee's till along for the ride—people said he eloped all the way to Latin America, and I'm inclined to believe it: for all his faults, Lyonchik did have a romantic strain; he had vision and a love of adventure, which, after all, were the things that made him fun. (Once, when drunk, he confided to us that his grandpa was a Gypsy who the Germans hung for a stolen chicken—at the university it was believed that Lyonchik's ancestor was a partisan almost as legendary as Kovpak and died a hero fighting the Nazis. Lyonchik played this spiel like a saxophone for the whole five years of Komsomol meetings at the university.)

Who knows. At the bottom of his rat's soul he may have been dreaming of a Gypsy baron's grandeur—of having his villa, acquired with the Komsomol dues, guarded by swarthy and jolly saber-toothed cutthroats in Che Guevara T-shirts, instead of the bored and shapeless Ukrainian cops who all look like farmhands so much more than pirates. Maybe his hot blood yearned for the beat of salsa tunes, and the vision of a cocoa-colored ass barely covered with feathers beckoned to him from across distant oceans, like the longed-for reward for all of his Komsy ratting, which, as it later turned out, he could have saved himself the trouble of doing because it did nothing to help the Soviets in the end—or maybe that was precisely why he eloped: because unlike the rest of our Komsy-to-business-converts who've already filled our parliament, he was ashamed of his past. Whatever the reason, Lyonchik disappeared, leaving us in possession of his apartment with a Venetto mattress on the floor (so thoroughly permeated with sperm and

vomit that we had to throw it out)—a place of our own, our own
house, a hundred-point lead in this crappy business, all thanks
to Lyonchik, may the old goat have peace wherever he is. And if
he's still alive, may God send him a whole swarm of chocolate-
skinned girls, and may the bullets of Colombian partisans miss his
old goat head. (Many of them are also Marxists and fight for the
Communist revolution, so if they take Lyonchik hostage, he, worse
comes to worst, can always become their political commissar and
recite to them on steamy tropical nights the decisions of the last
Soviet Communist Party Congress if he hasn't forgotten them all,
the program of the USSR's development to 2000 included. Or he'll
teach them to sing "Lenin Is Young Again." As you would expect
of a Gypsy, Lyonchik Kolodub was incredibly musical.)

I can almost hear Lolly's voice right now, telling me sensibly—
like a cool, tender hand on my feverish head: Why are you making
such a big deal out of it? And I am, my golden girl (because you
are my golden girl, have been, are, and will be, no matter what lies
ahead of us), making a big deal of it, and I don't even know why.
And I can even tell myself, plain and simple (don't know if I could
ever tell you, though) if I wanted to have something to be really
proud of, I should have nailed myself, damn it, like Jesus Christ to
the cross, to our doomed thermionic generator seven years ago. I
should have lived on bread and water, quit smoking, told Tatyana
to go where the sun don't shine with her constant whining about
how she's got nothing to wear (I hope she finally caught herself
some fat dickhead after we split; she was still pretty enough for
that), bitten off a piece of some foreign grant for the lab, worked
eighty hours a week like a bulldozer, and forgotten about the rest
of the world—but finished the project! Like that. Then I would've
shown myself what you showed by resigning from your channel:
resistance of the material. I would know then that I couldn't be
bent, that I'm capable of standing my ground. Instead, I split.

I could've been a scientist—a real scientist and not just another
PhD in physics. But I've already missed the age of brilliant ideas—
those all happen before thirty. Bohr developed the model of the

atom before he was twenty-eight, Einstein published "On the Electrodynamics of Moving Bodies" at twenty-six, Bell invented the telephone at twenty-nine. It's a good age: you're starting to know what you're talking about, but you aren't scared yet because you don't believe you can lose. A constant upward ascent. I used it up on building my business. My best years, right here—in this office, in these catalogs. In this damn log: two Russian copper coins in good condition, fetch up to twenty-five Euros a piece at Russian auctions, if, of course, one gets lucky. And why shouldn't I—I'm a lucky motherfucker, ain't I?

What I've never told Lolly is that as a second-year student I caught the eye of Strutynsky himself, God rest his soul—and that was the same as falling into the hands of a living god. When the old man shuffled into the lecture hall, always in his dust- and chalk-powdered suit, everything froze as if a basilisk had just entered. We, young bucks, had no clue back then that we bored this legend, with his scornfully drooping eyelids, to tears: the distance that separated us could only be measured in light years, if at all. And Strutynsky wasn't a teacher, and did not know how, or feel inclined, to begin to breach that distance. What he did know how to do—magnificently—was to spot, through those leaden eyelids, like a mythical Viy, those in the massive class before him who had the potential of breaching that distance themselves one day, who could rev their thought to the speed required.

There were three of us like that, that year—Gotsik, Zahar, and myself—and that's who he taught, collecting quizzes from the rest of the class and giving them to us to grade. It was in his seminars that I first experienced that dazzling exultation that comes from the energy of a thought set free—and it's never come back as powerfully since. The brilliance, the clarity when chaos begins to make sense under the quickening assault of your thought and finally—poof!—turns into the slim crystal of a formula—there's nothing else like it. A complete loss of self and a sense of omnipotence at once—you step out on a break reeling like you're drunk and feel sweat running down between your shoulder blades. Skydiving's got nothing on it.

So I do know how it felt to them—Einstein, Bohr, all those dudes who could. The whole thing is in not letting your assault slacken. In knowing how to keep it up. For years, if need be, that's the thing. For years.

Instead, I split.

It's been a long time since I dreamt of complete, perfect solutions—and I used to, they came for a while even after I left the lab—as if my unemployed thought, evicted from its home, moved to the basement of my mind and kept stubbornly running her Singer sewing machine there: night after night formulas lit up on my screen (I still remember that cold metallic glow from below!), appeared, as if spelled out by an invisible hand, bloomed like seaweed, like underwater flowers, one time a whole scheme came together in space as if made out of snowflakes, like the fairytale about the Snow Queen; and in my dream I somehow knew that the space was four-dimensional, but didn't remember the proof itself in the morning, only retained a general impression—of spellbinding, freezing beauty. Or maybe I did remember but didn't write it down—because what would I've done with it? The day then dropped into my mind like a dirty sponge and erased everything it didn't need without a trace. Fifteen years ago Strutynsky used to say I had a unique cognitive apparatus—I interrupted him with a question in the middle of a lecture and the old bloodsucker's eyes flashed like laser-beams: "Vatamanyuk," he said, fixing me with an enamored stare that made me blush, "you have a unique cognitive apparatus." The glory of that moment lasted me until I graduated. It sputtered for a long time, that apparatus—spinning empty, like an engine without fuel. Fading oscillation, a faint SOS signal, dying, dying ... I doubt it could be revved again to cosmic speeds now.

Gotsik's now a postdoc somewhere in Minnesota; Zahar's top management at a German trade firm, develops their strategy. Or maybe Danish, I don't remember. No physicist came of him, that's a fact. Nothing's ever come of anyone doing science in their free time. Science is not your folk art, be so kind to observe.

Maybe I could get a stand-up routine going: Old whore crying over her lost chastity? In the subway, with that ocarina accompaniment?

To tell myself, straight, what I'll never have the guts to tell her about myself: Adrian Vatamanyuk, you're a loser. Yes, you're only thirty-four, and you've accomplished certain things in this life, you eat your bread with butter and even caviar, have a business and like it (love it, in fact), own an apartment in Kyiv—one of Europe's most expensive cities, let's not forget, and a small capital—have friends, and finally, the most important thing, the love of your life. Your defeat is looking quite successful. Indeed, so successful that no one, except you, can see it.

It is nested so deep inside me that it's long ceased being a foreign body. It's become part of me.

I didn't break down. No, no one broke me. I got scared. And my breaking point was truly the day I caught myself looking for a cigarette butt I could pick up and put in my pocket. I'd seen our engineers finishing someone else's before—the guys would "disinfect" them by running the filter ends through a match flame. Half of our class had fled into business already; rumor had it some of the faculty had turned to small "shuttle trade"; someone had seen Assistant Professor Rybachuk at the flea market with spare parts and burnt-out lightbulbs (which people bought to screw in at work, after taking the good ones from work home for themselves)—although not in Kyiv itself but in Irpin: there was a "professors' flea market" there for those who still would've been ashamed to have anyone they knew, let alone a student of theirs, come by their spread. It was only later that our professorate caught on to the notion that grades, exams, and diplomas were also commodities for which one could charge students money without having to stand out in the cold or even to leave the building; and back in the nineties the country still roiled in a violent chemical reaction whose outcomes carried some to the top and sank others to the bottom.

There, at the bottom, in the increasingly visible deposit were accumulated the paupers, the hoboes with dollies and plaid oilskin bags the size of suitcases, people with no age, with dead eyes and faces that looked like they'd been sewn from linen crumpled damp and never ironed out. A few years ago, at the door to Pantagruel, I was assaulted, with demented roaring and open arms, by one such half-decomposed Lazarus fresh out of the grave; with horror, I recognized him to be Sashko Krasnokutsky from my class—we'd solemnly declared ourselves milk brothers once, after we'd found out we'd both slept with the same ever-willing lab tech from the radio physics department, Ilonka-the-Barbie.

"We'd sucked at one tit!" Sashko had roared happily at me then, and his roar hadn't changed since his student days at all, still sounded like a bike without a muffler, only it wasn't so easy to tell that it was, in fact, Sashko, that was doing the roaring: he was missing front teeth, and kept slurping up his spit. There was something caricaturish about our run-in at the restaurant, from which I'd just rolled out all fat and glossy like the bronze cat they had by the door—stuffed with a good dinner and a half bottle of Beaujolais Villages—and here was this toothless monster like something dug out of a trash heap slapping me on the shoulders with the choking roar, fit for the loony bin, "Huw'sh it shakin, bud!" This could have looked like a prank, like a skit based on the well-known joke about the two old classmates:

"And how's your life?"

"I haven't eaten in three days!"

"Hey, man, that's no good; you gotta make yourself do it!"

Only a purposely bad skit, crude and grotesque, as life always looks when it aims to imitate folklore and other literature. Plus there was one "but," one departure from the text: Sashko wasn't about to complain to me about not having eaten for three days, not at all. In fact, he seemed to be completely oblivious to the dramatic contrast between us and went on babbling as obliviously and cheerfully as if it were he and not I who'd just finished some young Beaujolais, and about three bottles instead of half.

From his lisping I more or less gathered the poor slob played the stock market, and played himself clear out of his home, the oldest story in the world. Basically—went after wool and came back shorn. But the horrifying thing was that Sashko wasn't pretending or bullshitting when he gabbled about it in a casual, could-happen-to-anyone tone, chuckling now and then as if this were something amusing and unimportant—and next stammered enthusiastically with his toothless mouth about his "exshellent proshpects." Never mind that the only prospect he could've been hoping for was a good nursing home: he really could not see himself from outside. Apparently, at some point on the descending slope of his life, he shut his eyes and checked out, refusing to watch the horror of it once and for all, and probably saw a completely different version of himself when he looked in the mirror—the one who used to walk around with his pockets stuffed full of condoms and banged Ilonka-the-Barbie, who eventually married her department head and went with him to the Sorbonne.

I gave him a twenty on some face-saving pretext, even though he didn't ask for money, and he was so happy that I thought he'd latch on to me like a tick after that, whine for my telephone number and so on, but he said goodbye quickly with the air of a man late for a business meeting and trotted off through the park. A little later when I drove down Zolotovoritska, I saw him duck into a bar on the corner, saw the tense expression of his back (exactly that: the expression of his back), and that's when it finally dawned on me where he lit out for in such a rush: the bar had gambling machines.

It was as if someone had shown me an alternative version of my own life. What could have happened to me if I hadn't one day, watching for a cigarette stub underfoot, seen myself from outside and been horrified: Holy shit, is it that easy? Snap, and you're on the trash heap and several generations' worth of survival experience—of those packed off into camps, stripped of their property as kulaks, deported, the heroes of Grandpa's tales about Karlag, all their long-forgotten skills, "I saw me a stub with a line of red lipstick and broke from the ranks after it"—defrosting in you as they'd been taken out of the freezer?

I remember the exact spot where it hit me—on Shevchenko Boulevard, not far from the University subway station. Like something shook me out of a coma, and I looked around, stunned, slowly recognizing the place. In moments like this, your mind, for some reason, always fixes the place like a postcard: it's late fall, slush, drizzle, dim streetlights; street stands line the Botanic Garden's fence, and the garden's dark presence looms below, the massed domes of St. Volodymyr cathedral in the brown sky above. It was as if I were seeing it all at once, from above—the gigantic, steep Kyiv slope down which I was being carried like a parachutist; I felt this downward motion in my body as it sometimes happens in dreams—down, into the dark, scraping against the spikes of the fence and the naked branches of the Botanic Garden.

All young and brilliant, the winner of every academic competition and Strutynsky's own pet, I was plummeting, going down without any resistance, pulled into the last residual sputtering of a stopped machine, only this time the machine was real. My research lab was in agony; our entire system of research institutes was in agony; all our applied and fundamental physics, chemistry, astronomy, and biology, that had spent the previous half-century feeding and clothing themselves off the accumulation of increasingly more perfect means of destruction—and now that only the Russians, of all Soviet heirs, had the privilege of killing anyone—had come to a grinding halt. So our jackals feasted on the scraps from the Russian's table—falling over each other to pawn off deathly junk on whatever Asian/African fiefs were buying, so they could beat one another to buying live giraffes for their dachas, dialing the fuck out on all our science for decades to come.

What solar batteries, you moron!—I almost groaned out loud, right there in the street, seeing, as clear as on a graph, the remaining trajectory of my motion: lower and lower, down into the deep-water murk, with a thin line of tiny bubbles, into despair, the hopeless peddling-piddling of whatever came my way (I'd already sold two of Grandpa's cigarette cases and eaten through the get). Everything inside me rebelled, every little cell squealed, "No!" And my entire fucking unique cognitive apparatus that had been hitched to the thermionic generator hammered feverishly, revving out of inertia, and dragged me in the opposite direction—up, clinging to every alternative I hadn't bothered to consider before. I called my cigarette-case guys that same night.

I didn't slam any doors as Lolly did. I, when you think about it, didn't quit anything abruptly, the smartass that I am—like all Galicians, Igor would say (he's one of those who'd binged on the Brothers Gadiukin band in their day and came to believe, once and forever, that Galicians constitute a special breed of people). Officially, I can always go back; officially I'm still a PhD candidate in the Semiconductors Department. Weekend scientist, that's me. People think you can do that. That it's like an office manager's job: you come in, turn on your computer, work however long, shut it all down, and walk away—free as a bird. Some clients, when they learn I'm a scientist, and a techie to boot, look at me with new respect: that's an extra layer of cool. Shit that's cool. In moments like that, I feel like a male prostitute who's killed his patron and is now peddling her things. No one except me knows that I had to bury a part of myself—forever; that's it, lights out, it's all gone. That I live with my own corpse. As do all my peers, actually, only for some of them it's worse. For most of them, to be precise.

I took Sashko Krasnokutsky, who lunged at me out of the darkness and then fell back into it, to be a fortuitous—that's how selfish I am!—sign from Providence. A visual aid illustrating what it was that horrified me that day on Shevchenko Boulevard—and that I did well getting horrified. Sashko's arc led down, mine—exponentially, up: E to the nth degree. That's how it seemed to me then.

For a while, it even soothed the constantly stinging pain of dull dissatisfaction with myself. I recognized this pain in others, too, especially from the way people drank, the way they celebrated a contract, the way they worked so hard to prove to themselves that "life is good" that they ended up face down in their salads. Hell no, I told myself: two cognacs or three glasses of dry wine, and not a drop more. Plus the swimming pool, plus the gym. I was always bright-eyed and bushy-tailed at the time—a big cheese, like that heron among the birds. The only thing I missed—my dreams: I didn't remember them anymore. Nothing to do with alcohol—just, a part of me went cold like an unused room in a house.

And unused rooms, as is only to be expected, are where ghosts move in.

"Adrian Ambrozich, yu hev a meetin et haf past faiv."

Yulichka emerges at the door, barely covered below the navel by her new maxi-belt. Where'd she get the idea that she's got legs fit to be peeled to the root like that?

Out, you moron!—I barely keep from barking, but the pure love of truth keeps my mouth shut: my secretary is no moron. Instead, I do something I'd never in a million years expect from myself: I get up, go right up to her (her perfume's rather nice), bend down, and run my hand over the entire length of her satiny-black-hosed, calvary-bowed thighs—she could press them together and you'd still fit your head between her knees—bottom up, all the way, to her crack, to her very pubic bone sheathed in her micro-skirt, and squeeze it so hard that my brave Yulichka hisses. Hisses but doesn't give in, what a trooper, take one for the team. That's what I thought—a G-string. And it doesn't cut in?

"Thank you, Yulichka," I say, leaning her away from me like a tin soldier, but not letting go of her nether regions. "By the way, I've been meaning to tell you—would you mind buying yourself a suit? An English one, you know, a traditional cut, a bit conserva-tive—just the thing for the antiques business. Remember that old man who'd promised us a cuckoo clock? Where'd he disappear to—did you, by chance, scare him off with your, *mmm*, glamorous outfit?"

"I'll call him back," Yulichka mutters as if hypnotized, throat caught, voice softened.

"That'd be great," I say just as nicely, and let her go. The whole interaction holds about as much eroticism as if I'd held on to a doorknob for a while, but it still makes me feel a tiny bit better: nothing improves one's mood like a spot-check of female deployability, even if you've no use for it whatsoever. Well, at least now my secretary'll remember that it's not all gold that's wet. Staff development, that's it. It appears I'm also a petty tyrant, who'd have thought.

"That's the only comment I have—otherwise, you're doing a wonderful job," I grin, friendly as a crocodile, as she disappears behind the door—not to cry in the bathroom, I hope. I don't want girls crying because of me. And I shouldn't be taking it out on my subordinates. It's no one's fault I took a left turn at Albuquerque, as the cartoon goes.

And at "haf past faiv" I do, in fact, have a meeting—with my, generously speaking, expert. Half past five, both hands drooped down—a moment when time is impotent. Half past five, Adrian Ambrozievich, half past five. Fie on you, bite your tongue!— Granny Lina used to say. Am I turning superstitious or something?

In fact, the difference between me and Sashko Krasnokutsky was not that great: we were both moving further away from ourselves, from whatever was the best in us—meaning, we were both heading for the bottom. Because the bottom is not scavenging in trashcans—the bottom is precisely this: rejecting whatever's best in you. The arc of my descent was more comfortable and smelled better, that's all. And if you want to talk about signs from Providence—that was one, without a doubt, manifested as clear as could be, short only of a statue talking. Or a burning bush. Only I, self-satisfied moron that I was, was liable to blow off a direct fiery warning from a thorn bush too. The dumbest thing is I did not recognize myself in Sashko—did not see that I lived a lie I told myself, just as he did. Did not see that we were both sick with the same illness, only in him it had reached the symptomatic stage and in me it had not. Something shoved it straight into my face, and I blew it. I should've seen Sashko as a magnified projection of myself, and instead I fanned my tail and turned up my nose like a snob: I ain't my brother's keeper. And he's my brother, milk-brother, isn't he—we held on to the same tit. Whose keeper am I?

Every man's natural need—to be a keeper, to protect that with which God trusted you, to hold your place in this universe—with arms, if need be, and to the end. Oleksiy, the security guard, once told me that when his child was born he understood, for the first time, a line he'd remembered since school, from some classic author—*I'll shoot if they come*. That author had some scoundrel land-lord saying this when his land was being taken away from him, or something like that, or maybe that's just the way it worked in the Soviet textbook—that the landlord was a scoundrel, and maybe in fact he was a good guy. At any rate, the way Oleksiy said it sent shivers down my spine. The last thing I'd expect of the guy was such artfully crystallized philosophy. The man's plain as a door, younger than me, a former cop—left his post after he and his bosses locked horns over something—loves his wife beyond belief, glows all over when he talks about her, quit smoking when she got pregnant. And built them a house in his Obuhov, where his parents live—everything like in that song. His own house: wife and child. And the dad who keeps a Kalashnikov under a bench somewhere—in case "they come." I shake his hand now every time I see him now, something I didn't use to do. I could count on the fingers of one hand the people I've met who have the courage to live their own lives. Their own, and not just whatever came their way.

"I'll shoot if they come"—it's perfectly lucid; it has the beauty and clarity of a simple solution. And I didn't shoot because no one came for me—I came for myself. And now I'm "shooting" to keep the tax rats away. Fucking hero. From, shame to say, a whole line of soldiers, as the song goes, keep the shrapnel coming down the line; Ukrainian rebels don't retreat in a fight.

Lolly did gasp with such delight that first time we met: "You're Olena Dovganivna's grandnephew?" The way she looked at me—I went faint (from that first glance—in sickness and in health, till death do us part): She looked at me with the same thrill of recognition as Strutynsky once had when he said to me, "Vatamanyuk, you have a unique cognitive apparatus." You are the only two people—Lolly, don't take offense for my lumping you in with the old gnome; he was a great man and a great scientist, God rest his soul—who saw in me something *greater* than myself. Something, entrusted to me by fate, that demanded *effort*: the unrelenting assault, the stretching of my neck till sweat ran down my back to grow tall enough to measure up to that greatness inside me. You saw something I had to reach for. You and no one else.

We met right about the time when I stank of self-satisfaction like a whole duty-free store at an international airport. Thought myself a heck of a cool cat. Riding that same wave, less than a month after my run-in with Sashko outside of Pantagruel. Since then, Lolly and I have gone to that little park on Zolotovoritska a million times, to the café across from that casino-bar with the machines where Sashko trundled off to hoping to win his life back with the twenty I'd given him, and we go to the opposite side, too—to the Cosmopolitan, and the pub on the corner: we've stomped all over that spot, spun our presence like spider webs around it, but I've never taken her to Pantagruel. The woman of your life—what a cheesy banality you'd think, straight out of a cabaret repertoire, a bad restaurant chanson—you'd never say it out loud unless you were a total moron. But whoever originally thought this up was no moron. Every banality, it seems, is just a truth that's been too often repeated—like a mantra, until it lost all meaning. It doesn't stop being a truth—it's just that now everyone has to discover its original meaning, worn off from frequent use, anew. The woman of your life—the one who gives you back your life. Your own, the way it was supposed to be—if you, asshole, hadn't flushed it down the toilet. If you hadn't split, refusing to maintain the effort.

Denga, altyn—I go back to the same line, read it and do not understand what I've just read. Nope, I'm no use at work today.

How old is she? Dad asked about Lolly, when we came to record his memories (and all that footage, the entire archive, almost two years of Lolly's work is now just going to rot because

the channel owns it!). I told him she was five years older than
me. (Actually, six and a bit—I don't know why I felt compelled
to understate the gap.) I waited for the old man to bring up
Mom—maybe not up front, as in, she reminds me of your mom
(although Lolly does resemble Mom a little; she, too, has something of an alpinist in her, knock on wood), but for him to recall
the story of his own life's biggest love because that would've
meant that he accepted Lolly and understood how serious this
relationship is for me. Instead, he went all soft and sentimental,
though somehow missing the point: oh, he responded, delighted,
"You've always liked older girls, remember you were three and
the neighbors' little girl was four and a half and you went around
telling everyone you guys were getting married? Tailed her
everywhere she went, gave her your teddy bear—remember?"
I remembered neither the girl nor the teddy bear, but still got
all sentimental myself: it's always nice to confirm that time is a
relative value, that a person does not change in any fundamental
way over the years, and that blondish rug rat in the old photo
with pieces of string tied around his plump little wrists and the
current knuckle-dragger of six foot six, two hundred and five,
are one and the same, after all.

When I later told Lolly about the girl with the teddy bear, she
had a good laugh, and then said, once again astounding me by
giving voice, unerringly, to my own unspoken thought, "Do you
think it's possible your dad was actually thinking about himself—
about something he himself remembered from when he was three
years old, from that night when they roused him to kiss Aunt Gela
goodbye—*that's* what I was asking him about. What if his mind
had just stayed on that track?" She's so smart, my little Dr. Freud.
The woman who enters your life and pierces it through, literally,
like a threaded needle—gathering, threading the bits and pieces
scattered through time into a complete picture that had begun to
stringing itself together long before you came to this world. The
woman who can reach *deeper* than your own memory—and that's
why, with her, you always know who you are.

The first sign she was The One: Lolly gave me back my dreams. Turned on the lights in the unused rooms. Doesn't matter if some of those dreams turned out *not to be my own*, as if during my absence, while I was obtusely stuffing my mind with tax reports and client co-optation strategies, looking first for an intelligent accountant, then for a good lawyer, followed by reliable experts and reliable bribe-takers in the city government, and other shit, of which there was so much that the mind could not keep up and suffered from chronic constipation—while I was doing all that, someone else had moved into the unused rooms. Someone I don't have a clue about, have no idea why he's wandering around in there with his flashlight like in an old-timey picture show, showing me pieces of some unknown old movie, or what this has to do with me and my family. That it does have something to do with us I can guess by the fact that the family, too, has been frequenting my dreams—but in a bizarre way, as if in passing: Great-Aunt Gela walks through me as if I weren't there and speaks to Lolly directly, like I'm no longer their *go-between*—alright, that's fine, I'm not jealous, but it's upsetting a bit, you know, who's whose blood? Whose dad got pulled out of his bed at the tender age of three for a goodbye kiss, and then taken to Kazakhstan in the cattle car, on dry rations alone, so that when the convoy gave Granny Lina her half cup of water at stations, she held each sip in her mouth and had the child suck it out along with her spit? (Dad himself does not remember that journey, but he talked about it as though he were reading from notes—the way he heard it from Granny.)

"So one could say," Lolly said to Dad kindly, sympathetically, in the tiny living room, where he sat before the cameras stiffly as if in a plaster corset, afraid to shift his pose, between the Hutsul rug crucified on the wall and the hutch with the few unshattered remains of the old Korets china set (under the camera lights I was suddenly blinded by the pitiful squalor of these trappings of a Soviet home where I grew up, pieced together painstakingly from the splintered-off fragments of the old world), "that you were, essentially, persecuted as a child solely for the fact that your aunt fought in the nationalist resistance?"

Dad made a small embarrassed sound: he didn't find the designation of a "persecuted child" especially appealing—he would've preferred to cut a decidedly manlier figure before his daughter-in-law-to-be, and he surprised me by telling the story—I almost wondered if he weren't making it up on the spot, at least I'd never heard it before—of how when they were already in Kazakhstan, in the settlement, he, a five-year-old runt, rushed to defend his mom against a guard, sinking his teeth into the man's arm until he drew blood. "He got all mad, 'You,' he spat, 'Bandera spawn, we'd do better to shoot all you fuckers'—but he let Mom go!" Then Dad laughed, pulling together the dense (so much denser now, I thought) wrinkles from his entire face, glowing just like his five-year-old self—thrilled anew with his first display of masculine valiance—and I saw he was telling the truth.

"You never told me this," I said later, to which he, still elated, responded cheerfully, "Forgot all about it myself, don't even know how it came back right then!" That's how I discovered that I am not the only one for whom Lolly can turn on lights in unused rooms. It's her gift—drawing out hidden information from people, like pushing a button: Click!—and the light goes on. ("You should've been a detective," I joked—"Yep, like Columbo!" she played along. We've already developed our own repertoire of set phrases and words whose only purpose is to replace touch because you can't really live your life in each other's arms—that's what loving words are for, to hold each other with them—and now we'll have to strike some things out of this repertoire, so as not to put salt into her wounds—my Lolly's no longer Columbo.)

Incredible how much of this kind of stuff, long forgotten in our family, she's brought back into the light in this way of hers. And it was all gradually coming together—all the disconnected facts I remembered from what Granny and Grandpa told me, fragments of recollections, episodes unattached to dates, people who had died long ago or were scattered around the world—all this was settling, piece by piece, into a chronological order, into bins sequentially ordered by year. (I was thrilled, of course—I never had the time to organize the family history, but now I've come to regard the fact that Lolly was delivering it to me for free as an inextricable part of our life together, as a family. And now the foundation's sliding under this life, too, the thing that had made us first accomplices and later lovers was being taken away.)

And still for Lolly all that wasn't enough. There were times I'd say, listen, don't you think you could call it good already— you've got four generations of the Dovgans down pat, good as your own kin—and she'd just shake her head: all this I've put together so far may not even get used, for a thirty-minute film—if it's to be any good—you need a good thirty hours of footage, and twenty-nine of that will end up on the floor, and I'm still missing—she'd be snapping her fingers in the air—the main twist, the answer, that! The answer—to what? In those moments I felt myself to be the go-between. As if Lolly, by some mysterious trick, had leapfrogged over me in time, had jumped over my back and landed in the place of Granny Lina, the main keeper of all our family's stories.

Only Granny Lina ran out of time. After Grandpa's death, she'd been meaning for years to write down her memoirs, even got a special thick notebook bound in dark-green, fake leather. Dad and I encouraged her every way we could, but nothing ever came of it: after Granny was gone, all we found in her special notebook were a few pages illegibly laced with columns of dates and initials that looked like an alphabet of a dead language or a cipher of a wiped-out spy ring—like all Dovgans, Granny Lina did not like writing; even her letters, always short, reminded me of doctors' prescriptions.

One thing I did always like about them though was her unchanging form of address—"Beloved Adrian"—which once allowed me to pass them off in a summer camp as letters from a fantasy girlfriend. In psychology, Lolly says, this is called transference—or maybe sublimation if I'm not mixing them up again.

But I really loved Granny Lina, and I believe she loved me, too. It was she who sang to me before sleep when I was little; she could sing just as well as Mom, only all her songs were unlullaby-like, tragic—I recognized one of them later, when Zhdankin sang it in 1989 at the Chervona Ruta Festival ("black furrows plowed, and the bullets sprout, sprout, hey, hey ...")—as if Granny, sitting next to my little bed, were mourning someone. It was only later that I learned that Adrian was supposed to be the name of her second son—my uncle, due to be born in exile, but who was born prematurely and laid down in an unmarked mass grave on the steppe where Temirtau now stands, next to the banished adults, camp prisoners, and Japanese POWs.

The city they were building was later called a Komsomol project, like all Soviet cities built by prisoners, and it's still burning up the sky somewhere in the middle of the Kazakh steppe with its forest of yellow smoke plumes—"foxtails." Temirtau, the city of metallurgists, with the highest cancer mortality rate in the world. "Some get medals, some get proud, some get the city Temirtau," Grandpa often repeated the local saying, and might as well been reading his obit, because thirty years later Temirtau cancer caught up with him, too—but at least in his own bed, and not in a ditch on a foreign steppe.

I don't even know how Granny had come up with this name, Adrian. It wasn't in the family—in the whole last century I don't know anyone who was called that. Dad was named Ambroziy in honor of Grandfather Dovgan, Granny's father and my great-grandfather, who in the Polish days was a rather famous doctor in Lviv—one of the few Ukrainian doctors whom the Poles, like the Russians, otherwise big fans of the "blending of the people," never did kick out of the city and into some ethnically Polish lands—he must've really known his doctoring stuff, that gramps. Accordingly, the second son should have been named after the grandfather from the other side, Iosyp. Iosyp Vatamanyuk—sounds fine to me. Or, did Granny think that was too plain, too country? On the Vatamanyuk side, all men for generations have been Mykhailos, and Grytskos, and Vasyls, like Grandfather's younger brother, the one who perished in Kolyma.

Grandfather was the first in his family to go to Gymnasium; he passed his exit exams, the matura as it was called—"done turned a gentleman" by the standards of the day—ironically, the same year the Soviets came. He was a good student, but did not receive a distinction because of this one Polish professor, he said, who couldn't stand the sight of Ukrainian students, and humiliated them every chance he got. And Grandpa, on top of that, once openly refused to sing, at some official occasion, the Polish military march from 1918—and at this point in the story he'd always whine, incredibly off-key, "We-e-e the first briga-a-de, ri-i-flemen campa-aign," making the march sound like goats bleating to illustrate his point more convincingly.

Were I in that Pole's shoes, I'd get mad, too, when I heard that. Although the thing that stunned me most when I was little was how one could just declare to the teacher, out loud, "I won't sing the occupier's songs!"—and only pay for it by losing a stupid A somewhere on your atestat. (In second or third grade, I spent some time seriously contemplating repeating this experiment on our choir teacher, who called us up one by one to squeal without accompaniment before the whole class, "Vast is my Native Land," but I ultimately decided not to venture beyond shooting spitballs through tubes—really disemboweled ballpoint pens—during her lessons, all the rage at the time.) And when in '39 the Soviets came, that very first autumn in Grandpa's town they put to the wall everyone who graduated with distinction, line by line according to the Gymnasium's rosters—Poles, Ukrainians, Jews, not sorting who was "genteel" and who was "peasant," everyone whose atestats had that summa cum laude that Grandpa, thanks to his Ukrainophobe professor (I wonder if they shot him, too) never got.

As Granny Lina used to say, there's no bad that doesn't come to good. Had Gramps kept his peace and been a good boy, he, too, would have gotten a dose of lead from the Soviet government for his distinction, just so he wouldn't go around being smart. Go figure, then, how you're supposed to live—singing like they tell you to, or, better, putting your foot down, saying, I won't and you can all go to hell?

He and Granny met later, under the Germans, when Grandpa was already in the underground—but they were still kids, basically. Although, people back then seemed to mature sooner than we do now. Such a romantic story it was, like in a movie: Grandpa with a briefcase full of OUN leaflets got caught in a raid, and Granny Lina just happened to be there, in his way; he whispered, "Help me, miss!" and she got it, instantly, and threw herself into his arms, pretending to be his girlfriend, and, before the Germans got him, took his briefcase and got home without any trouble at all. Germans didn't search girls, wasn't their custom. Granny used to say she didn't even remember what he looked like really—only that he was decent and had brown eyes, which turned out to be blue. How, one has to wonder, did a seventeen-year-old girl know how to act in that situation, who taught her? Gramps, never one to gawk, managed to ask for her name before they hauled him off, and found her after they let him out. By '45, they already had little Ambroziy, my dad.

But still—why am I Adrian?

It's sort of disturbing to think I will never find out. That I don't have anyone left to ask. That there are things people didn't tell you before they ran out of time—departed for destinations much more distant than Latin America, way beyond the coverage zone, and the church in its role of mobile service provider has long thrown in the towel: no hints, clues, or leads—you're on your own. They abandoned you, the keepers of your secrets—naked, not a thread to cover yourself with, and you're just doomed to spin in this world, your whole life like shit in an ice-hole, basically knowing and understanding nothing about yourself. They did deal you a few cards beside what's written in your medical chart under Family History (cancer—well, at least it's not schizophrenia), and you play life the best you can, but blindly because most of the cards come face down, and you never know if the one you're drawing next will be an ace or a single six. Come on, man, come on, you hear from all sides, knocking on doors, breaking through your windows, come on, no time to think.

"Adrianabrozich!"

The knocking—it's Yulichka. Does a man here ever have a chance to focus and finish a decent thought? What's that goose screaming about?

Yulichka stands at the door, holding on to the frame like she's being pursued by gangsters in an action flick—spooked, her face drooping, and for that reason really resembling a goose.

"What happened?" I ask as sternly as I can manage. "What, are we being raided? By the Red partisans, perhaps?"

Yulichka stares at me with her yellow goose eyes: she's lost. Of course, she never met Lyonchik Kolodub; she came later, when he was already gone. For an instant, I feel intensely sorry that no one remembers him anymore—the last romantic from the tribe of Komsomol rats, and I don't even have anyone with whom I could share the insight that just now occurred to me: that Lyonchik must have run all the way to Latin America, not after cocoa-skinned mulatto girls, but after the shadow of his Gypsy grandfather, the unfortunate partisan chicken thief. To seek there, among the slackers just like him, blissed out on the world's best pot, his lost ideal motherland: red-cockaded soldiers, Kalashnikovs over their shoulders, firewater at their belts, and Lenin so young and so fair. All good Komsomol men go to Latin America after they die. Shit, am I getting so old no one in my circle remembers the friends of my youth?

And only then do I grasp the fact that someone has really scared Yulichka, and I finally rise from behind my desk—crack the ceiling of my own thoughts with my head. (Mom once taught me that a man must always rise in the presence of a woman, but seven years in Ukrainian business relieved me of all the good manners imparted to me in childhood.)

"What's going on?"

"Telefon!" Yulichka exhales noisily, and it scares her even more: the word drops too inappropriately for her stormy entrance, and I've already put her down on the appropriateness front today. "I don't knou, Adrian Ambrozich ... Veri strendzh kolls ..."

"What do you mean, strendzh? Like threats?"

It appears I still have a pretty good grip on my voice (the slight hoarseness can be written off to my sleepiness)—enough not to betray a sickening shift in my stomach—with a chill filling the gap that's opened up. That's the last thing I need today. Could I really have crossed someone? Me, barely a stringer in the bush leagues? I'm just the dregs, a bottom-feeder not even worth the bother.... But how, what could they want?

"Yulichka." I come around the desk, take her hands (icy cold, like a frozen chicken) into mine; I'm all shelter in the storm now, her good daddy. "You just calm down, okay? Everything will be fine," I assure her, already with complete certainty, and believe it myself—as if I were casting, through some incomprehensible leap in space, my protective spell on Lolly, not on her. "Let's take it slow: Who called, and what did they say?"

"I ... I don't knou." Yulichka makes a visible effort to focus. "I don't anderstend, it's oll so strendzh.... Several taims in a rou—it ringz, and wen I pick ap—hissin, very laud, Adrian Ambrozich, I've never herd anysin laik zat! Crackle, haulin, laik wind in ze wires.... Clicks, and somesin laik," she looks at me cautiously, "laik mashin gun shutin...."

"And do you know what mashin gun shutin actually sounds like?" I ask lightly, to calm her down, while my mind quickly cycles through the possibilities. Doesn't sound like wiretapping—and who the hell would ever want to bug my phone, what am I, some political bigwig? Although I wouldn't put it past those bastards, they've all gone insane with the elections now. They say every summer camp around Kyiv is packed with hired guns from Moscow that our mobsters have brought in to have them win the elections for them. So what if one of those "working groups" that sits up all night hatching increasingly outlandish scenarios suddenly got the itch to tap, say, every tenth name on the voters' list? Or maybe, hmm, what if it's Yulichka's nerves? That's weird, I never noticed any trouble; she's such a sensible miss, always has a plan for ten steps ahead, an ideal secretary really.

"Zose were gunshots, Adrian Ambrozich." Yulichka pulls back her thawed little paws and fixes her skirt, apparently recalling the talking-to she got earlier today. "Don't iven sink, I'm not gallucinatin. And I knou wot gunshots sound laik—mai first boifrend worked for Savlohov."

Whoa now! Now it's me who feels like a total moron: this fact of Yulichka's biography is news to me. A gangster's mistress, no shit. Surprise, surprise. How old was she then—seventeen?

"And where's that boyfriend of yours now?" I ask, very nicely.

"At ze Woods Cemetery," Yulichka answers politely, like at an interview.

Of course, where else? I'll have to give her a raise—I'll never find another secretary like this, that's for sure. A floozy who, having come to Kyiv from Melitopol (or Mariupol—where *is* she from?—it's all the same anyway), lands in a gangster's bed—that's nothing unusual, even, in a certain sense, quite natural; but that after all the shoot-outs back then, when, sometimes, you'd go to a store for a loaf of bread and it'd be full of cops and dudes in black face masks lying on the floor, and some of them ain't moving, those were the days!—that she didn't end up at "ze Woods Cemetery" or walking the streets herself—that takes some serious wits. And luck, too, and that's not the least important thing in business, not least at all. So this means Yulichka, too, got lucky. Like me, like all of us. Except, of course, those who didn't.

For the first time I notice that Yulichka, under her highlighted, porn-starlet bangs, fluffed like cream for cappuccino, has the face of a dramatic actress—someone for heroic roles, big-boned and willful, the Cherokee-cheekboned face of a mature woman. It's as if she's been out of focus for me before, and now everything's come into place. She's a trooper—one of those who'd chew through a steel wire, if need be.

"Okay, so what you are trying to tell me, my heroic Melitopol princess, is that someone was trying to get through to us while semiautomatic weapons were being fired off behind his back? A client calling straight from a hunt, perhaps, from a reserve or something?" They've carved up the whole country into those reserves already, the bitches—we almost drove into one with the guys once, just outside of Trahtemyrov, ten miles from Kaniv. Had a mind to check out this one bay on the Dnieper. Vovchyk raved the whole way about how he'd gone there back in the day for hippie camps, and how it's beautiful, out of this world, and what insane energy it's got—Hetmans' old lands! What we found was a wire fence and turnpikes welded shut, and gorillas with AKs over their shoulders who sullenly grunted at us to "Keep drivin'!" Only in the next village, which looked like something from a nightmare—graveyard quiet, not a thing stirring—a permanently terrified woman whom we barely got to talk to us, finally whispered that it's now a preserve where they breed wild pigs, and where "the bosses" come in black jeeps to hunt, and that those pigs dug up her whole vegetable garden, and we should go drive out of there as fast as we could "or they'll kill you and no one will find you." And now some assholes like that scared my Yulichka, too—"Must've called straight from the pigs' den, no?"

"If it had bin laik zat, I wudn't hev got scared."

Yeah, that sounds about right. She doesn't look like she would.

"Adrian Ambrozich, I anderstend you don't beliv me.... Zis was somesin else.... Zere were voices too."

"That must've been at the station. You just got connected into someone else's call."

"Like hell I did!" Yulichka explodes in the unmistakable tone of a truck-stop girl. She can't help it; we all, in moments of emotional upheaval, revert to our native vernacular, and no secretary course can fix that. "Zat was no fuck—" she slams on the brakes at full tilt, correcting herself, "no conversashen et oll—voicez laik militari orders, dogs, a mashin gun burst, and in ze end a blast.... And it waz laik wind houlin ze hole taim, we never had such horribl connection, even wiz Avstralia wen, remember, zat avstralian

Ukrainian bot an aikon from us? It did zis three or for taims in a rou, I can't even tell how much taim passd. And zen—zen a woman's voice, right in ze reciver, straight into my ear, veri cloz.... Zat's wen I got scared. In Ukrainian ..."

I give a purposely loud whistle (don't whistle indoors, Grandpa used to say, you'll call up the Devil!). "Well if it were 'in Ukrainian' no wonder you got scared!"

"Adrianambrozich, you shudn't laf from me." Yulichka looks at me with unfriendly coolness, like at a sick man who might be contagious, and I decide not to make fun of her "from me." "It's non of mai biseness of course, and I don't really anderstend wat I hev to do with zis at all.... I didn't recognaiz ze voice, but it waz completely clear." She belligerently thrusts her Cherokee chin at me. "Forgive me, Adrian."

Has she lost it? She's lost it, hasn't she? What is this nonsense?

"Forgive me, Adrian," Yulichka repeats, as if to an idiot. "And somethin about a chaild, laik she's expectin a chaild, but I didn't remembe, got scared, can't ripeat exactli...."

"You're sure you're not imagining it?" I say automatically, because I know she's not imagining it. And I can see she's not pulling a prank on me—and I can tell she knows she's got me, although she doesn't know which part of what she said did it. Her eyes flash with triumphant vindictive satisfaction: this is her moment of power over me, only she doesn't know how to take advantage of it, and how to make this moment last longer—women never know how to do that, the bed is the only form of power they know, and if a woman doesn't turn you on, she'll always be nowhere with all the other advantages she has over you because she won't know how to use them—and thank God for that.

What if she's shooting up in the bathroom on the sly? Or doing acid?—and then, as an ideal secretary, she hallucinates more or less professionally on the phone? Only why would her auditory hallucinations be in unison with my own thoughts—why would we be on the same brain wave, completely in sync, as if we were connected as closely as I've only let a single woman become connected to me in my entire life? At first, the thought singed me, a blazing shot of horror through my brain, that it was Lolly asking my forgiveness, saying goodbye to me forever because she was expecting a child from another man (The one she'd flown to Holland with, to eat lobsters on the beach?)—a theory just insane enough to be instantly discarded. No, this was something else, something even crazier.

Yulichka broke into my thoughts as though she'd been summoned by them, as the universe's direct response to the claims and complaints rumbling in my head like so much intestinal gas, and I believe that she really heard something and got scared because she did not know she was tuned into my brain waves, only I can't make heads or tails of any of this either, and do not find this tuning in particularly enjoyable—the same as if Yulichka had penetrated my dreams: such things are only pleasant with someone close, and this Mariupol Amazon is no one to me, nothing, a secretary, no more. Well, that's what you get with a perfect secretary, is the sarcastic retort that pops up in my mind: she can even take calls from the other world!

The other world? Why—the other world? Or is that Adrian who was being asked to forgive precisely the "chaild," the one Granny Lina expected in exile? And it was Granny's voice that materialized in Yulichka's phone, summoned by my remembering? But how exactly could it materialize—and with dogs, machine guns, and explosions to boot? I'd forgotten my radio technology, crap. I'll have to dig around in the literature. I wonder if sound can, say, in a highly resistant medium, get stuck in time? But, for how long—half a century? Total bull. Or maybe I'm one of those, what are they called, somnambulists, and Yulichka and I are under some kind of collective hypnosis? Like in those Moscow sessions that were all over the zombie-tube in the late eighties: stadiums full of people, a gorilla-like psychotherapist in the middle of the field, and a string of hypnotized folks before him, flailing their arms and shaking their heads like a team of demented soccer players—no wonder a country like that croaked soon after. Calm down, Adrianambrozich, calm down now; don't let yourself get rattled over nothing.

Easy to say, calm down: I feel like I've been caught in an invisible fishing net and it's dragging me somewhere where my feet don't reach bottom. In such cases, the only sensible way to proceed is to let go and quit jerking around, because aside from wasting your energy, the jerking does you no good. This presence in my life of some invisible outside force that keeps making itself known, like in *those dreams*, does not demand *understanding*; and that's the thing Lolly cannot seem to recognize, my diligent toots, like a straight-A student who firmly believes that every problem has a solution and she just needs to find it. No, this force demands only *obedience*, and the best thing you can do, once something like this has claimed your life and is running some sort of a unipolar current through you in an unknown direction, is simply to submit to it and let it carry you like water, ride it like surf....

When Mom died I was too little to know anything about this, but I still remember, a whole year before her death, being gripped and torn, so I sometimes couldn't fall asleep at night, by waves of suddenly surging dread that Mom would die. They say it often happens to teens, and there is nothing mystical about it—the usual prepubescent rollercoaster. But the sense, from back then, of doors opened onto the cosmic cold and the draft of a strange will blowing through them—a will stronger than anything I could have imagined then or could imagine now—I kept this feeling. I remembered it like a dog remembers a scent. And so when it comes again, when the doors creak open—I recognize it.

Only I don't know how *to obey*.

(If back then, when I was twelve, I hadn't let Mom go on that last trek to Goverla, if I'd latched on to her clothes and screamed, "Don't go!"—would she be alive now? Although, on that actual day I didn't have any sense of foreboding, no one did—not even Dad.)

I cannot let go because the fear for Lolly grips me. An irrational, instinctive fear—the dread that I won't recognize the moment when I need to latch on to clothes—hers this time. The fear of being under fire from all sides, like those wild pigs in the preserve: you don't know where to aim when they come.

Or *who* is coming.

Still, what if the "chaild" is actually me? And it's Mom who was asking for my forgiveness? (For what?) Lolly, Granny, Mom, Great-Aunt Gela—so many women already hold me in their net, ensnare me with their presence, and now Yulichka wants a piece of that action, too—like they've all conspired behind my back, sending each other their secret signals. Women, of course—they have to be more sensitive to any drafts stirred up in the universe; they, with their monthly bleedings, must be well familiar with this anonymous force that takes you over unilaterally leaving you to simply change your pads obediently. Women ought to be wise as snakes; they ought to be the ones showing us the right way to live, so why are they always so damn helpless?

Calm down, Adrian, keep it down man.

"Well, that's quite a story." I smile at Yulichka with Olympic composure. "I think I read this somewhere, or maybe it was a movie—this guy comes to a new town, checks into a hotel, and just like you, right then, overhears someone else's conversation on the phone. And in the conversation they're making plans to kill someone, so the guy then spends the rest of the movie trying to decide if he should go to the police—but he doesn't know any names, or dates—so he'd just look like an idiot. Alright, sweetie, is that all? No one else called?"

Yulichka coolly flutters her heavily mascaraed lashes at me. I recognized this same tense mistrust from the guard at the Tax Inspection office the other day—a hick who's convinced that the whole world is just waiting for a chance to rip him off—when I tried to tell him a joke. The poor sucker didn't even smile. But the mention of her immediate professional duties produces its usual effect in Yulichka, like a "sic 'em" command to a police dog, and she sets obediently to reporting who else called while I, here in my little alcove that's loftily referred to as the office, was indulging in my philosophical meditations instead of doing work. (Which was, actually, the right idea: when reality starts to leak, there's no better way to show it who's boss than to plunge into the piddly, routine stuff, like organizing my acquisitions log—only it looks like our reality is leaking for real this time, despite my attempts to derail it.)

"End you hev a meetin et hav past faiv," Yulichka reminds me for the umpteenth time.

I assure her, with somewhat exaggerated gratitude, that even Julius Caesar couldn't hold a candle to her. Because while holding five things in your mind at once is pretty impressive for a man—we men are all single-taskers; we can only focus on one thing at a time, but fully and to the end (and if you couldn't, and split, that's your own problem)—no man, let him be ten times Julius Caesar, your namesake, by the way, could ever dream of keeping track of as many things at once as do you, my priceless, for which you earn my awe and respect!

Uf-f—the emperor's namesake, lips still pressed into a displeased crease, slips back out the door where the bell just happens to have announced someone's arrival (probably just a stray window-shopper). Thank God. Now I can loosen my tie and gulp some water straight from the pitcher…. What I'd love to do now is my yoga routine, the best thing for restoring composure—just to drop into forward bend and hang there a good five minutes or so, like a shirt on a clothesline with arms hanging, so that blood comes back to my head and my mind becomes correspondingly clearer. Doesn't look like I have time for the whole routine—how long do I have before the meeting with my so-called art consultant? (Another lummox who can't focus on one thing, never mind he'd spent his whole life waiting for the chance to do just that. Dabbling in freethinking in other people's kitchens, amassing in his mind a veritable archive of rare and arcane knowledge, and collecting in his tiny Khrushchev-era apartment the complete set of albums published by the "Art" press that's not worth shit to anyone now. A guy who wanted to write, one day, once freedom rang, a fundamental work on the history of the Ukrainian underground, and when said freedom finally did ring, boomed, in fact, louder than anyone had ever expected, the only thing he turned out fit for bragging was a treatise for students about his friendship with dead Grytsiuk and Tetyanych. And if small hustlers like yours truly weren't tossing him bones every so often, he'd still be walking around with kefir in his net sack. All of them, those Soviet-bred "brilliant intellectuals," turned limp and shapeless on the free range, like jellyfish taken out of the water. In bright daylight all their submarine gloss turned out to be a mere optical illusion, a side effect of the atmosphere of social paralysis so prevalent then, which was the only thing that made it possible to mistake impotence for a kind of spiritual aristocratism. So we'll have our half past five today—a meeting of impotents from two generations.)

At our modest dinner, I will ask the professor to certify with his distinguished signature the authenticity of a pretty dubious Novakivsky. (I'm almost a hundred percent sure that the work is not by Novakivsky, but by one of his students. It will do just fine for the rake who's got his eye on the piece—he's already abused his privilege to move half the National Museum into his lair, enough's enough!) And once the dear professor, after a bit of posturing, agrees (he's never once refused), I'll also ask him, for dessert so to speak, a little extra after the main business of the day, to find Yulichka a spot as a distance student in his art history BA program (which is why the poor thing's been lunging at the end of her leash with diligence—reminded me five times about this meeting!).

This entire, well-rehearsed ritual of ours, in which he acts the impoverished aristocrat who's bringing me, the obtuse nouveau riche, the light of science and knowledge, and I pretend to eat it all right up, is in about forty minutes. I've time to spare, only it's already rush hour; the streets are jammed, Kyiv's been choking like a deathbed asthmatic lately. The way you have to crawl through downtown now, you'd rather run cross-country in a gas mask; and what the fuck, I ask you, are we feeding a mayor for? A cell phone, obviously, is not something the professor would have, can't warn him if you run into a jam, so it's better not to be late and not to make the old man nervous, the easier to work him at dinner. Alright, he-rre we go, back and up—temples tingle pleasantly as if filled with champagne, the dark wave falls noisily away, rings fade from before my eyes. Consider me fit to roll out in public—triumphantly, like a brand-new BMW from the garage.

See you later, Yulichka. (Yep, gawkers—a young couple, the miss in a muskrat fur coat, welded to the cabinet with the Soviet porcelain, and Yulichka, like a Cerberus-bitch, looming nearby, acting the guide but actually watching they don't steal anything. I don't need to stay; if they feel like buying a porcelain vixen or a young pioneer in shalwar, Yulichka'll handle everything on her own; she's a bright girl. She'll be priceless once she actually learns a couple of things.) I embrace the whole group with one mighty smile as I walk by, and that's how they remain imprinted on my retina, the trio, with three heads turned toward me, like a magnified copy of something manufactured by the Konakiv Porcelain Factory—see you later, goodbye, go to hell.

And only when I am in the car putting the key into the ignition do I see that my hands are still shaking.

"WHO ARE YOU?"

This comes out by itself, like a breath. How naïve—there are never answers to questions like these. I don't even know if it's a "who" or if there is more than one, maybe a whole platoon studying me through their crosshairs from the invisible afar. Before, there were only dreams. Now a phone call. That's closer, warmer, as in the children's game. They are coming closer, rapping on the window, breathing on the back of my head, into my face, with their dogs, their explosions, their bursts of machinegun fire, forgive them, Adrian. *Brr.* No, warmer is clearly not the right word—the hell it's warmer. It's like snow poured down your spine.

Let me sit here just another minute, I ask "him"—"them," head resting on my fists atop the steering wheel. It's not like I'm afraid to be driving right now. I just can't quite figure out how I'm going to bore again, like a dull corkscrew, into the exhausted flesh of this deranged, wildly sprouting city, into the falling dusk and the crawling current of hoarse cars, through the drifts of dirty snow piled by the curbs, cars sometimes buried inside them, and past the water-filled ruts splattered with flashes of reflected lights along the sidewalk, accompanied by the squealing of car horns where traffic begins to coagulate into clots, which make you squeal out loud. And all so that I can arrive on time to a place where I will lie and be lied to, so that I can later lie somewhere else and get some money for it—Lord, what a waste.

Lord! You see what a fuckup I am—I've nothing to show You in my defense. I did not spend sleepless nights thinking of how to make this world a better place—although the world would, probably, become a better place if solar power got even five percent of the time people spent on gas pipelines (like that gas will flow forever!—go to Dashava, look at what's left when gas wells are sucked dry). But I'm not one of those who breaks through walls. And I didn't do much laying of life for friends—once only knocked the teeth out of a rake. Our asshole union organizer went after the weakest guy in our group and worked him over on the kolkhoz trip so hard the guy had to be taken away in an ambulance. Turned out to be a diabetic, didn't actually have to come with us, could've gotten excused without a fuss, but was ashamed before a girl he liked; after they'd taken him to the ICU, I went up and socked that capo right in the mug like every one of us wanted to do, because if no one did, we'd all have felt like accomplices later. Afterward, though, I often shook hands with other scoundrels knowing full well they were scoundrels, but their scoundrelism had nothing to do with me at the moment, and what could be worse than that?

Be hot or cold but not tepid—that's what You said, Lord, and I've been tepid so many times in this life I can't stand myself. Whatever gift I had, I flushed down the toilet, and I don't know how to love my neighbor like I should because I know I haven't given so many folks their due that I can't even count them anymore. And I'm not even sure that I actually love people—not friends, or family, but people. I love objects; that's true. I love things made by human hands—that may be the only shred of physicist that survived in me.

When I unscrew the lid from an old watch and spread it on a velvet cloth, like Grandpa used to do, the miniscule nails, perfect, like living beings, the clever mechanism carefully tucked inside, as if in a small nest, it's like a warm soft paw touches me from inside. These things are still alive; they breathe—unlike the ones sweeping us under their mass-manufactured avalanche today. And although I refuse to change the world myself, I still love this substance that somebody else's hands had once tamed, in which one can still glimpse the folded trajectory of another's thought like the light of a dead star. Gold sand, a sparkling trail. Sweat between shoulder blades during a break between classes.

Look—Grandpa showed me when I was little—a transparent-blue dragonfly, a reed, a sun-drenched splash—look how perfect the dragonfly's fuselage is, you couldn't dream of making a thing like that! Old things still have that same thrill that rang that day in Grandpa's voice—a human's joy at being in the presence of the perfection of living forms. The joy of overcoming chaos. When all these things die out, crumble, move from antique stores to pressurized museum chambers, this joy will vanish from our life together with them. Then we'll be completely stuck in a sanitized, dead space filled with radically different things—ergonomic and anonymous, like disposable needles. And what'll be left for us to do then but eat our own shit and scream that God is dead?

Lord! Yes, I'm a fuckup, and yes, of all You've given me, I only managed to keep a few mere crumbs from slipping between my fingers, but if there is any truth in my life, it's in the fact that I *did not betray* them, not one from the army of those anonymous crafts-men who had the ant-like persistence to transform the world, bit by bit, passing it on to me the way it still was when I was a child. My store is just my way of trying to keep that world alive for just a little bit longer, against the avalanche. My way of being loyal—tepid maybe, fucked up, yes. But at least in this I am not lying.

And the woman I love—and I know you see I love her, Lord. I've never loved anyone in my life like I love her. I really could die for her if it came to that; she feels this in me, this ability of mine—to be loyal. Maybe that's why she loves me, the fuckup.

Keep her, Lord—no matter what happens to me, if something really were to happen to me, and all these specters storming at me from their other worlds are for a reason. If they've set to shake my soul ("I love you hard and shake you harder," Granny Lina used to say to me when I was little—or was it Mom who said it?) until that poor soul drops clear out of my body like the pit from a cherry—to heck with me, whatever, only I beg you Lord, keep this woman because I love her!

How strange, moisture between my fingers.... Could I be crying?

I raise my head. It's gotten dark, and the sky above the city went out like the screen of a giant computer—only the artificial keyboard light remains, a neon-pale blaze above the roofs—the nocturnal aura of the metropolis. And—here you go!—right before my car, two elongated golden rectangles have fallen onto the snow, stretching across the entire well of the yard from a second-floor apartment window. Like God's smile, I swear, like a sign of consent.... If an angel in white robes had alit right now onto the hood of my car and nodded soothingly, meaning, everything's fine, dude, don't sweat it—I doubt I'd be happier to see him.

For some reason I am always moved by the light falling from a window at night—like a promise of a sweet mystery. Or a vision from a forgotten dream. I've even come to love the yard of my Troieschyna apartment block ever since I saw that lacy light from the barred windows at night—and what, you would ask, is so special about that? But there it is, glowing-laughing, and I can't take my eyes off it—thrown onto the snow, like a stained-glass window in church, the tall gold-haloed window. It has to be tall, like in church, and in old-Kyiv townhomes, and our Lviv ones also have windows like those—and it seems any moment now a woman's shadow would appear there as though on a movie screen, retreat, then surface again, hold still leaning against the frame, like she's is waiting to spot someone invisible below. And as if a trail of some-one's footprints sits darker than the night on the white steps to the building's door, and makes my heart squeeze with something never fulfilled and so dear—my beloved yard, the rejected Kyiv Secession of the cement-boom era—no, cities, like things, also have souls, and all the generations of barbarians, our own and the ones now invading, cannot shake it loose.

For a moment, everything grows still, inside and around me. As though everything were falling into its proper place, and I, too, were in my proper place. Here, behind this dark window, also barred, facing the yard, is my little alcove; here is my store, and I am an antiquarian. And I know already that I will remember this moment forever—stopped, torn out of the current, like a swollen drop suddenly filled with weight.

Forgive me, Adrian.

I've forgiven. I've forgiven everyone. I hold no grudge against anyone. Do you hear me, Mom?

The first chords of Queen's "The Show Must Go On" suddenly thunder gravely, from here, from inside the car, and they make me jump like a blast of the archangel's trumpet. The next instant I realize the sound is coming from my cell, which has fallen out of my pocket and is lying on the floor—I reach for it, knocking my head against the wheel, absolutely certain that I am about to hear Mom's voice. I'm certain I will know it at once, even though the only thing I can seem to recall is an age-distorted recording on the ancient Vesna recorder's reel. (An amazingly low, rattling contralto recites Mavka's final monologue from Lesia Ukrainka's "Forest Song"—"Ah, for that body do not sigh"—and unless you knew that Mom had just over a year left, that strange voice would not evoke any special emotion.)

Okay, okay, God, where's that button—"does anybody kno-o-ow what we are living for"—at last, a direct link, at last I'll hear what they want from me and what I have to do—a direct link to my fate.

"Puss, where'd you go? I've called twice already," says my fate in the dearest voice in the world that makes everything inside me come instantly back to life, makes blood run through my veins afresh, and I giggle, consoled, but, strangely, disappointed. What a log head, how could I've forgotten that this is Lolly's new personal theme song? She's got it on repeat all day long. Although if you ask me, you'd do better climbing gallows than going to any shows to that tune—but my funny girl put her foot down, and says I don't understand.

"I'll be home soon, Lolly. I've got one more meeting to sit through. Should I buy anything? We have bread?"

This is real happiness—when you can ask her these simple, everyday things, and drive home at night with a grocery bag in the back seat, and see, still from the car, the light in the fourth-floor window (a rectangle of light on the asphalt), behind which she's rooting around your apartment, or sitting at the computer, or listening to Queen—and at any moment her shadow may appear on the curtain, as though on a movie screen, and hold still, leaning against the frame: Did someone just pull up below? It's me, my love. I'm here, four flights leaping over every other step—and I'm with you.

"Actually, I'm still in town myself, Aidy, just got out." Lolly speaks as if she were walking on an icy sidewalk, looking for the right place to plant her foot. "I had a meeting with Vadym."

"And?" But I can guess from her voice already: bad news again.

"Not good, puss. Not good at all."

She'd thought that with his help she could put a check on those fuckers planning to sell women through TV. Did she get nowhere with him? Or was it something worse?

"Dead end, wasn't it?"

"Yep. Deep ass. Actually, I wouldn't mind a drink."

"Now, that's a wise decision! Let's do that. I'm meeting my expert at half past five at The Cupid. Just go there!"

Damn that expert, and that bloodsucker client who can't live without a Novakivsky on top of everything he'd already stolen, and

Yulichka with her freaking career—now, when I just need to hold my girl, hug her shoulders, because she's about to cry.

"Won't I be in the way?"

She'd never asked that before, she didn't have this meek—heartbreaking—resignation to being shown the door if she were in the way—the Daryna Goshchynska people recognized in the street and asked for an autograph could only be in the way when *she* chose to; she had *the right* to be in the way.... Lolly, if only you knew how sorry I am—with a lump in my throat....

"You ask that again and I'll beat you up!"

"With a fist?" She seems to warm up a bit, sensing a game.

"Why a fist—a boot."

"Is that, like, not to leave any bruises?"

"Sure. How could one leave bruises on such a nice butt?"

"You friggin' aesthete!" my sad girl finally chuckles. "Alright, I'll pop into a hunting store on the way; take a look at those boots."

"You can't use those. You want the military ones, tarpaulin."

"You perv. What are they, stronger?"

"Sure. Strength and beauty. Two in one."

Another chuckle, then:

"Puss?"

"Hmm?"

"I love you."

And that's it, and I don't need to know anything else. Such a bright, solid wave of warmth. I grin like an idiot to the golden rectangles on the snow, and the grandly overturned cubes of the trash bins deeper in the yard, like a stage set for a Greek drama. And look, Lolly—too bad you can't see this!—look at the offended dignity of that humongous black cat crossing the yard toward the overturned stage set. Who could ever make such a perfect creature go out in the cold, his whole manner begs, as clearly as if the words were spelled out in the air above in a comic book bubble? I'm so full of feeling, I honk sending him dashing away, all that dignity instantly forgotten, like a small-time thief caught red-handed. It's so funny; I can't help laughing. Lord, how beautiful the world still is, and how beautiful it is to be living in it. My dear girl, fear nothing, no one can do anything to us, just keep loving me, you hear? Just don't leave me alone.

"Who're you honking at there?"

"I'm saluting. In your honor. Now I'll just go twist my Mykola Semenovych into a German knot, so he won't be in our way, and place his mortal remains at your feet."

"You seem to be getting pretty aggressive. Is that because night's falling?"

"Lolly. You little wonder, my Lolly, I miss you already."

"You're the wonder. Alright, I'm going to The Cupid."

"And I'm flying. On wings of love. Wheels up already."

"Wheels? Is that what they now call it?"

"Fie, you shameless wench."

"Be careful, the roads are slick."

"I will, I promise. Mua."

"Same to you."

My fingers aren't shaking anymore—turn the key and my trusty Golf tears off the spot with a happy squeal, as if it got bored waiting for me. At the street exit, under the arch, where I have to brake, the cat, flat to the ground, like a yogini, head pulled between his shoulders—didn't get very far!—watches me with a mistrustful gaze much like Yulichka's. Takes all I have not to wave at him through the window: So long, beastie!

From the Cycle Secrets: **I Killed Her**

They're humming along, Aidy and this weaselly looking gentleman with a mournful mouth and thin colorless hair interspersed with bald patches (What's his name? I forgot already.); Aidy pulls out a file folder, rustles papers, and the gentleman produces his glasses and perches them atop his nose—all this as if behind a glass wall. I can't, I don't have it in me to listen, to participate in the conversation. I just sit here guzzling my wine like water, and every so often, when the gentleman blinks at me uncertainly from under his glasses, I convey the peaceful nature of my presence with a wrung-out smile—the habit of controlling my face for the camera helps. I wish he'd go already. His shirt collar is soiled.

"Why aren't you eating anything?" notices the solicitous Aidy.

Why? Because I feel sick to my stomach already, and without any food. It would be just physically difficult right now to swallow pieces of another creature's roasted flesh. Bits of some innocent calf that went under the ax in the bloom of his youth. It'd be like dropping boulders down into my stomach where they'd remain lying, dead weight forever. I smile silently, this time apologetically, and reach for my wineglass again—like for the rail in a rocking subway car (this place is just as crowded and smells exactly the same, too—of wet clothing and cigarettes). This is how people drink themselves to death.

Vadym wouldn't have given me the meeting if he had known what I wanted to talk about. No doubt about it: he'd have hidden and wouldn't have answered his phone. He's been avoiding me lately anyway—did he possibly think that I hold him accountable for Vlada somehow? Right away, as if to justify himself, he rushed to tell me about Katrusya—that he'd seen her just the other day, and had taken her to Switzerland for a skiing vacation; how nice of him. As if I didn't know about this already, from Nina Ustýmivna. He just kept on talking, as if afraid I'd interrupt him. About what a big girl Katrusya is already, and how one German boy had a crush on her up there in the Alps. Only N.U. had told me other things, too: that, besides Katrusya, he'd also taken his masseuse, Svetochka, on the trip. Well, life goes on, you can't mourn forever, can you? A man accustomed to a monogamous relationship would perish like a zoo animal set free in the wild—someone has to take care of the orphaned guy. Fine, let him have Svetochka. Although I don't think she makes appropriate company for his stepdaughter. (I generally try to avoid thinking about what kind of creature Nina Ustýmivna will raise that child to be—I know all too well what it took Vlada to get out from under her mother's influence back in the day. If she actually ever had—if it's even possible.)

For God's sake, what, what did this Vadym have that put such a spell on her?

Aidy, noticing that my glass is empty, wordlessly refills it from the bottle—Aidy knows what to do around the sick, a rare gift for a man. No, he just loves me, my sunshine, my bunny rabbit, and I'm an ungrateful beast. I'm so sorry that tears of contrition suddenly well in my throat, tickle inside my nose: Aidy, my love! What's this threadbare old weasel still doing here? When's he gonna go already? Shit, what am I—how'd I get drunk so fast? And the roof of my mouth is already numb, as if cowled with a metallic film; I need to get a bite, I do, a piece of bread with butter would be best—the fat neutralizes the alcohol, which I learned from Sergiy way back when. Or was it someone else?

The worst is that now I can't get rid of this wretched, rotten thought—like when you snag your hose, and it runs and runs, and you can't put it back together—what would Aidy be like if I died suddenly? Would he go feral, look for a replacement, too? Well, at least I don't have a child, that's a plus. And I wouldn't leave paintings behind—it hasn't occurred to anyone yet to do a televised retrospective, and thank God for that: a TV show dies the second the credits end and the commercial rolls. It's the same with a person: as soon as the grave is filled, commercials start rolling, the recently departed becomes an information product, and there's no way to tell truth from lies anymore. And the more time passes, the less hope there is. Like finding those paintings of Vlada's, from the Frankfurt flight, something for which Vadym, in his own words, "doesn't have time right now." Of course, the elections are around the corner, don't I understand? No, I don't. Kill me, I don't; and I shall not: How could you have lived four years with Vladyslava Matusevych and not have the slightest idea who you'd lived with?

To be fair, Vadym did sponsor the posthumous show at the National Museum, hired a curator—the best one, he bragged (according to Vadym, he always gets the best of everything!), but, in this case, actually just the most famous. I tried (and failed) to convey to him that the two were not the same. It was at that show where I first caught the whiff, like stale breath from a painted mouth, of this vulgar, mercantile tang that had never clung to Vlada when she was alive: the thunderous rock band at the entrance was out of place, all those musicians in aviator helmets, who later cruised through the galleries with benevolently stoned grins; and so were the Gothic-looking damsels with baskets of roses, which they, for whatever reason, strew all over the floor (a creative touch of the fashionable curator who knew how to blow up a budget); and the video, sliced like salami from the footage of the various European museums where Vlada's work had appeared, was also somehow distastefully pretentious, like a promo for a travel agency. And that's exactly how it played: "Where is that? And that?" the ladies inquired of their companions, with lively interest—much livelier than for the canvases displayed on the walls—as they crowded before the screens, lined up as if for a glamorous photo shoot, some with feather boas draped across their shoulders to match their gowns. As is always the case at art shows, there were among them a few truly beautiful women, and everyone singled out a model with her linen-white hair in a pony-sized tail as a real, honest-to-goodness prostitute from Crimea, from a Yalta hotel, or so they claimed.

The prostitute, or whoever she was, quickly got drunk on the free wine and danced a solo for the helmeted rockers—she was marvelously supple, as though performing a pantomime. I really liked her, actually, and I think Vlada would've liked her too: the prostitute was, in fact, *real*. Otherwise, it was a bizarre audience, like a mixed salad of diplomats, politicians, officials, bankers, artists, journalists, who filled the rooms and melded with the paintings on the walls in a colorful shimmer that seemed to produce a new chemical compound, an amalgam with the paintings, and in this way seemed surreptitiously to *displace*, to falsify, Vlada. Vlada who was no more, and about whom this audience, truth be told, couldn't care less. I saw almost none of her friends there, none of the people who simply loved her—perhaps because they were not VIPs—but I did see a few of her artist colleagues who would've gladly drowned her in a puddle with their own hands while she was alive—and enjoyed every second of it—and who now were just as happy to be talking to the proffered dictaphones about their many-year friendship with Matusevych, cropping the edges of their verbal group shots to make themselves appear not only of the same stature as the deceased, but also just a little taller. And someone had already uttered—and kept repeating—the word "generation," and a thing repeated enough, as everyone knows, ceases to be a lie.

Not to be found among the guests was the aging Rita Margo, "Saint Rita," the universally known concierge at the studios on the Pechersk hills who was always ready to entertain little Katrusya while Vlada painted, or to run to the store for milk for Vlada herself—anyone who accomplishes anything in art has a guardian angel like this one. Mostly invisible to the public, they are unfailing, self-denying shadows, all those editors–makeup girls–gaffers who are rarely mentioned in brochures and catalogs except in tiny print somewhere in the back where no one would ever look, while in fact they are the ones holding it all together, the ones who glue together, like swallows with their own spit, the whole edifice with the glorious name in foot-sized letters on its facade. Vlada always said that Rita Margo was the ideal "artist's wife"—apparently comparing her to her own mother, who had spent her whole life in that role never having had any particular qualifications for it; while Rita Margo, with all her qualifications, did not have the fortune of an artist husband and was not, it seems, fortunate with men in general, except for her blind son who sewed or glued something in the invalids' co-op.

At the show, N.U., although much withered after Vlada's death, still looked presentable: a black dress, black lace shawl, the wife and mother of artists—alas, both dead. She, for one, liked everything; everything was exactly the way she'd wanted it: "Dara," she exhaled at me in the bathroom with sincere elation. "Just think, we've got *six elected representatives here!*" I was just dabbing my makeup with a napkin in front of the mirror, and pitied her as much as one would have pitied Rita Margo's blind son had he appeared suddenly among the guests, but at the thought that in these six damn elected representatives (Vadym's legwork!), she saw the meaning and justification not only for her own life, but also for Vlada's, I wanted to cry. Such a feeling of desolation swept over me; I wanted to cry, not to unload it, but to wash it all out, just as I wanted to cry now—without any hope of ever stopping, a quiet drip, like drizzle "Les saglots longs / des violons / de l'automne," pardon the French, Nina Ustýmivna. Ever since I left Vadym's office, I've wanted to cry exactly like that—like the long sobs of autumn violins—and that cannot be allowed under any circumstances. Better to drink.

Oops, looks like I just devoured the butter meant for the whole table—how rude of me!—the weaselly looking gentleman makes for the empty butter dish with his knife, and his shiny physiognomy, which could also stand to be dabbed (Why is he perspiring like that when there's such a draft from the door, I shiver every time it opens?), spells blatant disappointment: something's been snatched from right under his nose again, as has happened to him throughout his life! Aha, so that's where this mournful mouth of fortune's redheaded stepchild comes from—been getting the short ends of sticks all his life. But why sweat like that, I wonder? His hands must be moist, too. Now I recall I didn't shake hands with him when we were introduced; instinctively avoided him, only nodded. I see I get sort of mean when I'm drunk. This is new; I don't remember being like this before, but something in me, I swear, has quit feeling sorry for everyone—my sorry-meter must be busted. Aidy waves at the waiter; Baldy sits back in his chair and laughs—a piddly, weaselly sound, *he-he-he.* As our cameraman Antosha used to say, run for your life 'coz you're getting sober.

Back then, at the show, I couldn't shake off the sense that Vadym actually couldn't care less about all those paintings, since the woman who'd made them was no longer there. He needed Vlada alive and warm—and Vlada was gone, and the works that were left behind must have caused him pain just like her clothes in the closet. All those whimsically artistic dresses that she, when she'd had more time, made for herself, and the later ones, hand-picked from designer boutiques, a whole flock of chic outfits in diverse styles—traditional, sporty, avant-garde—but all belonging together by virtue of something elusively Vlada's own, like exotic birds that alit in Vadym's apartment on Tarasivska from places she went without him: the pale-pink Milano flamingo with large gold buttons; the blue-black Parisian blackbird of a short trench; the stern, closed-neck, cardinal-red Ralph Lauren dress from the other side of the ocean, bought when she had a show in Chicago; and something else unendurably, tenderly blue, tropically undulant that looks so great on a blonde and instantly fired off the flash of her hair in one's memory. How could a heartbroken man ever live with that menagerie, which, as soon as one opened the closet door, screamed the absence of its owner at him?

This belonged to the Problems-That-Had-To-Be-Solved category, and Vadym solved it in one fell swoop—called a team from a thrift store and, in a matter of hours, they packed up the whole flock in plastic bags, like a dismembered corpse, and hauled it all away to an undisclosed locale. "You must always give the deceased's clothes to the poor," Vadym declared didactically when I gasped at the news, "You ... what ... gave it all away?" "And you ... what ... wanted some of it for yourself?" he shot back with morose scorn—meaning, do I also count myself among the poor? (Vadym enjoys disarming his opponents by humiliating them—he is good at it.)

"There were dresses she designed in there, Vadym, that's also her legacy; they could've been exhibited." (I purposely deployed an argument that ought to have sounded convincing to him, used the language of tangible reality, a language I learned long before I met R. and could be quite fluent in if need be.) A show of her designs—why, what's wrong with that?—and if I did secretly *want* not just "something" but her entire wardrobe to be kept intact, so what? What if I did want to put glass over it and bury it, dig a little hole in the ground just so I could know that the feathers she dropped do exist somewhere, are kept safe, and that one could come to that place, slide open the door to the ground, knock-knock—and the revealed secret would shimmer, its colors playing in your eyes, a living smattering of brilliant shards: here is Vlada like a bird in the red closed-neck dress, face half-turned; and here's the lilac dress, and there was a little amethyst-studded hat to go with it; and that's what she wore when I saw her for the first time (I remember I'd had time to think, who's this Snow White? And in the next instant she was stepping in close to me, uncoiling from the bottom up with her head tossed back, like a cat about to leap into a tree, "Good evening. I am Vladyslava Matusevych."); and here's the chiffon scarf that flies off in a gust of wind, gets tangled in her hair (it's August, the café in the Passage, and her pale face opens up in the piercing nakedness of a leafless tree, like that of a monastery novice about to take his vows)? Even if this was what I truly wanted, I was not about to advance such arguments to Vadym, and he didn't know me well enough anyway to take them seriously: such arguments, pulled from the totality of our inner lives, always sound unconvincing and pitiful; Aidy's the only one to whom I could ever confide anything like this, with others it's better to swim closer to shore. How far did Vadym swim out, one wonders?

"That's not how you do a show," was all he grumbled at me then; he was obviously not going to admit that there was anything offensive, as far as Vlada was concerned, about so categorically getting rid of her things (out of sight, out of mind!). He organized *his* show not long after—the way *he* saw fit. Much to Nina Ustýmivna's delight. Maybe he should've married her instead of Vlada?

They do now make a kind of a family, with Vadym cast as Katrusya's weekend dad. And Svetochka cast as his help. Katrusya does with Vadym exactly what she does with her labrador, Putty, named after the Russian president: makes a show of jerking his leash—his tie—in public so as to leave no doubt in anyone's mind that this massive and, as she sees it, all-powerful dude is hers alone; she calls him Vaddy the way her mom did and teaches him various useful tricks, such as toting around her skiing gear or anything else she wishes to have toted. Not bad for a teenager—one day, when she grows up, this damsel will avenge us all.

In response to all that, Vadym just huffs like a Gypsy bear, and not without pleasure, and N.U., misty-eyed, beholds the idyll. Vadym, if you think about it, got himself a pretty cushy gig—for one lost woman he gained three, a full set: Katrusya for emotional attachment, Nina Ustýmivna for spiritual understanding, and, of course, there's Svetochka with her permanently engaged massage organ, where it is always so nice to stick his worked-up dick. Especially if it makes itself known at an inopportune moment—say, when Katrusya, the innocent child, climbs onto her Vaddy's lap.... Although I highly doubt that a thing like childhood innocence even exists in this post-sexual-revolution generation.

Irka Mocherniuk's kid has already enlightened his mom about sex—it's when a mister and miss kiss each other where they "go wee-wee"—and suggested he and his mom do the same, right there in the bathtub, when Irka was giving him a bath before bed.

Irka said the thing that shocked her most was the way he looked at her at the moment: wily, askance—like a man, "exactly like a man, Daryna, you wouldn't believe it!" Grandpa Freud, wherever he is now, is rubbing his dirty hands together in satisfaction, and Katrusya's already, what, thirteen—high time to, as the national bard did, herd her lambs beyond the village on the lea.

Gosh, now I'm feeling like I can't breathe—wasn't there water on the table somewhere? Aha, I see—the water's been appropriated by the bald weasel; he's moved it close, to keep it handy. That's fair: I take something he wanted (butter), he takes something I want (water), and in such manner a balance is maintained in the world, and it (the world) continues to spin. Spins, God damn it, so fast I'm seeing black.

"Excuse me ... may I have some water?"

The sound of my voice makes the glass wall between us crack, and noises spill over me from the general hubbub of the café like knives from a sack, discrete and separate: the clatter of plates in the kitchen, the desperate creak of the front door, the sharp soprano, like a car alarm, at the next table; the bald weasel, in an unexpectedly theatrical, self-regarding baritone, accustomed to people taking notes (Is he a professor or something?) cuts in, too. "Of course, of course, right here, with great pleasure." He'll even pour it himself. He's making a fuss, reaching across the table (revealing the moistly darkened armpits of his already dingy shirt—it's obvious he's worn it before today); how solicitous of him! Aidy's sitting next to him in his elegantly unbuttoned sport coat, calm and sharp like a snow leopard; it makes my heart flutter just to look at him—this ability of his to maintain an utterly natural benevolence in the most artificial, contrived situations. Who would ever think that he's the conductor of this show? It always puts me in a state of mute awe: Is this possibly the same man with whom I made love the night before? Whose cells are probably still swirling somewhere inside me like tonic bubbles? "Oh, I see, it's Perrier.... Thank you very much, that's enough.... Pardon?... No, you're not mistaken.... Yes, on television, quite right, *Diogenes' Lantern*." (Oh God, do I have to go through this now, too?)

Baldy oozes grease (And why did he want to eat more butter?) from every pore like a miracle-working icon dripping myrrh, and suggests, with subtle didactic superiority (He's got to be a professor!) that I consider featuring a unique subject, unfortunately not yet popularized by the media: the heroes of Kyiv's artistic underground of the 1960s and '70s, a whole little-known stratum of our culture, and what a rich stratum indeed! The professorial baritone assumes an elegiacally restrained tempo, as if preparing to launch into a popular lecture right here and now. (Oh, please, I couldn't possibly take that; it's too much to suffer in my unemployment: to listen, especially to something interesting, and not have a way of retelling what I hear. To know that I won't be telling people about this from the screen anymore—that I'll just swallow it all right here and here it will stay, sitting in my stomach, an undigested boulder. And instead, they'll have the *Miss New TV* show steamrolling across their screens.)

"You're right, Grytsiuk alone is worth a show," I nonetheless acquiesce meekly: Vlada considered Grytsiuk a genius; she used to say he was one of the best sculptors of the twentieth century.

My sage gentleman darkens for a moment, unpleasantly ambushed by my omniscience—what if it's his dearest hobbyhorse and he wishes to possess the secret knowledge alone? But he instantly regains his composure and grins indulgently, "Myshko, *he-he*, Myshko Grytsiuk, poor thing.... It was harder for him than for all the rest of us—he was a repatriate, after all; he was used to the free world, although he'd grown up in poverty back there in Argentina.... One had to teach him so much, and he still never got accustomed to many of our realia."

I see, so it wasn't so much a lecture he aimed to bestow upon us as a monument to himself, with Grytsiuk and all the other dead rolled into the pedestal. Only the TV cameras are missing (and I'm supposed to supply those). The expression on his myrrh-oozing countenance, meanwhile, makes it clear without any doubt that even if one of the best sculptors of the twentieth century, Mykhailo Grytsiuk—or for my interlocutor, simply Myshko—was still predominantly a sum of endearing weaknesses (his socks stank perhaps), his weaknesses were utterly forgivable, especially among friends; don't take it personally, bro, we're all family....

A "generation," sure—as that excessively fidgety painter kept saying at Vlada's show, arranging his fingers into a teepee—only he looked more like a rat. Why is it they all look like animals to me—rats, roaches, weasels—am I going off my rocker here? A hallucination à la Goya: packs of creatures with animal heads root around, twitching their noses, peering into butter dishes—first they mauled the ones who were worth anything and now they feast on their bones.

The old poetess's mug surfaces in my mind, the one I once had to listen to as she put curses on the terrible Soviet regime—which failed to arrange her jubilee reading the year Stus was sentenced to the ten years that would kill him. She had the same mouth—bitterly insulted, talking with slurps of spit; they passed up her bowl, too, at feeding time, only the old woman wanted no mere spotlight for her bowl, like our art historian here, but a crown of thorns, and she twisted my arm to get one woven for her. Back then I also got fiercely depressed and drank to get drunk just like this, and not very far from here, either—at Baraban, the favorite watering hole of journalists, where I won't go again because I don't want to run into people I used to work with and watch them hide their eyes. And see what animals they begin to resemble.

And then a very strange thing happens. Maybe I am really already drunk, but for some reason it rattles me, literally, with a shiver, this coincidence—like the repetition of the same figure in a dance: of the place, the time (back then it was also winter, there was snow on the ground), and the characters, that old hag and this bald weasel, the oppressive sorrow for the waste of my father's life I felt then—and the sorrow for Vlada's life I feel now. Then, as now, I carried a death for a life that no longer really mattered to anyone but me, and now, as then, I am drawn, as though by a magnet, to the same spot, the same downtown crossing, into a café where I sit at a table just as I did then, and drink in an effort to dissolve, if only a little, that indigestible sorrow (like a swallowed boulder) in a scorching torrent of alcohol—because this sorrow demands it, not for nothing do our folk songs always speak of drowning our sorrows, if not in mead and wine, then deeper, in a river or a sea—because if you don't thin it with something, it will, by its own solid weight, squeeze liquid out of you like whey from cheese, in a quiet tear-drip without end, like an autumn mist, until it squeezes out all your life juices and you petrify, becoming one with it, becoming it—this insupportable sorrow, a boulder, a pillar of salt.

I have seen women like that—among the mothers who lost their children, the ones who got them back from Afghanistan as "Cargo 200," in coffins welded shut and who fell against the zinc boxes, scratched them with their fingers and begged to know, "Baby, baby, are you in there?" They are the women who, twenty years later, remember their vigil at their sons' faceless coffins and their urge to throw themselves atop them as they were lowered into the ground as their last hour of being alive.

Nina Ustýmivna, it appears, is at no risk for anything like this; she said she'd cried out all her tears already, but she still drips periodically, still has to put a hankie to her reddening eyes every now and then when you're talking to her—so she mustn't have cried herself dry yet. She's still got plenty of liquid, even her Zodiac sign is Aquarius, the life-giving element. And Vadym's not even worth mentioning—he is not the keeper to something that's gone to the ground. But Goddammit, shouldn't someone make it her work to find a story in Vlada's life? You can't just let it break and scatter like a string of pearls from a torn thread, can you? No human life should scatter like that, because it would mean that no life was worth anything, not anyone's; if that's the way it is, then why are we all still taking up space on the planet?

Again, this taste of insoluble sorrow on my lips—the same as three years ago—and tomorrow the hungover heartburn will parch my lips just like it did then—soda and salt. And this recasting, three years later, of the same plot with different actors in the original roles, strikes me, for some reason, as something incredibly significant, filled with an all but mystical meaning. Lord, what if our whole lives are made up, without us ever noticing, of precisely such repetitions, like a geometric pattern, and that's where the answer is—the main secret locked in every human life?

Two brightly lit episodes, like windows at night, three years apart, as though placed on a twist of one invisible spiral that links the "then" and the "now" with a single, pervasive meaning. Throngs of other encounters and episodes huddle in the time between the episodes, and maybe some of these will also repeat someday just like this, and pushed by the invisible coil to the top, will flash with the same searing intensity of memory revealing their, as yet indiscernible, meaning—the way a dark shard of bottle glass flashes when you hold it up to the sun: the effect Vlada sought to achieve in her *Secrets*—amber, thick as buckwheat honey, stitched through with a pulsating golden thread. The world, after you've seen it like that, appears at first gray and faded like in an X-ray room. Now I could tell Vlada what she'd spent ten years searching for: not a technique, not a color—but this unseen coil that threads through time.

But Vlada is gone, and there is no one to tell. In that gray and faded X-ray–room light, Aidy and Baldy, cowled in bluish drifts of smoke, nod their heads like puppets in an animated film and pursue their incredibly boring, hiccup-inducing, vacuous game—rolling words to each other like balls on a pool table.

"You, Mykola Semenovych, absolutely must write about this."

"My dear boy, I've long had all the preliminary research completed, all that's left to do is sit down and write. But *you* know how busy I am...."

"Uh-huh, and here I am taking up *your* precious time! But I must, and you must forgive me—where else would I find an expert like you? And, actually, that's all I've come with, I won't delay you any longer—I'll just leave you the documentation so you can take a proper look at it later, and just write your conclusions whenever you have a spare minute."

"You're leading the old man astray, you realize that?"

"Why astray, Mykola Semenovych? You've said it yourself—the possibility of Novakivsky's authorship is fifty-fifty, the experts' opinions may very well conflict, some will say yes, and others will say no. What's so wrong if saying yes, in this case, happens to benefit you and me directly?"

"Oh, I've long known you as the demon of temptation; ladies must find you irresistible.... Speaking of which, why haven't we toasted the fair lady at our own table yet?"

The fair lady—that would be me. That's my role in their little movie. I smile and nod, my head on a hinge, while Baldy (standing up, how else, officers and gentlemen, and Aidy rises too—reluctantly, like a teen forced to entertain a small child, shooting me a look that's both conspiratorial and indulgent), with unexpected thirst, as if he'd been kept away from it for ages and then finally set free, drains half a glass of cognac in a single gulp, displaying again the wet underarms of his unfortunate shirt; and it's obvious that he doesn't actually want to go anywhere—that he has none of this hyper-important business to attend to, has nothing, in fact, more important and dearer to his heart than sitting like this in the populous warmth of a café, enjoying the good food and drink someone else is buying—and having an audience to boot.

To talk and talk, that's the most important thing. To knead his life with words, to give it shape like a thinly filled pillow. The Ukrainian underground, the little-known stratum of our culture, Myshko Grytsiuk and I. Pound, pack—stuff—his life with the meaning he's talked into it: as long as he's talking, and for some time afterward, the shape holds—even if eventually, inevitably, it all crumbles back into its original form. So he has to keep talking. And that old poetess hag who tossed her dyed curls at me like a starlet in front of a sugar daddy—she also wanted to talk up some other life for herself, different from the one she'd already lived, which was happy and worthless. To install in it, retroactively, the coil that it didn't have.

Fuck, it's not my job to be forever feeling sorry for everyone! I grab my glass again, because what else can I do? Especially since the two of them just drank to the ladies, so it's like they drank to me and now I should respond in kind. I can't just sit here like a log—I should drink to them, return the favor: to your health, and all the very best to you too, jolly good fellow. Shit, what jolly good fellow? This is no birthday—more like a wake. My wake for Vadym, that's right. For Vadym who can do nothing, because he's got the elections. No, worse: for Vadym who turned out to be Vlada's defeat—the pothole that caught the spinning wheel of her life, a Harley Davidson speeding along the highway.

"No, no, I don't want any cognac, thank you."

Aidy says that he has one more little favor to ask, on the fair ladies' topic, of this Semenovych, a matter in which he could be of great help, not to Aidy himself, but to one young woman—and Baldy pricks up eagerly, ears and nose, like a weasel smelling a chicken house. "Aha, and what is the favor?" That he is not being gotten rid of just yet, that the feast goes on, is enough to make him happy. Instead, it is me who stiffens up unpleasantly: What young woman?

Aidy's always taking care of something for someone, always helping someone, and all these young girls who're running loose out there, throwing themselves under every more-or-less financially secure dude, like Anna Karenina under the train, they've no decency, no decency or shame whatsoever; I can easily imagine a Barbie doll like that, fresh and tight, just out of the box—oh no, I'd better not! This is also new; I don't remember having such textbook jealousy fits before, and tonight I've already caught myself several times being irritated by that exceedingly vociferous look-at-me soprano at the next table—with her jungle of luxurious hair that makes you want to put your hands in it—it's a chestnut Niagara like in a shampoo commercial; at least Aidy's seated with his back to this Niagara—but here we go, this is full-blown paranoia already.

I see—the young woman Aidy is talking about is his secretary. Sure, of course I remember her, met her once (forget princess, she's a pavement queen, brash and wily, not his type). Secretaries, masseuses, interns, assistants—come to think of it, what a wide choice a solvent man has of young women thirsting for a better life! And what a kick I got at first from being assigned to that same market category on sight by waiters, hotel clerks, or steward-esses (I saw the way one of them looked at me when R. stroked my thighs under the tray table on that Amsterdam flight) when I appeared in public with R. somewhere people didn't know us—how bewitchingly fun it was, God, what a turn-on! A constantly giggly, champagne-bubbly arousal: a queen at a masquerade, dressed as a shepherdess. Yes, boss, as you wish, boss—a wildly sexy game. I want you right here and right now. The silence of his driver who took us to the airport—a professional silence, impenetrable like the Mottled Hen's golden egg that no one could break—you pay a premium for such silence, such folks don't give interviews (and, oh, how I wish they did, and wished back then, too, the journalist in me never quit doing her job!).

When the world takes you for a whore but keeps its mouth shut, or grins politely, like that hotel clerk who presented R. with the room keys (although it was I who did the talking, while R. just breathed noisily at my side because his English is nonexistent, and there's one more category I could be placed into—an interpreter), it sort of gives you the social sanction to do exactly what, as they believe, this breathing character is paying you to do. Your sexual act, thus, begins, essentially, at the check-in desk, and by the time you reach your room in the impatient, pulsing-like-a-bulging-vein silence of the elevator (where a Russian or a Turk, infected with the atmosphere, nails you with a fiery look as he steps out on his floor, letting it be known that he could take care of you no worse than your companion—it spreads like electricity, men always flare up like lights on a string when they see a woman being led to a good fuck, and this erotic illumination is also part of the show), you quite simply must, as soon as the door closes, drop onto the bed and get to business. So, you're an interpreter now, let's see you interpret this.

There's something of an orgy in this almost-public sex that is being watched through the walls by dozens of eyes—the sex of the information age, sex without privacy, as if at a stadium with crowds of fans: floodlights on, olé-olé-olé-olé, go-go-go, and sco-o-ore! And the result: a couple of vacant, mechanical orgasms and the inevitable popping up of the same postcoital question in your mind. Why the hell am I doing this, exactly?

And on the flight back—already knowing, after that morning with the hotel-window view of the wet roofs below, that I urgently need to break things off with R.—I just had to spot one of those tight Barbie dolls, not long out of the box but already not quite fresh, slightly spoiled by a touch of second-handedness, turned out as unambiguously as if she were wearing a uniform: loose, tar-black hair down to her buttocks, gold chains, silver stiletto heels that made her a head taller than her companion, who looked like he could be thrice her senior. They took the seats immediately behind us, and the man—also, I figured, a big wheel that flies everywhere with his own masseuse (the doll didn't quite have the goods for an interpreter)—instantly dove into some Russian pulp, some Hitler-Stalin-Zhukov potboiler with a hot-red cover. (Bright, they like everything bright, pop-your-eyes-out bright; they are forever hungry for bling, these children of gray factory developments and mining towns.)

He spoke to his companion exactly once during the entire flight, when the stewardess came by with the drinks. "You want a beer?" The way I talk to Barsik, "You want some scraps?" And it was as if I'd seen myself and R. in a distorting mirror—aped by this couple who embodied the essence of the rich-man-and-his-slut genre so much better than we; they were almost kitschy (for what is kitsch if not a genre's essence stripped of any individuality?) and seated right behind us, as if to fulfill the express function of visual aid, illustrating the next step on the evolutionary ladder.

Unlike myself and R. (whom I intentionally allowed to pay for that whole trip, so I could wallow in the feeling like the proverbial pig in mud), the kitschy couple was not playing a game, was not pretending to be a boss and his sex servant—that's actually who they were, and no erotic sparks flew between them. Zilch, nada, you could see nothing, flying or otherwise, aside from vacant, self-congratulating vainglory: the boss took pride in his young mistress, decked out like a Christmas tree. She—in her gold chains, silver stilettos, with her shopping bags in her luggage, a whole trip she could boast about to her friends, eliciting their unending envy; the two had no other motivation for copulating. Sex, at their evolutionary station, was dead—as ours would have been, too, if I didn't insist on playacting someone else's life.

I understood then what R. meant when, elated after one of our conjugal acts, which, as far as I was concerned, did not command any special elation at all, he allowed himself to venture into a frankness that was not, generally, characteristic of him, saying in Russian (he always slipped into Russian in intimate situations), "You are so … bright—in everything. I've never known a woman like you."

But Vadym did, didn't he? He did live for more than three years with Vlada; that's not counting the months she waited, however taken she was with him—forget taken: she was head-over-heels in love with him. (Somehow, after everything that's happened, I'm loath to acknowledge that part of her life, as if I'd be humiliating her by doing so. But back then, even the way she moved changed, became more cat-like; it was as if she were stroking everything she touched, rubbing, with an inaudible purr, against the air itself as she walked, as though against a man's bristly cheek—when such an invisible soft cloud of someone else's touch envelopes a woman's every motion, it is the surest proof that she is most certainly loved and in love, and not merely physically sated, and Vlada laughed then and said, happily, that being in love, as it turns out, is a rather deleterious condition for making your way in the world, because instead of telling the extorting cops off like they deserve, you smile a languorously tender smile and they rip you off like their own mothers.) Despite all the feverish heat in her actions back then, she hesitated long and hard, before she finally took the step of transplanting herself and Katrusya into Vadym's newly acquired apartment.

Vadym had just divorced his previous wife (whose tender mind ostensibly cracked under the weight of the wealth that descended upon it without any warning, and she went cruising for a safe harbor from one shrink's office to the next—well, why not, it does happen to the wives of the nouveau riche) and bought himself the entire topmost floor in a noble old building on Tarasivska, with the mind to build a penthouse on the roof.

I think what finally swayed Vlada was the chance to play with that big space: Vadym had agreed to let her decorate the entire two-floor apartment according to her own designs. And now Svetochka makes her home in that apartment, decorated by Vlada's designs. Svetochka goes to the same bathroom where Vlada once sat me down and made me up ("Let me make a living portrait of you, Daryna, it's something I've always wanted to do!"), and I saw myself in the mirror as I've never known myself and grew scared. (It was too unlike my image for the TV screen—that strange and ominously beautiful, vespertine face, as if carved out of the night by the light of a bonfire, with long, Egyptian eyebrows, and lips that were ultra-dark, as though sated with blood—a face you instantly want to put out, like a fire. It's suicide to take it out in public. This can't be. Matusevych, what have you done to me? I'm not like this!) And on the same shelf where Vlada put down her brush ("Wait, don't wash it off just yet, I'll take a picture"), Svetochka now keeps her toothbrush and contraceptive cream. Although, no, a Svetochka like that probably has an IUD installed, to spare her man any inconvenience whatsoever. And a dolphin laser cut into her pubic hair—wasn't it yesterday I saw an ad for a beauty shop on our station? Fifteen minutes of airtime, welcome, fellow Ukrainians, for a mere 500 Euro, and no problem: a dolphin forever.

That is really mean of me to think.

And unfair on top of that: How could I possibly know what's going on between them? I've never laid my eyes on that Svetochka. She may be a perfectly kind and generous soul. Poor Svetochka—sucked into the vacuum of the just-renovated, nouveau-riche apartment: an apartment like that simply cannot stay deserted for long; it must inevitably, sooner or later, draw a body into its orbit—to root around, move from room to room filling in the excess of space, to clatter cups in the kitchen, turn on the TV in the living room, forget to raise the lowered seat on the toilet, and leave, in the mornings, in the bedroom with drawn curtains, the pungent whiff of female genitals, so sharp against the smell of sperm (of which quite enough has already spilled onto the lonesome bed). Nothing wrong about it, it's quite natural; this is merely the law of large apartments. These are the apartments themselves, by virtue of their gravity, commanding people and fates: a home, once it's built, always places its own demands on whoever inhabits it; and he who remains to live alone in such a big dwelling finds himself in an undeclared war with the place, in which he sooner or later will be defeated (because dwellings last longer, they outlive people), and then compelled to get out, and should thank his lucky stars if he manages to do so in one piece.

Why did I never make a show about this? It would make a great show, even a series, and it'd have been a piece of cake to find a sponsor, a construction firm, for example. I could call it *Personal Interiors* or, say, *The Personal Home*—about how our homes rule our lives. Now that we have crawled out of our Soviet-brand hives and begun cocooning ourselves into our own nests, it is the perfect time. It's too bad I didn't think of this earlier, and now it's too late. Your whole life can pass like that: blink—and you missed it. Those evacuees from the Chernobyl zone, the villagers who went back against orders—they still knew what a home meant, and probably could have told the rest of us, but I, when I made my Chernobyl film, didn't appreciate this angle, missed it, wasted it. Moron.

I know another home like this—endowed with its own will—
that would be worth telling people about: it's in Lviv, the townhouse that used to belong to Aidy's grandfather, the one where
his granny and Gela Dovganivna grew up. Aidy told me how when
he was little his granny took him across the entire city from their
neighborhood of proletarian high-rises to what used to be the
professors' colony up the hill behind the Vynnyky Market, to show
him—look, Adrian, this is our home; these were the windows
of the girls' room; this is where Great-Aunt Gela and I used to
sleep. After the war, the house was given to some KGB type—a
"liberator" and, I bet, "a fighter of the OUN gangs," who eventually drank himself to death, fell out of a second-floor window
(the girls' former room perhaps?), and broke his neck, ostensibly
in a fit of delirium tremens. Only I believe it was the house that
spat him out—chewed him over for several decades and finally
spat him out—the liberator's children made short work of selling
everything off and emigrating when the Soviet Union fell apart,
but by then Aidy was studying in Kyiv and had no intention of
returning to Lviv.

Aidy (who has long completed his studies) raises his eyebrows at
me sensing a shift of mood: Is something wrong? (He and Baldy are
swilling their cognac in masculine seclusion now—they've come
to an agreement and it must be toasted.) No worries, everything's
fine, I reassure him with a silent nod. Everything is really perfectly
fine; oh, if only you knew how perfectly fine you are, my beloved
snow leopard—what a joy it is to watch you and be ravished by
your calm, unhurried confidence: the poise with which you move
through life has nothing in common with the impenetrable daft-
ness of those who turn over big money in full certainty that they
make the world itself turn. And I know now, I figured out what it
is that makes you so unlike all those types. I could stand up tall
and declare it to the whole café—listen up; Daryna Goshchynska's
had a revelation: it's your home giving you shape!

That house in Lviv, lost three generations ago. It's like those
little metal molds—fishes, stars—that I used to pack with dough

to make cookies with my mom when I was little: you were packed into the house just like that—when you were still pliable, at an unconscious age, and the hardy frame of that house, where you always knew you could go and see the windows from which your young grannies once gazed at the street, is there, invisible inside you. It keeps your spine upright, *that's* where all your grace of natural—unrestrained—dignity comes from. This can't be bought, or cultivated, or trained—this is given like a problem's condition, there are things in this world that a person can only get this way—by being given them. Or not. One can build a house, top it with a penthouse even, but it takes more than a single lifetime to learn how to carry that home with you.

You are shit, Vadym. Good Lord, what unadulterated shit you are.

This sentence comes together in my mind suddenly and of its own volition, like a barrel lid rumbling shut. (At the next table, the high-pitched soprano squeals again—damn, she's loud, should be singing Mozart or something.) I have to smoke. The curious part: no more internal squishiness, none of that drizzly whining of the drunken French fiddler. It's all gone, shut off. Like a sudden change of weather. Simply: the man with whom my friend had once fallen in love turned out not to be the person she'd thought he was. A crappy and rather trivial turn of events, basically. Of which the crappiest part is that the friend has moved on to a better (one hopes) world, and the man who had once babbled to me incoherently in an empty apartment—"I killed her"—goes on presiding over great flows of money from his office and responds to my claim that his class brethren, his fellow minders of, perhaps, the very same cash flows, intend to use television as a means of netting girls for the sex trade, by telling me he has more important affairs to attend to. Affairs of state, damn it. Of the state.

"Fuck this state, Vadym" (and representatives therein, I added mentally) "if things like this can be the norm!" At this, Vadym, sniffing offendedly, advised me to be realistic. Translated from representative-speak: quit being stupid. But—that's a chore, as

Aidy's dad says. Once a person's stupid, you can't do much about that. One could, I imagine, have put her wits to work and figured out, in advance, that the sex business, for Vadym, does not constitute a good enough reason to rush to anyone's rescue. That, when he himself needed rescuing from the Misfortune-That-Had-To-Be-Endured that had so unfairly befallen him, he must have tried, besides Svetochka, any number of professional masseuses for his orphaned dick, and found them precisely on the same market that the *Miss New TV* show is intended to supply.

Everyone makes use of prostitutes, sure—that is to say, everyone who can afford to—why should our elected representative be any different? Is he a man or what? It's a man's world, sweetie, nothing to be done about that, nothing to be done, and you just have to be realistic. The more Svetochkas out there, the easier it is for solvent men to endure everything they are supposed to endure. To bear their cross and be pillars of the state—the poor thing's about to keel over, like the tower of Pisa.

I'd better stub out this cigarette. I'm getting lightheaded.

I asked him about Katrusya after he said that—how's she doing at school? Does he keep track of that? Vadym thought it was my way of changing the subject and started telling me, happily, how he picked her and some friends of hers up from school just the other day. Quite a sight for a pervert's imagination: this big-screen, well-massaged, tightly fleshed at the nape, and everywhere else, Humbert Humbert in his Land Cruiser, smack in the middle of a whole flowerbed of sweetly aromatic Lolitas—girls at that age still smell almost as divine as babies, of vanilla or something like that. I'd give anything to know if fathers ever get erections at the sight of their pubescent daughters. Right, like anyone'd admit to that ... Vadym believed (and if Vadym believes something, then that's the way it is) Katrusya had an easy time with her studies; she could get all As if she tried just a bit harder, but (he believes) it's not the most important thing. Of course not. And does she watch TV? Vadym still wasn't catching my drift. You know—what would happen when Katrusya watches this beauty contest, girls, you know, need such things, especially at her age: to have a universally accepted standard of beauty before them, something to aim for—and then around eighth grade or so, she'll want to send in her own picture to be considered for the contest.

"But you'll warn her, won't you?" Vadym smiled with the charming immediacy of an adult talking to a child, and I was simply floored—floored, and for a moment fully capable of believing women could find him attractive, even a woman like Vlada. The smile was absolutely genuine, a good, beautiful smile. He wasn't being dishonest or cunning—he really did not see here a Problem-That-Had-To-Be-Solved situation. And if Vadym doesn't see it, then it's not there at all.

I did not ask him, after that, who would warn all the other Katrusyas around the country—the ones who do not go to the British Council School and for whom television is their only window to the world. And I did not even tell him that I resigned from my channel—why? Clearly, the media and everyone involved were low on Vadym's priority list at the moment; the imminent election tsunami meant something different to him than it did to us, mere mortals—something hard and tangible, some stupendous redistribution of cash masses in the direction I'd be lucky to guess. Only I'm not inclined. In any case, I've no doubt that for him things will turn out just fine; Vadym's not used to losing. It's only with Vlada he got beat. Got away, that one.

What if she did want to get away from him—only didn't know how? What if she'd also had her own morning looking through the window onto wet roofs—when she had to force herself out of bed with the new day pulled over her head like a bag and realize that her life took the wrong exit somewhere, that this was no longer her highway, and she had to grab the wheel and twist, back up, back up. Only it's very hard to do when you live life at the speed Vlada did. Her motor revved till the scenery flew past like a ribbon.

She did. Of course she did—my proud girl who quivered as though set on top of a tightly coiled spring. Proud people who are accustomed to being the ones giving support to others are so bad at sending out their own SOS signals that even when they call you at two in the morning and complain about insomnia, about an irrational fear—if I fall asleep, I'll die—you do not hear the signal. And even when you can see, having spent five hours straight under the watchful guard of her boyfriend, as if he were ordered explicitly not to leave you alone for a single minute even if his bladder should burst, that something is very much awry indeed, and things are not as good as they'd just recently appeared—you still don't allow yourself to think that the love glow this couple radiated not so long ago could have been no more than a ghost light, leading a trusting traveler straight into the bog. You do not allow it because you know, in your heart of hearts, that to think so would be to insult your proud friend, because she herself, teeth clenched, must have fought an unimaginably exhausting, life-sucking war before she could admit it—her defeat—to herself.

Now I am absolutely certain that's exactly what happened.

Now—after today's Vadym, who has already heroically turned that page ("She was the best thing in my life," he'd said over Vlada's coffin, and had I died, R. would've said so over mine) of his life and returned to himself—the way he was before Vlada, BV, because people like him do not change and no new experience can turn things upside down inside them; now all the little incidents that had once scraped on my attention as dissonant, accidental splinters line up, in hindsight, into a regular pattern. There was one thing Vadym and Vlada had in common, and it was this thing that like a wrench thrown into a turning gear caught Vlada, brought her to a halt: they both had it living in them and motivating them their entire lives—the fear of defeat.

It was that fear that, ten years earlier, made her break up her marriage with Katrusya's father (who, ultimately, did not manage to do anything better with his life than to emigrate to Australia, where he, according to different sources, either worked as a night guard or babysat kangaroos). It was that fear that made her hair stand on end when, in the fall of 1990, we were smoking the one cigarette we had between the two of us in the little park on Zolotovoritska—right here, across the street, where the casino now stands (the spot I've been circling since— for fourteen years already—as if under the sway of gravitational pull)—and the hot wind of tectonic shifts blew self-published (on Roto Printers back then) leaflets at us, and the bitter coffee from tiny chipped cups scorched the roofs of our mouths. "We had no youth, Daryna."

We did, Vlada, we did, that was it—our youth, and our country's youth that was being born out of the tidal roar of the Independence Square, of the boys with seraphic faces and white hunger-strikers' headbands, not one of whom, back then, had yet thought of paying for being prepared to die. And they were really prepared to die, and those who haven't died, only got themselves to blame.

Yes, my Vlada had that fear, of course she did, however deep it sat—a genetic fear, inherited from her mother, from Nina Ustýmivna. Or perhaps even older than that—from those grandparents of hers, the Komsomol activists who, in 1933, lit out for the city from the famished country and became teachers at a workers' night school, and thus did not die together with everyone else in their village—and who knows at what price. And it was because of this fear, which did not allow her, in her own eyes or in the eyes of her jealous community, any right to err, that she got stuck with Vadym for so dangerously long in that stage when you work through your days as if they were wet dirt on a shovel, because in place of your extinguished love, or whatever it was that appeared to have been love, comes emptiness—and into emptiness, always and inevitably, like black water, seeps death: I'm afraid to sleep. I'll fall asleep—and die.

Shit, now I remember! She even told me, sometime that summer, before our interview, a dream she had—told it to me in detail. The dream was about Vadym, but I only remembered one image from it. (You generally don't remember other people's dreams very well; they're like the plots of movies someone has retold you but that you haven't seen yourself.) In the dream, Vadym took her somewhere, to a hill, gray as the surface of the moon, and the hill began to slide from under her feet, and she saw it was a pile of concrete sand—really, what could be deader? I think there were even crows in that dream—black, fat, and glossy.

Why couldn't I have told her then: Vladusya, my dear, cut the cord and run as fast as your legs will carry you—exactly like you did ten years ago; follow your own design, that same mind-boggling pattern of yours. I know you can, you've done it before, and you know when it's time to go under the knife—and to hell with him, this husband of yours, and with his—actually your—penthouse, with its glassed-in floating clouds, mirror surfaces, and white leather ottomans; all that, literally heavenly beauty, with the eternal view of the sky, you could charge admission to that place, that was a heck of a job you did, but to hell with it, tear it from your heart and run. Run because this man, whose one other woman has already gone round the bend, alarmingly, in the loony-bin direction, is clearly dangerous; there are men like that—packed hard inside into an unassailable mass of self-satisfaction that we mistake for strength, and everything they touch, they kill, even sex. Such men like power, and it comes to them easily, because when someone's plowing ahead with such unassailable confidence, it is very hard not to think that he is the one who has seen the light and will, if you follow him, show it to you, too—hard to believe that such a juggernaut carries with it nothing but itself. But it's now that I'm all wised up—I knew nothing back then; it was all before I met R., and I was as stupid and naïve as a bunch of parsley. Dara—Dolly—Folly.

Why is the word death of feminine gender in our language; where'd this nonsense come from? Death should be a man; a woman's death, at least. That's the way the Germanic people have it, I think, they've always been better mystics than we. Spoken by a man, "I killed her"—it even sounds better, more convincing, than when a woman says, "I killed him." When a man says it, it doesn't admit any levity of interpretation. *I killed him with that one phrase*—men don't talk like that. Or, *I killed him with my silent disdain*—you're kidding, right? He doesn't give a hoot about your disdain, if he even noticed it. What does he notice, really?

I know nothing about the war that may have been raging between them her last autumn, when Vlada was so rapidly withdrawing from us all, cloaked in the cold, otherworldly glint of estrangement, like an acolyte soon to take her vows—I know nothing, and will never know anything more. And Vadym doesn't know either—I doubt he suspected even then what role he'd been destined to play in her life. (He did get rattled a bit with a chilly draft of recognition when she died—in those first weeks, when he drowned his grief in drink and, like a buffalo, stampeded at nights down the Boryspil highway as if he wanted to catch the runaway and bring her back—but he did not let that recognition rattle him any looser, and no more drafts from the other side will ever get to him again.)

No one, except the dead person herself, can see her death in its entirety. See how it evolved, how it ripened, day by day, like a fruit. The living can only observe, from their side, the result: how the overripe fruit drops from the branch under its own weight. And only the dead, herself, knows how things got that far.

***

"Let me make a living portrait of you, Daryna. I've always wanted to."

The bathroom—impeccably stylish rather than luxurious, without any nouveau-riche bells and whistles, all those Roman therms and gold leaf—still smelled of recent renovation, of paint and varnish, and the smell resembled the air of Vlada's studio a little. Perhaps that's what put her in the working mode, made her hands itch to pick up her tools (painting, she loved saying, is first and foremost manual labor, a craft!). She worked differently from the way makeup artists usually did: seated me facing her instead of the mirror, did not talk to me, did not comment on anything she was doing, but instead brought in a tape deck and put on Queen, "The Show Must Go On."

The longer I sat there, offering my face to her with my eyes closed, the stronger chills that ran through my body. Brushes, multiplying against my skin like a swarm of butterflies, tickled my mouth, temples, cheeks, eyelids; I was being transported to a different place, disappearing, changing form like a sculpture in the artist's hands. The music blared inside me, and from there, from the darkness of roaring halls, broken glass poured down my veins, a battle call breaking to the surface—like a challenge to life itself—it thundered: the show must go on! And Vlada's breath on my face froze like the breath of a tightrope walker hovering above the abyss of a great dark hall: this was no game, no inno-cent playing at dress-up and do-over, but something as ominously desperate as what Freddie Mercury must have felt in the flight of his own voice—she wanted to bring something important out of me, show me something that mattered a great deal to her; and when that scorchingly bright face finally hit me from the mirror, with the long Egyptian brows, the blood-dark lips (the face of a pagan goddess of war, a priestess of a bloody cult, something about it threatening, witchy, something that made you want to stomp it out, right away, like a fire, go back to the ranks, to the polished TV-screen picture that can reassuringly tell you the brand of the anchorwoman's suit), I recoiled, terrified. But at the same time I couldn't take my spellbound eyes off this strange mask, marvel-ing at how, aided merely by the masterly blended colors, it grew out of my own features. Incredible. Perhaps only in dark, low-lit windowpanes, with the texture of the details smoothed away, can human faces be as magnificent as this, and afterward it was in dark windowpanes that I'd glimpse this strange face on myself—and shudder every time. By then the emotional overload was making my whole body shake, all but teeth clattering, and all I could manage was to hide behind a nervous chuckle, like a village girl behind her sleeve: "Matusevych, what have you done to me? I am not like this!"

"Then you were like this in a previous life," she answered, very serious, "you just forgot."

"You think?"

In response, she stepped in closer, with that balletic move of hers, upward from below—and kissed me on the lips, running her tongue between them, which brought them, with a gasp, right back to life under the rolled-on lipstick, the feeling back in them again: her little tongue, in comparison to a man's, turned out to be incredibly soft, tender, like an oyster pried out of its shell. I forgot how long it had been since I was kissed by a woman—at school, at summer camp?—and thought to myself, stunned: so that's what we girls feel and taste like, some lucky bastards those men! Vlada withdrew and stood in the mirror beside me—a bloody smudge stained her lips like the hand mirror in that famous painting of hers, *Contents of a Purse Found at the Scene of the Accident.* "Now wait, I'll take a picture of you."

And I stayed there waiting, trembling a little—had she told me to slice my wrists at that moment, I would probably have done as she said. But she only brought back her camera—and casually, without aiming, shot off, like a good machine-gunner from the elbow-grip, a whole clip, *click-click-click.* "And now, the hardest"—and she stood next to me again, with that bloody smudge across her mouth, holding the camera aimed at the two us in her stretched-out arms, *click-click-click.* A double portrait: the artist and her (nibbled) model. Or, perhaps, not the model, but the work? No, it wasn't the model, or the work either. For her, I was something else in that incarnation, a bizarre impersonation of female strength, which she no longer felt in herself. And I remember well the strange alarm that stirred in me when she was aiming at us like that, with both hands, at face level, as if it were a gun muzzle and not a camera lens.

Those pictures remain in her digital archive—Vadym hasn't destroyed that yet. That's what he says, at least. I don't know if I would like to see them now. "Doesn't matter," Vlada said, when we looked at the pictures together—"no photograph can ever give you what you get when you look at the thing in flesh, and color photography especially is all smoke and mirrors, bull and opium for the people." And she was right: The pictures were very impressive but something crept into them that wasn't there in the mirror—theatricality. We looked like a pair of masqueraders, and my witchy mask no longer mesmerized as powerfully—some magic had gone out of it. This is why, Vlada professed contemplatively, painting can never be replaced, not ever, not with anything. "That's okay. I'll use this. I'll do something with these. I just don't know what yet ..."

And I did not tell her that she'd already done something—to me, only I also didn't know yet what it was. Washing my face in the bathroom later—with dull regret, as if an unfulfilled promise had breathed so near and passed me by, only brushing me with that one touch on the lips, and then slipping between my fingers (only living beauty can evoke such an aching sense of loss—never the one on canvas)—I felt my knees buckle under me. Just like that, literally, as if the tendons suddenly turned to mush and lost their grip—and up till then I thought "straw legs" was just a figure of speech. Had there been a male artist in Vlada's stead, everything between us would've discharged into clarity by means of immediate sex, and that sex probably would've been divine. One of those few times, count them on your fingers, that you remember for the rest of your life—with a complete release from the body such as one experiences in the midst of religious ecstasy, when, as I seem to remember Papa Hemingway wrote, the ground swam, although that was nonsense, too, because there's no ground left in sex like that, neither ground nor sky, neither up nor down, and love has nothing to do with it. Although I did have one time like that with Aidy, but then I've also had one with Artem—that time in the archive, when I first saw the photo of Dovganivna with her comrades and it came over me right on the spot, and that's when it all started, my life changed.

But Vlada was not a man, and the two of us could not rely on such simple resolutions, programmed into us by Mother Nature herself. Something else, then, was between us, something more unsettling, something akin to the link between a new mother and the fruit of her womb—she gave birth to something in me that night. She set something free, like a large dark bird.

And this remained our secret, one for the two of us—we never talked about it again, didn't have a chance. Until the day there was no longer anyone to talk to.

How could I have given her the strength I myself did not know was in me?

***

"B-beg pardon, I didn't hear you—what was t-that?"

Baldy asked me a question or something. And I tuned him out. Coz I'm drunk. Drink-dong-drunk … I hear bells ringing somewhere, a tinny-tiny little sound. No kidding, I'm drunk, good and drunk, who'd have thunk. Somewhere there was a stage at which I should've stopped and lingered, and I didn't notice how I rolled straight through it. Overdid it. And butter won't help no mo'.

Baldy was asking whether I am bored. Oh, sure, he needs an audience; he wanted to preen before me, too. And I just tuned him out; how uncivil—did not hear a thing, *nada*, of what they were talking about.

"I'm n-never bored."

"Oh, then you are a very special woman. One of a kind—your health!"

But I am bored looking at you, mister. Do you have any idea how boring you are to look at? You're all so boring, like someone'd just pulled you out of a washer. That's exactly what you're like: soggy and wrung out. And you probably imagine yourself all clean and squeaky, right?

"It's time we got going," Aidy says. The big sweetie, he's a bit tipsy, too. And all that alcohol has clarified some things in his head, too: that the only way to get rid of this character is exactly this—to get up and leave altogether. He won't go by himself, unless someone throws him out. And Aidy can't throw anyone out for anything. Aidy doesn't like humiliating people. And thank God for that. Thank God.

Baldy shoots hungry looks all around him, as though he wants to swallow the whole place in one gulp before he leaves, and take it with him, in his gut, like a smuggler carrying diamonds. And sighs sorrowfully, woman-like: *oho-ho*!

"As old Taras once wrote—"

Who? Baldy quotes with great pathos—although he talks all the time as if he were quoting someone anyway. His generation still uses quotes like scholastics use the Holy Scriptures, sat out their whole lifetimes behind other people's backs.

"First drink down—makes you spry / second—worry on your mind / third one—now your eyes glow / thought after another follows!"

"Taras Shevchenko wrote that?"

Aidy and I ask him to repeat it, and he does. I love it—like it was written about me. The clinical picture spread out, plain and simple. If only I'd stopped at that third drink—while the eyes still glowed. Aidy hands his credit card to the waiter, and Baldy pretends he is too engaged in the conversation to have noticed this delicate moment. (He'll ask insincerely later: How much do I owe?—and pretend to be surprised, just as insincerely, that the bill's already been settled; these old suckers always do that.) He tells me the great bard wrote this on a wall somewhere while he was carousing in a tavern. You know those poets maudits. Although it's still better than "les saglots longs des violons." For some reason, this conclusion prompts a surge of patriotic pride in me. (How did I ever get so drunk?)

"It would be good to write it on the wall here somewhere, too," Aidy contributes, as he always does, a dose of constructive pragmatism. That's right, this is supposed to be a literary café; no less, they even have some moldy hardbacks huddling on the shelves over there—what idiot would ever want to read in this light? Thought after another follows, that's very well said indeed.

And, out of some deeply sentimental gratitude to this old art-worm for the aptly supplied quote—as if this quote, for reasons past comprehension, took us to some deeper level of mutual understanding in this place and at this moment, before we got up from the table and parted ways (Will our paths ever cross again, or have they separated forever already?), as if the quote sent us into the throes of an intimacy so urgent we needed to fall into each other's arms at the feet of Myshko Grytsiuk, whom Vlada considered a genius—in a word, that drunken daze that makes the proletariat, after the umpteenth, by the great bard unforeseen, drink, grab whatever's handy and crush it on the tablemate's skull, I open my mouth and blurt, "Did you, by chance, know Vladyslava Matusevych?"

Done, it's out, can't take it back. And instantly the face I see before me is no longer weaselly—it's a hyena's maw. *He-he.*

"You know, for me it was enough to have known her matinka, *he-he*!"

"Nina Ustýmivna?" I'm not being obtuse—I'm slamming on the brakes: something's coming at me that I do not want to hear, and there's no way to swerve around it.

"Exactly, exactly. Ninél is her real name."

Ninél? Yes, indeed, that's right, Ninél—a name once fashionable among the Soviet bureaucrats, "Lenin" spelled backwards.

"I knew Matusevych Senior, too. He wasn't actually without talent, as a painter, but that bitch, pardon my language, just drove him to the grave. We used to call her the praying mantis among ourselves, *he-he* … the spider female that turns the male into protein after the act.… She, by the way, was a beauty, a nuclear blonde; you know—you could bury her alive, and she'd dig herself out with her bare hands, *he-he*. God spare me from a woman like that."

Something in his voice, a grating note, tells me he is not married. Or long divorced. Could've figured it earlier, not rocket science: his dingy shirt, a general dusting of neglect—it happens when a person has long lived alone and doesn't have anyone to look him over on his way out. His only consolation—how bad things can be for the married. Especially those who marry beautiful blondes. Vlada also always said that her mom had been a beauty, and I always kept politely quiet: I think the real beauties remain beautiful in old age, and I wouldn't say that about N.U.

"The fact that Matusevych never fulfilled his potential as an artist," Baldy continues to gloat, "was all Ninél's fault, much more so than the Soviets! She couldn't get him the Government Award, that's true, although she packed him off to the Central Committee more than once—to confess the mistakes of his youth, and he still didn't make it to the special-rations ranks, *he-he*... I'll finish the cognac, with your permission. No use leaving tears at the bottom— Your health!

"About me, she wrote a denunciation in '73—to the Union's political committee and the Art publishing house, whence I was promptly expelled, after that report of hers—for ideological immaturity. And that was the beginning of all my trials and tribulations. Despite the fact that I was a young specialist and they had no right to expel me." (He is talking as if this all happened just yesterday, the resentment raw in his voice.) "Right before that I published in ..." (*Bla-bla-bla*—he names a periodical from back then, *Socialist Painting* or *Swine Tending*, I forget instantly) "my article ..." (he rolls out a pretentious multiclause title that whizzes straight over my head and might as well have been in a foreign language) "they called it the generation's manifesto, the debate in the Union was oh-so-stormy—the last, you could say, stir of freedom."

"You mentioned a denunciation."

"And the denunciation, *he-he* ..." (he's all but rubbing his hands together, so pleased is he to be opening my eyes to the bottomless pit of human depravity) "the denunciation was that beauty's way of getting back at me for criticizing her husband, among other things. In that article of mine I wrote that he was more successful in his nonfigurative works than he was with the builders of the Chernobyl Nuclear Plant, and that was absolutely true. Except that he'd already been raked over the coals for his nonfiguratives, and it was time for him to distinguish himself. It was a critical year, you know: there'd been one wave of arrests already, Zalyvaha got time, Gorska was killed, a whole bunch of people got expelled from the Union, blacklisted—and Ninél, you know, she was used to comfort, to status; she wouldn't have taken kindly to being the wife of a persecuted, starving abstractionist. So she packed him off to paint 'men of labor' at the Chernobyl Nuclear Plant Project...."

"Good Lord, why to Chernobyl?"

"Eh, you, young bucks!" Baldy is all but melting, blissfully, like a living block of butter. He is in his element—the guide to the past, where we are foreign tourists, mouths agape. "They just started building it, right then! All the papers blared about it; poets were falling over each other to sing the peaceful atom on the Pripyat's shores. It was a win-win subject: it's not the great leaders you'd be painting again, you know, but men of labor—just like Courbet did—and at the same time you'd be manifesting the correct understanding of the government's and the party's policies. Back then, you must remember, few knew—it only came to light after the accident—how dangerous a project it was, that nuclear plant. And that the Ukrainian Academy of Sciences, no matter how deep in Moscow's pocket it may have been, did not, in the end, give its approval to build the plant in such a densely populated area—only in Moscow, they didn't give a shit, pardon my language, about some stupid Ukrainian hohlys' permission.

"It was so ordered—and off went the campaign, and everyone ran to get in line for a creative road assignment. And Matusevych Senior, too. He slapped together a whole series, painted in the realistic manner, of course; it was his first official show. He did have a few interesting uses of color here and there; color was his strength, and you can't escape yourself at the drop of a hat, just like that—but overall it was a sloppy job, such blatant socialist realism. If they'd given him the award then, it would have been a giant leap for him ..." (he spreads his arms, to make his point more visual) "clear to being crowned on the other side of the chessboard, straight into the establishment!" (The establishment seems to drop onto my untouched plate next to the veal filet that's gone cold, and Baldy blinks at it in passing, with visible regret.)

"That's what Ninél counted on—and not without good reason. Many careers were made like that at the time—after the best and the most talented went underground, like I did ..." (no, I didn't really hear that last bit, that's the alcohol finishing my thoughts for me) "the gaps had to be filled somehow. And, sure thing, all this rubbish pushed its way to the top, and the age of the talentless began. But, so that the difference would not be quite so obvious right away, they still mixed in a few of the old beaten-and-denounced; the ones who demonstrated contrition— as long as they were clean on the KGB count, of course.... And they were only too happy—Brecht was fashionable then, and he has Galileo say that it is better to have your hands stained than empty—remember? Many thought so, too: alright, let me get a little dirty, but in exchange I'll have a chance to do something, in art, in science.... But it didn't work that way, *he-he*! All of them, those who went from the underground to the officialdom, met Matusevych's fate—and never created anything good again! They were left empty-handed, *he-he*."

So this, then, is the main justification for his life? And for his own empty hands, which, by his reckoning, are superior to the hands of those who ate better than he did back then, and he wants someone to recognize this. He must make a good professor, actually—he has a way of drawing you in. So much so, in fact, that I've sobered back up to that third-drink level: thought after another follows.

And here I am, sitting across from him, some quarter of a century his junior, with my own clean hands, like Pontius Pilate's—and feel my blouse sticking to my shoulder blades, and notice the stench of my own armpits very clearly; it's not a hallucination. I, too, am beginning to sweat like him, beginning to ooze, his mirror image on the other side of the table, liquid from every pore. He also drips out of sorrow, I instantly realize and feel, for a moment, remarkably perceptive—a protracted sadness like that, over many years, can make one cry, or it can make one sweat. Looking at him, I see my own future. Myself—in another quarter century, when I, too, won't have anything left except persuading the grown-up youths (those I manage to latch on to) that I am better than my colleagues because one time, long ago, I didn't want to soil my hands, and disappeared from the screen. And I'll have nothing in those hands of mine, either, when those grown-up youths ask: And who exactly are you, miss, and what have you accomplished? Not one more worthwhile thing—just like him.

It all goes around in circles, I realize, horrified (and repulsed by my own indomitable smell)—in circles, over and over again, the same thing in every generation, only the costumes change. It's a special kind of trap: a whirligig of ruined lives. A Ferris wheel: you'll get off where you got on. I can't breathe; I'm going to be sick. Aidy, noticing or sensing something (my smell?), covers my hand with his comforting palm—thank you, love, yes, I understand, it's time to go, but I have to hear this man out. Hear everything. To the end.

"So Matusevych, then," the professor carries on his tale, losing most of his oratorical flourish (apparently, *he* is immune to my smell) "had, at the time, a perfectly realistic chance of improving his lot, and Ninél spared neither time nor effort for this. Wore her own soles off making sure he'd get nominated—and why not, he was practically clean on the KGB count ..." (How exactly, one wonders, does he know that?) "a few trifles here and there perhaps, a bit of this and that, dissident acquaintances in his past, but who didn't have those? The important thing was not to keep them up, and at that, Matusevych was rather abundantly experienced! When he got married, he broke off all contact with his own family—lest someone remind him that his uncle fought in the insurgency. He didn't even go to visit his mother—this, by the way, also upon Ninél's insistence; she just couldn't be too safe, that lady."

"Wait a minute." I sober up all the way to the first-drink level. "What uncle in UIA? Wasn't Matusevych's family from somewhere around Khmelnitsk?"

Khmelnitsk region—that's where Vlada went when she was little to her grandmother's, her father's mother's funeral, where she heard the wailing that she remembered for the rest of her life. And that was her only memory of that grandma, because she did not, in fact, ever see her alive, not once.

Baldy magnanimously aims the shiny circles of his glasses at me (and now he reminds me of Beria). "And did you imagine there was no UIA in the Khmelnitsk region?"

"Was there?" Aidy perks up.

"Was there anywhere it wasn't?" laughs Baldy, a downright homey laugh (his tie has slipped askew). "I come all the way from Sumy, and I remember how my mom hid partisans in the German days! And then when the Reds came, I was told to keep my mouth shut about it, not a peep, because it turned out that partisans they were, alright, but not the right kind … not the Soviet ones. And where Matusevych was from, in Podillya—that was basically Bandera's backyard!

"But they had to have forgiven him, that uncle of his, long before; Ninél was there at his side, a living, breathing proof of rectitude—she came from the privileged, an apparatchik family, her father started in Party work all the way back with Stalin…. So then, she had a clear plan—to push her husband to the top. And here I come, *he-he*, a greenhorn, truth-seeking idealist, and plain out declare that Matusevych is rubbish as a Socialist Realist, and that he's wasting his time doing something his heart isn't in."

"Isn't that a bit of a denunciation, too?"

This slips off my tongue before I can bite it—I'm not quite sober yet, after all. But now, in the pause my words abruptly throw open—this silence is bottomless, and so are Baldy's eyes as he stares at me, rendered instantly speechless, as if I'd just hit him with a right hook to the chin—in this silence that rings in my ears as though the entire café has also been stunned, lights changed and sound turned off, I finally sober up completely, the daze gone without a trace, like it was never there. Hang on a second. Who was it that looked at me with just such frightened eyes not so long ago? And why did Baldy get so scared?

Aidy is first to come back on line—with an amiable chuckle: he's getting a kick out of this; he's admiring me and doesn't hide it—he can afford to admire me, how awesome I am, how quick my reflexes are. And, since Aidy is the one who is bankrolling the evening, Baldy reacts to Aidy's signal—and engages again, although he has to force it, creaking and screeching like a rusty machine, flexing the muscles around his mouth: *he-he-he.* I already know who it was that looked at me exactly like that not so long ago—with the same dread, a cornered animal's hatred: it was my boss. During our last conversation, when I accidentally, just like this time, reminded him about the dead body buried on his conscience. The reaction's identical, down to a T; the facial expression's exactly the same. C'mon, mister, you're weaseling around, skirting something—you've got something to hide, haven't you?

"*He-he* … you, my dear, don't quite grasp the times, do you?" he declares, choosing to resume his magnanimous tone, and partially succeeds, only a few dry sparks crackle under his glasses in the wake of his momentary short circuit. "People took my article as a breath of fresh air! The journal still dabbled then in freethinking, for old times' sake; it was the last little island like that, but after Ninél's denunciation the publishers had their air shut off too. Ninél, you see, reasoned somewhat along the same lines as you just did, *he-he*...." (Vindictive, aren't we? Put the jab right back where it came from.) "Well, you can be forgiven on the grounds of ignorance, but you know this women's logic of yours. Women always rush to defend their own, in this they're much like Jews ..."

And anti-Semitic, too?

"There are all kinds of women out there. And Jews, as far as I know."

Aidy grunts his approval again—resigned to the prospect of not getting out of here as quickly as he thought. He nods to the waiter to clear the dishes from our table, pulls out the cigarettes he already put away in his pocket, and lights one up.

"Could I have one, too?" Baldy asks, suddenly, and unexpectedly.

He hasn't smoked all evening. Means I really got to him. Got him good, looks like. *Ha!* Am I Columbo, or what? Time to take the initiative: "So, if I understand you correctly, Nina Ustýmivna decided that *your* exposé could harm her husband's career, and responded with a preemptive strike?"

For a moment, he doesn't say anything—as if he were experiencing that strike again.

"A stab in my back," he says after the pause, drawing on his cigarette with the greed of an old smoker, his Adam's apple bobbing hungrily—and I see how worn he is. Soggy and worn. And old. "It was a stab in the back. She, essentially, ruined my life, your ..." he mocks with a caustic smirk, "*Nina Ustýmivna.* Unlike her, an apparatchik offspring, I had no protection or patronage whatsoever. They wouldn't think twice about giving me time—and not on political count, mind you, but for a criminal offense. Vagrancy or hooliganism—like they did with everyone who didn't have a famous name—workers, students, all the political bottom-feeders ... not a mouse would peep. Do you even realize what it was like ..." (his voice swells with an altogether theatrical pathos, it appears he's getting himself worked up again) "to be fired because of a political accusation, for 'ideological mistakes'? Can you imagine at all how an art historian might survive in 1970s Kyiv if no one would give him a job? How he might feed his family?" (Here I could have pointed out that I myself had once been a child in a family like that, and that our family, after they locked my father up in the loony bin, was fed by my mom. But I doubt it would trip him up—he appears to persist in the conviction that he is the only man in the world ever to have survived something like that.) "What it means—to beg around for small jobs? To write reviews under other people's names for twelve rubles a piece and consider yourself lucky when you could?" (Something similar may very well be in store for me in the near future, but I don't want to bring that up.) "My wife left me. She couldn't stand it after a while; she, too, wanted comfort—as Shakespeare said," he twists his mouth as if for another *he-he*, but this time no sound comes out, "Frailty, thy name is woman."

Shakespeare, Brecht—all this is also a kind of nouveau-riche gilding, like in their McBathrooms, all these quotes he pulls. He is not lying—he's just bizarrely off-key, as though he were playing his solo on an instrument in need of tuning. Or is it this iresome pathos of his that's ringing flat in my ear? You can't deny it: their generation used up our national stockpile of pathos for centuries to come, didn't leave us anything that could sound natural. Like Vlada making fun of her mother: "Nous sommes les artistes, maman!" Nina Ustýmivna, it's you again, Nina Ustýmivna.

"And you call it a preemptive strike! Perfidy's what it was, my dear, common human perfidy! The instinctive response of a cannibal who bites off the head of anyone who dares stand in her way, and moves on without a second thought!" (I wince unwittingly under this verbal barrage—as if it were Vlada who had to listen to all this instead of me.) "She chomped down her own husband, too, and didn't even blink! He never did get that award, not then, not later; they didn't let him to the very top," again he twists his mouth gleefully. "The competition was too stiff for Ninél, too tough for her to bite, and she broke her fangs, her resources were not immeasurable.... Bet my reputation—on that, the lady left her brand for many years to come. For a while there I was simply crossed out of life—in a dead end! Do you understand? Dead!"

"And that's when you were recruited by the KGB, wasn't it?"

He remains just like that, mouth not quite closed, halfway through an inhale: a freeze-frame. I can't help it—it's my professional proclivity for dramatic effects: as if I really lived inside a mystery series, where I'm also in charge of creating drama, and every time my trick works I get a small professional satisfaction. Aidy, my audience (the only one I have left)—also my view from outside, the director's voice from outside the frame, the cameraman on the other side of the camera, and the makeup artist with the powder brush at the ready (how quickly did I invest him with the powers of all my old overseeing authorities!)—makes a short, glottal noise that could, if one were so inclined, be taken for applause. He's so sharp, mind like a steel mathematical trap, that he's instantly put together all parts of the equation, and even if either one of us still wondered whether I have, in fact, divined the correct solution or stuck my chalk, at random, straight past the blackboard, one glance at Baldy is enough to erase all doubt: he looked as though all his sweat had instantly dried up all over him. A sudden change of seasons: a night of frost—and everything's stuck.

Oh, I guessed it all right; I bloody well did. He shouldn't have counted on my ignorance of this topic—I have, like it or not, done hundreds of interviews, with very different people. I've got my own personal Google in my head. I even know how much they were paid, these small-time rats on the take like him, for their monthly written reports on what their charges blurted out after a couple drinks—sixty rubles. A nice number, twice Judas's fee—I bet some wit made it so on purpose. Enough money, when push came to shove, to get you by. So he did.

He is right about one thing: it's true I cannot imagine how he lived. How he hung around, for years, showing up uninvited at other people's homes, at the old-time wooden annexes, not yet devoured by the new developments, at the attics of underground studios to glean his shred of borrowed warmth. How he slurped the borsch the women set before him and drank the cognac, the cheap Armenian stuff—there wasn't anything else back then, berated the Soviet government, viewed the men's works and pronounced his unwritten judgments on them—with great feeling, I bet, peppering them with quotes, honing his style—and sweating the whole time: oozed murky liquid from all his pores like under-pressed cheese, under the weight of his secret task. And then trudged home—and worked everything he'd heard into a story for his captain. I can't imagine a life like that. Or how one could endure it for years.

He'll write nothing about that "little-known stratum of our culture." He won't ever write it, no matter how eager he makes himself sound for Aidy. I could tell him this right now, right to his face, absolve him so he wouldn't suffer any longer; let him stop sweating under his uneased burden, once and for all: he won't write it because he's already described all those people—in his reports. He's already made a story out of it—the one others demanded of him. And this story has stayed with him, has short-circuited his memory. Because it's always like that with the story; I know it from my own experience: you remember people, alive or dead, not the way you once knew them, but the way you told others they were. Doesn't matter whom you told—whether you were speaking to TV viewers from the screen, or to a KGB officer in a room with closed doors: you can't make a different story from the same material, zero out the first one, new text over the old. The material's burned. Burned, charred, turned to ash, leaving but one trace—the bitter taste of resentment, the eternal sense of having been robbed of your due, the mouth etched into a mournful arc.

He had his story taken from him, taken away. It was done with his consent, with his own hands, and there isn't anyone to blame now. Maybe he really would have died if he hadn't agreed—it was those who didn't agree that died. And those who lived now have no tale to tell us because they'd already told it once. And, unfortunately, not to us.

They should be telling us another story now—a story of taken stories. The story of their defeat, but no one wants to do that. Vlada, too, probably never heard from her mother about that episode with Baldy—and would Nina Ustýmivna even recall it herself? People often forget the evil they've done unto others, but retain forever the antipathy toward those they've wronged—reasons for this are found and fit into the puzzle later, retroactively. Vlada may have heard Baldy's name at home, spoken with a bit of scorn, with a magnanimous chuckle, as one commonly speaks of ambitious losers, and may have thought him one. And somehow I find this unfair and hurtful—as if they'd cheated her, my Vlada.

As if everyone, all of them, cheated her and were cheating her her entire life, since she was little—all of them driving her, together, into the ditch.

I am tired. Good Lord, this day's got the best of me. Was it only this morning that I was getting ready to meet with Vadym, rehearsed in my mind the prosecutorial speech I'd prepared about the girls' show, made sure to choose the right jacket and turtleneck—the same ones I wore to see him in his apartment on Tarasivska, the day Vlada died, counting on the outfit triggering Vadym's Pavlovian reflexes, engaging subconscious machinery of memory and guilt? What an idiot!—like men even notice what a woman is wearing unless they intend to rip her clothes off.

God ... it's too much for one day—feels like this morning was at least a week ago. And the intoxication's passed, blew clean out, and I'm cold. I've got this chilly shiver running down my back—I might be getting sick; it's flu season, and there's this draft from the doors.... And, please, there's no need to be yelling at me—I'm already tired beyond belief, and can't possibly muster the effort to react to any stimuli, except maybe if he picked up a knife and went ahead and sliced me into halves like the circus woman in the box, only I doubt I'd come back together again—Aidy, can you do something about this? Why won't he stop yelling at me?

And look how red he's turned—crimson, poor thing, the whole bald spot flushed like a jug of cherry liquor split under his skin. God forbid he "took a conceit," as Aidy likes to say, meaning, had a stroke.... Only separate phrases break through to my awareness. ("Who's the injured party here? What, was anyone injured because of me? No, no one can say that; go look as long as you want, you won't find anyone!") His monologue refuses to coalesce in my mind; it splits and shatters. Plus he is yelling, and I have trouble with yelling even when I'm fully awake—yelling in falsetto now—no longer a baritone—with hysterical girly modulations, which are also somehow fake, as if he'd memorized in advance the right way of screaming his indignity when he is suspected of collaborating with the KGB. Or maybe, in all those years of leading a double life, he lost the ability to speak spontaneously altogether—just forgot how you do it, say what you think, without prepared notes in your mind? ("It was me they threw out on the street like a dog, and it's your Ninél's fault! Hers and hers alone! You can't ever deny it!")

Aidy coos something soothing to him, as he's done the whole evening—now would be a good time for me to make amends, curtsy peaceably, maybe even apologize, say I didn't mean anything like that at all, tell them I want to go home now—stop, enough, enough of these memories, the ripping open of old wounds, of this eternal Ukrainian self-destruction. Aidy slaps his hands on the table like he's slamming all the demons I've summoned back into the boards—enough, time to step out; it's stuffy here, the ventilation's crap, and it stinks like dirty socks—he can be squeamish, my Aidy, only it's not socks, I think, detached as if in someone else's mind: it's the stench of decomposing souls. I've been reeling them in all day today, drawing them in like a thread on a spool—first Vadym, now this character, and if this is the new journalistic investigation that I've assigned myself to, I don't want to touch it with an ten-foot pole.

And that's when Baldy bursts open with a new, no longer false, undeniably honest sound: hurried, the last blubbering argument from the shut-off tap, the triumphant cry of well-aged hatred. "But God sees it! He sees it all! Walked over dead bodies she did, and dead bodies she got—or did she think it would always turn out her way? Thought she'd have her bed of roses—first with her husband, and once she drove him to the grave, then with the daughter she'd make into a Big Artist? Vladusya the genius. Yeah right—stamped out a bunch of those folksy paste-jobs of hers, Ms. Cookie-Cutter. Sure they played in Europe, what doesn't? It's been a desert for God knows how long. The Brits give out their Turners for shit you wouldn't believe, and everyone here's just happy to play along—fancy that, a world-famous artist, drives a sports car! Not very far she didn't! Now her old matinka gets what she deserved!"

The next sound is that of a chair falling. It's from under me—and I, on my feet, loom over the defiled table, like Lenin over a pulpit in an old Soviet movie, and yell, choking, at the lenses of those Beria glasses, something barely sentient and incredibly pitiful, something that begins with "How dare you" and instantly makes me want to disappear from the face of the earth. And when Aidy emerges from the ensuing brouhaha, from the snowstorm of the waiters' white shirts and the dense smatter of faces that have turned to look at me, when he rises to his full monumental height and waves his arms like a conductor over the orchestra pit where the band's gotten drunk and is now banging out a loud cacophony, I cede my pulpit to him and flee in a most undignified manner. Tripping and painfully slamming my hip into a corner of a chair or a table, blindly ripping my coat off the hook—out, through the doors with their desperate squeal of hinges, into the rancid, soggy, oily gloom the streetlamps are swimming in, down the stairs, coughing and slipping, to the thump of my own boots—and only on the sidewalk, where I stop, do I notice the napkin clenched in my hand: When did I snatch it, and what for, I wonder—was I going to throw it into Baldy's face?

Night, snowdrifts, streetlamps fringed with mist, clouds above Prorizna running fast, so fast, unwinding into streaks of smoke above the bluish glow from the moon. When I was little, Mom and Dad used to take me for sled rides at nights—they'd hitch themselves to the sled and run down the long winter street, and one time I fell out of the sled on a turn and just lay there, in a snowdrift, a well-padded bundle. In the minute or two it took my parents to realize what had happened, the whole universe came crashing at me, alone—like an astronaut out of his ship, in open space. I remember the sky above—a star-dotted blackness—and the incomprehensible, cosmic silence, the likes of which I never heard again. When my parents returned, noisy and laughing, I already knew the world was different from what they were trying to make me believe it was. That a person was alone in it. And that to cry—something I remember they were very surprised I didn't do—was futile. There was no one to cry to under this sky.

I don't know how much time has passed—maybe a minute or two—when the quick scrunch of snow under a familiar step calls to me from behind my back—*slush-slush*, the thick vapor of breath, the dear smell of a tobacco-scented coat, aftershave, warmth, skin—home. Keys jingle. "Baby, don't—here, get in the car before you catch a cold on top of everything, come on."

And only now—after I turn to him, bury my face in his chest, in his dear smell, clawing through the soft fabric of his scarf, between the lapels of his cashmere coat, pressing, burrowing into his whole self, as if digging deeper into the ground to escape an artillery attack—do I finally let all my tears run at once, all of them, accumulated, it seems, over twenty years—from that day when I cried into Sergiy's chest, the first man to whom I opened up. I let loose with a single blast, as if the cork were knocked out of me with one terrible, hiccupped sob, and the weeping that had sat all day in my throat like barking, breaks out. Like dogs barking.

Mama, Mommy. Aidy, Aidy. Don't let me go.

***

"You asleep already?"

"Uhm-hm..."

"You're kind of different with me now, you know?"

"Uhm-hm?"

"And when you enter me ... inside ... it's somehow different ... I don't wait for the climax anymore, you know? It's just, you're inside me, and that's it. Like in a dream. Or like breathing."

"Is that good or bad?"

"You silly. Good, of course ... it's good. Go back to sleep."

"Come to me."

"What, again?"

"Yep. Again and always. What were you even thinking putting this shirt on?"

"Listen, do you believe that? What he said about Vlada's mom?"

"That she ratted him out? I think so—why else would one hate someone else's wife like she was family?"

"No, not that. The part about Vlada's father—that she killed him? Do you believe something like that could happen?"

"Your feet are still cold, you little goose. Here, let me. All kinds of things happen."

"Have you ever been with a woman like that? One who is killing you, and you know it—day after day?"

"I forgot. I forgot everything that was before. You've got the wrong guy to interview."

"What do you mean, wrong guy? Who else am I gonna ask now?"

"You're funny. I want you. All the time. Can you believe that?"

"No, listen … earlier in the day even, when I left Vadym's place, I was thinking the same thing about Vlada. That she had no other way out, with Vadym. That it was like a tunnel, you know, where you can only move forward. What if it's always like that: When one spouse dies, it's always the other's fault? No wonder they didn't much care for widows in the old days … or widowers, either."

"Mm-m."

"No, I mean it. The one who survives, he or she, sort of, didn't hold on to the other—let them slip. Let death have them, you know?"

"Hush. Don't think about that. You and I will live happily ever after and die on the same day."

"Really? You promise?"

"Cross my heart. Worse comes to worst, we'll blow ourselves up with one grenade."

"Why did you say that? About the grenade?"

"How should I know? I was asleep, remember?"

"You poor thing!"

"Yep. You're the one who roused me—and instead of getting down to business, took me to task about who I killed."

"I love you. Here, put your paw right here, uh-huh, that's good ... I know you didn't kill anybody. Honest."

"Cross your heart? You believe me?"

"I do believe you, Aidy."

"Let's sleep then."

Room 6. Adrian's Last Dream

And we will dream the same dream.
The same dream, my love—only we will be watching it from
different ends.
Where are you, Adrian? I cannot see you.
I'm here. Don't be afraid. Give me your hand.

At night, the wind howled and wailed in the vents, mournful like the clamor of the lost souls it drove through the dark, host after weeping host. The giant firs at the entrance to the bunker flailed their boughs, clawing at the air, and for a moment Adrian thought dozens of hands were pushing the branches apart, splitting and cracking their way through the forest, and heard in the howling of the wind a distant echo of foreign voices calling to each other and the baying of dogs. But it was only the wind—*lem wind*, as the Lemko people from beyond the Curzon Line called it.

They—who had wandered the entire summer in a wasted, deserted land, among the villages burned by the Poles, where only feral cats, remembering people, ran out to greet them—believed that air could hold echoes of voices that had once rung through it, and insisted that the wind often brought, mixed with the smell of the charred homes, the clamor of a great human mass—children crying, cattle bellowing, engines running—all those unmistakable sounds of a twenty-four-hour deportation, which in reality happened already two months ago.

Every time, Adrian patiently explained to them that it was not physically possible for a sound to exist without its source and even used a stick to draw on the ground the range of fading fluctuations. But, of late, he himself experienced such auditory hallucinations more and more often: his nerves were wearing thin, which was bad because ahead of him loomed the entire unbroken winter like a wall that could not be scaled—only dug under, crawled beneath by the patient marking off of days, one at a time, on the calendar in the bunker.

"I'll craze!" he thought suddenly, in a flash—and got angry at the thought, jumping onto the trunk of a fallen spruce, slipping under it, hugging it with his arms and legs, delighting without shame in the joy of his body roused from immobility, each muscle awake (pure sport, a child's game—he could've just as easily walked on top of the log, sweeping over his tracks with a handful of fir brush). His body responded, engaged, instantly recalling its long-forgotten skills, the deeply buried spider-like four-handedness of a mountaineer, which a long time ago, in a different life, had carried him over mountain gorges on Plast climbing trips; this was *the same* body, limber and lithe, and it was a blast of true delight to move it ahead like this, bear-fashion, under the log, trying not to disturb the feathery cap of wet snow on top. Instantly sweaty, warmed from inside with a healthy heat, dry as a fire's, he crawled to the spot where he was to leap down into a quick, nonfreezing stream—the "warm-run"—pulled himself astraddle the log and drew a triumphant breath, looking over the whole wooded gulch, lit by the snow's glow in the predawn dusk.

And that's when it struck him, sharp as the proverbial stick in the eye, the thing they'd feared: the snow had betrayed them. The first, fleeting, phantom November snow—as soon as the wind changed and breathed warm from the south—didn't hold, it sank and opened above their underground bunker, a thawed-out window of dark earth, clear like a circle of breath on cold glass.

Even from where he sat, he could see the rusting of last year's leaves in it. Aw, for the love of tripe!

The wind "spilled" them, undid all their conspiracy. Even a child would know that under that patch of earth people lived and food cooked—on a tiny gas flame that smoldered for three hours to make a pot of gruel. Rot it. This bunker was never any good. He didn't like it from the moment he saw it: not dug deep enough, shoddy (loose earth kept falling from the ceiling with a rustling noise, over and over, grating on their already ragged nerves) and fatally tight for the five of them. But at the moment they had no other choice but to stay and wait. And now he was walking away to the city, leaving his comrades to the mercy of fate—and the southern wind. By noon it should thaw more, speckle other open spaces with the same ice-hole blackness, and mask their hiding place anew—the air he drew in was humid, only the wind had to hold. Nothing to be done now—dawn was near. He had to go. Over the same wet snow.

He freed one hand from his overcoat's sleeve and with a quick motion, like his mother used to do whenever he had to travel away from home at night, made the sign of the cross over the bank, which seemed to have held its breath in the predawn stillness, with the black stain against the white.

And plunged into the creek.

"De-vil's winds! Accur-sed winds!" That's how Geltsia recited the poem for them—she knew myriad poems by heart, while he had forgotten everything unnecessary that he had ever learned and could not stop marveling at her, making her recite again and again, so he could exist in the presence of her voice, whose sound in the darkness packed thick enough to cut with a knife the breath of four lice-ridden men (and she—She!—had to breathe their miasma), spilled like cascades of silk, seemed to glow like silver. And that's Tychyna? Really? The same one who now writes odes to Stalin and the kolkhozes?

Ever since his Gymnasium years he loved no poet more than Ólzhych, his "To the Unknown Soldier"—that was about him: his life. But Ólzhych had been tortured to death in a German concentration camp by, they said, none other than Willie Wirzieng himself, whom Adrian was supposed to liquidate back in Lviv in '43. Twice he tried, and both times something had stood in his way—that Gestapo man must've sold his soul to the Devil; the Huzuls say about such people that they have "help" ... Adrian buried Ólzhych for himself then, together with the guilt about the failed missions; nothing in the world could make him recite one of his poems now. Even to Her. No, especially to Her.

De-vil's winds. At least it's safer to travel in this wind: his steps cannot be heard in the woods. Although it's not just his steps that cannot be heard—those *other ones*, if they came, wouldn't be heard either.

He once had the alias Beast—a long time ago, back with the Germans. Later, when Beast got on the GB wanted list, he had to change his alias, but, thank God, did not lose Beast's sense of danger, which had kept him alive through the years in the underground and now whimpered inside him like a squashed pup: the wind carried the smell of a raid.

But after all, he thought, trying to reassure himself, wading in the free water of the warm-run (he would walk another two hundred yards, just to be sure, as far from the bunker as possible, so he wouldn't betray its location with a stray footprint)—after all, this was no surprise: this raid covered the entire district and had been going on for more than a week already; it was the reason why they had to halt in the woods in this opportune makeshift bunker—still a ways from the village where they planned to winter.

The village turned out to be occupied by a Bolshevik garrison, which went searching house to house; several families, their courier informed them, had been taken right away in the middle of the night, and people lurked in their yards like shadows—at night, no one put any lights on, except in the village council building, the former parish house (the priest with his family having been shipped off to Siberia the previous winter), where the Reds sat in their meetings with the turncoats all night long and drained, for bravery, buckets of homemade booze they'd looted earlier in the day. The villagers quickly surmised that drink was the Soviets' preferred currency, and there was hardly a home left that wasn't at work brewing some; but it didn't protect people from being robbed, because, in addition to the alcohol, the others, like locusts, swept up everything within their reach—in a widow's home where an insurgent hideout had been prepared, they skewered the whole pantry with probes and when they didn't, thank God, find the hideout, they took the single thing of value that was in the home—chrome leather for a pair of boots. They're the horde, said the courier with unconcealed contempt; he was an older man who'd been with the partisans for a long time and knew very well that in any decent army, just as in the UIA, looting was punished by firing squad—but, he added, at least this time they weren't setting homes on fire.

They no longer had need to torch villages as they did right after they came, when they treated the Western Lands as enemy territory—and sent whole villages to Siberia with only the clothes on their backs, murdered people on the spot without trials, raised them on bayonets, tied them to horses, sliced pregnant women's stomachs, and raped girls in front of their mothers' eyes. Now Stalin had called off those orders, now this was territory they considered *theirs*—and demanded obeisance and duty: seven metric centners of grain per each hectare of land, regardless of whether it was arable, four hundred liters of milk from each cow in a barn—just like the Germans before them, only the Germans didn't trouble themselves by lying so shamelessly, never promised the Jews the happiest life in the world as they herded them into ghettos.

There was already a kolkhoz in the village: back in August, in the heat of the harvest, when everyone worked around the clock, the garrison rolled in without warning, toting a Ukrainian lobcock from the Eastern regions, who, waving his submachine gun, rounded up all the men into a fold, locked it, put soldiers around it, and said none who don't sign up for the kolkhoz come out alive. They started coming out, with hands in the air, on the third day, when they had to drink their own urine.

And so the new Molotov Collective Farm was founded. The grain that had already been harvested was confiscated with the announcement that only those who work for the kolkhoz would receive some back, fifty grams for each so-called workday—pure scorn, people said, what this world's come to, worse toil they'd never endured, even as serfs a hundred years ago with Austria, may it rest in peace! But bread was still taken away; those villagers, the poorer ones, who didn't manage to hide theirs, now received assistance from the ward—out of the reserves meant for the insurgents. How long those reserves would last was something Adrian had to find out. In two days, one of his management adjutants was due with a report, and then he'd have the complete picture. Fortunately, back in the spring, when the hungry from Greater Ukraine and Bessarabia rolled into Galicia like thunderclouds, the Supreme Commander ordered the UIA to release part of the strategic reserves of grain they had won back earlier from the Germans, so they had enough to help the hungry and, according to the courier, last until the new harvest, so the people weren't yet really affected by this kolkhoz.

The lobcock received an oral warning: the local Security Service detail picked him up for an hour-long conversation when he was traveling through the woods with his wife. There was some unpleasantness: the woman panicked at the sight of the banderas popping out from the bushes and fainted, and the husband later had to send her to spend a month in Lviv in the Kulparkiv clinic—to help her nerves. The man himself had cooled off since then, the conversation made its impression: he'd become decidedly nicer to people and even warned the warden about the current raid, but he still wasn't trusted in the village—neither he nor his poor wife, who returned from Lviv, the courier said, all sort of beaten down, like a hunted rabbit.

Adrian was irked, as always, when he heard of innocent women being harmed—but in the same instant, he saw, as though sketched out in charcoal, Stodólya's face, every muscle still; and it seemed he could almost hear the hidden ticking of the man's thought, like that of a time bomb. Did that woman really see doctors in Lviv, or did she go through GB's schooling? It was precisely the rabbits like her that often turned out to be the most dangerous informants—they were so terrorized by the GB that they lost their minds, became unpredictable. And Stodólya was an expert in that. This was *his* war; he fit into it perfectly. Adrian could only be grateful for his good fortune with Security. And he was very fortunate indeed. Wasn't he?

It was a strange condition, dreamlike. For the seven months since he left the infirmary after being wounded, he'd been living as if dreaming with his eyes open (only in rare moments when he was, as now, alone, he could see all three of them at once, from outside—himself, Geltsia, and Stodólya, whom she called Mykhailo)—and marveled, impassively, as if in an ether-induced haze through which no thoughts could reach to the deep layers of living pain, half-consciously: How could this have happened, and why did it have to happen?. And in that dream he did, in fact, have many occasions to feel grateful for his Security Service, thrilled at every successful mission, of which, knock on wood, they'd had quite a few. It had been a busy summer, the summer of the Lord's year nineteen forty-seven, when the movement faced the joint special forces of USSR, Poland, and Czechoslovakia, a giant red octopus spread over three countries, and they didn't waste this summer, nor did they mar their honor and oath.

He and Stodólya did work rather well together—like two mountaineers roped together, each one outdoing himself to prove his worth to the other. They fed each other a sort of constant reciprocal charge that kept them from giving in to fatigue, kept their minds sharp even after a sleepless march—like that time in the middle of summer, when they had a rendezvous and Adrian arrived not having slept for three days: he was shutting down as he walked, falling, for a few seconds at a time, into a dark well while his alert body continued to move on its own. Stodólya's people were also exhausted, and Stodólya had eyes like those prisoners their boys had fought off down by the town of S.—bloody like meat in an open wound, with eyelids drawing pale circles on his blackened face when he blinked. It wasn't Stodólya, but Adrian who noticed Stodólya's guard sitting down to clean his weapon and said to the man—straining as if to shout from under a mass of water—make sure, friend, you don't have a bullet in the stock. And it was good he said it, because it turned out he did. And Geltsia was there; he remembered the way she looked at him. Was happy then and not only because he prevented a grievous accident—there'd been a few already in their territory, two riflemen had died after getting wounded like that, cleaning their weapons when they'd lost their vigilance to fatigue—but also because he kept his, and She saw it. And Stodólya did, too. Lord, how he slept then—catching up on the whole summer.... And afterward, wolfing down hot grits, abuzz with new strength and energy that were flooding his body, Adrian told them how he and his unit mowed down a hundred Reds just a few days before—those crowding a clearing in a hollow like a herd of sheep brought to slaughter really—how they could barely keep their machine guns loaded, sweeping at them from the brush.... Even the usually tight-lipped Stodólya said he wished he could have been there.

No, they really fit themselves to each other quite well—you couldn't have come up with a better personnel match if you tried; no great mind in General Staff could have devised this on purpose. Adrian wished sometimes there was an organizational adjutant he could pat on the shoulder, whoever it was that had brought them together like this, be it even the Devil himself. And more, somewhere at the bottom of this months-long, eyes-wide-open dream, he felt a pulsing vein, a warm-run of secret pride for not having yielded last spring to a moment of weakness, for having overcome himself—and not having asked to be transferred to a different territory for personal reasons.

Because it did occur to him at first. He could not conceive how he would work on the same territory with the other two. Friend Dzvinya, friend Stodólya—the thought made the hair on his head ache. Once he even tagged along with Woodsman's people when they went to a village wedding—he'd never done that before, even when an insurgent family was celebrating a marriage and asked him to come—dragging himself out in public like a lout, hoping for a temporary distraction. But at the wedding the girls seemed to sing for his ears alone—like it happens with a fresh wound: no matter how you turn, you'll manage to worry it, moan through your teeth—"Now eagles fly to drink from that well, now that girl stands under a wedding veil ..."

In that instant he saw it clearly, as though through a brightly lit window at night: Geltsia weds Stodólya, and the one officiating is Father Yaroslav! He didn't notice how he crushed a glass tankard in his hand—only saw it when the blood mixed with his uzvar drink and ran into his sleeve and people around him raised a fuss—"Hey, pity-pity, loved the girl since he was little, loved her since he was little, loved but didn't take ..." Two things stopped him then: first, that it would not have been easy to find anyone to replace him, especially at the moment, in May, when the place boiled like a hell-cauldron—no one starts redistributing troops in the middle of a battle!—and second, second was that Stodólya had saved his life. Carried him, wounded, from under fire, on his own back.

He had to love Stodólya like his own brother. That was the task he had set for himself—never mind that Stodólya, armed with silence like a dynamite cruiser (always, after he was gone, he left upon the others' memories an impression of a much larger man), did not make it especially easy to love him.

Stodólya had saved his life.

And Stodólya was the man She loved.

Geltsia.

Friend Dzvinya.

(She protested, knotting her little brows, while her eyes flashed from under her frown with irrepressible joy at seeing him again, because he was her joy: her youth, Lviv, the first tango at a People's Prosvita Hall ball, "I have time, I will wait, should you find a better one"—well, she did, didn't she? For the first few moments, the play of light and shadow on her face, like on the surface of a mountain lake on a breezy day, blinded and deafened him; he drank her with his eyes like precious, thirst-quenching water, and did not comprehend what she was saying: "I'm a *friend* to you like all other men!"—and then she lowered her voice to a whisper which broke, with a small ding, a secret string, invisible and taut inside him: "Or we could address each other by name … Adrian?")

Can dreams possibly be this clear? So you understand everything, so precisely—as if you're watching a film with voiceover?

This is not a dream.

What is it then? Who is this man?

I don't know. He is dead.

How could he possibly be dead? Don't you hear how alive he is? Only, something is tormenting him. Something too big for one person.

Could this be why he cannot die?

"Mourn you have, my fair sir," a Gypsy woman clucked at him at the fair in S., latching on to the sleeve of his gimnastiorka and pushing her face up close to look him in the eye. "Moi, such fair officer sir, and such mourn has you!" her low voice rang hypnotic, from deep in her chest, but to him it seemed to mock. "For your mourn, I'll read for naught, just so you know what to watch for"—something about her reminded him of Rachel, the memory rose in his body and screamed in such a yearning spasm of desire that he bolted from under those eyes of hers that were pointed at him like two black craters framed by their blazing whites, tore away roughly, like a real Soviet captain—and barked over his shoulder, in Russian, "No need!" He wanted no witchery; he never wanted to see into the future, especially right before a mission, and that day in S. they managed their mission gloriously, broke apart a whole caravan in their Soviet uniforms—"Documents check!"—sending the trucks that carried weapons on a detour to an ambush, and then another unit neatly potted the general's black GAZ-M20 that zigzagged among the trucks loaded with people and goods leaving the fair. The Bolsheviks already knew that the banderas did not attack where there were civilians and hoped to slip by in this manner, only they didn't know we had people among the peasants riding those trucks, so they heard the "Down!" command precisely an instant before the machine guns opened fire from the forest, and no one outside the GAZ-M20 was hurt. Inside it, the driver and the emissary general from Kyiv were killed, but the one the boys were after, a major from the regional GB they wanted to interrogate, was lifted from his hiding place under the backseat, where he lay curled up like a babe out of cradle, alive and unharmed, and, over the course of the summer, this major gave Stodólya, man by man, the GB agent network across the entire region.

On several occasions during that time, Adrian found himself in a state of a strange arrested amazement toward Stodólya: he watched the man hunt down the octopus fanatically, pin it in, methodically, from all sides, setting his traps so tight a mouse couldn't slip through, and then with one or two sudden strikes, sever the writhing tentacles with an expert surgeon's precision. He witnessed more than the mere thrill of the hunt, as in combat such calculated, multistep operations obviously gave Stodólya his own, special satisfaction; and when, after each success his peculiarly molded face, dark as though burned from inside, with its close-set eyes and the protruding, slightly hooked nose (wolfhound, flashed through Adrian's mind again: once he gets a hold of someone, not a hair will fall without his permission!) would assume for a short time a contentedly sated expression, lit with a quick, cunning squint—rebel, blast him!—and Adrian, however much he thrilled with their victory, felt somewhere deep in his heart discomforted as one feels in the presence of a rival who has an advantage. And this vexed him, and spoiled the joy.

On one such occasion, Stodólya loosened up so much that he allowed them all to be photographed—this was unusual indeed because Stodólya was religious about secrecy and fastidiously controlled circumstances in which any of the rebels might accidentally be caught on camera—and now it was he himself who permitted the courier to bring a photographer to the forest, from three villages over. The photographer, however, was reliable, checked many times and thoroughly instructed about where and how he was to hide the negatives; he took a picture of all five of them—Adrian, Stodólya, Geltsia, and the two Security Service guards, Raven and Levko (the young man with rosy cheeks whom Adrian warned about cleaning his weapon).

Right before that, Stodólya's unit eliminated one of GB's provocation groups that had been operating on their territory since winter, terrorizing civilians, and Stodólya, usually gloomy and short-spoken, uptight and buttoned-up, was openly celebrating, letting the success soften and thaw him. He told Adrian how long he'd been hunting those bandits—he found two traitors in that GB group, guys who'd been born around here. A year earlier, GB had taken them alive and recruited them in jail, so during raids they spoke like locals and the horrified peasants believed that it was really "our boys" who went on a rampage, and wished they could now hide underground themselves, not knowing what was going on and where they could turn for protection. But as luck would have it, the bandits made a mistake: got, as was their custom, drunk, and when killing a teacher's family one night, dressed in the rebel-style mazepynka caps and embroidered shirts, failed to notice they hadn't finished off a twelve-year-old boy, left a witness.

At this news, Stodólya's eyes flashed with that predatory, quick flash of wicked triumph, instantly hidden by his characteristic squint, giving Adrian the feeling of a creeping, unpleasant chill that told him they were different: Stodólya spared no thoughts for the murdered family, and the wounded boy, in his mind, had played his part once he relayed the information and gave them the lead. Stodólya enjoyed the revenge itself, knew how to enjoy it. And not the way one enjoys winning a complex combination in chess, but almost lustfully, like love. Adrian did not know how to do that. The hatred toward the enemy, by itself, did nothing for him; he didn't know how to savor it.

That was the first time it occurred to Adrian that Stodólya outdid him in something important. Or maybe that's what a real counterintelligence officer was supposed to be—immune to sentiment. When a village courier, a very young girl, sitting with them around a campfire, blurted out, like a little kid, that she dreamed of studying to be a doctor one day, "when we have Ukraine," she touched a nerve in all of them: Raven remembered how, in Polish times, he dreamt of becoming a barrister, defending the wronged; and the rosy-cheeked Levko, when he was little, acted in theatrical performances at Prosvita and everyone said that he would make a fine actor, but what kind of job is that for a lad? Adrian tossed in his two cents with a story about how he surprised himself when he discovered he could use trigonometry in battle after having been best in his class at it in school. Only Stodólya said nothing. As if he had no life other than the one he had now, none in reserve and none he wished for.

Another time they started talking about the assassination of Colonel Konovalets in '38, and how differently, had he been alive, the Ukrainian card would've been played between Hitler and the Allies during the war, with an incomparably more winsome outcome for us. Stodólya regarded such high-minded speculations with open scorn, saying that such politicking nowadays was no more use than mustard after dinner, and, of course, he had a point; but the assassination itself, its technique and execution—with the bomb camouflaged as a box of chocolates—aroused his genuine curiosity.

"Colonel let his chocolate get him," he grumbled, curtly, not as a reprove to the departed for having been fond of such high-society luxuries, as one might have expected to come from a peasant's son (although Adrian never did know for certain whether Stodólya really was a peasant's son, had no concept of what education he might have had—Stodólya never said anything revealing and kept his true identity a secret), but more with disappointment that even a great man such as Colonel Konovalets could have had a weakness, even one so tiny—hardly worth a haw—and one could hear in his voice the lesson he extracted from it and learned like *Paternoster*: that you dare not have any weaknesses the enemy could exploit.

That's who Stodólya was—a man without weaknesses. And that's why he was disliked in the underground.

And feared a bit, too: Adrian wasn't the only one Stodólya kept on edge.

From the day they had themselves photographed, when they celebrated eliminating that provocation group (every tentacle severed like that gave them, for a while, an illusion of breathing more freely), another conversation stuck in his mind, one that fell like a spark on straw and, word after word, flamed up into an almost serious quarrel between Stodólya and Geltsia. They were talking about the hungry that were coming from the East—for some reason, the locals called such people "the Americans." Levko, of the rosy cheeks, had gone to the city to reconnoiter, dressed in woman's garb ("You should see what a fetching wench he makes!" Geltsia laughed), and had seen, at the station, a freight train full of these people: they climbed down from the cars and fell right on the spot to rest, having no strength to drag themselves any further. Close by stood a canvas-covered army truck, and soldiers picked up and tossed into it, like logs, those who could not get up again.

Adrian remembered Gypsy from Slobozhanshchyna, one of the men with whom he had made acquaintance in the infirmary: he, too, had told of similar things happening in '33 in Great Ukraine. When kolkhozes come, the Easterners then said to the Galicians, you'll see it with your own eyes. Geltsia, agitated, told a story of her own: one spring she had to wait out raids in a different territory, stayed at a homestead with a reliable family, with the cover story of being their niece, when one day a very young girl, from somewhere around Poltava, wandered into their yard asking for work. "You mean that's what she'd told you," Stodólya interrupted, seemingly beside the point; it was obvious they had argued about this before, and now he was taunting Geltsia on purpose by treating her like a child (in response she merely glared at him from under her knotted brow, a single affected glower that pulled Adrian's insides into a knot).

"The girl was called Lyusya," Geltsia continued.

What kind of name is that? Oh, it's short for Lyudmyla ... a fine name, thought Adrian—it warmed him with some long-forgotten radiance, this name that could belong to a little doll, Lyusya-Lolly-little dolly, white lacy frills below the hem of the dress, fragrant girlish hair plaited into thin braids, the glossy silk of it in his hand. (Long ago, when he had just started at the Gymnasium, a young girl in a sailor suit appeared in the gates of the building next door every morning, with hair plaited into two thin braids—and, giggling, hid behind the gate as soon as he approached, until one time she lingered, stepping forward bravely and informing him, with the composure of a grown woman, in Polish, "Mama washed my hair, would you like to feel it?"—and offered him her bowed head, smooth, acorn-glossy with a little groove in the middle, pale like a June bug's maggot, which he could not keep from touching, ran his finger over it—and was scorched, for the first time, by the silky defenselessness of woman, little doll, lolly, who trusts herself to you as innocently as nature itself, like a chrysalis that knows nothing yet of how fragile it is, pulled from its underground nest.)

"I told her," Geltsia continued, "we had no work at the moment and we didn't keep hired hands, and when she heard it she suddenly went all aquiver like a sick chicken, it scared me—my owners were having a pest on their chickens right then ..." and, catching Adrian's look, interpreted it in her own way: "Please let it not surprise you, I have mastered all farm chores already; I even know how to muck horse stalls! Only I don't have the knack for milking," she added, honestly. "So I ask her—and she's so famished, so wasted, all eyes—'Miss, are you unwell?' And she tells me that she's tugged there all the way from Poltavshchyna, that they have terrible hunger there, already ate their dogs and cats, and at home she left her mom and little sister Olyunka who cannot get up anymore, born in '39—turns out, and I didn't know this, Stalin forbade women to have abortions before the war."

"Sure," the boys chimed in, "he had to re-sow what he'd mowed in '33!"

"Ain't got enough of his own stock to people Ukraine—but he needs someone to work!"

"And to war for him too—they don't spare their people at all! Look at the herds they drive at us—like lambs to slaughter."

"In the mountains, after they had two hundred of their own killed in a battle, they poured gas on them and burned the whole lot."

"You're kidding! Whatever for?"

"You know why—to hide their losses. So the number'd be smaller."

"And how's that supposed to work—two hundred living souls gone from the face of the earth and what—no one'd cry for them up there in Moscow-land?"

"Like the Bolsheviks care! For them, a man's life or a chicken's, 'tis all the same."

"And when they first came in '39, some buffleheads in our village were so happy—they made it out, you see, that when it said the Bolshevik Party was krasnaya raboche-krestyanskaya, it meant Christian and for that reason krasna, fine. Asked of those: Where are your chaplains?"

Someone laughed, spoons clicked faster against the canteens, and Geltsia remained quiet, her eyes fixed on a single invisible point, as though she was overcome, for a moment, by that ancient, viscous fatigue that makes one fall out of the conversation or forget about a bullet in the stock, and at once something exploded in Adrian's head, lighting, like a flare, the dark vista. He remembered who it was that wore that sailor suit—it wasn't that little Polish girl next door, no, it was a different, older girl: down the steep Krupyarska Street the hoop rolled, bouncing on the cobblestones and throwing off dazzling flashes of the late afternoon sun, and a shaggy red cur chased, barking, after it, and up flew the kicked-up pleats of the sailor-suit skirt—"Lina!" Geltsia called and, turning to him, said with loving pride, "That's my little sister." He did not remember the younger girl's face. After looking at Geltsia, it remained on his retina as a bouncing flare, like after looking at the sun—he only remembered how when she ran up to them, breathing hard, the tiny hillocks of her breasts rose under the sailor blouse and that fresh, apple-crisp waft of a young body that he always associated with Geltsia and the Dovgans' home—the scent that is only found in homes with growing daughters.

He understood: Lyusya from Poltava and the little sister, Olyunka, she'd left at home reminded Geltsia of her own little sister—where was she now, the younger Dovganivna, for whom (now he remembered this, too!) he used to buy éclairs in the Mikolyash Passage, not yet bombed into dust then, in the center of Lviv—what had this blood storm done to her?

Since the spring of '44, when the NKVD ordered the families of insurgents arrested en masse, small children included, every one of them carried inside the same burning wound, the knowledge that it was not just their own lives alone they offered to lay down—as the Gospels say, for their people, because that's what they'd chosen freely, and their yoke was their freedom, and their burden was light—but that they also condemned, inadvertently, their loved ones to following them into suffering, into torture or Siberia, or at best—if they fell in battle—to the sight of their mangled, vandalized bodies—stripped naked, girls' breasts or men's genitals cut off, a trident carved into the dead forehead—and mothers and fathers unable to mourn their children or to bury them but bound to say, as they turn themselves into stone, not thrice but thirty-three times, like Peter, if he could bear it: I do not know this man. I do not know this woman. Mama, forgive me.... (And they forgave—they all forgave, only not all of them endured: the mother from Kremenets, when they stood her up before the bodies of her six sons, also said, "I do not know them"—but never spoke another word until her heart broke under the burden of six-fold grief, and the mother fell dead next to her children.)

It was easier for him: His mother and father were in Siberia already, and his mother never saw his brothers—arrested in '41— dead. In the pile of massacred bodies the Bolsheviks left when they retreated, the family could not find either Henyk or Myros.

One could choose to think they survived (and that's what Mother believed), that they were safe somewhere, abroad, on the other side of the ocean.

He understood—and smiled at Geltsia from across all the past years at once, the way he smiled at her on that long-ago day when he stood at sunset on Krupyarska awash in the apple-crisp aura, the fresh air of young girlhood.

"And then—did you help those Poltava girls?"

Their eyes met—and such a depth of gratitude was in her gaze that he felt his entire chest flush with heat: she needed him, after all!

The men grew quiet and she spoke again, and he saw it all as though with his own eyes—he saw the girl Lyusya. He knew that type of Poltava girl, beautiful (Geltsia said the girl was beautiful) with the beauty of antique statues—tall, majestic as Roman matrons, with classical sloping shoulders and profiles destined for Carrara marble. He'd glimpsed their breed in the refugee waves more than once: The steppe-borne daughters of Ceres, Amazons, Kozak women—how dare the demons of the twentieth century turn them into highway beggars? Geltsia (bundled in a kerchief up to her eyes: "If any strangers came to the house, my story was I had toothache") had fixed a bowl of thin gruel for the girl, fearing that fresh bread with milk might hurt her after she hadn't had any for so long, and then took her to the pantry and filled a sixty-pound sack ("Took both of us to stamp it down!") with wheat flower—of the stores reserved for the insurgents ("I wrote out a quittance for the warden, a very nice man, he just said, 'We don't keep count of that,' said he'd have given her of his own grain, and flagged a wagon right there, to take her to the station, to get on the Zdolbuniv train"). And it was there, in the pantry that it happened: As they went to pour the grain into the sack, Lyusya from Poltava suddenly froze, her face changed.

"She was looking at my hands," Geltsia said, guiltily raising her delicate, so unmistakably intelligentsia-bred fingers, and Adrian felt his stomach knot again in pity at the sight of them: they were fit for a typewriter or a radio, but to muck stalls?

"She knew you?" Levko whistled.

"Told you so!" Stodólya cut in, with a kind of venomous satisfaction. "Hands and lingerie—how many girls already got caught on that!"

"I took off my underthings when I changed, and I was going to soak my hands in brine-water and rub them with ashes—it makes them look like you'd farmed all your life, never fails. But, it's a chore—so I hadn't had the time! So we are standing there, the two of us, looking at each other: I know that you know that I know ... and then she started crying." Geltsia's voice gave a suspicious din, like cracked crystal. "Fell to her knees, grasped my hands, kissed them. I yell 'Get up, miss!' and she, 'I won't tell anyone! I won't tell a word to anyone, I swear to you!'"

She stopped, fighting the emotions. The men were silent, too.

"And that's when she told me that as soon as they got off the train the MGB picked them up, right there at the station.... Kept them for half the day telling them horrors about the banderas and instructing them, when they go to the villages, to watch and report if they notice anything special.... Fed them pea soup for that."

"And if they'd given her sixty pounds of flour, would you've vouched she wouldn't tell on you?" Stodólya asked dryly.

This was no longer a man teasing a woman he loved; this was a superior analyzing the situation for the benefit of the younger riflemen, and Adrian, who had no grounds on which to intrude upon Security's business, could only listen as any other accidental witness and concede, in his heart of hearts, that Stodólya had a point: Geltsia behaved in that situation dangerously indeed, she could have gotten caught herself and implicated her hosts. (Someday, when we win our Ukraine, we'll build a monument, somewhere in the Carpathians so it'll be seen from far away—a monument to the rural families that helped us, and went into Siberian exile for us, and died by the hundreds of thousands, but never once, not at one door said to us: go on, boys, God keep you, go on your way because we have children and want to live. No, instead they said: it's one God's will for all, what he gives you, children, we'll take ourselves. You're laying your lives down and we won't spare you a piece of bread?)

Still, despite all the rationalizing, he felt that Stodólya pursued not so much Geltsia's old (before she was under his command?) mistakes but something else, something more important perhaps, something unsaid: quite simply Stodólya did not believe any of those strays, even if they vailed before him—just as he did not believe anyone he couldn't check and verify.

That was the most important thing.

Whichever portions of the world were not subject to his control represented, for Stodólya, enemy territory where there was no room for sympathy. Adrian had met other men who lived by the same notion—there used to be more of them when the war first began.

This was Poland's legacy, he thought: for twenty years Poland handled us as tools, with a condescending, speak-to-you-through-the-teeth certainty that the Rúsyns were not people but pigs, and honed and tempered us to respond, like a good ax, symmetrically, in kind. But Poland fell and was forever banished from these lands, and so did Hitler's Reich that had come armed with the same blind scorn for us, the üntermensch, and now came Moscow that knew no people at all—they gave no more thought to blowing their own into ashes than strangers. Tens of armies and hundreds of tribes had stampeded through Ukraine (from the happy Italians, handsome lads and inept, take-it-all-just-leave-me-alone soldiers who would've gladly given us all their ammunition if we'd let them go home without a fight, to the motley swarms of narrow-eyed nomads that erupted from the depths of the Asian steppes—like a new European invasion of Genghis Khan's hordes, except that, for some reason, so many of them wanted to join our side when taken prisoner, almost as many as from among the Red Army Ukrainians). And over the shattered borders, through the smoke of the pyres, we glimpsed the Great Ukraine, the dream of our fathers, and learned, on our first marches east, from it, crippled and tortured in ways we never imagined, what neither Poland nor Germany could teach us: that there is no free country without free people, and he who forces his will upon others imprisons himself.

And when our military force, like a swollen river, reached the floodmark and began to spill into vengeance, and fires swallowed the manors of Polish colonists in Volyn and Podolia, we found another force that dammed the rush that careened toward blind retribution: the pontiff of St. George's Hill, and with him the stigmatic martyrs in the underground put up a halting hand holding a cross and begged our people not to stain their holy weapons with innocent blood in the face of the Lord; and the Supreme Command spoke to us through its Third Congress ordering us to be *reborn* for the struggle ahead—because our force is called to serve not vengeance but liberation, and he who wrongs the unarmed, imprisons himself.

And we were reborn; we recast ourselves in the furnace of battle; we tempered ourselves into steel, shedding the irresolute into the winds of the crisscrossed frontlines—the accidental avengers, the forcibly mobilized, all those who had grown weary and yearned for the plow more than the sword and who valued life above freedom; only death's volunteers remained, the bridegrooms of death—a noble metal that rang clear as a bell. And when the Soviets came, hanging us publicly in the squares (and quit as soon as they realized who they were dealing with), every such execution fed our strength—our boys stepped up to the noose with their heads held proud and high, called out to the crowd with their last breath, "Glory to Ukraine!" and the human sea rumbled, swelling with the wrath of forced silence, and at night dozens more ran off into the woods to volunteer and win themselves a death like that—a death of free men. And we already knew: for every force that enslaves, there will be another, greater force—German for the Polish, Russian for the German. Only the force of liberation has no match: it is the one and the same and combats all tribes and peoples, however many there are on this earth.

Our new war is no longer fought by the doctrine of Von Clausewitz, whose books we studied in underground training—not for a bridge, or a railway station, or even this or that inhabited locality. And although we do maintain our ward administration in all Western Ukrainian lands, we can't afford to keep paying for it with growing losses and deportations the enemy chooses when they can do nothing else to us, because in another ten years of this contest the Soviets may just win for themselves a Ukraine without Ukrainians, as the Poles had already done with our lands beyond the Curzon Line. We stand against Moloch who stops at nothing, but we are the ones who are called to account to the thirty million souls of the nation whose freedom we have vowed to win. We fight for nothing if not for people's souls, every day and every minute, and in this war we have a singular right—to die. And the right to lose is not ours.

All this Adrian should have said to Stodólya—but didn't. Didn't know how to say it. Such conversations were ill suited to Stodólya—he was too certain of his own strength. He was stuffed full of it like a strongbox with dynamite. A rock of a man, that Stodólya, hard as a rock wall. Listening to him upbraid Geltsia—it was like he turned her into an inanimate object, a lecture prop, an SMG taken apart and cleaned for the benefit of rookies who've yet to see fire, and she sat there blushing all the way down into the collar of her gimnastiorka and didn't dare breathe a word in her own defense (after all, Stodólya was her superior, and she was his secretary)—Adrian worried above all that she would burst into tears. (It was afterward, much later, that she confided to him that she had lost the ability to cry in the fall of '45 when she lost her most intimate friend—the girl had a wound to her stomach and she, Geltsia, then still Zirka, sitting up with her waiting for medical assistance, let the exhaustion put her to sleep—and awoke when she brushed against her friend's already cold body; she showed him photographs of that friend—a thin-faced, dark-haired girl, pensive as if in anticipation of the near end. The deceased some-times have that expression not long before death—as though their flesh, already sentenced by fate, wears thin, becomes threadbare, and lets through the imminent otherworldliness. Geltsia looked at the photograph, too, along with him, and her eyes, although red from lack of sleep, were dry.)

He did find a chance to edge into Stodólya's diatribe, break up his verbal offensive with a few apt lines, ease the tension in the room—he had the knack for it. The underground had given him much experience in getting along with people of all temperaments. He reminded all of them together, in the world's calmest voice: we have the order of the Supreme Command—feed the hungry. And that's it. Period. No use flogging a dead horse. They are our brothers and we are saving Ukraine's next generation. And another thing: if we won't give a hungry man a piece of bread, how are we different from the Bolsheviks who feed only the ones they choose, their handmaidens—some with pea soup and some with the caviar from officers' rations? Stodólya's face grew even darker at that, but he said nothing. And then the courier came with the photographer, and they went to arrange themselves for the picture—he on one side, Stodólya on the other, next to Geltsia.

A sort of effervescence came over everyone then, and they laughed and joked with the photographer. Geltsia did, too—as though there had been no unpleasantness whatsoever.

Maybe he just didn't understand women? Maybe she actually liked Stodólya's annihilating upbraiding, being dragged over the coals by a tank like that—maybe she liked it when he showed that he was in command of her? And when Stodólya reproached her for carelessness—was it his way of showing her that he cared?

He knew nothing about that. Had no experience with women. Where would he have gotten it?

At that wedding in P., when he crushed a glass goddard in his hand, something else happened that he preferred not to recall: the alarmed womenfolk rushed to stop his blood, all but falling over each other, and in the end he found himself somewhere dark on a bed of hay with a fiery-eyed young wife who had fussed over him most of all, rubbed against him with her breasts, as if by accident, winked and made eyes at him, and finally teased him into an angry muddled confusion—alright, if that's the way you want it, I'll let you have it, you're all the same! In the dark, through the hay, the woman gave off an intoxicating smell of sweat, mixed with the scent of the fire from the hearth, and whimpered with pleasure under him like a little dog, thin and high, on a single note—*ee-ee-eeh, ee-ee-eeh*. Outside, in the distance, the chorus of girls' glass voices pealed the same song, the same record stuck on a gramophone inside his head: "Hey, pity-pity, loved the girl since he was little, loved her fine since he was little, loved but didn't take...." And then came the moment when he realized, with disappointed, unquenchable irritation, that it was not Geltsia that he'd been yearning for with his flesh all this time, it was Rachel. Rachel who had nursed him back to life and did so in such a manner that any common woman after her simply had to seem bland to him. He all but cursed out loud at the unyielding, unavoidable, unclean whirlpool that had trapped him and dragged him further and further away from his love, and he promised himself, right there, barely having unplastered himself from the generous, sultry woman, that this would be the end of his romancing, once and for all. He couldn't be allowed to think about women, couldn't be distracted by them, and certainly couldn't entertain any dreams of personal happiness—not until the struggle was over.

Unless, he quickly tacked on, leaving himself room for maneuver, there was a miracle.

But none came.

Afterward, he asked to keep that photograph of the five of them for himself—the only photo he had of Her. He never had any others: back in their Lviv days, she did not gift him any. They weren't engaged, after all—they were friends, comrades from the Organization of Ukrainian Nationalists' Youth Network, and later, under the Germans, comrades in the underground, and that is who they remained. He never once kissed her—they hadn't had the time together for that. Even in his dreams she vanished every time he drew close, in the agony of bliss, to her radiant face.

The fact that this face was now Stodólya's to kiss—that Stodólya could, with the same panzer-force as he talked, crush her entire delicate figure, made even smaller by the uniform, fragile like a chrysalis, with the mass of his thickset, tight-jointed body (he had to be heavy, not for nothing did he always leave the impression of being larger than he really was ...), that he could bore into her with the lover's careless cruelty, and everything that happened between a man and a woman in private could very well occur between them—all this had plainly failed to reach Adrian's awareness, as though he had an impenetrable shutter closed on that part of his mind.

In the photograph he *saw* it—as clearly as if it were real. As if those two were making love right before his eyes. That photographer must have come from the mólfar, the witching tribe—pagan worship was still alive in the country around them, the girls here wore wormwood under their clothes as protection from pishogues, and fern flower still bloomed in the heart of the woods on St. John's night, and Adrian's bodyguard, Raven, believed it, too. Or maybe, the war was the reason—the war that had roused not only people, but spirits? On their march to Volyn, rumors of various marvels swirled around them: that at the Pochayiv monastery on the feast of Assumption, Our Lady cried living tears before the people, while in the cave below stirred the silver coffin of St. Job Zalizo, the confessor to Duke Constantine of Ostrog, and, in Ostrog itself, Constantine's voice was heard above the ruins of his castle, as it had once been prophesied to awaken the spirit of our people down to the twelfth generation. And every night in the fields around the village of Berestechko roared the invisible battle from three hundred years ago—sabers rattled and clashed, horses neighed, and the wounded screamed so you could hear each man's lonely call for help, and in the year of our Lord nineteen forty-two this, obviously, could not portend anything good. But at least then the church still endured and gave people comfort and help. Now, with the NKVD men running the churches and the batyushki they installed questioning peasants who came to confession about any guests "from the woods" who might visit at night, one had no one else left to believe but the mólfars.

That was a mólfar picture. He could find no other explanation. This was the way people's faces appear when a spell was cast on water—to make everything hidden rise clear to the surface. A single glimpse at his own visage (it jumped out at him, the first from the whole group) made Adrian remember the Gypsy woman from the fair: so *this* is how she saw him! The witch didn't lie, it was truth she spoke—he had sorrow. A beast of a sorrow; pox on it. In the picture it could not be hidden. Like the smell that wafts off a man on the day of his death—as when, say, seven men are in a bunker together or camp to wait out the day in the woods, and all of a sudden one of them starts to reek of earth: that's a sure sign that he'll fall before sundown. If he'd spotted among his men anyone with eyes such as he had in the photograph (didn't even look into the lens, the wretch!—looked somewhere to the side as if listening to a distant choir of glass voices, *hey, pity-pity!*), he'd take that poor slob and send him posthaste somewhere quieter, up to the mountains, to rest. Or, better still—legalize him: men don't war for long with eyes like that. He felt bad about this mishap before Raven—the boy, just like Stodólya's Levko, came out really well, while Adrian's face seemed covered by a shadow cast by nothing. He looked a lot swarthier than Stodólya on the other side of the group—only the whites of his eyes glowed. Like a Gypsy's. Or had the witch in S. put this jinx on him, to teach him a lesson?

Generally, there was all manner of wrong with the light in that picture: it fell seemingly from nowhere, obeying no optical law. By itself, the light of the summer day that glimmered here and there in the background could not possibly create this effect. If he didn't know better, he'd say they had the picture taken in a church, not in the woods, but in a nave, where sheaves of slanted glow come streaming down from above, from under the invisible dome, streaming—and refracting around Geltsia.

Geltsia in her oasis of light looked as though she was rising through the air to float above the rest of them—it wouldn't have surprised him to see that she did not touch the ground with her boot-clad little feet—so fair and serene, and smiling such a mysterious smile, as if she knew she'd been put there to watch over the men, but this was not for them to know, and for that reason her life-giving—he wished to drink it with his eyes and never stop, for the rest of his days—beloved smile that he had never seen before, had not quite come out, was halted halfway, only touching ever so slightly her daintily tailored lips, but not quite changing her expression, and her precious—nothing was dearer in the world!—clear-eyed face appeared to be lit from inside, as if Geltsia herself were the source of the fantastic light brought forth by the mólfar's Fotokor, and the sheaves of slanted glow streamed and shifted to her and from her at once, creating, the longer one looked, the effect of a living, pulsing shimmer.

And with this radiant shimmer, Geltsia sheltered, like Our Lady of Pochayiv with her cloak, the impenetrably dark shape of the man who stood next to her—and one could see they were selfsame. In between them there was no line that divides human bodies. Never mind that they stood not touching one another, but half a step apart, and Geltsia held her disciplined left hand on the grenade at her belt, jutting a resolute cautioning elbow in Stodólya's direction, as if precisely to emphasize the official distance between them.

But there was no line.

They were one, just as it said in the Scripture: "Therefore shall a man shall leave his father and his mother, and shall cleave unto his wife: and they shall be one flesh."

He saw it for the first time—it hit him like an electric shock and the shutter fell in his mind.

Why *him*? Rot it all to pieces, why him—what does he have that I don't?

For an instant—for a single short instant, but yes, he did, although he wouldn't confess it even to save his immortal soul—he hated Stodólya. Everything about him—at once: that grim

face of his with its hooked nose that jutted forth like an ax, the
Red Army cap pushed down almost over his eyes, and the way
he stood there with one foot forward like he owned the place—
the rascal, you couldn't help but admire him: "at ease" as all
of them, but still alert, watchful, as they all should be—like a
loaded bundook full-cocked, like a wolf on hunt, ready at any
moment to leap up and tear into a stranger's throat—and Adrian
felt hot with shame for his impulsive outburst. Dog your bones,
brother, this guy carried you under fire on his own back! It was
this man's efforts that dismantled the enemy agents' network in
three districts; this man's intelligence service worked like a Swiss
watch and knew of the Bolsheviks' plans five minutes before
the Bolsheviks themselves did—so what if he could not, did not
know how, to let go of his abundantly tight grip without need?
Adrian could indulge all he wanted in his nostalgia for the old
warfare, in which the enemy came bearing arms, but that warfare
was, indeed, over, and the one that was left for them to fight was
incomparably harder: the housewife who put GB-supplied poison into the bread meant for the insurgents, and that batyushka
who interrogated his flock when they came to confession—they
did not bear arms—they *were* the arms, weapons of war in the
hands of the enemy who wished to stay invisible. So was it really
any wonder that Stodólya, constantly dealing with the darkest
sides of human nature, had learned to treat people as tools to
be used to achieve his goals?

Including the woman he loved?

Because Stodólya did love Geltsia. Adrian saw how he followed
her with his eyes, how his face changed when their eyes met. On
her name day he presented her with cyanide in a sealed, lightproof
blue vial—he didn't have any himself, such a luxury rarely fell into
their hands, wherever did he find it? A few people Adrian knew
resorted to arsenic, but it was not reliable—the Soviets could always
keep them alive with a simple stomach lavage. Except cyanide,
nothing was reliable: the last bullet you kept for yourself could

jam, a grenade could fail to explode. Adrian was happy to know that Geltsia had a vial of certain death, pure as lightning, sewn into her collar. He was grateful to Stodólya for that.

And still, looking at their group in the photograph—looking at them all from outside for the first time, as though he had been asleep before and just awoke—he clearly felt unease, like the ticking of a bomb.

TICK ... TICK ... TICK ... TICK ...

The unease emanated from Stodólya. The trusty Stodólya, solid as a rock wall. The Stodólya to whom you could yield—or die.

It could not have been easy for her. It was *his* life she eased, *his* power that she softened with her light. How long could she bear this double burden—the underground's and the husband's?

He felt the same unease again when they were informed that Stodólya's winter bunker fell. Fell in the middle of October, when it was already too late to build a new one. They were lucky they hadn't yet stocked it with a winter's worth of food and hadn't transferred their typewriter there. There had to have been a traitor, the courier said; around the same time, in the same territory, a Security Service courier girl got turned in by her own boyfriend—the gump believed the GB when they promised they'd leave them in peace as soon as the girl parted with the underground. When the girl said nothing under interrogation, they nailed her tongue to a board—right before the boy's eyes. He may have been the one who somehow found out about the bunker and spilled it, but there was no way to find out: he lost his mind.

Stodólya and Dzvinya were left without a bunker. Someone had to share quarters with them. Only no one was in a big rush to winter with Stodólya: four months in a bunker with him was no picnic.

And, with a sudden sickening feeling in his stomach that usually occurs when you are staring into the black eye of a gun barrel, Adrian realized—he would do it. He asked the courier to wait and wrote a ciphered dépêche to Stodólya. With his secretary and bodyguard—Adrian's own bunker had just room enough for five.

***

"Geltsia! Lolly, oh … are you here?"

"Shhh … can you hear it?"

"What?"

"The wind …"

"Listen. I was dreaming about that again."

"Me too."

"What?"

"Don't shout. You cried out in your sleep."

"What did I say?"

"All kinds of very intelligent things, only really loudly. You woke me up. You were talking in your sleep—but in full sentences, like you were reading notes."

"And what did I say?"

"That the set of memories is finite."

"Really?"

"I've no idea what it means, but you repeated it several times."

"Wow. That's something … anything else?"

"I couldn't memorize everything, Aidy. Something along the lines of everything that happened to us already happened to someone else before. The set of memories in the world is finite. A girl that lets you smell her. Who is that?"

"Marynka. We played together behind the trashcans, and she let me see her pee. Let me run my finger along her groove, down there."

"Little slut."

"No, wait … I remember what it felt like to touch her—like silk. But why would she be speaking Polish?"

"You don't speak Polish."

"It was in my dream. Only it wasn't my dream; it was his dream. That other man's. The dead one."

"Did the dream have a different girl in it?"

"The girl may have been different, yes, but the memory was the same. A finite set. Actually, that's a thought! It's great that you woke up and heard me—I wouldn't have remembered this on my own."

"It's my new vocation—a night secretary. I'll be turning on my dictaphone before we go to bed and keeping track of your dreams."

"No, really, Lolly, what if it's true? What if the set of human-kind's memories is really finite and everything that is happening to us now already happened to someone else before? Then, in principle, this is a set that can be measured—theoretically, at least, you could pack all the memories in the world into a dozen hard drives, you know? It'll be the only reasonable explanation for all that déjà vu, no?—just a shred of someone else memory getting caught in your mind, like a speck of dirt in your eye ... a couple hundred kilobytes, that's all ..."

"Sweetie, you've gotten me all messed up with your kilobytes. Now I can't remember anything I dreamt myself."

"Neither can I—it's all bits and pieces ... but a finite set—that's a great idea, Lolly! I've been thinking about it, just couldn't find the answer—and it's right here: if different people's memories match, not because of the experiences they share, but by the random-numbers principle, like, you know, cards from the same deck, when sometimes you draw four sixes in a row—that's a different picture...."

"The photograph!"

"What? Why?"

"You said picture and I remembered: there was a photograph. In my dream. The same one, of Gela in the woods."

"No kidding?"

"Yes, I'm pretty sure ... a picture of a woman taken not long before she died. Vlada, when we shot that interview with her, in the Passage, for a moment had eyes like that—as if no longer hers. And I also, for some reason, remembered Aunt Lyusya, my mom's sister—you haven't met her, she died in 2000 ..."

"Of what?"

"Breast cancer. She had this tremendous will to live, believed to her last day that she would get better. Mom was with her, and she said when her heart stopped, she had this baffled expression on her face, like—what, this is it? She looked like that in the coffin, too.... She was a very strong woman, one of those, you know, that hold the family together—way out of Mom's league in that respect. After the war, during the famine, she went after bread somewhere to your neck of the woods, schlepped a sack of flour all the way back from Zdolbuniv, no one knew where she got it.... That flour fed them through that hungry year—and Mom was so weak with hunger she couldn't get up. Later, when Mom left to study, Aunt ferried food to her in Kyiv too, every Sunday.... But what made me think of that?"

"Must be that kind of a night. With the dead in our dreams. Means it'll rain, no?"

"That's not funny."

"It's not supposed to be. Here, be quiet a sec. Can you hear that?"

"What?"

"The wind."

"No ... isn't that the fridge?"

"No, be quiet now. You'll hear it howl. Come to me. Here ... Lolly, my Lolly ... my apple-crisp girl ..."

***

A bird cawed once, waking. Another one clapped its wings against the wind from atop a spruce and answered with a sad cry. (He would say—couriers calling out to each other.)

Did it hear a human walking, or was it a sign of nearing dawn?

He had to leave the forest while it was still dark. He had to walk through the city in broad daylight in his officer's overcoat with ripped-off stripes like the ones commonly worn by discharged Red Army soldiers—who were clean-shaven and even sprayed with the tear-inducing acidic chypre (all Soviet military men seemed to take baths in the stuff; what is wrong with those people?)—all in order to meet, practically in the enemy's own lair, in an old apartment building already half occupied by the new "owners," a dying man who had no right to die until he told him what he knew.

His father used to go out like this in the dark too, in rain and snow—to administer the sacraments to the dying. Little Adrian would wake to the creak of the plank floors and the shuffle of steps behind the wall, and would see a golden stripe of light creeping under the nursery door. Something groaned in the big stove and the wind wailed in the chimney; younger, sounder-sleeping Myros and Henyk puffed together, like a pair of hedgehogs, in the dark under the down blankets. Outside, black furry forms shifted behind the windows—the men set out because someone needed them. And a sweet, minty chill squeezed the boy's chest from inside because he knew that one day he would become one of those men and would also set out somewhere in the middle of the night, because such was the duty of men.

And now he had to set out, had to reach the dying man while he was still alive. Had to take from him information that determined the course of hundreds of other people's lives. Was this, then, not a sacrament?

"See you later," he said when he left; that's how they always parted in the underground. See you later—never Farewell!

"God help you," breathed the watchful darkness in response, in four distinct voices, the way his mother used to bless his father with the sign of the cross when he set out, and later blessed all her sons, one after the other: God help you! Geltsia and the boys— they were his family now; he had no other. His entire past was with him now, from the earliest years of childhood—the entire length of his life wound onto the bobbin of his sleepless, tense, twenty-seven-year-old body.

He carried it all. Had to carry it all the way there and back, intact and unharmed. Knew too much to fall. And would know even more on the way back.

The other man, the one fighting death at this very hour, also knew he didn't dare succumb until he passed on his secrets. Adrian was on his way to relieve him of the burden of his earthly duties—to release him unto death.

Was this not a sacrament?

He didn't know who the man was, was afraid even to think of that (it had to be someone he knew, someone from the regional command)—only knew the password to enter: "Do you have Brits to sell?" And the answer: "Yes, but only size 10."

Brits—English chrome boots, not more comfortable but decidedly better looking than the American military boots and, for that reason, especially loved by the small-time thugs who'd flocked "in Western" Ukraine from all over the Soviet Union to grab whatever the comrades hadn't already stolen—would actually come in handy: his own boots, a German trophy, were worn out. They had served him well though—not once did he trip or stumble on forest paths.

The forest grew thinner, sensing its edge. In the hum and groan of the wind, Adrian's sharp-tuned hearing distinguished the drip and slide of melting snowcaps from the tree branches: it was getting warmer. Snow no longer cracked like gunshots underfoot; with every step, he found more cushion from last year's leaves, moss, and mulch under a thin dusting of white. New snow, especially when wet, is the most dangerous—not like dry powder. Worse yet—old snow caught under a crust. But this—even if he left an accidental footprint in the dark somewhere—would soon hollow out, collapse, wash away. By light, *they* won't find anything. Unless, maybe, they bring dogs. But then again, they train their dogs to the smells of a rural home—and he stinks like they do, of chypre. Reeks to high heaven—exactly like all dog bosses with red stars on their caps.

So why did he feel so weary-hearted, why?

He had dreamed something bad, that's why. And he could not remember what it was.

Couldn't even put shards of that dream together. Of one thing he was sure, though: the dream boded ill. And this feeling—that in the dream he was entrusted with a terrible secret that touched on the fate of many people, and he lost it, like a nervous rookie on his first courier run—would not let go of him. The beast that lived inside him lost its bearing and pawed at him, restless, not certain where the danger was coming from—from the raids in the forest behind? From the city ahead? And was it he himself that was in danger, or the friends he left in the ill-fitting makeshift bunker?

In Von Clausewitz's *Vom Kriege*, he once underlined something that struck him as especially apt: four elements constitute the atmosphere of war—danger, tension, chance, uncertainty. This was the formula he always chose to begin the course he taught at junior officers' schooling: when you have a ready formula it becomes incomparably easier to act. Was he not well used to uncertainty? To the feeling of danger that filled the air? What, in heaven's name, was happening to him—all he had done was *forget a dream!*

And yet he felt disarmed.

He stood at the edge of the forest—awash in the inky-blue clearness that quickly, too quickly, with the swiftness implacable to any human prayer or curse, thinned the November night (somehow, all his riskiest missions, just like all the most significant collisions of his life, always happened in November)—and felt a nasty, uncontrollable tremor rise from the depths of his sleep-deprived body and swell in his throat, unstoppable like vomit. He tore off one mitten, fanned his fingers in front of his face—but it wasn't light enough yet to see if his hand was shaking. Dog your mother! Had he gotten so he was afraid to step out of the woods?

Stodólya. Stodólya was the reason—Stodólya wrung his memory dry of dreams. From the instant he woke, the man weighed down his consciousness with the full mass of his presence (oh yes, he was constantly aware of Stodólya's presence as of an external force!) and stole that portion of Adrian's attention that was supposed to keep his dreams afloat. Stodólya was heavy; he left no room, not the tiniest crack for anything that was not him. He was *stronger* than Adrian, yes, that was the thing. Finally, he'd said it to himself. Stronger than himself, Adrian Ortynsky (aka Beast, aka Askold, aka Kyi), Ukrainian Insurgent Army Lieutenant, the region's administrative adjutant, decorated with the Bronze Cross of Service and the Silver Star.... None of which meant anything against this simple fact: Stodólya was stronger.

And Geltsia knew it.

That's why she'd chosen—him.

A woman, of course, she was a woman in everything—how do they say it in French?—a woman par excellence. And you can't fool a woman; a woman sees the strongest man way before his commanders—and more surely than the men he commands. Stodólya had will enough to bend, not dozens, but hundreds, even thousands of people. The sector was too small for him—he'd do well with the region. Or even in the area's Central Security Service Command. One day, if he doesn't get killed, that's where he'll go, most likely. While he, Adrian Ortynsky (Beast, Askold, Kyi), always felt best in open combat—and when it ended without losses. Hated nothing more than sending people to their deaths. And that's why, however much longer he had allotted to him, he would never rise to regional command.

For some reason, he remembered the story Levko told him the day before—a story that was more like a confession. Levko did have an artistic temperament, and Adrian liked him: the boy was sensitive. Of them all, Levko was the first to feel uneasy—as soon as they stepped into that bunker to wait out the raid. He joked and bantered but it all came out somehow nervous, and Adrian could feel it: he and Levko, whom he had once prompted just in time to check for the bullet in the stock before cleaning his rifle, were connected by that special, wordless link that occurs between the rescuer and the rescued—the one Adrian could never sense with Stodólya. When they found themselves alone, Levko started talking as though he'd been waiting for the opportunity for a long time. He told Adrian how they had to liquidate an MGB major they'd captured during the operation in S., one they'd lived with in the woods for six months, until he gave them every single agent he knew in the territory. That major was great help—he cooperated willingly—and in the six months they spent together they all got so used to each other that near the end they didn't even guard him anymore. Where would he escape to anyway, back to his Bolsheviks? To be court-martialed and shot?

When Stodólya gathered his Security Service troops and announced that the operation was completed and they no longer needed the major, it became so quiet you could hear a pin drop. They knew more about the major than about each other. They knew he was a Ukrainian, from around Zaporizhya, that he'd been mobilized to NKVD when he was very young, that he'd brought his wife and child to Lviv with him, that he had an elderly mother back in Zaporizhya to whom he sent money every month—they knew lots of things. Stodólya asked if any one of them would vouch with his life that the major could be left with the underground. That if they kept him, he would pledge allegiance to Ukraine and would fight on our side. None of them were ready to do this; the silence held. Stodólya asked if anyone would volunteer for the liquidation. No one did. Stodólya then chose two men, who later came back as good as dead themselves.

The major told them that he hadn't expected any other end for himself. That he was a military man, too, and understood. Even though he wasn't a military man—he was from the NKVD, which meant he, too, must have had to shoot at an unarmed man with a blindfold over his face. Service like that makes men into no-good soldiers: they can't fathom that the gun barrel can just as easily be turned on them, and when they first chance upon such an impossibility, they lose all human semblance on the spot; it's hard to watch. But in the six months he had spent with them, the major also changed, had been reborn—and faced his death as an officer should, as if he wished for nothing more than to earn their respect, to be seen as their equal. He said under no circumstances were they to send word to his wife, because it would only put her in danger from the bureau. It was better for her to know nothing and receive his pension with a bonus for death in service. He asked them not to blindfold him. And for a smoke. They smoked, all three of them. Get on with it, boys, the major said.

That wasn't a liquidation; that was murder. Everyone knew it. Those two boys fell soon afterward—first one and then the other volunteered for "dead missions," the kind from which no one comes back. They were looking for death, Levko said. What they had done broke something inside them. Levko said this without judgment, as if he were speaking about a random bullet or a change of weather—in no way did he intend to discuss with Adrian his commanding officer's actions, which he did not doubt; something else tormented him, and Adrian saw what it was: Levko blamed *himself*—for not having vouched for the major at that decisive moment. For not having had the courage to step forward, click his heels, look Stodólya in the eye and say, "I vouch for him." And to hell with what comes next.

He was a good man, Levko—and it pained him that he had not had the courage. That it was his, Levko's, faintheartedness, and his faintheartedness alone, that cost these people their lives. All three of them.

"You are not a coward," Adrian told him. "But it is good that you're afraid of being one. A man is always afraid of something; only fools have no fear. The question is what are you afraid of more? Then your greatest fear snuffs out the lesser ones—and that is true courage."

This was an idea Adrian cherished; he'd had it since long ago, since the Germans, when he first took part in an attack on a Gestapo jail: the idea that courage, true courage in which you never falter, is simply a question of the hierarchy of fears—when you fear dishonor and a traitor's brand more than death (and more than that, most of all, so much your blood turns to ice in your veins, you fear Shevchenko's poetic warning: "You'll perish, vanish, our Ukraine and no trace will be left on earth"—nothing more horrible could befall you than bearing witness to that, and no force in the world could ever stop you from fighting to avert that horror). But he couldn't be certain Levko understood the word hierarchy. Although, really, he was saying it all just to say something. Not to be silent. Talking to shut up his own conscience. Because, had he been in Stodólya's shoes, wouldn't he, Kyi, have given the same order?

It was like he comforted Levko in Stodólya's stead. And Levko did cheer up a bit, brightened like a finch brought in from the cold (looking at him made Adrian think, for no particular reason, shame about your rosy cheeks, brother; winter'll paint you green like potatoes in a cellar ...). And it was only now, as he waited at the edge of the forest for the clouds that raced across the sky, swiftly unspooling into ribbons of smoke, to cover the moon and allow him to come out, that the conversation came back to him, like a bitter heartburn after a heavy supper, and he thought, coldly and clearly, yes, he would've given the same order but under his command Levko would have *found the courage* to step up. He would have clicked his heels and said, hand to the peak of the cap in salute, "Permission to speak, friend commander, I vouch for him."

And to hell with what comes next.

Adrian was now finally awake, completely. Inside he felt empty, like before stepping into the line of fire. With a quick sharp whine, time came together, squeezed like a Moscow harmonica's bellows—into the streaming minute, a singular chink open for immediate action. And that disgusting tremor inside faded, went still. And his hands weren't shaking.

He was free.

Around him, his land breathed in the quiet of the night. The spirits of the woods who had watched over him guiding him through the thickets, stood behind him. This was *his* land—his strong-as-death love pulsed like invisible light in the dark. Those who had come to stomp it down with their boots had no such strength. Could do nothing to him.

He felt the angry glee enter him. The berserk heat that comes in battle and—if you have luck—on a mission, fills your body with

dreamlike ease, with the tease and tickle of danger that arouses
and intoxicates more irresistibly the more boldly you deny that
danger, until it retreats, tamed, because you showed yourself to
be *stronger*. Ahead he could see the white field—no, not white but
already speckled, welcoming him with black wet inlets of thaw;
his mind—a white knight in icy armor—observed from outside
his body, watch in hand, and the watch ticked loudly, calculating
the minutes measured before his turn, and somewhere in space,
or perhaps inside himself, an invisible hand wound up a barrel
organ for a bawdy kolomyjka tune, tighter, tighter, don't crack the
spring—no, that's a twig cracking underfoot, like a girl who's done
waiting. "To the mountains go white sheep, up higher and higher,
I slept with a partisan and I ain't yet crying...." He grinned, noisily drawing in a full chest of sharp forest air, stretching his lungs
like an accordion's bellows in anticipation of a dance, cruel like
a wolf hunt. Only it wasn't him anymore—it was a demobilized
Soviet Army captain, Anton Ivanovych Zlobin, dispatched, with
magnificent documents and a Nagant revolver engraved with his
name, by the grain supply department to finalize grain collection
in the district. *Alright, motherfucker, let's go!* said Anton Ivanovych.
And crossed himself.

Let the games begin.

Adrian's Lost Dream

Why am I creeping, half-bent, along this wattle fence with no end in sight?—the weaving glistens wet, as though varnished, and drops of water leave earthbound trails on it here and there, like tears on the wrinkles of an ancient face seen up close—a thaw, it's dawning, patches of flimsy threadbare snow like moth-eaten wool grow lighter on the black ridge as my foot finds them, spellbound, obedient, to avoid stepping on the white—

—that's a rule we have, sweetie, like in hopscotch: "Don't step over!" Jump on each square, miss none, to get to the main nave of the heavenly sky—here I am, Lord!—but watch out, don't step on a single line, because each line is a line of fire, and he who steps over is out of the game—boom, dead!

And then can't reach the heavenly sky.

Has to start all over again from the beginning. Again and again—until he comes all the way.

I am ready. Ready to do it all over again if they kill me now.

You still have time. And you have all eternity before the heavenly sky. Because the Lord gathers all who'd been killed in one place where the living cannot go—turns their shoulders to the sky and their faces to the earth from which they'd been torn too soon—and from that secret place of our Lord they watch over you: they war when you go to war, make sure you don't stray from the path, and send you letters you don't know how to read …

So they're watching me right at this moment? Igor, Nestor, Lodzio, Roman, Ash, Myron, Lisovyi, Ratai, Legend, all the boys who left me here alone—I can sense their silence as it fills the air, it hangs above the ground as though a whole platoon is studying me through their optical aims from an invisible cover, and when I raise my arm to fire my weapon they all hold their breath as well, so that my arm steadies, and when my voice warns me an inch before death—is that they, too?

They, they ... but you already knew it. Ask something you don't know—you have time for one more question.

Okay then. I've never said this to anyone. I would like to fall in Kyiv, like Lodzio. On the apostolic hills where my nation began. Where the Dnieper's blue and the churches' gold are our ancient colors before the heavenly host. Where the glory of our princes and hetmans roared—and from where our forefathers marched to the peal of St. Sophia's bells to defend it. I never came that far—and I so yearned to go there, to see it all with my own eyes, that's why I chose Kyi as my alias—

Your blood will be in Kyiv. You don't need to know more.

Who are you that you say this to me?

Black furrows plowed, plowed, hey, hey. ... Black furrows plowed, seeded and plowed, and the bullets sprout, sprout, hey, hey ...

I know you: You are Grandma Lina! Oh, Grandma, I am so happy it's you—only where are you, why can't I see you?

I'm no grandma, man. I am the land.

The land? Yes, I see it—black dirt, not furrows—just mud, you leave tracks on it, too, so I must watch my step, step so the snow won't creak underfoot, rouse neither men nor dogs, leave no trace on softening, rich soil. I see my breath knit through the air before me; I cover my mouth and nose with a wool scarf, and it's instantly wet inside it; now tears brim in my eyes, my ears are full of wind, my eyes and nostrils full of moisture, the thaw, the thaw, everything runs, everything drips, champs, slips, screams—what?

It is the land bubbling, soaked with blood—heavy, swollen with blood like the walls of a woman's womb: fecund, brewing, gurgling bog; she can't take any more blood; she oozes it like black beestings—she is asking to rest; she is asking for winter ...

Like a woman who bleeds in vain and bears no children? Yes, I see—it's the time before winter, the darkest of seasons, and the land although wet, has no smell; it is going numb, entering sleep ...

The winter that's coming shall be long, so long it will seem eternal. Only the women won't cease giving birth. Remember that.

I don't know who you are, but listen—I cannot remember things I do not need! I have a mission, and I must come back alive, and no one will write down for me what I am soon to hear. I will have to archive it all in my head, down to the last comma, the dots above the i's ...

What you are soon to hear you will no longer need. And what you might need you will not hear.

What's that supposed to mean?

You'll understand when the time comes. And now the wattle fence will end, and you'll hit your knee on a stake.

Bugger! There it is, a stake alright. How did I miss it?

This will be a sign for you. So you would remember when you wake up on the other side of this long winter.

So I am asleep?

No, soldier. You are already gone. Look—

The earth! Sweet beloved God, have mercy on us—the earth is falling from above. Is it the bunker or the world that's collapsing? So much of it, Lord, I can't get out from under it; it is heavy; it stifles me, covers me. I can't see the light! It is dark ... dark ...

Sleep, soldier. They'll call for you when the time comes.

***

Written on a pack of cigarettes on Adrian Vatamanyuk's bedside table:

> *Blood will stay in Kyiv*
> *Women won't cease giving birth*
> *You won't need*

***

Two policemen in winter shearling coats passed him by without a second look. For a minute, he was overcome by the sense of being invisible—as though he'd been transported, in flesh, through a well suddenly opened in time, into a different November morning, where another, German, patrol passed just like that, not seeing him, as if through thin air, and the feeling made the world around him shift and begin to slip, a door taken off its hinges. This didn't last long, two heartbeats at most, but he flushed: it'd been too long, darn it, he'd forgotten how to walk in the city.

The city, however, had not changed—those who now ruled it by day knew only the work of ruin. In the cities they took—just as in homes abandoned by owners on a moment's notice, with embroidered tablecloths on the tables and family silver in the drawers—they repaired, fixed, or tidied nothing; they didn't love the cities they took and didn't understand that any place, be it a city, a home, or a bunker needed someone's hands and heart to live. All they knew was how to wield their threatening presence to paralyze anyone who had hands and heart to put to this task, and wherever they made camp they brought with them, like rot, a cheerless air of unsettledness, discomfort, and poverty.

The heap of rubbish where the Germans had blown up the synagogue hadn't been cleared—only sagged a bit since he was here last summer: people must've been stealing the excellent Austrian brick from it, pilfering it piece by piece. In the window of the pharmacy on the corner, a bust of Stalin had appeared: a sign that the local pharmacist who had supplied the underground with medicine was gone, arrested. Closer to the center, there was more Stalin: a portrait on the former German administration building, a portrait on a school—and everywhere the eye tripped on red streamers and lengths of red fabric with white lettering, strung across streets for their holiday tomorrow: "Long Live the Great Socialist October Revolution!"

The most notable change was the construction of a jail—the only project the new power had begun: through the gates, opened to let in a five-ton truck loaded with bricks, he hooked, out of the corner of his eye, and reeled into his memory a sliced-off view of the yard, and deep in it, under the dirty pink wall, the color of

Soviet ladies' undergarments (the Poles at least had better taste and didn't adorn either women or jails in such a nasty color!), lined up in rows, like piglets at market, were reddish sacks of precious cement. Uncovered, he noted with spite: everything with them louts is like that—just dropped in the middle of the yard, under rain and snow, can't keep things straight even around their prison! Not for naught it is said—if it's everyone's, it's gone. Like what happened around Drohobych to the cattle left behind when they'd shipped everyone off to Siberia. Six thousand head, with nowhere to keep them and nothing to feed them, because the silage they'd also left under the rain all rotted—they rounded them up in the district center and slaughtered them, as if enacting some ancient nomad funeral rite in which the animals shared the fate of their owners....

But they *are* nomads—the voice inside his head reminded. Of course, who else—Batu Khan's horde come to ravage our cities and villages, exactly like it happened a thousand years ago, only this time it's reached far beyond the Carpathians, across the Vistula and Oder ... Flagellum Dei, Scourge of God. The man walking toward him on the other side of the street, dressed in a civilian gray Mackintosh and a hat with a navy band, seemed somehow familiar to him; he turned his face to the wall and crouched to tie an ostensibly untied shoelace, turning—to no avail—that vaguely familiar face over and over in his memory, as if straining to push through a locked door that refused to budge. He could feel with his shoulders that the man on the opposite sidewalk also slowed down, and he regretted his slipshod disguise, resented Anton Ivanovych Zlobin for not wearing at least a mustache like all Soviet military men, even retired ones (it would appear that the shaving of one's face and the perfuming of oneself with chypre constituted their entire repertoire of personal hygiene, since, according to our girls who worked in their military hospital, they didn't have much use for toilet paper, as the scraps of newspaper that hung on a nail in the water closet there remained undisturbed for days on end). As he assessed the distance to the closest doorway into which he could dash, he noticed, out of the corner of his eye, a dark spot on the sidewalk, but then his Voice gave the order "Go!"—and when he turned his back to the wall again, the man in the gray Mackintosh was no longer there. Instead, a single crow stood on the sidewalk, covered like a brand new gun with a moist oily gloss, and leered at him saucily, askance—as if she had something to say to him.

Pish! He almost spat as he would have in the forest (the Soviets, though, spat in the streets openly, right where they walked, and equipped their official offices with a fixture never seen in the Austrian or Polish days—special bowls for spit, like at a dentist's!). This was the second time he saw this crow—no, couldn't be, this had to have been a different one—the bird had greeted him at the edge of the city, on one of those boggy little lanes lined with thoroughly country-like homes behind wattle fences. His attention, strained to its limit, fixed every little detail—yet he still couldn't identify the man in the gray Mackintosh: had they really met before (Where?) or was it merely an illusion, a coincidental similarity of facial features that raised alarm in him?

This was why the city was dangerous—it was a bottomless and unpredictable reservoir of *the past*. The woods—they were the opposite. The woods had a short memory; the woods, like the partisans, lived in the streaming moment; every storm that blasted through erased the contours of the land you knew by touch just a day before, blocked your path with a fallen tree, a slipped slope; a twig you broke as a sign was torn off by deer or bears; cuts you made on tree trunks scabbed up like blisters on your own skin, and went black, blending into the landscape; heavily trodden campsites were soon overrun by shoots of new grass, studded with a generous sprinkling of buttercup and anemones; blood you spilled seeped into the ground without a trace. Adrian would be hard-pressed to find the bunker where he'd spent the previous winter although he dug it, as conspiracy rules prescribed, himself, with his own two hands; perhaps only the peasants who'd grown up grazing their cattle in those woods and knew the area's topography like their own homes in the night—just as he, Adrian, could take apart and put back together a Mauser in three and half minutes without light—could etch into their memories, without fault and for all eternity, a spot at the edge of the village where someone made a money cache or buried archives in milk cans. Except no one ever divulged such information to peasants, and those who did *know* how many steps to take north by the azimuth from the dried-up hornbeam tree or the third rocky outcrop from the right often perished before they could pass the secret on to another confidante. How many of them were already there, slowly rotting underground, our abandoned secrets?

The city was a different beast—inside its walls, the city closely guarded the entire mass of time lived in it by its people, stashed it, generation after generation like a tree growing new whorls. Here your past could pounce at you from behind a corner at any moment, like an ambush no reconnaissance could ever warn you about. It could explode in your face like a time-delay bomb—with an old Gymnasium professor of yours, miraculously not extermi-nated by the Germans or the Soviets, or with a former friend from the German Fachkursen, later recruited by the NKVD, or simply with someone who had once been a witness to an old fragment of your life, which was, at the moment, of absolutely no use to you and thus subject to being expunged from your memory—but not from the city's. Because this was the city's job—to *remember*: without purpose, meaning, or need, but wholly, with its every stone—just as to flow is the job of rivers, and to grow is the job of grass. And if you take the city's memory away—if you deport the people who'd lived in it for generations and populate it, instead, with relocated squatters, the city withers and shrivels, but as long as its ancient walls—its *stone memory*—stand, it will not die.

Adrian walked down the street and felt the city oozing the past from every pore, sap from a pine tree. It trapped him like a fly with his little feet sinking into sticky amber goo—he felt as if he were walking on the bottom of a lake, against the resistance of many atmospheres. It may have been because at the moment he wanted nothing more than to run, as fast as he could. His time, tied to the time of the one who was fading like a dying candle and who waited for his friend Kyi to whom he could pass on the secrets he'd guarded until his last breath, was running out. But friend Kyi could not run. The city hung on him, weighed him down with stone on all sides; it clung to him with the tar of dozens of eyes he could see, and hundreds more he couldn't. Lord, how much easier things were in the forest.

I've done become a woodsman, he thought with a city dweller's instinctive pride in this accomplishment and with a growing anxiety about how much of it was apparent to others (so far, he checked, there was no tail). And right away, the next idea caught up with the previous one, clicked against it, like balls on a pool table: so, *they've* really driven us from our cities, from our memory's terrain—into the underground of history, the twilight zone....

"Documents!"

"Please."

A captain and a lieutenant, well-fed and also in good shearling coats; another fifty meters behind them, a woman with a market basket approached. The rest of the way was open; the space he left between them as he handed over his documents—piece by piece, not all at once—would be enough for a freely swung cross-in, edge of hand against Adam's apple above the collar, the two of them at once; he punched equally strong from either side.

"Looks like he's on a road assignment, tovarish Kapitan ..."

"Last name?" verifying the papers actually belonged to him.

"Zlobin, Anton-Vannych."

At the sound of his undeniably Russian pronunciation—a local could never fake *that*!—both finally, as if on command, relaxed, brightened up.

"Where are you from?" the captain asked with unexpectedly human curiosity; Adrian saw in close-up, as if through a Zeiss telescope, his pale eyelashes and thin, watery skin grained with freckles, breathed his smell—shag, leather shoulder belt, chypre ...

TICK ... TICK ... TICK ... TICK ...

"Lvovzagotzerno, tovarish Kapitan."

"That's not what I mean! Where'd you fight?"

"First Ukrainian front," he said, icing with hatred, feeling the pistol against his side under his overcoat, and in his stomach—the tightening knot of anticipation, because at any moment, any moment now the alien past could rush at him, and he wouldn't know what to do with it: he was confident in his Russian only with short, chopped-up sentences, even though the original Anton Zlobin, known by the alias Lisovyi in the Insurgent Army, always praised his pronunciation.

"And I was at the First Byelorussian!" the captain said, thrilled for no particular reason. "Did we cross paths in Berlin, by chance? It's just your phiz looks so familiar."

"I was done fighting at Sandomierz."

The woman with the basket passed them and, not looking back, hurried along as if someone were after her.

"Got laid up in hospitals for a while after that."

"Well, it's no picnic here either," the captain said by way of boasting—or maybe complaining. "The banderas are keeping things hot alright." He clearly wanted to add something else, but stopped and waved Adrian off with the carefree, comfortable gesture of a person not afraid of leaving himself open to a throat jab. He offered Adrian's documents back as if to say, sorry, brother, just doing my job, and in a flash of sudden insight that is the sole provenance of ancient, well-tempered hatred—the kind that doesn't fog your mind with black madness but hardens, year after year, into a heavy amalgam that melds you with the one you hate like two lovers to death—Adrian realized that the captain also longed for the old warfare. For his First Byelorussian front, the brotherhood of battle that he must have experienced there, and that the reason he tarried with needless yap was that he felt much better then and there, than now and here. And now he would remember him, Anton Ivanovych Zlobin wounded at the First Ukrainian front; now Adrian would have one more person who knows him in this city. Rot your bones to pieces, tovarish Kapitan.

He kept walking, and about ten meters before the intersection he needed, that same crow materialized on the sidewalk before him. Turned her head every which way and stepped from one foot to another like a whore in high heels. He didn't give a doggone about signs and such nonsense, but this was a bit too much.

"Shoo!"

The crow bounced once, heavy and awkward, like a woman at term, then again, and lifted into the air, wings rustling, and then landed, a few steps ahead, atop a cracked mascaron head above a doorway. Adrian thought he saw the mascaron wink at him. Was it just a tall tale or can crows really live to three hundred years old? And this same one could have flown above the battle at Berestechko? The ominous bird stared down at him as if it knew something. Where had he seen this unmoving gaze before? Like a snake's, the Queen of Snakes ...

TICK ... TICK ... TICK ... TICK ...

As he turned the corner, he spotted the gray Mackintosh at the other end of the street again (Could it be the same one?) and made a sharp turn into the first available gateway, and stood still, waiting. A woman dressed in a whole pack of silver foxes walked by with a small boy—"How many times do I have to tell you— No!" scorched her high, screeching, self-assured voice. Must be a commissar's wife. Claws clicking on the cobblestones, a dog ran by—there's a creature that doesn't need to be afraid anymore.... Minutes dropped, loud as drumbeats; somewhere in the building a radio came on. The gray Mackintosh still did not show. If he was a tail, he was an incredibly sloppy, amateur one.

Come *on* already, for God's sake!

Here it is finally, Kirov Street. Kirov! All streets now renamed after some Bolshevik commissars, new scabs on old walls.... From here, it's the sixth door on the right. One, two ...

"Watch out!" boomed in his head.

The morning street looked empty, lying in wait. And, like in the children's game of cold-warm-hot, his alarm grew with every step. He could actually hear it, the sound of alarm pushing from inside at his temples. Something was wrong, and the something was right ahead of him. Dear Lord, please let him be alive, please let me come in time, Lord Almighty, please keep him living…. A small old man with a cane shuffled out of the third door and began to close it behind him with a protracted, teeth-grating screech. Four, five … he saw every doorstep at once, polished to a silky gloss by thousands of feet, saw every crack in the sidewalk, the moist gleam of the cobblestones, the sugary trim of snow along the curb, and the dark specks in it, burbling with thaw-water, and the tear-streaked, cracked (Why doesn't anyone fix it?) clay gutter at the building's door. And—three curtained windows on the fourth floor: safe to proceed.

Here are the doors, the sixth doorway, a lion's head with a ring in its maw, a gold maslin handle. Heavy. His mouth instantly dry. Lord, please let me not be late. Fourth floor, apartment eight.

Stairwell—dusk, pale light from the pseudo-gothic window facing the yard. If need arises, he can flee that way. Silence uneasy, ominous. But no, a door slams overhead. That's lower, on the third floor. Someone coming down the stairs, the planks groan and creak: a man.

Adrian hastened his step to have his back to the window when he meets the man—he'd already advertised himself plenty, no need to parade his face before the neighbor as well…. From above, a pair of boots descends, then navy uniform breeches—a policeman! A major. Well, that'll beat your grandmother! Jeepers. Steady now, don't look away, keep straight at him, open, bold, schlagfertig …

TICK … TICK … TICK … TICK …

But the policeman, much heavier and slower, also plows straight at him, silently like a somnambulist, his entire body blocking the way, like a boulder; he snuffles with the previous night's vodka heaves and poor digestion; he blocks Adrian's path as if he wants to embrace him—and looming, with all his shoulder straps, stripes, stars, and belts, exhales unexpectedly quickly, quietly, hoarsely into Adrian's face.

"Number eight?" he asks.

Adrian is silent.

"Leave, it's a kapkán. They arrested everyone last night. "

"Thank you," Adrian manages to peel off through his dry lips, then jumps astraddle the rail and slides down in a blink. He's out in the street, in the deafening, blazing day, faster, faster—but not too fast, he can't run, watch out!—puts distance between himself and the sixth door, Kirov Street, all the while waiting, with his back tuned to every sound, for someone to yell "Halt!" after him like a shot of the starting pistol. But nothing happens, it's all quiet behind him; there's no chase, no stomping boots; two more blocks and he'll turn onto a more crowded street that runs to the market; he'll mix with the passersby. Holy God, Holy Mighty, Holy Immortal have mercy on us....

Why wasn't there a curtain pulled back in the middle window—the agreed-upon signal in case of failure? They didn't have time? Someone prevented them? Or, worse, the worst—were they betrayed? Kapkán—the word stuck in his mind and lay there like a rock in the middle of a stream, cracked into its two syllables, two blows with a Tatar cudgel, *kap-kán*—but man, do you have luck! Thank You, Almighty Lord—three and a half floors below the trap, two minutes before the fatal knock on the door, three-one-three, "Do you have Brits to sell?" He'd have dropped like a ham hock into stew. God bless that major—whatever'd come over him? With girls, it's been known to happen—sometimes moskali saved them by warning them like this, but a man? Must get a message to our people at the police, let them find out what kind of a major they got themselves here.... "They arrested everyone last night"—whom, how many? Was the one he'd come to see among them? Had he had the time to shoot himself, or was he taken alive? Waited for friend Kyi, but got another kind of visitor altogether, the uninvited kind—if only the courier had come the day before, a day, just a day earlier!

Adrian all but moaned through his teeth, his old wound aching in his chest: as if it were he who was being dragged, unconscious, and tossed like a sack into the "black raven," as they called police vans ... "You, black raven, why'd you circle ov-er the hum-ble he-aad of mine" went the doleful ballad, drawn out like your own guts slowly pulled by a well crank, when friend Lisovyi sang it around their campfire, the former Red Army captain, Andriy Zlobin, who perished in the Carpathians and to whom Adrian owed his papers (they only changed Andriy to Anton, but that was nothing in comparison to what it would've taken them to manufacture good legal papers otherwise). And now it came, the "black raven"—not for nothing did the stupid black bird haunt him But no, you bastards, the day has not yet come when you could take Kyi alive! But who, who was it? He didn't know even their aliases. A wounded man, dying—that's all the courier communicated. And what if they'd taken him alive?—they'll nurse him, to be sure, patch him up in their hospital and then torture him until he tells them what he was supposed to tell Adrian.... And right from under his nose, rot it!—the MGB snatched away the secret that couldn't be confided to a single other person on the territory, the secret he'd walked eighteen kilometers (and now had to walk as many back!) to hear, and now could only pray to God that they wouldn't get to it, that it would perish, vanish forever, go into the ground together with whoever was its keeper...

"Beg pardon!" he blurted in Russian when he shoved past another man. Closer to the market there were more people; he couldn't keep the same pace without drawing attention to himself, and he spotted behind him—this time beyond any doubt because it was much closer—the gray Mackintosh and the navy-banded hat.... Whoa, brother, you're a slob to shame all slobs, who tails like that? His mouth was still dry, but his heart had returned to his chest, and his reason worked coolly and clearly as though placed outside of his body. Under different circumstances, he'd have had good fun losing that tail, would make a sport of vanishing without a trace, but now he felt unavenged wrath choking him, high in his throat where it had risen, by the law of communicating vessels. As soon as the first, dark wave of fear ebbed—he was still in that state where the body, like a

well-oiled machine, acts of its own accord as it does in dreams,
in love, and in moments of mortal danger—and before he knew
what he was doing and could rein himself in, in blatant denial
of all logic of safety that demanded he remove himself, now, at
once, far from the city, he was making a show of turning onto
another street, almost tripping into the arms—Beg pardon!—
of another fur-wrapped missus who instantly ogled him with a
purely feminine hunger—some other time, lady; I've no cash
on me today!—a quiet and usually empty street where he knew
a very good doorway, with narrow latticework like in a confessional—and he was feeling an urge to confess to someone, a
powerful urge indeed! He didn't care if it was broad daylight,
as long as the dolt didn't lose him again.

He was right: after just a few moments, he could hear hurried steps clattering from the same direction he'd come from—
clickety-clack, check it out, the comrades make a fine racket when
they walk, and we, when "the red broom" swept its hardest, were
compelled to parade through the woods barefoot so a mouse
wouldn't stir—clattering close and then stopping, hesitating, not
far from the darkened doorway. Has he lost sight of his object or
what? You poor bastard, who sent you off like this, a calf into the
woods? Alright, come on, here, brother, a little closer, don't be
scared, step another step, davai-davai, as your handlers like to say
as they give you a helpful prod with the gun barrel....

The other man, as if hearing Adrian's call, obeyed and moved
ahead—that's it, good boy!—and when the gray Mackintosh,
uncertainly spinning his head about in search of a trap door
through which his object may have disappeared, aligned with
the doorway, Adrian sprang in a single noiseless lunge out the
door, and the rest took a matter of seconds: a short confusion, a
sob from a terrified human throat, like a muffled caw, cut short
before it could disturb the quiet of the city morning, and in the
dark pend, shielded from the street with the narrow cast-iron
grating, Adrian pressed the newcomer close to himself, feeling
the man instantly freeze against the gun poked into the small of

his back, and spoke to him over his shoulder, lips almost brushing the man's frigid cheek.

"Do not move. Who are you?"

"I ... *khhhh* ... I ..."

What a buzzard! Every time he found himself among civilians, Adrian had to remind himself how retarded they were in comparison to the guerillas—like gramophone records set to play on slower speed.

"I ... *khhh* ... I am a teacher, sir ... from P."

The deuce take it! An amateur snitch was the last thing he needed.

"Then why are you here, in the city? Why did you follow me?"

"I came to the school district office, for a meeting.... Our principal left middle of the year ... I recognized you. I'd seen you at a wedding in our village last spring."

This same face—only without the hat, with large, flaggy ears—now surfaced, clear and bright, in his memory, ensconced on the other side of the wedding table: the man had a fine singing voice, a tenor, resonant as a well, "Hey pity, pity, loved the girl since was little...." Adrian slackened his grip a bit, but did not let go; to an outside observer, this must have looked like an embrace, two men hugging each other in a pend in the middle of the day. Must be drunk.

"Did you intend to renew our acquaintance in this manner, professor?"

"I thought ... your photo is up there ... by the police ... I saw it this morning ... I thought you might not know ..."

A photo? By the police? "Help find this bandit"?

"Your phiz looks so familiar," said the captain who checked his documents. That would be why. He felt like laughing out loud: apparently, he's on the wanted list (What price did they put on his head?), and he's strolling through the city, not a care in the world, right under the noses of an entire garrison, the day before the Great October Socialist Revolution, when the Bolsheviks are especially vigilant—and not a feather ruffled, not a hair raised?

The invincible, elusive Adrian Ortynsky—as if cloaked by Our Lady with a magical cloud that makes his enemies look right past him.

And instantly he was covered with sweat: that was too much luck for one day! It must have been the smell of chypre that made the Soviets not see him when they looked at him, and not one of them had sensed him a stranger. Except maybe the major in the stairwell—he had to have recognized him; he saw his face up close, beyond doubt....

TICK ... TICK ... TICK ... TICK ...

He had to flee—he had drained the well of his luck to the bottom and the dregs were turning to vapor as fast as his Soviet cologne: he could already sense his own smell emanating from him like heat from a stove—the heavy, sylvan, animal smell of an unwashed body.

"Thank you very much, professor." He stepped back, pushing his pistol under his overcoat. He believed the man now: no agent would be foolish enough to tug after him—just report him to the nearest patrol and end of story. "Please accept my apologies for being so uncivil to you."

"No harm done; no worries.... This worked out well, actually; I was, pardon me, perspiring, following you—I couldn't figure out how to come close enough so that no one would notice." As any civilian would, after the shock of encountering a gun, the man, although he kept his voice down to a whisper, turned instantly and uncontrollably chatty. "And yesterday I had such fright, God forbid!—we set out for the city, on a wagon, through the forest, and there'd just been a fight right there, and the moskali stopped us, and put two wounded into the wagon, our folks, from the woods, a man and a woman...."

A fight? Near P.? That's Woodsman's territory, with the infirmary.

"When was that?"

"Late, it was dark by the time we reached the city."

"You wouldn't know the hour, would you?"

"No, not exactly ... I don't have a watch; moskali took mine two years since already, and I haven't earned enough for a new one yet."

"Anything you can tell me about those two?"

"Both young ... probably married ... the man died on the way. That made them very angry; they cussed like God forbid.... The one who was their boss yelled, "We need him alive!" And the woman was still alive when we pulled up to where their cars were ... pregnant, about seven months. She moaned so, poor soul; I just kept praying that she wouldn't go into labor on the way.... She's dark, swarthy like a Jewess ..."

The day went dark before Adrian's eyes—as if, with a heavy hop and a rustle of wings through his mind, a black bird took flight from the edge of his sight. No, no, it was impossible; it wasn't true; it could not be ...

"Can you remember anything else?"

Something in his voice must have changed, because the teacher blinked at him in a kind of awe—the first time he looked straight at Adrian, at the man who, a minute earlier, had thrust a gun between his ribs. Apologies, professor. It could have been worse, much worse. More than once at night, unable to see clearly, we've shot our own.... But, for the love of Christ, please, anything else, professor? Give me just another detail. A handkerchief, a shred of her underwear. So I would know, so I would know for sure. The man—that must have been Orko. Lord, please make it so it isn't true.... Seven months pregnant—and it's November now ... somehow he lost his ability to count and started folding his fingers one by one, inside his pocket, like when he was little and Mother taught him how to tell from his knuckles which month is long and which is short: May, June, July, August ...

"I can't remember," rustled the teacher timidly. "I didn't look very closely, I was scared ..."

He was scared—and still he followed me through the city to warn me; he trembled; he hid—but followed.... Adrian felt a lump in his throat. He wanted to shake the man's hand, but didn't dare, was held back by the years-old underground habit—never offer a hand.

"How did you know she was seven months?"

"Be darned if I know! Could've been eight. Just the way she looked—my wife gave birth not too long ago."

"Congratulations," Adrian said automatically—and then understood the meaning of what the man said: he had a child. "A boy?" he asked, not sure exactly why—as if he couldn't leave just yet, as if something held him in front of this man, a last hope or a promise, some delayed message. "Or a girl?"

"A boy!" The teacher's face glowed in the dark. "Little rascal, three kilos and a half! That's already the second one God gave us, the older turned two on the Feast of the Intercession."

"God bless your family," Adrian said. Like he was caroling for the man. Like this was Christmas, the greatest of all feasts, when above cities and villages and snowbound bunkers an invisible light pulsed through the night and underground, like in Roman catacombs, kolyada, the Noel, boomed, a great buried bell lighting the faces of all who had come together with the glow of the good news: the Son of God is born! He, too, received the good news today—he, too, was to have a son born, and exactly on Christmas: November, December, January, nine months exactly, mysterious are your ways indeed, Lord—while we war and perish, somewhere in the darkness of women's bodies new lives swarm, grow, hasten to light, into the world, to the unceasing, bloody birth feast, the Christmas of our nation that carries on and on without end in sight....

Villagers began singing a new carol: "Did you people hear sad news again—into chains they bound our dear Ukraine...." King Herod's servants walked through the snow like Brueghel's hunters, looking for newborns—somewhere, a crusted rag the color of rust in the cradle of an emptied Lemko home was a six-day-old baby shot at close range, and young men with submachine guns who had caroled at this very home not too long before—Lord bless all those who are in this home!—Thank you, boys, blessings on you, too!—ran outside and vomited into the snow—joy to the world, joy to the land. Down, down the carolers' hands runs the red wine, brims in goddards, spills from bullet-ridden, bayoneted skulls, but the women—they must be mad; they pay it no mind; they cling to us like roots that trap our feet, begging for love so they may bear children in pain; and God is on their side, because who, really, would remember and count the murdered newborns of Bethlehem when the whole world rejoices with the new joy, and the living from everywhere come bearing gifts for the one child that lives?

And that is good, that's the way it's supposed to be—let him live, let him grow big and strong—someone will grow, someone will hide in mangers, in thickets, in caves, in a forgotten village at the edge of the woods while Herod's hunters walk and walk through the snow, single file, falling upon homes in the night, tearing the living from their warm beds—two hours to pack, two loaves of bread for each soul, and only the clothes on your back. Officer, sir, can I please change the baby?—davai-davai, hurry up, go!—and the wagon with two not-quite-shot lives, the woman and the child in her womb—Lord, is it really my child?—bumps over forest ruts and potholes to where the prison opens its gates for them—and the prison grows, swells, gains the strength to contain the rebel blood inside it, and tomorrow the sun rises again like a pregnant woman's belly over the skyline, as if the whole earth writhed in pain but could not bring forth its Savior, and a voice is heard in Rama, lamentation, and weeping, and great mourning—Rachel weeps for her children, and would not be comforted, because they are not ...

He had more questions to ask—the man had to have noticed something else!—but he remembered himself: there was noise in the yard behind them, someone had left the building and was walking toward the gateway. A young, dancing walk. The walk of a person who hadn't yet given birth to anyone. Whose body still believes in its own immortality.

"O-olya!" a woman's voice sang out, as if through a silk veil, slicing the quiet from above.

"Stay behind," Adrian whispered. "Ask for directions, like you're lost. And, God forbid, do not follow me—you can't be seen with me."

"May God bless you," he added or maybe just meant to add. If there was an answer, he did not hear it.

Ahead of him lay eighteen kilometers in which anyone could recognize him. The hunters walked in the snow, well-fed whippers in new shearling coats and snug leather shoulder-belts, surveying the field through field glasses—and the dogs lunged at the end of their leashes, baying, choking, barking their lungs out, and scuffed the ground madly with their back legs, kicking up fountains of black mud into the sky. The beast did not err; the beast had guessed it all as soon as he stuck his nose out of the bunker at dawn: the warm wind from the south carried on it the smell of a raid, a hunt—and he was the one being hunted.

***

Do you see it?

I see it.

He is coming.

Yes.

Don't be afraid.

I am not.

It's just a dream. We're dreaming the same dream.

Is it really possible? For two people to dream the same dream?

It is. My grandma and grandpa had it happen to them once, in Karaganda. It's actually quite simple: I'm dreaming you, and you're dreaming me.

It is, isn't it? So strange—how simple things can be in a dream; it seems it couldn't be any other way.

That's because in dreams things are the way they really are. And in daytime—the way they appear to us.

Then I really love you. Now, in this dream, it's so obvious it doesn't require any further proof or evidence. I can't see you in this dreamscape; you're somewhere aside, close by, like a part of me—I can only feel there's another, separate life beside me, and I love it. And I know it's you. It is you, isn't it? You? Is it you? ADRIAN?

***

"Adrian? Where'd you go? Why did you turn on the light?"

"Go back to sleep... I just have to write this down, or I'll forget ..."

"Write what down? The covers are all bunched up—how'd that happen? What time is it?"

"I don't know. Four."

"Did you feel me love you? While we were asleep? In our dream? And you just had to wake up."

"There was something else there. Let me think."

"Come here, we'll think together."

"Damn it!"

"What?"

"My knee ... I just touched it ... it's like bruised or something. What did I do? Last night it was fine."

"Did you hit the bedside table? You've been jumping up and down all night. Let me see."

"How bizarre. How very bizarre."

"No, no bruise ... Does it hurt when I do this?"

"No, not really."

"What about here?"

"It's like it's inside somewhere, really deep. Muffled. Really weird."

"Well, go back to sleep then. You scared me and I lost my dream again. All I remember is that I loved you very much for some reason. Why would that be?"

"That's good. You just go on loving me. Love me all the time."

"And what do you think I've been doing?"

"Man, I am in luck."

"We're both in luck."

"Uhu. Madly."

"Oh ... Aidy ... Aidy, I love you. No, please don't stop ... oh, God ... oh, you, you're my ... my ... my ... —my love ... my beloved ..."

"Here, let me wipe your tears. Put your head on my shoulder ... like that. Just like that."

"That's even better than in my dream."

"It's what comes after."

"Actually, that's exactly what it is ... because when I'm with you, I always see something. New pictures every time—like a movie ..."

"You're my picture. The best in the world."

"I only wish you could see what I see ... I wish I could show you. That would be some kind of a movie!"

"So what was it this time?"

"A flash. Just a flash, but incredibly bright. Like a searchlight straight into your eyes after coming out of a dark cellar. And a blast ... a mix of terror and thrill, like flying out of your body. I wonder if it's like that when you die ..."

"The way you moaned ... it scared me a little."

"It really seemed a lot like dying."

"You know, you just helped me understand something."

"Something about your infinite sets again?"

"No, about that dream of mine ... I realized why there's no fear of death in it, in any of those dreams ... even though they're all, in a way, about death. Strange, isn't't?"

"You little fool ..."

"Baby, what is it now? Why are you crying again?"

"Because I love you. I love you so much I don't know what to do with it."

"Shhh ... don't cry. Here, do you want me to hold you and rock you?"

"Jeez!"

"There ... I'd rather have you laugh."

"Go ahead, tell me. What about the fear of death?"

"Nothing, that's the thing, it's not there. I don't think he was afraid of death at all, that man. I think he was always ready for it. And that's what made all the pictures in his head so sharply focused, intensely physical. It's the same as in ecstasy, you know? When you said the thing about leaving your body, it made me think of this."

"Oh God. No, it can't be …"

"What?"

"No, nothing … just a guess. I think I know who that man was."

"For real?"

"More or less … you wouldn't recognize him, would you? In a picture?"

"No more than myself without a mirror."

"Well, then it's moot. No use thinking about it."

"About what?"

"That flash. Nothing, forget it. How's your knee?"

"Quiet now. Not a peep. You've healed me."

"Aidy?"

"Mm-hm?"

"Do you think it's really us? Or are we dreaming ourselves?"

"I don't know, Lolly."

"Sometimes I get this feeling … promise you won't laugh at me?"

"I promise."

"I get the feeling that we got someone else's love. Someone's once unfulfilled love—you know, like the imperfect tense in grammar."

"Well, then it was meant to be."

"No, listen … once when I was little, really little, when we still lived in Tatarka, this one girl moved out from our apartment building. The whole building got blighted; they moved us out not long after that, too, but this family was the first to go, and the whole building helped them. The truck came and parked in front of the gateway; people carried furniture out of the apartment—the same armchairs we used to pounce on together—I can see them now in that girl's living room.... Outside, under the sky, they looked like pulled-out teeth. They let me hold the lampshade they'd had above their dinner table, with a wire frame, you know, bright yellow with little tassels."

"I know—vintage fifties."

"Uhu, everything they had was old ... taken out of place, it stopped being a lampshade—I could pull it over my head, and it'd be a hooped skirt, like a princess's.... And there was this one thing I couldn't stop thinking about ... we made a secret a couple days before, that girl and I. We were very proud of it, too. And so I stood there and all I could think was, now she is moving out and what's going to happen to our secret? You see, she'd forgotten all about it. She'd moved on to other things. Maybe if we'd had a chance and snuck away, just the two of us, to dig up that secret and pledge our undying friendship over it, everything would've been different. More melodramatic. Or, if she had bequeathed that secret to someone else, given me permission to show it to someone else after she left, to another girl ... but nothing like that happened—our secret just died; it was so clear. It died because she forgot about it. The same thing happened to it as happened to the armchairs and the lampshade—it lost its defining purpose. It was still in the same spot as the day before, and perfectly undisturbed, but it was no longer a secret—just a little pile of buried rubbish. Are you listening?"

"Uhu."

"And I remember this very un-childlike gloom came over me. A child—she feels the same things as the adults, you know, just doesn't have the words for them. It was like I saw all at once all those secrets we'd made and then abandoned and never checked on again—how they all were somewhere underground. All our sealed friendships, tears, pledges ... our little lives under glass like exhibits in Mom's museum. A giant museum of abandoned secrets. And people walked right over it; they didn't even know it was there, right under their feet."

"The museum of abandoned secrets—that's nice. I like it."

"I don't feel like I've been making much sense...."

"No, I understand. You are trying to say that you and I are together because we accidentally dug up someone else's love. Like one of those secrets that got left behind."

"Yeah ... something like that."

"But don't you think it's also possible that whoever made it may have, as you put it, bequeathed it to us?"

"I'll tell you what I think. I think that man was in love with Gela. And she did something wrong. She made some terrible mistake that messed up everything. And it still hasn't been fixed."

"Now, that's just your imagination ..."

"No, it's a hunch. A woman's hunch, trust me on this one. It's always us, the brilliant and the beautiful, who make the kind of royal mess no plain little mouse of a girl could ever dream of. It's true. You know why? The risk is higher: plain little mice don't get nearly as many chances to imagine they can control someone else's fate."

"Never really liked those plain little mice ..."

"That's the problem right there! You all want the brilliant and the beautiful. Do you think that makes our lives easier?"

"Oh, you poor, long-suffering, brilliant thing ..."

"Finally, about time someone felt sorry for me. At least I'm alive—for now."

"And warm too. Damn it!"

"What?"

"My knee!... Got it! Lolly, I remember! I was crawling along a wattle fence somewhere on the outskirts of town, and ahead, in the city, lay a betrayal. I was supposed to kill the traitor, Lolly! That's what I went to do; that's why I was called! And I didn't even learn his name! I learned nothing!"

"This was all in your dream?"

"And I bumped my knee—against that fence!"

"You're kidding?"

"Nothing to kid about, girl! The pain made me remember.... And you, by the way, were there too—you spoke to me."

"Me? And what did I say?"

"Wait, it might not have been you after all … Granny Lina, maybe? In any case, it was a woman's voice; I'm sure of that. A woman that's very close, very dear to me. It couldn't have been Mom, could it? Shit, I can't remember.… All I see is this soggy plowed field right in front of me."

"And you don't remember what she said, the woman?"

"Wait, I wrote it down as soon as I woke up! It should be here somewhere.… Here, got it! On my cigarettes."

"Let me see. Jeez, that's some chicken scratch."

"I wrote in the dark! 'You won't need.'"

"What does that mean?"

"How should I know? It's all gone now. 'You won't need'—no kidding, that's like a joke or something.… 'Blood will stay in Kyiv.' Don't remember that either. 'Women …' what about them?"

"Give it to me."

"A prophesy of the Oracle of frigging Delphi: The words are all there but make no sense whatsoever! Like you said about that secret of yours: a pile of buried rubbish …"

"'Women won't cease giving birth.'"

"How's that again?"

"'Women won't cease giving birth.' That's what you wrote down."

"Sure. Is that supposed to be like $E=mc^2$?"

"That's not as stupid as it seems."

"What does that have to do … you've got to understand, that dream was a warning—a warning that for some reason was left unheeded. Who was that traitor I had to kill? And someone was supposed to die because of him—the dream is still leaving marks to make someone, anyone remember that!"

"Listen. We've got to stop this. We're both going nuts. It's like Macbeth with the witches—he also kept trying to decipher their prophetic message, and look what happened to him. It's not like we're going to find out anyway. I'm done, sweetie. I quit. Turn off the lights, it'll be light outside soon.…"

"Lolly?"

"Mmm?"

"Are you asleep?"

"I is."

"Alright then. Good night."

***

What happened still didn't make sense to anyone.

Stodólya disappeared.

As simple as that. He'd left the bunker before dawn, soon after Adrian had left, to go to the village to get some food and just disappeared. Hadn't come back.

Hard as Adrian tried to look elsewhere, Geltsia's eyes found him wherever he turned—ghastly, completely black around the huge pupils, corners swelling with blood. He had seen eyes like that once—on a hare he'd shot, and they had gone glassy afterward, turned dead. Those eyes of Geltsia's grated on him, demanded an extra effort of him while his thoughts raced in every direction at once like mice in a barn. Geltsia hampered him; he wished she weren't there.

The thing that didn't make any sense was that they still had food—not much, and only groats, which you couldn't just eat by themselves, but Geltsia managed to boil grits even in these make-shift circumstances, and they could've lasted another day or two! And they still had a bit of anti-scurvy herbal tea—no sugar to go with it, but so what, he would've loved a cup of that tea right now, forget the sugar, as long as it were hot, but it was a chore—so he had to make do with the cold grits when he came back, and now his weighted-down stomach made noises like someone was moving a room's worth of furniture in it; this, too, was irritating. Darn it, even if they had to go hungry for a little bit, what's the fuss? To not eat is to not shit—can wait for a bit (as they cheered themselves up when Geltsia was out of earshot): wouldn't be the first time their stomachs saw their spines; you'd chew on bark and leaves in the woods sometimes just to make your mouth, hot as a dry skillet, fill with spit again, to fool your body into humming with sweet warmth—rebels are old pals with hunger. Whatever possessed Stodólya to take off in such a rush to get food, not even waiting for Adrian's return?

Wrong, wrong, something here was wrong and he could feel it, and the boys could feel it, too, and this unspoken torment mixed with anxiety wormed into their souls like an itch drawn out over a fire—like when lice, feeling the heat, crawl out from under your skin, and it's better to endure the honest scorch to your fingers held over the blades of flame than to bear the crawling that bores into your brain.

And Stodólya, of all people! The one who was draconian about maintaining conspiracy, the one who had the authority to court-martial others for the smallest infraction—and who knows how many he had convicted already. It wasn't all enemy blood he had on his hands. His motto was, "Do not trust anyone, and no one will betray you." Now it occurred to Adrian that whenever Stodólya said that he did so with a sort of condescending scorn, like he was challenging them—like he was *warning* them, up front, not to trust him, and he found it entertaining that no one braved asking him, up front: So, do you mean we shouldn't trust you either, friend Stodólya? An ancient paradox, from the Gymnasium logic class: the Cretan said all Cretans are liars, so did the Cretan tell the truth? The paradox cannot be solved: according to Gödel, every system of axioms contains a statement that cannot be proven within that system. But when you find yourself inside the system, the realization of it sends your shaken world helter-skelter and all things leave their usual places like in the nightmare where you're crossing a frozen river and suddenly the ice begins to crack under your feet, opening a black abyss.

If you start seeing a traitor in everyone, even in the comrade who'd carried you out from under fire on his own back (Was that really what happened? Or was it only an elaborate ruse, orchestrated on purpose like those NKVD barrel ambushes with staged fire to fool the victim into believing that our boys had fought him off from the Reds, so that the grateful soul would tell them every-thing they couldn't pry out under torture? How can you know what really happened if there are no witnesses, except Stodólya, of that fatal May march left alive, and you yourself were unconscious?), if you don't trust anyone, and see the enemy's traps everywhere, then how do you not lose your mind, how do you even go on living?

Could Stodólya have lost his mind? Maybe he couldn't take it anymore, nerves failed him, he'd gone mad—and no one in the group noticed? No one stopped him?

Bolsheviks went mad like that, and not infrequently. They had people shoot themselves; leaders throw themselves out the windows. Adrian had long ceased being shocked by that: ever since he saw, in combat once, how when some of the Reds turned and ran, their major, small and narrow-shouldered, a gnome with grotesque wings of shoulder straps, chased after them and shouted, "Halt, motherfucker!" while firing at the running men's backs, and did fell a few before Raven, first to shake off their com-mon torpor (because none of the rebels had ever beheld a marvel like that—an officer shooting his own men in the back—before), mowed the gnome down with a short burst from his machine gun. Adrian remembered well their common impulse of *sympathy for their living enemies*—up till then he'd only felt sorry for their dead, when they found them lying in the forest uncollected, in foreign uniforms, with glassy eyes staring at the sky ("Why did you come here?" he chided them, mentally), and it occurred to him that the garrison's atrocities and their constant, self-obliterating drinking, their monstrous explosions of irrational rage (somewhere they skewered to death a man who'd come into the forest for firewood, somewhere else they opened fire on children sledding from a hill and killed one) must have come from more than their sense of impunity alone ("We can do anything!" barked one of those drunken Ivans when villagers came to complain to "Officer, sir" that "you can't do that"). It must have come from the fact that in a land boiling with partisan warfare these people had been turned into tiny, inanimate screws—and they had broken under the strain just like screws: the nightmare ice cracked and split under their feet all the time, and behind them shuffled some major of theirs, in big shoulder straps, ready to shoot anyone in the back at any minute. And the major, in turn, had his own superior behind him, and that one his; and this went all the way up to Stalin: everyone was afraid of everyone and no one trusted anyone. And this was the fundamental formula that they carried with them wherever they went like a mass lunacy—to make it so *no one could trust anyone.* So no one would love anyone—because trust is only possible among those who love one another. That's what they wanted from us; this would be their victory.

And now, on top of everything else, he felt angry because he sensed in himself and the boys the same noxious virus—the corrosive poison of silent suspicion. He didn't allow himself to think the worst, but the thought was already inside him, inside them all—injected into their blood like that "vaccine" given to people arrested in K., after which the GB, for no apparent reason, let them all go home, and, within a month, all seventy who'd been vaccinated succumbed to a mysterious illness. A man's utmost humiliation: to feel that you, without ever noticing, gave in and now act exactly the way the enemy wants you to act, against your own will. And everything that used to give you strength—friendship, brotherhood, love—begins to fall apart from inside, eaten away by doubt. You begin to do the enemy's work for him: you break up the ice under your own feet, throwing your pickax in time to the beat of your heart.

Or, maybe, Stodólya simply didn't risk walking back through the woods with knapsacks once it got light, and stayed to wait for nightfall somewhere?

Where could that be? Not in the village, surely?

And why not? The warden could have hidden him. There was still hope; they just had to wait for the night. Anything could have happened.

Adrian knew that while he had been gone, in the city, the others had already talked to death all the likely versions of what happened—and that his return gave them new energy, enough for another round. Really, all kinds of things happened at war. Under different circumstances, meaning if Stodólya had been there, he would have told them about the policeman he'd met in the city, three and a half floors below the appointed door. "Leave, it's a kapkán...." And now he won't. Not ever. Even if Stodólya, God willing, does come back, alive and well—he still won't tell them. Only in his report, to his anchor in General Staff. Don't believe anyone, and no one will betray you.

No, that's not what the anchor had told him, a long time ago, in Lviv, back under the Germans, during that dark time when our people fell utterly without explanation—when Gestapo shot down OUN members right in the streets, picking them out from among passersby as certainly as if the Germans carried their photos in their pockets, until it turned out they did, in fact, have photos, and more—that back in November of 1939, in Kraków, at a joint conference of Gestapo and NKVD, the Soviets had turned over to the Krauts the lists of political cases they'd inherited from the Poles, so everyone who'd joined the Organization under the Polish rule was obliged to disappear, go underground: "Remember," his anchor had said then, "even if I betray, you never will." And he remembered—because at those words, goose bumps sped up his spine. He remembered it for the rest of his days: he was the sentinel who didn't dare leave his post even if he were there alone.

He wasn't alone—yet.

Levko and Raven's faces, concerned and alert in the shape-shifting flicker of the gas burner (Geltsia went to brew some tea after all—it was the only reasonable thing that could still be done to maintain the illusion of unshattered order), moved him to an unfamiliar, painful tenderness—as if these boys, a mere seven or eight years younger than he, were his sons. If God had given him a son, he'd wish for one thing and one thing only—that his child grow up to be like them. They'd been taught from a young age that work and prayer are life's foundation, but what they'd really learned was to tell good from evil. And that's the only important thing, the most important thing that a father must give his child—God takes care of the rest.

Adrian felt he was growing lightheaded and his eyes were beginning to tear up—probably because there was so little air to breathe in the bunker. And Geltsia's presence impeded him—he couldn't look into her bloodstained, wounded-hare eyes; they pierced right through him. As if in accusation, as if to say, in plain language: you never liked him—are you happy now?

Happy he was not. Honest to God, was not. Wanted one thing—to know the truth. Either this or that. Either dry solid ground under his feet—or ice water closing over his head, but either one or the other, finally. Anything but this nightmarish cracking of ice where things should be solid. To wake up, finally, from his seven-month dream through which he'd been marching blindly with his eyes open. Marching because he loved this woman. She looked at him with all but hatred now, and he still loved her.

No, the boys said, there'd been no shooting—if there'd been a fight, they would've heard it, noise carried far. There was, thus, hope that Stodólya was still alive.

Still, they had to get themselves out of this bunker. Adrian was sure of that. The bunker smelled like a grave to him. Had from the beginning.

Hence, they'd drink their tea and would have to spend the night in the woods.

Geltsia looked at him out of her terrible blackened eyes as if she didn't understand what he was saying. Mater Dolorosa, flashed through his mind, irritably. She did not like sleeping on the snow; she once admitted to him that for her it was the most unpleasant aspect of the partisan life. For a woman, it really must be uncomfortable—when everyone sleeps under the same waterproof cape, fitted against each other like spoons in a drawer, turn all together, and a half-awake chap is liable to grab hold of some body part that doesn't belong to him—but at the moment he worried a lot more about how they would keep themselves warm during the night. There'd been too little snow for them to pile onto the cape as insulation, and things could get tough if the night dipped far below freezing. Geltsia would have to lie in the middle, and they would keep her warm; they'd protect her, they'd guard her from the cold. And what if Stodólya did get caught by the raid?

The water still refused to boil. Let me breathe on it, Levko offered, and Raven chuckled something supportive—they were showing themselves they could still joke. Or perhaps the still-young energy in them, like in young animals, took over; well, that was not half bad. Not half bad. We've got another fight or two in us yet, boys. We'll *keep things hot* for them as that captain said. He stared at the lifeless little pot—come on, boil already!—and a different vision rose before his clouded eyes: a stubby oblong metal box sat on the burner, and the water in it wobbled a little, and glowing sparks of tiny bubbles rose from the bottom, growing more numerous and dense until they sheathed a pair of surgical metal pincers, readied for an operation. That operation didn't happen either.

What?, he startled: Geltsia called his name. Instantly, he was scared—really scared, to a cold squeeze inside his chest—What is it, am I asleep?—and all his fatigue disappeared, at once, as if surgically removed. He was focused again, ready for action—only his heart beat faster than normal. The doubt, that's what had worn him down, burdened him, taken away his strength—that accursed doubt. He needed a moment, a moment....

Geltsia wanted him to come outside with her. Signaled it with her eyes.

And this, too, had already been; his body remembered it: going out of a bunker into the night after a different woman, his heart pounding, and him not knowing himself, knowing nothing except the nearness of her presence, stepping toward the moonlight—only then it was spring, and now pale spots of snow lay under the firs, and in the graphite sky to which both instinctively turned their faces once they'd climbed out, gulping the open air and space with all their senses, the naked branches of hornbeams hung black against a murky, chalk-dusted moon. It was quiet—the wind had died down, and only the free warm-run's muffled babble rose from the bottom of the ravine. Adrian had time to realize that of all of them Geltsia left the bunker most often; he'd noticed it yesterday—it must be that time of the month for her, and the bunker, without a latrine, was not meant for long stays. And that was when he heard her voice, the voice that instantly shook him clear and sober of his revelry in the night's open air—it spoke as if from under stone.

"I'm to blame. It's my fault."

In the firs' dense shadow he could barely make out the stain of her face. Were she to take another step back he wouldn't be able to see her at all. And this, too, it seemed, had once been—where? When? She suffered and he could do nothing to help her.

"He went for me ... the food was for me. He wanted to find me some milk."

Milk? What did milk have to do with anything? It was as if she were speaking a foreign language that refused to coalesce into meaning in his ears. He thought he heard a twig break somewhere in the thickets—or did he?

"I should have talked him out of it. I told him it would pass ... the malady. It's the early weakness; it always passes."

He still didn't understand—he only knew she wasn't there, with him, in that moment, wasn't with them all, and that's why she irritated him, like a voice cutting against the choir's harmony—she was separate from them, locked in this obtuse hull of hers. Her anxiety had a different color, different density. So she is ill?

"It's not an illness," Geltsia responded to his unspoken thought—gently brushed aside the man's crude clutch extended toward her in the dark; a new note appeared in her voice—soothing, self-assured, maternal almost—her voice glowed again, albeit not as brightly. "It happens often ... in the fourth month."

It happened. The blow fell onto him softly, like a lump of snow from a spruce. In the Hutsul highlands he once saw a master slaughter a lamb, after talking to it for a long time, all but whispering into the animal's ear until the little thing obediently lowered its head as if agreeing to accept its end. He saw himself as that lamb now.

So, that's how it is, he thought obtusely. So that's why. As if he slammed, at full speed, into a dead wall, but the momentum kept his legs moving: so that's how it is. That's the thing. But then again—he felt strangely relieved, as if someone put red-hot iron through a wound inside him and let the pus out: Stodólya went to find some milk. Left, without explaining himself to anyone, because his wife was pregnant and needed nourishment. Well, he probably would have gone too, if it were him. Would've crawled on his hands and knees, even right now. Would've kept crawling as long as he had air in his chest.

She interpreted his silence in her own manner.

"I can bear it, Adrian."

That Adrian resounded inside him like a twist of steel in an open wound. She could've addressed him by his alias right then, could've given him at least that one drop of mercy. But she couldn't think about him: he was here, right before her, alive, unharmed, and free, and he was not her child's father.

"I won't be any trouble. And when my time comes in the spring, I'll go have the baby up in the mountains. It's all been arranged; I have an address."

She was apologizing; she saw herself as the only one to fault for what had happened. And at the same time, she emanated such unbending fortitude that Adrian's breath caught in his throat: it was as though she'd grown taller in the dark. He did not know this woman, had no inkling of her strength. "They can't do anything to us!" flashed in his mind with wild, rabid joy, a blast of awe like one inspired by a mighty storm—a sudden, almost superhuman pride for *our women*: no one can ever do anything to a nation like this. We'll overcome it all, all! He stood at attention instinctively, as if he were about to salute her. Geltsia, Lord. The same delicate violet of a girl, tiny feet in soft lace-up boots, the petals of her tracks scattered over the snow—he'd once stood at her door, stood there all night long, having forgotten himself with happiness. Geltsia, Geltsia, my only one, why are you not mine?

And instantly everything inside him collapsed, leaving a sickening vacuum. He remembered where and when he lost her—remembered the dream that had haunted him all these years, ever since the Polish prison: the two of them dancing in a darkened ballroom, somewhere in Prosvita or the People's House, and at some moment Geltsia vanishes—detaches from his arms and dissolves into the darkness. Just as she would, if she took a step back now, be lost in the gloom of the forest. In his dream, he ran madly all over the great hall looking for her and could never find her; the hall grew bigger and bigger like a dark drill field without end, filling, along the walls, with the dead who kept coming—those who had departed, as the song went, for a different, bloody dance—to break Moscow's shackles off Ukrainian hands. And he, too, joined the bloody dance—he died in the infirmary; he hung on a cross, and the centurion struck him between the ribs with his spear where the bullet had entered, and Geltsia was the merciful sister. No, she was Magdalene in an overcoat lined with living raw purple, like ripped-off skin, with its hem folded back, and no matter how hard he called for her, she did not hear him and did not look toward him, and the centurion promised him with a malicious chuckle that he'd see her again, moy-ye, see her good and right! And the merciful sister was a different woman, Rachel. And he loved her, too.

"Dark, swarthy like a Jewess. Pregnant, about seven months...." And Geltsia now—four? It suddenly struck him: this meant that when they had that picture taken, she already had the new life living inside her! It coalesced into a pool of light before his eyes, in the space where he sensed, more than saw, her fragile figure between the fir branches, that picture, illuminated like a Byzantine icon by her semi-apparent smile: the smile women smile when they carry a secret invisible to others under their hearts.

He was overcome with a queer urge to place his hand on her stomach—and instantly, the next thought was: How nice would it be if it weren't Geltsia's but Rachel's stomach—then *he'd know for certain*? But he didn't have a chance to finish that thought, didn't get to comprehend what it was that he would've liked to know for certain, because from the darkest bowels of his soul rose, menacing and unstoppable, like a pregnant woman's urge to vomit, the thing he'd been kicking around in his mind this whole time, on the whole eighteen-kilometer return trek from the city, moving his feet without getting anywhere, trying in vain to stomp out the poison of suspicion already injected into his blood: *the picture!* His photograph displayed at the police station, his phiz that the teacher from P. recognized, having seen him but once half a year before—that picture must have been recent, which meant it could only have been *that same one*, from their group photograph. The one in which he "had mourn"—a shadow on his face like soot, the whites of his eyes bright as sin: nothing like his regular self, a highway Gypsy. No one could ever recognize him if they hadn't seen him before—the shadow fell from nowhere like a Gypsy curse and disguised him. The GB had nowhere else to find an image of Kyi; that was the only one taken of him in the last three years—the one Stodólya had made of them all last summer.

How did they get it?

And *who* revealed the location of Stodólya's bunker in October? The courier girl didn't do it. That's why the GB nailed her tongue to a board. And he knew how they did it: they'd bring in one of their doctors during an interrogation, and he'd pretend to offer medical attention to whomever they're torturing—he'd feel the pulse, take the temperature, even wipe the victim's face and put salve on the wounds. And then he'd ask the thoroughly reassured prisoner to stick his—or her—tongue out and say "A-ah!" And the others, as soon as the tongue was out, would jump in and put it in a clamp. Then they can torment their victim to death if they want without having to worry about hearing her scream, or curse, or die with the last "Glory to Ukraine!" You can do whatever you want to a person with their tongue in a clamp.

No, not quite. Can do whatever with the body, but not with the person. That girl did not tell them anything.

But *who* did? *What* compromised Stodólya's bunker?

Put your hand on my forehead, he asked her silently—She, with Stodólya's child in her womb. Cool me, clean me, set me free. Let this poison out of my soul; tell me something else I don't know. Tell me how he kisses, how you part your knees for him, and how he enters you as your husband, and what you feel when he does; tell me the words he says to you—I will bear it all, as long as it is *true*. Tell me so I don't have to suspect you, too. In his memory flashed, with a burn of pain, their happiest hours in the underground, when they sang all together. Their singing and their communal prayer—those were hours of otherwise inexpressible unity, so resplendent and inspired were the faces of friends, such fires burned in their eyes. Stodólya never sang. He wasn't musical.

Somewhere close, but outside himself, he could hear the chronometer ticking: his consciousness, distanced from his pain, sober, cruel, and implacable, like a knight in icy armor timed him, counted his minutes. TICK … TICK … TICK … TICK…

"Let's go back," he said, surprised by the sound of his own voice, the way it came out of his throat. "It's time to leave this bunker."

He thought he felt her shrink, draw back. As if he'd hit her (she'd told them about the time, during a raid on the village where she was staying, dressed as a peasant, when a captain had hit her on the face and, before she could realize what she was doing, she instinctively struck him back—her mistress then threw herself at the captain's feet in panic, assuring him that her niece was "born stupid" and they believed her: for them, it was the only possible explanation for why an unarmed person would respond to being hit by hitting back). Alright, he thought, it's your turn to strike. Hit me, stomp me, don't spare me, hate me if it'll make you feel better—it doesn't matter anymore; someday, if we survive, I'll set things straight with you, but now we have to save ourselves. Black hunters were walking through the snow, black dogs were running, pulling the men along behind them, their leashes so taut they sang—he could feel their choking breath at the back of his neck. The anxiety that had been smoldering inside his body like fever now gathered itself, acquired a shape and a contour, pointed outside like an antenna trained on the village—and Geltsia, like a child too preoccupied with her little owie, was deaf to it all; really, women can be quite obtuse sometimes.

He forced himself to speak again. "Thank you for telling me."

"I didn't want to talk about it around the boys."

"I understand. And now we should go back to them."

"Do you not believe me, Adrian?"

He felt like laughing out loud. Only a woman could ask something like that. He could have repeated her disappeared husband's commandment: "Do not trust anyone, and no one will betray you." Could have said he trusted that she was, in fact, pregnant. Why not? Could tell even judging by how often she had to go outside. He'd read his share of medical texts; he knew the symptoms. Although no, he couldn't say that, could never have said that to any woman. And that wasn't what she was asking about anyway.

So, instead of all that, he blurted, "And who am I supposed to believe?"

It sounded unexpectedly rude, like a teenager's outburst. Exactly like a teenager from a ragtag neighborhood, and it made him blush—at least she couldn't see that in the dark!—and then he heard her respond with a muffled sigh, a bitten-down sob of relief, like the touch of a breeze that brought him her smell through the firs—the blonde smell of her hair that he remembered so well from the days when they were like Marlene Dietrich and Clark Gable on a ballroom floor: long unwashed and uncurled, pulled into a greasy knot at the back of her head. It only smelled stronger, more piercing—of cut wildflowers, of hay before a storm—of Her. And he made a quick wish then: if the other one does not come back, be mine! Be mine, until I fall, until my last breath, until the last bullet that waits for me.

And she, revived by his sincerity, seemed to awake and spoke with new urgency—to make her point, beat it to a pulp. "Mykhailo is an extraordinary person, Adrian! None of you really know him …"

Mykhailo. Stodólya, Mykhailo to her.

"He once said he can do everything that the Bolsheviks can, except better, and that's why he always outplays them. He won't let himself be caught, you'll see!"

She's always been like that, Adrian thought, ever since the Youth Assembly—always pushed through to the end, to reach whatever goal she'd set for herself. And he stood there like a dolt and let her go on talking.

"All any of us knows is how to die for Ukraine; that's the only thing we're good for. And he belongs to the breed of people who will build it up one day, after we win it."

"That could be," he said. But what he thought was that's how it actually is. And it's always been like that, since the dawn of creation: those who love their land above all are the first to die for it in battle. And if they have luck—not the plain soldier-variety luck that he still had, knock on wood, but the gambler's luck of a historical player that puts him in the right place at the right time so that their blood follows whatever suit leads in the worldwide political game, played far above and beyond their heads—then their blood brings to power those who love power itself and know how to hold on to it. And Stodólya was one of those people; that was true. And the Bolsheviks were, too. If they ever need an independent Ukraine in order to hold on to their power, they will build it just as zealously as we now fight for it in the underground. When Stalin needed to pry Ukraine from the insurgents' influence in '44, when the whole country was united behind them, he allowed Ukrainian ministries of defense and foreign relations to be created. And when the Supreme Liberation Council demanded from the Allies that we have a government in exile, Stalin also outmaneuvered us by making Ukraine the founding member of the United Nations Organization. And even though it was all just for show, formal attributes of a country that does not, in fact, exist, one day we'll make use of it all ... Kyiv wasn't built overnight.

And he also thought: in these circumstances, living from one day to the next, he wouldn't have dared have a child with her. And Stodólya did. So he did not live day to day—he kept a longer count. And that, too, somehow underscored the truth of what she said.

Meanwhile, she'd gathered speed, she flew now like a bicycle down a hill, unable to stop, possessed by her lust to win him over to her side by whatever means necessary, to make it so he would share her faith in the man whose seed she carried in her womb.

"The Bolsheviks won't kill him; they want him for themselves! They had offered to take him into their intelligence school, and after—to send him to Yugoslavia as an agent. They didn't even want any information about us from him—only for him to work for them. And he outwitted them then, too: rubbed his palms so he could show a fever and get into the infirmary, and then managed to organize his escape from there."

"Did he?" he said. "I didn't know this."

The bicycle just hit a rock at full tilt, but she never noticed the rattle, din, and clang of her words crashing: so Stodólya had been arrested? (He really didn't know anything about the man!) If so—he had to have passed a security check with the highest levels of the Service; they must've turned him inside out there. But still, for some reason, this thought did not comfort him: all the separate little splinters he pulled out one by one—the disappearance, the photograph, the loss of Stodólya's bunker, his past arrest—were coming together of their own accord, were aligning themselves into a geometric progression, and connections appeared between them where none had been evident before. Every new circumstance landed with a more alarming screech because it took on the combined weight of whatever had come before it, and this new sequence of elements skewed the whole picture further and further away from the image Geltsia had in her mind. I have to write a report to the Supreme Command, he realized. Just write it all out, as it is. And with this, part of the burden shifted off his shoulders; he felt better—it's always easier when someone else has to make the decisions, someone other than you. He stirred impatiently, felt a wet scrape of a fir branch on his cheek, its myriad minute claws—he was in his proper place again; he knew what he had to do.

"Anything else, Miss Gela?"

"Don't say 'miss' to me, Adrian. Please."

"I apologize. I didn't mean to offend you."

"Because it sounds like you don't take me seriously."

And this is just the beginning, he thought. It'll only be worse later—if they get a later.

"I'm sorry," he repeated. "And now please, go ahead, I'll cover the tracks."

"Let me do that."

"Some bullet-head you are!"

"There," she laughed—a sprinkle of light in the darkness, "that's better! Much better than 'miss.' I just wanted to make wee-wee down by the stream."

"I'll wait for you," he said, moved by this sudden intimacy, such as they'd never shared before. He remembered an illustration in some thick anatomical volume: a semicircular dome full of innards, the riveting and simultaneously repugnant female belly and uterus inside, an oval aquarium with a bigheaded mollusk, pressing the bladder from above.... He tried to imagine what that would feel like, that pressure, shuddering as if he'd felt a wet toad in his pants, and for the first time realized that her condition meant something completely different to her than it did to him—that all this time her body knew something he would never know, even if he'd memorized all the books in the world. This something existed outside their struggle's logic, in utter disregard of it, as if it had come from a different planet. And that's the way it'll always be, he thought in awe, listening to her descend heavily (she did sound heavy, the rhythm of her step had changed), like a she-bear, down the rocky slope, taking time to choose where to plant her feet (and the one who was

in her seventh month already—how did she move?)—*swoosh,
swoosh, swoosh.*

Everything went quiet for a little while, and then he distinguished, over the measured babbling of the warm-run (his hearing
strained, pushed like a radio receiver to the very edge of its range)
the sound of louder, self-propelled, and somehow very jolly purl,
and this sound suddenly clenched his throat in a wave of intolerable, melting, animal tenderness. In the same instant, as a dark
accompaniment, the bass hum of free current with the violin solo,
he became aware, to his horror, of muscles contracting below his
stomach—his body awoke and remembered the other one, the
one he lost, hammered in his temples, screamed with its every
cell to will back the insatiable luxury of that one spring night, the
intimate, selfsame yielding of moist flesh like earth that brims with
the juices of life, the fiery contour in the dark—as though these
seven months had never been—he couldn't hold on to separate
faces, they came together in his mind and melded: the barely visible stain of Geltsia in the dark between fir branches; the white
face, like a round of sheep cheese, of Rachel thrown back to the
moon, upper lip bitten down. He was blind; he simply wanted to
embrace the Woman, a pregnant woman with a taut round belly.
To squeeze his head between her milk-laden breasts, to breathe
in her smell.

Sobs shook him hard, once, like wind over a dried tree—dry
sobs, tearless like a soundless scream. Like the mute roar of a beast
with its tongue nailed down.

Swoosh, swoosh, swoosh—she was coming back. He could hear
her heavy breathing: she was short of breath. He felt happy to have
her coming back and to have her miss his moment of weakness.
(He watched yellowish circles swim in place of the fiery contour,
as if someone had thumbed him on the eyes.)

"It's beautiful in the forest right now, don't you think?" she
exhaled into the back of his head in a single spasm, like she'd also
just cried. And instantly sensed the change that had come over

him—a woman must sense these things, as a doe senses a deer buck, from afar. As long as she doesn't decide to touch me right now, he thought. Anything but that soothing touch of her hand. As long as she doesn't, I'll bear it. He faltered a bit as he stepped aside to let her pass and remained standing like that, feet wide apart, his hand instinctively planted on his gun, as if prepared to defend himself.

"And did you know," she suddenly laughed very softly, and it was almost like a touch, only not the kind he feared, "that my Lina is also a mama? Three years already!"

"Who?" he asked, confused.

"Lina, my sister!"

Her sister? Oh, yes, she has a sister …

"She married a very nice young man, one of ours, a student at the Polytechnic. And they already have a little son, named Ambroziy—in honor of our dad."

"Aha," he said. "Congratulations," thinking, who was it that I already said this to today? Quite a day I've had—full of other people's children. Lina? That little girl in a sailor suit that used to run around with her dog? She had that comical way of blushing whenever he brought pastries for her, as a present. He held back a big fir branch, so that Geltsia wouldn't have to bend too low. As they walked, her quiet twitter continued to envelop him like the stream's babbling: she'd visited her family recently, in October, when she was in Lviv on a mission. They still live in the same house on Krupyarska; the house now belongs to the Soviets, and they'd been moved to the ground-floor room. They all went crazy when she rapped on the window that night—they hadn't seen each other for three years! And the boy is very handsome, looks like Lina—she'd taken a good look at him while he slept.

"We talked about you, too. Lina was very happy when I told her you were alive. You were her first love, did you know that?"

"No," he said, "I did not know that."

Life was full of things he didn't know. But it did not matter anymore, he did not change his mind, she didn't convince him. They had to get out of the bunker. The clock was ticking.

"She was head over heels in love with you. In Gymnasium, she had a picture of Clark Gable pinned above her desk—with his mustache covered up, to make him look more like you. I think she was probably a little jealous of me."

Oh no, he thought, I won't fall for this. Does she mean to soften me up with this? A covered-up mustache—what notions women have sometimes! They've always fallen head over heels for him, that's the son of a bitch he is: women have always fallen for him hard and fast, lined up wherever he went and threw flowers (or more than that, some threw themselves) at his feet—all except one.

His soul no longer perceived the meaning of what she was saying (she's gone lost her wits for Mykhailo; it's like she's lost her bearing without him and doesn't understand anything!). He only thought, at the pace of a ticking clock, of sparks of tiny bubbles rising through wobbly water, boiling the dark outline of fear: she's playing me; she's playing me however she pleases, like a piano, and I am letting her. I am responsible for a woman who has more power over me than I do over her, and this is bad, it is no good at all, friend lieutenant. A tremor he couldn't control started small inside his exhausted body—like a fire in a house. He focused on the prospect of hot tea, hoping it had finally boiled.

"Adrian."

She stopped—like music that's been turned off. They stood opposite each other, a step away from the stump that masked the lid to the bunker, and in the darkness he could feel the crown of her head level with his lips. Here was a woman made to his measure—the one such woman in the world.

"I wanted to tell you. There may not be a chance later. I am very grateful to you. And not just for listening to me right now. For everything."

He was silent, a lamb under the cudgel.

"You are like family to me. Like the brother I never had. And always wanted, for as long as I can remember."

"Thank you," said friend lieutenant, alias Kyi. "Go ahead, Dzvinya."

***

You'll never betray me?

I will never betray you.

Don't leave me.

I will never leave you.

I don't have anyone closer than you.

Me neither. I don't have anyone at all, just you.

And the other man?

There never was another. Forget it. It wasn't me.

Are you sure? How do you know you won't change your mind? That if he comes back and calls you, you won't lose your head again and run to him?

I know because I don't like the woman I was with him. I don't like her. What motivated me then, what pushed me into his arms—it wasn't mine. Wasn't his either. I saw a completely different man when I looked at him—a man created by my want from the hard losses, unaddressed complexes, and collective desires of my people. I thought him strong. Someone capable of determining the fate of many. Because it's always been foreigners and their lackeys who determined the fate of many in our country. A Ukrainian security agent, a Ukrainian parliamentarian, a Ukrainian banker—people of power—this has always been an unattainable dream: an embodied dream of our ancient collective rightlessness of "its own" native force that would protect and defend. I thought him strong. But he was only cruel.

To you? To you, too?

Let's not talk about this. Don't.

Okay, we won't.

It was all like a dark pall. But I thought that's the way it was supposed to be.

My poor girl.

What can I say? Taking cruelty for strength is the most common mistake of youth. Youth only knows life by the intensity of its own feelings—a continuous explosive fortissimo with a foot on the pedal. Youth knows nothing of that supreme sensitivity, the true sensitivity of the strong that denies cruelty; youth has no inkling of the force with which a barely audible pianissimo can strike under your heart. Women make this discovery with the first butterfly quickening of a child in their wombs.

And what about men then—do you think them dumber?

You love war. And war is not conducive to refined sensibilities, it keeps pressing on their pedals, intensifies them. It's that same fortissimo, all the time—until you go deaf.

You are unfair.

I am a woman. I want to feel the butterfly stir and see God's presence in it. God is constantly present to us in small things—in a shape of a leaf, in the thin lace of new ice along a shore. In the miracle of miniscule nails on an infant's fingers. War makes one deaf and blind to all that.

You are being unfair. War is also a way of seeing God manifest. Perhaps the most direct way. And the most terrible, as it should be—it is a fearful thing to fall into the hands of the living God. Omens in the sky, comets, messages spelled in fire, voices of spirits, descending angels, renewal of churches that will collapse under bombs tomorrow—every war has its own metaphysical history. And none have yielded as many martyrs as this one. And we are mere tools in it, rocks in God's sling.

Adrian. Tell me, will this war ever end?

The war never ends, my girl. It is always the same—only the weapons change.

Is it you telling me this? Or that other one, the dead man?

Are any of us alive?

No! Don't say that. I don't want it. And these are not your words at all!

Don't forget—it's a dream. We're dreaming this, and words can flit into this dream from wherever they please—like dust into your eyes.

I know where these words come from. I remember the painting that went with them, *After the Blast*—one of Vlada's, who is now dead, too. Weren't these her words—about a strong man her imagination created out of fear of losing? What is she doing here? Why is Vlada in this dream?

It'll end soon. You have to bear it for just a little longer. We have to squeeze just a little farther through that narrow, dark shaft—we've got a bad bunker, with a straight entrance, and the entrance should always be angled, you should build it zigzag, so that when they throw in a grenade, no one inside gets hurt.

I don't see the shaft. I see myself step into water, into a stream. I am washing my legs and dirt runs down my skin.

Maybe the dream has split at some point into separate branches, and now you're seeing something I'm not? But water—that's good. It's good that the dirt is washing away.

Such clear, black streaks on bare thighs ...

That's everything extraneous coming off. The soul's being cleansed, remains itself.

I love you. And I will never betray you.

You know, I was so jealous! For quite a while, I just never admitted it to you. Those lobsters you ate with him were stuck in my throat.

It's washed away, all washed away like it's never been ... I see a little girl smiling, laughing, a blonde little girl, two years old or so—and somehow I know she's mine ... I'll have a girl?

A girl! Of course, it has to be a girl, how did I not see that? A girl, of course, a little Geltsia with tiny blonde braids ...

And where is the boy?

Which boy?

The one who'll protect her. Every girl is meant to have a boy like that—a husband, a brother, someone else…. Why do I not see where he is? Has the war taken him, too?

What if he's already been born? He's among the living and that's why you cannot see him?

And there's no one alive in this dream?

Only you and me, Lolly. This is our dream. And we cannot change it …

***

"Banderas, surrender! Come out!"

Shouted, in Russian, into the vent. Above, dogs bayed, boots stomped—many boots, the commotion made the dirt fall from the ceiling, the sound growing like a shell's whine through the air: higher, higher until it falls, explodes, buries them.

"Come out, Kyi! We know you're there!"

The four looked at each other. The flashlight lit Levko's face as the color drained from his cheeks and it turned sallow. Like Geltsia's. And Raven's.

"This is it," the voice said inside Adrian's head—with heretofore unknown calm. And instantly a bubble of long-awaited relief burst inside him: finally! And then his whole being rebelled against it: no! He licked his lips—the lips were also someone else's, separate.

Who? he mouthed without a sound, but everyone heard because they were all asking the same thing in that instant: Who brought the raid?

Or did he bring it himself? Did the dogs pick up his trail, all the way from the city?

"Come out, bitch, or we'll smoke you out!"

Oh, so they have gas. They've got it all—gas, dogs, all the force in the world. His throat caught in a spasm of hatred, like a burst of machine-gun fire he mentally sent up the vent. For a moment, he couldn't see, a dark veil over his eyes. He gestured; Raven understood him first: the papers! Hurriedly, they began to empty their knapsacks, shred photographs; Raven struck a match, the fire blazed, sent flares dancing across faces, shadows along the walls. Adrian thought he saw Geltsia's teeth chatter. He didn't feel the heat either; wouldn't have felt it if he put his hand into the fire. He did, however, feel, with his whole body, the cold of his pistol, suddenly heavy—the pistol was doing the thinking for him, choosing its aim: temple or under the chin? He stepped under the vent and shouted, head up, "Go smoke your mama out the barn! Where's the one who brought you here?"

"What'd you want him for?"

"Get him here; I want to talk!"

Up above there was muttering, low, indistinct over the dogs' racket, in several voices, light moved in the crack of the vent. They'll negotiate, he realized; they want me alive. Personal commendations, promotions, decorations, vacations—they are drooling now, like those dogs, they won't want such prize getting away from them. Talk, buy time for the archives to burn. And then fight it: grenades through the shaft and go. There's always some chance, he's been in worse straits. No, he thought, not like this. Lord have mercy on our souls, but Geltsia must remain; she must live. Rachel—that's my sin, let me atone for it now. Let one of them survive. I am now like Orko in the fight yesterday—a guard to a pregnant woman. If it was really Orko—but it's all the same, whoever it was: he was now all of them—all who had perished, blown themselves up in bunkers, burned themselves in haylofts, fallen to bullets, coloring the snow red under them and grasping the grenade's pin in their fingers' last twitch—the endless dark ballroom where he danced, his danse funèbre gathered itself, like a fist, into this underground hideout and thousands of the fallen thundered, marching in his blood. Your blessing, Lord.

Something moved close to the vent. Now, he thought. He seemed to feel the breath coming from above, and the breath mixed with his own, like two people sleeping under one cape. Suddenly, his body shook with a long, fierce tremor, more intense, almost, than love's, and sticky sweat covered his forehead. He had never been so appalled before.

"Friend commander—"

It was Stodólya.

Geltsia gasped behind him, a thin short noise, a baby-bat squeak. Above, the barking was cut short, turned to whimper—someone must have kicked the dog, so he'd keep quiet. The boot, give him the boot, always the boot.

"Let her out," said the one who had been Stodólya; no one had ever heard him speak in this voice before, it slithered over Adrian. "Let Dzvinya out, friend commander, let Dzvinya come out."

A noise made Adrian turn around. Dzvinya, who had squatted to throw documents into the fire, had fallen backwards, hit her head on an SMG propped against the wall, and now lay across the bunker's floor, the fire lapping at her boots. This is hell, he thought, watching the boys drag her aside; I'm in hell. This is what it looked like in the picture of Judgment Day in the old wooden church where his father used to serve Mass: tongues of fire wagged, sparks sliced through faces, and devils in reddish-gray haloes bared their hungry fangs at you from below. Hell is feeling appalled forever, without reprieve. He didn't know this before. Before, he was happy.

Smoke made his eyes water.

"Better you come down here," he shouted, fighting back the cough. "Your wife has just fainted, she needs your assistance. If your masters will let you, of course."

"This is not what you think, friend. I swear—"

"You've already broken one pledge you'd sworn. Don't trouble yourself."

"Let me talk to her!"

"I'm afraid I can't help you. Ask the ones you've sold us to."

"She's guilty of nothing!"

"All the worse for you, then," he spoke almost mechanically, as though knocking out the standard insurgent verdict on a typewriter: "We order you to remove yourselves from such-and-such village within forty-eight hours, and similarly from all Ukrainian lands. There is no place for people like you on Ukrainian land. We warn you that failure to carry out these orders will ..."

Stodólya used to be the one who carried out such verdicts; now he, Adrian, had taken his place. "You'll just have to live with that. The judgment of Ukrainian people will find you."

I'll do it myself, he promised himself mentally—I'll give you a load of lead when we start the fight, and with such cold satisfaction, it'll be like squeezing a boil. And that's when he realized how he would do it—instantly, as if he saw it in a flash of a photographer's magnesium.

"Smoke! There's smoke, comrade captain, they're burning something down there!"

"Kyi, don't be stupid, turn yourself in. Your pal here—he's smarter than you!"

He knew how he would do it; he felt an amazing clarity in his mind and body. You're yet to see how the banderas surrender. You wanna see it—I'll show you. Something white to hold in his hand—a newspaper? The boys leaned Geltsia against a wall; her head fell to one side. As long as those above don't stuff the vents shut, so the fire doesn't go out ... Levko kept slapping her on the cheeks; it would be better to leave her alone, let her not wake.

"The Soviet government is doing you bandits a favor, and you're turning up your noses at it?"

He pushed a few more photo shreds into the fire with the toe of his boot: a merry-eyed girl's face with her smile torn off, a pair of peasant hands folded in a lap. Somewhere in there burned the picture of the five of them together. He'd tossed it in after shredding it. Ashes alone must remain. Ashes alone, everything must burn to dust. Not a name, not a sign, nothing after us. Only our blood for you, Ukraine. A new, unfamiliar excitement alit in him, growing brighter and hotter as the fire that swallowed their archives. Someone was coughing; he wiped his eyes and saw a smudge of soot on his hand: It was his own hand but he could not comprehend it.

"Should we burn the newspapers, too, friend commander?"

"Leave them. Let them read."

"Come out nicely, Kyi, or are you done living?"

"And who would you be to order me around like your pig herd?" he shouted, listening to the movement above ground. Just as he thought, they were taking positions on the ground behind the trees, away from the entrance in case grenades came flying out of the bunker; Stodólya showed them where the entrance was. "Or are you all pig herds yourselves? Then go fetch me Colonel Voronin, I'll talk to him!"

"Yeah, sure! No colonel for you—I, Captain Boozerov, am in charge of this operation!"

He thought, there, my death introduced itself. From a thousand possible anonymous faces it had chosen this one. And I wished so much for this to happen in Kyiv—and I never got to see the city. That's a shame. That was one thing he regretted, a single thing, and the regret was already too small to touch anything inside him. Lord, help me. This is the last time I'll ever ask You.

He heard a bolt click: Levko sent the bullet into the stock. And stood up, for some reason—the low ceiling kept him half-bent and he stood like that, pistol in hand, as if holding the entire earth on his shoulders and swaying a bit under its weight.

"Friend commander ... friends ..."

"Hold on, Levko," Adrian said. "While we're still armed, it's no good rushing into the next world without taking a few Bolshevik souls with us. Captain Boozerov's already in a hurry, can't you hear it?"

"Kyi, surrender! I'm giving you five minutes to think!"

"Grenades?" Raven asked hoarsely, ravenously.

Adrian looked at Geltsia. She was awake. She sat, unmoving, and shone her eyes at him straight through the darkness. For a moment, all sounds disappeared and the only thing he heard was blood ringing in his ears. A high, dangerous whine.

"Forgive me, Adrian."

She knew, he realized. Knew that he loved her. She is here, with me. Hand in hand. My love, my happiness. Wonder lurched inside him, tore free, and burned high and even like a torch.

"May the good Lord forgive you," he answered in Father Ortynsky's voice. "And you forgive me, Gela. And you forgive me, boys, for however I sinned before you, Raven ... and you, Levko ..."

"Lord forgive ..."

"I forgive you, forgive me, friends ..."

"And you forgive me ..."

"May the good Lord ..."

Awkwardly, like strangers, they kissed each other: each was already alone with his or her fading life and the touch of another's body struggled to reach their awareness—a stubby cheek, a hot cheek, a cold one, a wet one.... That's Geltsia's, he realized: she is crying, her tears returned. Tears ran down her cheeks in grooves or moist glitter, and he suddenly regretted not having had the chance to shave one last time—felt like he was leaving a camp untidied.

"I said five minutes, Kyi! Did you hear me?"

He heard fear in that shout. Now's the time, he thought. Like in that fairytale where the shrew kept asking the girl to dance and she tarried and tarried, until the roosters called. Only the roosters won't call for us, and help won't come. His clock was about to stop; the hand counting seconds almost ran its last circle. The thing for which he'd been preparing himself all these years was rising before him as a humongous, menacing wall, more magnificent and menacing than anything he had known before. Even the feeling he had when stood in formation in 1943 with four Insurgent Army companies, just sworn in, and sang "Ukraine's not yet perished," could not match this. Nothing could. And no matter how much you prepare yourself for this, you can't ever be ready.

"Dzvinya, you stay," he spoke. "Stay here. Come out later ... when it's all over. That would be best."

She opened her mouth spasmodically, as if about to yawn. And instantly the sharp pity he felt for her—for leaving her alone, tearing her away, as though he were ripping out of her, full of love, his aching flesh—caught him and entered him like a knife under his ribs—and he shuddered, scorched by the boundless, infinite mass of life that was hidden inside him.

"They already know everything you know—from him," she said as if to justify herself. "It won't do any more harm if you turn yourselves in."

Only then did he see the pistol in her hand.

"Shoot me, Adrian. I beg you."

"No!" he said.

"For the love of God, do it. I'm afraid my hand will err."

"You must live."

"I don't want to."

"Gela," he said.

She jerked her chin sideways, in torment, as if not having the strength to complete the gesture of refusal. "I don't want to … carry his blood," she whispered the last words.

He didn't know what to say to that. He was not a woman. The life force that was in her differed from the one he felt, the one that urged him into his last battle. He could only repeat, "You must live. You can bear it, Gela. You're strong."

"I don't want to surrender to them. I have grenades, too, two of them, in fact." At once and without words they all remembered how they gave her an RGD grenade for her name day in September, and she must've remembered it, too, because she sobbed, or perhaps chuckled nervously. "Goodness, I clear forgot—I've got Christmas presents prepared for you all!" And next she was tossing some bundles into the gathering darkness from her knapsack—mittens? socks?—something white fluttered and fell like a wing. Scooping up heat from the cinders, she caught it, shook it out. "This one's for you, friend commander, will you wear it? Lina, my sister, asked me to give it to you. I was saving it for Christmas."

It was a shirt—a blazing white shirt with dense embroidery, lush as a row of marigolds, down the front. The kind girls embroidered for their betrothed—and the sight of it made the three men's breath catch in their throats. The shirt glowed in the dark as though alive; it wanted to be worn into marriage, not into death. And suddenly Adrian knew why it was there.

"Geltsia, bless your heart!" he said, no longer surprised by anything. Everything was the way it had to be; life, aimed at its end like a bullet sent down the stock, ran smoothly along its course as though guided by a supreme will, and everything fit into its proper slot. And the little girl in the sailor suit, who had, without knowing it, embroidered his last weapon, was also there and looked at him with love. He would use the shirt to come out.

He explained his plan: he would announce they were giving themselves up. He'd come out first, under a white flag—this one, he took the shirt into his hands, but it had no smell: he could no longer perceive smells, could only sense the smoke. He'd use the shirt to hide a grenade—they won't see it until they close around him. Then, with three blasts at once, they'd be able to destroy at least a dozen enemies. More if they were lucky.

And Stodólya with them, he thought but didn't say out loud. That was his last mission, his alone, not to be delegated to anyone else: he had to kill the traitor. He dared not die without it; he wouldn't be able to look them in the eye in the other world. And Geltsia had to stay here, in the bunker; Geltsia had to live. Someone had to raise our children.

"Friend commander." It was she again, only her voice had changed unrecognizably, became low, as with a cold. "Allow me to go with you."

But he wasn't listening—a giant dark wall was rising before him, bigger than anything he had ever scaled before, and he said to the one who wasn't letting him go, who was tethering him to life, "No," and stepped up to the vent.

"Wait!" Her hair had come loose; she looked deranged. "Listen to me! They've come for you, friend Kyi, but *he* has come for me!"

The men looked at her as if they'd seen her for the first time.

"He'll survive," she said; hysterical notes rang in her voice. "He'll slip out, he's wily. You won't be able to do anything to him. The Area Council of Security Service Command is in two weeks, and he'll go there—with new troops. And that'll be the end. Lord," she almost cried, "don't you understand that *you* won't kill him? You won't fool him with your show, and he'll escape; he'd escape even if you had a bomb here instead of your grenade and took half a garrison with you! I have to come out. And first, just like he wants! That's the only way he'd believe you—if I'm standing next to you!"

Silence. Through the ringing in his ears Adrian thought he heard thin children's voices singing in chorus, far away, a carol.

"She's right," Levko said quietly.

Three kings came from an East-ern la-and, put pre-cious gifts into the Vir-gin's ha-ands ...

She was right, Stodólya had come for her. Stodólya also knew he, Adrian, loved her, and counted on it—that he wouldn't let her die. She was right; she knew him best. She was right, that was the only way—to come out together; to perish together.

I didn't want this, thought Adrian Ortynsky as he collapsed with inaudible din, shattered into pieces, into myriad slivers of his own life, all visible at once and up close like lit windows at night through a field glasses, like a snowstorm splintered into myriad snowflakes—he didn't want this. But his will was no longer there— *Not what I will but what you will. Get up, let us go. See, my betrayer is at hand.* The choir of angels reverberated, the ringing in his ears grew—somewhere far ahead, on the other side of the impossibly dark wall they were to scale, rang St. Sophia's bells, the bells of Heavenly Ukraine for which they were setting out. *Greater love hath no man than this, that a man lay down his life for his friends.* Yes, he thought. Yes. She was right.

He nodded. Very slowly—everything around him instantly became very slow so that no trifle escaped his attention, not one snowflake that swirled before his eyes—he could see them all; he could hold everything at once somehow: the ribbed ebony handle of Raven's SMG, the convex gleam of buttons on their jackets, the crimson remnants of the fire like an ashen bruise over a wound, and the rounded snouts of grenades, sitting dark, alive in their hands. Six grenades between the four of them. Not bad at all.

"Agreed," he said.

And then he felt it stir in the bunker—the breeze of tension that always comes before battle.

Geltsia made the sign of the cross over him, and he also saw the gesture distinctly, like a snowflake under a magnifying glass: his mother made the cross over him like that, when he left home for the last time. He wanted to smile to his bride in death—this was, in a way, their wedding, and the chorus of tiny voices that made the invisible glass sphere of his life crack with a slow ringing sang the wedding hymn for them—but he could no longer smile. Instead, with a senseless, bear-like lurch he suddenly pulled them all by the shoulders together as though he were about to dance the arkán with them here in this tomb—the ancient dance, the warriors' dance in which a single, many-headed body spins in a locked circle, and feet stomp the ground with a single force, faster and faster, and the chain gathers speed, arms on shoulders, shoulder to shoulder, the eternal male dance of their people that's been holding the circle together on this land with an inhuman effort, ever since the days of the Horde, holds the circle that others keep breaking with blood and torment, and it takes more torment and blood to renew it, to find the strength and stomp your ground. It's mine! I won't give it!—here's our circle, we are together at last, my girl, this is it, this is our wedding dance; it was once interrupted, but everything's now set right. We are together again; we've found our music; we've only the finale to play—play it cleanly, without a single fault, because it can't ever be played again …

The last twitch of the hand counting seconds—and the clock stopped.

"We surrender!" Kyi called out from underground. "You win!"

He still heard the noise of movement above—when they skittered, ran up there, barking orders—but he was already thinking with his body alone, wrapping his grenade with the wedding shirt: *She* will walk two steps ahead; I will pull the safety pin out of the grenade. Those above shouted for them to come out with arms in the air, and he pictured their fear—gray, as if a pack of excited rats swirled around the bunker, not entirely sure of its prey, and the rats had to be soothed, so he spoke—or rather someone else spoke from him while he listened—"There's a woman here who requires medical assistance ..."—and these words were as right, mindless, and singularly precise as his movements, and were received by the others as a command. Because he, Kyi, had taken command over them in this moment. He roused them onto their feet, already happier, already weaker; their minds' focus shifted from the imminent order "Fire!" to a new hole in their shoulder-straps: *Ha, we win, the pussy talked them into it!*

This was something they understood, something that accorded with what sent them out trudging through snow and muck in other people's lands and putting to the torch the cities and villages they'd come to hate: some pussy, a fat ration, and everyone afraid of you—they already believed their luck, they were straining their necks and rubbing their hands together, these simple organisms, lower vertebrates that know only the most primitive instincts and destroy anything they can't understand. Although created in God's image, they never did become people, and he felt no hatred for them—hatred had already left him like all other emotions that used to constitute his being—but among them was the man whose heart he felt inside his own like proud flesh, like a second, black heart that continued to beat in this hour, and he had to cut it off, tear it out by the root, excise it. Through the lifted lid flooded the white blaze of military searchlights, blinding them with steam and cold, trained on the bunker and the black female shape rose in his sight, endlessly slowly, in stopped time dammed like a lake with the invisible dark wall before them, and stepped into the light—the cold, devilish light meant not to brighten but to blind—with her arms up in the air, to give him a few extra seconds to regain his scorched-out sight.

His hand squeezed its death grip on the grenade.

What illumination. What quiet.

He was looking from above, from aside, from the night sky—and saw himself: his body stepped out of the bunker holding the white bundle in his hand raised high above his head—and a noise came from nowhere, from the firs as if the forest sighed its farewell, and the cloth wing opened above him in the searchlights like a beating sail as tens of eyes boiled to it.

The world stopped breathing, the Earth held its spin.

He saw the muzzles of machine guns aimed at him from the dark and the figures behind them—below, by the stream, to the sides, among the trees—saw the face of the shepherd dog barking his head off, straining his leash, and Geltsia's profile two steps before him, and the trajectory of her gaze clear as on a ballistic graph—a hyperbola reaching down and behind the firs from where the light beat on them and where a cape stood stiff like a monument, and shapes clustered together. There!—and saw the stillness that came over the scene and lasted for a single endless moment melded into the pause of creation—when only he and Geltsia moved among all the figures frozen in the forest with the lightness of somnambulists on the edge of a roof, turned inward to listen to a musical rhythm audible to them alone—this was enough for him to gain his advantage, exactly as he wanted.

"Him! That's him!"

They no longer paid any attention to the woman.

"Throw down your weapon!"

He dropped his submachine gun.

And that's when they ran to him. Came into motion just as slowly, incomparably more slowly than his consciousness, transported outside his body, commanded—like a pile of black fallen leaves whirling into his eyes. The back of his head felt the burn of hot breath and the dog collar's clang, the hand that was holding the sheaf of light separated from the cape, and the light was coming closer, splitting, along the way, into several distinct figures, and the face that pounded inside him as his second heart—the living, real face with the hooked ax of a nose pulling it forward, the wolfish face with close-set holes for eyes—swam into focus, blocking the light before him: it was coming straight at him, contorted with a wild spasm of terror and joy, and it took him a moment to realize that it wasn't coming at him; no, it was coming at her—at the woman who stood beside him, who, in the rhythm of their inaudible wedding dance, already took her decisive step back before the storm of black fallen leaves.

"Glory to Ukraine!" he said to Stodólya. And relaxed his fingers curled around the grenade's handle. The world, deafened, clicked drily, and a white veil flit as it fell—his wedding shirt's wing.

"Grenade! He's got a grena—!"

"Motherfu—"

"Oh God!"

"Down!"

He did not hear the explosion. Or the two that followed, almost in sync. He only saw the flash, the terrible flash, dazzling beyond what a human brain can endure—as if a thousand suns exploded at once, and the Earth flew up in a single sky-high black wave. He had time to lean forward after his hand offered his enemies the released grenade like a heavy ripe fruit on its open palm. His muscles filled out with the weight of their burden—but everything ahead was already cut off by the blast, and it was only his body that moved for that split second that a body already vacated can propel itself forward before it collapses obeying the force of gravity, while the film, overexposed by the flash, continues to rustle its blank frames inside his skull.

"Gela," he wanted to call.

But he was no more.

Room 7. The Road to Zolotonosha

The Last Interview by Reporter Goshchynska

Who is he, really—Vadym?

He sits across the table from me, heavy and immovable. He always sits like that, wherever he is, as if he were at home where he owns everything—things, and people, even this unsettlingly empty restaurant, like the setting in a Hollywood horror flick, where he has brought me, after he called, in the middle of the night. It actually looks very much like he owns it, because when we came the doors were locked; he pushed a button I hadn't seen and as soon as the doors opened, went straight in, not waiting (and not letting me go first, how rude!), pulling the scarf off his neck (Armani, 100 percent cashmere), saying to his door-opening lackey over the shoulder, as he walked, "Valera, have Mashenka lay the table for us." He didn't ask for the menu, nor did he ask me what I would like, or whether I would like anything at all, and now here he sits, across the table from me, in the large empty room, like Ali Baba in the thieves' cave (it *is* a cave: black lacquer, black leather, backlit surfaces—the all-too-familiar mix of ostentation and grim industrialism that lacks charm but passes for glamour in our latitude). He is capacious and amiable like a shaved, whiskerless walrus, and his breathing is a bit heavy and irregular, as happens to well-nourished men past their prime: an early shortness of breath that, if you're not used to it, might be taken for erotic arousal. Did Vlada like it perhaps? Or maybe he didn't breathe like this back then, with Vlada?

"Stay out of it," he says, looking at me without expression in his eyes, vacant like this restaurant of his (when'd he have time to buy it?). "There are serious people involved. You don't want any part of it."

Serious people. Meaning—those who, should you get in the way of their financial interests, might just whack you, another Ukrainian journalist disappeared without a trace. Or you might end up dead in a car accident, or found dead in your own apartment, a suicide. A woman who could not, for instance, get over being fired, why not? A single woman (the boyfriend is not mentioned in the police protocol), without children, all her life in her work, got a pink slip—and that's it, she couldn't take it, lost her will to live. And the best thing—no one would even think twice about it: a childless woman is a perfect target, keels over without a thump.

How nice of Vadym to warn me. And I, truth be told, after that ill-advised conversation we had, started to think nothing would get to him. And he, in the meantime, did some legwork, took the time to ask around—how kind of him. There are serious people behind the *Miss New TV* show, people whose names no one will ever read in the credits. Like the names of the girls who will come to Kyiv for the contest's preliminary rounds and never make it to the screen, girls who will make it to a completely different place. Not necessarily to foreign brothels even—but right here at home. Someone has to welcome the EU sex tourists and thereby raise the country's attractiveness-to-foreign-investment ratings; someone has to give a donor a blow job while he is speeding home in his SUV from the meeting at campaign headquarters. Serious people, serious business.

Crying's the last thing I need right now, but my nose tickles treacherously, and I begin to breathe hard, like Vadym, hard and fast. We sit facing each other, the two of us, and snuffle like hedge-hogs on a narrow path. We must be quite a sight. But, dear God, what a nasty feeling this is—to know a crime is about to happen, and not be able to stop it.

How much does it cost—one girl? Those who trade in people—how much do they charge for a soul? Why do I not, after ten years of hard-boiled journalism, know these figures? And why can't I now bring myself to ask Vadym, who must know?

Who in the hell is he—Vadym?

All I know is that in his previous life, before he became a serious person himself, he graduated with a degree in history, from Kyiv State U. A useful department it was, history: full of country boys straight from army service who paraded around in double-breasted navy suits with Komsomol pins in their lapels and signed up to rat for the KGB for the love of the game. Now the boys are all well past forty and have a new and improved uniform—an Armani suit and a Rolex on the wrist, a real one. And chauffeur Vasya in the SUV—a distant relative from the native village. Who are all these people, and how did they come to manipulate the lives of millions of others—including mine?

"Have some sausage," Vadym says, nodding at the plate of cold cuts. The slices—beet-red, blood-black, rusty-brown with whitish curlicues of fat—look in the glamorous light like Gothic porn—an installation of vulvas post-coitus. I think I'm going to throw up. Wordlessly I shake my head. Vadym, oblivious, hooks a forkful; a parsley sprig drops from the folded red flesh and remains against the backlit tabletop like an exhibit in a natural history museum. Vadym's always had a good appetite—a sure sign that the man knows how to enjoy life.

I taste the wine: a 2002 Pinot Noir from an Italian winery with an unpronounceable name. A sunny year, Vadym assured me when his lackey brought out the bottle swaddled in a napkin and, following a commanding motion of Vadym's eyebrows, proudly presented it to me, like he was a midwife holding up a newborn for the mother to see. Vadym, as is his custom, is drinking cognac, but he knows his wines. People like him know many inessential things that nevertheless make life undeniably more pleasant. Would their life be utterly intolerable without this pleasantness—like a petrified turd under the milk-chocolate cover of a Snickers bar? The long-forgotten face of R., the way he looked after sex, pops up before my eyes, and I take another sip. Indeed, the wine is superb.

"The opposition won't do anything about this," Vadym explains, moving more food to his plate. "This show won't make a loud case, and it's not good enough for an attack-ad campaign—not much there to work with. This close to elections they want heavy artillery. And your show's just games, small potatoes."

"Human lives, actually," I remind him.

Vadym grows momentarily surly, as if I'd said something tactless, and sets to work on his salmon. I've noticed this habit of his before: not responding to an unpleasant remark as if he hasn't heard it at all. As if the other person farted in public. This is what power really is: the privilege of ignoring anything you find distasteful.

"And if that's how things are," I go on farting, "then what's the difference between your opposition and the goons that are running this country?"

Vadym sizes me up with a quick, short squint over his plate. (Where did I recently see this triumphant look—like a card player dealt a good hand?)

"And what, in your opinion, should it be?"

"It's only in Jewish jokes that you answer a question with a question. I thought we were serious."

Vadym smiles mysteriously, then says, "The same difference, Daryna, as always separates people: some have more money and others have less."

"And you think there are no other differences that separate people?"

"In politics—no," he says firmly.

I can see he is not joking.

"I'm sorry, but what about ideas? Views? Convictions?"

"That was good in the nineteenth century. In the twenty-first—been there, done that."

"That's how it is, huh?"

"And you thought?" he retorts, mimicking my intonation in jest—he's got quick reflexes, like a boxer—and dabs his lips with his napkin: he has large, sensuous lips, almost cartoonish, and they make it hard to notice, at first, what a strong, willful face Vadym has. "All those ideologies that in the nineteenth century set the course for politics for a hundred years ahead have given up the ghost by now. Nationalism is the only one that has survived. And that's only because it relies not on convictions but on emotions."

"So did Communism! It relied on one of the most trivial human emotions of them all—envy. Class hatred, in their parlance. Because you can't make everyone rich, let's make everyone poor so there isn't anyone to be jealous of! Isn't that the way it worked?"

Vadym does not like being contradicted.

"That's the way, but it ain't. Remember Marx? Ideas only become a material force when they've gripped the masses—remember that?"

"Let's say I do, so then what?"

"So, no one ever said what came next. And that was the most interesting part, and the Bolsheviks were the first to catch on to it—Lenin really was a genius.... *How* do you get an idea to grip the masses? The masses never did, and never will, give a flying fuck about ideas, pardon my language—the masses don't want ideas, they want bread and circuses. Like in ancient Rome, and that's how it's always been, and that's how it will always be. It's just that, until now, no society has ever been able to give the masses a steady supply of what they want, the economics weren't there. Developed Western nations today are the first to have come within reach of the ideal: a well-fed citizen sitting down in front of his TV after work with a beer. The running of the country is conducted entirely behind his back; he is only shown talking heads on TV, the floor of the parliament—where people are making speeches, debating, working hard to sway his opinion—and he develops a sense of his own significance, a sense that he matters, that he has a say. So every now and then he goes to vote, casts his ballot, persisting in the illusion that he was the one who elected all those people into office, hired them, that he rules the country. And he is quite pleased with himself—and a person who is pleased with himself will never rebel. That he only cast his ballot for those he saw on TV most often, and at the best angles, never occurs to him. And if it ever does, he'll dismiss the idea on the spot, because it threatens to topple his comfortably ordered world. Do you follow? You don't seem to be eating anything ..."

"I had dinner already, thank you. So what about those ideas that grip the masses?"

"What I'm telling you is there aren't any left in big politics. That's the thing, Daryna. Have some cheese. They're all illusions of the pre-information age—all those socialisms, liberalisms, communisms, and other what-have-you.... The nineteenth century still believed all that—in the last twitches of Enlightenment. But, you can write four-letter words on a wall all you want—it's still a wall, and everything's still behind it. Take the Second World War—it was a clash of two socialisms, the Russian against the German, and who now remembers that? What ideas? Who gives a damn? The masses are not ruled by ideas—they are ruled by certain complex emotions, but even those are not so complex that you couldn't predict and model them. Self-satisfaction, envy, resentment, fear—you've studied psychology, you know this yourself. And ideas in politics—whenever politicians really needed the support of the masses—always had the same function as slogans in advertising: they're triggers."

"Meaning—they affect the subconscious?"

"You got it. They mobilized certain complex emotions and locked them into a short circuit. Like with Pavlov's dogs. You said it right, just then: Communism was a mobilization of envy. Thus, your core constituency is the socially disenfranchised; that's the base you can count on. Everyone knows the best pogrom squads are made of those who'd grown up being pogrommed themselves. Bolsheviks made good use of the Russian Jewry before they secured their power. You mobilize the base with envy, with the desire for revenge—and intimidate the rest, the passive majority, terrorize them to nip resistance in the bud. And that's it; you don't need no ideologies after that."

"Are you trying to tell me that was the Bolsheviks' original plan?"

"That, or something else—what does it matter? The main thing was that Lenin made the brilliant discovery: it's not an ideology that constitutes a material force—it's political technology!" Vadym enunciates the last word with such gusto you'd think it were edible. "You can feed the masses whatever hogwash you want—today one thing, tomorrow another, and the day after something different yet, without any connection to what came before. Today we're dismantling the army, tomorrow we're shooting the deserters; today we're recognizing Ukraine's independence, tomorrow we're installing a puppet government with our bayonets; today we're giving land to the peasants, tomorrow we're taking it away. Any maneuver can be justified by the political goal of the moment, and the masses will keep eating it up. But—only as long as you keep pushing the same button. That is to say, engaging the same complex emotions. And you can keep pushing it till kingdom come if you not only have the means of enforcement in your pocket, but also the media—and Lenin didn't even have television! What you can't do, under any circumstances, is change the button or the whole machine will explode. Gorbachev tried it—and you see what happened?"

"Vadym, you lost me. Are you talking about political history, or the mechanisms by which criminal groups co-opt political power?"

Vadym cringes, but in a friendly way: he heard my fart this time and is letting me know that in the company of serious people it will not be tolerated.

"I am talking about effective politics, Daryna. Have some cheese; it's Brie, good stuff, fresh.... Politics is by definition the struggle for power."

"To what end?"

"What—to what end?" Vadym asks, confused.

"Struggling for power—to what end? To come to it, get it, and sit there? Chase away new contenders? Or is power still a means of implementing certain, forgive me for belaboring the point—ideas? Certain convictions about the way your nation ought to develop and, more generally speaking, about how we can all collectively dig ourselves out from the pile of shit your effective politicians have piled on the human society? I'm sorry, I know I'm spouting banalities here, but I do feel like I'm missing something."

We have never had conversations like this before, Vadym and I. When he called me out of the blue at ten at night—"Hello, Daryna, Vadym here, gotta talk"—and stunned me by declaring he was coming to get me, I could imagine anything (my first thought was, something's happened to Katrusya) other than this lecture on the fundamentals of political cynicism in an empty restaurant. If what he really wanted to do was to warn me, he could have done that on the phone. And yet somehow I am not surprised; I am playing right along, dutifully posing my questions. As if I were interviewing him for the cameras. (Do they have security cameras, I wonder?) As if one day I were going to bring this interview before Vlada who stands, an invisible shadow, between us: she is the one who left Vadym to me—like a question to which she failed to find an answer.

Vadym finishes chewing unhurriedly, dabs his lips with the napkin again, folds it neatly, and puts it down beside his plate. Then he raises his eyes to me—a statesman's weary gaze, a mix of boredom, lenity, irony, and pity.

"Do you think that Bush lost sleep over saving the world? Or Schroeder, after he stuck his country on the Russians' gas needle? Or Chirac? Or Berlusconi?"

"What's gas got to do with anything? Even if they're all rotten bastards it doesn't automatically mean that ..."

"Whoa, now!" Vadym cuts in, beginning to enjoy himself. "What do you mean, what's gas got to do with it? Power is access to energy sources, my dear! Fuel is the key to world domination—always has been, always will be."

"I seem to remember hearing this before, somewhere—the thing about world domination ..."

Again Vadym squints at me with the directed gaze of an attentive, always internally focused person. (Where, where did I see this look? Night, darkness, reddish reflections of fire on people's faces ...)

"If Hitler's who you have in mind, his case is actually the best proof that having an idea can only undermine a serious politician. Really, ideas are counter-indicated. Of ideas, poor Adolf, unfortunately, had plenty—and believed in them, to make things worse."

For an instant, I despair: it's like Vadym and I are speaking two different languages, using the same words that have different meanings for each of us, and I don't know how to disentangle myself from this confusion. And he is on a roll, words are spilling out of him, and he is clearly enjoying the process—how smoothly and evenly it all comes out.

"It was from the Bolsheviks that Hitler learned the most important thing—the technology of manipulating the masses. And the button he found was good, too: national resentment, the Weimar defeat complex. Plus the same envy of the socially disenfranchised that the Bolsheviks exploited. And there he had it—the German nation of workers and peasants, and on an order of magnitude more successful, by the way, than the one the Russians had built. If Hitler hadn't had a brain-fuck, excuse me, on the idea of winning world domination for his beloved German people—and that's a totally demented idea; no *people* can dominate the world, only corporations can, and that's how it has always been and always will be—if he hadn't had, to put it simply, a bunch of idiotic fantasies in his head, history would've have taken a different course. And the US today would mean no more than Honduras. Or, say, New Zealand."

"So what then, Adolf fucked up?"

Vadym does not share my irony.

"Exactly. Fucked up. There was a reason Stalin couldn't, until the very last moment, believe that Hitler would attack him. He couldn't fathom that a politician of that stature could turn out to be such an ideological dickhead, like a green student radical or something. They could have—couldn't they?—just divided the world into spheres of influence as they'd agreed in '39, and everything would've been fine. A lot less blood would've been spilled, too. Back in my university days, I wrote my thesis on the Battle of Kursk—I tell you, that was a horrific business: if you didn't know better, you'd think the only thing either side cared about was how to kill more of its own soldiers. There you have your ideas."

"Is there any chance it might matter *what* those ideas are?"

"Whatever you want them to be, Daryna! In politics, all they do is stand in the way—they're noise. Trust me; I've been handling this shit for years. And without gloves," he clarifies as if this were some especially sophisticated exclusive he were giving me. "We're on the verge of a new world order—the status quo that emerged after World War II has long been pushed to its limits, the Yalta epoch has exhausted itself. Think about it, you're a smart woman. Do you honestly believe that toppling the Twin Towers was the homespun work of a handful of demented Arabs from nowhere? And that Bush, who, by the way, has old family business ties to the Saudi oil sheiks, went into Iraq to save the world? And the apartment buildings blown up in Ryazan when Putin needed to send the Taman Guards to Chechnya, a division recruited from that same Ryazan—is that not the same scenario? Only they did a sloppier job in Russia, and everyone knows that those explosions were FSB's handiwork. But it's too late now; the deed's done. The way to the Caspian oil pipeline's been cleared—Georgia's still fussing underfoot, but it'll be its turn soon. Now one of your journalist people over in the States is making a movie about September 11—trying to prove the whole thing was a political provocation, and that Bush knew about it ahead of time ..."

"You mean Michael Moore?" I remember I saw the headline on a news crawl somewhere—about the film's presentation at the Cannes Film Festival, where I am no longer going. "I wouldn't think you followed that kind of news. So, is there a hypothesis about *who* engineered that provocation?"

Again, a quick triumphant flame flares up in Vadym's eyes—as if he himself were one of the provocation's authors. "Who it was, Daryna, no one will find out for the next ten to twenty years. Until the new redistribution of the energy-source markets is over. And that Moore guy won't prove anything to anyone, mark my word."

"Why do you think that?"

"Because—again—it's too late! The button has been pushed, the masses mobilized: they were shown very real horror on television, and they got scared. Bunched together into a herd. And no journalistic investigation can now convince them that that was precisely the goal—to have them bunch together into a herd and put their fate in the shepherd's hands. On the contrary. Now, the more American blood is spilled in Iraq, the more trust there will be for the administration because it is the hardest thing for people to admit that their loved ones died for nothing. Nothing glues a nation together like spilled blood: the USSR was sealed in the same way—by the Great War. And Bush, you can be sure, will get reelected for a second term this fall. That's the reality, Daryna. And all the talk about liberal democracy, or the Party's dictatorship, or whatever—it's all crap, forget it. The politics of today is an amalgamation of the experience of twentieth-century superpowers and the experience of the marketplace, of advertising. An immensely powerful combination, if you know how to use it."

"Precisely. Orwell wrote about it, back in the day."

Vadym ignores Orwell like another fart.

"This is a very serious shift, Daryna. A historical one. The masses no longer choose an idea, or a slogan—they are choosing *a brand*. And they're not doing their choosing rationally either— they vote purely with their emotions. Bread and circuses? Here you go—public politicking itself becomes a circus! What are presidential debates if not the same old gladiator fights? September 11 is the most successful reality show in history: every soul on Earth who could find a TV set watched it. Putin is a TV superhero now, and seventy percent of Russian women have erotic dreams about him. In Stalin's days, they threw people in jail for dreams like that. A public politician today is a showman first and foremost, the registered trademark of the company behind him."

"And the company—who is that?"

"A corporation of those who do the actual governing," Vadym answers calmly. "The world has always been ruled by such corporations. Only the post-information society is much easier to rule than societies were sixty years ago. He who ensures the best show for the masses wins. He who, to put it bluntly, puts the picture into the TV. Meaning, ultimately, whoever has the most money. And that's that."

"You really believe that?"

Vadym smiles. He does have a really nice smile.

"Believing belongs in church. And Daryna, I am used to dealing with things that are real. You just remember that history is made by money. That's how it's always been and will be."

An unpleasant chill begins to fill me, like in a dentist's waiting room when I was little.

"The Soviet Union had enough money to wipe its ass with it," I tell him, mustering as much crudity as possible. "And fat lot of good it did them."

"Whoa there one minute!" Vadym exclaims, astonished. "Half the world under control—that's not good enough for you? You couldn't swing a dead cat in the twentieth century without hitting Soviet cash! Take even what happened in '33—Stalin got the West right where he wanted them when he flooded the world market with all that genocidal Ukrainian wheat! And remember, it was the Great Depression—d'you think Roosevelt just happened to roll over and recognize the USSR exactly then? There's your fat lot of good, right there. In '47, Moscow sent grain to France in silk sacks, and French Communists waved those like flags at the elections: look how the working class in the USSR lives! All those Western Communist parties, leftist movement, terrorism, Red Brigades, all the rumbles in the third-world jungles—do you think it all fed and clothed itself? No, dear, the hand of Moscow could be very, very generous when it needed to be. And not a single peep from anyone—so, alright, they let a couple dissidents out, and maybe the Jews stood up for their own, but that's it; that's your entire Cold War right there ... Americans can tell themselves they won it all they want since it makes them so happy—but they're living in a fool's paradise. In reality, if oil prices hadn't collapsed in the eighties, and if the Politburo hadn't started squabbling, you and I would still be living in the USSR. You can be sure about that."

He is talking like a sports commentator reflecting on the rise and fall of some team like Manchester United, and in that regard I also hear something else in his voice: the time-tested ardor of a soccer fan, a boy's admiration for the forward—the same intonations with which old retired military remember the USSR. There are so many of them—people who are always ready to see all kinds of good in any crime as long as it goes unpunished.

"That's exactly what I am not so sure about." For some reason, my voice goes low; shit, could I possibly be nervous? "I know nothing about any squabbling in the Politburo, but as far as I can tell, if one were to try to find a single reason for why the USSR collapsed, it was under the burden of its own lies. All of it, accumulated over seventy years. Because virtual reality—it is this thing, I'm here to tell you, that can hit back very hard if you play with it for too long. You can't keep lying and maintain your own sense of how things really are at the same time. If you keep ordering a certain picture on TV, you eventually start believing it yourself. Inevitably. And that's the end of any, as you call it, actual governing—exactly what happened in the USSR. And this Politburo of yours, a corporation of senile old men ..."

"It's not mine," Vadym grins, warming a glass of cognac in his paws. "But it does fit the definition of a corporation, I'll give you that."

That's praise—as if he were assessing my performance in his mind, like a judge at an art show or a violin recital. Putting pluses in some imagined columns next to my name. And this, for some reason, really pisses me off.

"So then, this *corporation* of yours was made up of zombies who'd zombied themselves so thoroughly they knew nothing about the country they ruled! They thought Armenians were Muslims—remember that big shot from Moscow who let that drop in Nakhchevan? The FSB still can't bring itself to believe that Ukraine is independent—they keep waiting for their made-up picture to come back on. Governors, my ass! Like blind butchers in a slaughterhouse.

"Some folks I know interviewed Fedorchuk not too long ago—the head of the Ukrainian KGB under Brezhnev, he's living out his days in Moscow now—with not a soul to talk to, his son shot himself, wife also committed suicide, and to him it's all like water off a duck: like they'd catapulted the dude to Mars decades ago, and he just stayed there—spent all his life in virtual reality. By the way, it was on his watch they packed my father off to the loony bin.... And do you know what this mummy remembers before he dies, the most important thing in his life? That he put up a new departmental apartment building for the KGB in Kyiv: made sure all his cronies had a place to live! My jaw dropped when I heard it: what kind of a Gestapo chief is that? I thought he'd at least lash out at the nationalists he used to fight, you know, regret that he didn't quite finish them bastards off, since now they've brought the great country down. But he couldn't care less—the only reality he had and still has is this one: a departmental apartment building. A family corporation, like the mob. Beyond that, the world doesn't exist for these people; that's how they see it—like a picture they chose for themselves, and on which they can push the delete button if they want to. Not much by way of ideas there, you're right! What kind of government can there be with ideas like that? You're a historian, Vadym," I resort to my last argument (like all serious people who didn't start out as goons, Vadym likes pointing out his former "civilian" vocation).

"You don't need to be reminded how that corporate country burst, like a soap bubble, every time it came face to face with a reality on which it couldn't press its delete button. That's exactly what happened at the beginning of the war, only Hitler helped them out that time, by turning out to be a worse zombie yet—folks took a good look at what rolled into their backyards and went to fight for real. And in our own memory—when Chernobyl blew up: an idiot could see that the system was on its last legs, an idiot would've known people should have been evacuated from the contaminated area. But these zombies herded children to the Labor Day parade in Kyiv, and the KGB was running around like the proverbial chicken with its head cut off, desperately recruiting new finks because it ran out of the ones it already had ... pressing the same old buttons, as you say. Lies can get you to the end of the world, but they can't bring you back, thank God. You can't keep raping reality with impunity; sooner or later it will take its revenge, and the later it comes, the more terrifying it will be. You don't kid around with these things, Vadym!"

All of a sudden, Vadym starts laughing—with his entire body at once. His monumental bust in its Armani suit coat shudders above the table like Etna, with subterranean jolts; his face contorts pathetically, as if he were chopping onions, and looks so comical that I, too, can't help smiling—making both of us look rather stupid. Vadym nods to a long-legged, long-necked, and black-clad young woman who has appeared, like a miniature giraffe, out of thin air next to our table. "Ice cream, Mashenka."

From his mouth, this comes out as warmly as "sausage" did a bit earlier. Mashenka, before disappearing, shoots me, from the height of her triangular face—a Cubist's dream—a professionally manufactured smile, a mirror image of my own momentary grin, and, at the same time, a sharp, wary look of the territory's mistress who is about to leave an untrustworthy guest alone with her male: this is mine, don't touch it. Wow. Did he really find the time to put his stakes down here, too? She's pretty stylish, Mashenka is; she could've been a model … wow again. What about the massaging Svetochka now?

"At least you still have taste," I tell Vadym vindictively, following his little black giraffe with my eyes as she leaves the room.

He pretends he didn't hear, and pours me more wine. He does stop laughing, though. Only breathes heavier and louder than before. Exercise, you need to exercise more, Vadym—what kind of shape are you in, breathing like that at your age? While Vlada was alive, he and I always used to be a little caustic with each other, but back then I wrote it off to the natural jealousy every man feels toward his wife's girlfriend, an owner's reflex—so now I keep pushing. "You own this restaurant, don't you?"

"What if I do?" Vadym replies, looking slyly around the brightly lit, black-lacquer cave and squinting like a cat that's trying to get you to pet him. "Do you like it?"

Now, this is a look I remember exactly where I've seen before— that's what my boss looked like when he waited for me to praise him at his housewarming, signaling at me with his eyes across a giant room full of people: applaud me now, go ahead, applaud, confirm to me that it hasn't been all in vain—give my marathon swim through shit its long overdue justification.

So is this what Vadym's brought me here for—to show off his new acquisition, to get my approval—you're on the right path, comrade? Now I finally catch on to something I should've caught on to long ago (for the smart woman Vadym believes me to be, I can sometimes be incredibly daft): for him, I have replaced Vlada in the bar-setter's role—if I approve, she would have approved, too. And then everything's okay, and Vadym's life is back in tip-top shape. That's what he wants; that's what he is trying to extract from me. He doesn't miss a beat, this guy. He's a bull!

Do you have to be a toothless old hag to stop falling into the same trap—to stop mixing up *strength* and *resilience* in men? In every war there is but one law: the strong die and the resilient survive. There's no special accomplishment in that, no credit to be given them; it's the genetic programming they were born with—to survive: like the lizard that grows back its tail, or the earthworm that regenerates its lost segments. Vadym, who so recently appeared to be utterly annihilated by Vlada's death, has put himself back together like the damaged Terminator—by disassembling his dead wife into the various critical functions she performed for him and redistributing them to other women: N.U., Katrusya, several Svetochkas and Mashenkas, to each her own, like in Buchenwald, and only the niche of the bar-setter ("How am I going to live now? She set the bar for me ..."), the one to whom you bring your life like homework to be graded, to receive, in return, a clear conscience and untroubled sleep—this extraordinarily important niche in every Ukrainian man's life has been, for Vadym, unfilled, and he must be feeling a constant discomfort emanating from that spot. No one will tell him the truth now—he's got too much money for that. But I—I'm always there. I'm Vlada's closest friend, and I want nothing from him; I'm the perfect fit. And should I be inclined to blurt out something contrarian—well, that's exactly why he's given me, completely for free, his very valuable piece of advice: keep quiet.

Now I am supposed to pay him back for this favor, tit for tat, a fair trade! I am supposed to applaud his new acquisition without interrogating him about where he found the dough for the new glam digs (especially right now, when the powers that be are taxing everything that moves to fund their anti-Yushchenko campaign, which is beginning to look like an actual war and not just a publicity war, and Vadym's ostensibly part of the opposition, if I'm not mistaken, so what fairy godmother waved her wand and conjured this restaurant?). I should praise the interior design and Mashenka and whatever else, whip up a bunch of compliments and ensure for him the aforementioned clear conscience and untroubled sleep. And I should not, God forbid, ask what the hell he wants from this fucking restaurant, and why, once he had money to spare, he didn't put it—toward his dead woman's memory, as she had dreamed of doing ("when I have real money, Daryna ...")—into any of the squalid pig-farm barns our museums have become: the National right here, for one, where to this day they can't give what survived of the Boichuk School the space it deserves; or the Hanenki, out of which you could, if you fancied, lift a Velázquez or a Perugino as easily as canvases out of a crashed car—oh, the list goes on and on! That's what Vlada would have told him. But I won't because I don't have the right to. And he knows that. He knows, and waits, and squints with pleasure in advance—like a cat about to be scratched behind the ear by the mouse he's caught. How can you not love the guy?

"You, Vadym, are an amazing piece of work."

He instantly takes this for the compliment he feels due, swallows said compliment like a morsel off his plate—gulp!—and brightens up so sweetly that only a complete bitch wouldn't feel disarmed. "You shouldn't have turned down the dinner! My chef has three international diplomas, beat a French guy at a contest in Venice last year."

Dare I hope he is not about to take me to view those diplomas?

"As I said, I've eaten already."

"And now you're missing out; you can be sure about that. You have to join me for dessert, at least."

"Uhu, as my granny used to say, 'you haven't eaten an ox until someone saw you do it.'"

"Mh-hm," Vadym agrees, either because he doesn't get it or because he didn't quite hear me. "Our grandparents lived through some real tough times, what can you say...?"

And that's why now we take such pride in what we eat, I think but do not say out loud—1933, 1947—it's all stowed away somewhere inside us, coded into our cell memory, and the children and grandchildren, delirious with the sudden abundance of the nineties are now busy growing new segments, like the earthworms—catching up for everything uneaten in the generations before them. Only it's as if there's been an error in the genetic code, a mutation that's been selecting for the most resilient, the best at chewing and digesting, and it is now they who fill our city with the petrified refuse of their gigantic intestines: restaurants, bistros, taverns, pubs, diners, and snack bars multiply at every step like mushrooms after the rain, only dentist's office marquees can compete with the eateries in their intrusive density, and if one were to stroll around Kyiv with nothing particular to do (only who now can go strolling like that, with nothing to do), one might very well think that people in this city do nothing but eat, eat—and have their teeth sharpened so they can eat some more.

R., too, took great pleasure in talking about the delicacies he ate in Hong Kong, and the ones in the Emirates, and others in New York, in some stratospheric establishment where they don't even give you a menu you just order whatever comes to mind, and don't ask about the price. "And do they really just get you whatever you ask for?" I asked him. "They certainly do," R. assured me with dignity. "What if it's an endangered species? Komodo dragon brains? Siberian tiger steak? Or something more environmentally friendly, perhaps—charcuterie of donor kidneys, chopped out of some Albanians or Mongolians no one bothers to count?" R. laughed. And when I asked him, up front, how many starving people could be fed for the price of that one dinner, he took offense and called it bigotry. Although he, unlike Vadym, wasn't even a bit heavy.

This is who they are, these serious people—all those who, after the Soviet Union's collapse, rushed to rake in never-before-seen capitals, first as cash knitted into their undershorts, and later as transfers to offshore accounts—this is who they are: the descendants of a pogrom. The kind of pogrom modern history couldn't fathom, and which, for that very reason, it failed to see or acknowledge when it happened in its own time, simply pressed the delete button. And now it is too late, they have arrived—the ones who, as Vadym said, make up the best pogrom squads. They have arrived and will take revenge on the new century for the mounds of deleted corpses from the past, spawning similarly deleted mounds of new corpses, and never suspecting that they themselves constitute a mutation—a tool of revenge. Flagellum Dei, the scourge of God (where did I just hear this phrase?). They have magnificent teeth, brand new titanium implants, and are insatiable like the iron locusts of the Apocalypse: they have come to eat, and they will eat until they burst—until their titanium teeth grind everything in their path into dust.

Suddenly I feel so tired, as if all the air had been let out of me. As if he'd sucked me dry, this Vadym—although it is not at all clear how he could've managed that. A growing ache buzzes at the back of my head; I try to hold it straight. The black-giraffe Mashenka brings ice cream in silver flutes—his own ice cream, made in house, Vadym continues to brag, from that same wonder chef.

"Taste it, you won't regret it. Have you ever had homemade ice cream?"

Rich, thick-enough-to-cut-with-a-knife ice cream, yellowish like cream, does have an unusual taste—like the taste of country cooking: something filling, dense, unrefined and fragrant, from an era before plastics. One helping of this is enough to keep you full for a day. Obediently, I say this to Vadym. He nods like a professor happy with a student's answer on an exam.

"Now this, Daryna," he suddenly says didactically, "is the reality."

"What—the ice cream?"

"And the ice cream, too." He is no longer smiling. "All this," he looks over his cave again, "and many other things. The ice cream, by the way, is all-natural, made with real milk. No chemical dyes, no GMOs. You know what gee-em-Os are?"

"I've seen that abbreviation before ..."

"Genetically modified organisms. The ones that are winning a growing share of the world's food market and our national market as well. Soy beans, potatoes with scorpion genes ..."

"Good Lord, why scorpion?"

"So the bugs won't eat them. And they don't. But we do, all of Polyssya has been planted over with those potatoes. Western importers are dumping all this shit on us with no restrictions or controls whatsoever; another generation—and we'll have the same problems with obesity as Americans do today. And in a few more generations on such a diet we might very well start growing tails, or, say, hooves, no one can tell for sure which in advance."

"Come on, that's straight out of Hollywood!"

"Yes!" Vadym responds, inexplicably encouraged. "Now we're getting somewhere. You were so full of fire and brimstone when you were talking about reality and how one doesn't kid around with it, you almost had me. You're good! You nailed it, as if from the screen. But what is it—this reality? To listen to you, it's a ... a ..." he hesitates for an instant, uncertain outside his regular vocabulary, "a fetish. As if reality existed separately, all by itself."

"Doesn't it, though?"

"For some village grandma—it may very well indeed. But you, of all people, ought to realize that reality is manufactured by people. And you can't draw the boundary anymore between what you call reality and what's been manufactured," he slows down again, looking for words: he is not used to abstractions, "realities that have been manufactured by people."

"Simulacra?"

Damn that silver tongue of mine! This is not a word Vadym knows—and for a few seconds he studies me with the unblinking antipathy of a redneck whose first instinct is to suspect treachery every time he runs into something unknown. (This momentary clash—as if he and I had rammed into each other at full tilt—makes me instantly dizzy; the world, shaken, lurches into motion like sloshing water, and a queer sense of someone else's invisible presence flickers by, a near presence, somewhere by my side, where I don't dare turn my suddenly aching head.)

"It's postmodern theory," I hear my own voice say, also as if from somewhere beside me. "Media, advertising, the Internet—they are simulacra. Phantom phenomena that do not bear a direct relationship to reality, but together constitute a parallel reality, the so-called hyperreality. A famous theory—Baudrillard wrote about it. He was French."

"See!" hearing that he, by himself, came to the same conclusions as a famous Frenchman, Vadym regains magnanimity. "That's what I'm telling you. Just then, when you didn't believe me, you said, Hollywood, and that's perfectly normal, that's a normal reaction. It's harder now to believe the truth than something made up. Any truth is the result of so many complicated moves and connections, with so many of those moves hidden, that a regular guy could never dream of making any sense of it. And something made up, a fiction—that's what they call a slam dunk, every time. And the more information there is out there, the more regular people will favor simple solutions."

"Occam's razor?"

"That's it. Tell the public that Kuchma ordered a journalist killed because the man had criticized him—and everyone will believe it. Because that's what dictatorship always looks like in movies. But if you tell them it was a special operation of several intelligence services, one whose geopolitical significance for the region could be compared to that of the Balkan war—and people'll look at you like you're nuts."

"So was it really an intelligence operation?"

"Doesn't matter!" Vadym cuts me off, lips holding back a smile that threatens to slither out like a worm, and that same sensation, of a rocked vestibular apparatus, undercuts me again: a splash, a giant mudslide, the solid ground under my feet slipping apart like fissured ice.

He is bewitching me. He is bedeviling me, like a professional seducer, so that I won't know what to believe—this must be how he gets all the women: by robbing them, step by step, of their footing, turning the ground beneath their feet into shifting gray sand like in that dream Vlada had, and once he has, all that's left for his bewildered victim to do is to throw herself onto his broad chest: he is a wall of a man, the solitary rock among a fog of phantoms! A powerful erotic move, to be sure, but where, damn it, have I met a man exactly like this before (*not* R., R. was simpler)—with the same calmly assaulting manner of persuading and subjecting others, even with the same cunning glint of insanity in his eye? (A patient in a faded grayish gown whom I saw looking at me, a fifteen-year-old, in the yard of the Dnipropetrovsk loony bin, grinning as if he knew everything about me—all the worst, the stuff that would never in a million years even occur to Mom who went twaddling on about something pathetic; neither would it occur to her that a visit to my father could evoke in me any feelings different from her own, and that I, boiling with tears of rage, stood there thinking that my mother was a fool and my father had abandoned me, had betrayed me for the sake of his own, terrible grown-up business that was more important to him than I was, and had become this helpless desiccated old man with murky eyes. At that moment, I hated them both, with all the fervor of teenage resentment, and that's when it hit me, head on, blinding me—the look of that other character who grinned as if *he had read my mind,* and I went cold—and only later saw what it was he held in his hand tucked under the loose hem of his robe.)

"Take another example," Vadym pours out more of his sand. "The White House announced that Iraq had weapons of mass destruction—and everyone believed it. And never mind that they still haven't found those weapons—and, most likely, won't. They'll be morons, of course, if they don't; if it were the Russians, they would've planted some right away, and then no one would ever dig up what actually happened. There you have your reality. And you say—bad governors. No, my dear, the effectiveness of a government must be judged according to the tasks that the government sets for itself. The stuff that goes out to the public—that's not an indicator, you can't pay attention to that."

He lied to her, I suddenly realize. He lied to Vlada. I don't know how, I don't know what about, but I know it as clearly as if the right switch finally flipped in my mind and the light came on: he lied. And was perfectly effective at it—Vlada lived with this simulacrum for three years and did not notice it. Only close to the end did she begin to suspect something—all her works from the last year of her life were full of a growing premonition of a catastrophe. Her best works, the ones that triggered such a fit of anger in Aidy's artworm (I still blush at the recollection of that ugly scene). And not in him alone—few in Ukraine appreciated Vlada's *Secrets*, something about the series transgressed the boundaries of the acceptable.

An intimate knowledge of darkness—that's what they contained. Her *Secrets*—of darkness made home, warmed by a feminine hand—adorned with flowers and decoupage, like a wolf's lair hung about with elaborate patchwork quilts, her *own* darkness. Mixed media, the mysteriously shimmering collages by the girl who stood at the edge of the abyss and looked down with a child's thrill—until she got dizzy. As I am getting right now.

He is shrouding me in his language, this Vadym—it's like a cloud of marijuana smoke. I can't contradict him: I do not, in fact, know anything, let alone have any of the intimate familiarity, about all that hidden machinery of big politics that he keeps hinting at—with passing, shifty references I can't quite grip; I have no logical crutch I could lean on to help myself scatter this verbal fog—I am only sensing a fundamental *untruth* hidden in it, and this hypnotic cocoon in which he is ensnaring me is paralyzing my will, as though taking away my command of my own body. The bifurcation point, a phrase from Aidy's vocabulary, shoots through my mind: this is the point at which women undress for Vadym. Or tell him to fuck off.

And, pretending that Aidy is watching me (and I am savoring, in advance, the story I'll have to tell him when I get home), I improvise a husky, deep chuckle—in the big, empty dining room, it sounds more defiant than conspiratorial—"Why are you telling me all this, Vadym?"

Oh, what a look he gives me! A man's look, sizing me up, taking direct aim—a look that'll make your knees buckle!

"Are you bored?" he changes tack abruptly.

"No, but it's late already."

Music begins to play, low. "Hotel California," an instrumental version. Mashenka must've put it on. Must be the way they do things here: put on music for dessert. It triggers the necessary complex emotions in the current object of wooing. Like in one of Pavlov's dogs.

"Have you got someplace to be?"

"Just tired you know."

"You'll sleep in tomorrow. You're not getting up for work, are you?"

Such a lovely place, such a lovely place, such a lovely face ...

"Pardon?"

"Didn't you resign? You don't work in TV anymore. You don't work anywhere, do you?"

God! It's like my plane drops into an air pocket. Uncontrollably, my jaw drops: what a brilliant tactician he is! One could see what got Vlada, especially in contrast to Katrusya's father, the newly minted Australian kangaroophile who'd spent the entire span of their marriage on a couch in front of the TV.

"You are well informed indeed. So you weren't making your inquiries only about the beauty pageant?"

"Does it bother you?" he glows modestly: it's always nice to knock your neighbor down a rung or two, lest she think too highly of herself.

"You could've just asked me—I'm not making a secret out of it. Or do you perhaps think that I could have gone on working there? In full knowledge of what they were doing?"

I hear how weak that sounds—like I'm making excuses. In this game, as in any kind of business, the what is not important, and neither is the how—the important thing is who got there first. A lead automatically means a better position. Vadym got ahead of me when he found out about my resignation behind my back—and now I'm forced to justify myself, and my obsession with that despicable beauty pageant begins to look not entirely unimpeachable (Could it be retaliation by a disgruntled employee perhaps, instead of simple righteous indignation?)—and he is looking at me like that Dnipropetrovsk nut, as if he knows something about me that's so dirty I'll never be clean again. As they say in American movies, anything you say or do can and will be held against you.

From this moment on, Vadym owes me nothing; the moral advantage is on his side. And all I'm left to do is applaud his brilliantly calculated timing—and prepare to hear what else he's got in store for me: this is no longer my interview, I'm not the one asking questions, our roles have reversed.

"What are you thinking of doing next? Have anything in mind yet?"

"I don't know, I haven't thought about it."

"You better start. The clock's ticking. The reshuffling of the media market is in full swing, the cushiest gigs are up for grabs right now. Closer to the elections you'll be looking at leftovers and rejects."

"Somehow, I don't feel compelled to get reshuffled to accommodate the elections."

"What else do you want?" he asks, surprised. "An election cycle is an injection of money! Good money, Daryna. It's like in the ocean where at different depths different currents begin to form, some stronger, some weaker. This is your chance to ride the one that'll take you to the top. Later will be too late. And you, I'm sorry, won't be getting any younger either."

Knocking the last stool from under me. Bingo.

"So, do think about it. I, by the way, might be able to put someone with your experience to good use."

So this is what we've taken our sweet time getting to. All this was mere exposition for the main plot, and the plot comes now—

plain as nails: I am being bought. I am unemployed: naked and available. On the block.

And for some reason, I'm terrified. Inside, a sickening chill blasts just below my breasts—as if *they* have come for me. (Who? The human figures with wolf heads I imagined were behind the door of my bedroom when I was little, Goya's monsters, mad paramedics, machine-gunners with dogs?) As if all my fears that until this instant had been scattered across my life like shadows on a sunny day rose at once and stood to their full height, leaned all together against an invisible divider and flipped my life to the other side—and now it seems there has never been anything in it, except these fears, not a glimmer of sunshine. Catacombs, dungeons. An artificially lit cave. (Someone will throw the switch now—and it will turn dark, and I'll never find my way out of this darkness; I will remain here forever, for Vadym to do with as he pleases.)

"I mean that show of yours, about unknown heroes," he says suavely. "Diogenes' something …"

"*Diogenes' Lantern.*"

"Oh yes, lantern. Was he the guy who went around with a lantern looking for a man? Not bad, only you got too clever there; you gotta keep it simple for the common folks. But the way you created those heroes out of nothing—that was awesome! Super professional work."

"Thank you. Only I wasn't making anything out of nothing. They were all amazing people—every person I ever made a show about."

"Whatever. You know how to package a person—how to turn some Joe Schmo into a cult figure. You've got, as they say, the sales pitch. I still remember your show about that priest who keeps an orphanage and how those retarded kids call him Daddy …"

"Not retarded. There was only one kid with Down syndrome."

(The boy with Down syndrome was already a grown, stout, wide-shouldered youth with the cognitive development of a two-year-old—he laughed, pushed to grab on to the shiny eye of the camera, and hooted, again and again, the same line from a VV song, "Spring comes! Spring comes! Spring comes!"—and somehow was not in the least bit repulsive to look at, made so, perhaps, by the presence of the priest who adored his charge with a real fatherly tenderness, as though he could see in him something invisible to the rest of us. "Let every thing that hath breath praise the Lord," the priest said, and it came out sounding especially beautiful somehow, so that I, the sentimental cow that I am, got all teary-eyed: every creature born to this world has the right to live and be happy praising the Lord, and what ever made us think that some of us are better, and others are worse? And then I remember that Vadym has a son from his first marriage—from that woman who lost her mind, and he sent the boy to study in England: to an orphanage, one could say, only of a different kind, a five-star one. Whom does that boy call Daddy there?)

"And are you aware of the fact that later, when the local elections came around, three parties fought each other for that priest's endorsement?"

"Can't be! I'd never ..."

"Exactly. You'd never. You made him a public figure, a moral authority. Who was he before you discovered him? Just another ragtag village priest, without voice or power. And then you made your show—and he's a spiritual shepherd! Pilgrims from the whole region mob his church; bigwigs roll up in SUVs, bringing their children. We'll do as Father says! And you say it wasn't out of nothing!"

"You have a strange way of looking at things, Vadym. My role was not at all as critical as you see it."

"Oh, stop it. Modesty, as a friend of mine says, is the shortest path to anonymity." Vadym pauses to give me the opportunity to appreciate the joke and when he doesn't get a reaction (my head's humming like a power substation), winks at me: "And you were a star! And could remain one."

"You want me to help you create heroes, is that it?"

He looks at me almost gratefully—did I save him from further verbal exertion?

"Precisely."

Another pause. A kind of very slow approach—millimeter by millimeter, so as not to startle his prey, except that his breathing gets louder. (I heard a man breathe like this once, the two of us were in the same train compartment: I woke up in the middle of the night because he, breathing like a horse, was very carefully, so as not to wake me, pulling the covers off me before dashing back to his berth, the instant I, scared to death, stirred and mumbled something as if still half asleep.)

"A political project. Image focused. We'll put together a strong team, with first-class foreign experts; you'll love it. Naturally, they will all work behind the scenes. What's needed is a public face, sort of like a press secretary. But it can't be just a pretty face; it has to be someone who knows what they're doing. Someone from inside the kitchen, so to speak."

"And what will that kitchen be cooking?"

He nods in approval: we've finally gotten to the heart of the matter.

"This information cannot be made public yet. In the elections, besides the two main contenders—from the establishment and the opposition—there will be a number of technical candidates."

"Meaning what?"

"What—the usual. Candidates who are there to divert votes from the front-runner."

"From Yushchenko?!"

Now I really don't understand anything. Isn't Vadym a member of Yushchenko's coalition?

"Give me a break, Daryna!" he cringes, and I shudder: it's Vlada's phrase, part of her vocabulary, that's where he got it! "Yushchenko, while we're on the subject, is also, you could say, a technical candidate. In a way ..."

"What on earth are you talking about?"

"I am talking about the fact that things are much more complicated than they appear to you. Than what they look like from the outside. And even if Yushchenko wins, although that's more than doubtful, his victory won't be the end of the game that's going on, you can be sure of that. Yushchenko got propelled to the top by a whole series of favorable circumstances, he's always had luck; you might say he's charmed." At this last word, Vadym's voice twangs with a barely audible note of envy, like the ding of chipped glass. "But there's no *corporation* behind him. The ones backing him as a viable candidate today are all the disgruntled ones, the ones Kuchma left standing with nothing when he divvied up the property. And a coalition like that, as you can surely see yourself, cannot last. If Yushchenko does manage, by some miracle, to win, all hell will break loose—the ones who ride his coattails to parliament will waste no time wresting the steering wheel away from him."

"And you decided not to wait until after the elections?"

Lord, my head hurts!

"And I," Vadym doesn't take offense, only swirls the cognac in his glass unnecessarily fast—with a short, slightly nervous circular motion. "I attempt to take a broader view. And to benefit from any outcome. And I would advise you to do the same. What does it ultimately matter if it's Kuchma, or Yushchenko, or someone else, or the next guy? You can't teach a pig to sing. Think about it, who are we, really? A former colony, with no statehood tradition of our own, knee-deep in shit. A transit zone. In the current global scheme of things, that's our only asset: we are a country conveniently located for transit. And that's where we can earn our commission—and trust me, it's not pennies. The future outlook is not too shabby either, if one knows how to use one's head."

"What kind of outlook do we have if no one cleans up the shit?"

"You're not paying attention," he chides me. "I told you, the Yalta era is about to end. The balance of power in the world is changing; new players are coming to the stage ... China, possibly India. And until the new trade balance shakes itself out, Russia and America will keep dragging us back and forth, like dogs in a tug-of-war. Neither will let go—the bone's too big. We've always been a trading card in the big countries' games anyway; it's a function of our geography. Except that only a few of them in the past century realized that Ukraine is nothing less than critical for any serious political ambitions—Lenin knew this, and, by extension, Stalin. Today, the Russians understand this much better than the

Americans. Europe's not even worth mentioning—they're off the field, and it's not a given that they'll ever get back on it, aside from falling into the Kremlin's sphere of influence."

"You're kidding?"

"Not the least bit. Gazprom already owns a good half of Europe. They have Nord Stream lobbyists in every European government. Everyone, Daryna, loves money. Especially the big kind. Especially when the one paying it is someone you used to fear. That's power. Money, you know, is not just banks—it's also cell-phone service operators, and Internet providers. You see what I'm saying? As soon as those losers in the EU implement electronic ballots, you can write Europe off. Politically it'll mean no more than some Kemerov region; they'll have all their leaders chosen in Moscow. So the stakes are quite high, Daryna—it's a big game. And in the scheme of this game, we are the testing ground for new manage-ment technologies. The ones that will determine the fate of the world in the new century. Try to see it that way."

"So what, we are a kind of a shooting range? Like in World War II, and with Chernobyl? Your big players come play here, see what happens, and then bury us again—till the next time?"

"A range—that's well put. Here's to your health!" He holds up his snifter to let the cognac flash in the light. "You have a way with words. History's secret range. Not bad at all, it's got that something ... I bought this book the other day, by a British guy, about Poland, a thick one." He stretches his fingers, a pair of sausages, to show me. "It's called *God's Playground*. I liked that, too—I think that's even more fitting for Ukraine than for Poland."

"Then it shouldn't be God's. Should be the Devil's. The Devil's Playground."

(Devil's Playground, yes—where the best are the ones who perish. The ones who expose themselves, who stand up from the trenches. One can't expose oneself on the Devil's Playground—can't step into the floodlight's beam, unless one plays for the side that's sitting in the bushes with the sniper's rifle; on the Devil's Playground, one can only make good if one lives the way Vadym says: get low and watch where the strongest current will run—and swim in it. You are a wise, wise man, Vadym, aren't you; you've got it all figured out ...)

"Why do you have to be so dramatic," he mutters, and an absurd hope that he is simply drunk flares up in me—that he is just drunk, that's it. Look at how much less cognac there is in the bottle; I didn't even notice how he'd siphoned all that out. This may well be merely the ramblings of an intoxicated man. Damn it, why is my head crackling and hissing so much—like a cell phone with a weak signal! No, drunk he is not.

"Now, a range—that's well put!" He sticks to his tune. "That's exactly what it will be. Just you wait and see—there'll be a whole bunch of interesting new tricks launched for the first time in these elections! Someday, they'll write textbooks about it. Post-information era government technologies—that's something! It's like when they first split the atom. In the beginning, no one could see what possibilities that opened up either. This'll be an interesting year for you and me, Daryna." All of a sudden, he rubs his hands together with such a youthful, hungry lust for life, like a teenage boy after a swim that I, taken by surprise, miss my chance to react to his "you and me."

"Let's have a drink! *Let's drink, honey, let's drink here, they won't pour on the other side....* What's that, why didn't you finish your ice cream? Watching your girlish figure?"

"Drink to what, Vadym? To whose victory?"

"Ours, Daryna, ours! Let those Yankees and Ivans tussle all they want; our business is to make profits! The first round in this game went to Russia: after the Gongadze case, the Kremlin's got Kuchma right where they want him, totally under their control. Now they're betting on the Donets'k contingent, they do business together; they're one crew and all that, I'm sure you know this. Going back to the Soviet days. And the Americans bet on Yushchenko—with the goal of keeping Ukraine in the buffer zone. And we shall wait and see how well it works for them."

"And all the people who actually live in this country—the way you see it, they aren't a part of this game? We've no will of our own?"

"Whose masses do, Daryna? Name one country. Or do you, by chance, believe that bullshit about history being shaped by the people? Don't make me laugh; we don't live in the nineteenth century! Seventy percent of people, according to statistics, wouldn't know their own opinion if it bit them in the ass—they just keep repeating whatever they've heard. People are stupid, Daryna. That's the way it has always been and always will be. People eat up what's put before them. And you belong to the elite who have the opportunity to do the putting. So, please, do me a favor, don't take that for granted."

He squints—quickly, conspiratorially—and again this flicker, like a shadow across the surface of the water (and I'm underwater; I am *under* the whole time; what gills do I have to breathe?) and a flare-up of another senseless hope: what if it's a sign he is giving me (Before whom, in front of what third party or surveillance camera?), a sign that all this is not for real, that he is pulling my leg and I shouldn't believe a single word he says? "Do not trust anyone, and no one will betray you"—was it Vadym who said that? (When?) But instead, he grows more solemn.

"So when it comes to serious money, Daryna, only Russia is prepared to invest in us. That's the reality."

In my mind, I shake off the water—droplets sit cool under my skin.

"The foreign experts you mentioned—those are Russians?"

"What does that matter?" he shrugs. "I am offering you the most interesting work a creative person could have, and right up your alley: take a dark horse, Vasya the gas-station-guy, doesn't matter who, we can talk about that later.... You take him—and make him a hero! A leader! A cult figure with his own myth—you guys can figure out what that myth is, brainstorm something together. You're creating your own hero, like the Good Lord from clay—how beautiful is that? And in the people's memory that Vasya will remain the man you made him. It's like a whole new kind of art, right there! And with the widest appeal—even cinema can't come close."

You couldn't say Vadym spent four years with an artist for nothing.

(Art, Vlada used to say, contemporary art, is first and foremost the making of one's own territory, a discrete exhibition space where no matter what you brought in, even a urinal, would be perceived a work of art: modern civilization has allocated its artists a niche in which we can play with impunity, letting off steam, but from which we can no longer change anything in the accepted way of seeing things.)

"That's not art, Vadym. Art is what you don't get paid for."

"Whoa there!" Vadym even leans back in his chair. "And when Leonardo da Vinci painted the Sistine Chapel—was he doing that for free now?"

"Michelangelo."

"What?"

"Not Leonardo—it was Michelangelo. You're getting it mixed up with *The Da Vinci Code*."

"So Michelangelo, whatever. What's the difference?"

"From the client's point of view—none. The same job could have been done by someone else. They were only paying for a canonical treatment, nothing else. That airy lightness that blows you away, and you don't even know why—that's just a bonus, it may very well not have been there. Art is always a bonus. That's how you know it when you see it."

"Give me a break." Vadym is visibly irritated by our detour off topic. "That was a different time, so of course the commissions were also different. The church is also a governing corporation, and, while we're at it, it was the most powerful one of its time. Take a broader view, Daryna! Everyone does this, not just politicians—every person tries to create a legend out of their life, if only for their kids and grandkids. It's just that not everyone can have this done professionally—that takes money ..."

And another splash, and again I am underwater. Why didn't it ever occur to me to see things the way he talks about them? Aidy's professor at The Cupid, the old poetess who shook her dyed tresses before me so proudly—they are losers, amateurs who simply did not have any money, and so were trying to buy me with what they had: their thinning tresses, gossip, lies, the peeling gloss of worn-out fake reputations. And there was more, more—crowds of random faces spill out of my memory as if from the opened doors of an overstuffed closet: bosses of all kinds, administrators, directors, princes of tiny local fiefdoms, all performing their greeting rituals for me—television's come!—in their offices. They click through my mind frame after frame like a newsreel from a military parade: the suits—gray, charcoal, black pinstripe, gray herringbone (one such bundle of tweed with suede elbow patches still calls me, keeps inviting me out to dinner)—rise energetically from behind their desks cluttered with telephones; a front-desk Mashenka brings in the coffee; and, after a short prelude, every one of them turns the conversation to his monumental contribution to one thing or another, blows himself up into a hot-air balloon, bigger and bigger, ready to fly up to the stratosphere, and stoops, and bows, and fawns over his goods. And then there were the high-fliers, the unacknowledged geniuses, the inventors of perpetual motion machines, and the victims of incredibly convoluted intrigues who couldn't wait to fill my poor ears with assurances that their story was the one that was going to make me famous world over (the breed that, fortunately, has collectively diverted to cyberspace with the arrival of the Internet, like water finding a break in a dam).

Lord, how many of them, in my years of work on TV, danced around me like savages around an idol, with tambourines, hollering, flowers, and toasts—all to sway me to turn them into the fantasy heroes they wished to remain in people's memories? Like electrons wrenched from their natural orbits by some tremendous explosion, all these people, even when they managed to find perfectly good places for themselves in this world, kept smoldering with the secret conviction that those places were not really *theirs*, and that they were really meant for a *different*, amazing and remarkable, life, which had either been taken away from them or was not yet apparent to everyone else—and that's why they needed an apostle, an advocate, a sculptor with a mass-media chisel who would help bring out the contours of the masterpieces hidden in the shapeless bulk of their biographies, someone who would chisel away everything redundant, and reveal them to the awestruck and speechless world.

They've always been swarming around me, these wrenched-from-their-orbit electrons who dreamt of becoming simulacra. Only I used to treat their presence as an inevitable cost of doing business—like the dark side of the moon, a gloomy shadow that trails every vocation—this was just what you got for being a journalist, you couldn't help it.... Now, when my own center of gravity has shifted, under Vadym's assault, onto this other, dark side, I see for the first time, in close-up, *the way* the whole army of them, with Vadym at its helm, sees journalism; it turns out they weren't the shadow at all—they were my profession itself, its essence, its bare and hard core, cleared of all extraneous layers: *advertising.*

Not information. Not the collection and dissemination of the information that helps people develop their own views, as I had believed until now. (To journalism students at the university, when they asked me what my gold standard of reporting was, I always said, watching their young faces turn puzzled and surprised, Chornovil's underground *Ukrainian Messenger,* which he published in the 1970s—I can name no reporting more chemically pure than that.) But in fact, my shows are in the same class with commercial breaks: I am an advertiser; I advertise people. Others advertise beer and sanitary pads with wings, and I advertise people. Shape them into attractively packaged legends. That's my specialty.

And that's all there is to it, as Vadym says.

"Excuse me?"

"Twenty-five grand," Vadym says. US dollars. A month. Until the end of the election campaign. And sits there looking at me, eyes narrowed. (What color *are* they?)

I must be really good at advertising people. I am also, it would appear, good at controlling my face before the camera: he doesn't seem to be able to read anything from it.

Looks like he is a bit disappointed.

"Hotel California" is ending; I hear the last chords. My head is pounding so hard that muscles throughout my whole body reverberate with pain. And inside—it's empty; the fear's gone. It's the strangest thing: I am taking this round—compared to the previous one, in my boss's office—incomparably more calmly, as if it were all happening to someone else. The reactions I do experience are peculiarly physiological—pain, nausea; the emotional machinery seems unplugged, as if my body has taken on the entire burden of this conversation and I, myself, am playing no part in it. As in a dream.

Wait. What dream was like that?

The pause is getting long (a commercial break without content, the screen burns vacant, and someone's money is going down the drain as the purchased airtime ticks on: TICK ... TICK ... TICK ... TICK ...).

"What do you say?" Vadym gives up. Gives up first. So I am stronger than he is. And Vlada intuited it correctly when she painted me a maiden warrior to the accompaniment of "The Show Must Go On"—she had the right instinct: to seek in me the fulcrum she needed to leverage this man up and free herself from under him. It's too bad I proved such a coward back then, got scared, flailed, and clucked "I'm not like that!" I did not recognize, I couldn't see. Could not see anything, stuck my head in the sand: I *needed* everything to be just fine in Vlada Matusevych's life—for my own peace of mind. I, too, betrayed her; I'm as guilty as Vadym before Yushchenko. I ran. I deserted. I abandoned her.

What I'd most like to ask Vadym right now is whether he has seen those photos in her archive—the ones of the two of us, me in the witchy makeup, in the style of the early Buñuel heroines, Vlada with the bloody lipstick smeared across her mouth. But I won't ask him this: even if he had found them, he wouldn't have seen anything in them. And would not have understood anything.

So I ask something completely different—what he least expects to hear. "Why me, Vadym?"

And he looks away.

"Why did you choose me, of all people?"

(Softer, someone at my side seems to prompt—softer, more intimately, less steely ...)

"Money like that could buy you any of the super-popular faces from the national channels," I rumble low like a cello or a bandura, an intimate, chest-deep timbre (of course, the voice is key, folks knew it all the way back in the time of the fairytale in which the wolf runs to the smith, *smithy-smithy, cast me a voice*—how's that not an electoral technology?). "My show's not that popular, it wasn't even in prime time, never made the top ten ..."

"People trust you," he answers simply. He has chosen to be sincere. Good move.

"Oh. I see. That's nice to hear."

A pause. TICK ... TICK ... TICK ... TICK ...

"And that's it? That's the only reason?"

"Well," he smiles wide, his most charming smile yet, "that and then again—we're family, aren't we?"

We *would be* "family" if I agreed. That's what he's after—this is it, finally. We would, and the trafficking would vanish between us—delete, delete. Vlada would also disappear—the Vlada I remember. Vadym would've bought her from me, together with her death. The way he's already bought her from her mother, and is now buying her from her child.

Now, this is really slick. Not just slick—it's awesome, it's brilliant, it's all but enough to have me sitting here stunned, breathless, with my jaw dropped again: regardless of the ends a man's intellect is pursuing, the sight of said intellect at work is always as irresistible to women as female beauty is to men. I applaud you, Vadym Grygorovych. What was it he said—"history is made by money"? It's only logical that this should apply to the history of an individual life as well—all one needs is to choose his witnesses well. Buy the right witnesses, as in any decent lawsuit. Because every story is ninety-five percent about who does the telling. And he knows that I know this. And I know that he knows that I know …

For an instant, I short circuit, a spasm grips my throat, and I am blind with hatred for this self-satisfied face with its pink-lipped mouth lined with white ice-cream residue—but the hatred, too, is somehow *not my own*: I watch it inside me as though I were filming it. Somehow now I need to switch to his language—and I find I do speak it; I know how they talk, these people.

"I understand you, Vadym. Now look what we've got here. You say people trust me. If I agree, then after all these … interesting experiments of yours, one thing is certain—they won't trust me any longer. Even if I commit ritual suicide, samurai-style, right on camera, people will say—eh, a publicity stunt. I won't make any more heroes; I'll have to retrain. You say profit. Fine, let's do the math. Twenty-five grand a month, how long do we have before the elections—six months? Okay, let's say seven. Twenty-five times seven—a hundred and seventy-five. You are proposing that I sell"—(And here I break pace for a second: sell what? My country, which foreign secret services aim to shove back into the hole it hasn't been able to dig itself out of anyway, going on thirteen years already? My friend whose death is on my conscience too, and whose memory is now on my conscience alone? No, none of that will do)—"sell my professional reputation"—(there, that's better)—"for one hundred and seventy-five thousand dollars? For the price of a one-bedroom apartment in Pechersk? That won't cut it, Vadym. I did spend ten years earning it, you know. And you, as my father-in-law says, want to pay a penny for a handful of nickels."

The father-in-law (and Aidy's dad does say that) is a bonus, pure art: Vadym's never heard a whiff of any father-in-law, and it won't sit well with him—it tells him he missed something (and I'm not as naked and defenseless as he'd thought, someone must've covered me). The smile remains on his face as he left it there, and now looks as untidy as an unmade bed. He licks his plump lips, his eyes wander around the big room, as if he were trying to remember something, and then he pulls out his cell phone, flips it open—until now the phone's been off, that's how important a conversation we are having—and finally refreshes his smile, bringing it now to a waxy ripeness.

"I remembered this joke about the Place Pigalle ... a really old one, from back in the student days," he starts.

"The one about women who can't be bought, but are very expensive?" I smile, too: so there won't be a raising of the price, it's nice to deal with an intelligent man. "What did you think? That's exactly how it is; there's deep wisdom in that joke.... You know something else they say? An honest reporter only sells out once. This is not one of those times, Vadym."

"I am sorry to hear that," is all he says. Says it from the heart—he really is sorry.

"Me too. You know why?"

"Why?" he calls back, an echo.

The Show Must Go On. The pain is making the world before my eyes congeal into a yellowish gloom, and I focus hard on the bridge of Vadym's nose, it's all I see before me, the bridge of his nose, this one fixed point to which the other parts of his face drift slowly, distorted as if filmed under water. Freddie Mercury's voice ascends somewhere inside me like a bird set free from the dark spilling broken glass into my veins, invisible brushes multiply on my skin, tickling my temples, cheeks, eyelids—I see myself through the eye of a hidden camera, and the camera is Vlada's: click-click-click. I grow still in the face, holding my breath, and feel myself suddenly grow more beautiful. I feel the flicker of fire under my skin, feel my features grow smoother as in lovemaking, feel my lips darken as they fill with blood—Vadym's the only spectator of this show, but I am not doing this for him ... smithy-smithy, cast me a voice, and now the cello comes in—a low, chest-deep timbre that no man can resist.

"Why? Because this whole scheme, Vadym, looks to me like one monumental screwup ..."

"Is that so?" echoes the bridge of the nose.

"Uhu. These big shots of yours cannot possibly be really good professionals. I suspect, in fact, they are nothing but really good swindlers."

"What makes you think that?" the bridge of the nose, says, startled. He is scared. So, he's got his own money tied up in the deal.

"How should I explain it?" Now it's my turn to play, like a stage magician juggling knives, at being privy to secret knowledge. "There's this thing—we professionals," and I lean into this word with my voice as if pushing against a locked door, and feel the door yield under the spell, "call strength of material." In his language, professional is a magical word, the object of a savage faith, an element of a religion in which the world consists of human demigods who rule it, the masses that provide the gods with a steady supply of ambrosia, and professionals, a breed of creatures somewhere between priests and useful Jews, who huddle in back storerooms like shadows in Hades waiting for the gods to reach down and tap them to carry out their operations. A professional's position is duplicitous: on one hand he is, most certainly, the help, a whipping-boy runner, but on the other he does command a dose of respect, as a carrier of secret information, which the gods themselves, for lack of time, cannot master. So in this way, he has an upper hand on the gods, and who knows how he'll decide to play it, and that's why one has to be careful around professionals, as one had to be around soothsayers and witch doctors in the Middle Ages. One must listen to a professional, especially when he or she delivers a warning, and Vadym is very much listening, my cello call streams straight into his yawing ears. "A *professional* is born the moment he learns to sense the strength of his materials. Learns to intuit the limits of his pliability. Working any substance is always a contract, like with a living being—up to here I burn you, oxidize you, mold you, and you go along with it. As long, of course, as I am not trying to make knives out of glass or teapots out of paper."

"More to the point," Vadym breathes.

"Just think about what I said."

A professional's language, just like that of a soothsayer or a witch doctor, must be obscure enough to elicit respect. A political technology, as Vadym says.

"Think how much more complicated this becomes when your material is people instead of brick."

A pause. Loud breathing. TICK ... TICK ... TICK ... TICK ... It feels like I'm working through an algorithm that's been pre-programmed into me—I barrel ahead without hesitation, without thinking, with a speedy, dreamlike ease, hitting every open target.

"These people are hacks, Vadym. These professionals of yours. They're puppet masters, snake-oil peddlers. Taking on a scheme as farfetched as this—to win elections in someone else's country by means of massive PR campaigns aimed at someone else's electorate—that's as bad as promising you paper tea kettles: they're demonstrating their total ignorance of the material. It's unprofessional, stupid, arrogant, and ignorant. You can't treat your material like that. It turns on you."

A pause. Loud breathing. TICK ... TICK ... TICK ... TICK ...

"It explodes. Or cracks."

His face—I feel it throb, pulse inside me like a second heart—gathers again to the focal point of his nose, as if distorted by a bent mirror.

"It's the same with people, too."

TICK ... TICK ... TICK ... TICK ...

"That's what I call reality. That which lies beyond the limit of pliability. The part that we can't measure because we can't see it—or only five percent of it perhaps ..."

"Five even?" he shoots back, ironically: numbers have a soothing effect on him; with numbers he's safe, back on his own territory.

"Five percent is the statistical deviation ... in accidents, the X factor. They say there are always five percent more survivors than the theory of probability would've predicted."

The face across the table from me remains impassive, only blinks as if against the wind. How did she have sex with him—was she on top? He must be so heavy, unwieldy, like a strongbox full of dynamite.

"Watch out, Vadym. They'll leave you a royal mess, those quacks."

And, suddenly and to my own surprise, I realize instantly that this is true. That things won't go their way. Won't go their way at all, ever, no matter what illusions they peddle. This comes as an inexplicable certainty, unshakable, clarion-clear, as if all I had to do was speak it, and here it is, summoned, like the "Sesame" that opens a cave—it came and parted the solid rock before me; it broke the spell, and now it's clear that things cannot be otherwise—that whatever malfeasance Vadym intended toward me is nothing but stuffy, creepy smoke, the miasma of a mind unhinged, moon-blindness that obscures everything *unyielding*, all that can't be bought or eaten. How could these people, blinkered, and with nothing but the sewage of streaming dollars under their paws, possibly hope to bring down an entire country full of mysterious, unquantifiable life? That's just a glitch of the matrix in their ailing heads, a mental affliction—like hell they'll get it!

The man across the table from me, by contrast, has no certainty of this kind, on either side of the scales, and I can see it: he is left alone at the mercy of his own mind, submerged, as if into his own miasma, into his own calculations that he is so afraid to get wrong, his snappy faculties busily sniffing over the warning he's just received, weighing whether it merits a revision of his well-composed, multilevel equation, or if it can be brushed off, deleted, in which case he would also have to delete me as an authoritative source right along with it, and that's more difficult. I am still a professional and, once I've been offered a certain amount of money, I can't be crossed off the books just like that. They are held hostage by their own money and the hyperreality they have created; these people are physically incapable of admitting that something they paid for, or were about to pay for, could turn out to have no value whatsoever, because this would mean they'd been had, and that, by definition, can never happen to gods.

The man across the table from me is throwing sparks, at this moment, like a faulty telegraph wire—a short-circuit, a cognitive dissonance: he must accept one of two things—either he's just fucked up royally with me, or he is looking at the prospect of fucking up even more royally in the game I just refused to play— and that's it, a dead-end; this dilemma has no solution within the framework of his system.

And now I *remember*—as if a new picture finally breaks, easy and free, independent, onto the surface of the one I persist in keeping steady before me with a superhuman effort of my throbbing brain—a picture that has spent the entire evening fighting its torturous way up through my long-suffering mind: a déjà vu, the recognition of a once-seen, completely different face—sharp, eagle-nosed, and thin-lipped, protruding like a wolf's snout with close-set eyes—but it doesn't matter that the face is different, because now I know *where* I saw it before. It emerges in my memory now, a giant dark mass, like a whale surfacing, bringing with it the image that I've been groping for, blindly, for so long—*that dream* of mine, the one dreamt two weeks ago, on that wild night—the night that would not end, as if Aidy and I lived several lifetimes in that single night, on the verge between dream and wakefulness; my beloved tried to run after someone, shouted that he had to kill the traitor, and I was his land, the moist, sloshing darkness that kept him afloat.

I don't remember how many times we made love. I was exhausted. I was plasma. I was a runny mass; he melted me completely, down to the most secret nooks and crannies. I was dying and could not die, and then it finally came, and I saw death with my own eyes and recognized it, the white flash of it that I'd known once before: a thousand searchlights aimed at me, a new sun exploding in the depths of the cosmos, the birth of a new planet. After a night like that one could go a year without sex. No wonder I hadn't felt like any for two weeks already, that's never happened to me before—it was as if we opened the doors to something beyond that night, and that otherworld poured into us more than we could hold, and, aside from our all-night vigil of lovemaking, all that stayed with me were fragments of our conversations when we lay, in the ebbs, spent but still in each other's arms, and kept mumbling things, interrupting each other like drunks, desperate to scoop up and somehow hold in our words what was already seeping back behind the door. We were dreaming the same dream; the magnitude of memories is finite—the girl in a sailor suit, Aunt Lyusya with a sack of western flour, the childhood secret abandoned in the yard in Tatarka, Aidy's notes on a pack of Davidoff cigarettes about blood in Kyiv and women who would not cease giving birth—but these were all just words, impenetrable and flat like lids, and the other dimension we had glimpsed beyond them was already hidden from us again. And although in the morning I, too, carefully wrote down all the details I managed to retain, the entirety of it had hopelessly and irrevocably disintegrated.

But now it surfaces again, to prove that it didn't disappear at all—it bobs up for a single, short sliver of a moment, in the fully renewed, searing sharpness of color it had that night, as if I were looking through a camera zooming swiftly in, framing the night, the woods, human figures cut out from black cardboard, set against a blood-red fire, and right there, smack in the focal point—got it!—a protruding, stern, and stiff face, like a wolf's snout, not so much handsome as commanding with the sculpted perfection of its features, with eyes purposefully narrowed to Tatar-like slits, so you can't even see what color they are, and someone beside me (a woman's voice) prompts with the name Mykhailo! and in this single glimpse—because in the next instant, the ocean's smooth surface closes back on itself, and the dark mass of the whale's body vanishes below it—I *recognize* him. I recognize what I've known ever since that night: *this is the man who caused Gela's death—just like Vlada's.*

This is what she wanted to tell me in that old dream of Aidy's, my radiant girl, my radiant-eyed Gela Dovganivna—when she took Vlada's seat at the table in the Passage. They *knew*, Vlada and Gela both, what I did not know: they had been cheated the same way—by loving the force that destroys life while that force pretends to be the power that rules it.

And just as I grasp this, it's gone. What's left is Vadym turned the color of a beet in his sloppy sportcoat and droopy lilac tie—there he sits, chair turned sideways, holding his snifter of cognac in his hand, and breathing over it so hard you'd think he were waiting for something to hatch from it. And that's it. And even my head—thank God—does not ache anymore, is clear as a bell now. And neither do I feel tired, not at all—although it must be bloody late by now, close to one in the morning ...

And with the lightest touch, very gently, so as not to alarm him, I push, just as he recommended, the button he was trying to buy from me—he must be vulnerable to this pressure now; he is without defenses, without his usual inch-thick armor.

"Vadym," I am not asking—I'm pleading; not a prosecutor—an accomplice: "Why do you think she died?"

He startles, blinks at me, and looks down right away.

"Don't torture me, Daryna. I've racked my mind thinking about it."

"Were you fighting?"

Despite what I feared, he does not bristle or go on the defensive—he is subdued like a little boy before his mom, when he knows he is in trouble. (So my warning did scare him; so he does have something to be scared of.)

"That's the thing ... if only I'd gone out with her that day ... or sent a driver at least ..."

But she didn't let him. Maybe she didn't even tell him where she was going. Maybe they were no longer talking as friends, were not talking to each other about anything at all—a two-level, 3,600-square-foot apartment has plenty of room to keep you from running into each other, and she left unannounced, without a "Bye, honey, be back in an hour"—just bolted through the front door, like a gunshot, and that was the last memory of herself she left him; the next time they met was in the morgue.

"She was about to leave you, wasn't she?"

He looks at me with a growing alarm.

"She told you?"

"Yes," I lie.

I know how it can be; I've been there—with Sergiy, and with other men—know what a breakup is like when it takes you a long time to find the courage to do it. I know what it's like when you have to force yourself to drag your own body from point A to point B like a corpse, automatically putting it through the motions it has learned by rote; what it's like to have a heavy, impenetrable cloud of thoughts hanging constantly over your head, thoughts you've done laps around, the same track over and over: "How could this be?" and "What do I do now?" And then you stop suddenly in the middle of the apartment as if someone had ordered you to freeze, trying to remember vacantly, what did I come here for? Things are a little better when you lie in a bathtub and the water slowly washes away the solidity of your body together with the thoughts wedged in it. And another thing you can do is go for a drive, especially outside the city, on the highway; she used to love that—she said that was her way of resting: a monotonous motion, the even ribbon of asphalt unspooling before her eyes, the soothing flicker of trees on the sides of the road, rain against the windshield, the measured back and forth of the wipers, the rain, the rain.... Of course she went alone; she wouldn't have taken a damn driver in a million years—one would have to talk to a driver....

I can imagine how it was. How it all happened. I don't even need to go there, following her tracks, as Vadym did—I just know.

And he knows that I know.

"Don't torture me, Daryna," he says. From his heart. And adds, "Life goes on anyway, you know?"

As if he weren't the one who spent the last two hours lecturing me about how he is the one shaping that life, without inviting me to join him on mutually advantageous terms. Apparently he sees no contradiction here, no cognitive dissonance this time: he simply dives instinctively into the current that, at the moment, lifts him from the shallows with minimal losses—while keeping his controlling interest intact, of course. One can be quite certain—

he'll double-cross his FSB crew, too. And pull his money out of the scheme right in time—he will take my advice.

When someone turns to truisms, it's a sure sign that it's time to wrap up. Life goes on, most certainly, who could argue with that? I look at the man across the table from me (*I thought him strong. Someone capable of determining the fate of many. The embodied dream of an eternally rightless nation of its own, native force that would protect and defend them ...*) and feel my lips curl, as if in a mirror with delayed reflection, into that same meaningful smirk of the loony-bin nut: I know where I've seen you before. But you—you don't know me.

He expected absolution, and my silence unsettles him.

"By the way," he says, pretending he's just now thought of it, "how are you doing money-wise—have something to live on?"

Now it really takes all I've got not to laugh in his face. Bless your cotton socks, you could've thought of something funnier! Or is that it—he can't?

"Don't worry. I do have someone to keep me."

Then what is it you want, you fucking bitch? his eyes all but scream, hating me. Any rejection of money, in his system of coordinates, is equivalent to blackmail, and my behavior points at some hidden threat that he absolutely has to neutralize—and without delay.

"Not R. by chance?"

So he knows about R., too. That's no surprise, really, since he had contacted the channel's management and assembled a file on me; a pile of dirt on a future partner is also part of the controlling interest package.

"No," I shake my head. "Not R."

"If you wanted, I could buy your pictures from them ... the ones of you with R." And he grins, as if he'd seen them himself.

And if he had?

"I don't give a damn, Vadym."

The amazing thing is that I don't, in fact, give a damn. And finding out that the new management of the channel has armed itself with the pictures that R had taken of me in various revealing poses (and didn't he say to me back then, "Don't be so sure!") utterly fails to produce the effect Vadym counted on. I just don't care—and that's it. As if it truly weren't me—as if I hadn't been the one sprawled naked under the flashes, with a strap-on, smeared with sperm. You can wallpaper your whole office with those pictures if you feel like it, boys—you won't get to me.

"They wanted to cover their bases," Vadym explains, not yet believing that the bullet he's been saving for so long has missed by so much. "In case you decided to make a fuss about that *Miss New TV* show …"

Aha, so my dear ol' boss must've really felt compelled to hustle, bless his heart. He threw everything he had to plug the hole in his wall. I wonder what kind of story about me he intended to spin based on those pictures? Actually, come to think of it, I don't wonder—not even a little bit. Don't even feel like flexing my imagination in that direction.

Instead, something completely different occurs to me—with the same dreamlike ease, as if someone else had determined my actions and all I'm supposed to do is leap off the cliff—a plunge, arms at my sides, head first like a swallow, into the dark-blue abyss below …

"If you really want to thank me for the consult, Vadym," I measure out a pause with just the right dose of sarcasm, "then there's something else you can buy from them for me."

Happily, eagerly, he pulls his BlackBerry from his coat pocket and personally writes it down, running his stylus over the screen—he'll do this, he promises: the materials for my unfinished film, for *Diogenes' Lantern*, yes, that one. Working title—"Olena Dovgan." He really will do this for me, I've no doubt—he'll rescue Gela and all my other Dovgans from that vipers' nest: look at him perk up, his hands suddenly moving with an unusually solicitous busyness. It's hard for him to believe that he'll get away from me so easily, that he can buy my silence so cheaply: I will never again speak of why Vlada died. What we both know will remain between us.

He has no idea that it is Vlada who at this instant is buying, with his hands, my film. The film I now know how to finish, by myself, no matter how much it will cost: I know now what has been missing. And Vlada's death, too, will be in the film—it's the only way I can tell the truth about her. And it doesn't matter that the man who caused her death will have a different face in the film—the face of the man, the farthest on the right in the old rebel photograph. Because aside from the factual truth, grounded in names and faces, there's a deeper truth of the stories lived by individual people, a truth invisible to strangers, one that cannot be made up or pretended. One that lies beyond the limits of pliability.

And, as if it had just been sitting there waiting for the right moment all this time, a cell phone rings. My cell, I hadn't turned it off, and I already know who it is, and my facial muscles melt involuntarily into a smile while my lips squeeze out a mechanical "Excuse me" to Vadym.

"Lolly?"

"Aidy!" I holler, so loudly the whole room seems to echo, as I break out from the dark underwater cave into the light of day. "Aidy, I'm here! I'm here, I'm okay! Don't worry about me, I'm on my way out already; I'll be there in twenty minutes!"

"Thank God," he exhales loudly into my ear, my love, my man, Lord, how happy I am to hear his voice! "Alright, kiddo, get on the road. I've got all kinds of stuff going on here …"

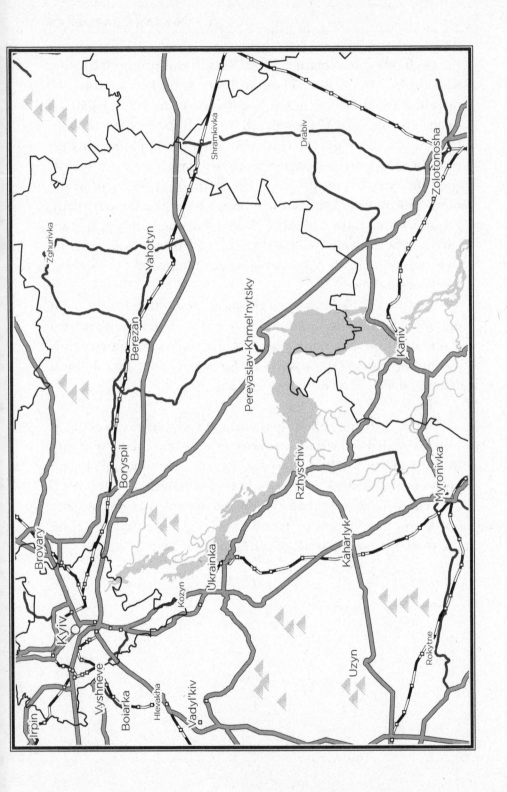

Forgive Me, Adrian

"Brew us some tea, could you please," Lolly asked.

"Chamomile? We've only got chamomile left; I didn't have a chance to buy anything today."

"That's fine, let's have chamomile." Then after she sipped it, like a gosling—hardly any, as if forcing herself to swallow—she put the mug aside and smiled: "We're like a pair of geezers—sitting here with the wrecks of our lives drinking chamomile tea before bed. We just need some aches and pains to complain about to complete the picture."

Had to have been that fat rat, I thought, that Rep., the bastard, who'd gotten to her with the women-of-a-certain-age talk, the whole now-or-never shtick, up or out. As a client of mine used to say: under forty, it's enough for a woman to be pretty; after forty, she needs to be rich—and made eyes at me, even though the old battle-ax had ticked past forty back when I was in middle school. And Yulichka must have just sat there, listened, and made another mental note.

"You did everything right, Lolly. You did great; I'm proud of you."

"You know," she said, brightening, "my mom used to say that about my dad, in those very same words: that he did everything right. Weird, isn't it?"

Lolly has changed. Matured? Knowing her and the way she, the straight-A student, reverberates in response to every blow life deals her—taking it as an instance of cosmic injustice—I was afraid, at first, to dump the entire truth into her lap the way it had landed in mine: here's what happened, my love; we're in deep shit because my secretary has taken me for a thirty-thousand dollar ride (and I've been an idiot; I've been such an idiot!). But when my girl, with her gaze turned wondrously inward, told me about the dinner she had with that fat Rep. rat, it totally blew me away, so my own screwup instantly diminished in importance: Are you kidding me? This is *war!* Unannounced, secretly creeping, real GB war, and no one has a clue about it—everyone's got their noses stuck in their own shit and can't even see what's going on out there!

I ran around the kitchen, smoked one cigarette after another, and shouted that something had to be done; we can't just let a pack of hometown goons hand the country over to the Kremlin, lock, stock, and barrel, just because they think they can, and that this Vadym was an old Soviet rat for sure. I know his breed; I've seen more than my share of them—the ones who first cleaned out the Komsomol and Party purse and then made a beeline for politics where they could clean out everything that was left in state owner-ship. What was it you said he traded in, kerosene? You know what it's called? Agents of influence, that's who they are—the agents of GB influence, every last one of them, on the Kremlin hook, all these former rats, bitches, fuckers; we should've run the lustra-tion back in 1991, that was the only way to get rid of these Soviet cancers, and now look how they've spread!

I felt a kind of uplift in my rage—a certain purifying relief from having found a more deserving object of scorn than Yulichka, who'd been running schemes with my competitors behind my back—I'd shaken off the nasty feeling of having been robbed that had burned me all day, and felt myself filling with a pure, ethyl-alcohol-like civic outrage: Who do they think we are, these bastards? Do they think they'll get away with this? I opened my shoulders wide and stood up tall facing a *real*, worthwhile enemy, one with whom you *want* to cross swords—while Lolly, by contrast, remained amazingly composed the whole time, as if she weren't really surprised to hear my news (I've always suspected that she disliked Yulichka). She asked succinct, businesslike questions and generally appeared quite calm—as if all the blows that came this evening fell, for her, onto an invisible protective pad. She used to behave differently under stress. When she was resigning from the studio, she went around all but shaking. But something new has emerged in her; she is somehow distant: she even spoke without triumph or melodrama about how elegantly she undid that fat Rep. My poor girl's nose has sharpened to a point and grown pink with exhaustion; the lamp above the table cuts deep, unmistakable, graphic lines from her nose to her lips—without makeup, she is always so dear, so sweet I get shivers inside when I look at her, but only now do I see how much she's worn away in these last few days, become all ether, even her face has grown longer and gaunt. She no longer looks like a teen, I thought. For the first time since we've been together, I felt that she really is older than me—and not by a mere six years, but by a much greater, immeasurable distance.

"Let's go to bed, love"—I could barely stand up straight myself, and wondered, what happened to being nineteen, when I could party all night like the Energizer bunny and in the morning grab a breath mint to blunt my hangover breath before running to class all bright-eyed and bushy-tailed?

"Uhu," she nodded, "let's," and raised her eyes at me, and they suddenly pierced me through all the fatigue, the mental numbness of the late hour, and the burnt-to-cinders adrenaline; they went through me with a living music as though they'd gained a voice and sang—her eyes glowed with tenderness, and obedience, and sadness, and something else so inexpressibly feminine that I a felt a lump rise in my throat.

"Can we go see that man in the country tomorrow?"

"If you want to," I wheezed in the voice of the old Mafioso from Tarantino's *Reservoir Dogs*. God damn it, I was so moved I just about broke down crying right there. The next morning, I planned to go to Boryspil anyway, to see that country hick Yulichka had expropriated—to find out the details and assess my losses (a cuckoo clock, a walnut credenza, what else did that witch hand over to Brey & Co. behind my back?)—but I'd intended to go alone; I'd never gotten Lolly involved in my business before.... The business, however, had never been subjected to anything like what Yulichka did to it. I'd warmed a snake on my own chest, as they say.

This, essentially, is the thing—as it became clear once the ball of initial shock had a chance to settle a bit, to steep, loosen, and unravel into separate strands of damage: where I suffered financially, where I suffered morally, where the firm's image was damaged, what pieces I had to pick up first to try and patch at least some of the holes—this is what cut me the deepest—that I had warmed a snake. Of all the damage, of all the holes, the breach of trust is the most painful, and there's no way to fix it. Such a great secretary, my irreplaceable assistant, my right hand! She was so perfect I wanted to pinch myself. And she was always informed of all my plans, damn it, and damn it again! How could I have missed it—the little bitch's been swindling me for six months? And I just ate from her hand when she fed me the story about the man's heirs, a son and a daughter, who got cold feet and convinced their old man not to sell any of his stuff. She was all seriousness, so preoccupied—"Gosh, Adrianambrozich, wat are wee goin to do, thei refius to sell nou?"

"We have to make them a better offer," I said like an idiot. "We've no other choice." And the interested parties, it would appear, made Yulichka a heck of an offer indeed: when I called the guy myself, he wouldn't even speak to me—know nothing, sell nothing, changed my mind, go to hell—he honestly did not want to talk to me, like someone had really riled him up against me or just told him a boatload of lies about me, but at the time I still didn't suspect anything. I've no idea how I found it in me not to betray myself in any way, to keep my cool today (actually, yesterday already) when my bank director, an old and loyal client, complained to me, with a veiled reproach, that he'd seen a new piece at the minister's home, a Secession cuckoo clock, and heard that this marvel'd been found right here, not far from Kyiv, in a village next to Boryspil—meaning, how'd you miss it, you moron, right under your nose? That hit me like a truck. The trusting, softhearted Adrian Vatamanyuk, friend of small children and animals. And Melitopol prostitutes. And after I just gave the bitch a raise and got her a tuition-free ride to a degree in art history—go, sweetie, get educated; we'll get ahead one day ... fucking A. And how, as the textbook puts it, should one go on with one's life? How should one be building up one's business, or anything else for that matter—if one can't trust anybody?

And the funniest thing is that Yulichka's whole scheme would have come to light sooner or later anyhow: a cuckoo clock is hardly a needle in a haystack on our pathetic market, where it's a like a village, where everybody knows everybody else—you can't keep a secret like that for long—but the greed must have gone to our little schemer's head. The chance to bite off a piece of pie she'd never dreamed of ... I do wonder what commission Brey's people offered her, how much she sold me for?

Essentially, these two things are no different: selling a person or selling a country. Lolly's asleep already, but I go on talking to her in my head: the difference is purely quantitative, Lolly, not qualitative. The single difference between your Vadym and my Yulichka is the scale of operations: your rat charges more. And that's it. It's just that there's us, my love—and then there's them: those who serve something greater—and those who serve themselves, trading in what's not theirs (and I shouldn't call them whores—prostitutes, at least, peddle their own, anatomically inalienable, goods). It's like a pair of enemy camps, and the line between them is like the line of fire at the front. This may be the only line between people that actually matters. A division that can never, under any circumstances be overcome. A thin line, unseen to the naked eye—and there are turncoats who've crossed it, but also the ones who lost their lives to it, as always happens in the line of fire. And it's not clear of whom there's more.

This just occurs to me, a belated response to your already half-asleep confession, when we were getting up from the table: go ahead, you go to the bathroom first—no, you go; I'll have a smoke here. You said, "You know, I understood this thing about Vlada and Gela, too, the mistake they made; it's your dream from a year ago. I've cracked its code: they had the same death."

"What do you mean, the same death?"

"Well, not literally, of course, but they both died for the same reason."

"I don't know, sounds to me like you're really reaching there, toots."

"No, it's true, Aidy. I just haven't figured out how to put it into words yet, but you'll see when I finish that film; I will finish it, just let me get the footage from Vadym …"

For a moment, I confess, I thought you were beginning to ramble with fatigue, and I got scared for you about *your own* old fear, which you'd, apparently, injected into me without my noticing (because in love you exchange everything, to be sure, from sweat and microflora to dreams and fears). Your father was in an asylum. What if there really was a reason? I remember I went all cold inside—and that's when you said this thing that has lodged inside me and goes on churning like a small engine someone forgot to turn off, propelling one new sleepless thought after another: "She, meaning Gela," (or did you say Vlada?) "*mistook the other for one of her own*, and you can't err like that in love. In love—it's deadly."

You saw it in your own way, too, in your woman's way—this line between us and them. You saw it as it relates to men and women—where it's like a species barrier that must not be crossed.

"Can't do it in love," you said. "And what about sex? Can you do it in sex?"

You see, toots, I actually have, ever since we got together, stopped seeing other women as women. I'm not kidding. It's not like I don't see the inexhaustible variety of women, their butts, and all the other things a normal dude sees around him—I do, and quite clearly, but none of it feels like a cause for action anymore. I just don't want it, and that's it. As if there were a single woman left in the whole wide world—you—and the all the other members of your sex, they're just people. So when Yulichka paraded her G-strings and miniskirts in front of me, I sort of felt sorry for her: like a child whom some bad people taught to put on this show, and who wouldn't get it if you tried to teach her that she's a big girl now, and it's not appropriate to act like that. But, to be completely honest, I can't be sure that if you hadn't come into my life, I wouldn't have done the merciful thing one day and kindly fucked Yulichka in my office—to be humane, or whatever, given that the poor thing is always begging so hard.

Vasylenko banged her; he's the one who brought her to the company. He'd take her to the bathroom in the middle of a day, too. I remember I grumbled (because I didn't like it, there's a proper time and place for everything, damn it) that it must've been Lyonchik Kolodub's Komsomol whoring that infected our office with some airborne virus that compels the corporation's director to unzip his pants when we need him to be thinking with his other head—not for nothing is it said that spaces retain the karma of their previous owners. There was a reason all the Party's district committees were always housed in former bordellos.

But soon enough it turned out that Vasylenko's acquisition could do more than wear skirts that end above her panties and bend over in bathrooms—the Melitopol (or Mariupol, I can never keep it straight) orphan had a well-oiled brain, too, and was already taking accounting (or secretarial) evening classes somewhere and quickly became not just our secretary (three hundred dollars a month plus bonuses), but a true comrade in arms: whenever we, the three of us back then (Vasylenko, Zaitsev, and I) discussed any new projects, Yulichka was unfailingly there to assist and, more often than not, would make a useful suggestion right at the moment when we were about to go for each other's throats.

As long as Vasylenko was there, she felt very comfortable; even the time I pointed out to her that she had semen in her hair; she just smiled at me winsomely and said, Oh! (And that, by the way, was the only time when I felt the tiniest urge to unzip my own pants and ask her to repeat the procedure with me, purely for sport, because how am I worse than Vasylenko?) I don't know if she rolled over for Zaitsev, too. Apparently, as far as she was concerned, once my partners departed in search of better hunting grounds—from the very beginning, they were both interested in making money much more so than they cared for antiques; they didn't care what they sold—and I remained the sole owner of the business, with her as my secretary (five hundred dollars a month plus bonuses). I was the one who was supposed to take her to the bathroom. And since I didn't do that, she decided to teach me a lesson.

What do you say to that, Lolly? What do you think about that theory?

I know, you won't say anything because you're asleep already—you've sunk yourself under the blanket (you have a very cozy way of curling up there, under the covers, and without you, my own bed now feels like a hotel one) and zonked out, as if unplugged. Very still, only making a small noise as you breathe regularly into the pillow—funny, like a bunny rabbit.

Sitting up with you now, while you sleep, with the nightlight on, I catch myself smiling. Like I've smoothed out inside a little. "Sleep, one little eye, sleep, the other," Mom used to say to me when I was little, kissing me before sleep: a fairytale charm. Sleep, my brave girl, you did everything right; you held your ground, and I am really proud of you. But I can't sleep, despite how tired I am: I've wound myself up, and smoked too much—burned through three packs almost—to a wheeze in my chest and my heart pounding just under my Adam's apple. And tomorrow I have to be rested and fresh as a daisy, and the pressure—to go to sleep, damn it, and right now—only sends my nerves into overdrive. Classic insomnia, the professional ailment of Ukrainian entrepreneurs. Most of my colleagues have given up the fight with alcohol (three fingers of cognac before bed—and you sleep like a baby, Igor assures)—and some have moved on to sedatives, which is no good at all. And the ones who deal in really big money call in even heavier artillery. Things keep going this way, and people at parties will soon be asking each other, who's your dealer, the way they now ask, who's your stylist?

So we'll go visit that cuckoo dude tomorrow, alright. I checked the map—it's really not that far at all: right after Boryspil, after the exit to Zolotonosha. Zolotonosha, such a nice name—means gold-bearing. Dude was a gold mine indeed. A Klondike of a dude. The same stretch where Vyacheslav Chornovil crashed—and Vlada. Still no one knows if it was an accident, or if he was murdered—that was also right before the elections, exactly five years ago, and the old camp general, as they called him, was rumored to be thinking of running for president.

That story looked bad, it looked really, really fishy: a KAMAZ truck knocks the car with the future presidential candidate off the road and then vanishes into thin air—that's textbook Russian. And it was right after that, it seemed, that things went south in general—as if with the death of the camp general, an important spring finally snapped in our society, and we lost, as Lolly puts it, the strength of the material. The journalists didn't bat an eye at the time. I remember one rookie even made a big boo-boo in the media when he wrote something along the lines of, good timing for the old man to die. If he'd hung on much longer, he'd have risked becoming a caricature, like a retired Don Quixote—which looked bad, like a young high-flyer's dancing on an old fart's grave—and not long after that, the rookie himself crashed, only without any KAMAZs involved: he and a buddy of his smashed into a tree when they were driving home drunk from a nightclub. Fate, you could say, really rubbed that one in. Better to refrain from dancing on graves as a general principle.

What was that joke my banker told me? This lady has to walk through a cemetery at night, and sees a man, and asks him to see her to the gates. No problem, he says. Thanks, she says, I'm really scared of dead people. Sheesh, he replies, surprised, why would you be scared of us?

That's not as silly as it seems. I'll have to remember to tell Lolly the joke in the morning.

Not scared, no. But we've pushed them completely off our radar, the dead—we've come to ignore them, plain and simple. And it's not sitting well with them, looks like. In the old days, people knew how to live with their dead, invited them into family homes for Christmas and so on.... One dreads to think how many have been added to the other side in the last century—the dead that no one mourned. One can very well imagine they're about ready to revolt against us. A mass uprising, the Great Revolution of the Deceased. What if they do rise up from the graveyards one sunny day and take to the streets?

One thinks such happy thoughts in the middle of the night, doesn't one?

We should buy flowers when we go tomorrow, put them on that spot on the highway. I wonder if it's even marked in any way....

Better go make myself another cup of that chamomile tea. Now I know why old people drink it—they also suffer from insomnia.

Suffer indeed. At this very hour.

The thought puts me on my feet. All this piddly shit you do, waste your life on, only for your own family there's never enough time ... I'll just go ahead and call, right now. Why not?

I shut the bedroom door behind me (sleep, one little eye, sleep, the other), and do the same with the kitchen door, turning the light above the table way down, so it doesn't shine into my eyes; I noticed this a long time ago: people speak softer in low light, instinctively keep their voices low. Two closed doors and a hallway between me and my girl—I don't have to worry about waking her.

Man, I smoked the hell out of this place! Rooms where people smoke a lot and for a long time, especially when warm, smell not of cigarette stubs or smoke, but of decay: not quite of cadaver yet, but of the stage right before that. A unique whiff of rot: it instantly calls up, on its associative heels, the aromas of whoring, wet dog, and alcohol from the night before. Boy, have I smelled too much of that. And how many people have I seen off to the graveyard already?—the ones with whom I hung out in this atmosphere of uncouth smell that no AC can filter out; back when we were all young, this was the smell of our jolly poverty, the air of Soviet dorms and sophomore parties—and later it turned out that our money stank just the same. Vovchyk, whom I met all the way back at the Sinny market, died of a heart attack at thirty-five; Yatskevich OD'd one day; people said Red (I forgot his real name) coded, he always drank like a fish. Kukaliuk even had me over to his dacha—a brand new two-level, but it also stank just like that, only even more rotten, sweeter, with cigar and weed thrown into the mix. Kukaliuk complained that some politician double-crossed him so that he now owed everyone, like land to a kolkhoz—and next I heard Kukaliuk fell out of a train he'd never taken in his life.

I throw the window open and suck the prickly night air into my nostrils. I may be losing it to insomnia, but for one instant, I clearly catch the moist smell of the animate earth—a sign that it has already awakened, that somewhere in its depths juices are brewing, running, getting ready to shoot up tree trunks ... the first sign of spring.

Gosh, it's quiet out there. Not a single window lit in the whole neighborhood.

I put on the electric kettle. And pick up the phone.

One, two, three beeps ... on the fourth one, the receiver comes to life—see, I knew the old man wouldn't be sleeping!

"Hullo?" He sounds stern, displeased—who's this loser calling in the middle of the night?

"Hi, Dad."

I can hear the TV murmuring indistinctly in the background and can picture my father as if he were in front of me—standing in the hallway of our tiny Lviv flat (the phone's in the hallway, the TV in the living room), in his broken-in felt loafers with the heels folded in, the bookshelves behind his back packed with old magazines he can't bring himself to throw out, and above his head—heck, I forgot what's up there—a coat rack?

"Oh, it's you," my father says. "Howdy."

As if I weren't four hundred miles away but just walked through his door, the way I did when I was fifteen. I took my shoes off in the dark, tiptoed in my socks through the hallway ... and froze at the kitchen door. Dad was sitting at the table with the nightlight on, reading—it was obvious he had not gone to bed at all. Howdy, was all he grumbled at me—and went back to his book, a bit embarrassed even: as if each of us had gotten caught in the middle of something he did not want the other to see. (I was in love with a girl, my first love; I think he'd guessed as much....) And now he is also working hard not to show how happy it makes him to hear my voice—he can't show he is dependent on me in any way at all. Only now, when he is over sixty, and he's got high blood pressure, diabetes, and podagra, his reticence has a completely different meaning. For the second time tonight, I feel my throat catch.

"I didn't wake you, did I?"

"You wish," he protests vigorously. "You know I don't go to bed so early."

Early is before three in the morning. He won't fall asleep until it's begging on dawn, and might sleep three or four hours. He does not call this insomnia; he still puts on a tough show, loath to admit any old-age ailments, pretending that this is just the schedule he's set for himself: he is a busy man, works until late, and spends his nights after work assembling the family archive (Lolly's idea). Plus, he is very engaged with politics, naturally, like all people who are growing old alone.

"I was just watching Channel Five ..."

Recently, this channel, propped up by the opposition in the run-up to the election, has become for Dad what Radio Liberty used to be in the Soviet days.

"Have you heard what these goons are up to in Mukachevo?" And in the same breath, he spills into my lap everything he's just heard on the TV (which meanwhile goes on muttering in the background, the effect of which is a surreal experience of something like simultaneous interpretation), about how in Mukachevo the powers that be are calling a special election, to replace the current mayor with their own puppet. I'm left making sparse grunts to evince my continued attention, not showing that I have heard all this before—and more than once. About the Carpathian forests, cut down by "those goons," and that the catastrophic floods that wreak havoc on Transcarpathia every year are nothing but a natural consequence of their criminal lumbering, and how the current mayor, who was determined to reel "those goons" in a bit, was prevented from even running in these elections by having his paperwork stolen, and now the quiet resort town of Mukachevo is suddenly swarming with packs of homicidal-looking men in leather jackets—they're being brought in by busloads, from who knows where, they stroll around the town like they own it, make trouble in its bars and restaurants, and intimidate the locals, so that folks are too scared to go out after dark anymore; it's terrorism, pure terrorism, and the indignity makes my dad younger, as if in the course of speaking to me he's lost about thirty years.

"What do they think they're doing, bringing back the Stalin days? That's plain the way the Soviets used to run their elections in '48! Bring a garrison to every village, herd folks to the ballot box with Kalashnikovs. Some folks still thought it'd work the way it did with the Poles: if we boycott the elections, they won't be legitimate. That was before they figured how this new power does business."

The kettle, as if heated with the fire of Dad's speech, bubbles up indignantly. I can't help smiling. He doesn't know this, of course, but Dad is mimicking me—an hour ago I was raising hell just like that in front of Lolly. She's right when she says that when I grow old I'll be "a carbon copy of Ambroziy Ivanovych." Been a while since I last called. I've been busy. Been even longer since I last went to Lviv …

"This, Dad, is what they now call electoral technologies."

I pour boiling water into my mug.

There will come a day when I can no longer just dial a number like this, day or night, and hear my father's voice. For a moment, this future void gapes before me, as if someone snatched away my blanket while I was sleeping, and left me exposed to the cold. I get up to shut the window, while Dad—alive and well for now, thank God—continues to expose the 1948 vintage of Russian electoral technologies.

"You know what else they did? As your gramps used to tell it, they'd bore a little hole in the booth's ceiling right above the spot where the chemical pencil lay tied, and let a stream of chalk dust pour from that hole the entire time. When a man came into a booth and bent to lick the pencil to put whatever in the ballot, that little stream of white dust would land right atop his head. And it's winter, February, everyone's wearing hats ... stepped into the booths with their hats on, too. The booths are private, as they're supposed to be—no one can see anything, vote however you please! Cross that one candidate out if you please, or put a clean ballot into the box: It's a free country! Guaranteed by Comrade Stalin's constitution. And on the way out, everyone who had white on their hats—the ones who put the pencils to use—got snatched onto a truck that stood ready in the backyard, and went to build Communism in the tundra. That's the kind of elections we used to have, kid."

"Cool," I admit.

Really, that's quite a technological trick. I think Conan Doyle has a story kind of like that: a locked room, a fixed spot for the victim, and a hole above it where a poisonous snake comes out. Dad doesn't remember it, but offers to look it up: he's got Conan Doyle on those shelves, an old Soviet edition.

"Do look it up," I agree, because now I'm curious, too. I'll have to tell Lolly tomorrow where these political technologies of the information age take their root. He didn't have anything to boast about, that Vadym of hers, it's not like his boys have come up with anything new. Maybe they just can't come up with anything new period—and that's why they're hunting for people like her? Then the Church is right: evil by itself is impotent; its power comes when it co-opts the weak into its service....

Not a groundbreaking insight by any stretch, and, correspondingly, it's not especially valuable, but for some reason it gives me the same boost of consolation as the smell of the awakened earth from the window a minute ago: I *can think* again! Can think—and not just shuffle endlessly, like a bug in a trash heap, through the causes and consequences of Yulichka's scheme, with my mind trapped under the pile of lost dollars—an intellectual activity that neither adds to one's common sense nor makes the world more comprehensible. It's like my system's been reloaded: I feel like myself again. Meaning, I feel like the same moron I was before.

And on this wave, as though slightly dumbstruck by relief, I blurt it out in one breath—everything I had no intention of telling him whatsoever, and probably would not have told him in daylight, when things change their proportions—how they tried to recruit my girl today. Without naming names, of course—I'm not that stupid—but most certainly with numbers: twenty-five grand a month; that's the kind of rates they run these days, Dad.

The TV set in the living room grows quiet, and I can hear in the receiver my father's heavy breath. Very close, with a slight wheeze: he, too, must be smoking too much.

I don't often share things like this with him. Back in the day, he was so proud of my accomplishments in physics, so openly glowed with joy when I came home during breaks and sat down in the kitchen to draw for him the scheme of a thermionic generator. And now there's nothing I could ever do to give him back that fatherly pride. We have both been long and reciprocally silent on the topic of my research career: he no longer asks about the progress of my dissertation—he stopped after the one time I lost it (because his questioning was beginning to sting) and snapped at him in that same kitchen, that I don't live *my* life to pay him back for what was taken from *his*. He did not say anything to that then, shuffled away to smoke, and I noticed, for the first time, how he shuffled when he walked—like an old man. There are, indeed, things that are better left unsaid. Because Dad would have probably made a good scientist—had he gotten the proper education in his day.

His cognitive apparatus was very much in order—enough for me to get some of it, too. It's not his fault that when he graduated from high school, he fell into the just-instituted quota for admission of the locals to Lviv's universities—the notorious "twenty-five percent." It was the sixties; Khrushchev liberalism was over, and admission committees, especially those at universities "with clearance," were beginning to take a closer look at the applicants' bios. No one would open a door into fundamental physics—military research, basically—for a "Bandera spawn." Dad's single chance was to go to study in Russia—many did exactly that, and that was part of the authorities' plan: that "the Westerners" not admitted at home would leave, dissolve into the mass of the Soviet people, somewhere out there on that sixth of the world's landmass that made up the geographical Soviet Union. And that was how, little by little, "the fire of Ukrainian bourgeois nationalism" would be dispersed.

But Dad did not leave. I think Grandma must have exercised her influence. For her, Russia was exile, the waterless echelon, the drunken guards, the rail line you rode for three days without seeing a single village—she and Gramps learned firsthand how such lines were laid: a dead man for every tie. She left her own unborn son somewhere among those dead, and she would not, having come back from there alive herself, hear of sending her oldest child back voluntarily—her son who lived. That's the way it must have been, I believe, and I never asked about the details.

When it was my turn to take the entrance exams for physics, it was somehow understood that I had to go to Kyiv—as long as it wasn't Moscow. Only recently, at Lolly's prompting, have I begun to see our family—first the Dovgans, and then the Vatamanyuks—not as discrete portraits in a family album, as I did before, but as a connected network of links, like the Internet; only recently has it occurred to me that it was actually Dad who drew the lot of paying with his life for the life his parents had had stolen from them. Except that Dad never spoke of it like that, and may never even have thought of it like that—until I ripped into him that time (and I could've kept my mouth shut. I'm such a moron; I knew better already!)—and certainly would never stick me with the bill for all of it.

He eventually graduated from the Lviv Polytechnic, where Gramps had also gone—as a distance student, when he was already working at the factory—but a research career was out of his reach at that point. In my own career's rocket-propelled launch, amidst the ruins of the Soviet system, he must have seen a triumph of historical justice—our family's conclusive victory over the power whose mission, for all these years, had been to reduce us to dust, of the gulag or any other variety. He was reborn then, for the first time since Mom died—he was full of plans, even became more tolerant politically, justifying the economic chaos of the early post-independence years, first by the Soviet legacy and then by the lack of any national experience, in the business of self-governance. And even though he found many things about which to boil and rage then also, he generally believed that the country was headed in the right direction. The main thing was—we were free!

My exit into business must've come as a serious reality check for him. I don't know how he learned to live with that, and do not intend to ask him. Ultimately, one learns to live with anything. And if I happen to be bent right now, at three o'clock in the morning, on giving him a synopsis of the lecture on current politics delivered to a famous journalist in a restaurant by an elected member of parliament, it's not in order to make my old man see the shit around us more clearly or to have him console himself with the fact that his son is not the worst of it. That's not the thing.

I just like telling him this. I like saying out loud "Daryna says," like a secret we now share, a family secret: as if with those words, I was drawing a circle of light around all of us together, the three of us (and a golden rectangle falls from our window onto the darkness outside). As if by doing so, I was entrusting Lolly to him—for him to love. For him to be proud of. To be proud, not of the fact that his son in Kyiv lives with a famous journalist but of her, in her own right.

"And that, Dad, is how things are."

He does have a wheeze in his chest ...

"You've got to make this public somehow," he finally responds. "So people will know ..."

"How could I make it public? Who'd publish it?" I'm a bit upset to see his thoughts turn elsewhere. "Somewhere on the Internet is all I can think of. But even there, there are already ways to have information buried, with that same money, and you don't even need to deal with censorship—just hire a spam brigade and in an hour they'll pile so much junk over what you posted that it'll just disappear like a needle in a haystack!"

"If you don't want anyone to find a letter, put it with all the other letters?" Dad replies. "Wait, that's from Conan Doyle too! Or Poe?"

"There you go. They haven't come up with anything new."

"Then you have to print leaflets!" he determines, as business-like as if he'd spent his entire life doing just that. "And give them out where there are people—in squares, at stations ..."

Actually that's a thought. Why didn't I think of that? Of all things, leaflets I can still do. And if I got my boys involved ... I could talk to Igor, to Modzalevsky, and Friedman ... call Vasylenko, for old times' sake. They've all had it with tax inspection, everyone's had it with all this shit; the elections were our one hope that things would change, and if they're wanting to cut off our oxygen on that front too and roll the whole country into concrete ...

"We'll be doing something, Dad."

For a moment, I feel uplifted. As if the clock were turned back to the days of the Student Brotherhood, the fall of 1990—the university deserted, a note on a classroom door—"Everyone's gone to the revolution!" our tents on Independence Square—hard to believe, but back then it was still called The October Revolution Square, the self-published leaflets I used to give out at the metro entrance, the run-ins with the cops—the whole of that scorchingly magnificent autumn, like a blast of hot air into my face. Why do we so rarely remember it? For the single reason that our then ringleaders wasted no time selling out to the then Communists and now sit together in the Supreme *Con*-sel?

But we did rouse Kyiv then—we did *put fear into them,* at least enough to make our Communists sign the declaration of secession from the Soviet Union in August of 1991—like hell the Union would've fallen apart anyway, even if Ukraine hadn't split off! We rocked the boat. And in ten months, the sum of the forces we applied worked, broke the course of history—remember how Kravchuk screamed at us back then, spit flew from his mouth, the day factories went on strike and hundreds of thousands of workers took to the street under our banners: "I'm not afraid of God or the Devil, and I won't be scared of you!" Never mind that scaring him could not be further from our minds back then; we were just thrilled to see our little pebble start an avalanche—and now some fat-ass will tell me that it was all his oil that did it?

I don't know how Lolly managed to hold her tongue; she was there, too, in October of 1990. We were probably standing just feet apart from each other in the same crowd.

"Darynka asleep already?" Dad asks, as if hearing my thoughts.

"She is."

He's never called her Darynka before.

"Burning the midnight oil, are you?"

"Yeah, a little bit. Had a lot of work today."

"That's good," he concludes, not paying attention. And adds, with a belated explosion of surprise, "But gosh darn it, how could people turn rotten so easily?"

"Easier than you think," I say, with great conviction thinking of Yulichka again (damn her!). "If it were only the politicians! Daryna says there's no one left from their echelon—every colleague she could vouch for is no longer in business."

"Keep her safe," Dad suddenly says. "You keep Daryna safe."

Whoa.

I am mute as an ox suddenly. And completely lost; I don't imagine he means that Lolly is in any kind of danger: Dad's not one to panic and not an alarmist. He was the one who taught me, when I reached the age of street fights, never to threaten anyone, that only the losers threaten, but you must be ready to strike if someone messes with you, and if you can learn to keep this readiness turned on inside you at all times, no one will mess with you—lessons he carried with him out of his street-gang Karaganda childhood and for which I will be grateful as long as I live. And only after a moment or two, does it come to me, so simple it sends a chill down my spine: it was Mom he was thinking about! The one he loved—and whom he, as he sees it, failed to keep safe.

What if it's always like that: When one spouse dies, it's always the other's fault? The one who survived somehow didn't hold on to the other—let them slip.

You don't understand squat about your own father until you meet the woman with whom you want to have children. It has never occurred to me before that he might feel guilty for Mom's death. But right then, he said it as if he were asking forgiveness: keep her safe. Keep her, once you've found her, don't let her slip away, because there's nothing worse if you do ...

To hell with how late it is, this is a solemn moment—there aren't many like this between us, and perhaps you don't need many in your entire life—better to appreciate *the gold they bear.* And only now that Dad and I have become equals, now that he has finally put *my love* next to his own in a private hierarchy, do I feel a terrible sadness for Mom. Not that I miss her, but that I feel a sadness *for her*—for the mysterious girl who remained in the photographs and whom my memory, shredded into fragments, can no longer assemble into a whole: a funny biscuit-shaped chignon on her head, as was the fashion at the time, a headscarf tied coquettishly over it, in track pants, carrying a humongous—how did she ever manage it?—backpack (and she carried me, too, just like that, an extra twenty pounds attached to her only in the front like a backpack she couldn't take off—we do put women through all kinds of hell). And everywhere, in every pose she had the same poignant gracefulness of *an accelerating* motion interrupted, the ominously unfinished elegance of a sharpened pencil or a flying arrow: when the precision of the lines determines the vanishing point without deviation, and if the vanishing point cannot be seen, the impression left is unsettling, anxious. Where was this girl always running, aimed so intently? (What did she come for, why did she leave so quickly—never having lived to her intended vanishing point?)

And she was always running—she chased after something all her life, didn't settle down even after she became a mother, as happens to most romantic girls. Well, at least it taught me at an early age that I'd never replace the entire world for any woman.... The Plast scouts were banned back then; Mom, being an alpinist, went hiking and took climbing groups to the mountains for sport. She used to say to Granny Lina that in the mountains one is closer to God, and that before every expedition she'd dream the exact position of stars above her future campsite. She also sang in a choir that eventually got disbanded for "religious propaganda"—they sang carols—and knew by heart what seemed like everything Lesya Ukrainka ever wrote, "Oh, for that body do not sigh." How was she supposed to live with all that in the hopelessness of the Soviet seventies? A heartrending, incomprehensible life dropped, as if from a cliff into an abyss, into an utterly inanimate time—like a bird that'd flown in through the wrong window.

I am sorry for the *incompleteness* of Mom's life, and in comparison, seen from afar, our lives—my own and my dad's—appear regular, like everyone else's. And they *are* like everyone else's, that's the thing: it's the same—for everyone. I don't see a single complete life around me: they're all somehow off, crooked, whenever you take a closer look. The only difference is that on this incompletion scale Dad and I are somewhere in the middle, and Mom is closer to the starting point. Much, much closer.

And someone has to pay for everyone's incompletion. The law of equilibrium, no?

I always knew I could never hurt a woman. Never, in no way, not one. I always felt sorry for them: I saw all girls as ethereal, ever-vanishing creatures marked on their foreheads with a secret touch of death. The fact that boys are also mortal, and with, actually, a much greater statistical probability of mortality, I only came to appreciate later, in adulthood, empirically—yet it did not affect the way I perceived the world. I was so sorry for Yulichka, too, the poor little slut. And—I can't help it—in my heart of hearts, albeit infinitesimally—I still feel sorry for her.

And that, Dad, is the rub.

Except that I don't tell him this, of course.

"Consider it done, Dad," is all I say, like that mafioso in Tarantino's *Reservoir Dogs*. I could've added, as the security guard at my building puts it, "I'll shoot if they come"—and I wouldn't have been lying, but it would've been too much, a whiff of that teenage boasting that, as he had once warned me, was the last resort of losers.

"You've changed, you know," Dad says unexpectedly, startling me.

"Me? Meaning what?"

"You've matured ... gotten more serious, like. And thank God because I was afraid you'd turn out a flake. You were a bit spacey, you know. Grandma, God rest her soul, kept worrying you took after Stefania—she kept thinking you were too delicate for a boy."

"But I thought Grandma loved Mom ..."

"Of course she did, how couldn't she?" he replies, taking offense at my obtuseness. "But one has nothing to do with the other. Boys are one thing, girls another ... Grandma did not have a daughter, so she delighted in Stefania as if she were her own. But a boy is a different matter entirely."

"Oh, I see what you mean."

Things are getting a bit foggy in my head (sleep, one little eye, sleep, the other), and I don't grasp right away that Dad is talking about me from the perspective of *his own time*, speaking from the apartment where virtually nothing has changed since I was little—except maybe there's more dust and the upholstery is more worn. And that reality of his is also a part of me—and likely not the worst, and to keep it safely attached to my mental file, all I have to do is let Dad set the course for our conversation and just go with the flow, picking up the cutoff ends of his thoughts: he chops them short because they are obvious to him, and he thinks they're obvious to me as well. As he sees it, I still inhabit the same reality he does, one which contains a set of quite specific, commonly known requirements for a boy. And the most amazing thing is—I do understand what he has in mind.

"Well, we all know Granny had her own standards."

"Our lads"—that was her standard. Whenever Granny Lina said that, it was clear she did not mean my dad and me but totally different lads who were light-years ahead of me, and possibly even of him. The same impression was left on me by the silver-toothed old men, all with identically unbending, stiff military bearing, who used to gather occasionally at our apartment while Gramps was alive—to argue about Kim Philby, the Cambridge Four, and other things I did not understand. All of them had been through prisons and camps, but did not seem to mention that much around me, did not seem to talk much about the past in general—they were more interested in current politics and in when the Soviet Union might fall apart, while I, at the time, was mostly interested in girls, Depeche Mode, Formula I, radio circuits from the *Young Technician* magazine, and other earthly delights, and only came to appreciate the precision of the old men's forecasts when the Soviet Union did fall apart.

Strangely, the old troops did not speak out even after that. It was only from Lolly's digging that I managed to put some of the pieces together—and eventually figured out that Granny and Gramps must have been working for the underground right up to their arrest, in 1947, only the KGB never found out: they were deported as family members, "for aiding and abetting," "for Gela," and they both had all their own teeth—they never had any knocked out during interrogations. The old Areopagus that came to visit them, just as it must have come at nights to the townhouse on Krupyarska decades earlier, had to have known more, but the men, all of them with the silver replacement teeth that Granny and Gramps miraculously never needed, went to the grave, one by one, never having betrayed their secrets. And when they said our lads, they had the dead in mind—the ones who had fallen and whom they held in their mind at all times as if standing at attention before them—and that's how they carried their unbendable, military bearing through until the end.

And I was growing up surrounded by dead women—I throbbed with a lasting, ever-present caution: What would Mom say if she could see me right now? Great-Aunt Gela, too, somehow imperceptibly resembling Mom (the two of them, with time, have melded for me into a single entity), wearing a large round, white, lace collar, a bit like a bib, watched me from atop Grandma's writing desk. Out of a 1941 filigreed frame: the picture was taken the day that Gela, wearing this very bib, arrived from Switzerland, where she had been studying to become an engineer back in Nazi-occupied Lviv—"to gain Ukraine." In October of 1990, at the height of our strike, Granny Lina (she was in the hospital already) sent me that photo from Lviv, along with the one of Gramps. She took it out of the frame, sealed it in a plastic bag, and sent it with some man on the train. And was gone herself before the year's end.

Granny may not have drilled me into a soldier with unbendable bearing, but she did accomplish something else: gradually, without me noticing, she pushed Mom, the way she had been in real life, out of my memory and replaced her with the image of another woman, shrouding even Mom's death in an aura of heroism that was borrowed, as I understood only later, from another life—and another time. Whenever the name Stefania was spoken in our home, everyone would fall reverently silent for a moment—as if we were remembering a great heroic act. Or at least that's how I always thought of it when I was little. I even made up a story for myself, which I came to believe and told my friends in perfectly good conscience: that my mom had died on Hoverla saving beginners who only survived thanks to her. This sounded heroic, almost from the same department as our lads, and that there was nothing especially heroic about a mountaineer's death in the mountains, that it only proved that a person couldn't very well stand her bland and slow life down in the valley, were things no one ever said out loud.

Granny did with her daughter-in-law's life as she saw fit—as she saw necessary. And it was as if Granny's own dead sucked Mom into their fold, vacuumed her in, and dissolved her within them. Made her for me, forever, indiscernible, leaving me only that piercing pity for all the girls—like small birds, who'd accidentally flown through the wrong window into this world and at any moment would flit through the smallest available opening.

And dreams—they left me those, too. The dreams. This is mine, no one can take it away from me: the ability to see in my dreams what's invisible during the day, it's from my mom; it's my legacy from her—the girl "not of this world" about whom I have no more stories to tell.

Dad, on the other hand, fresh and chirpy at three in the morning—invigorated by the chance to fill a sleepless hour with all the memories he's bursting with all the way over there—could talk about *his* mother until broad daylight: even now, thirteen years after her death, Granny Lina remains inexhaustible. She is the ever-present fourth member of our family circle in the middle of the night—here, where the emptied tea mug glows white in the lamp's circle of light and the woman I love sleeps behind this wall: she, too, was brought to me by Granny Lina. Reached over from the other side and got her. Reeled her in with the same bait, Great-Aunt Gela …

And that, by the way, is exactly how things worked.

She is in charge here. She made it all happen. Made all of us happen. She, Granny Lina. Ms. Lina, as the neighbors used to call her. Polina, Polyenka—as the Moscow women she met in exile called her. My own grandmother, Apollinaria Ambroziivna Dovgan, may the good Lord rest her soul. Put everyone where they belong. What a woman.

I have reached that stage when you don't feel tired because you've lost the sense of your own body altogether (except that raising it off the chair requires an effort beyond anything imaginable—you'd sooner just fall asleep right on the spot!) and your mind is operating on an oscillating, revved-up frequency, and thoughts and impressions, mixed together, rush through it in a single fiery current you have no hope of quantizing. But this incredible sensation, intoxicating and effervescent—like what a marathon runner feels at the eighteenth mile, when you get a second wind and endorphins come gushing from who-knows-what secret reservoirs in your brain; when everything that had been so obvious that it blended right into the wallpaper—suddenly flares up, all at once, as if at sunrise, and all you can do is wonder: how did I not see this before, how all of us, our entire family, the way we are, have been shaped by Granny Lina—and her alone? Like the Easter paska breads, big and small, that she didn't allow anyone to touch—always kneading the dough by herself in the kitchen, shaping them and settling them into the oven herself, and all we were required to do was step around the apartment lightly and refrain from jumping or stomping, lest the paskas cave.

From somewhere else, somehow I remember this sense of awe (pride, admiration) upon seeing a person so close to you (a woman! a weak creature, as you'd gotten used to believing ...) suddenly rise before you into a magnificent, grand figure, while you just stand there like a tree stump (woods, snow, fir branches ...) and reel with wonder: How did she manage that? She is so small. (Grandma's head barely reached my chest.)

"That brown notebook," Dad's voice scrapes its way into my awareness, "in which she made notes for her memoirs ..."

The slight cognitive dissonance finally shakes me awake.

"The brown notebook?" I ask, surprised and almost conscious. "Granny's? The one with the cryptograms? I thought it was dark green, wasn't it?"

I would have sworn it was green. I can see it as if it were in front of me: the dark-green cover and a couple dozen pages inside, laced with mysterious acronyms—like the code of a compromised intelligence service.

"You clear forgot!" Dad bristles. "I showed it to you the time you came filming—a brown notebook, a thick one, with a calico cover. I've got it right here on my desk!"

Maybe when moving from one time to another there's something like the refraction of light when it enters a different medium—and that's why old objects change their shape and color in our memories. (Then what about sound? What would happen to sound, to voices sounded long ago?)

"Speaking of which," Dad says into the receiver from his small corner of the world, still illuminated by Granny Lina like the light of a dead star, "would you happen to recall a comrade of hers who had the initials A.O.?"

"You're asking me?"

Jeez, how does he think this works—that we're the same age? I couldn't remember a single of those old guys' first names, forget the initials. Although, wait, maybe if I think really hard …

"A-O," Dad spells out clearly as if to someone deaf. "Or also, Ad. Or."

"Ad. Or.?" I echo stupidly.

"I'm certain it's a name," Dad says proudly. "I've already deciphered two names from her notebook: Krychevsky—he is that friend of Grandpa's that died in Norilsk, during the uprising—and old Banakh, the doctor, do you remember him? He visited when you were little, came all the way from around Sambir—they wouldn't let him live in Lviv after the war."

"I am just a Sambir lad, Mother's sick and Father's dead. I'll go sing, and I'll go dance. I am here to raise hell …" my mind fires off a couple of lines from an old street song, instantly swallowed by a blast of machine-gun fire—ha, missed me, didn't you, dog your mother?

"No, Dad, I don't remember."

"Neither do I!" he says, interpreting my answer his own way. "And it comes up quite a few times in Grandma's notes—sometimes A.O. and sometimes Ad. Or. And the Ad. Or. is sometimes spelled without periods, as one word, Ador, so it's like in French—je vous adore, I adore you. Same root as adoration. Doesn't look like it's an alias; I do think these are someone's real initials, but I can't remember any of their circle who'd fit. Whom could she possibly have coded this way?"

"What if you're thinking of the wrong people? This could have been an admirer of hers back when she was a young girl, and you're just fixated on the war; you want to keep the shrapnel coming …"

"Nonsense! She's got whole chains of events spelled out with these initials! Like formulas. You just listen. I'll read it to you … hang on; let me grab the notebook …"

Swoosh, swoosh, swoosh—he shuffles off away from the phone, the heels of his loafers slapping against the floor, before I have a chance to say anything. If I end up not getting any shut-eye, Lolly will have to take the wheel in the morning. We're having some serious fun with this night, the old man and I—catching up on all our unspent hours worth of talk at once. Or, to be more precise, it's Granny Lina who's having fun with us. How much longer does she have in her?

"Here." Dad reappears noisily in the receiver, fumbling with something. I hear the rustle of pages being turned. "Here, found it! 1944—Grandma had a separate page for each year and, looks like, filled each page in gradually, as she recalled what happened that year. Here you go: Meeting Iv.—she means Ivan, your grandpa; she has him as Iv. throughout … then, capital B, Briefcase. That's how they met, during a Nazi raid …"

"I know. Grandpa dropped his briefcase with leaflets into her arms, and she then carried them all the way home, right under the Germans' noses, through the streets."

"That's right! And just after this briefcase, in parentheses, like a comment, she has G. with A.O. to, and then a cross, meaning death, then PZK and the date, in Latin letters—November 1943. P-Z-K—that's an acronym, German most likely … PZ was how they referred to the police, K for Kommandant. But there's a cross, too, which means it was a person, a Christian. Looks like a PZK died that November of '43, maybe he was a German … they could have had a raid after something like that…. In any case, G. and A.O. were both there, and looks like it also involved a briefcase with leaflets in it …"

"Or a gun."

This pops out of me totally by itself, as if someone else thought it. While Dad was talking, I was thinking of nothing, only saw the entry in Grandma's notebook scrolling out before me like a news crawl on a monitor: *Meeting Iv. Briefcase (G. with A. O. to †PZK. XI 1943)*.

She was going to write where she learned that trick with the briefcase: from G. and A.O. This is no cipher—just notes she made for her outline, which she, unfortunately, never fleshed out. But I have heard a story sort of like that before—about a briefcase, with a gun in it, and which, for that reason, needed to be gotten rid of, and also with the Nazis, and in the street, and in the middle of the day. Or did I see it in a movie?

"Or with a gun," Dad concurs, rustling pages; he is focused on his own ideas. "Or here, here's another one! 1947, October. G.'s last visit. This has a whole string of initials, and separately, among them, Ador lives—see, here she has Ador!"

"And who is this G.?"

"What do you mean, who's G.?" he's asks, stunned, taken aback by the depth of my idiocy. "Gela, of course!"

Sweet Jesus! Dad—he's still working on preparing material for Lolly's film—we never told him that the show's over. He knows nothing—neither about the pre-election acquisition of Lolly's channel by Russian investors, nor about Lolly's unemployment. He only watches TV, so the only information he has is what they say on the air.

And how could I tell him now?

"You probably oughtta go to bed, Aidy," Dad determines sympathetically, having interpreted my slowness in his own way. "You go turn in, and I'll play around for a bit longer."

As if I am still the eight-year-old boy who lost his mother, and he, who promised to be both Mom and Dad, is wishing me a good night standing in the door of my bedroom—before he goes back to the kitchen where he will stay up late solving the problems in the take-home math exams for well-connected students, the main source of supplementing his engineer's wages. At eight, I could not yet understand that his promise to be both Mom and Dad meant not remarrying—and he did not remarry, he kept his word. Granny Lina did implant in him some of her generation's unbendable resolve.

I would give anything to be able to hug him right now—to grab him in a bear hug and hold him close, my lonely, aging dad, who has podagra and diabetes and smokes too much, and has a wheeze in his chest, and flakes of dandruff on his jacket (when we went to film in Lviv last year it was Lolly who noticed it, said to me: you should tell your dad about anti-dandruff shampoo)—if he were here, that's exactly what I would do, although our family has always been sort of ashamed of any displays of male sentimentality. Grandpa and Dad, caught in a fit of tenderness, would at most ruffle my hair, or slap me on the shoulder, meaning, it's all good, pal, hang in there! And if he were here, it would've been enough, after we hugged, to slap him on the shoulder in silent understanding: it's all good, old man ... so he would know that I'm here for him, that he can count on me.

I know I'm not a very good son—although I'm considered to be good because I regularly send him money. But a good son—that's not money, or even taking care of one's father when he begins to need help. It's having the balls to accept your father's legacy and everything it means and make the honest payment for it with your own life—without trying to jump off that train. Maybe it takes time. Maybe it takes years and years to *become* a son—biology alone doesn't cut it.

"I only asked you about this," Dad explains apologetically, as the vision I had of him in his spot of light over in Lviv, backed by the bookshelves with old magazines and dusty pennants (pennants! I remember them now—the pennants! and the trophies—the trophies Mom won—that's what's up there on top!), now goes out of focus before my suddenly moist eyes, "because this Ador must somehow be connected with Gela, so I thought maybe Darynka could use it.... It might be important ... and I don't even know if it's a man or a woman."

"Probably a man," I force myself to say. He doesn't need to know anything; let him sleep easy (sleep, one little eye, sleep, the other). "Or. must be Orest, no?"

My voice sounds normal. Almost.

"Nope, can't be," Dad perks up. "If it'd been Orest, it'd be first! Grandma kept the same order of initials throughout; she's always had ironclad order in everything! First the name, then the last name. Or. has to be the last name, but this Ad. ... could be anything—Adam, Adela?"

"Adrian," says someone else for me, in my own almost-normal voice—and I feel the unleashed word fly through the receiver like a rock thrown into a deep well, an incredibly deep well like a dark shaft ...

> cutting the air with a whine, and while I, above the
> curb, wait
> for the sound of it hitting the water, cold goose
> bumps crawl up my legs... *Whoosh!*
> A splash, bubbles, circles on the surface of the
> water, a slowing down of movement,
> a change of medium, a passing into another time,
> "Forgive me, Adrian."
> *Crackle, houlin, laik wind in ze wires.... Clicks, and*
> *somesin laik laik mashin gun shutin ...*

Miss Yulichka. Comrade-in-arms, my right hand, Mata Hari ...

A fluctuation of air is all it is, I say to myself. Sound is simply fluctuations of pressure that fade exponentially because they cannot last forever: the first law of thermodynamics. The fluctuations cannot remain because they are not recorded on physical media—not anywhere. There is no virtual, open-access audio library of once-sounded voices out there. One cannot welcome visitors to a museum of children's secrets.

I know all this. But I also know that "Ad." is him. Adrian. The one after whom I was named. My godfather, in a certain sense.

I just know it, and that's it.

"You're right," Dad says. "How did I not think of that?" And he instantly moves to the next level, like in a computer game, "In Temirtau, when she was pregnant, she kept saying to me, you'll have a little brother, Adrian. She was so certain it would be a boy. And she was right, as it turned out."

She wanted to have this name in the family, I think to myself. She wanted the name to belong to our family—as the man who had borne that name was supposed to belong to her.

"And when you came," Dad unspools his tale, "as soon as we got word we had a boy, she greeted you: Adrian! I can hear her the way she said it, now—it was like she … exhaled it. Sealed it."

"Uhu." What else can I say? That to name both her son and grandson after some unrelated guy, a woman must have once really wanted to have that guy be their father and grandfather? I don't see any other reason—but maybe I don't really know women?

She must have loved that man very much, my Granny Lina. Only he loved another—Aunt Gela, her precious sister.

"Now, Stefania, she wanted our boy to be Ostap," Dad mumbles on like a somnambulist. "And if we had a girl, she wanted to name her Lesya. And I thought to name the kid after Grandfather—Ivas, or Ivanka…. But Stefania agreed with Grandma right away: Let it be Adrian! We could see it really mattered to her."

Of course it did. Both in 1950, and then in 1970, when I was born, it mattered just the same. Twenty years changed nothing. In her own way, however she could, Granny Lina also spent her life trying to set right something that had not come to be. Something that was meant to happen—but did not.

"Do you have any idea who it might have been?" Dad asks. A touch fearfully, as it feels to me. Now he is the boy who is afraid of losing his mom: the image he'd had since he was little has suddenly come alive, like a statue that's drawn a breath and is ready to leave its pedestal and set out in an unknown direction—and I bite my tongue before I let my ready answer roll off of it: I've seen him.

For a split second, the unspoken words billow out from my lips like bubblegum—and then burst inaudibly: poof, and they're gone. And it's not true, anyway, because *I* haven't seen him—I've only seen pieces of footage from inside his head. (His later-to-be-exploded head.) My beloved has seen him. No, my wife—from the night the two of us dreamed the same dream, something has changed between us: she is now inside my life, like a part of me. Apparently, this is exactly how married people experience themselves. And this is the change Dad meant when he said I've matured.

"He died, Dad," I say out loud. "In battle." And because this sounds suddenly curt, as if I were suggesting that this dead man be buried and forgotten posthaste, I add, "At the same time as Aunt Gela. With her."

"Oh, I see," Dad sighs—relieved, it sounds to me. "Then it all makes sense," and catches himself, "but how do you know?"

"From Daryna," I say. Since that's basically how it, in fact, is.

"She's a trooper." Dad reaches for the highest praise it was ever acceptable for a man in our family to give.

"Yep. Something like that."

"Alright then ... you go now, go to bed, son."

He is letting me go—and I understand: he wants to be alone now with his newly gained knowledge, to roll it over in his hands, hold it up against the light, work it into his previously undisturbed picture of the past until he can't see the seams. He might have to move some things around in that picture in order to do this; that's not out of the question, things have to be cleaned up as always happens when one brings a new piece of furniture into a well-lived-in room. This is indeed work that takes time, and I understand him perfectly.

"You oughtta turn in too, Dad. The notebook can wait till tomorrow."

"Uhu."

But of course he won't; he couldn't possibly—he'll go sit right back down and read it all over, picking out, with his new eyes, the A.O. and Ad. Or. from the web of Grandma's acronyms, like one glowing light in a dead string. Who knows, he might get at something else this way, light by light ... Lolly's method.

"Thank you for calling."

Wow, it really got to the old man.

"Don't mention it. I'm sorry I don't call as often as I'd like ... been totally buried at work."

If only you knew, Dad!

"Of course, of course, like I don't know how it is," he mutters on. "Sure, it's a chore. Nothing to be done, though." And, as if plucking up his courage, he exhales from somewhere very deep, all the way in his gut, "You've got to make your own buck, since your father left you no means!"

And this bursts with such fierce, ancient bitterness—like the pain of defeat, for years unmentioned—that it cuts me to the quick, makes me draw in air sharply, through my teeth.

"Dad, why would you say that? Did I ever ask you for any?"

And how exactly did you pull off the trick, I want to ask him, of keeping that unwavering old Galician mandate buried inside you well into your old age: a man must provide for his family! Some people these are? You'd think they didn't spend their best years in slavery to the "Union unbreakable," but lived somewhere in Switzerland or at least in their old prewar Poland, where there was no shame in owning a townhouse one paid for, because one could, still, honestly earn enough to *pay* for a townhouse instead of stealing it. How could they keep the two together—spend fifty years waiting for the Union to fall apart, and yet somehow believe the entire time that a man could live in it according to Grandfather Ambroziy's standards—a man must provide for his family!—and not go rotten?

I could have also added that I know only too well who did manage (and how) to accumulate certain means for their children. I have to deal with these children of Soviet apparatchiks—the current politicians, government officials, and—less often—bank directors (few of them are smart enough to be in finance) much more often than he can imagine, because they are the ones who constitute the lion's share of my clientele: they were the ones who, armed with their stolen capital, were the first to begin collecting what used to be my ancestors' property. It doesn't matter how many times I've tried to remind myself that a collection, no matter who owns it, is always a collection—a way of preserving things that otherwise would have been destroyed, or the more valuable of them smuggled out of the country. And until the country, from which for centuries people have pilfered anything that wasn't nailed down, learns to value its own inheritance, I can help to keep what has survived—twig by twig, crumb by crumb, like an ant—safe and at home. Despite all such self-comforting, this kind of clientele remains the most distasteful part of my job, and I try to separate, in my mind, the collections from their owners, and add to the collections for the collection's sake, just so it'll be there.

Or does Dad think that I somehow begrudge him not crossing the line to cooperate with the KGB, not growing fat and stealing his own share, with which he could have secured for me the opportunity to be doing physics now instead of making my own buck? Well, I don't recall many offspring of the Soviet elites among our physicists; the few that dabbled in science have long split to rake it in at gazproms and naftogazes.

And God knows there is much else I could have said to him to make him stop feeling *guilty* for having honestly worked like a dog his whole life and not being able to provide for his son, because there is no fault of his in this—this is … it's really beyond the pale. But a wall of my father's deaf and stubborn silence rises in the receiver like a concrete dam—the kind of silence that deflects every possible argument well before it can be leveled; no words of mine can reach him. Any words I might say would be too small. It doesn't matter that I never asked him for anything—he failed, in his own eyes, to fulfill the obligations he had taken upon himself. And I have no weapon or tool that could crack this petrified pain in him.

So I retreat.

"You ever think of cutting back on smoking, Dad?" is all I say.

"No worries!" he responds, unexpectedly chipper, apparently happy to hear the topic change. "You can't fell me with an ax!"

"Yeah, that's what you think … I can hear it all the way over here—'the box of whistles playing,' as Grandpa used to say."

We exchange a few more routine lines—fading fluctuations, an exponential process.… He's right, it's time to sleep. Now—I can feel it—I'll go out cold as soon as I put my head on the pillow, just like Lolly did earlier. And will sleep like a log, without dreams.

"Tell Daryna," Dad reminds me before he hangs up.

"About what?"

"About Adrian, what else?"

"Oh, yeah. Sure, I will."

"Good night then. You all take care of yourselves now, okay?"

"You too, Dad. Good night. Sweet dreams."

Click.

Beep-beep-beep …

I sit, holding the receiver, now mute, in my hands, and stare at it as if waiting for something else. A thought pops up—a last bubble of oxygen from the bottom of the well, stirred up by the rock: if I ever have children, I'd like a girl—they have it a bit easier in this world after all.

Dude, time to sign off, you've still got the whole day to figure out tomorrow. Or rather, the whole day today.

And the day after. And the one after that.

Alright. How do I get to my feet again?

From the Cycle Secrets: Untitled/ Ohne Titel/Sans Titre

"**W**here did you get this?" Daryna asks.

"What?" the cuckoo yokel replies, half-spooked.

Just about had it wit' dem all, he did. Dey'd come and talked up such a storm you couldn't hear your own self think. Da other ones, dose come before, bought da clock and sideboard and wanted the other clock too, dat littler one over dere dat father brought from the war, when da wife put her foot down, said I ain't gonna let you clean me all out—dey didn't wag dem's tongues for nothing, one-two, counted off the dollars, loaded up da things into dem van and gone oft! Dese new ones catechize you worse than cops, God forbid.

But, he's no fool; he's caught on to which way da wind's blowing, right off. If not for dis skirt he'd seen on TV, he'd of told her boyfriend to go stick it and dat'd of been end of story. Wouldn't of listened to nothing. Clear as day, he's that antiques-Yulka's boozer ex who'd called here before, and tried to get him. Da one who scared the daylights out of Yulka, so she asked to not come to her work and meet up in da park instead. Looks like he couldn't suck anything off of Yulka no more, so he'd gone found him a new one.

She's not bad to look at, either, he's done well.... What'd she seen in him? Tho, you wouldn't tell he's a boozer just by looking at him, and his hands don't shake yet. Must be a heck of a fucker— milks 'em all dry, and dem girls probably thank him afterward.... Heck, I got nothing to complain about either, thank God. Do one a good turn myself if da chance arose.... No helping it—he squeezed the antiques-Yulka in the mudroom after she'd let him pinch her tit. She'd of let him hold it and ball it, too. She clucked right back at him, and stuck her hand into his pants, and said, Wow! You could tell she'd took a shine to him right off, back when he first came to her store and she took him out to an expensive diner, said, if my boozer turns up now we'll have no peace....

Young girl like dat, they always got eyes for a man with some 'sperience, 'specially if she'd got burned already once. But—dat's all bygones, old news. And he's a family man hisself: might get hungry somewhere else, but likes to sup at home anyhow. Dis one here—she's quick as a fox, look at her eyes sweep over this whole place here! Now dey think I'm s'posed to tell em like at confession—who, and what, where'd it come from?

"Where did you get this?" Daryna repeats.

"What?"

"This," Daryna says, rising from her chair, and walking, like a sleepwalker, across the room with one hand outstretched in front of her.

Seeing the change in her face, Adrian springs to his feet, too, as if she really were a sleepwalker stepping along a ledge and could slip to her death at any second; the yokel rises after him, drawn inexorably into the same flow of motion, as though they were all in a wind tunnel. And this is how the procession presents itself to an ample-bodied wife, in a stretch T-shirt and a bra one size too small, who appears at this very instant in the doors between the room and the kitchen: the three of them, spellbound, moving in the same direction, one after another, as if in a slow-motion game of tag—and what are they all after, it's just a wall?

"This," says Daryna, coming to a halt against the wall and pressing her fingers to "this" like a blind man who's just recognized a dear face under his fingers.

Adrian can't see what it is—Daryna is standing between him and whatever object has arrested her, her hand in place, not moving. Before he got up, he was sitting with his back to that wall, and did not get a good look at what was pasted over it—a deep colorful blob, a poster or something.... As soon as he'd stepped inside the house, he quickly and professionally sized up the decor and the furnishings, and his spirits lifted:

this may not be a gold mine, but there was wool to be shorn off this yokel yet.

One is surrounded in this home by such a noxiously packed and savagely motley mix of bric-a-brac from the last two generations that Adrian would not be surprised to spot an antique gramophone from a Stakhanovite grandfather or some other marvel like that. And while there is no gramophone in evidence, and neither are there any of the oilcloth wallrugs with swans on them that have recently become such a hot item, most of what is here is 1970s junk—the peak of this rural boss's prosperity no doubt.

Displayed, museum-like, behind glass in a monumentally cumbersome hutch is a gilded Madonna dinnerset; also present are the most impractical Bohemian crystal ashtrays in the world, chaste as virgins and heavy as icebergs, and right next to them (Adrian could barely keep from smiling)—a painstakingly cross-stitched picture of hunters at camp from Perov's painting. The hunters are draped over a Samsung TV, on top of which—now we're getting somewhere!—stands an old stone clock, a splendid piece, a German Manteluhr with a carved oak facade, likely by W. Haid (make sure to check the back), Third Reich, 1930s or '40s, definitely a trophy. The yokel's ancestors must've done well for themselves in that war if that's what they managed to sneak back home—as Daryna's mother says, one man's war is another man's bonanza.

Experience has taught Adrian that such rural honchos (those who in the Brezhnev era had clawed their way to where they could steal)—kolkhoz administrators, farm managers, warehouse managers, machine- and motor-pool directors—did not hold on to things that were actually old and instead rushed to replace them with whatever was new and "city," naming their daughters Ilona and Angela rather than Katrya or Mariyka. He figures the yokel had daughters by the heap of *Cosmopolitans* and *Teens* on the bookshelf and the glam advertising posters that are plastered, it seems, over every inch of bare wall, hitting one, like ammonia, with the acrid whiff of the present.

Apparently, the family isn't doing well enough to replace all their furniture with the newest set from an Otto catalog in one fell swoop, and the most current symbols of material comfort were fit into the Gypsy-caravan density of their home bit by bit, patch over patch: a monstrous multitiered chandelier of several hundred crystals, a faux leopard skin on the floor in front of the couch. It isn't hard to understand why the yokel decided to part with the old clock and the credenza (How on earth did it fit anywhere in here, you can barely turn as it is?), but there can be only one reason why it took him until now to do so, the one Adrian chose instinctively as he formulates the best strategy for negotiating with the man: he is loath to part with his stuff.

All these things, accumulated in his home over decades, must be, for this man, the "goods" that he would be very sorry to see go, evidence of his former special status in the village. He probably thinks that all his stuff is still worth astronomical amounts of money—the kind that, in his day, neither a dairymaid nor a tractor driver had, and still do not have today. Puckered up tighter than a snare drum, the yokel sits on his pile of junk like a gnome, imagining himself the master of treasures uncounted. A type like that would actually sooner refuse to sell anything than give an inch on the price. So in a certain sense, Yulichka did not lie, or, rather, like all competent liars, she built her lies on half-truths: the yokel really did turn her away at some point, didn't let her strip him of everything that had any market value—he let her have only the most valuable objects, because at the end of the day, a few tens of thousands of US dollars, a few suitcases full of crisp new Benjamin Franklins present a temptation no gnome can resist (and afterward he probably whined that he let it go too cheap ...).

Focused on the business at hand, Adrian missed the colorful picture in the far corner of the room, so packed with ads and posters that it looked like an iconostasis—deciding instead to ignore it and intentionally sat with his back to it. The blob held no antiquarian interest and would only distract him from the conversation, because (now, looking at Daryna's stiffened back, he remembers this clearly) there was something about it that did draw one's eye, much more so than an airbrushed poster. It's not a poster at all, in fact. What *is* there?

"What about it?" the yokel answers cheerily. The woman's tone got him a bit scared—she's gone all nervous, and he's got no desire to get mixed up in any stories or anything. "You like it?"

She turns to face him, her lip bitten down hard, and the way she looks at him scares the man for real.

"Where did you get this painting?"

"And is dat, 'scuse me, any business of yours?"

"It is, very much so," Daryna says, hearing her own voice return to her as if from a great distance: it is calm, but quiet, and very, very slow, as if spun at a lower rpm, like on an old turntable—the last time she heard this voice was in her boss's office.

"The author of this work is a friend of mine. The police are looking for this painting. They've been searching for four years."

"It's Vlada's?" Adrian gasps.

Daryna nods. Her lips are trembling. "Her signature's even on it. Only it's been cut off ..."

The movement continues: now all three of them are huddling in front of the painting, like seals caught in one net, in a narrow gap between the couch and a massive mirror-faced mahogany wardrobe, which, apparently, replaced the old walnut credenza (most likely Art Deco, but possibly even older than that; in any case, that trophy was locally sourced from a landlord's estate and redistributed by the Bolsheviks). Each tries to push the other away or peek over their shoulder at the painting—and the yokel is the most enthusiastic of them all, as if he's never seen the painting before and it wasn't in his own house that it hung. Pinned to the wall the same way rural folk used to pin up their oilcloth rugs with swans on them—unframed and unmounted, a snakeskin, the Frog Princess's pelt shed and splattered with colorful blood, used here to cover a hole in this improvised iconostasis, between the dazzle of a glossy blue seascape from a 2001 calendar and a silicone blonde, smiling a pearly toothed smile and holding, in her hand, as triumphantly as if it were the Russian flag, a toothbrush with a dollop of Aquafresh on it. That's quite a sizeable hole, and a nonstandard one, too—the canvas is cut to size to fit over the whole gap, at once.

Daryna holds her fingers to the sliced-off edges of the canvas like a surgeon to the edges of a wound. It's a collage, she thinks, feeling sensation drain from the tips of her fingers—they just went ahead and made themselves a collage, the best they could. In the past, rural families used to compose these using family photographs—framed them and hung them up in the main room in between the icons; she's seen this in the abandoned homes in the Chernobyl zone: grandfather, grandmother, a group shot from a high-school graduation, wedding pictures with the maid of honor and best man in red sashes, a boy in a Soviet Army sergeant's uniform, a whole iconostasis of the many-sized and many-colored (from black-and-white to Kodachrome) kin; and in the gaps between the pictures—which must grate on a rural eye like patches of untilled land—they would carefully paste in strips of colored paper, sometimes even decorative cutouts. That was the place Vlada's work took here. What was left of her painting, to be exact. A piece that had once been a collage, composed according to the very same principles of this primitive aesthetic—and now returned to its source. Collage to collage. Ashes to ashes.

"Dis here?" the yokel fumes. "Come on! I can drawr better dan dat myself!"

Any idiot could, he boils genuinely, in his mind, irked that he let himself be intimidated so easily—big deal, splatter up some paint so it gets all wrinkled up on itself. Lioshka-the-tile guy, the one who did the loo, could do a better job of it—he puts his heart to it, never was dat he didn't line it all up nice and tidy, smooth as a baby's bottom! Dis stuff here's all puckered, what's dere to stare at? What's dere to be going searching for it? Wanna play chicken? Well, I ain't one to let anyone piss on my parade; I ain't born yesterday, thank the good Lord!

"Hang on just a minute, sir," Aidy interrupts, having some-how—the yokel can't tell when—edged him away from the subject of the discussion and ceased to address him directly; were he not so consumed at this instant by going from defense to offense, the yokel would very well begin to doubt whether this character is indeed the worthless good-for-nothing the antiques-Yulka had told him he was: the yokel knows how bosses talk and ought to have recognized in Yulka's "boozer ex's" calm ease a boss's pro-fessional habit of moving people around without resistance, like pawns on a board, in order to achieve a result important to all, that is demonstrated in the army by ranking officers from platoon commanders on up—but the yokel hasn't yet caught on to what, exactly, result these two are shooting for, and this man's question, asked of the woman, fails to sound important to him.

"Where did you say you saw the signature?" Aidy asks.

"Right here," Daryna points. "She always signed this way—VlMatusevych, without a dot."

"I see, yes … it's cut off in the middle—you can see the 'u' but the 's' is questionable …"

"This is hers beyond any doubt, even without the signature, Aidy. No need for an examination—this is one of the works that was flown in from Frankfurt. From the *Secrets* series. I saw them all, remember, at her workshop, before they went to Germany for the show. And there are slides; it can be identified."

"Who has the slides? Vadym?"

"Nina Ustýmivna. She is the legal heir, until Katrusya comes of age."

"Splendid."

"I just can't remember the title right now. It should have been on the other edge, there on the left, but that part has all been cut off … this used to be about this wide," she spreads her arms like a fisherman showing off the size of his catch, "and it was taller too, I remember the composition well."

"I cut it to size," pipes up the wife.

Her appearance in the kitchen door has gone unnoticed, and at the sound of her voice all three turn and stare at her with various degrees of shock; before speaking, just in case, she's crossed her arms defensively under her breasts, which are already spilling out from her overburdened bra; and her thusly proffered bust, taken together with her powerful neck and arms, looks magnificent in its way (rolls of fatty dough around the edges of her undergarment are thrown into high relief under her Lycra T-shirt). She puts this bust before her like a shield—evidently picking up on her husband's alarm—and is rushing to his rescue before the old fool can screw everything up from here to Tuesday.

She'll do the cutting alright, Adrian thinks, contemplating, not without interest, this menopausal socialist-realist milkmaid in front of him. She'll cut all sort of things. He quickly exchanges glances with Daryna, and pulls out his business card.

"And you must be the lady of the house? Pleased to meet you."

The shield is shattered—the wife takes the business card, but does not know what to do with it, and walks over to the shelf where her eyeglasses sit—to read it over. Daryna gets the chills—it's the familiar shiver that runs through the body in the presence of death, like a short circuit—and she keeps silent, afraid that her voice will fail her.

"So where did you say you got this painting from?" Adrian casually inquires of the wife, as if continuing an interrupted conversation.

"Found it *downa track*!" she cries out, almost pained that such a trifle could cause such a ruckus. "It just laid there in the mud, so we took it—why waste? And the spots that got mudded up—I cut those off. It just laid there downa track, ina rain. Been a while now, four years since—right, Vasya?"

"Could be more," Vasya confirms with gravity, happy to have reinforcements. Might all blow over yet, and dey won't ask too much questions.

Where?—Daryna starts to ask, but figures it out before she speaks: "Downa track" is down the road, meaning on the dirt road that runs from the main highway to the village.

"You mean, on the highway?" Adrian asks—he didn't understand the woman either.

"Yeah … I mean, no," the wife stumbles. "Ona turn," she waves a mighty discus-thrower's arm in the direction of the mirror-faced wardrobe, "dere, where you go from track to asphalt. I mean *the highway*," she corrects herself quickly and solicitously, demonstrating the traditional strategy of Ukrainian rural politeness: adopting the language of one's interlocutor. "Wherea tree-line ends, ona knoll, ona very turn … that's where it all got skittered around."

And as soon as the last words leave her mouth, she panics, and her honest blue eyes for an instant go all glassy, like a celluloid doll's. But it's too late: the word's been spoken, and it can't be put back.

"*All?* So what else was there?"

Now it's the husband's turn to rush to the rescue. "A bunch of stuff. A car must of crashed dere, looked like." He does, just in case, hide his eyes.

"There's accidents there alla time!" the wife picks up his line cheerfully. "Would you believe it, no more'n three months passes before someone gone crashed there again! And thank goodness when it's not to death." Judging by her intonation, she finds those accidents far less satisfying than the ones that actually are "to death." "And this year, there'd beena crash already, not long since, a month, right, Vasya? Showed it in TV, you didn't see it? A whole family slammed to death in a Honda, ana baby, too!" This sounds all-out triumphant, like Beethoven's *Ode to Joy*. "Ana woman, they say, she was 'specting, too, just think … coming from Pereyaslav—and hit a Mercedes …"

"Not a Mercedes," her husband corrects her, "a Bee-Em-Doubya!"

"Same difference!" the wife laughs, flushing with excitement. No, sir, Adrian thinks, she's not in menopause yet, she's got all her hormones alive and raging, just look at her go! "I don't tell them apart, Mercedeses or Bee-Em-Doubyas, I just know was some big cheese driving!"

"Big cheese, phew!" the yokel snorts with scorn. "Sure ... teenage punk more like it, one of dose that bought hisself a driver's license but Daddy couldn't pay for a brain to go with it. Dem, when dey drive, think dey god and king, and don't need rules, 'coz all the right lawryers sittin' in his pocket. Part, sea, let shit pass! He went to pass on the double and jumped into incoming traffic. Must of been in a great hurry—well, he ain't hurrying now."

He reports this without any glee, only with the legitimate satisfaction of a man who likes things to be fair. The woman, on the other hand, delights in the topic and can't wait to savor more details of this reality show—it is, after all, much more interesting than any soap opera, and these visitors know nothing of it, "And two years since we had a real big crash, a whole rig flipped over! Five cars slammed to pieces, right, Vasya? Took them two days to wash alla blood off the asphalt."

A ripple of cold shiver shoots through Daryna again. Blood, she didn't think about blood. She didn't go to the site of the accident, did not see Vlada's blood....

"Dat's a special spot over dere," Vasya nods. "Chornovil died here at our corner, too."

"Oh yeah," the wife echoes, proud as if she'd personally contributed to the event. "Folks put wreaths round that cross over there, alla time—d'you see it? You came from Kyiv, didn't you? That was a bit over that way, toward Kyiv, after a turnoff to the Kharkiv bypass."

Time to put a memorial here, Daryna thinks. This place is like Checkpoint Charlie was in Berlin. Only this one'll give you a real thrill—it's still operating. And these two could be the tour guides as living eyewitnesses—they'd do a heck of a job. Again she sees, as if in rewind, the highway stretching away from her—only not the dry one she and Adrian drove earlier in the day, but the other, from four years ago, with the lonely Beetle speeding along: the road is silky-black, flashing with the nebulae of puddles, the cloud of water kicked up by the car falls onto the windshield and the hood, streaks of rain meander down the glass. The road is empty, not a soul in sight, the signs float by—Pereyaslav-Khmel'nytsky 43, Zolotonosha 104, Dnipropetrovs'k 453, Thank you for keeping the shoulder clean—rain, rain, and tears streaming openly and freely, and the windshield wipers sweeping back and forth, and back and forth again, like two scythes over a hayfield.

Adrian's voice reaches her as though through water. "Couldn't they put rails along that turn, at least, if that's how things are?"

"It won't help." The yokel shakes his head.

"It would make it safer than it is now!"

"Won't help," the yokel repeats with unshakeable fatalism. "Dat's a special spot."

"What if you brought a priest out to consecrate it?"

"Dat'd be a whole lot of consecratin' to do."

There's something about the way he says it that brings on an awkward pause, the way it happens when a conversation slams on the breaks at a crossroads trying to decide whether to go on or to make a U-turn and head back. The woman ventures, "There ona other sidea track, back ina starvation, they hada grave ... drove bodies froma village there and buried em. We, when we were kids, useda run over there in spring—to look: where it's shallow, the dirt settles and sometimes human bones come up ... humongous grave, they say it was! It was later they rolla asphalt over it."

"Over a cemetery?!"

"Dat's no cemetery!" the man cuts in, almost as if he's angry. "Who'd go 'bout settin' up a cemetery back in da '30s? Dey just piled dem all into a hole, covered it with dirt, and left no signs. Da old people, dey just remembered da place, da ones who're still alive."

"Yeah, the old Moklenchykh woman, who died last year, she useda go there every spring the week after Easter to light a candle ... she'd just put it down ina dirt, and it'd burn. Once it burned all day till night, remember, Vasya, we seen it alla way over here through our window."

"You got no better business dan bringin' dat up?"

But it's too late to try to rein her in.

"And once, when we were kids, tha boys found a skull over there and kicked it around to play soccer ..."

"Now you're full of it!"

"Fulla what? What?" The wife pouts and again assumes her defensive position, arms under bust. "You count 'em: Lionka Mytryshyn—that's one!"

"Lionka was drunk ..."

"Were you dere drinking with him? And even if he was, then what?" she objects, not in the least concerned by the mild inconsistency of her dual objections. "Just think," she turns back to her guests, "boy served in Afghanistan ... the one who founda skull. Graduated military school, got the rank already, and no bullet could get him! And then came on leave to visit his parents—and bam! Drowned. Went to a pond for a swim ..."

"He was drunk, I'm telling you—dat's why he drowned," her husband persists. "You people just live to wag you tongues ..."

"Didn't end with that, did it tho'? Allose boys who kicked the skull back then with him—all toa last one, none of em alive! Kol'ka Petrusenkiv smashed to death on his motorcycle; I was still in school then. Fedka got trampled over by horses one day when he was drunk—took him three days to die ina hospital, poor bastard, and Vit'ka Val'chyn—that's way beyond even ..."

"Dat's a separate story altogether."

"Just think—man dranka poison for Colorado beetles!"

"Drunk, wasn't he?" Adrian inquires stupidly, having fallen, unwittingly, under the spell of this macabre graveyard litany.

"Nope, was not, dat's another thing with him: got mighty insulted. Ninka, his neighbor, went missing a wallet, so she went after dis Vit'ka. Meaning, like he took it. And he got mighty insulted. Drank da poison at work, went home, and says to his wife, Valya, I'll be dying here. Folks rushed to call da ambulance, but 'twas too late, dey couldn't flush him."

"Ana wallet later turned up!" the wife triumphs. "Ina pasture. Ninka herself dropped it, the scatterbrain!"

Daryna feels an urgent need to sit down. Her legs have suddenly turned to straw; this has happened to her before. When? Yes, of course, that night in Vlada's bathroom, when she was washing the warrior-maiden makeup off her face.

"So what's dat soccer got to do with it? Like dat's what killed dem! People talk nonsense—just to wag dem tongues!"

Somehow, the yokel finds his wife's mystical interpretation of the story decidedly unnerving. That's weird, Adrian thinks—he's the one who first brought up "dat special spot." Or, perhaps, the man himself kicked around human skulls when he was little—and, like most, remains receptive to the idea of a metaphysical payback only for as long as it is *someone else's*—never his own car that crashes on a defiled grave? As long as it is strangers' blood being washed off the asphalt—that's a reality show, same as on TV. But when it's folks from his own village who are found guilty on the same count, that means you yourself aren't completely safe and secure either, and that is something you shall deny with vehemence, right, Vasya?

"Razing a church—dat's another matter, I get dat," Vasya proceeds to reason, businesslike. "Dat—yes, den—things happen. Dat's better left alone, of course ... Father said when dey had da church razed in dem village, all da ones who lent a hand dere—all were gone before da year was out! One fell to death right away—dropped off da belfry where he'd climbed to rip off da shingles. So da belfry just stood dere like dat—unstripped—no one would go up dere, until later, in da starvation already, dey trucked some soldiers in. But dat's a church! I get dat, dat's different. A skull—dat's just a skull, of someone dead, and dat's it!"

Daryna has sat down on the edge of the couch and is hugging herself to contain the trembling. "Too many deaths." That's what Vlada said to her in the dream, the one in which she was looking for "a bill of ward" for those deaths. So that's it! That's how things are.

Another ripple of chilly shivers runs through her: the angel of death has gone by. The conversation she had with Vadym the night before, still undulled and uneroded, still living on in her memory, now stuns her with its macabre absurdity, like a madman's grimacing or kids playing soccer with a skull: it's cheekily caricaturish, grotesque incompatibility with everything that is now happening here in front of Vlada's work. Daryna feels, all but physically, the dense heat the painting radiates—like a fragment of skin that's just been ripped off a living being. Biker girl, life was her racetrack, and she was always the winner ... to hell with all those victories, they're not the point. How could all those bloodsuckers have missed the most important thing? You were a genius, baby. It came out of you with this uncontainable force; you burst with it. And how is it that no one had your back?

"Too many deaths." You're right, absolutely—there are too many. Perhaps, when there are so many deaths piled up in one place, and there is nothing to ward them (And what should be warding them, what kind of a bill?), their accumulated mass creates its own gravity—and draws in new ones, again and again? Like an avalanche? An avalanche—of course!—only this is from an earlier history, of the Kurenivka neighborhood in Kyiv: in the fifties, the city had Babi Yar paved over too—they built a dam and for ten years straight pumped loam pulp from a nearby brick factory into the biggest mass grave in the world, to leave no trace of it. They even built a stadium and an outdoor dance floor on top of it—and in 1961 the dam broke and a forty-five-foot wall of mud wiped out an entire neighborhood in thirty minutes, burying hundreds of people—no one had their backs, either. And the bodies that washed out of Babi Yar rushed down Kurenivka to Podil together with the living who were swept up in the flood.

As a girl, Daryna had heard her fill of horror stories of the kind this woman loves so much: about a child's hand torn off and left in her mother's grasp when the child herself was ripped away by the avalanche, about a pregnant woman, trapped alive in a cement bubble. Babi Yar rebelled, adults said, only back then one said such things in a whisper. In a whisper and with a pillow over even one's cradled phone: Soviet superstitions had it that you could be listened to through your phone even when you weren't talking on it. And then the stories of it slowly faded—survivors dissolved in the masses of newcomers, the city grew, and the newcomers never learned about the flood. They just went to play soccer in that same stadium, Spartak, which was so quickly built up again.

The dead were the ones who took you, Vlada, weren't they? Other people's dead—exactly when your own life shifted and slid, losing its footing? They are strong, the dead; they can do things. Oh yes, they are strong. Lord, how strong they are. We couldn't dream of matching them.

This jolts her again. The woman will think Daryna's got the hiccups. Or a concussion. One thought follows on another's heels, in a series of spontaneous discharges, uncontainable like labor contractions or vomiting; after another surge, Daryna's mind suddenly achieves final clarity: she knows now how it all happened then on the highway, "downa track," at the Pereyaslav exit. She knows what the yokel's afraid of—because he is afraid, has been the whole time, from the moment she recognized the cut-down canvas, glancing at her when he thinks she doesn't see it, and then looking instantly away, like he's been burned. Even though she, with no qualms whatsoever, does not take her eyes off him, as if they were each other's dearest people in the world about to part, as if she were hoping that at any moment he might work up the courage to tell her everything he has to tell her, to the end, even though she's already understood everything and does not need his explanation. It's only Adrian who hasn't yet figured out how Vlada's painting found its way to this home—so she wills herself to knock down the barrier of disgust, releases her jaw, which has been clenched the entire time, and asks the yokel, unexpectedly loudly, as if speaking on camera, "Did the two of you search the car together?"

Now it's the yokel's turn to be jolted by electricity. For a second, he's covered in a cold sweat: Moderfucker, he thinks; now I'm fucked! And—for what?! Dat's da worst of it—get caught over nothing! Go ahead, be a good dad, give your daughter a house-warming present, damn it! And said to da wife—don't take it. It's not worth da trouble, but no, she'd put her foot down—it's pretty, she said, real pictures, in frames, like they sell in stores in Kyiv for big money, put it up nice in Ruslana's new flat. Dey all gonna be sitting pretty now, and Ruslana, too, when dey get us for robbery—hell on a fucking stick, to get caught on such crap!

And such an intolerably bitter sense of resentment for this outrageous injustice fills the yokel that instead of defending himself, he shouts out, straight at Daryna, almost desperately, as only an innocently wronged man could shout to a woman with such maternal eyes, "Like dere was anything to look for in dat car of yours! Nothing but dese here pictures!"

In the silence that follows, a fly buzzes loudly somewhere under the ceiling: it's spring, Adrian mechanically observes, as he regards the yokel with new curiosity. The spring will show who shit where. What is it that the cops call the dead bodies of the missing they find in the spring? It's something lyrical, oh yes—snowdrops. Goddamn, the dude sweeps crashed cars, then. And this mustn't be his first time either. And really, no reason for good stuff to go to waste—and the dead don't care anymore. That's why he went into such a huff over the tale of the avenging skull, the delicate soul that he is. Impressive. No wonder he and Yulichka reached an understanding.

"Where are they?" Daryna's voice trembles. "Where are the rest of the paintings? There should have been five—where are the other four?"

Their hosts glance at each other: a pair of schoolchildren who've been caught smoking in the bathroom. Adrian wonders if the dude has connections among the local cops. The cops might be in on the action, too—the law doesn't require photographic records for highway accidents, so they're free to pick over the fresh carrion. Why not? It's their loot—money, jewelry ... one man's war, after all. Adrian blinks automatically at the Haid mantel clock on top of the TV (quarter to noon): a respectable, well-made clock, straight from somewhere in bombed-out Königsberg or Berlin. Let anyone try to prove, after the fact, that the victim was wearing jewelry. And who would try to prove that—the victim's grief-stricken family? Time to reclaim initiative, Adrian decides.

"A bad story you got yourself here, Vasyl Musiyovych." This time Adrian leaves no doubt about his police-inspector intonation, and the yokel, who's been half ignoring the "boozer-ex" all this time, experiences a stab of confusion. "A really bad story. The police have been looking for these paintings for four years already; the accident made quite a stir in the news; it was on every channel. And the painter, the one who died, was not only a close friend of Miss Daryna," the pair of schoolchildren obediently, as if following a teacher's pointer, move their eyes to Daryna, "but also the wife of an elected representative." Adrian says Vadym's last name and watches, not without glee, an intense—he's all but got steam coming out his ears—thought process manifest itself on the yokel's face before being replaced by an expression of genuine pain: aha, he's getting it—he'll have to kiss the pictures goodbye; no way around it, no matter how loath he is to part with them.

But the wife reacts faster.

"Well, who knew what was ina car! It sat turned upside down ..."

Daryna freezes. Adrian can feel her thoughts as clearly as if it were his own brain being bombarded with electric shock; another instant and he'll lose it, let it rip; only his worry for Daryna helps him to keep his cool.

"But don't you know that you had the duty to call the police and the ambulance? What if she were still alive, inside that car? Consult the Criminal Code, ma'am!"

At the mention of the Criminal Code the woman shudders but does not back down.

"Well, it was all just skittered ina mud!" She takes a new angle, now pleading. "Just think, that's a whole load of trouble. If we hadn't took it, it'd of been ruined anyhow!" she's finally found her lifeline. "It was rainin' so hard you couldn't see your hand, right, Vasya? If it'd laid there some more, the paint would of come straight off. This way, I saved them pictures, you see."

She steps up to the canvas and runs her hand over it, with a sense of ownership, as if smoothing out a rug she's selling, and shoots Adrian a sly sideways look (unlike her husband, she intuited Adrian's status right away). In different circumstances, Adrian would have smiled at this—just watch her go!—but at the moment he is in no mood for comedy. The yokel catches on, too.

"If you want to take this picture, I won't mind ... what about you, Galya? Let 'em take it, right? We don't need it dat much. Only how do I know you're telling da truth? Can't just anyone come over and start grabbing whatever he fancies."

Adrian understands they're now haggling. The pair has realized they're in trouble, but will keep kicking until the end, to try to get out with some sort of gain for themselves—if I can't eat it, at least I'll bite it. They don't know how to be any other way; otherwise, they'd be as "mighty insulted" as that poor bastard that drank the poison for Colorado beetles. Only these guys won't go drinking poison—they love life too much.

And that's when Daryna begins to laugh. She is not hysterical, nothing like that, she just can't help it: the redneck's last sentence, together with his offended look, gets stuck inside her and keeps spinning there, producing, with every turn, a new wave of raging hilarity—"can't just anyone come over and start grabbing whatever he fancies"—and she is shaking with laughter like a loose-bolted old truck on a dirt road; she is a rattletrap of unglued muscles and tendons, oh my goodness, wiping tears— rewind and rewind, again like contractions or vomiting, "can't just anyone come over"; she can't breathe, and the thing is the phrase loses none of its effect with repetition; it remains, to Daryna, insanely funny, and she cannot stop, even though no one else is laughing, and she herself could not possibly ever explain what's so funny about it, but God, she's about to burst—her panties are wet already, and tears are running down her cheeks like streaks of rain down a windshield; the redneck and his wife are a blur in her eyes, "can't just anyone come over and start grabbing"—and she jumps to her feet, shaking her head and choking on a new fit of laughter, waves at Adrian, meaning, it's fine, she's fine, she'll be back to rejoin the company in just a minute, she just has to laugh it all out....

At this moment, the one who cannot *not* be watching the two of them through the mangled, swollen, and poster-clogged eye of her painting on the wall must clearly see Adrian and Daryna caught together, at once, in a lightning-quick flash of déjà vu.

As Adrian watches Daryna dash out the door, grabbing her purse on the run, he recalls a recent scene exactly like this one, at The Cupid—a stunning coincidence, like a repetition of the same movement in a dance, almost a rewind, but not quite; something has changed, because something always changes, and the elements of "then" and "now," so brightly lit in our awareness, though they do call back and forth to each other with all their apparent congruity, like a repetitive geometric design, are still never one hundred percent identical. This time, Adrian realizes, there's no need for him to run after her—she really will come back in a minute, as she said she would; she is fine.

Daryna's déjà vu, however, comes to her as a direct extension of her negotiations with Vadym the night before—still warm, still swirling in her mind in shreds of dirty foam: in the yokel and his wife's naïve determination to bite off a piece of the action, no matter how small, and hide it in their cheeks, even when backed into a dead corner, Daryna recognizes the same element of a behavioral matrix she encountered the day before, the same "election platform"—to get off the shoals in a way that allows one to keep the controlling stake. And in this very instant, as Vadym and the cuckoo yokel become in her mind a single entity, the laughter that took her over lets up like a sudden spring downpour—as if she'd heard a joke that stopped being funny after it was explained—and Daryna, still shaking her head in amazement (Can you believe this?) feels for a pack of Kleenexes in her purse, sniffing, and pushes at a white plastic door, decorously hidden in a niche, on which a stenciled peeing boy glows proudly like polished brass on a military uniform.

The bathroom smells of sweat and perfume: this is a well-off home, built to every city standard. From the mirror above the sink a woman she has seen somewhere before but doesn't recognize right away looks back at Daryna: a clown or Lady Dracula. No—rather, a silent movie actress washing her face in the dressing room: the shoot is over, the role's been played. (The terrifying beauty with fire hidden under her skin who once flashed up from under all that artful makeup is not coming back—and there isn't anyone left to make her up anyway.) Her mascara is smeared into dense, predatory black fans around her eyes, and those eyes themselves, still not quite conscious, as if drunk with laughter, radiate, in contrast with their grotesque frames, a glowing, uncanny detachment, as if focused on something unseen. Something beyond reach.

A sudden understanding intrudes upon Daryna: I am not alone, she thinks. Who else is here? Who is with me?

She runs the water and puts both hands under the icy stream. What bliss, what boundless joy—just water, even when it's merely coming from the tap, like this. The living water, the same as that which flows in the Dnieper. Or do they have their own well?

She bends over and catches the stream with her lips, drinks, swallows, and drinks more as she once saw a pigeon drink from a fountain where he perched: beak open hungrily, his whole body feasting on every sip. Or was it a dog? Lord, there's so much life all around, and—dear Lord, what unthinkable things we do to it.

She raises her head and looks at the woman in the mirror: the Revlon lipstick smudged around her mouth as if she's been kissed—like on a compact mirror in a purse found on the scene of the accident. That was a painting, that was a photo, *I'll use this somehow, I just don't know how yet*—wet streaks run down her chin, hang there like tiny stalactites of sweat, her wounded lips move, and on her skin, she somehow feels her own breath as she whispers, "I did everything as you wanted, Vlada. Everything. I will take them back. You go now."

"I got him to sell me the clock, too!" Adrian announces.

"You should be in the right lane," Daryna advises, focused on the road. She's allowed him to take the wheel because he is now in better shape than she is, but she hasn't relaxed; she's alert; two heads are better than one, and the Lord helps those who help themselves. "What clock?"

"The one that they had sitting on top of the TV, you didn't see it? A prewar piece, German-made—a trophy! He said his father brought it back from the front."

"Sweet. And my gramps brought back a piece of shrapnel in his chest, which killed him within a year. And two cans of American meat stew from his rations—he didn't eat it, saved it for the kids, as a treat."

"You can't compare. Didn't you see, they have a tradition? Runs in the family."

"Oh, look, another cemetery!"

"That one's new, clearly."

"Yeah…. Look, gas and food—do we need to fill up?"

"You know I wouldn't mind filling myself up with something. How about we stop after Boryspil somewhere? All these Petrivna's-and Mariyana's-type places don't inspire much confidence in me; there'll be better places closer to the city."

"After the interchange? Sounds good. I'm hungry too. Could eat a horse, actually."

"That's from an overdose of emotions in a single twenty-four-hour period."

"If you say so. But you know, I've still got no clue what got me back there—what was so damn funny about anything?"

"A normal defensive reaction. But you wouldn't believe how agreeable they got after that! All warm and fuzzy. The wife started asking me right away if you were the one she'd seen on TV. They were so scared; they must've thought you were about to broadcast them to the rest of the world. It worked even better than Vadym's name. They cracked on the paintings without any fuss—said their daughter has them. So you, my dear, basically made the breakthrough in high-level negotiations. For which you shall receive a special commendation."

"In the form of a big smooch? Hey—you should go ahead and just hire me as your secretary! At least I won't rob you."

"Can you start today? If you really mean it."

"Are you serious?"

"Absolutely. It's perfect, isn't it?"

"But I know nothing about antiques, Aidy."

"I'll train you. No problem. You won't even have to go to college."

"I see you're skimping on me already."

"I'll be your dream boss! You'll see."

"I don't remember you ever propositioning me like this before ..."

"Do you now appreciate the seriousness of my intentions?" He smiles but receives no smile in return. "Do you know, by the way, how Yulichka got him? He told me this at the very end, when we stepped out for a smoke—turns out she claimed that she was the owner from the beginning. Like it's her gallery, and she's this hotshot businesswoman who's being stalked by her ex-husband, an alcoholic maniac. Meaning, me."

"I've always suspected she was a crook."

"But not this big! And I kept wondering why the dude disappeared and how she, with her bulldog grip, let him slip away. First she called me to say we got this diamond in the rough—and I, naturally, squealed like a little girl, said I was on my way and she should keep him there—and by the time I swooped in, the dude was gone. She told me this whole story about him being late for his bus. And proceeded to handle him behind my back from that day on."

"Why did she call you at all?"

"She must have wanted to make sure that this particular hide was worth tanning, you know? That this was the right moment for her to go in on her own. And I was so thrilled, I blurted it all out—that we'd never had such luck before ... which, by the way, is the sacred truth: that yokel's cuckoo clock, turns out, was also from his father, and also a trophy—from Schwartzwald! That's the top manufacturer, goes back to the eighteenth century. That's where they all came from, the cuckoos—Schwartzwald in Germany; it was only later they got called Swiss clocks, after they started making the body in the shape of a chalet ..."

"Watch out! He's got his turn signal on!"

"Yeah, I see him. Come on, jack, turn already!" Adrian honks at the gray Mazda in front of him. "And the yokel, when he decided to sell the clock, just went from store to store and asked—to see who'd pay more. That's how Yulichka got him."

"Well, they're meant for each other. A fine pair."

"Indeed."

"You got the daughter's address, right?"

"Yep. And I got the number in my phone too, the dude called her on the spot. She lives on Berezniaki, Davydov Boulevard. Name's Ruslana. I thought it'd be Lolita or Angela or something."

"Ruslana's not much better ... and Aleksei Davydov, by the way, was that Kyiv city administrator who was in charge of liquidating Babi Yar."

"You're kidding?"

"Not even a little. They just never got around to renaming that street from the Soviet days."

"No shit. So it was on his watch that the dam on Kurenivka broke?"

"His alright. The project, of course, came down from Moscow; he was just the one who implemented it ... for which he was recognized accordingly. That's how it goes, Aidy."

"Makes me wonder—is anyone ever gonna set this country straight?"

"'Tis a chore, as Ambroziy Ivanovych says."

"And Granny Lina used to say, call it a chore and treat it like your job. I called him yesterday, by the way. My dad. He sends regards."

"Thanks."

"He is still putting together materials for your film. He's dug up some interesting stuff. I didn't tell him that the film won't happen ..."

"The film will happen, Aidy."

He looks at her sideways, blinking.

"It will," Daryna repeats, with the unshakable certainty of an ancient Sibyl in her voice, so much so that Adrian gets goose bumps. "I have not a shred of doubt about that now."

Adrian doesn't say anything. He keeps his eyes on the road.

"You don't see it yet, do you?" she says softly.

"Don't see what?"

"Remember the tape of my interview with Vlada? The one in the Passage, the one you dreamed later, only starring Gela?"

"Not very clearly. Why?"

"In that interview, Vlada promised to give me one of her paintings as a present. From this very cycle—*Secrets*. You'll just come over and choose one you like, she said."

"And then she died. And you didn't have a chance to go and choose one. Lolly, I understand how much you regret not having a single tangible memento of her. Pictures or video—that's totally different, it's not the same as the things a person leaves behind that she made with her own hands. I understand this very well...."

"You don't understand anything. I did have a chance to choose."

He blinks at her again. This woman will never cease to amaze him.

"It was this very work, Aidy. This one, the one we took back from them."

"Can't be."

"This very one. Only intact, not cutoff, of course."

"Are you certain? Are you sure it's not just something you think now, in retrospect?"

"No, there's no mistake. I recognized the painting right away, the moment I saw it. It's her present. Vlada's. She's the one who brought me there. To the place where her *Secret* was buried. Except for the two of us, no one knew about the painting she'd given me."

"God almighty."

"Nah, it's simple, really. She was a very neat girl. You know, one of those people who always picks up after herself and hates to have unpaid debts. I think she is closing her earthly accounts. She is fulfilling all the obligations she took on. Apparently, she cannot leave until she's done. I mean, leave for good. You see?"

"Uhu. Looks like she's not the only one either."

"Yeah, I can't get these 1933 dead out of my mind ..."

"A road over a mass grave, how about that?"

"Well, almost every village this side of Zbruch had a pit like that, but not every one of those has cars driving over it, thank God."

"Horrible story with that skull."

"You know what occurred to me as she was telling that story? The place of the skull—that's Calvary in Latin!"

"Lolly. My Lolly."

"What?"

"Nothing. Hey, you know what—come be my secretary?"

"And we'll go around together buying up trophy mantel clocks from the descendants of the 'liberation army' and selling them to the new breed of pillagers?"

"Nope, wrong answer. Try again."

"Sorry. Don't get me wrong, Aidy, but that's what it looks like to me ..."

"You know what I would really like to have?" Adrian says. "What kind of a shop?" he is not looking at Daryna; his eyes are fixed on the road. "Not a boutique—boutique is a bad word, too glam, something for the new little Russians—a shop. One that would carry things that are no longer made. Good, necessary things—from a Singer sewing machine to a hand press for rolling your own cigarettes. Clever everyday things that one could use today. Things that were meant to serve a long time but have been made redundant by industrial production. You would agree with me, wouldn't you, that tons of women out there would be thrilled to make clothes for themselves and their kids instead of wearing something made in China. And how many people would smoke honest tobacco instead of this trademarked trash!" He nods at the pack of Davidoffs next to the gearshift. "And so on ... that sort of thing. And next door to this shop, right behind the wall—I'd have a few repair shops. Like the ones on Khreshchatyk, you know, in the courtyard next to the McDonalds, where we went to have the clasp on your necklace fixed last autumn. Good, honest repair shops. Staffed with serious men who'd spend their time giving new life to all these things. So that people would buy them not just to show off, but because they want them. And would go on using them."

"A store called Utopia, no?"

"Let it be a utopia. Let it be a dream. Call it what you want."

"And put up a handloom in there, would you please? That's for me, personally. I've always wanted a real homespun dress."

"No problem. I'm ordering it as we speak."

"I like this game."

"It's not a game. You said it yourself—it's a utopia. That's better."

"Actually, I think you'd pretty quickly attract your circle of dedicated customers."

"I think so, too."

"And you'd find other followers, too. Maybe you'd even start a brand. Like those Swiss Freitag guys, only yours is more ambitious."

"See now?"

"And then one night, a bunch of boys would roll up in SUVs and burn your utopia to cinders, with all its wonders inside. As soon as their sales of made-in-China shit drop."

"Eh, maybe they would and maybe they wouldn't. You don't know until you try, right?"

"This is a very nice idea, Aidy. I mean it."

"You like it?"

"I do. And you know who else would've liked it? Vlada. She'd have been insanely in love with it. It's her style. She brought me a Freitag bag back from Switzerland, as a present, that big black one ..."

"Are those the ones they make from old truck tarpaulins?"

"Yeah. Vlada loved them so much, you'd think she made them herself—it wasn't so much the design for her as the idea. The rehabilitation, as you put it, of honest craftsmanship. She considered herself a craftsperson. She always said so, even to the press.... Oh, Aidy, I'm so sorry you didn't get to know her!"

"I am sorry it's impossible to know all the good people who are already gone."

"The two of you are very much alike in a way. Very much. You both have an abundance of some essential spiritual vitamin that I chronically lack."

"Man, you must be hungry. We're almost there; just a bit further there'll be a nice little place. In a forest, under pine trees."

"I'm serious! I may not have put it the best way; I'm sorry, but that's only because there's too much stuff coming at me all at once ..."

"Try not to fuss so much. You're vibrating like you're plugged into the wall. You're jumping up at every car we pass. Baby, don't."

"Aidy. Listen. I'm thinking about this one thing. A bad thing, a terrible thing. I've been thinking about it the whole time, since that woman told us about the grave. I'm afraid to say it out loud even to you."

"Don't be."

"It's about Nina Ustýmivna. About her parents, actually. About Vlada's grandparents."

"What do they have to do with anything?"

"I'll tell you. Listen. Vlada suspected that back in '33 they worked the hunger. They were redistributing property, going after the better-off farmers, the kulaks—and it was somewhere here, around Kyiv. That's where Vlada's grandfather got his career started; it was only later, when the starvation began, that they were transferred into the city itself. They never spoke of it at home, of course, but Vlada accidentally overheard something somewhere once. And it matched their bios. She said her grandmother, when she was already a distinguished—for outstanding service to the country, what else?—pensioner chasing kids from the apple trees in their yard would, if she got really angry, call them kulak spawn. That was her worst cuss word."

"You're a two-faced and evil folk, you the kulaks who've been thrice-cursed!" Adrian recites with pathos.

"Good God, where's that from?"

"Ukrainian Soviet poetry, of course. Stuck in my mind since high school, I don't remember who wrote it. Didn't you guys cover that, too?"

"Jesus, Aidy, don't you understand what I'm saying?"

He puts his hand over hers.

"Of course I do, Lolly. Don't think about it. You shouldn't."

"But it's unfair!" Daryna all but moans. "Why did she have to …? Why did it have to be her? That she'd be the one, on that very spot … Aidy, she was so full of light, if only you knew! One of the best people I've ever met in my life …"

"That, Daryna, is not for us to know," he says, flipping on the right-turn signal, causing Daryna to glance back instinctively to make sure the road is clear. They turn off the highway and, kicking up gravel with a great noise, pull up to a small roadside restaurant. "You've said it yourself—Golgotha," Adrian says as he pulls the key out of the ignition, and in the silence that descends upon them, like a healing compress on a burning forehead, they remain, her head on his shoulder, his lips touching her hair. "And Golgotha," he utters, barely audibly, "is, among other things, death for the sins of others. Also, you could say, a way of tidying up, of leaving things clean. Someone has to do it when too much stuff piles up. A way of purifying the system, according to the law of large numbers: many, many small Calvaries …"

He kisses her behind the ear and raises his head.

"I tell you what, Lolly. Think simpler: a deeply depressed woman went for a drive, not even knowing where, on an empty road, just went for the sake of going. Her reactions were dulled, the road was wet, it was raining, and then a critter ran across the road in front of her, a dog or something…. She slammed on the brakes at great speed, the car swerved, it was probably pretty slippery too—and that's it. Shoulder, ditch. The end."

She raises her head, not taking her eyes, wide and childlike in their incredulity, off him. "Is that what you really think?"

"No," he says. "But it doesn't make the least bit of difference—neither what I think, nor what you do. Or anyone else. The statement is unprovable within the system. It's a Gödel theorem. And now, let us go and eat something. As long as we remain within the system, we certainly have to keep doing that."

Finally she smiles—he's managed to make her smile for the first time after that fit of hysterical laughter.

And only on the path from the parking lot to the porch does he notice that she is carrying a white plastic bag bulging with the edges of a canvas rectangle wrapped in several layers of newspaper.

"Oh no." She shakes her head when she sees him looking at it, and smiles, a bit sheepishly this time. "Say what you want, but I'm not leaving it in a car again."

Room 8. Blood in Kyiv

And just like that, it's spring outside!

The sun blasts from everywhere, like an orchestra that's been waiting, bows poised, for me to emerge from the SBU archive as its signal to launch into a thunderous fanfare—a moist glow with a little blue mixed into it blazes from every crack, every gap between the buildings, and every puddle on the asphalt, and the asphalt along Zolotovoritska gleams like a freshly bathed seal's back: while I was having my audience with Pavlo Ivanovych Boozerov, the world got rained on! Wet tree trunks drip with sweat like the bodies of happy lovers, a whole new stream sprouts cheerily out of a downspout, and the faces of passersby—who had been looking increasingly oppressed and gloomy of late, as though the imminent elections were bringing with them a front of oppressive air into the city—have acquired the silly and joyful expression of those missionaries who call out the good news about Christ in courtyards, in Russian with an American accent, without a clue that they're about twelve centuries late bringing this news to us; and new grass is so vigorously bright on the lawns it makes you want to turn into a rabbit and hop over to nibble it, and the buds on the trees have been instantly transformed into a visible stubble, into that translucent goldenish mist that envelops the trees in a gentle glimmer like the fuzz on a newborn's head. Life does, yes, it does have its bright side—as, for example, in Kyiv, in April after a thunderstorm! How did I not hear it roll in? It must've come down in torrents—the puddles are still rimmed in white foam—I heard absolutely nothing ... it's totally soundproof in there, like a dungeon.

And it is a dungeon, that archive of theirs. Artificial lights, eternal dusk. Coming out feels like breaking free from a bomb shelter.

Two characters, clearly from the same building, smoking on the sidewalk, look up as one and follow me with their eyes. They might be from a different building, too; there's some sort of a bank next door. Bank employees have the same eyes as the rank and file of secret services. And the same manner: false friendliness and a cold secretiveness. They all looked at me that way—everyone we passed as Pavlo Ivanovych escorted me out: down a hallway, up the stairs, another hallway, another set of stairs, all the way to the check-in turnstile. Return your pass, please. Of course, or else, God forbid, I'd keep it for myself and then what? The signature of the SBU check-in lady on that pathetic piece of paper would be acquired by foreign intelligence agencies?

There are things that do not change. Names of countries, monuments, language, money, uniforms, military commands, even ways of waging war—these all change. But secret services do not, they are always the same. Always and everywhere, in every country. One out of every six men convicted in the USSR after the war for working in the Nazi police had been an NKVD employee before the war. Had it been, by some bizarre set of circumstances, the American and not the German army that invaded the Soviet Union back then, these men would've gone to serve the American democracy—and the American democracy would've been just as happy to have them. Because there are things that do not change.

Alright, now I can finally have a smoke myself. Draw in, as they say, life deeply. Catch my breath.

No dictaphone, Pavlo Ivanovych told me, no records. And never a mention of him as a source, under any circumstances. That's what he was taught, back in KGB school, and secret services do not change. It doesn't matter that this ban makes not a grain of sense—except that it creates extra obstacles for me. I have to find a place to sit—around this corner on Reitarska there's a cozy little café—and write down, before I forget, the most important parts of what he was so kind as to tell me. Although, the thing of it is, Pavlo Ivanovych cannot tell me what is most important, the thing that's burning me the most, and where I had most hoped for his help, because he does not know what he is guarding. And none of them who work in that building know—and it doesn't look like they ever will. No one will ever learn exactly which portions of the Ukrainian archives were taken to Moscow in 1990, and which were burned later, after the declaration of independence—in those fall days of 1991 when we, young and stupid, marched happily along Volodymyrska in front of the no-longer-scary, dark-gray ziggurat and chanted "Shame!" And inside, in the courtyard, people were hard at work—they were burning "material evidence," covering up their tracks. During the months of September and October, Pavlo Ivanovych said. My dear Pavlo Ivanovych. An old friend of the family. He, dear soul, was one of those who did the burning.

Who was that clown who once quipped "manuscripts don't burn"? And somebody else picked it up and now people keep repeating it like they've all drunk the purple Kool-Aid—as if precisely to cover up for the burning brigades.

My legs, of their own volition, carry me toward St. Sophia. Alright, I'll take a walk; I'll take a detour—exactly a cigarette's worth, and then I'll take Striletska back to Reitarska and come back from the other side. And while I'm at it, I'll see if the lilacs next to Metropolitan's Palace have opened already.

It's not like I didn't know that archives were destroyed—no, I've known that for a long time, since back when Artem told me. But I had no concept of the scale of this destruction. And all these years, until today, somewhere inside me there lived—of course it lived, how could it not?—a comforting certainty that one of the iron-coated safes on Volodymyrska held *the source* of those four fat folders knotted with strings that sit in Mom's attic, like secret minutes from the Molotov-Ribbentrop meetings. And that some-day it would all "surface," as my Pavlo Ivanovych puts it, it would all come to light—the storm in government offices, the criminal renovation of the just-opened Palace Ukraina, the head architect's suicide, and among all that—the fate of one common fighter for the slaughtered project: engineer Goshchynsky.

I did really believe this—that it was all out there somewhere, kept safe, sealed, waiting for a volunteer to come one day and dig it up. Doesn't matter when, even twenty years later. Or thirty, or fifty. I knew I could not become that volunteer—it would hurt too much to read all that. It would be too hard to turn the origins of my life over again—like working wet clay with a shovel ... I don't want to, I do not. Seems like digs like that do require a kind of historical smoke break—to catch one's breath, to take a one-generation-long detour. Children aren't much use for this, but grandkids are perfect: Two generations is exactly the right distance, a systole-diastole, a rhythmic breathing, the pulse of progress. It's enough to know that it's all basically out there somewhere, waiting for its time. That's what we've been taught, this is the underpinning of all European culture—this firm belief that there are no secrets that won't sooner or later come to light. Who was it that said it? Jesus? No, Pascal, I think it was ... so naïve. But this faith has been nurtured for centuries; it has sprouted its own mythology: the cranes of Ibycus, manuscripts don't burn. An ontological faith in the fundamental knowability of every human deed. The certainty that, as they now teach journalism majors, you can find everything on the Internet.

As if the Library of Alexandria never existed. Or the Pogruzhalsky arson, when the whole historical section of the Academy of Sciences' Public Library, more than six-hundred thousand volumes, including the Central Council archives from 1918, went up in flames. That was in the summer of 1964; Mom was pregnant with me already, and almost for an entire month afterward, as she made her way to work at the Lavra, she would get off the trolleybus when it got close to the university and take the subway the rest of the way: above ground, the stench from the site of the fire made her nauseous. Artem said there were early printed volumes and even chronicles in that section—our entire Middle Ages went up in smoke, almost all of the pre-Muscovite era. The arsonist was convicted after a widely publicized trial, and then was sent to work in Moldova's State Archives: the war went on. And we comforted ourselves with "manuscripts don't burn."

Oh, but they do burn. And cannot be restored.

Our entire culture is built on faulty foundations. The history we are taught is nothing but the clamor—increasingly deafening and difficult to disentangle—of voices out-yelling each other: I am! I am! I am! I, so and so, did this and that—and so on, ad infinitum. But the voices resound over burnt-out voids—over the silence of those who've been robbed of their chance to cry out, I am! Over those who had their mouths gagged, their throats slashed, their manuscripts burned. We don't know how to hear their silence; we live as if they never existed. But they did. And their silence, too, is the stuff of which our lives are made.

Goodbye, Daddy. Forgive me, Daddy.

A clump of winos with beer at a kiosk, foreign cars parked right on the sidewalk ... I turn off onto Georgiiv Lane, which will take me past the baroque Zaborovsky Gate—there's never anyone going this way.

In the fall of 1991, they burned "fresh kill"—that is, recent cases, Pavlo Ivanovych said, from the 1970s and '80s. So there isn't much left from that period. He told me this as if in anticipation of my unspoken question—even though I came for something completely different and wouldn't have had the guts to raise this topic anyway: after all, it was Aidy's, not my, family, that had brought me to Pavlo Ivanovych. I talked about the film, and asked Pavlo Ivanovych to be my expert consultant. With an acknowledgement in the credits and everything. The compensation is modest, but I pay by the hour—just like in Hollywood, yes, sir. I already filed for incorporation—VMOD-Film (VMOD is Vlada-Matusevych-Olena-Dovgan, but no one needs to know that) and sent grant applications to a dozen foundations; I brought the paperwork with me, and was ready to show it to him. I am assembling my team, yes, sir. Starting with him (but he doesn't need to know this, either). And all for nothing: Aidy's query went nowhere, Pavlo Ivanovych said.

Nothing, they have nothing in their archives. Nothing but their clean hands. And, of course, flaming hearts, as their founder Comrade Dzerzhinsky bequeathed them.

They don't even have a complete catalog of their holdings. And how could it be created now, after the black-market trade in archive materials became, in the 1990s, SB employees' all but main business?

"One could take practically anything. It's still not especially hard," Pavlo Ivanovych added modestly.

"Yes, I know." (I've taken my share out of certain archives, why should the SBU one be any different?) And, naturally, there were individuals interested in acquiring certain documents. Oh yes, of course. And they were prepared to pay. Yes, of course, I understand. I just kept nodding with an intelligent expression on my face. My long-standing conviction that one day everything would come to light and Tolya Goshchynsky's truth would not disappear from human memory when I am gone was collapsing noiselessly under the attack of his words, like the Twin Towers on a TV with the sound turned off.

Nothing, there is nothing. I can go ahead and reassure Aidy: there will never be lustration in this country—there's nothing left to lustrate. But they built a new facility, well done. A wonderful facility, with high-tech storage areas—climate- and humidity-controlled and full of all kinds of other bells and whistles—to house the archives that, basically, do not exist. A new facility to store the black box with who knows what left in it. Unswept scraps, sacks from the 1930s arrests that never once got opened in the last seventy years. They sat on these sacks of stolen loot for seventy years—well done. Now that there are no living witnesses left, they can start opening them—slowly, one by one, without any rush. There is enough to keep all of them, those who work in this building, busy until they retire, and their successors too. Just imagine how the poor things had to hustle back then, in the fall of 1991, to pull out from this mess whatever had to be burned posthaste!

"They are the Tenth Bureau," Pavlo Ivanovych said. "The archive service: select, proven cadres."

So, does this mean he was also once a select, proven cadre? And is still proud of that? And Aidy and I thought an archive appointment for a KGB officer was like a mission to Mongolia for a diplomat....

I was all sincerity and openness. I nodded like a wound-up bunny; I chuckled like an extra at a Comedy Club broadcast. And all for naught: There wasn't a case with that name, Pavlo Ivanovych asserted, they didn't find any. They did look, he gave me his officer's word (apparently, the word of a secret services officer, in his mind, is still worth more than a journalist's or a businessman's!)—they looked, but they did not find anything. Dovgan Olena Ambroziivna, born in 1920, was not found among the operational-search case, or among the agents' files. He is very sorry. He may well be genuinely sorry, and not simply because he's just lost his chance to appear as a film consultant and to make a buck along the way. He did genuinely want to do something nice for me: I must be one of the very few good deeds in his life, in his entire select and proven service career. His one "onion," like in Dostoyevsky. Although it's not like that's exactly what he was thinking; it must've just felt nice, as he looked at me, so pretty, lifted straight from the TV screen and placed into his office, to remember the young, and also so pretty, Olya Goshchynska, whom he had once saved from being blacklisted when it did not cost him anything. It's nice to feel like a decent man—meaning, translated into the language of Soviet realities, one who, when required to do a despicable thing, did not take initiative.

So I believe him, my Pavlo Ivanovych. I believe his officer's word. They did really look and they did not, really, find anything. "But one should not lose hope," Pavlo Ivanovych said. "It is still possible that the case will one day turn up somewhere." I didn't really understand what he meant by that—another perestroika in Russia, perhaps, after which the re-reformed FSB would again open its archives for a short time, or the possibility that the case might be lying in a drawer in one of their senile veterans' apartments, and would turn up on the black market after said veteran dies? Or on the antique market, why not—didn't Aidy find Polish love letters from before WWI in a secretary desk once? Manuscripts don't burn, as everyone knows. A wonderful slogan for the burners' union.

"And what does this mean?" I asked.

"Agent cases were the ones opened for people who were arrested," Pavlo Ivanovych explained. "Was your, e-er, relative arrested?"

"No, she died in the resistance. In a battle with a team of"—I almost blurted out "your guys"—"MGB forces."

"Well, there you have it," Pavlo Ivanovych said with satisfaction. "What do you expect?" Stunned by his logic (there's formal logic, there is female logic, and then there's the secret services logic—to confuse and befuddle until the opponent loses his or her mind), I couldn't even react right away.

"And that other thing, the one you mentioned before, the operational-and-something else, what is that?"

An operational-search case, Pavlo Ivanovych explained to me as if to a proverbial blonde, is initiated for an object of an operational search.

"So, there isn't one of those, either?" I asked, now totally having a blonde moment.

"No," Pavlo Ivanovych shrugged. The aging, heart-sore Pavlo Ivanovych with the eyes of an Arab stallion. Or an Arab terrorist.

You see, I kept at him, worrying him like a limp dick. I just can't wrap my mind around this—how could a person, because of whom an entire family had been arrested and deported, just disappear from the National Security Bureau's archives? Her family, after the deportation, was even issued by the MGB a certificate of her death, with the date—November 6, 1947—on it.

"This means that when she died, the MGB must have at least identified the body and documented it accordingly, doesn't it? So there must have been some kind of a case, no?"

"You're right, this does not add up," Pavlo Ivanovych agreed. "When did you say this was? Oh, in '54—well, many things did not add up then. They made quite a mess...." And then he proceeded to tell me, asking me not to mention his name, how the archives were destroyed, in several planned waves, the last of them in the fall of 1991. And the first—in 1954, after Stalin's death: they freaked out back then too, and rushed to burn "material evidence." And an epidemic of suicides swept through the senior leadership back then, too, just like it did in 1991. Pavlo Ivanovych made it sound like a report about natural disasters.

"So are you telling me that Olena Dovgan's case may also have been destroyed in 1954, after it was used to produce the certificate of her death for the family?"

"Anything is possible," Pavlo Ivanovych agreed.

"Then, how would you explain *this*?" I asked, pulling the photograph out of my purse and putting it down before him, as if before a psychic. Or a witch.

"Is this she?"

"This is she."

"Hm," Pavlo Ivanovych said, studying the four men and the woman in the UIA uniform with a professional eye, "this is a good picture." That was not a judgment he made about the aesthetic properties of the photo, its angles or composition—he was assessing its usefulness for operational purposes: the recognizability of the five search objects, lined up and photographed before Pavlo Ivanovych was even born. (Or had he been by then? He is the right age, about sixty, and Mom also said he was born after the war ...)

"Where did you get this photo?" Now, this sounded like an interrogation question.

"From an archive," I said honestly, "only not from yours—from an academic institute's collection. How could it have made it there, how might it have, as you say, turned up?"

"That's a good photo," Pavlo Ivanovych repeated and put it back down.

"Yes," I said, getting annoyed by this irrelevant demonstration of his GB professionalism, which includes, among other things, the ability to avoid inconvenient questions, and pointed with my finger at the man who loved Gela. "Look, this one, he even looks a bit like you, really, he does! Too bad this shadow got cast on his face here, but still, there's something ..."

Pavlo Ivanovych gave me a strange, quick blink: like a condor, not lifting his eyelids—eyes like a pair of jet stones. I blurted out without thinking, "So someone looks like someone else, big deal, the world is full of people who look like each other." (I've even heard this theory that every one of us has at least one living double somewhere else on the planet, a trick of genetics.) And, the weird thing is—under the immovable condor-like, or maybe snake-like gaze of his (the eyes of an Oriental beauty, he's just a damn Shahrazad, isn't he?)—something in my mind clicked and revved up: "I've seen him somewhere before," Aidy had said after he went to see Pavlo Ivanovych at the archives that first time, and I laughed then and quoted from *The Lost Letter*, "Listen, dude, where'd I see you before?" It must be that such an exotic appearance provokes bizarre déjà vu in people all by itself. Mom also said he looked like Omar Sharif, or whatever that actor from back in her day was called, and I would've said—Clark Gable from *Gone with the Wind*, which was not a movie they showed people in Mom's day, only a Clark Gable adopted for an Oriental taste, as if edited by a Muslim censor to fit a location with palm trees and minarets. Or what if that's a whole separate type—The Man Whom Everyone Has Seen Somewhere Before, and they need people like that in the secret services too, better to confuse the public?

In any case, I wasn't taunting Pavlo Ivanovych, as he seemed to think—I simply pointed out an obvious thing that ought to have flattered him: his face does look a little like that sad-eyed handsome man's in the picture—the man from my dream, the one Aidy suspects to be his mysterious namesake who passed through his family's lives like a stunt-double in a movie, never having identified himself (an "Ad. Or." Aidy says, although I countered right away that he can't be his namesake because "Or." has got to mean "Orest," and only later wondered if perhaps I said that because of the movie *White Bird Marked with Black*, in which the young Bogdan Stupka, for the first time in the history of Soviet cinematography, played a Bandera follower who was not a caricature, and was named Orest).

But Pavlo Ivanovych, apparently, was not in the least bit flattered by this comparison because he informed me, rather sternly, that his father served in that area—and precisely in the "antibanditism" department, how about that? I felt my jaw drop. And his father was even severely wounded in battle; it was a miracle he survived. "Oh," I said, not knowing what else to say. "He remained an invalid for the rest of his life," Pavlo Ivanovych lamented. I went ahead and made a sorrowful face, too, feeling like it was now he who was taunting me: it was *my* father who had been made an invalid, and not without the help of the very agency in which the Boozerov dynasty so distinguished itself. And since we're on the subject of fighting "banditism"—it was *my* father who went to war against it barehanded and never came back—against banditism without quotation marks, the one that had taken over half the world: enthroned, institutionalized, ruling. And here was Pavlo Ivanovych seemingly stacking our parents' fates in the same file, seemingly saying we should be friends: the two invalid-father orphans, hello, Mowgli, we be of one blood, ye and I....

I asked if Boozerov Senior still lived. "No, he died in '81." And again I felt as if Pavlo Ivanovych expected me to say back to him, oh, and my father passed in '98. As if he were purposefully challenging me to turn the conversation to my father, something he didn't dare do himself, challenging me to a game with incomprehensible rules, like the Easter Day knocking of one painted egg against another, to see whose father is stronger ... but I said nothing. My exploded faith in the ontological indestructibility of every truth stuck out of me in all directions, charred steel, and the site of destruction was cordoned off with yellow police tape: Ground Zero, do not cross. And afterward, for some reason, I felt sorry for him—my self-appointed Mowgli, Pavlo Ivanovych Boozerov. The invalid-father orphan.

I toss the cigarette stub into a puddle, to the great ire of a flock of sparrows (such tiny little nuggets—and what a ruckus!). I come up on the Zaborovsky Gate, to which they don't bring the tourists, bricked shut for three centuries already—with its wildly curled baroque frieze and a colonnade sunk into the surrounding wall. Across the street is an oncology hospital; its patients enjoy a view that's perfect for the contemplation of the eternal: a sealed gate, No Exit. Abandon hope.

I do wish Aidy weren't in a meeting right now.

Should I call my mother, perhaps? No, it'll take forever to tell her everything, and it's not the kind of conversation one has on the street anyway. Pavlo Ivanovych did not neglect to send his greetings this time either, even asked me if she still worked in the Lavra, the Museum of Cinematography. "No, she is retired." "Really?"—Pavlo Ivanovych was surprised: in his mind, he must have fixed Mom as a younger woman. Must have fixed her the way she looked, and not by her date of birth, from the file. He must have really liked her. She got lucky. And, by extension, so did I.

It's only Dad who didn't have any luck. That's just how it worked—he didn't get lucky, and that's that. Actually, if you think about it, Pavlo Ivanovych's telling me about his invalid father was a sort of underhanded apology—peace, what can you do, that's how the cookie crumbles. Some get lucky, others don't. Let bygones be bygones, and we'll now be like peas and carrots. I really have no complaints about Pavlo Ivanovych personally—quite the opposite. There's something likeable about him. Something even vulnerable, in its way.

But the thing is that there was another person who did not get lucky that time—the one of whose posthumous truth my father became the keeper, until he perished himself: the man who created the magical palace of my childhood fairytales, and then hung himself—right in time not to see his creation crippled. He, then, he is the one with the worst luck of all, although this really has nothing to do with Pavlo Ivanovych; this, in relation to him, is a pure and simple natural disaster. And Pavlo Ivanovych probably never thought about that man at all, and forgot how that whole story began, so isn't it better just to erase it from your sight, so as not to complicate your already complicated life? Delete, delete.

It is at this point that something ursine inside me rears up on its back legs and growls: Hands off! I won't let go! I wonder why it never occurred to me before that I, basically, spent my entire journalistic career doing what my father gave his life for—defending someone else's essentially deleted truths? I gave voice to the lacunae of intentionally created silences. We are of different blood, Pavlo Ivanovych and I.

A KGB dynasty, that just blows your mind. Our family's second-generation KGB man—just like the family doctors people have in Victorian novels: from one generation to the next, from mother to daughter.

It's a profession: creating silences. Forging voices, layering the fake ones over the ones that have been stifled—so that no one could ever discern the muted truth. We have different professions, too, Pavlo Ivanovych and I—with directly opposite goals. No wonder we couldn't reach an understanding. No matter how hard he tried.

It's like when a bruised spot regains feeling after the immediate shock of the impact, only to fire up with pain later, when you think everything has turned out okay: with every step along the peeling, not-for-tourists St. Sofia wall, stained with damp patches and indelible graffiti, I succumb to an increasingly corrosive sense of disappointment. A feeling that I've erred in something, like I screwed up, missed something important, let it out of sight.... And lost a truly invaluable consultant for VMOD-Film, the single person, perhaps, from the entire KGB corps whom I needed, who was—literally—written in my stars, as one's most important friendships and loves are written. How many things of the kind you'd never read anywhere must he have learned from his late father, the "banditism fighter"! Things you'd never dig up from the archives, either: the most toxic "material evidence" of the Stalinist era, the evidence that might very well make the slaughter sprees of the Khmer Rouge and of Comrade Mao's cannibals look like training exercises for a volunteer militia—that kind of evidence, no doubt, flew into the fire back in that first wave of panic, in 1954, following The Leader of the People's death. How did he say these were marked in their registries? "Document destroyed as one not constituting historical value"? Crap, I've gotten so used to being recorded, I can't be sure I remembered everything right. Those fighters did not leave memoirs behind, either, for perfectly understandable reasons—but they may have told their children some things, and Pavlo Ivanovych is certain to know a lot more about that era than he wishes to reveal to me. Even if he is not aware of anything specific concerning Olena Dovgan who died on November 6, 1947. Or the man who was the cause of her death: I pointed him out in the picture, too—the last one on the right.

I came at it from the wrong angle. I counted on being able to see, finally, once I got my hands on Gela's case (which, for some reason, I had also imagined to be a fat folder with strings tied around it), a clearly and precisely documented, *factual* skeleton of her death, with the first and last names of everyone involved, that would give me the springboard from which I, without much trouble, could edit my footage (Vadym did get it for me from the studio) and show on the screen, as if turned inside out, the whole story as I know it—know it anyway, without the SBU archives, but by feel, through my own life; through Artem's basement and its rickety desk; through Aidy, Vlada, love, dreams; by the same blind and unerring method through which I know the truth about my father's death.

Except that, no matter how certain this knowing-for-oneself is, it must be firmly attached to the commonly known—facts, dates, and names—if it is to become public knowledge. When did she get married; who was he, the man standing next to her in the picture—an undeniably married couple; and most importantly, how did it come to the betrayal that poor Aidy spent an entire night hunting for in his dreams? And what did it look like from the MGB offices where the operational plans were developed, and where the records of interrogations were kept and bound (They had to have been!) into someone's as-yet unlocated folder with the label "Agent case" (That would be the one, yes?)? Without this factual dimension—even if it's only five percent of the material, it is essential as yeast is to dough—Gela's story cannot become a bona fide document, but will remain as it is—a story that belongs to the one telling it. My own story—lame-assed docu-fiction.

And I can't put it together only as I see it; I can't turn my own life inside out, make it into a movie for wide release. I can't show how Gela summoned me to tell about her death: how she tossed it to me from her photograph, like ball lightning—a white flash, the blast of hundreds of spotlights in the instant of an accidental orgasm in an uncomfortable position, on a rickety desk, in a basement of a certain academic institute—how she connected her life to mine like a torn-off wire and, like a skillful radio operator, cleaned the terminals. I can't put Aidy's dreams into the film—or even that last one that we dreamt together (even though I told Pavlo Ivanovych the name of the last man on the right, as it came to me in that dream—Mykhailo—without, of course, revealing my source; it was a gesture of pure desperation on my part—a name without the last name wouldn't get you anywhere even in the British archives, never mind ours). *I know* that the story of Olena Dovganivna's love and death that I have recovered is true because my own life vouches for it—but I can't bind my life to her case. Without a few critical pieces of documentation, which, let's face it, can only be supplied by the very country against which Olena Dovgan had waged her war, her story, in other people's eyes, would be no different from the movies my mom used to play in her mind after her conversations with Pavlo Ivanovych so as not to go mad. Facts, facts, Miss Goshchynska. Facts for the editing table, be so kind as to oblige. Names, passwords, safe houses, everything as it's supposed to be....

I manage to jump into an alcove just in time—a black BMW speeds up from behind me, from Zolotovoritska, tears past me like a tornado, splashing water from a fetid puddle upwards in a grimy arc that's as tall as me. Had I been on the sidewalk—I'd have been drenched head to toe. Jackasses! Rich jerks.

My having counted on Pavlo Ivanovych's assistance (and to know how little I need—damn it, I could fit it into a cigarette pack!) came from the same mythical certainty that everything hidden is really out there somewhere, just waiting for its digger. Essentially, I was counting on finding precisely the same kind of original source whose absence prevents the four string-bound folders in Mom's attic from yielding engineer Goshchynsky's buried truth. I had been certain that I only needed to recover Gela's case from the archives to have everything fall instantly into place—to have the last empty boxes filled. That the case simply *would not be there*—that the country against which Olena Dovgan had waged her war would manage, after its own demise, to outmaneuver both her and me by pretending that Olena Dovgan never even existed—for this I, the naïve cow, was utterly unprepared. I had been taught that manuscripts did not burn, hadn't I, and I was always a straight-A student. And now what? What am I supposed to do? Where am I to look?

A bricked-up gate. No Exit.

Daryna Goshchynska, you are an idiot. People have been screwing you over in a particularly cynical manner your entire life, and you did not even notice it.

And the funniest thing is—I can't help it that I do find something about Pavlo Ivanovych irresistibly likeable. Is this a variety of Stockholm Syndrome, or common gratitude? Because he is, really, my benefactor—it was he who, a quarter of a century ago, held my life in his hands: had he decided to score himself another star with my mom's case, I would've ended up in some godforsaken home for orphaned children. I'd be making my living at a beltway truck stop now. Or in the subway. I once went on a news assignment about what went on there at night, saw a peroxide blonde the cops pulled out from a storage room: she looked sixty and turned out to be younger than me—thirty-four. A black eye and arms poked with more needle holes than a sieve. The typical career of a Soviet orphanage graduate.

We're bound up together, Pavlo Ivanovych and I—and there's no avoiding it. But beyond that, there's something about him— although yes, he is second-generation, and yes he is Tenth Bureau, select and proven—something appealing in a very human way, something boyish, even vulnerable. It's no picnic, of course—having to watch, in your mature years, what you spent your entire life serving collapse: watching people pilfer left and right from the archive where you spent umpteen years like a chained guard dog. And for what?—while some quicker-witted Major Mitrokhin was carefully copying and stuffing into his shoe soles all that "material evidence" that was supposed to be destroyed as "not constituting historical value," and when the right moment came, sold it all to the Brits, and now sails his yacht on the Thames or somewhere like that, the bastard. And you sit, like a toad in a bog, in the dungeon on Zolotovoritska, guarding the stacks of gaping lacunae, and wait for your pension, which will be just enough to buy you a few fishing rods—and whose fault is that? There's something moving about this, I'm telling you, as there is about any human defeat. (Aidy is sure to laugh at me; he's already said I'm walking around all sentimental like it's the first day of my period....) Or is it that I just have a soft spot for losers? At least for Soviet losers—in that system, losers were the only likeable people. And now, I still pick the people whom you could call the losers of the new 1991 vintage, from the ruins of the empire—I find them more appealing than their high-flying colleagues who, at the right time, found themselves closer to the Party's coffers. Thusly is Boozerov so much more appealing than Major Mitrokhin. Even though Mitrokhin performed a historic act, and my Boozerov can't even supply me with a meager couple of certificates in exchange for hourly pay.

How are you not an idiot, Miss Daryna, Daryna Anatoliivna?

I pluck another cigarette from my purse and light up as I walk.

I gave it one last shot, back in Pavlo Ivanovych's office. There was still a small chance. A teensy-weensy little one, a rabbit's tail of a chance. I grasped at it as I stared, in my dead-end desperation, at the picture with the five young people standing in a row, dressed in the uniforms of a forgotten army, four men and the woman in a column of light—the picture I thought I knew like a lover's body, down to the tiniest mole, and yet I missed the most obvious thing: death! That's where the key might be. I've always only thought about Gela's death, separately from the others, but they had a *shared* death, one for all five, and it happened, if one could believe GB paperwork and dates at all, on November 6, 1947. And that, by the way, is a not just a regular day—that's the eve of the Great October Socialist Revolution's 30th anniversary, "the 7th of November is the Red Day of the calendar" as the children's poem went; they most certainly did not just pick that date at random—it all looks like a long-planned operation, primed for a big-occasion report to the higher-ups!

I'm old enough to remember those ritual pre-holiday, nationwide convulsions: reports from the miners and the steelworkers, from the workers of the fields and the animal farms—this is how much we have mined, milked, melted, and harvested for the Great October's 60th anniversary; and the workers of the jails and execution chambers must have also reported, correspondingly—this is how many we have arrested and eliminated, so this operation had been planned as a sure win in advance; the squad Gela's unit encountered had come for a certain victory. They had come after easy prey—after medals, ranks, vacations, engraved watches, and cigarette cases with ruby-encrusted Kremlins on them. They knew where they were going: someone had shown them. I could feel the trail of treachery quivering within my grasp, like a rabbit's tail.

"What if you looked by date," I asked Pavlo Ivanovych.

"How do you mean?" he asked, on guard.

"What if you just, you know, checked the Lviv GB archives for November of 1947? To see if there's a report about the liquidation, on the Lviv Oblast territory, of a five-member bandit group, four men and one woman, timed for the Great October Revolution's 30th anniversary—that's not a needle in a haystack, is it?"

Pavlo Ivanovych again blinked his protuberant eyes at me in that strange way of his, as if his eyelids twitched—and looked away immediately: "That wouldn't be here, it would be in the Lviv archives."

"No, Pavlo Ivanovych," I said, as kindly as I could, "it is here. It's all here, in the central archives—all the plans for the liquidation of the postwar resistance are here, the entire 'buried war,' almost a hundred volumes, code name Bear Den. If you gave me access to these files, I'd be happy to look myself. But you won't give me access, will you?"

"I've no authority," muttered Pavlo Ivanovych. My inside knowledge was clearly a surprise for him; he's new to this territory—a journalistic investigation—he's not used to it. He's used to dealing with a different demographic—harmless scholars no one cares about, quiet academic historians, acne-ridden students, and bespectacled postdocs who submit their inquiries composed in compliance with form N-blah-blah-blah, who receive the answer "the document is not found," and politely write it down as a research outcome—he is used to the absence of material strength. So I even felt a stab of professional pride: Don't mess with us! He'd look, Pavlo Ivanovych promised. It was at that moment that it crystallized—the impression I got that for some reason he really would rather not look. And if I called him back in two weeks, like he told me to, he would again shrug regretfully and report, with his officer's word, that he did not find anything.

Daryna Anatoliivna, Daryna Anatoliivna ...

Actually, now that I think about it, I must have picked up that vibe a bit later—when he was escorting me back to the entrance and, no longer having anything to add, kept talking anyway, as if someone forgot to turn him off—talked on and on, like sand out of a gashed sack. He even reminded me, for the first time in our entire interaction, of that captain with shifty black eyes who had once "interviewed" me in the chancellor's office before I began my pre-graduation field studies—they talk you to death, these people. Old schooling, done by the same old textbook, and what dickhead wrote those?

Pavlo Ivanovych, for some reason, started on his father again—as if he were still trying to play in the same sandbox, make his father friends with my hero, with the old man's former adversary, make it all nice; there was one thing in that whole verbal torrent that stuck out and stayed with me—it didn't sound like something Pavlo Ivanovych made up on the fly—that his father told him, in moments of sincerity (When he was drunk?) that he, Boozerov Senior, had "a lot of respect" for the banderas (this did sound like a straight calque from Russian), because the way they, the banderas, "stood up for their cause" was something "we" (one would understand this to mean both Boozerovs'—father and son's—colleagues) still had to "watch and learn." How about that?

Pavlo Ivanovych had said something similar about my mom, except not about the banderas but about her loyalty to her husband, that he would have liked it if his wife "stood up" for him like that—apparently he was having some trouble at work then, Pavlo Ivanovych was—and my poor mom was so proud of this KGB compliment that she remembered it for the rest of her life. I must confess, however, that I suspect this almost-dissident's (Heaven help us, were they all dissidents back then?) respect for the banderas on behalf of Boozerov Senior stems exclusively from the fact that they were the ones who crippled him: all these "banditism fighters," just like common bandits, respect only those who can kick their asses, and the harder their asses get kicked, the greater respect they feel for the one who did the kicking. But, so as not to ignore Pavlo Ivanovych's aspirations to fulfill the official presidential policy of national reconciliation completely, I mumbled agreeably that it seemed like at some point, while working on the film, I came across this name—Captain Boozerov, could it have been his father? But this, for some reason, did not make Pavlo Ivanovych happy, as I had expected it would, and he only said that his father retired in the rank of the major—straight from the hospital. Captain Boozerov, then, had paid a steep price for his promotion.

That's what I'll say to Aidy: I went after Gela, and got Captain Boozerov, damn it! (Really, though, where did I hear this captain?) And, okay, there's a miniscule, microscopic chance that Pavlo Ivanovych, for old times' sake, will be moved to look in the surviving part of the archives where I so helpfully pointed him. And will, after all, produce out of its dark depths the victorious report of a certain MGB anti-banditism squad written just in time for the Great October's 30th anniversary. And yet somehow, I find this very hard to believe. I failed to evoke in Pavlo Ivanovych the appropriate level of professional enthusiasm; I failed to recruit him....

I wonder how many people he recruited in his day, when he was still on operational duty? And now all their cases are sitting somewhere in his stacks, and he knows them, those people; he might be following their careers and could at any time pick up his phone, call someone like Aidy's professor who squealed at me at The Cupid, and express his wish for something practical in exchange for his silence. Not much fat to be had off an old professor like that, of course, but there're bigger fish—tons of them, whole schools of them that rushed, like salmon to spawn, into politics and government after 1991, to build up the country that had finally freed itself. And they, too, thought they had freed themselves—from the agreements they had signed with the KGB—they were giddy with freedom.... Meanwhile, Pavlo Ivanovych just sat, like a spider, in his dungeon and spun the threads of new dependencies. Maybe his life isn't as hard as I so charitably worried it might be, and by the time he retires he, too, will have, bit by bit, put aside enough for his own modest yacht to sail the Dnieper—and the climate here, thank goodness, is so much better than London's. And I foolishly thought I'd tempt him with my consultant's fees—two fifty an hour, money I don't even have yet. Come to think of it, I don't have any money at all. You're such a nitwit, Miss Daryna, Daryna Anatoliivna....

"Miss Daryna! Daryna Anatoliivna!"

Someone's actually calling after me, and I didn't hear it … I feel as if I've been caught in the middle of something indecent—it's always like that when people recognize me in the street: an instant transition, like being captured in the sudden light from the soffits, like being catapulted from the darkness of the audience straight onto the proscenium: Hoop-la, the thunder of the applause, you turn around, stand there like a pillar of salt, grinning a plastic grin; oh shit, are my trousers splattered with mud in the back?

A girl—plump, dark-haired, and pretty cute, an expensive leather jacket thrown open, scarf messed up on the run. She's breathing hard, wide-open eyes like plums, spellbound, she's glowing, so thrilled she can hardly see straight: She made it! As if she's run a marathon to catch up with me.

"Daryna Goshchynska!" She is not asking, but triumphing like a soccer fan who's spotted Andriy Shevchenko and can't wait to shout to the whole world about it, name, exclamation mark, pointing finger—*look, look!*—before her deity disappears or changes itself into something completely different as deities in every myth are wont to do.

"Ooff!" She's trying to catch her breath, hand on her chest— some rack she's got there, C-cup at least—she shakes her head, laughing at herself now—at her breathlessness, at having run, and having caught up with me, and at having me stand now here before her, and at it being spring, and at the downpour that's just passed, and at the sun shining—and I smile, too, infected, unwittingly, with this puppy-like burst of her young youthful energy: What a funny girl! Sweaty, flushed, clothes in a mess.

"I'm so sorry … I recognized you from afar; I'm so glad I caught you." She's still not taking her gawking black eyes off me, her plump-lipped mouth is stretched ear to ear; this must be the first time she's seen Daryna Goshchynska live: "I would very much like to invite you, may I? Here!" she exhales, full-chest. "Take this, please."

A white, or rather, a gray butterfly—a cheap booklet, on thin paper, like all free concert invitations.

"On the twenty-fourth ... in the Grand Hall at the Conservatory ..."

"Thank you." I react with my standard working smile now, and put the flyer, without reading, into my purse: I'll throw it out later, I get mountains of this junk every month, and the mail's not letting up yet—the news that Daryna Goshchynska no longer works on television has not yet gained national currency. It'll be a full year before my name is taken off all the mailing lists, and I must say something encouraging to the girl: "Your concert? Congratulations."

"It's our class concert ... for our whole year, I'm in the second half. Piano, it's in the program ... I have two pieces—Britten and Gubaidulina."

"Difficult composers," I nod knowingly, about to wish her the best of success, anoint her with a ritual blessing by way of taking my leave: go with God, child—but the child has no intention of giving up so quickly, she needs to pour it all out, since she's caught me, and, without giving me a chance to break away with another word, she bursts forth, like rainwater gushing from a gutter.

"This is my first serious performance, Miss Daryna, please come if you can, please. It would mean so much to me! It's so important for me, if only you knew." She clasps her hands prayerfully to her C-cup breasts, which protrude vigorously under her leather jacket and the fashionable short sweater under it, so that a pale strip of her belly winks every time she moves—the current fashion is meant for stick figures, and this girl—nothing to complain about—sports a good childbearing shape, but her hands—her hands are made for the piano indeed: large, with beautiful long fingers. And who wouldn't melt a little hearing this: "You are my hero, I watch your every show; I haven't missed one in two years! I even ran away from a date once, to watch it."

"Thank you," I say, waiting for her to ask me why the show didn't air last Wednesday; I have to change the topic: "That's very nice to hear, but running away from a date—that seems a bit much, doesn't it? Unless the boy wasn't anything special."

She wrinkles her nose, laughingly shines her enamored bovine eyes at me, and concedes that he was not anything special: a moment of female solidarity; we are both laughing. This is it, my audience. This is what I have managed to accomplish in my life. How many of them are out there, across the country, girls and boys like this? Lord, the letters I used to get! *This is* Diogenes' Lantern *and I'm Daryna Goshchynska, stay with us.* And they've stayed; they haven't even noticed my absence yet.

"As soon as Dad said you were coming to see him, I just couldn't wait ... I had a class at the Conservatory; I don't know how I sat through it, and as soon as it let out, I ran uphill! I tried to flag a cab on the way, didn't see any, and just kept running, the whole way ... I rang my dad and he said you already left! I didn't think I'd catch up with you!"

"Your dad?"

"Well, yeah," the joyous stream whirrs forth from the gutter unchecked and unstoppable. "I called after you back at Zolotovoritska, as soon as I spotted you from afar, but you didn't turn to look. And I recognized you right away, from the way you walk, the way they show you in your show's teaser when you enter the studio, you're unmistakable."

"I'm sorry, and who are you?"

The stream plugs up, the prominent eyes freeze in their sockets like prunes in whipped cream. "Oh ... I'm sorry. I, I didn't think...." Catching herself, she blushes even deeper—all the way to her ears now, "I'm Nika ... Nika Boozerova."

Never underestimate the value of professional training: all my facial muscles remain in their places. Well, well. Of course, how did I not figure it out—the same eyes like jet stones, the same plump lips, and the same high cut of the nostrils that makes them appear constantly puffed, and her body is built the same, too— she's short-legged and big-bottomed, a dark little pony, but a girl with hips like that can do alright for herself, much better than her dad. Pavlo Ivanovych can be congratulated on this improved replication of himself—a softened, more delicate version, not as

oily-spicy-Al-Jazeera cast as the original: the features are seemingly the same but the treatment is in watercolor, not in oil. "My
daughter," as he bragged at our first meeting, with the stress on the
first syllable. Nika, of course—Veronika Boozerova, a Conservatory
student, my fervent admirer. This is she, in person. Apparently, the
Boozerov family has decided to parade its full ranks in front of me
today—who do they have left, mom, grandma? Bring them all out!

"Aha," I say to the girl in the voice of an anti-banditism operative. "Very pleased to meet you."

"Me too," she blooms, malapropos, not having noticed how
much like an idiot I feel. So, that's why Pavlo Ivanovych took his
sweet time shooting the breeze with me—for her sake; he was
holding me back for his kid, until her class let out. But she is still
too young to appreciate such complexities; she, with the happy
enthusiasm of youth, is still filled to the brim with herself exclusively and her urgent need for self-affirmation (little princess,
Daddy's girl, and a late child to boot—Pavlo Ivanovych must've
been pushing forty). And she springs at the chance to unload on
me, all at once, everything she didn't spill along the way while she
raced after me with her booklet all the way from the Conservatory,
up the hill from Gorodetsky Street to St. Sofia (and that's quite a
trek, must be what, about thirty minutes, and all uphill, no wonder
the plump little thing is drenched!).

She reminds me, happily, that she has my autograph—in her
mind, this must constitute some kind of intimacy between us, a
sign of a connection—of course, I remember, the same loving
father solicited it for the child the first time he ever laid eyes on
me, must be nice to have such a loving dad! A strong, healthy one,
not an invalid. A dad you can be proud of instead of swallowing
every mention of him, mangled, as quickly as you can—oh yes, I
remember the feeling: the last time I had it was at the opening
of a fairytale palace, when my dad stood in the glowing crystal
foyer in a huddle with other serious men, and they all took turns
shaking his hand. I was still little then, but I remember; I know
what it's like.

Nika's Ukrainian is natural if a touch too literary, as with all children from Russian-speaking families, without any slang—a Sunday language, starched for going out, not for home use. Although, it could be that she is making a special effort for me, cleaning up her act: I am a different generation, an adult woman, and she is speaking to me the way she would speak to one of her professors at an oral exam. Asking me for her A+, the straight-A girl. A good girl, engaged, diligent.

Aidy's right, I have gone all sentimental like on the first day of a period—my eyes mist over as Pavlo Ivanovych's daughter, and Captain Boozerov's granddaughter, rattles off the list of the *Diogenes' Lantern* episodes that made the most indelible impression on her—changed her life, Nika declares a bit too dramatically but with clear-eyed candor. She and her friends discussed these shows; they have a whole fan club going. They even tape me (used to tape; what are they going to tape now?). Of course, these are students, I mentally subtitle Nika's nourishing babble for my ex-boss's benefit, or perhaps for addressing the new owners of the channel—who also act as producers of a sex-industry show—these are students, gentlemen. These are the young people; this is our fucking future, you motherfuckers, young people always need role models—"who's out there to shoot for," as a boy taxi driver once said to me, spitting furiously through his rolled-down window. Young people need to have before their eyes not only millionaire gangsters and their Lexus-driving sluts but also—Vadym had a good phrase for it—moral authorities, and that is precisely why my never-heard-of heroes and heroines that hold for you no authority whatsoever are for these children like water for parched land: they gulp them down with a hiss, and beg for more! And what gets me the most, what cuts me to the quick, is that Nika unerringly names all the episodes of *Lantern* that were most important, closest to *my* heart, as though running her fingers over the departed show's acupuncture points that only I could see, and by doing so, revives the pain I thought I had lulled to sleep. It is incredible how precisely this child is honed in to the same wavelength as me, and this wave washes me from inside, finally closing around my throat when she brings up my interview with Vladyslava Matusevych—she says she was still in high school then, and it was that interview that cemented her determination to devote herself to art. "Is that so," I manage to gurgle.

Yes, even though Daddy tried to convince her that musical performance is a profession without any prospects whatsoever and wanted her to go to law school. But Daddy is musical himself; he has perfect pitch and still sings sometimes in good company—he naturally has a wonderful tenor, Nika asserts so fervently as if it made all the difference in the world to me. As if I had visited her dad for the express purpose of assessing his natural vocal abilities. Now it is *my* turn—I recognize these notes in Nika's voice with unerring precision, I can't be fooled: Nika is making excuses, she is ashamed of her father's profession—she would much rather see him an opera tenor, even of the second or third roster. Really, how did I not think of this before: at the time of her childhood, in the '80s—and even of mine, in the '70s—the acronym Kay-Gee-Bee spoken out loud was already likely to elicit from other kids the same snickering as names of certain hidden parts of the human body, so standing up and announcing to the whole class where her daddy worked could not have added to little Nika Boozerova's popularity among her peers. It wasn't all that cloudless, then, her childhood....

"Your father's trepidation can be understood." I smile at her maternally. "Art is an uncertain business; only a few make their way to success, and law school at least guarantees a living. Especially when, like in your family, it's a legacy ..."

To this mention of family legacy Nika darkens and bites her lip—it must be a nervous habit she has, because her front teeth have traces of the lipstick she's swallowed.

"Well, not really ... Daddy, when he was young, wanted to take the entrance exams to Mechanics and Mathematics, he was really good at math, but Gramps didn't let him. And the musical talent—that comes with the Jewish blood ..."

Jewish?

At first, I don't know what to say: Nika and I truly belong to different generations—the freedom with which she speaks of her Jewishness can serve as a line of demarcation for an entire era. Among my peers, being Jewish was still a mark, something profoundly ambivalent and vaguely shameful, something even those with last names ending in -man and -stein were loath to admit to, and half-bloods hid like syphilis under the covers of their Slavic last names. And there was no game better loved by KGB-paid informants than teasing a Jewish grandma's grandson with anti-Semitic innuendo and watching him go pale, change in the face and chuckle along stoically like the Spartan boy with a fox cub chewing at his stomach—the other extreme from the opposite camp was an urgent, tentative, roundabout confession, to everyone suspected of being Jewish, of one's own Judophilia and love for the state of Israel (about which at the time absolutely nothing was known but which was loved anyway, long-distance, purely for the fact that it was not loved by Moscow).

And in my student years, I often said such things myself—feeling, however, every time, a slight awkwardness at this forced demonstration of basic human solidarity, like the feeling one gets from demonstrating one's health at a gynecological exam. To Jewish people, I think this must have been as offensive as any anti-Semitic barb. But the problem, as Aidy says, did not have a solution within the framework of that system and instead took care of itself later, after the collapse of the Soviet Union, when I simply stopped noticing who was Jewish and who was not, and what kind of Jewish they were, and who was whose grandma's sister's husband, and have internalized this not noticing so deeply, it would appear, that I now stand before Nika Boozerova feeling like the world's biggest idiot for the second time in five minutes: oh, so they are Jews!

So that's where Pavlo Ivanovych gets his Arab look, his near-Eastern charm, some of which, in a diluted form, has trickled down to his progeny—and when Nika turns her head, the magnificent prominent eyes, the tucked-up nose, and the plump-lipped mouth assemble instantly, like a 3-D image behind a stereoscopic picture, into a new kind of person: a Jewish girl, a mixed-blood—and what a comely mix it is!

"So, your grandmother must have been Jewish then?" I ask, now with genuine curiosity: this must mean that Gramps Boozerov managed to get married before 1937, before the great Jewish purges of the Party and NKVD. Afterward, Jewish wives were no longer fashionable among the fighters of banditism, and after the war, when they went after the Jews almost as zealously as in prewar Germany, a wife like that was a downright liability.

Something makes the girl hesitate before she answers, the expression on her cute face the same as her father's when he avoids giving a direct answer. The whole situation strikes me as pretty stupid: here we are, standing in the middle of the street, lined up against St. Sofia's wall, investigating the genealogy of Veronika Boozerova's musical talent! But no, there's something else going on, a different story that involves me, too: back in the '70s, when Pavlo Ivanovych curated Mom's museum, they didn't suffer Jews in the security services, not even half-bloods—by then the USSR was fighting Zionism, and those few-and-far-between Jews who remained in the corps had to have been so select and proven that they wouldn't cast a shadow at sundown—men like that would sell their own mothers to keep their positions, never mind some Olya Goshchynska, and Pavlo Ivanovych doesn't fit the type, something's not right here.... And Nika, although a product of a different epoch, also backpedals, tries to take her Jewish grandmother back, awkwardly, like a child pulling back her doll.

"Well, I don't really know for sure ... probably ... Gramps died before I was born, and Grandma didn't know either. They were pure Russians themselves, born and raised, from somewhere near Kuybyshev ... Samara, as it's now called."

"Oh," I say, totally lost now.

"Only we're not related," Nika says. "They adopted Dad from an orphanage."

Mowgli bursts in my mind, like a bubble, the spur of the old guess cutting in again. "Your matinka still alive?"—"And well, thank you, and yours?" Oh God ... how he recoiled—so obviously!—when I shot it back at him, so casually, back then, when we first met ... Mowgli, an orphan, so that's what it was, who'd have thought?

"Oh," I repeat, as if dazed. "I see."

Well, at least I—owing to Pavlo Ivanovych—was spared a similar fate ...

"What if we took a little walk, Nika? I was about to go into the grounds, see if the lilacs have opened ..."

Nika, instantly relieved, happily trots beside me, hanging devotedly on to my every word—now she'll tell me anything I want and will go on for as long as I want. Along Striletska, the puddles spread resplendent as lakes and pigeons totter across them in pursuit of females, cooing just like Nika into my ear. I'm getting a bit lightheaded.

"Daddy was adopted from an orphanage in Lviv when Gramps worked there"—I decided not to seek Nika's clarification of the exact nature of Gramps's work there—"Daddy does not remember his biological parents, he was too little.

"He doesn't even remember Lviv, he grew up a Kyivite—the Boozerovs were given an apartment in Kyiv when Gramps was discharged. In the heart of downtown, not far from here, on Malopidvalna, it's now worth half a million dollars," Nika brags—she doesn't really care what she is talking about as long as it's about her: she is showing me her life like her school report full of As;, she is playing her capstone concert for me alone, with a single piece on the program—The Boozerovs. From the top, one more time, please, Nika—one and two and ... on Malopidvalna?

"How convenient, that's really close to work for your father, isn't it?"

"Yes, Grandma said that she wanted to move to Crimea, to the south shore, to Yalta or Simeiz—the Boozerovs could choose.

Crimea was just being resettled at the time, but Gramps picked
Kyiv. That was after the war, in '48. In Stalin's times," Nika clarifies.

Yes, I understand. Her biological grandparents—the ones
Daddy doesn't remember—a Lviv Jewish couple, most likely, fell
victim to repressions. And, most likely, they were executed, because
had the mother still been alive, no one would have taken an infant
from her—Nika's familiarity with contemporary penitentiary pro-
cedures is also a legacy, although she is not aware of it.

Nika always feels like Lviv is her native city; she's felt it since
the first time she set foot there, back when she first went there
on a school-group tour. She felt as if she had lived there before.
Now she'll start telling me how much she loves Lviv; I bet this
number of hers plays especially wells with boys—even in the
Soviet days, Lviv was our last symbol of Europeanness, and today
the admiration of Lviv coffee and what's left of its Renaissance
architecture is a bona fide prerequisite for all intellectually ambitious boys and girls.

So, that's who Nika would like to be—a Lvivite with a pedigree, and one and two and ... stop, stop, let's go again from the
beginning: it's 1948—how could there be any Lviv Jews left? There
were still those who hadn't managed to escape to Poland, Nika
explains. But the Lviv Jews were wiped out by the Germans, back
in the ghetto, during the war, and when, did she say, was her daddy
born? January of '48? So how?

"Well, many of them returned later, in the Soviet times already,"
Nika says lightheartedly—many of those who had fled at the beginning of the war. Well, okay, that could be, all kinds of things were
known to happen—must have been a couple of poor souls with
pro-Communist ideas, and that was their undoing.

As far as I'm concerned, let her have her Lviv Jews if she wants.
"And the Jews, you know, they're all musical," Nika repeats with
an unsophisticated and totally goyish proclivity for superficial
generalizations. Well, certainly not all of them? Doesn't matter,
she and her daddy got their musical gifts from the Jewish side,
Nika insists—on her mom's side of the family everyone's tone-deaf,

not one of them has any ear-to-voice coordination. Is that so, well, then, of course.

Her daddy, Nika coos melodically, in tune with the pigeons, had actually suspected he was adopted ever since he was little, because older boys in the yard had often mocked him as a little Yid. Really, what a keen phenotypic observation for a child to make. Nika nods, missing my irony—"Grandma Dunya, actually, was also a brown-eyed brunette, but she looked different; they had Tatars in their family ..."

In a fit of generosity, Nika is ready to throw in Grandma Dunya as a bonus, but I delicately steer the kid back a couple measures: and one and two and ... "And how did you find out for certain?"

"And for certain," (Nika repeats this phrase with visible gusto, it must be new to her in Ukrainian and now she'll trot it out whether it's called for or not) "for certain Daddy learned when he was an adult already, in his thirties. Sometime around then. Someone at work, who envied him—because Daddy was moving up quickly and many envied him—wrote a complaint to the higher-ups alleging that he had relatives in Israel. This made quite a stir," (her speech more and more wiggles free of the school textbook's manacles) "for a while there it looked like Daddy would get fired." Oh, I can certainly imagine that, I remember those times. Yep, so they were running background checks on him and stuff like that—Nika gives her shoulder a disgusted jerk, as she walks, as if to shake off stuff like that, and bites her lower lip again: a very sexy little mannerism she's got. "Fortunately, Gramps was still alive then, and went to the appropriate offices and set the record straight. And for Daddy, too, while he was at it."

"And Pavlo Ivanovych," now it feels sort of weird to say his name like this, knowing that he is not Ivanovych at all, and maybe not even a Pavlo: the name, gray as a KGB suit, is instantly stripped of its living bearer, and becomes a handle one hesitates to repeat, like something indecent. "Did Pavlo Ivanovych ever try to find his biological parents?"

"Oh no!" Nika is shocked by my ignorance. "How could he?"

"Well, of course, but I don't mean back in the day, in the Soviet times ... now, after the independence; he could've done it, couldn't he? Especially since he works in the archives ... if they really fell victim to the repressions in '48, there might be a record, a trace?"

"But what's the point?" Nika objects sensibly, clearly rehearsing the arguments she's heard from someone else—from the adults. "They are not alive anyway; if they'd survived, they would've found him at some point in the last fifty years. People who came back from the gulag—they looked for their children ..."

But no one looked for Boozerov. So there wasn't anyone left to look. And if they had found him? Would it have made Pavlo Ivanovych, a KGB officer, happy?

"And those relatives in Israel—is that true, or ...?"

"Oh please!" Nika snorts. "They just made it up to derail Daddy's career. What relatives could there be if we don't even know the last name he had when his biological parents surrendered him?"

This strikes me as strange, but I know very little about orphanages; I've only made one show on this topic—the one about that village priest who adopted a few dozen homeless children, and those weren't cute and black-eyed like the baby the Boozerovs must have chosen one day—like a shiny tchotchke in a store window—but ones that truly no one else wanted, defective ones, born with handicaps. But this was in an independent Ukraine already, and who knows what kind of laws they had back in the USSR; I haven't researched that, so I better not say anything.

Nika and I turn the corner onto Rylsky Lane and walk past the windows of Kyiv's most expensive boutiques, under the eyes of bored security guards who stir to life when they see us—just enough to follow us with their eyes—the two women, one older and the other younger, one slim and the other plump—and decide which one they like better—the same way I use my eyes like fingers to feel out each pebble of leather on the purses in the window displays as I walk by (even the cheapest of them costs a third of my former salary!). And under the leers of this sleepy fight club that's pulled itself outside for a gulp of fresh ozone, Nika, a true straight-A student, instinctively straightens up, pulls her stomach in, and reaches to her temple to tuck a loose strand of hair behind her ear … looks like she's still a virgin, or at least really inexperienced. An obedient, diligent child, and that's the way she'll be in bed, too: tell me what I should do, and I'll be the best at it.

It's what they told her, I think to myself, vaguely—she hasn't decided anything for herself yet. She is still stuffed full of what the adults have packed into her, and it's Daddy who told her, Daddy has decided for her: the child doesn't need her biography burdened with some lost-without-a-trace Jewish grandmother. Or a grandfather, or whoever it was, so biblically ox-eyed. And at some basic level, one can understand Daddy's decision—when one remembers how thick the miasma of anti-Semitism was within those walls on Volodymyrska: that was the atmosphere that shaped him, and it must have been the same in the home where he grew up.

Gramps Boozerov, if he was a captain by the end of the war, must have been shipped in from someplace near Samara right at the peak of the purging of the Jewish elements, and from that point the orders stayed the same until 1991, so Nika could not fail to inhale some of that miasma herself. That's probably why the possible relatives in Israel hold no appeal for her; it's no asset. An exotic Lviv backstory—now, that's different: for now, it's just an ornament, body glitter that gives her extra charm in the company of her peers, but later, if her musical career takes off, she'll be able to put her lost-in-the-depths-of-the-gulag, Polish-Jewish ancestors to much better use, and better yet, because they are unknown, she could claim whatever pedigree she wishes—she could hint, perhaps, to a Western impresario, at possibly being related to Arthur Rubinstein, or any other famous musician who might have been a Polish Jew. It's an inexhaustible resource! She could choose from thousands of lives that were slashed short, just as Gramps Boozerov could choose from any one of someone else's suits in the wardrobes of Lviv's emptied apartments, any one of someone else's cities, homes, and even children—could choose *someone's life, already made,* and wear it as his own. She wouldn't even need to hire promoters or convert journalists to her cause: Jewish ancestors, vanished without a trace in Lviv under Stalin's rule, are ready capital. You just have to know how to collect your dividends. I could clue her in right now (she herself, of course, hasn't thought about it yet)—I could tell her about all kinds of our movers and shakers who are doing very well for themselves in the West peddling their freshly pressed Jewish pedigrees, the way Russian White Guard emigrants used to sell their estates, supposedly left behind in the old country, to the gullible French, and every Georgian in the camps was called a Count.

This must be the natural course of things: it is not the antiquarians or museum curators, but swindlers and profiteers who are first to descend upon the ruins, and they are the surest sign that life, as Vadym preached to me, goes on.

It's stupid, but I sort of resent Nika for her biological grandparents—for her not having gotten curious about them, not having made her dad untie a few of those dust-covered archival bags. It's stupid, she is still so young—her life still revolves around herself. She isn't even quite comfortable in her own body yet; she hasn't grown out of the phase where one fits oneself into the ready TV- and movie-supplied molds—she does not know yet what she's had taken away from her, does not feel the emptiness where the amputated part used to be. And her confessions make me feel ill at ease, as though she were brandishing at me a poorly set, naked stump of a limb—and was completely ignorant of the fact that it was not her arm.

"When did your daddy tell you? Did you know already?"

We have reached the square in front of the Bohdan Khmelnitsky monument, and Nika lowers her eyes, focusing on the granite squares under her feet as if contemplating a game of hopscotch.

"It wasn't Daddy who told me; Mom did ... Daddy told me later, after Grandma Dunya died ..."

She is evading again, the question is uncomfortable—and, adapting to her, because she is now slipping from my grip, I unwittingly adjust my step, too, and also try not to step on the cracks between the stones that pave the way to St. Sofia's gate. No stepping, as it was called in hopscotch—it's incredible how your body recalls—in a blink—these long-buried childhood skills: the way, on your walk home from school with the back-pack on your shoulders, you hop from square to square, without stepping, and the stone squares are wide, so you have to make one big hop first and then, skipping, two little ones, ONE-two-three, ONE-two-three, ONE-two-three.... And all of a sudden, Nika's youth, with all its unspent reserve of energy, engulfs me in a searing, apple-crisp wave, the near flame of her immortal girlhood knocks the air out of me, this effervescent ripeness of hers that could burst at any moment into a leap, a laugh, a chase, a game—a revelation. *This is the reason people have children,* darts through my mind, *with them, you live through all this one more time, and nothing can replace it!* How much older than her am I, nineteen, twenty years? If I hadn't kept safe with Sergiy back in the day, I could have had a girl like this too—or a boy—no, a girl's better....

And, instead of finishing Nika off with one final blow to the crown of her head (bent at the moment, as if purposely exposed, I can even see the whitish furrow where her hair is parted, like a chestnut's raw flesh), instead of asking her, pointedly, if she really feels herself to be Boozerov's granddaughter, and if she really never felt the urge to know what her and her father's real name was supposed to be, I surprise myself by asking, with a hungry, almost zoological curiosity, "How old is your mom?"

"Fifty-two," Nika says, raising her head.

A thirteen-year difference between me and her mother, not that much, really.

"Are you the only child?"

Yes, she is. I needn't have asked. I feel more connected to her with every passing minute—like with a stray kitten picked up from the street: the longer you hold it, the harder it is to let it go back into the urban jungle. Why is it, though, that I can't seem to find the courage to ask Nika if she knows that her dad and I go way back—that he knew about my existence before Nika was even born?

Because I, too, put on a show for her dad. I, too, played my capstone concert: look, here I am, the same girl you read about in Goshchynska, Olga Fedorivna's personal case, under Children. I am the daughter, with the stress on the first syllable, no, back then, they probably had it in Russian still, dotch. Darya, born 1965—here I am, look (a turn of the head), all grown now, a well-known journalist, come to offer you a job working with me on a film I am making.... The way you show off to the doctor who put your broken leg together: Look at me dance, doctor!—or to the school teacher who suggested you take exams to film school back when you were in eighth grade, to every person to whom you owe something in your life, knowing they'd be pleased with your all-As school report, because it's their achievement, too, they played a part in it. Played a part, exactly. If it weren't for Nika's dad's goodwill, my life would've gone down a decidedly more crooked path. But this doesn't mean that he, who lived his entire life under a stranger's name, and raised his only daughter with it, should find my archival digging pleasant—why on earth should he?

You cannot expect of people the impossible, Miss Daryna. Or, as Aidy's dad says, "Don't brag about your stove in a cold house...." Why would anyone expect the man who still goes by the name of Pavlo Ivanovych Boozerov to help me find my, e-er, relative if he never looked for his own birth parents?

And—what right do I have to judge him?

Nika, having broken free of the direction of my imaginary conductor's baton in our little conversation, is back on the subject of music, cooing about her studies, bragging about her piano professor—of course, I see: she, too, is reporting to me. I, too, am somehow, tangentially responsible for the choice she made. A living mollusk in a shell cracked open: naked, defenseless, its flesh soft and runny (on a plate, in a seaside restaurant; when was that?). And a kind of new, unfamiliar sorrow floods me—not the bitter-scorching kind that parches you into a salt flat; no, this one does not scorch, it is moist, and it makes me grow weak, soft like earth under rain. I heave with it; I swell to the very edge of my vision, another instant—and I'll burst with it, and it'll come pouring out through my eyes, nose: Nika, Nika, you poor girl, what have they done to us all?

We cross the square before the monument—pausing for a second, as always, where the urban axis reveals the sight of two constellations of cross-topped domes with the fortresses of bell towers, St. Sofia's and St. Michael's, and your breath, no matter how many thousand times you've seen it, explodes out of your chest in an uncontrollable *A-ah!* (the awkward upright trunk of the future Hyatt in its green mesh of scaffolding does not, fortunately, fall into the same line of sight)—and step into the gates as if into a pocket of silence sewn into the very center of the city: behind the ancient walls, the street clamor fades, and here even Russian tourists grow sort of subdued, as birdsong emerges, loud and triumphant, and the babbling, the crystalline babbling of dozens of streams from invisible gutters—you hear it so much more here than outside …

One's gaze flies up of its own accord, climbing the eastern wall of the cathedral spotted with patches of pink plinthite; Nika pauses for an instant, too, and then starts back on her topic again: the Germans swindled Gubaidulina out of the rights to all her works, got them virtually for pennies, but Nika will play the piece anyway, even without permission. It's not a big deal at a student concert, who'd ever find out, right? Of course. And we'll go this way, now, Nika—through the back, past the public restrooms, toward the old seminary: the old monastery orchard glows from afar with the softly goldenish froth of just-opened buds and the ant-like mesh of sunspots on the new grass.

On the corner in front of the restrooms a young Japanese woman, like a doll with an unbending back, is setting up a camera with a timer on a tripod, and we stop to let her take the picture— the woman turns to us, bows smiling like a cork-tumbler toy, thanking us with a mouthful of vaguely English mush and takes off at a teetering trot toward the clump of other cork-tumblers lined up against the cathedral wall. They all also mewl something, smiling with their mush-filled mouths, a red light blinks in the camera, the ballerina-backed lady gives a high-pitched yelp, must be to say, one more time, and trots back to the camera. And Nika and I walk on, as huge and awkward among these delicate creatures as a mama bear with her cub. It seems that for every square yard with a view there's a Japanese person with a camera, I tell Nika, but she couldn't care less about the Japanese, or their super-hi-tech machines (and our Antosha dreamt for so long of having a camera with a timer!).

Nika stares at me, lower lip bitten down, and I can again see on her large, childlike incisors the traces of the lipstick she's eaten. "Miss Daryna!"

I stare back at her: What now?

"Will you come to my performance?"

She is not all that self-centered, this girl. Not all that insensitive ...

"I will."

It comes out unexpectedly solemn, a line in a sugary melodrama.

And I know that I will, in fact, go.

***

"Why," Adrian asks, "did Olga Fedorivna not want to come?"

At the intermission, they opened the main doors, the ones that lead to Independence Square via a columned porch, and the thin crowd—looking more corporate than bohemian, made up mainly of the insiders, family dressed up as if for a wedding and friends and who keep excitedly calling out each other's names in the foyer—spills outside in two separate flows, for a break. Daryna and Adrian move along with the crowd; she's got her arm hooked through his elbow and holds on as though she were afraid of being left alone in this strange milieu.

"I don't know," Daryna answers, scanning the crowd distractedly. "She just said, 'I'm not going,' and that was that. Very resolutely, too, I didn't expect it ..."

Daryna imagined the outing as a family affair: Mom, she thought, would enjoy going out with her and Adrian for an academic concert, albeit a student one—she doesn't often get a chance to do something like that with Uncle Volodya; he is one of those people who always coughs in the middle of a most delicate pianissimo at the Philharmonic, and if he makes it to the opera, he always tells everyone how the box stank of socks (at our opera, the boxes do stink of socks)—and on top of that, or actually, most importantly, Boozerov is here, which, in Daryna's mind, ought to have held for her mom an absolutely irresistible attraction, greater than Ravel, Lyatoshynsky, Britten, and Gubaidulina put together. Daryna thought her mom would be as curious to see Boozerov face-to-face again after all these years as Daryna would be to watch them: a scene in a script written by life itself, only the camera is missing (she—daughter, witness, and accomplice—would act as a camera).

She liked this plot; she was already thinking which dress she would suggest her mom wear. Despite the extra weight that so vulgarly deformed her once-trim figure, her mom could still look quite presentable if properly packaged. The fact that Olga Fedorivna rejected the idea as soon as she heard Boozerov's name—I won't, I don't want to, end of discussion—that she refused to be cast in this film, Daryna thinks, with the bitterness of self-irony, in a way, did more to align her mother with Boozerov, in Daryna's eyes, than if the two of them were now standing here in the foyer exchanging polite small talk. Essentially, both had told her to get lost. Both refused her demand that they look back.

"That boy who played Liszt—I liked him," Adrian observes when they, having found a spot by a column, get busy puffing on their cigarettes.

"Liszt? Oh, that one ..."

"You could see he was really into it," Adrian elaborates. "The rest of them are so stiff, like they're in a military parade, these kids. But that one was different, he had the spark ... *Paa ... ba-ba-bam ... Paa ... ba-ba-bam*," he sings in a nasally sorrowful voice, rolling his eyes, to the tune from "Years of Pilgrimage," and Daryna can't help chuckling, looking at him with tenderness.

"Remember I told you about my trip to the Zhitomir region? To see that man whose address Ambroziy Ivanovych gave us?" she asks, seemingly out of the blue.

"That old geezer who was in the Kengir uprising?"

"Yeah, that one, but the uprising is not why I bring it up.... It took us forever to find his place, it's way out there in the boon-docks, out beyond the village—so we were driving around, stop-ping at every corner, hell knows where we're supposed to turn, and there's no one to ask—and here comes this little old lady in a padded coat, just marching across the field, at a good clip.... We ask her, where does so-and-so live around here? And she goes all suspicious: and what do you want with him? And we say we just want to talk to him, about the Kengir uprising. And she goes—hard, you know, like she slammed a door into our faces: That was ages ago! And marches off, without looking back. And later it turned out that old lady was his wife, the one who was also in the Kengir camp, and that's where they met each other, tossed one another notes from the men's barracks to the women's; you remember that, don't you? You saw the footage ..."

Adrian smokes and looks at the lights on the square—as if it were from there, through the noise of the traffic, that Liszt's lost tune were wafting over to reach him, a soundtrack. Years of pilgrimage, the very beginning.

"'That was ages ago!'" Daryna repeats with the old lady's intonation.

"Uhu," Adrian nods, and it is not clear what he is thinking about.

"That was how my mom said it: 'I'm not going.' She sounded almost angry. I asked, 'But why not, Mom?' And she said, 'I don't want to'—and that's the only explanation she gave me."

"It's only fun to go back to places where you won. Who wants to go back to where you'd been beaten, Lolly? And who wants to see the witnesses of your defeat again? That's not much fun, either."

"But I didn't think Boozerov was a witness of her defeat. Quite the opposite."

"It would have been if your father were alive."

"Exactly. I'd thought I could replace him in this mise-en-scène. I thought, for Mom, I was something she'd accomplished in her life, something she could show off to anyone. Rather self-important of me, wasn't it?"

"Can't say it wasn't," Adrian answers, purposely in the Galician manner, as he always does when he wants to soften the edge of his words. And smiles. Their eyes meet, meld together, and for an instant everything around them fades, is switched off—everything except an invisible circle of electricity that pulsates in the space around them and welds the two into one, until their two hearts skip the same beat, tremble with the same wonder, the wonder that each feels upon waking up next to the other: what a miracle it is that I have you, and what did I ever do to deserve it? And, because such self-generating (and self-locked) circles never remain unnoticed by those around them, since they radiate precisely the surfeit of warmth that makes life tolerable, the column where Daryna and Adrian chose to stand draws glances—the two of them become *visible,* as if held in a precisely aimed spotlight, a curious silence gathers itself at the next column where a whole pride of academic lions glows with its white manes. ("I've been in art since 1956," goes a snippet of overheard conversation.) And there, already hurrying toward them, across the entire porch on his stubby legs, is the one for whom Daryna kept searching the crowd—in the concert hall, looking over the orchestra-level seated heads, and at the intermission, in the chaotic churn of the crowd rushing through the doors.

"Good evening, young people!"

"Pavlo Ivanovych! Greetings!"

They are no longer surprised that he spotted them first: that's what he trained for, after all—but Pavlo Ivanovych's current appearance cannot fail to stun anyone who is used to seeing him in what you'd call the office setting. Adrian has only seen men like this—happily shaken, drunk on their own importance—among his friends, when they became fathers and proudly took juice and jarred puree to their wives in the maternity ward. Pavlo Ivanovych is literally glowing, not just emotionally—he's even broken into sweat in his generously cut, iridescent Voronin suit, even though the night is not nearly that warm; he's broken into a sweat and glows, as if glazed, which miraculously makes his magnificent head (his skin, in the light of the streetlamp, has acquired a clear olive tint) even more handsome, almost perfect, like the head of a lacquered idol with a disheveled mop of hair, spiked in two distinct places like the horns on Michelangelo's *Moses*, and his eyes burn with the inspiration of a biblical prophet: one can tell this is a big day for Pavlo Ivanovych.

Daryna struggles to strike the right note, feeling like a stranger at someone else's banquet: any words in such circumstances would be inappropriate, but Pavlo Ivanovych, obviously, needs no words whatsoever—their presence is enough for him to include them automatically among the circle of insiders who don't need to say anything, because everyone knows they are all in the same boat. When Pavlo Ivanovych shakes Adrian's hand, he does so with strong, honest, muscular gratitude, one man to another.

"Thank you. Thank you for coming."

He really is moved. It's good, Daryna thinks to herself, quickly, that Mom didn't come: he probably wouldn't even have noticed her, simply—couldn't accommodate her, too. Adrian is the first to find the right tone—businesslike and sophisticated at once.

"That's quite a strong class your daughter's part of." He nods at Pavlo Ivanovych gravely, like the lions at the nearby column. As if it were a soccer team, Daryna almost snorts. But, to her surprise, the words prove right, exactly the kind that a stirred-up dad is capable of hearing at the moment: in them is not only an assessment of the first part of the concert they just heard, but also a fan's anxiety (How will *our* girl look against such strong colleagues, will she hold her own?), a lifeline thrown to Nika in advance, in case of a less-than stellar performance (to lose out against the strong is, of course, so much more honorable than to outplay a bunch of slackers) and, most importantly, the voice of *expert* support, which Pavlo Ivanovych swallows with a neophyte's thirst. It must be, Daryna intuits, that he himself doesn't know much about music; it's just a status symbol for him, like the directors in Soviet movies who inevitably had Red Army officers of purely proletarian pedigree play grand pianos as a sign of their complete triumph over bourgeois culture. And in this unfamiliar world into which his child has set out, Pavlo Ivanovych looks at every initiated person like a new recruit to a colonel. The men exchange a few more lines—of co-conspirators, accomplices, members of the same club—and Daryna, relieved that Adrian has taken charge of the conversation, recalls suddenly her own appearance, thirty years ago, at a school performance: dressed as a snowflake, she danced and sang a song in English, "The snowflakes are falling, are falling, are falling," and her daddy, young, strong, and handsome, sat beaming in the first row, nodding his head in time with the music. Back then, when she was eight, she was still trying her best for Daddy, and the world was warm and cozy. What a pity that it all came to an end so fast.

Why did she come here? What does she have to do with these people?

She no longer knows. Why does this aging SBU-type, who has all but unraveled with the solemnity of the moment (just like a bad-mannered teen who doesn't know how to behave in public!), keep insinuating himself into her and Adrian's family? (At the moment, he is standing at a bad angle to the light, and she can see the white streaks of saliva, like colostrums, in the corners of his mouth—have your liver checked, or something, will you Pavlo Ivanovych?) He is comical in his inflamed paternal incarnation, like a yiddishe mame of Odessa jokes. Of course, how else? He's

from a "home," a foundling: people, who were themselves deprived
of parental love when they were children, will never learn to love
their children naturally; they will forever swing between extremes
like the color-blind forced to paint with colors, and what the hell
does she want with this stranger's life? Another life that she for
some reason has to fit inside her?

Doesn't she have enough of them already—other people's lives
stashed inside her, like in a safe to be kept in perpetuity. She's
done nothing but muddle around in other people's lives, and they
tramp all over her like on this square, demanding that she produce
from their strife and failure a spark of meaning they cannot seem
to achieve themselves; she has borne all this happily; she's liked
it, although there were some interviews after which she spent the
rest of the day in bed, feeling like she'd been run over by a tractor. But for these two—Boozerov and his defenseless (like a snail
without a shell) Nika, with her childish worship of Daryna—she
has no more room, sorry, that's it. It's too much!

These people have no connection to her; she has nowhere to
store their problems—and fails to see why she should be compelled
to do so. At this instant, Daryna thinks her mother did the wis-
est thing of all: what had been is gone; it's closed, and stored up
in the attic, and really what point is there in dredging back up
what's been buried for years? You can't go your entire life pulling
everyone who'd appeared in one or two episodes of it behind you;
no one's life is big enough for that!

She looks at Pavlo Ivanovych unable to overcome her sudden
dislike—those streaks in the corners of his mouth are especially
disgusting. Doesn't he understand that his girl has already grown
beyond the age at which one tries one's best for one's daddy—and
that no matter how much he fusses and beats his wings he can't
keep her under the glass dome of his warm and cozy world? At her
age, Daryna thinks angrily, I was already living with Sergiy—and
thank goodness, she, Daryna, chose well, because at the time there
were many more men eager to live with her than is recommended
for a young fool, feeling abandoned by her dead father and living

mother at once, who would have plunged into bed with anyone who'd mistake her for an adult.

Nika still has all these problems ahead of her, and one can be sure things will not go smoothly for her either: such unhinged daddies guard their baby girls like bull terriers, another year or two and it'll be Nika's singular dream to be abandoned by her daddy— a diagnosis completely opposite to my own, Daryna thinks—and freezes with her mouth open. *Oh shit, what if that's the thing—our diagnoses being opposite?* What if Nika actually senses in me what she herself urgently needs to survive and lacks completely—that very vitamin of early freedom (which I have digested successfully, thank goodness!)—and that's why she is pulled to me like an iron filing to a magnet?

Daryna feels faint, fears she won't stay on her feet. And instantly remembers what she has been trying to forget: her period is four days late. Her breasts are swollen, can't even touch the nipples, last night, when Adrian kissed them, she cried out in pain—but still no period. No, it doesn't look like the men noticed her dizziness. Daryna stubs out her cigarette. I cannot hold it all, she thinks, in desperation, there's too much of it! I can't put this story together even for myself, can't seem to gather up all the loose ends. Nika—my shadow, my doppelgänger, an antipode of my forced orphanhood. Yes, my orphanhood—because at fifteen a girl is still very much in need of a father, and at seventeen, too—to have him guide her into the world of men without bumps and bruises; until she herself becomes an adult woman, she needs him. Is it really possible—that Pavlo Ivanovych is making up with his own child what he once witnessed (And lent a hand to, didn't he?) taken from someone else's?

Now he seems to her to be manufactured from a super-hard material that does not let through any light: he has filled all the available space between her and Adrian, and stands there beaming shamelessly, like an infant in a bath—mad biblical eyes on fire, white streaks of saliva in the corners of his mouth. She wants to push him away—and in the same instant, with a kind of lustful, disgusted terror she senses his nakedness under that luxurious suit: he is drenched with sweat and probably hairy as a baboon. She thinks she can even detect his smell: a heavy, military smell—leather, sealing wax.... It's a dizzying, nausea-inducing intimacy—as if the three of them were in the same bed together, no boundaries between them. Is she now going to have erotic nightmares about him? Slope-shouldered, with a woman's behind, on stubby legs? Men like that are usually good and eager at love play. Lord, how disgusting, what's happening to her?

Finally, she catches Adrian looking at her with concern—and it's like all her glands swell instantly with tears of gratitude: she is a little girl again, and Daddy (Adrian) is sitting in the first row nodding his head in time to the music. My man, she flares up, the dearest soul in the world, I'd give anything to touch your hand right now. But the other one—hard, dark inside, solid, with the heavy military smell—is pushing them apart with his body. He has wedged himself between them (and here a vivid physical memory flashes through her mind—that he has taken this position from the beginning, from the first time they met: wedged between them, and with such unshakable self-assurance as if *he had a right to do so*). He fixes Daryna in the gaze of his magnificent Judaic eyes, half-covered by the drooping cowls of his wrinkly eyelids, and all of a sudden says something so ill-suited to this scenario—in which Liszt's lost measures spin and swirl around them in a neurotic dance (years of pilgrimage, Switzerland, pastoral symphony) together with the white-maned professorate that have seen better days, and the musicophile old maids who go to concerts to get their orgasms and sleepwalk through intermissions youthfully flushed—something so unexpectedly divorced from the young Nika, who is listening to her teacher's last instructions somewhere backstage right now, that at first Daryna thinks he has spoken in a foreign language.

"Actually, I have something for you. On that case that you inquired about."

Adrian and Daryna exchange glances quickly; the air between them crackles.

"You found it?" she asks, stunned. "You found what I asked you to look for?"

She doesn't dare say "found Olena Dovgan," as though complying with the rules once established by Pavlo Ivanovych: no names, no allusions, a schizophrenic secrecy, who needs it now? But let it be his way; this must be their reward—a thank-you gift for coming to his daughter's concert, a barter. This, Daryna feverishly thinks, must also be something they teach them in KGB school—that any relationship between people is merely barter: an exchange of favors. But what did he find, what is it?

"Did you really? Pavlo Ivanovych? You found what I thought might be there, didn't you? The anniversary liquidation report?"

"Not exactly," Pavlo Ivanovych says reluctantly: he is letting it out slowly, pulling their guts out, the sadist. "But I can shed some light on the matter. Choose a time ..."

"I'll come whenever you say."

"No, don't come to the office, that won't do." This now sounds abrupt, sharp, like a cry of alarm. "It's more of a private conversation. You know what?" He turns to Adrian, one man to another, as though struck with a sudden insight. "Do you by chance fish?"

"Should I?" Adrian responds.

Daryna laughs and listens to herself laugh from aside: no, everything's okay. Simultaneously, she realizes that the lions at the next column are not discussing the just-heard Liszt interpretation, but are talking about someone's recent concert tour—to Japan, it sounds like. "They have fish in abundance, whatever you like!" She hears distinctly the same dramatic baritone that's "been in art since 1956." "But it's pricey, more expensive than meat!"

She looks back at Pavlo Ivanovych—did he hear that or not? She knows it can happen like this: when life, either under the pressure of your own efforts or on an incomprehensible whim of its own, clicks on to an invisible track and rolls off all by itself, and it takes all you've got just to keep your feet moving fast enough to hang on, this is what happens—everything you run across, down to accidentally overheard snippets of conversation and advertising slogans, hammers home the same message from every direction, confirms the rightness of your course, as if put there on purpose, to make sure you get it. And sometimes, this can be funny, even very funny: the director with the full version of the script in his hands certainly does not lack a sense of humor. Fish, then. Alright, let it be fish.

"I, you see," Pavlo Ivanovych shares, "love to get out on the Dnieper when I have a chance, when I have time … on a weekend … to fish at night—it's the best kind of rest, you see."

Adrian nods thoughtfully. At the worst possible moment, the bell summoning the audience for the second part of the concert rings out from the foyer, and the whole of Pavlo Ivanovych comes into motion—from his rearing Mosaic forelock to the hem of his Voronin suitcoat (the bottom button, Adrian observes, unbuttoned, very civilian-like: did his daughter teach him?). He roils with impatience like an electric kettle, flares his nostrils, and turns for the entrance at full steam; he waves with a sudden unmanly, country-fair fluster at someone in the crowd that is rapidly congealing into a clot by the door, and instantly loses any resemblance to an SBU officer, or even just to a grown man, that he may have reclaimed in the last couple of minutes. I wonder where his wife is, Daryna thinks—she wouldn't have missed this, would she?—and manages to find, directed at them from the crowd, a frozen, even it seems, a bit scared (fish-eyed, of course!) look from an inexpressive lady, clearly not one of the musicophiles, dressed in a fashionable pink-tweed, fringed jacket that nevertheless does not look good on her at all; Pavlo Ivanovych, however, does not lose professional form and demonstrates appropriate vigilance just in time, managing (he's burrowed himself between the two of them again, and they are moving, three abreast, in the reversed current, back inside) to touch both Daryna and Adrian with his elbows and to nod, with every sharp angle he has in his body at once.

"My wife."

They acknowledge each other over the distance, mutely, as if underwater, and the pink, fringed fish stretches her lips into a smile the same way Nika does, only the mother, unfortunately, bares her gums when she does it—not the most photogenic sight. It would have been just fine if Mom had come, Daryna concludes, feeling somehow comforted. But then, on the other hand—why should she have?

And then she hears Pavlo Ivanovych's rapid-fire muttering above her ear—hypnotically similar, this time, to his daughter's dove-like cooing, "Come this Saturday to the South Bridge ... from the left, the Vydubychi side ... right around midnight, fish bite really well there ... and no one will bother us."

***

From Daryna Goshchynska's Audio Archives:
Night on the Dnieper. Boozerov.

Format: MP3
Sampling: 22 kHz
Bit rate: 88kBit/sec
Created: 04/27/2004
Modified: 04/27/2004

I didn't want to scatter the fish—so I didn't call out to you.... Voice, you see, it carries far at night—someone coughs on Trukhanov Island, and you can hear it all the way over here. Crawfish? Yes, boys trap them at night here ... and a ways over, beyond the Paton Bridge. You can buy some; they sell them for two hryvna a piece.

A drink?—of course, anytime! Good thinking that you brought some, it's an indispensable part of fishing, ha ... like tackle. I have some with me, here. In a flask. Would you like some? No? And you ... what's your patronymic? Adrian Ambrozievich? Yes, it's cognac. Transcarpathian. I always bring some when I go fishing. Here's to your health! *Bud'mo,* yes. We had this delegation from Israel once—took them to dinner at The Presidential, top-notch, everything like it's supposed to be ... and their interpreter did not know this word, he asked, whose "buddy" are we talking about? Ha ... well, *bud'mo*!

Uff. Have a pickle—it's homemade, marinated. I highly recommend it; my wife's a wiz at these.

Yes, we cooperate with them. With Israelis, and the Poles. Mainly on the Holocaust, we have the war period fairly well represented as it is. With the Poles, we also work on Starobilsk, where their officers were executed in the camp, the ones from Katyn group. Pardon, I didn't catch that? Sure, if we need something from them, they don't turn us down either ...

Oh, in that sense.

I know, Nika told you.

You know, she has the highest regard for you. Highest. She's an ambitious girl, thank God ... I've no idea where she gets it—I was never known to have any special ambitions, and my wife's the same. And you know—I'm happy to see it. I'm happy. Having ambition in life—one needs that. Yes, we hope so, knock on wood.... Her teacher praises her too ... her professor, I mean. Of course, one worries, how else? She's my only one, you see. Do you have children?

You must. Children, young people, are a must. Absolutely. Otherwise—what's there to live for?

Oy, stop with that talking, as they say in Odessa! Work—please. You know what they say: it's not like work will run away, and someone else can drink the vodka. Here, let's have another round. To your health! *Bud'mo!* Have a pickle ... homemade.

Yes, so that's how it goes.

And as far as my Jewish origins are concerned, I know everything I need to know already. I don't need those ... Israeli contacts for that.

Only, I must ask you—this is all just between us, okay? Not a word to Nika. She doesn't know everything, and she doesn't need to ...

Fuckin' ...! Lost it! That was a bite ... beg pardon. We should talk quieter, the fish—they're smart. Some, you know, grab the bait and don't even touch the hook. Like people.

That's alright though. We'll bring them, as they say, to light. Let me just hook a new worm …

Yes, according to Israeli law I am, basically, Jewish. The way they have it, one's nationality comes from your mother. If you're born to a Jewish woman—you're a Jew. But then my daughter is not, because her mom's Ukrainian. It's funny, a kind of a … zoological nationalism. I never understood this; we used to all be— Soviet people … alright, Russian, what's the difference. But what country we had! Everyone was afraid of us. Oh! Now it's coming, good things come to those who wait, as my father-in-law used to say. Fishy, fishy in the brook, Papa catch him on a hook …

And you are from Lviv, Ambrozievich? Well, then, we're compadres. I was born there too. Peace Street, former Lontsky Street … the MGB prison. Yes, that's where I was born. In prison. So the organization, you could say, is where I come from, my native land. For life. My native land and nationality … and my mother, the woman who gave birth to me—she also had a relationship with the organization. She was sent to infiltrate the banderas in '45 … with a particularly important mission. That's how it goes …

Only it's not a woman's work. God forbid.

I do know her name. Lea Goldman—that's how she was called. My mother, the woman who gave birth to me. In Israel, by the way, she is listed among the victims of the Holocaust. As perished in 1942 in Przemysl, in the ghetto. That's how it goes…. And you say—approach your Israeli colleagues. You think they, over there in Israel, would be thrilled to learn that in '52 they received compensation from the Germans for a person who actually survived on the Soviet side?

Of course, she died. And in the same prison even. But not until '48! That's a completely different story.

But please, I don't want you to think that I am, in any way, making excuses, so to speak, for Stalinist methods. Our side did not, of course, value people … never did. My father—the one who raised me—he used to say, we put to the wall people who, truth be told, should have been made Heroes of the Soviet Union. Obviously, we weren't fighting Hitler for human lives. And had Stalin struck a separate peace deal with the Germans in '42, it would have been the USSR eradicating Jews on our territories; the Soviet side promised Hitler as much at the negotiations in Mtsensk—in exchange for the Germans closing the Eastern front; these documents have been published already.... But that's, you know ... who knows what went on! We have what we have: my mother was supposed to die back in '42, from a Nazi bullet. And that's how they counted her in Israel, because it suited them better. The Soviet government gave her the gift of life. So, if you see things from the government perspective, was it so illogical to suggest she return the favor by working for us?

Nika doesn't know all this, she doesn't need to ... my wife doesn't know all this, either. You have to understand ... I've seen her picture. My mother's, Lea Goldman's. In her agent folder. Full face, profile. You know ... it's terrible. Especially in profile—it's Nika, exact copy. Sends chills down your spine, you know. Don't think me superstitious or anything. When you have your own children, you'll understand. Nika doesn't know, and doesn't need to ...

My father told me, yes. The one who raised me. Gave me life the second time, basically. That I survived, and grew up—it's all thanks to him. He made me a man. Made sure I had my own two feet to stand on ... I raised Nika to be that way too— she's always taking flowers to her grandparents' graves—at the Lukyaniv cemetery; they're buried at the Lukyaniv. On Victory Day, the Cheka officers' day, the week after Easter ... I wasn't even two months old then ... in prison. They had me in the juvenile criminal system.

Shhh! Nope, not biting, I just thought it did.

Well, if it's not biting, it's not biting. No use beating the dead horse, right? Let's have another round, so we're not just sitting here.... Your health! *Uff.*

That's how it goes. So I'm a lucky one as you can see. Knock on wood, where's a piece of wood here? A lucky bastard. That's what they said about me back when I was at the Institute. Yes, here in Kyiv, at the Red Army Street. I was the youngest in my class, signed up straight out of high school. Sure, at first everyone thought, you know how it goes, he's here because of his dad, a protégé … Father a decorated officer, veteran. None of them knew what kind of schooling I already got from my father. You couldn't get it in the Dzerzhinsky Academy. And I am grateful to him for it! Grateful, yes.

You know, I only felt I really understood him after he told me. Mom worried so much about it; it was such a stress for her … she had a weak heart already…. It wasn't easy on her, living with Father; she spent half her life deaf in one ear—he, when he got angry, hit her from the left, he had a heavy hand, may he rest in peace. But it wasn't easy for him either … to be crippled at thirty, that's, you know…. He could not have children after he got wounded. He was ferociously jealous, once threw an iron at her right before my eyes … an electric one…. Whenever she went out, he'd yell at her in the hallway when she came back, "Take your pants off!"—he was checking, you know … to make sure she hadn't cheated on him while she was gone. For the longest time, I thought that's how things were supposed to be. That everyone lived like that.

Are you cold?

Here, have a drink … by means of prevention, so to speak, it'll keep you from getting sick. Your health!

I sort of wondered if he were not my birth father—I thought, maybe Mom had another man before him. Like, this other man was Jewish, and they split up or something … children, you know, think up all kinds of things. And Father, by the way, fought all the way to Berlin, did Nika tell you? Yes, the entire war. A hero: twice decorated with the Order of the Red Banner. And then to spend years laid up in sanatoriums—what kind of life is that? For an officer?

Oh! Shhh! Aha! Got 'im!

I gotcha right here brother, don't even try it … a perch! That's alright, he'll go into soup. Let's get him in here, in the net—hold it out for me, would you please? Yes, to keep them underwater, fresh—see what beauties I got here? There. Thank you.

Yes ... so that's how it goes.

Turns out I really am a bastard. Only from a different woman. Who my father was is unknown. She never told them ... my birth mother. I was fifty the first time I saw her picture. These pictures, taken in prison—a person looks different in them than she does outside, you know. Especially women. Did you see our star, Yulia Tymoshenko—the way she came out of the Lukyaniv Prison? That's about the stage when you can take the pictures—when you can already see the way the woman is going to look in the camps. The eyes change ... the look ... but still, you could see she was a beautiful girl.... Lea Goldman. Davydivna was her patronymic. I understand she went by Rachel. She was just shy of twenty-three. I, soon as I laid my eyes on that picture, told myself: Nika must not see this, ever. God forbid. Especially that profile ... it just stands before my eyes.

That was a mistake she made, of course—not telling them who the father was. Worst mistake she could have made. If she'd told them, she'd have had a chance. Had she said anything, anything at all ... made something up, done something ... to cooperate with the investigation. They would have tried to use her again, of course—you didn't just write off people like that in Western Ukraine at the time. My father—Boozerov, that's what he said about it, he called it sabotage. It was criminal negligence to lose an agent with such experience. Two and a half years among the banderas—that's not nothing! In any case, the MGB would have let her live, that's for sure. Yes, they were angry at her, of course they were—they'd sent her into the enemy camp with a mission, and she'd disappeared! For two and a half years—vanished, as if the ground swallowed her whole, not a trace. Of course, what's the first thing they thought—that's she'd sided with the bandits ... but still, they would've kept her, agents like that were highly valued.

Beg pardon? Well, whether they trusted her or not—that's, pardon me, just sentiment, pink snot.... They didn't trust anyone!

There wasn't a single agent in Western Ukraine at the time who was trusted. And they were right not to, I'll tell you. Remember what happened with Stashynsky? Well, there you go. But you don't need me telling you this—your own families fought ... on that other side. So what if they didn't trust her! Until he or she is deactivated, an agent is active, on duty, you could say. That's what Father told me at first ... Boozerov—he told me that my mother was killed in the line of duty.... He actually may not have known everything himself, and if he did, he wouldn't have thought so much of it; they had a different view of things—men from the front, you know, those who'd gone through Germany. They were used to, you know, not being soft on the enemy. But this was different. She was Soviet citizen already. An agent with a special mission. Her death was a gross institutional error. She had to live. Two and a half years, so much information. She could have lived. If only she hadn't kept silent. That was the one thing she absolutely could not do. She should not have riled them up like that ... young men.

Are you getting cold? No? Mind the breeze, watch you don't catch a cold ...

Yes, they were interrogating her. And weren't doing it right. Now, my father—he was a first-class interrogator! Back when I was little, he'd put me through one of his wringers every so often—whether you wanted to or not, you'd tell him everything as good as under oath. And he had this way of twisting your ear—make you go down on your knees! Now, I don't want you to think he was some kind of ... sadist. I think, he loved me in his own way, was proud of me. Just—times were different, the methods were different.... And it worked, you know! It worked ...

That I survived is entirely his doing. His exclusively. However things were, you know what they say: she's not the mother who brought you forth, she's the mother who raised you. I was two months old when she ... when she passed. Not even quite that. Do you know what the orphanage mortality rate was for babies under a year of age? And I survived. It was only when he told me for the first time ... about my mother, and I was an adult already ... married ...

only then did I understand why he sent me into the organization. That was the right thing to do. He did well. Otherwise, I don't know what would've come of me ... I, when I was young, wanted to hang myself. They pulled me out of a noose ... in eighth grade.

Did you serve, Ambrozievich? Oh, after university ... a lieutenant? Which branch? Oh, that's where my father-in-law served, too, may he rest in peace. Go ahead, pour another one; no use just holding on to the glassware. To service! *Uff.*

You know, there is this concept out there ... they teach it in the military, too, from day one: understanding the service. A security services officer is always on duty; that's what we were taught ... what he was taught, my father—and he became cripple at thirty; after he got wounded, he couldn't have his own children ... so for him I was his last mission. For the rest of his life. That's service! Do you understand? Shtrafbat, penal battalion at home, so to speak. He guarded shtrafbats at the front, that's what he did, before he was sent into the Western. Guarded the men who had to pay with their blood ... Vysotsky has a song, remember? "We are not stra-ight up, we are *shtraf-bat/*we wo-on't be le-aving notes—count me a Com-mu-nist...." That's a good song, very soulful. Well, that's how Father saw me—I was in a shtrafbat. Paying for my birth mother ... who died. Escaped, basically ... forever. I saw the agreement in her file—the agreement to work for the government. Written in her own hand. And—not a single report afterward! Not a single one. An utter failure. Two and a half years, that's no joke! For every failure like that someone had to be held responsible....

No, I don't want you to think I'm making excuses for ... I don't even know if he knew it all ... Boozerov—if they'd apprised him of the situation, and to what extent ... but I understood his service! I understood why he raised me the way he did. When my mom, sometimes, would hide me from him, when I was little ... when he'd take his belt, his army belt with a brass buckle, and wrap it around his hand, like so ... he'd yell at her: "You," he yelled, "you stupid bitch, you don't know nothing, it's for his own good—it'll make him meaner!" That was his idea of education ... his methods.

Now, of course, we see it all differently. But that was a different time. That's what I'm saying; it all depends on your perspective.

I wanted to kill him when I was young ... once. After he twisted my ear at school, in front of the whole class ... forced me to my knees ... and made me apologize standing there like that, say I won't do it again—I was a troublemaker when I was little ... I still remember how quiet it was ... and everyone's eyes, the entire class looking at me ... ugh ... I ran away from home after that ... waited to catch him, with a shiv. That was back before I knew anything ... I was young. A boy ...

You must be thinking, what's the point of all this, right? Why'd I invite you to talk business, and then sit here, telling stories?

That's how I can tell you don't fish. Fishing—it takes patience, persistence. It's good training, you know ... same as tracking a target, basically. Everyone's always in such rush ... and in the end, the winners are the ones who can wait. And, of course, know when to hook—when you've got a bite, that is.

And they're not biting right now. Well, alright, we'll just wait. See how the float's moving? That's fry playing with it.

You know, back when I was a cadet, there was this one incident. I volunteered—went along with a soldier; they sent them out on these missions: gave a man a document marked Top Secret, three typewritten pages—they'd put it in a briefcase, lock the briefcase with a handcuff to the guy's wrist, put the guy into a jeep, and send him off—to us, one of our offices. And next to the soldier, there was this little red button—a "self-liquidator"... if in danger, the soldier has to press that button—and self-liquidate together with the briefcase. And I sat there and stared at that button the whole way. Couldn't take my eyes off it. That's why I came along ... I stared and thought: Now—or should I wait another minute? Now—or wait another bit? Rode a hundred and twenty five miles like that. And you know, it helped. I didn't have ideas like that after that ... for a long time. Knowing how to wait—that's the thing. That is the key. Another minute, another day. Someone will press your button for you eventually, so why hurry? Why jump the line?

No, it was intelligence that worked with her: blue bloods—that's how they thought of themselves. Everyone wants to think themselves better than they really are, don't they? They were trained in Moscow, in the Dzerzhinsky Academy. And here, in Ukraine—this was their finishing school, to train them for the dirty work, at detention sites. Beg pardon? I couldn't say I know about that—if anyone ever self-liquidated ... some might have ... back under Stalin, when there was still fear. In my memory, there wasn't anyone left who was stupid enough. And no one cared about those three pages—that was just, boilerplate, you know. Half of our archive, Daryna Anatoliivna, consists of boilerplate like that. The common, pardon me, bullshit. So please don't think that as soon as you find a document—that's it. Documents—they are written by people, you know.

Only please don't tell Nika.

Well, one never knows ... you might run into each other somewhere.

She is the only one I have. My wife—that's, you know ...

Nika, when she was born, weighed just over four pounds. And five ounces. I went to the milk kitchen ... fed her from bottle myself; my wife didn't have enough milk. Had it been a boy, I don't know if I'd have managed. It's different with a girl ... as long as I can stay on my feet, she'll need me.

So that's how it goes.... Another one? To our children.... You should have your own, have them soon, don't put it off, someone has to help the demographic situation in the country! I'm kidding, of course. Alright, here we go! *Uff* ... down it goes.... My father-in-law used to say, if work gets in the way of drinking, time to quit working. He, my father-in-law, was also from the military, rest his soul. Retired in the rank of lieutenant colonel, even made it to Afghanistan. And wished to be buried where he was born, in the Cherkasy region ... in the village both he and his wife came from. He and I went fishing there. He was such a character, you know ... always kept himself busy. He retired in '91—and became a taxi driver. A Soviet Army lieutenant colonel—working the wheel like a common cabbie! Why not? he'd say. I've got my own car; I'll make enough to cover the gas, and the passengers share cigarettes—so I'm ahead all around. That's the kind of man he was ... humble. That works better in the army; we had it a bit differently in our organization. He helped me a lot in this life. I was fortunate to have him. I'm lucky, I'm telling you.

My mother-in-law—she got bent out of shape a little when she learned I was adopted by the Boozerovs. With her, it was a simple, rural thing, you know—she wouldn't have people say she let her daughter marry a Jew ... a Jew, please! She got her daughter worked up against it, too. The wife got scared they'd ship me somewhere provincial, just to be on the safe side, and she'd already got a taste of the good life. Good thing my father-in-law didn't fall for it, set them both straight ... my wife and my mother-in-law, too. After Father, Boozerov, told me ... if it weren't for that, he may not have told me the whole story. But the way things went—he had to interfere ... reveal all his inside information, so to speak. Yes ...

I think that's what did him in. In a certain sense, so to speak ... cut him down. That fact that his life's work—everything he did, raising me—didn't do anyone any good. His service. I was a captain already. The youngest captain in Republic's entire KGB! If you see things from the government perspective, he really should've been made a Hero for that ... only no one appreciated it anymore. They used the old man up—and spat him out, forgot about him. And it was quite a shock to me—when he told me.

So that's how it all started ... because of the Jews.

Dear, dear Daryna Anatoliivna ... ask your matinka—she ought to remember, it was a colleague of hers. Yeah, yes. They worked at the same museum ... it was a Jewish woman who applied for emigration to Israel. And I was working with her ... talked to her. Spent two months talking to her, and all for naught. And how did you think it worked? That we just let them leave?

Ha ... we have a whole field branch there, in Israel. Even Vysotsky had a song, do you remember? "We missed our chance with Golda Meier's spot, but one man of every four is our former folk." A joke? Well, in every joke there's a seed of truth, as they say ... a grain. He cooperated with the organization too, Volodya Vysotsky did. What, you didn't know?

What did you expect? Of course, they were not trusted ... the Jews. There were cases when veterans from among them applied for emigration, even Heroes of the Soviet Union. So many scandals! Who knew it would all end ... so soon.

Aha! I got something! Come on, come to Daddy ... gotcha!

Darn it, another roach ... such a little thing, might as well throw him back in.

This moment here—this is the fun: when you've got something on the hook, but you don't yet know what it is! The most important moment, this. And back then I was still young, I hadn't seen real fire, so to speak, and pulled up with that Jewish woman a whole, pardon me, cabal.... She talked to someone somewhere—they had their networks working like clockwork to help their own—and they found a way for her to get out ... to slip off the hook, basically. They thought, you see, that I was also one of their own, only closeted—that maybe I changed to a Russian last name, when the government was fighting the rootless cosmopolitans. And such closeted people—they were rarely accepted into the corps, they worked as agents mostly, and worked hard. You'd work hard too, if, for instance, your mother was Jewish and your father was in the Nazi-sanctioned police! A schutzman, yeah ... you'd spend your life bending over backwards. Pardon? Well, we won't name names, these are respectable people now, in high posts. It's not important. So anyway, back then they decided among themselves that I must be one of those people—that I covered up, you know, some stains on my biography and got into the organization with a perfect record. They thought they'd found a weak spot, and that's where they hit—to take the fire off their woman and put me on the spot ... the best move. It couldn't fail.

Beg pardon? Oh ... that, you know, is just something that people think—that the KGB was omnipotent and no one could get around it. In fact, the organization was as much of a mess as everything else ... bureaucratic, backstabbing ... I, too, had to write an explanatory report to my bosses to account for the two months when I didn't get anything done. And then a thing like this hits—a complaint from your target, plus an anonymous letter—and that's it, you've been marked! The shadow's been cast: Jew won't cross a Jew, you know, and that I'm probably getting help from some Sochnut of theirs, their Jewish till ... for protecting my own from the KGB. What's the first thing? To cast shadow on a person—and you go prove yourself an upstanding citizen after that! Go prove you weren't double-dealing. That was a good, smart plan they had—they just miscalculated a bit. No one knew what really happened, remember ... I didn't know anything myself yet.

And I was in law school by then, about to get my degree. Long-distance ... got promoted to captain. Things were just starting to go well.

It was hard, you know ... it's always hard when you are not trusted. When behind your back, people are happy that you've stumbled, because there's a line waiting for your spot already. And at home—there was the same emptiness, nothing to lean against. The old man drank himself numb ... my father, Boozerov. That's how he told me—he was drunk; Mom just cried. He didn't live much longer after that. He had a hard time dying, too—he had a grudge ... against the whole world ... cirrhosis—that's not a walk in the park. Nika didn't know him; she was born later ... when he was already gone.

Are you getting a draft there? No? Your feet warm enough?

A stretch like that ... you don't want to go on living, don't want to go home at night. What's the point, you ask yourself? Just push the button, and that's it. I didn't know everything back then ... but it was a shock, a real shock. And the thing of it was—it was all like the world conspired to mock me, you know, that yes, I am a Jew after all! A bastard. And that my mother, the woman who gave birth to me, was also under suspicion, same as I ... in double-dealing.

It's like ... a curse or something. You start thinking these thoughts and ... God forbid.

This fear ... I don't fear for myself anymore, I don't want you to think that ... but it's inside me somewhere—since then, sitting there. In my gut. Thank God Nika doesn't know everything. She's got her own life. A clean slate, so to speak ... let it be....

I think Father didn't know everything either. But it cut him down. Finished him off, it did, that he had to go explain things— because of me. He had to go all the way up to Moscow, because here in Kyiv, people just looked at him like he was nuts. No one wanted to take responsibility for the decision, they were all too scared for their own hides ... and, well, they wouldn't miss a chance to bite off a chunk of someone else's. He was a stranger here. An outsider to the very organization he'd given his life to. Old fart who had no more influence anymore. So what, he was a distinguished pensioner? If all his service, everything he'd given his life to, just think—blew up like ... like feathers—from a single fabricated denunciation. How he yelled when he'd had a drink: Cursed ... Rats!—he yelled. He said that thing about the banderas once, I won't forget it as long as I live—that he envied them the way they stood up for what was theirs! For thirty years he hadn't spoken a word of it—and now it came back. I looked at him with new eyes then. That was before the '91 coup, you must remember, before all the changes....

It's all very complicated, you know. And you want things to be just cut-and-dried, nice and tidy! Like now—you must be sitting there, listening to me talk and wondering, what's all this about. Yes? I can tell ... everyone's in such rush, can't wait.... You want the archives opened, want your documents brought out to you on a silver tray, want them declassified before the fifty-year term runs out.... Do you know how many waves like this I've lived through already? And you with your film are just the same. And the consequences—have you thought about that? People's children, grandchildren. What have they done to deserve that?

Eh, Daryna Anatoliivna ... I very much would have preferred it that way—not to know everything. Sometimes, you think—here I am, I survived.... But for what?

Only Nikushka ... my girl. She'll always need me.

You're cold now? Well, that means we need to drink some more. My father-in-law used to say—"Let's save ourselves ... we're getting sober!" Come on, don't be shy.... Your health! *Uff.*

He was the one who rescued my family ... saved it, I mean. My father-in-law. Nika was born later. If it hadn't been for him, who knows how it all would have turned out. Such emptiness there was ... like a black hole ... such a dark stretch. At work—gloom, and at home—gloom. What's the way out? What could there be? Once you're in the system, you, my dear, have only two options—up or down! You don't get a third choice. Those are the rules. Until then, things were going up for me, but when they head down—you whole life goes down the drain. And I was only thirty! And not a glimmer of light at home, I had nowhere to go. My better half was pissed at me. She was afraid they'd pack us off to the middle of nowhere, where she wouldn't be able to buy the shearling coat she wanted ... from our chancery—she'd just put her name on the waiting list for one. My father-in-law later shipped in a whole container of those shearlings from Afghanistan, but those weren't the right kind for her, either, because everyone already had one like that—llama fur they were called, with those white tails like snot. Eh, why am I telling you this! All women are stupid. Sorry. That's what I thought at the time. Meaning—that that's what everyone's life was like. I'd never met a different kind of woman. And they only showed the Decembrist wives in movies....

So that was when I met your mom. That was a first for me ... in my experience. And, well, the last. After Stalin, they no longer used this method, but right at that time we got instructions to start again—"if the husband, then the wife" ... one woman got time that way—her husband was sentenced for anti-Soviet agitation, and she went to visit him ... to the camps. But—that was Fifth Department's turf; I never touched anything like that. Our job was to prepare the soil for them, so to speak, yes, I knew which way the wind was blowing; I read the instructions, too. All such methods were first tried out with us in Ukraine, and only then expanded to the other republics ... to the whole Union. Of course, it's illegal, but what can you do? You got your orders from above—go execute them! That's our job.

There was a time when this idea used to help me. Mobilized me. When I was young. Helped not to lose shape, not to start slipping ... spinning. Not to think ... maybe it would have been even better in the army. But—what's the point now? It's good things worked out the way they did. I am not complaining, and my conscience is clear.

Cognac for you? It's good cognac, Transcarpathian. Good for the blood pressure ... prevents hypertension.

Uff!

So peaceful out here! So quiet ...

You know, I had never met a woman like your mother before. Or after. Sometimes, that's the way it happens in life; there are such times when everything comes together at once, and it's just one thing after another. I had just learned about my birth mother for the first time ... and that she never told them who my father was ... didn't give them the name ... and then, when I was working with your mother—I understood, finally, how that could be possible. I believed it. I believed that it could happen. And that you could take anything for having been loved like that ... camps, prison, loony bin ... everything! You don't care. You could go out there onto the Senate Square, without a second thought—and be demoted for it, from officer to private. That's why the Decembrists came out ... that's how they could do it. And I was inside a different system. From the day I was born—I was born in prison, wasn't I? I knew how to put a person on his knees ... before the whole class ... I knew how to find people's weak spots. I'm not just telling you this—I was talented; it wasn't only the people who knew people who got promoted to captain by the time they were twenty-eight! But that's another matter.... The way those men were loved—no one ever loved me like that. And no one would have waited for me.

That's a big thing, you know—when someone is waiting for you ...

He was lucky ... your dad.

Ehh, Daryna Anatoliivna ... I don't want you to think that I ... I thought so at the time. The older I get, the more I think about this. There was a movie back then, in the '70s, about the Decembrists' wives, do you remember? I forget what it was called. It had this actress in it, from Kyiv—Irina Kupchenko ... she looked like your mom ... I went to see the movie again, when it was in the second run, and I was at the archives already. But that's another matter. Yes.

Beg pardon? Yes, they transferred me. Trusted me. That's to my father's credit—Boozerov's; it's all his effort. He renewed my ... background purity, so to speak—went all the way to Moscow, to his postwar bosses ... found everyone who was still alive—those who were informed of my ... adoption. Up till then, my service record was spotless—until that museum. And who'd have thought—a museum! You'd think it's a nice place ... quiet, mostly female staff ... and look how it turned out. So, I got transferred. From field operations, from working with people to working with documents. That was for the best, too, as it later turned out. In life, it's often like this—you think: this is it, I'm done, and later you see—it's even better. Because that was the second time in a row that I ... my second failure, with your mom—right after that Jewish woman. Except that with your mom, I did it myself; I made the decision. I didn't start the case on her, and wrote it like that in my report—that it would be a waste of resources, so to speak. Wrote up her profile. My boss read it—he got mad: "What are you doing here?" he asked. "Recommending her for the Communist Party?" But they put the brakes on it anyway, didn't pursue it any further ... changed their minds. And the hook was already cast ...

Nikushka hadn't been born yet then. She came later. And you were going to school already. You were such a skinny little thing, pale—I once saw your mom pick you up from school ... I wouldn't have recognized you now! No way. When I first saw you on TV, I thought—that can't be right ...

So, yeah, that's how it goes.

You know, in the army things are simpler, they have a clear line: there's home, and there's work. And the aggression is strictly localized in time: at seven a.m.—drills, you screw up—get a boot in your face. *Hic*! Excuse me ... so with my father-in-law you did better to leave him alone on weekend mornings. In NKVD, under Stalin, they worked nights—with the same idea—but in our times it no longer worked that way. My father, Boozerov—he was still old school ... he fought the banderas, after all ... fought with the dead, and it was to them he kept making his point for the rest of his life. Raised me to be meaner ... but careers weren't being made on aggression anymore; you didn't get ahead by being mean. Knowing you had been chosen—that's what kept you in the services! The feeling of being initiated ... to the services ... to the state's holy of holies ... a great state's, one that makes the whole world tremble! The might! The mystery of power, as this one man said, a director of a Moscow institute, he came to speak to us recently ... the mystery, yes! When you're young, it's hypnotizing; it can replace both home and family.... And then one blow like that—and you find yourself ... naked. Naked. And you don't, it turns out, want anything, nothing at all—only to be loved ... for someone to be waiting for you ... even to have you back from the loony bin. *Hic*! Knowing in what shape people came out of our loony bins and wanting you back anyway. I made sure I told her. Your matinka. I warned her ...

Yes, I did.

Sometimes I wonder who he was, my father. My birth father, I mean.... Why did she love him so much? My mother? She could have survived ... she was so young then; she wouldn't even be eighty now ... my mother-in-law's eighty-two ... she could have lived this long, too. How could she have done that? Sometimes you think—she was just foolish, a silly girl. She was too young; she didn't understand ... life ... and then I remember your mom ...

Olga Fedorivna, yes, I remember. And? How did her life go … afterward?

Well … that's good … good that it went well. Only, you know, when you have a daughter of your own … when you have your own children, you'll understand me. It's only in your movies that everything comes out so pretty. And I'll tell you from my experience: as soon as you read a document that's so pretty, so smooth, reads like Leo Tolstoy or something, not a word out of place—you should know it's fake … it's all fake, written for the reporting purposes. You can be ninety percent sure. Don't think that as soon as you have a document in your hands, you're done.

And you just wait, what's your rush?…. They're just starting to bite now…. Last Sunday I pulled a champ of a zander here, a twelve pounder! This big! Don't worry, I won't knock it over … let's put it over here, that bottle, closer this way…. *Hic!* Excuse me.

Have a pickle, it's homemade … my wife marinates them! You won't find another one like it. She's really stupid, of course, but runs a great house! Father-in-law's schooling. And Nika takes after me. Thank God. Some girl I have, no? Knock on wood … she's my blood!

My conscience is clear, Daryna Anatoliivna. And please don't go enlisting me in the shtrafbat. You think I don't understand? You think I'm too dumb to know? I've done my time, thank you. My father knew it too … Boozerov. He knew he got spat out. We all got spat out. Right, wrong … wherever you stood with the organization. All the same! Your father and mine, the same. Yes, the same! Only mine realized it first. Boozerov did. Long before the Union fell apart.

Hic! There's water right by you, would you mind passing? No, I'm fine; it's just to wash down my pill … thank you.

You know, I once heard this writer speak, she's the one—forgot her name—who wrote about sex … under field conditions … something like that. I don't remember exactly the way she said it, but the main idea was that if you're born in prison you grow up either prisoner or guard. No other choices, so to speak. And I disagree with that! I flat out disagree. I myself was born in prison—and what would have come of me if it weren't for him ... my father, the man who raised me?

No, you didn't understand. *Hic*! You can't just be so black and white.... What do you mean, either prisoner or guard? So what then, a whole generation is guilty merely by virtue of the time they were born? Those who survived—they're guilty? And they should all have hung themselves ... to come out clean, is that how it is? A noose around your neck—and you're out? Then you're a hero—fit for the movies? That's what you're doing, with your film, too. Okay, alright, I understand, let them be heroes—they fought ... for Ukraine's independence. We have independence now, times have changed—so we should honor them. Put up monuments and such ... fine. But why do you insist on digging in these ... deaths? On bringing back these death lovers? Is that a good example for the young people? Why do they need to know these things?

They need to live, Daryna Anatoliivna. Live! Not look back. You know what people say: the less you know, the better you sleep. I, for one, am very glad that Nika did not know old Boozerov while he was alive. My mom, our Grandma Dunya, may she rest in peace—she just bloomed after he died! Shed years. Lived another two decades. Raised Nika, had that joy in her old age ... Nikushka loved her too. She's always taking flowers to their graves at Lukyaniv cemetery ... we all go, as a family ... Memorial week, Victory Day ... and the Cheka Officer's Day, of course! I've given her what I could. She has what I didn't have. My daughter grew up in normal family! Like regular people have. If it were up to me—I wouldn't have told her anything at all, let her think she is Boozerova, like her grandparents. But my mother-in-law just had to get in there, the snake ... and what would you have me do? Tell my child that her birth grandmother hung herself in prison after three men raped her during an interrogation?

Yes, she did. Hung herself. In her cell, on her own braid. *Hic*! Used her braid to ... strangle herself. I myself didn't know until a couple years ago. I dug it out ... spent twenty years digging—to find that. Was that a good idea? You tell me, was it?

They were men from the front, my dear, men from the front.... You've got to understand. It was okay with German women in '45; war wrote it all off. And the banderas—they were basically considered as good as the Nazis: the Ukrainian-German nationalists, that's what they called them. The Germans had Ukrainian-Jewish nationalists and we had Ukrainian-German ones. That's the lot she drew ... my Jewish mom. If not Jewish during the war, then—sign here, please!—you're German afterward. And no one told her, poor girl, not to aggravate young men who'd conquered half of Europe, went all the way to Berlin! Wrote their names on the Reichstag. You know what the biggest thing was my father—Boozerov—saw written on a Reichstag wall? Letters this big! Excuse my language, I'll say it as it was: I FUCK YOU ALL!

Uff. Don't worry, alcohol has no effect on me. Sometimes I wish it did, I think to myself—what a waste ...

What did you think was going to happen? That I'd find piece of paper for you—and you'd have it all? They don't write things like that on those pieces of paper, my dear ...

The investigator? He was disciplined, yes. And those other two, as well. All got demoted in rank ... for two months. A suicide in prison—that's a severe breach, worse than an escape. How did she pull that off? A perfect escape. Escaped from me, too ... my own mother. Like in that song: "Dearest mother of mi-ne, tell me why you aren't sle-eping...." Sorry ... if only I knew where she's buried, I'd have carved these words on her tombstone.

And you come to me to see about your relative's grave. A grave! Where they took bodies from prisons, where they buried them—who's going to tell you? Those who did the burying are not talking ... if they're still alive. There was this veteran, from Russia—he came out not long ago—he was on the team that processed Shukhevych's body after the MGB killed him. A special operation; the team got extra leave afterward. They took the body out, burned it, and spread the ashes—in a forest, overlooking the

Zbruch river. There was no trace left to be found! Do you understand? No trace at all, and that's how they do it now, too ... in
Chechnya: after they secure a place—total erasure. You won't find
anything! And I won't find out either ... where my own mother was
buried. So now what? Huh? You can't tell me ... I'll tell you! I will.
When you have your own children—you'll understand. Because
a child needs to have a ... a place, a memorial, a cemetery in the
city, where she can go when all her friends go with their parents
and then talk about it at school. It's not like she's from somewhere
else—she's a Kyivite. These are her roots, basically. If you have
graves—you have roots. Grandfather, grandmother. Everything I
didn't have—I've given her. My daughter is not an orphan! When
she was little, I showed her the portrait on the headstone, taught
her to say, Grandpa, Grandpa—she still says it like that. And God
forbid ... God forbid ... *Hic*! Excuse me. No, I'm just ... something
in my throat.

Don't go digging in there! What do you want from it? Leave
it alone.

You think it's fear talking? Well, yes, it is fear! Fine, if that's
what it is. How do you live without fear? Everything will come
apart—look at it coming apart now! A whole state came apart as
soon as people stopped being afraid. I'm fifty-six, and I spent my
whole life being afraid: I was afraid of my father, of my bosses,
afraid to make a mistake at work. And now I'm done; I'm not
afraid of anything—myself, I'm not afraid for myself. If only you
could see how ... horrific. The braids she had ... in the picture
... my mother, Lea Goldman ... two braids, out over the front of
her shoulders ... black. Nikushka has such beautiful hair, too,
so thick. Grandma Dunya braided it for her, for school. No one
will see that picture. Maybe when she herself is fifty. When she
has her own children, grandchildren. If she is curious to know
... I saved the picture. Of the whole file, I saved the picture ...
I didn't show it to anybody. And I won't ... God forbid ... knock
on wood ... I'll knock on every tree along this shore, with my
head if I have to....

And pressing buttons—no, thank you! I've got a child; she needs me. My own mother didn't need me. She didn't think twice about abandoning a tiny baby, not even two months old, to be raised by strangers—fine! But my daughter needs me, my only flesh and blood. Everything I have—it's all for her! The grandparents' apartment, the dacha—my father-in-law basically built it with his own hands. She wanted the Conservatory—go ahead, child, do the Conservatory! We'll manage; while I'm alive, she won't want for anything! Let her study. God willing, she might make it … as some soloist, she's talented. And she's got ambition too, thank God, I gave her that, too—the confidence I never had; I was wolf cub. Whatever I could—I've given her! And as long as I'm alive, that's how it will be. My conscience is clear; I'm not guilty before anyone.

Oh, oh, here it goes, here it goes! Come on, sweetie, don't you fight it, I'm not that kind of a … hang on now … easy …

Fucking bitch! Ripped off the hook. A nice hook, too, made in Japan. You stupid fish, now you'll just go swimming around with a hook in your lip, till you die.

Darn it … such a shame. It was something big, too; could've been a catfish—they're wily! Or a perch. *Agh*, I'm sorry.

Is there anything left? In that bottle?

Alright, forget it—have another one! To our parents … and to my … to Ivan Tryfonovych Boozerov who gathered us all here today. Let him rest in peace … on the other side. If it's out there, of course—the other side.

The file? What file, Daryna Anto … damn it … Anatoliivna? There is no file under that name … Lea Goldman. Never was.

Or, yes, you could say that: it did not constitute historical value. You're a sharp cookie, miss. A quick learner.

Yad Vashem is where you find Lea Goldman, Daryna Anatoliivna. Yad Vashem, in Israel. She perished in the Przemysl ghetto, in 1942. Their whole family's there, the list: David Goldman, Borukh Goldman, Iosyp, Etka … Ida Goldman-Berkovitz, and Lea Goldman, too. And it's better that way—for everyone.

Take a pickle. Go ahead, have one, don't be shy.…

I'm not done telling you about Ivan Tryfonovych, though. I promised you, didn't I—about your case … about those who died … the
woman who died on November 6, 1947—just as you wanted. No,
Daryna Anatoliivna, I can't help you there—I couldn't find you a document like you wanted. But I'll tell you something else … about Ivan
Tryfonovych again; I think you'll find it interesting. Hang on just a second; let me get a new hook tied on here. Do me a favor, Ambrozievich,
pass me that little jar. Yeah, that one over there, so I don't have to get
up again … thank you.

Plop! I love that sound—"Fishy, fishy in the brook, Papa catch
him on a hook." Isn't this a great spot I showed you? So quiet—do
you hear it? Every rustle … you'd never guess you were in the center
of a city. It's because of the monastery, or else they'd have carved
all this up into developments long ago. A little further that way,
by the South Bridge, they've already got a few little palaces going,
did you see? You can't get to the water anymore—it's all fenced
off. I won't live long enough to save up for one of those, but hey.

Yes, so …

So I'll just tell you like this, without any documents. What
was it you said—"it's not a needle in a haystack"—was that it?
You were right; it's not a needle, by any means. So, dear Daryna
Anatoliivna … on your day of November 6, 1947 my father who
raised me, Ivan Tryfonovych Boozerov, was in command of a
combat mission on the territory of the Lviv Oblast. That's where
he was wounded, subsequently discharged. At the seizure of a
dugout bunker occupied by four, as they were called then, bandits, as we now say—partisans. Or rebel fighters—however you
please. Four: three men and one woman. And you were looking
for five, yes? Well, that depends … you could count them as five.
The woman, it later turned out, was pregnant. Yes. They found
out later, when they collected all the remains—it turned into a
bloody meat grinder there; Father was lucky he stood far enough
away. Of the guys who were out front, he said, there were only

arms and legs left, strung around the trees. Like in that kids' song, Nika used to sing when she was little, to a cartoon tune, "Off with your arms, off with your legs, out go the eyes, and we lay you to rest ..."

That's the story I have for you, Daryna Anatoliivna. A family saga, so to speak ...

Now, who those four people were and what their names were—I'm sorry I can't help you with that. Father, may he rest in peace, he might have remembered ... but there's no one left, except myself, who is aware of this fact from his biography. So it's all just between you and me ... among friends ... so that you wouldn't go looking for something you may later not be so glad to have found.

The documents are gone, long gone. I checked.

Well ... I suppose, you could put it that way—I made sure.

Well, what do you want from me? I had a young child. What good would it do for the girl to find out, when she got older, that her gramps—albeit adoptive, but still her gramps, as good as her own—the man who left us his apartment, secured our position ... everything we have, all thanks to him ... what good would it do for her to learn one day how he fought pregnant women?

And I'll tell you what: it's harder to build than to break. So much effort ... you spend all your life working, trying hard to put down some roots, make a home, a life—and to have it all ruined with a single blow, whoosh!—and down it goes? A single shove?

You don't want it, trust me. It's better this way ... for everyone. I'm the one to know.

"And now," Pavlo Ivanovych said in a surprisingly sober voice that made both Daryna and Adrian jump, "pull out your dictaphone. And erase this recording."

FILE DELETED

***

"I should have known it right away. From the first time I saw her. I can't believe how stupid I am."

"What are you talking about?"

"Gela, of course. The fact that she was pregnant. You could tell at a glance. The smile she had—a DaVinci smile, a Mona Lisa smile. That's what the secret was. She was pregnant. Now it all makes sense."

"I wonder—did Granny Lina know?"

"I bet she did. Yeah, she should have—it was October when Gela went to see them ... I bet that's why she went, actually—to tell her family. To share. Alone in the woods, among men, being pregnant for the first time—that's no picnic. And plus—of course!—she needed to make arrangements for the family to take the child. Her sister was already married; your dad was a toddler—they could have easily made it look like Gela's baby was theirs, their second. That's it, Aidy; that's exactly what happened! Any woman in her shoes would have run home like that, disregarding any danger, and no MGB would've stopped her."

"You women are something else."

"Why?"

"Nothing ... it never ceases to amaze me."

"What about it? It's very simple, really. Elementary, my dear Watson."

"Still, think how she kept silent about it her whole life ... Granny Lina."

"A fantastic granny you had. A beast!"

"Beast?"

"Yep. She's the one I should be making a film about, only no one would appreciate her quiet heroism, the feminine heroism—there's nothing *spectacular* about it."

"No, I mean, you said beast, and it rang a bell, somehow, in my mind.... Something linked to that word ... hmm. Well, that's alright, it might come to me later...."

"There's only one thing I don't understand: Why did he say four? Why don't they have the fifth man on their lists? He couldn't possibly have survived a bloodbath like that."

"Don't you think it's possible that our dear Pavlo Ivanovych did not tell us everything?"

"I don't think he was lying. No, love, I believe him. A gang rape, a suicide—that's not something a normal person would ever make up about his own mother, even if he'd never seen her."

"Operative word there being normal. Not so much with his background. God, if only we could play that recording! There were all kinds of things that didn't jive."

"Yeah, he threw me off royally, catching me with my dictaphone like that … I felt like one of those fish he kept yanking out of the water."

"You poor fishy! You worked so hard with that thing. My home-grown conspirator."

"Well, I knew that if I asked him up front he wouldn't let me record him. And it's not like I wanted to publicize what he said—it's just for me, to help remember things. I can't get over it—how did he figure out I was recording him? That I had a dictaphone in my pocket?"

"He smelled it! What if he really is—talented?"

"No kidding. Nika said he wanted to pursue mathematics when he was young. But he does have a beautiful voice, did you notice?"

"You bet. Our special attraction—a singing KGB man!"

"Not KGB—SBU."

"Same shit."

"I wouldn't say that.… But you're right; it sort of threw me off every time he'd start singing. Gave me the heebie-jeebies. It's like his whole self is patched together from different pieces, no? With the frame sticking out here and there. What kind of things would you say didn't jive?"

"All kinds of stuff. You can't quantize so much bull to the proper bit rate."

"Sweetie, could you please use words I can understand?"

"Sorry. He wore me out, that guy. The whole time, ever since I first met him, I have had this nagging feeling that I've seen him somewhere before—I told you—or if not him, then maybe someone who looks like him, and I can never see him clearly with this weird feeling in the back of my mind, the picture's always doubling up on me."

"Same here. Could it be because he's lived someone else's life?"

"There's that, too.... Who from his generation *has* lived his or her own life?"

"My dad. Your mom."

"They *haven't*. They *died*. That's the thing."

"Still, Aidy. You shouldn't compare his lot with anyone else's, God help him ..."

"Well, whatever, that's not my point, actually. The whole time he was talking I tried to figure out where he was going with it—and he's got more logic gaps in his tale than you can count; it messes up your algorithm. Take his mother, again. If she was in the Przemysl ghetto, then back in '42, it couldn't have been the Red Army that freed her, I'm sorry. She had to have escaped somehow—so how did she run into the NKVD? And what on earth possessed them to send her, a Jewish woman, under cover into Bandera's underground? Nonsense, it doesn't add up. And he just kept hammering on his 'she was a Soviet citizen!' As if every Soviet citizen automatically had to be an agent. Like fucking serfs."

"C'mon, that was just the natural logic of that government. That's what a citizen was for them—a serf, a subject. Like in the feudal days. You don't remember it—you were little then ..."

"Yeah, and the new government just thinks we're morons. Go vote for whoever we tell you to, and don't make a fuss. If you're not nickeled, you're dimed."

"Yep. Sounds about right."

"Are you feeling sorry for him, or something?"

"Why do you ask?"

"I thought you might be. He doesn't seem to bother you ..."

"Yes. Maybe. I don't know."

"Finally there's an answer that explains it all. Thank you."

"What are upset about, love? You're not jealous, are you?"

"Me? Of him? You're crazy!"

"No, wait a minute, you actually are.… Look at me, come on, you goof … now. What's wrong? Captain, my captain—what's bugging you?"

"I don't know, Lolly. It's … it's all weird. Weird. The whole time back there, he was talking to *you*—just you; I might as well not have been there, a fifth wheel, you know, the lady's escort. Someone to pour the vodka, sure, lend a hand. And the way you listened to him … wait, let me finish! I understand, he played a very meaningful role in your life. Your mother's life. But you cannot forget that it was an exchange and not just an act of charity for which you must forever hang on to his every word. You don't need to be a genius to see that your mom made something big click in his head, too—it's obvious. A gear without which he may not have survived at all. He's pretty hung up on the suicide theme, did you notice?"

"I did, sure. I actually think that's his greatest fear as far as Nika goes. Lest she find out that her grandmother killed herself, I mean.… He let something slip about a curse, remember?"

"Of course, and Nika's another thing.… He is making her your responsibility, no? Didn't you see—passing her on to you, so to speak, as your inheritance! For you to take her as your friend, or who knows what … your charge. By the same old curatorial logic, from the KGB. So basically, he and you have your own story. And I'm just sitting there, pouring vodka into plastic cups. Meanwhile, it was his old man who carried out my great-aunt's death sentence—and Boozerov has been aware of this ever since I first submitted my inquiry to the archives, last fall. But if it weren't for his daughter, the concert—like hell he would've told us this. Or that Gela was pregnant."

"You know, I can't shake that off—this must have been done in some office of theirs, right? The examination, the analysis of the remains.… It was someone's job to do that, can you imagine?

Collect the mangled bodies, sort them: ours over here, the other side's—over there ... the mother here, the fetus—separately, over there...."

"Hang on, you'll make me lose my point. It's not the different pieces, as you said, that are patched together—it's as if there were three different processes, and all of them nonlinear, oscillatory, a wave system—the Schrödinger equation. That's why he's out of focus, you know, that's why he sort of ... flickers—there are more dimensions than you or I can each individually perceive. Do you understand?"

"Honestly, no."

"Okay, did you take advanced geometry in school? Do you remember how to represent a three-dimensional object on a two-dimensional plain?"

"Draw three different views, from three sides?"

"Something like that. So what I'm saying, it's the same here. The world I—we—live in has fewer dimensions than we need to get an accurate representation of the process, so all we get is a set of random views, and not even a complete set. And the views you get don't match the ones I get—like, say, if you had the front view, and I got the plane view ... and I don't fall into your dimension, I'm not inside that field."

"Meaning what?"

"I'm just a go-between, Lolly. Like a semiconductor, you see? And occasionally, a catalyst. And that's how it's been for me the whole time, from the beginning: I function as an add-on to your project. *Your* project that involves *my* family and for which you needed a guide. A go-between ..."

"Weird ..."

"No shit."

"No, it's weird because sometimes I feel precisely the opposite. That it's my project that functions as a go-between—between you and me."

"And I've had enough of this going between. I want there to be the two of us, together, and no one else. I want to be your man, period. Your husband, not a go-between. Do you see the difference, or do I have to explain that too?"

"You goof ... that's who you are."

"I'm not sure, baby. I'm not sure."

"I am. You cover me. You have my back, all the time; you don't even notice it because it comes so naturally to you. This is why you got so worked up, too—because you took the whole Pavlo Ivanovych, the brunt of him, and now the aftershock of it is rattling you."

"Hm. You think?"

"Can't you feel it yourself?"

"I don't know.... He really got under my skin, that's for sure. Like I got some virus from him and it went running through my bones—smashing everything in its way ... bowling. And on top of that, I had to swallow it all as I listened. Just think: I've been working like a fucking ox for seven years, kissing up to God-knows-who, fighting for every little old tchotchke tooth and nail, trying to save at least a bit of our past, and underwriting the SBU's fucking budget with my hard-earned coin on top of that; and there he sits, paid, again, with my hard-earned coin—after he burned the archives! And the thing is—he's still convinced he did the right thing, and you can't get through to him!"

"Leave him alone, Aidy, others have gotten through already—left plenty of holes in him. He's a colander."

"Sure, someone tells you a sob story about his difficult childhood, and you're ready to feel sorry for him!"

"Someone has to do that, too, don't you think?"

"Yeah, yeah. Alright, don't take it the wrong way."

"I'm not. All I'm saying is he didn't have any other choice. None of them did—those who were raised on lies, with the natural course of life violated. Arbitrarily warped. Can you imagine what a flimsy existence he must lead—without roots, up in the air? A sort of a show that he plays for himself over and over and over. And there's no way to keep it going other than to guard, sledgehammer in hand, against the natural order of things reasserting itself, because if you miss a blink—it'll break through, like mud through that dam...."

"Yeah."

"His dam will break too, one day ... and sweep away the whole house of cards he's worked so hard to build around his child. It's leaking already—first his mother-in-law, then it'll be something else: the further his child ventures into the world, the more risks there are. That's why he's so afraid."

"So much wisdom. So much understanding. Where can I get myself some of that?"

"Why? You disagree?"

"You women just kill me ... just sit there, philosophizing, like it's all water off a duck's back!"

"It's all because you covered me. Shielded me bravely with your own body, you could say. Took the brunt of the negative-energy assault. Or, maybe more appropriately, of the informational assault?"

"You just keep kissing up to me ..."

"I'm not kissing up; I'm telling you like it is. You are my hero. My knight in shining armor. My Chip and Dale. My Ninja Turtle."

"Shut up. You're mean."

"But wise—you said so yourself."

"You know I've got a whale of a headache ... from back there, on the water."

"You poor thing. Take an Advil."

"Nah, a cup of hot tea—and off to bed. Lord. Some freaking day we had ... I have to say, you seem to be just generally super calm recently. Sort of distanced ..."

"I must be slowly developing the ability not to give a damn. What else can I do?"

"No, I'm serious. I noticed it back when you came home from your meeting with Vadym, and I was telling you about Yulichka. Things don't seem to get to you the way they used to; they don't affect you as much...."

"Is this a bad thing? That they don't?"

"Hey. Kiddo. What if you are pregnant?"

"Oy!"

"What's to oy about? What would be so terrible about that?"

"My dictaphone!"

"What about it?"

"I just saw this ... apparently, I left it on—after I erased the stuff.... Or did I not lock it, and it came on accidentally in my purse?"

"You mean, it was recording the whole way home?"

"That's what I'm telling you, look, it's on! It's still rolling ..."

"No shi—"

CLICK.

**

Daryna is sitting on the edge of the bathtub holding the test stick in her fingers—carefully, like a rare insect, a wingless dragonfly with a delicate blue fuselage. She sits and looks, unable to take her eyes off of it: to her, the strip seems to be alive. About to move. Or do something else to reveal itself, something completely unpredictable. Especially since, as the instructions claim, after ten minutes, the reading can disappear. Still, what she is seeing is beyond doubt.

It is real. It exists.

Two lines. Two blood-red vertical lines, exactly in the middle. Like a pair of tiny, very straight capillaries that have swelled up and begun to pulsate, instantaneously, and of their own volition.

Over 99% accuracy.

This has happened. And it cannot be undone. She can close your eyes, flush away the test, not tell anyone, and pretend for a while (How long?) that this did not happen; it was just an illusion, a mirage, a sudden instance of astigmatism, double vision. No one else has seen this; no one could testify that there were *two* lines.

But two is how many there are.

And this is indisputable. Regardless of whether anyone else has seen it. It just—is.

This cannot be replayed. She cannot delete it from her computer, she cannot set the clock back to the "time before," she cannot say to the darkness, where she cannot see either the director or the cameraman, "I'm sorry, I misspoke there, let's go back and record again from this point, here, yes."

It *is*.

Well, hello then, she thinks—a single breath of her entire being.

And instantly feels terrified.

Who are you?

Somewhere there, inside her, in an invisible cranny, in the self-propelling churn of her hot cells. (Are they actually hot? What is the temperature, pressure, the relative moisture of air in there? Is there even enough air?) Still no one, still not an existence. No machine can find you. But you already are; you are already there. Here.

Like looking into the wrong end of a telescope—a dizzying flight, an immensely long, spiraling tunnel with a golden speck of light at the far end, and coming from there, a moving black dot. She can't see its shape yet from this far away, but that's just a matter of time: its approach is irreversible, its velocity known.

Two red vertical lines on the narrow strip of the test stick. The first portrait of a future person.

Of her child.

Ripened: the word surfaces in her memory, something dropped there like a seed from what seems like a thousand years ago. No one speaks like that anymore—ripened—who spoke like that, Grandma Tetyana?

And right away—the next frame, scorchingly vivid, as if it's just been digitally remastered (Where does it all lie hidden, in what vaults?): little Darochka, Odarka, as her grandmother called her (and she didn't like it, pouted at Grandma: how crude!), listens, with a massive down blanket pulled all the way over her head (when you dive under a down blanket, you must tuck your feet under you right away and pull your nightdress over them, so as not to lose the warmth: the sheets are stiff and cold, the bed boundless like a snowy desert; in daytime a fluffed-up pyramid of sundry pillows towers on its expanse, pillowcases decorated with strips of embroidery and openwork, whose patterns are also imprinted in her memory as they were on her cheek when she woke up in the morning—you could run your finger over every stitch). The doors are open from the dark around her (a tunnel) to where the fire glows in the stove, where they are talking: her mom (she is the one who brought Darochka to visit Grandmother), Grandma Tetyana, and Aunt Lyusya. Grandma talks loudly as rural people, unaccustomed to whispering so as not to wake someone else, usually do, and Mom keeps shushing at her—every time she does, all three peer from their end of the tunnel into the room with the enormous wooden bed, where Darochka has hidden. Then Grandma Tetyana inquires—loud as a churchbell—"Is she asleep?" and the conversation resumes at the same volume as before.

Darochka is waiting for Mom to come to bed with her (then it'll be warm), and words she doesn't quite understand, the resonant and mysterious *ripened* among them—at first Darochka thinks it's about a plant, but then realizes it is not—waft toward her, churning her sleep like oars beating on water: "When I was ripened with you, it happened to me too," rises Grandma Tetyana's voice (a contralto), and Darochka wishes desperately that her eyes weren't so heavy and that she could grasp what it is they are talking about, but she can't—all she gets is a tinge of something unattainably mysterious and solemn, so solemn that Mom has forgotten about Darochka and says something to Grandma Tetyana in a lowered voice, while tossing one new log after another into the stove, to keep the fire going, like in Darochka's fairytale rhymes, burning high and bright, and Grandma goes on "and I knew I'd have a girl because I had a dream...."

A dream? She's had no dreams. No special dreams at all—except *that one*, Adrian's last dream in which they were together, in the same movie theater the whole night—breaking out of it, every so often, as if for a smoke out in the darkness, surfacing to the light of the nightlamp. She remembers that light shining on Adrian's head as he bent over the bedside table, the hair at the nape of his neck, a few backlit ruffled strands of it when he sat up to write himself a note, barely awake; and the recollection instantly makes the room go misty before her eyes, as they swell with tears of tenderness, and without realizing it, she spreads her knees like a cello player and touches herself where her yearning furrow took the fallen seed: it's Aidy's; it came from him. It's his.

That's when it happened. Now she feels like she has known this from the beginning. From that very night. Oh, that night. In the mirror above the sink, Daryna sees her lips stretch in a spontaneous spellbound smile. How could such profusion of life be contained in such a short amount of time? Years packed tight, like electrons in an atom's nucleus, something else from nuclear physics that Aidy explained....

Love me. Love me all the time—and together, knit indivisibly into one, grown into each other, we enter the same tunnel, the same movie theater, and leave it together, too, wincing at the daylight, unable to tell which limbs are whose, and before that, you were inside me again, while I slept, thrust after thrust, the film rolls; don't leave me; it's moist, fertile, fecund; we melt the snow below us; the ground washes away; we are lying in a pool of tears on the bare surface of a sad planet where everything once went wrong and must begin anew—bacteria, amoebas, the first man and the first woman, a new era, did you see? Yes, I did, they all died, and we return again to the place where the same movie is being played for the two of us, the film rips into white flashes inside the single mind knit from our two minds, machine-gun fire goes right through me, the fiery bullets explode inside me, a cannonade.

How many times did it happen that night, seven, eight? He was the one who counted, then laughed in the morning that he couldn't keep track, either; and she remembered everything as a whole, a single roiling river, hot as lava, that rolled and rolled carrying her with it.... How much life they were given in a single night! Their wedding night. Their wedding, that's what it was—the night of their wedding. Their marriage—to the toll of someone else's deathbell.

A family now. Forever.

They married us, Daryna thinks, speaks the thought to herself from beginning to end, completely, for the first time—gives voice to the idea, which, until now, merely stirred inside her, a half-guess afraid to become words: those who died that night in the bunker, married us. They *knew*.

The tile floor feels cold beneath her feet, and she pulls her nightgown over her knees, unseeing.

It's pointless now, as it always is in moments when you realize that something irreversible has happened, to let her mind ramble, feverishly shuffling the deck of circumstances this way and that, to pull and tug at them like on a purse caught in the subway doors: How, why, it can't be, how could it possibly have happened—she's been swallowing those pills, expensive as hell, religiously, and by the calendar, too, it seemed too early? What went on between them that night could not be contained by any calendar or pharmacological formula—companies fold, factories go under. *That* was stronger.

And now she has it inside her.

Hello, then.

Everything happened of its own accord. Everything has been done for her—she has no say in it, no will of her own. Someone else's will is at work, however—whose?—and all she has left to do was to obey it. Accept it. Lie under it.

She is a bit stunned with this new feeling—and at the same time, deep in her heart, strangely flattered: as if she's been jerked forth from the ranks of indiscriminate figures lined up on a drilling field, pointed out by the commander in chief himself. On the other side of the field, a fire burns in a stove in the darkness, and the three Fates—Mom, Aunt Lyusya, and Grandma Tetyana—turn to look at her with the same expression on their faces: the serene, all-understanding, and unclouded look that is brought to women's faces by the knowledge of the hardest and most important human work on earth. They turn, peer: Is she asleep? Awake? She's awake already—come on then, come over here, to our side ...

How many of them are out there, on the other side, disappearing into the darkness, no longer visible to her eyes? An army. An unseen, uncounted underground army, the most powerful in the world, one that pursues its war, silent and determined, over centuries and generations—and knows no defeat.

"Women won't cease giving birth." That's what Adrian wrote down on the pack of cigarettes by the light of the lamp that night. Someone said this to him, in his dream. Someone told him to remember it. He wrote it down and wondered later what this might mean and why such an obvious truth should have appeared in such a near-death dream—a dream about war, to boot.

Here's the answer. In her hand.

An army, yes. A second front. No, the *other* front—so much stronger than the first.

The two red (growing darker already) vertical lines on the test strip—this is her draft notice.

The only thing she can still do—the only thing still within her power and under her control—is to desert. This option is always available, with every draft. The black dot's movement from the distant light at the end of the tunnel can be stopped; there is a way—she could blow up the tunnel.

Even a year ago that's what she probably would have done, Daryna thinks, deeply moved, as if in response to events happening to someone else ("distanced" she involuntarily recalls hearing Adrian say, and this additional evidence of his presence inside her prompts another wave of warmth to fill her). Even six months ago, less than that—when was this?—yes, at Irka Mocherniuk's birthday: the women sat in the kitchen, and Irka kept lighting up and then stubbing out her just-lit cigarette in alarm ("What am I thinking!"), smearing her mascara on her cheeks and telling them how she's been trying to get pregnant with her new boyfriend, and how it's not working, and how she madly, desperately wants to have another child; Igorchyk is a big boy already, and she just can't help it—she's got this urge to squeeze and kiss every baby in a stroller she sees in the street—the same eternal female talk around a fire, where each one chimes in with her own "and that's how it was for me" by means of counsel, and everyone wants to hear it, the principle that was borrowed and then appropriated, without acknowledgement or credit, by Alcoholics Anonymous. And all of a sudden, they all ganged up on Daryna, like a flock of hens, pecking at her from every side: What about you, Sis, what are thinking, you're thirty-nine already, don't you know they automatically put every baby born after thirty in the high-risk group; you don't live in Sweden in case you haven't noticed, so what's the matter, what are you waiting for, what do you mean "I don't want to," what do you mean you're afraid? Everyone's afraid and everyone pushes them out, you're just stupid!

And she, backed into a corner, answered honestly and, to her own surprise, as clearly as if she'd been reading prepared text for the sound mixer, that her own survival cost too much for her to dare take on the responsibility for someone else's. She remembered these words because after she spoke them, for a moment, there was silence, the girls went quiet. Not because they granted her point, Daryna sensed, but because this was a line from a different script. From a different front—whose existence they, of course, acknowledged, and which they were perfectly willing to treat with due respect, but which really, secretly, somewhere in their very heart of hearts, they did not take seriously: they knew something more important.

Even a year ago—yes, quite possibly. She'd have tortured herself for a couple days, wavered, cried—and then she'd have gone to get an abortion. Although back then she had, among other things, a secure job with a full benefits package. Now she has to fend for herself. And without any especially exhilarating prospects, truth be told. She ought to be pulling her hair out: Of all things, a baby's not what I need right now! Forget me—hell knows what's going to happen to this country in six months!

And yet, somehow, all this no longer seems important. Instead, it all feels exactly like lines from a different script.

This is important: *She doesn't have it in her* to blow up the tunnel. This she knows for certain. The mere idea of it, detached and foreign, from a previous life, starts a drum beating under her skin and the wind howling in her ears, like bursts of machine-gun fire punctuated by explosions—Daryna shudders and looks at her arm: it's covered in goose bumps. How strange that this is her arm. That these are her feet on the tile floor. That it is her thigh—so large—draped over by the shroud of her nightgown.

Her body, as her will, no longer belongs to her—it is *no longer her.* It ceased coinciding with her. It was meant for one more person, turns out, from the very beginning. A vessel. Ripened.

Because all this has already happened before—she has seen the tunnel explode. She saw it from inside, the way no ultrasound machine or any other contraption can show it. She and Adrian were shown this—no, only she was shown this that night, he did not see it—"The way you moaned … it scared me a little." — "It really seemed a lot like dying." No, even before that night, earlier, she was shown this right away, in the beginning, when she first glanced at the photograph in which a young woman in a rebel army uniform, squeezed between two men as between the millstones of fate she had chosen for herself, glowed at the camera with her otherworldly motherhood: a white flash like a thousand suns exploding at once or spotlights fired up in the dark of night—and the earth flies up in a towering black wave. And that's it, the end. The tunnel is buried. No one will ever climb out.

Only the tapping from below—indistinct, uneven, going on for years, decades: someone wants to be heard, someone is not giving up, someone is calling to be let out …

I was wrong, Daryna thinks. All this time, the entire eighteen months (Is that how long it's been already? That's how long we've been together?) I believed that Gela called me to *her* death. But she didn't—it was the death of her child.

That's what was tormenting her.

But eighteen, or even twelve months ago, the then Daryna Goshchynska—a well-known journalist, the host of *Diogenes' Lantern*, a successful self-made woman who posed for covers of women's magazines and represented a status trophy for men who are driven around in company-owned Lexuses—would not have understood something like this. She had to change first.

They, the dead, helped her.

Over on the other side of the field, where the fire burns, the darkness begins to lift slowly, and behind the backs of her three Parcae, Daryna sees Gela. She sees the women of Adrian's line—the ones she knows only from his family photos: Mom Stefania (this is the first time Daryna addresses her that way, in her mind—up until now she was always Aidy's mom) and Granny Lina and Great-Grandmother Volodymyra, Mrs. Dovgan, and some other ladies, from the '30s, '20s, teens, the beginning of the past century, with little cloche hats pulled down over their eyebrows, silk bands, tall laced boots—of course, they are all related to the one who is inside her, he or she is theirs, too, their blood; they have a claim—and they mix in with my Grandma Tetyana and Aunt Lyusya, as if for a wedding photo together.

How could it be, Daryna thinks with quiet astonishment (if it is possible to be astonished quietly—but she can; she is adapting to their ways, to the unclouded, all-understanding serenity of those dead victors who finally won their war)—how could it be? Why didn't anyone ever tell her that it all began so long ago, long before she was born—that one famine year when Aunt Lyusya got from Great-Aunt Gela that sack of flour that kept Daryna's mother alive, that that's when they had met, these two women who have now become family, only Aunt Lyusya did not speak of this to anyone until she died, she had promised not to tell—and did not?

But how do I know this, where does this certainty come from, this sealed, spellbound knowledge—was this also in the dream *that* night? Gela did not choose me—Gela simply followed her flour to find me. She followed the tracks of the life she once saved—in exchange for the one that had been cut short inside her.

Well then, hello. Can you hear me? Do you have any idea in there, inside me, how many people had to work—and how hard!— to call you forth from the far end of that tunnel?

You know, I've seen you. That's what I now think. I clearly remember *that* dream having a child in it—a little girl, maybe two, no more, with Gela's golden braids. She was smiling, laughing at me, and I told Aidy who was also there to see her: I'll have a girl.... Why did you laugh? Were you happy to see me? A blonde little girl—like the Dovgans, their blood. Aidy's built more like the Dovgans than the Vatamanyuks, too, only he's not blonde ... *I had a dream.* Grandma Tetyana, how I wish you were still here—back then, thirty years ago, I was too young to go sit at the stove with the women, tossing logs into the fire—could Mom have remembered what dream it was you had before she was born, whether it was the same as mine? You had two little boys ("lads" you called them, Grandma Tetyana, country-style, no diminutives)—the three-year-old Fed'ko, a year younger than Aunt Lyusya, and the other son, who stayed only a few hours, not living long enough for a name—both were gone in '33, my unrealized uncles, may they rest in peace. And girls ("gals" as you called them, Grandma Tetyana)—they're tougher, hardier—"lustier" as you used to say, Grandma Tetyana, people don't speak like that anymore....

Well then, hello.

Daryna puts the test aside (the lines have turned beet red, but are still there) and feels her legs: ice-cold. And she didn't even notice when she got cold. A new, unfamiliar anxiety for her own body commands her—for this vessel's fragility, whose full extent has been revealed to her it seems, only now, for how easy it is to harm—and she starts rubbing her stiff legs energetically:

Should she go put on a pair of warm socks, or would it better to just jump under a hot shower—and how hot, precisely, should it be? Lordy, myriad questions pop up from nowhere, stuff that'd never crossed her mind—it's like landing in a foreign country where you don't recognize anything except the McDonalds. She knows nothing, absolutely nothing; she needs to read up on this right away, at least look stuff up on the Internet before she goes to see a doctor, and by the way, where should she go? She doesn't even know that—she'll have to ask the girls.

**

The same day, around noon, while Daryna is still on the Internet (she's had an idea for a new column in a women's magazine—why the topic of pregnancy is so unpopular in our culture?), her cell phone rings.

"Hullo, honey."

It's Antosha, her former cameraman. A voice from her previous life, no longer a stab of pain but of quiet sadness that sooner or later smoothes over the anguish of any loss: that was a nice life she had....

"Hi, Antosha. Glad to hear from you."

"You're lyin'. What's the joy hearin' from an old knuckle-dragger like me? Yurko says he saw you the other day on Davydov Boulevard with some mensch—he still can't get over it. Went off his feed."

Kyiv—always a small town. On Davydov Boulevard—that must have been when they went to visit Ruslana, to see Vlada's remaining paintings. Nina Ustýmivna's lawyer came a bit later, so Yurko must have seen them when they were getting out of the car—why didn't he call out to her? Still, it feels nice to hear Antosha's words, nice to know she's been seen with Aidy and the studio is now buzzing with gossip—she used to love that sophomorically careless, permanently simmering, as if on low heat, atmosphere of studio banter, jokes, flirting, "follies," and parties people spent weeks planning and then months remembering. Kids, she thinks. Grown, sometimes aging kids whose job is a serious game of virtual reality.

"Don't be jealous, Antosha," she says, surprising herself with the maternal notes in her voice. "I still love you."

"Alright, let's say I believe you. What are you up to these days?"

"Oh, you know … odds and ends. Whatever comes my way …"

"A decent living?"

"Still better than the nation's average. What's new on your end?"

"Good for you. Our chickens came home to roost. Whole flocks of them."

"Must be a chore to clean up after them?"

"You've no idea, Sis. Knee-deep in guano doesn't begin to describe it. Censorship's worse than in the Soviet days. I've got the same ol' feeling of eating shit again—got twenty years younger!"

"You're not that old yet, Antosha," she says, realizing that Antosha has called her to vent. "Don't write yourself off before your time." (I should really shut down the computer and focus on the conversation, she thinks, regretfully—but make sure to bookmark this site for future moms first.)

"Heck, I'm not the one doing it; I've got help. But I'm getting too old for brown-nosin', Dara. You know what ol' Lukash, may he rest in peace, used to say, the one who wanted to go to jail in Dziuba's place, except Dziuba then confessed, and Lukash just got fired from everywhere …"

"Of course I know who Lukash was—what do you think I am, a total idiot?"

"Well, this was back when you were still walking under tables and I was already working, and I remember how every word he spoke became urban legend…. So when people asked him how things were going, he'd say, 'I might be flat on the floor, but I'm not kissing any boots.'"

"Nice. I'll have to remember that."

"Yep. I'm feeling a little like that myself—not kissing any boots; I'm not a boy anymore to be getting bent over like that. Let their new snot-crop do it, they've hired a bunch from the boonies—give them three hots and a cot and they'll suck on anyone's dick."

"That bad, huh?"

"Worse than bad, I'm telling you. Total beck in ze Yu-Es-Es-Arr. For the news, we get instructions sent down every day: what to cover, and what words to use, and about what to pretend didn't happen. If you'd just insert 'our dear Comrade Brezhnev' here and there, you could recycle your calendars.... In addition to yours, they shut down three more shows."

He lists them and Daryna gasps—all were original programming, the kind that used to make their channel different from others, so what's left? "Did they close Yurko's show too?"

"They changed the format. No more live air. For anyone, wholesale, even talk shows will broadcast in recording lest someone blurt something undesirable. They're gearing up for the elections. Instead, they bought Russian programming—cop shows, soap operas, you can imagine."

"Are they launching the new show then? They had plans for some grand contest for young viewers—*Miss New TV* or something ..."

"Oh, the whore school? I didn't know you'd been apprised. No, they decided to hold off in the run-up to the elections, wait until after. Rumor has it, someone leaked to the opposition that it's bankrolled by the porn-industry sharks, and the money trail goes all the way to the top, and the administration has no interest in another scandal; they know they'll have enough egg on their face as it is. Did you catch the Mukachevo story?"

"Yeah, I did."

So, Daryna thinks, Vadym drew his own conclusions from their conversation. The opposition—of course, he is a member of the opposition, isn't he? Probably made a pretty penny on the whole thing, too: the new owners of the channel would pay for his silence regardless of whether this came to them as a friendly warning or a piece of light blackmail. The important thing is that they've held off with the show: stepped on the brakes, didn't pursue it any further—Pavlo Ivanovych's voice surfaces in her mind (file deleted)—and the hook was already cast.

Now she, too, has saved someone. Some nameless girls—the way Pavlo Ivanovych once saved her. Only, unlike herself, these girls will never find out what danger they were in. But that doesn't matter—she's done her job. In the run-up to the elections. Everything is now being done in the run-up to the elections, as if the end of the world has been scheduled for this one particular country, a plan for its final and irreversible subjugation by some dark forces. But it's impossible, something in her protests: it's absolutely impossible, how can anyone think this'll happen, have they all gone insane—she's having a child, for God's sake!

"And you won't hear a peep of it from our broadcast," Antosha drones on. "Not a word about Mukachevo, everything's hunkydory everywhere, the percentage of fat in butter is growing daily. Long story short, Dara, tell you what: you done good to cut out when you did. You, old witch, always had a nose better than a bloodhound—for people, for situations ... we were just talking about it with the boys yesterday."

That's a compliment: she can almost see this conversation as it occurred in the smoking room. When you work with men, you don't get to hope for any word of appreciation spoken to your face—they're always watching you, waiting for you to make a misstep or just to lash out in irritation, something they can write off, among themselves, to your PMS or, better still, to your not getting any (and how would you know, she always wanted to ask these self-appointed he-men—have you fucked me?), and to restore, in that manner, their male dignity, which is chronically compromised by the presence of an independent, beautiful woman in any role other than that of an office girl. Over the years of working with them, Daryna has mastered a system of signals that must be constantly deployed, as though on a highway in hazardous conditions, to show that she is not crossing the white lines, not aiming to cut into "their" space, and depends, time after time, on their aid, being the weaker sex that she is, and only rarely, oh how rarely—she could count those occasions on the fingers of one hand—did she hear them give voice to what every last one of them must have secretly known: that she was the brains of the channel, its soul, and not merely its showy face, which could, with appropriate promotion, be just as easily replaced with someone else's. And here it is—she's lived to see it—belated, almost posthumous recognition sent in her wake. Nose better than a bloodhound's—that's their way of appreciating her now that they've had a chance to regret not quitting with her, the whole team together, when they could (and they could have, they had their chance—and it would have set precedent for their whole guild, and it would've been easier to get funding for VMOD-Film now!). Nose better than a bloodhound's. That's what it's now called. Well, guys, I won't turn it down.

No point belaboring this—no sense multiplying essences, as old Occam taught, and as Antosha likes repeating; Antosha, who always defends the basest among all likely motivations for anyone's actions, maintaining that his chance of being wrong lies within the range of statistical error—and Daryna swipes Occam's razor at him.

"Is that proper language? Mind your discourse, Antosha!"

"Well, I didn't go to discoursing school, hon. You know, I'm a humble man—a shooter, as we used to say in school ... but, fuck me, I've had enough. I've eaten so much shit in my Soviet days that when the same Komsomol-GB rats throw me back into it and go 'give me ten!' it makes me want to hurl, and booze don't cure it anymore. Plus, one can't be drunk his whole life!"

This is somewhat surprising, coming as it is from Antosha who always and everywhere had been the first to inquire whether drinks were included.

"So what, you looking for a job?"

"Yep. That, by the way, is why I'm calling you. Come on, out with it, is it true that you've bought out all the footage we got on Olena Dovganivna?"

Not I, she thinks. Vadym simply solved that problem too, while he was at it. He chatted with the guys, did them a favor, looked out for himself, and, well, didn't forget her consult. Plus, threw her a bone to make sure she'd shut up, would never again drag Vlada's skeleton out of his closet. No wonder he turned it all around so quickly, and without her having to remind him.

"Where'd you hear that, Antosha?"

"Not like it's rocket science. Who other than you would want that stuff? It's obvious whose little fingerprints are all over this. Spit it out, Sis. You got it?"

"I do."

"You witch," Antosha drops his second compliment in a row, with genuine pleasure, like a dollop of cream into her coffee. "And what are you going to do with it?"

That's a good question, Daryna Goshchynska thinks. A very good question indeed. She would love to know the answer. Now that the life, passed on to her down the line from Gela Dovgan, smolders somewhere inside her, a not-yet-visible spark, and at this thought a smile rolls out, by itself, onto her lips: what if she went ahead and said into the phone, as she did to Adrian about an hour earlier, "You know, I'm pregnant"?

(No, that's not how I told Adrian. I said, "You were right, you know," and he knew it instantly from my voice, from the way it strained to contain the triumphant bulk of the secret knowledge that cannot really be shared with anyone, even with you, my most precious, my love, you whose touch I yearn for, while you, on the other end of the city, are choking on the uncontainable shock of this new joy, while I long for it like for a drink of water on a scorching day. It would be wonderful to have you by my side the whole time, holding my hand, but what I would like best right now is to fall asleep—sink into long, translucent daytime sleep, blissfully unhurried like rapid filming, like smoke rising from a fire in a summer orchard—languor-sleep, doze-sleep, the sweet stillness of the body stripped of will, with the mind dimmed like a lamp not quite turned off—sleep through which I could still sense your presence—you working in the kitchen, you out on the balcony, carrying something from one place to another, nailing, moving things—making a place for the baby, perhaps? Noises that blend with the lisping of rain outside and the whoosh of tires on wet asphalt, with flashes of sunlight that swim around the room from the balcony door when it opens, then closes—and then you dive in with me, under my blanket, hugging me from behind, and purr in a low voice so that even asleep I can feel how hot I am, how your penis instantly hardens pressing against my buttocks—my dreams will be here cut short and will later resume at the same point; the mechanic from the ancient club of my youth will glue the film back together, and on this parallel reel that has been running before my eyes the whole time, without ever obscuring the room around me, with its shifting light, the breath of the man I love and the rain outside, there will be Gela—it is with her I most want to share this; she is the one I want to call and say: come—

and now she finally will come to me—by herself, without any go-betweens: now, that I can finally understand her, now that it's not only she who needs me, but also I who need her—need her more than my mom, more than a sister or friend, more than any other woman in the world—

I will tell her she carries no blame. That she is now free. And also will tell her the war goes on, that the war never stops—now it is our war and we haven't yet lost it—

and will ask her: Gela, you see things better from where you are, tell me—it is a girl, isn't it? Will she be happy?)

"You know," Daryna says into the phone, "she was pregnant."

"Who?" Antosha's voice asks, startled.

"Olena Dovganivna. She was pregnant when she died."

"For real?"

"Uhu."

"Get out. How'd you find out?"

"From the son of the old GB man who was in charge of the raid."

"Fuck me. Pardon the discourse. His old man told him? I thought they'd signed papers like in Afghanistan—not a peep about combat operations, if anyone asks—you brought candy for the kids ..."

"No, you're right. It is the same with the GB, but his kid dug it up on his own. As an adult already."

"Wow. Where did you find this guy?"

"Right here in Kyiv."

"Mind-blowing," Antosha says. She can hear him light a cigarette; his excitement spreads through the network. "Awesome. Shit ... listen, Sis, so I was right? You're gonna finish this film? By yourself?"

"Already got incorporated. As my own—don't laugh at me—film agency. Am now hunting for cash."

"I knew it! I knew it. I know you, you old witch ... you! I'd smother you. In my arms. Tenderly. No. Hats off. Kiss the fair lady's hand, my respect, my total respect. Goshchynska, you sly wench, take me in, will ya?"

"I ..."

"You know you'll have to shoot more footage! You got that offspring on record yet?"

"No, he refused. It was a private conversation."

"All the more so!" Antosha exclaims, delighted: he is comforted to hear that she hasn't recruited a new shooter. "D'you think those twenty-four hours we shot are gonna do it? Fat chance!"

"Twenty-three forty," Daryna corrects automatically, not yet believing her own ears.

"All the more so! Doesn't matter. How much of that is rough, come on, turn on your brain now, how much of that will end up on the floor? And now that you've dug up how it all ended, with that firefight in which she died, you can't do without that scene—with or without the dude, you've got to show that somehow. Never mind all the other stuff.... How are you going to patch it all together, without a cameraman, who are you kidding? Meaning without me, the magnificent; it's basically my film as much as yours! Come on, Dara, what do you say?"

"Antuan, have you not heard me? I've got no money to pay you!"

"You mean, like, at all?" he sounds unapologetically sarcastic: the fact that she was able to get twenty-four hours of footage back from the channel appears to have instilled in Antosha a rock-solid faith in her omnipotence, the financial kind included. "Hon, you just think, how much do I really need? It's not like you're starting from scratch. I've got my own camera, and for editing I'll talk to the boys at Science and Nature, they're living on bread and water there and would make us a great deal. You do have to cover travel, to shoot on location, somehow, but that's not much.... You've bought the footage out of there—that's the thing, and you did it!"

This is precisely what she's been missing—words of support from someone who knows how it's done from the inside out, first-hand—professional support, the guild behind her, the brother-hood. Their company. Their community.

I'm gonna bawl, Daryna thinks. How deeply, it turns out, this got wedged inside her—the resentment from last fall, the insult of the boys all plugging their ears and covering their eyes at her departure, each of them already burrowing deeper into his own hole. Antosha, who would have guessed? Antosha— Occam's Razor—the old wino with his eye eternally askance at any show of uncompensated enthusiasm, like a country-man looking at a political agitator—is he really with her? It's true, they've always had an ambient sort of bond, of that easy, unforced kind that emerges when two people feel good working together—and laughing together. That's not an afterthought (at meetings and on location they always sat together, exchanging comments and snickering); it's important, it keeps you warm. Antosha—despite all the cynicism of his act—is a warm person, but for him to give up a sure meal on the table and follow her, on a whim, into the wild blue yonder, it is not enough to be warm; it's biblical—either hot, or cold, and she feels almost as ashamed, as if he'd suddenly proclaimed his love for her: he's broken the stereotype. So this film means something for him, too? Something more than the number of shooting hours, remunerated according to a contract?

"I can still manage the travel, Antosha."

This, actually, was what she and Aidy decided—so that if she didn't find a sponsor, she could finish the film by herself, out of pocket, only they didn't count on having a cameraman. But this was before she learned about Gela. She needs a cameraman, oh yes she does, and it would make her happy beyond words to have Antosha do it; he's a wiz at his job—one of those last Mohicans, old enough to have witnessed the glory of filmmaking in the Kyiv-school tradition....

"So there!" Antosha triumphs. "What else do you want? You know I don't take up much room; I'm skinny and don't eat much, as long as I've got enough for a drink, I'm happy.... You'll be saving on me!"

"Will you work for food? I can feed you. Like Lukash. They say that's how he lived in the '70s—whenever he'd visit whichever writer-neighbor of his, they'd go, 'Oh, Mykola, perfect timing, we were just sitting down to dinner, come eat with us...'"

"Yeah, that was their way of justifying their own fat mugs. Alright, woman, don't fuss. I can always find a gig; there's life in this old dog yet! One commercial can keep me on the road with you for a month, working for food alone, if that's how skimpy your operation's going to be."

"I'm not skimpy. If I get a grant—and there's hope—I'll pay you."

"I knew it! I knew it. Slave driver. If I don't get you by the balls, I won't get snow in winter out of you," Antosha sounds cheerier: the official part is over, and now he can go to the bar. "So what's next? When do we start?"

"I didn't know you were such a romantic soul, Antosha!"

The deal has been struck, and Antosha knows it, so he can allow himself to get serious and drop his usual hayseed tone.

"Dara, I am fifty-three. And, like everyone, I have my breaking point. You can tell yourself all you want that it doesn't matter who it is running behind with your camera—spit it, wipe it, and don't give a fuck where it goes from there, the stuff you shot, 'cause, like, it's not your problem ... but what am I going to tell my son? 'Serve, my boy, as Grandpa did, and Grandpa didn't give a shit?' That's from my army days, sorry...."

"He's in his last year, isn't he? Will graduate this summer?"

"Yep, from the same ol' rez. What's out there for him? Being the escort boy for the goons? I'd rather he didn't tell himself one day that his father had been a total cocksucker all his life. I'd rather leave something behind. Something that could make him proud of me one day."

"Antosha," Daryna says, feeling her throat go numb. "Antosha. We'll make a kick-ass film, you and I. You'll see."

"Of course," Antosha agrees.

"I promise you. Even if no one ever buys it—you'll show it to your kid."

And Daryna will show it to Nika Boozerova. And Katrusya, she must see it—even if she's too young to understand, she'll remember it. When she grows older, Daryna will explain. They grow up so quickly! Children—those living clocks and all we can do is try to earn their forgiveness at some point in the future. And this person who will come (a girl? with tiny blonde braids?)—how will Daryna look her (him?) in the eye when they meet if she doesn't make this? Her film. And Antosha, he is right: the film is his, too, and not only because he worked on it. It was Antosha's eye, always, no matter how hungover, that unerringly found the best angle, that was hiding behind the camera during every one of those twenty-four hours—Vovchyk, her show's director, had also done a ton of work on this, but what happened to his work has always been, for Vovchyk, "not his problem." He didn't have any trouble letting his employers have the final word about that. Antosha has not betrayed his work. He just hasn't, and that's it. Is this what Aidy, when he's appraising all that antique workmanship, calls, with such purely masculine, guild-like pride (we women can never quite say it the same way)—a master?

"Of all the shit to worry about right now, why would you pick whether anyone'll buy the thing?" the master grumbles. "I was just so happy, you know, when I heard you got the footage out of there. Good job, Dara, I thought, you stick it to those bitches ... 'cause I'm telling you I've had it with them. You know me—I'm basically an ox: you can hitch me to the plow forever, and I won't even moo; I'll just swish my tail at the flies ... the Ukrainian temperament, we're all like that. Until they bend you beyond the breaking point. And then it's the end of the line: the ox stops and you can forget your plowing. If you'd just told me you already had someone else lined up, I would be quitting the studio anyway. I'd go wherever, to hell and back, doesn't matter. 'Cause what these bitches are cooking up there, it's fucked up, I'm telling you. And the people have no idea, they don't get which way the wind's blowing."

"You did. And I did. And I know others who did. And how many are out there that we don't know about? It's a big country, Antosha. They can't just bend it however they want."

"I'm sorry about *Diogenes' Lantern*," Antosha suddenly says. "Real sorry."

"Uhu."

"You were holding it, you know. The lantern. And one could see there were people in this country.... And now all you see is shit crawling out from the woodwork and nothing else. Why should it be so, Dara? Why are they always putting us down? All the time, look at any time in history, it's the same thing all over again—someone's stomping us into shit, so deep we can't even see ourselves. Is that some fucking karma we got, or what?"

"Devil's Playground," she recalls. "That's how someone put it to me recently. I mean, he said God's, but it's actually the Devil's: he's one of those people, you know, for whom these concepts are interchangeable, God-Devil, up-down, left-right ... depending on the situation, what kind of a hand they get."

"Uhu, and they seem to be fucking everywhere … and what are you gonna do about it, huh?"

"Make a film," Daryna says. "Make a film, Antosha. What else would we do?"

***

It will be a film about betrayal, she tells Adrian when they are walking back through Tatarka from the restoration workshop. Daryna asked to come with him to see how they cleaned old icons.

"About betrayal? But we still don't know the identity of the man who led the raid to the bunker; we only have our speculations—so whose betrayal, which?"

"Any. Of one's country. Of love. Of oneself. Betrayal as a road that leads to death, but we've talked about that already—someone has to pay for every betrayal, one way or another, to restore the cosmic balance of forces that it violated. The greater the betrayal, the greater the sacrifice."

"So when are you starting?"

"Tomorrow. I invited Antosha to have dinner with us, to discuss the changes to the script, he might think of something—there're three of us now! There *were* three of us anyway. Without Antosha. Well, the little one hasn't made the team yet."

"Is that why you turned the place upside down today—you were going through your stuff?"

"Yes, and you know what I found? On my dictaphone, remember, it kept rolling in my purse on the way back from fishing with Boozerov, it recorded our entire conversation—at the very beginning, there's a bit of Pavlo Ivanovych talking."

"For real? How could that have happened?"

"Beats me—maybe the button got pressed, inside my purse, all the way back at the river, when he kept trying to send all that fish home with us. You can't hear exactly what he is saying, so it's just this irritating drone, as if from behind a wall, *boo-boo-boo*, persistent, like it's trying to break through and just can't, and it's just the timbre and the intonations, nothing else; and you know, it gave me such a strange feeling, this voice, distilled like that to the pure essence of sound—as if I had heard it before, the same intonations, they were so dreadfully familiar, as if they belonged to someone very close ... I'm not making this up, trust me. I didn't even have it in me to erase that bit, even though it's nothing to do with anything. And you know how it ends, the recording? With your voice—you asking what if I were pregnant. The first time you mentioned that. So weird ..."

"Adrian shrugs: What's so weird about it?"

"I don't know," Daryna slowly answers, thoughtful, as if still under the spell of that other voice—"I must be getting superstitious."

They stop at a crosswalk. In the openings between buildings, the dusk, already pricked with streetlights, smoldering, bluish and ashen; the windows of the top floors flash with every shade of fire; and, in the dusk pooling below the red signals at intersections, the taillights of passing cars glow mysterious and sweet, like pomegranate seeds.

"Look." She touches his elbow.

"At what?"

Look at how magnificent the city is in this light, she wants to say; this is the only time when you can sense its rhythmic breathing—when all the dirt people tracked in during the day is extinguished by dusk, and even the noise seems muffled, like when you instinctively lower your voice in low light; it does not last long, this time, half an hour perhaps—it is a change of rhythm like shifting gears or catching your breath: the tired masses of working folk, worn, an inexorably uniform look on their faces, head home to their concrete shells, and restaurants-theaters-bars have not yet taken on the next human wave, with its fresh charge of excitement. And in this interval, if you catch it just right, you can sense *the city's own pulse*, those anxious currents of waiting, pleasure, and dread that thread through it—an inaudible music—and feel numb with the love for this city, so defenseless in fact, and hear the trees grow through it, unstoppable, fearsome—the cottonwoods on its boulevards, the apricot trees and the cherries in the cubical canyons between its high-rises—you can feel their explosive, autonomous force, the same *will to grow* that is now inside me, and that is not given to anything made by the human hand (we do not notice it during the day, but should people abandon the city, the force of the trees would break free and run rampant without constraint until the eyeless ruins of buildings begin to sink in the boiling woods, in the wild primeval thickets, the same as the ones from which the city once emerged, some two thousand years ago). If only she could film the city like this, caught at just the right moment—for the film's opening. Despite the fact that it's not, at first glance, connected to Gela's story at all.

And, she tells Adrian, she would like to film the restoration workshop they'd visited. It resembles his dream shop of antiquities a little, the Utopia he told her about: with its unhurried, taciturn men in leather aprons, filled with a special inner dignity, with graphite-black fingers and an assured, almost genetic confidence in their way with objects—an atmosphere of unworldliness, so uncommon in the modern world, and, to an accidental visitor, all but church-like, and inseparable from honest work; the atmosphere she remembers from Vlada's workshop, and up until recently one could glimpse it in the last relics of ancient artisanry: cobblers' kiosks, TV repair shops, countless basement rooms smelling of wax and turpentine, where men fixed umbrellas, locks, eyeglass frames, and just about everything that could be fixed.

This disappeared in our lifetime; we watched it vanish, these pitiful remnants of the once-powerful Kyivan commonwealth, wiped out by the Great Ruin of the twentieth century: smiths, coopers, crockers, tanners, and lorimers, the once-glorious guilds that for centuries built up this city, founded churches and schools despite every alien tsar and magistrate—men who sat just like this in their tiny workshops two, and three, and five hundred years ago, and took with gravity into their hands the things people brought them, pronouncing their verdicts once and for all, as only men who know the true and good price for their work can. Not the price people pay at the market, but the one that is measured by the sum of expended life: the number of dioptres added to their sight over the years, the wheezing in their turpentine-laced lungs, their skin burned from constant heat, the high-contrast map of their wrinkles. The absolute concentration and surgical precision of movement with which a restorer, looking through a magnifying glass, dabbed away layers of age-old grit from a spot on an icon evoked in Daryna a downright sacramental reverence—a feeling remarkably similar to the one Gela's story aroused in her. But this is also something she cannot convey to Adrian—she doesn't know how to explain to him what these images could possibly have to do with a film about resistance. Except maybe as a metaphor for her own archival work—for her method (if that's what it was): this persistent, ant-like, unwavering, peeling off of layer after layer, inch by inch....

This is also resistance, Adrian thinks. Daryna's got it right. To work the way these restoration guys work—in utter self-dedication, for miniscule pay, purely out of devotion to what you do—that is resistance in its purest form, the essence of resistance, like that voice stripped of words down to a bare melodic lament. She's got it right. An intelligent woman must, after all, have a leg up on an intelligent man because she is endowed with this additional perceptiveness, one we lack—one that stems from her sisterhood with every living thing, regardless of place and time....

A passing trolleybus blows a used ticket at his feet, and he bends down, moved by a sudden urge to pick it up, see, as he used to do when he was little, if the number is lucky, but he misses it: the ticket flies off, mixes with other litter at the edge of the sidewalk. *There's another thing I will never find out*, he thinks, and shrugs, surprised at himself: I must be getting superstitious, too.

Aloud, he tells her that what he loves most about the city at dusk is its quiet courtyards—and gold rectangles of light from the windows cast onto the snow.

"Onto the snow? Why snow?" This surprises her a bit.

"Well, it doesn't have to be snow," he concedes, without real conviction; it could be on the asphalt. For some reason, he doesn't want to talk about this anymore, and she understands it—their thoughts, in the warm, exhaust-laced air of the spring evening, flowing in and out of each other, like intertwined fingers. The light turns to green and they step into the crosswalk like a pair of well-behaved children—holding hands and not even noticing they are.

***

VMOD-Film
Written by Daryna Goshchynska
EXT. CITY – NIGHT.

In the courtyard behind a city high-rise, on the playground, a girl sits—she's squatting like a young child, but there's already a frozen, unchildlike grace in her pose. The playground is empty: it's getting dark; the little ones have all been taken home; the girl is already too old for the sandbox, but still too young to be part of the next shift, which will soon arrive with their glowing dots of cigarette tips in the dark, the strumming of their guitars, and the bursts of silly laughter or a girl's squeal ripped from the hubbub, or the tink of rolling glass—the chaotic, Brownian splashes of puppy-like youthful sensuousness that will make a late passerby shy and hasten to reach his door.

Later still, in the short hours of night, when everything grows quiet, the couples will arrive, and some retiree, kept up by his insomnia and arthritis, will come out on his balcony for a smoke without turning on the lights, and will catch below a moon-glazed glimpse of flesh freed of clothes, a white stain—a breast, a hip—and will get angry because now he won't be able to fall asleep until morning for sure. But all this will be later sometime—it's all yet ahead for the girl who squats very still at the playground.

It is growing dark, the apartments' windows light up one by one, and the girl can barely see what she's got in front of her: in a hole dug into the ground (it rained the day before, the earth is moist and sticky, and easy to dig with a toy plastic scoop someone left behind in the sandbox); in a white frame made of apple-tree blossoms barely visible in the dark, a piece of silver foil, spread flat, catches what little light is left. What she is to do next, the girl doesn't know. And she doesn't have anyone she could ask, either. But she remembers her mother doing it, like this. She remembers, from when she was very little, that this is how her mother used to begin. The paintings came later.

Somewhere above, a window clatters open—the sound sends a pack of crows tumbling out of a nearby chestnut tree where they had already settled for the night.

"Ka-tya! Kat-ru-sya!" a woman's voice calls, echoing over the yard.

The girl startles, shielding the little hole she's dug up. Then she looks back at the building (in the lemony-green patch of open sky between roofs, an inaudible shadow glides by: a bat).

"Coming, Gran!"

Glass! This shard, right here. To cover the hole. And then you bury it, and stamp the dirt flat, smooth it over with the scoop so that no trace remains: no one must see what she was making here; God forbid, someone should find out.... Not now. Not ever.

The girl stands up and dusts the dirt off her knees.

T his book was conceived in the fall of 1999 and begun in the spring of 2002; over the next seven years, the book and I grew and developed together guided by the will of the truth that lay hidden in this story and that I, exactly like Daryna and Adrian in the novel, had to "dig up." This is why the traditional legal formula of the publishing world whereby "all characters and events in this book are fictitious and any resemblance to real persons or events are purely coincidental" does not fit: Only the characters in this book are purely fictitious. Everything that happens to them has actually happened to various people at different points in time. And could still happen. This, actually, is what we call reality.

Reconstructing the wartime and postwar events—the ones that are reflected in Adrian's dreams—was the most difficult and crucial task. Ukrainian, as well as European, literature is yet to develop a more or less satisfactory, adequate, and coherent narrative from that period; one is hard-pressed to find another time in the history of the twentieth century that has been buried under such veritable Himalayas of mental rubbish, packed over the last sixty years almost into concrete—the layers upon layers of lies, half-lies, innuendo, falsifications, and so on. Historical excavations of this period have begun only in the first decade of the new millennium, and in the course of working on *The Museum of Abandoned Secrets,* I was often delighted to receive another new message from fellow "expeditionists" spread all over Europe, from the British Islands to Ukraine, groups that, coming from different angles (different traditions, fields, and genres), have set to clearing up this logjam, Europe's largest and most difficult—the so-called "truth of the Eastern Front."

As I read, on the plane, Norman Davies's *Europe at War*, which I bought at Heathrow; watched Andrzej Wajda's *Katyn*, Edvins Snore's *The Soviet Story*, Ihor Kobryn's *Unity on Blood* (the first systematic attempt at presenting the thirty-year-long Ukrainian catastrophe of the twentieth century); as I encountered for the first time the memoirs of Nikolai Nikulin, published finally in 2007 after decades of "underground" existence, and those of a nameless woman in 1945 Berlin (*Eine Frau in Berlin*), and dozens upon dozens of new books finally giving voice to those whose truth had never been heard, I experienced every time something akin to the thrill of a volunteer who, as she works over an earthquake site, hears the same methodical chipping of pickax against rock all around her. The more of us who are here, the faster the rubble will be cleared—and the less poison from the bodies of those crushed underneath will seep into new generations.

When I began working on *The Museum,* purely Ukrainian publications that could provide the basis for clothing the skeleton of Gela Dovgan and Adrian Ortynsky's story were few and far between. The main documentary source I relied upon was the so-called oral history—the one preserved by being told. Thus, my first and deepest thanks are to the veterans—the witnesses and heroes of the tragedy that was the 1940s, who agreed to meet with me and be interviewed; each to his or her own degree has given pieces of their own lives to my characters. Some of these people are no longer with us, and I am deeply grateful for having had the chance to know them. Without them, this book could never have been written:

Bohdan and Daria Gablevych, Lyuba Komar-Prokop, and Ivan Shtul' re-created for me Lviv in the time of the Nazi occupation and the Ukrainian underground of the time; Oleksiy Zeleniuk (Pastor) and Romana Simkiv (Roma) gave me a tour of the resistance field hospitals; Vasyl Kuk (Lemish), Marichka Savchyn (Marichka), and Ivan Kryvutskyi (Arkadij) filled in dozens of gaps in the historical landscape. Irena Savytska-Kozak's (Bystra) help was nothing but priceless—it was precisely the three days I spent recording our conversations in her welcoming Munich home that finally "decided" Gela's fate; so was the assistance of Orest-Metodiy Dychkovsky (Kryvonis), with whom I consulted about the combat operations in "Adrian's Last Dream" (his analysis of that chapter is one of the greatest authorial joys of my life).

Archives were the other important source of historical information. As fatally disorganized as the Ukrainian archives are, they remain, for a writer, a gold mine of vintage details—things you could never make up on your own. My deepest thanks to Volodymyr Vyatrovych, director of the SBU State Archive; the indefatigable "guardian" of the Ukrainian Academy of Arts and Sciences in the US collection in New York, Oksana Radysh-Miyakovska; the staff of the National Museum of History of the Great Patriotic War of 1941–1945 (Kyiv); the Liberation Struggle of Prykarpattya Museum (Ivano-Frankivsk); and the library of the Lviv Academic Gymnasium, in affiliation with the Lviv Polytechnic National University (Lviv). I also thank my permanent field-expert consultants: Oleksandr Bondarchuk in physics, Dmytro Finkelstein in mathematics, Yevgen Karas' in the antique trade, and Bohdan Yuzvyshyn in forensics. A separate thanks to Vasyl' Ivanovych (Ivano-Frankivsk) for the gift of a field trip to the bunker "Groma" and the hideout "Boyeslava" when I needed the wintertime locations for Room 6. And, finally, I owe special gratitude to my first readers and critics, who supported me over the entire distance, and without whom it may not have been conquered at all—Rostyslav Luzhetsky and Leonid and Tetyana Plyushch.

In the course of working on *The Museum*, I wrote another book, *Notre Dame d'Ukraine*, which took more than two years; a variety of small routine projects took up, altogether, almost another entire year; and if it were not for writers' residencies which kindly accommodated me (God bless them!) I would probably still be working on *The Museum* now. Here is the list of the places where almost two-thirds of the novel was written—I owe each individual recognition: Ledig House (Omi, NY), Cerrini-Schloessl (Graz, Austria), Villa dei Pini (Boglasco, Italy), Literarisches Colloquium Berlin (Germany), Literaturhaus Krems (Austria), Baltic Center for Writers and Translators (Visby, Sweden), Villa Hellebosch (Belgium), Hawthornden Castle (Scotland), Villa Sträuli (Winterthur, Switzerland), Kuenstlerdorf Schoeppingen (Germany), and Villa Decius (Krakow, Poland).

I would like to give special thanks to the Baltic Center's director, Lena Pasternak, who found a room for me every time I, gone off the schedule again, called her with a desperate cry for help, and Ilke Froyen from Het Beschrijf in Brussels, to whose attention and understanding I owe my rescue in the eleventh hour of my novelistic odyssey (when there were already production deadlines I was about to miss). My heartfelt thanks also goes to my agent, Galina Dursthoff, who through all these years did everything possible to ensure I could work without disruption.

And finally I thank everyone who has patiently waited for this book, whether I've met you or not: you have also helped me write it.

RESOURCES

For those who need a bit of extra help navigating the historical context of the novel's episodes from 1943 to 2004, and after reading *The Museum* would like to expand their knowledge, I am providing here a list of widely available books (not archival materials or government publications intended for very small expert audiences) that I have found helpful.

Alekseeva, Liudmila. *Istoriia inakomysliia v SSSR: noveishii period.* Vilnius, Moscow: Vest', 1992.

Andrew, Christopher and Vasili Mitrokhin. *The Mitrokhin Archive: The KGB in Europe and the West.* London: Penguin Books, 2000.

Andrusyak, Mykhailo. *Braty hromu.* Kolomyia: Vydavnycho-polihrafichne tovarystvo 'Vik', 2001.

Blan, Elen. *Rodom iz KGB: sistema putina.* Kyiv: Tempora, 2009.

Davies, Norman. *Europe at War 1939–1945: No Simple Victory.* London: Macmillan, 2006.

Eco, Umberto. *Turning Back the Clock: Hot Wars and Media Populism.* Translated by Alastair McEwen. Orlando: Vintage, 2008.

Kosyk, Volodymyr. *The Third Reich and Ukraine.* New York: P. Lang, 1993.

Lanckoronska, Karolina. *Wspomnienia wojenne.* Krakow: Znak, 2002.

Nakonechnyi, Ievhen. *'Shoa' u L'vovi.* Lviv: Piramida, 2006.

Onyshko, Lesia. *Kateryna Zarytska: molytva do syna.* Lviv: Svit, 2002.

Poliuha, Liubomyr. *Shliakhamy spohadiv, 1944–1956.* Lviv: Piramida, 2003.

Pliushch, Leonyd. *History's Carnival: A Dissident's Autobiography.* New York: Harcourt, 1979.

Savchyn Pyskir, Maria. *Thousands of Roads: A Memoir of a Young Woman's Life in the Ukrainian Underground During and After World War II.* Translated by Tatyana Plyushch. Jefferson, NC: McFarland, 2001.

Sannikov, Georgij. *Bol'saa ohota: razgrom vooruzhennogo podpolia v Zapadnoj Ukraine.* Moscow: Olma-Press, 2002.

Shingariov, Vladimir. *Moskal' i banderovtsy.* Full-length manuscript published on *Gulyai-Pole*, December 2009. http://www.politua. su/moskalibanderovcy.

Viatrovych, Volodymyr. *Stavlennia OUN do ievreiv: formuvannia pozytsii na tli katastrofy.* Lviv: Ms, 2006.

ABOUT THE AUTHOR

Oksana Zabuzhko was born in 1960 in Ukraine. She made her poetry debut in 1972, but her parents' blacklisting during the Soviet purges prevented her first book from being published until the 1980s. She earned her PhD in philosophy from Kyiv Shevchenko University and has taught as a Fulbright Fellow and writer-in-residence at Penn State University, Harvard University, and the University of Pittsburgh. She is the author of seventeen books of poetry, fiction, and nonfiction, which have been translated into fifteen languages and have garnered numerous awards. Her novel *Fieldwork in Ukrainian Sex* was named "the most influential Ukrainian book for the fifteen years of independence." She lives today in Kyiv, where she works as a freelance writer.

ABOUT THE TRANSLATOR

Nina Shevchuk-Murray was born and raised in the Western Ukrainian city of Lviv and holds a master's degree in linguistics from Lviv National University. In 2006, she completed her graduate work in creative writing at the University of Nebraska–Lincoln. Since then, Nina has been working as a translator of Russian and Ukrainian literature. Her translations of Ukrainian poetry have appeared in *AGNI Online* and *Prairie Schooner*; she is a regular contributor to *Chtenia*, a quarterly journal of Russian literature. In 2010, she translated from Russian a novel by Peter Aleshkovsky, *Fish: A History of One Migration*.